People
of the
Lightning

People
of the
Lightning

Kathleen O'Neal Gear
and
W. Michael Gear

A TOM DOHERTY ASSOCIATES BOOK
NEW YORK

This is a work of fiction. All the characters and events portrayed in this novel are either fictitious or are used fictitiously.

PEOPLE OF THE LIGHTNING

This book is printed on acid-free paper.

Maps and interior illustrations by Ellisa Mitchell

A Forge Book
Published by Tom Doherty Associates, Inc.
175 Fifth Avenue
New York, N.Y. 10010

Forge® is a registered trademark of Tom Doherty Associates, Inc.

Library of Congress Cataloging-in-Publication Data

Gear, Kathleen O'Neal.
    People of the lightning / Kathleen O'Neal Gear and
W. Michael Gear.
        p. cm.
    "A Tom Doherty Associates book."
    ISBN 0-312-85852-3 (hardcover)
    1. Man, Prehistoric—Florida—Fiction.   I. Gear,
W. Michael   II. Title.
PS3557.E18P47   1995   95-34746
813'.54—dc20   CIP

First Edition: November 1995

Printed in the United States of America

0 9 8 7 6 5 4 3 2 1

To
Harold Arthur O'Neal,
one of the greatest storytellers of all time

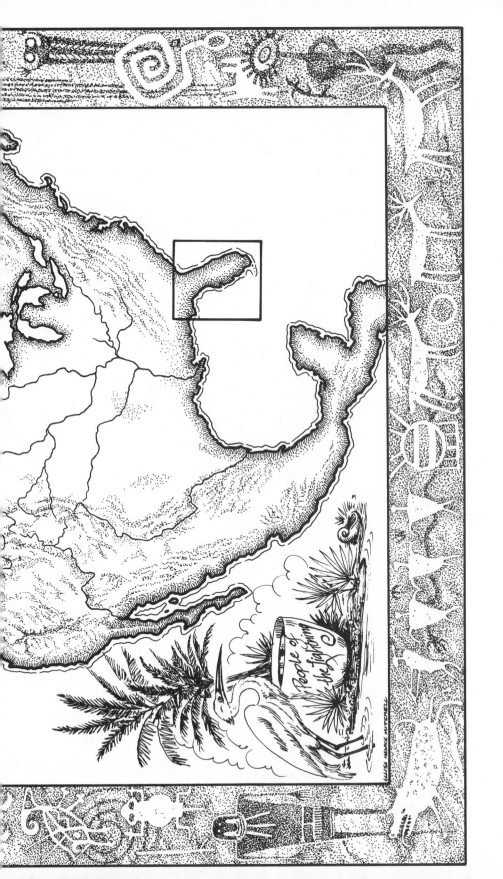

People of the Longhouse

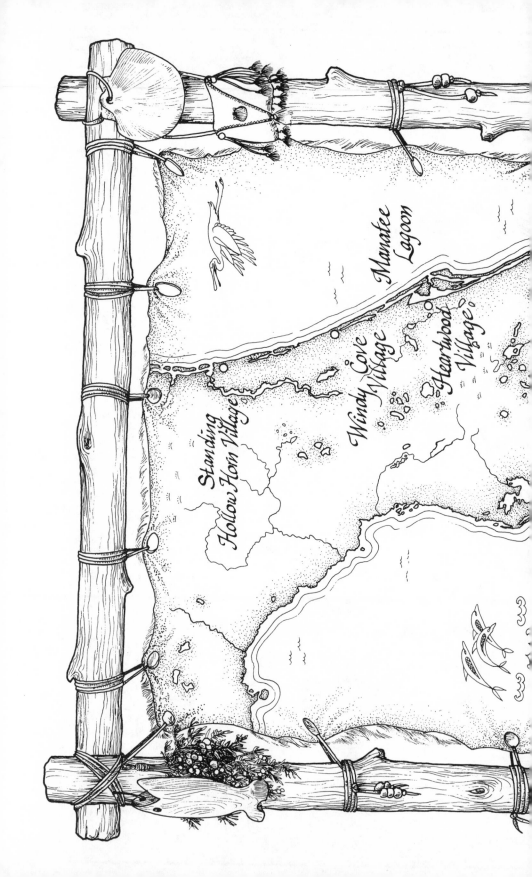

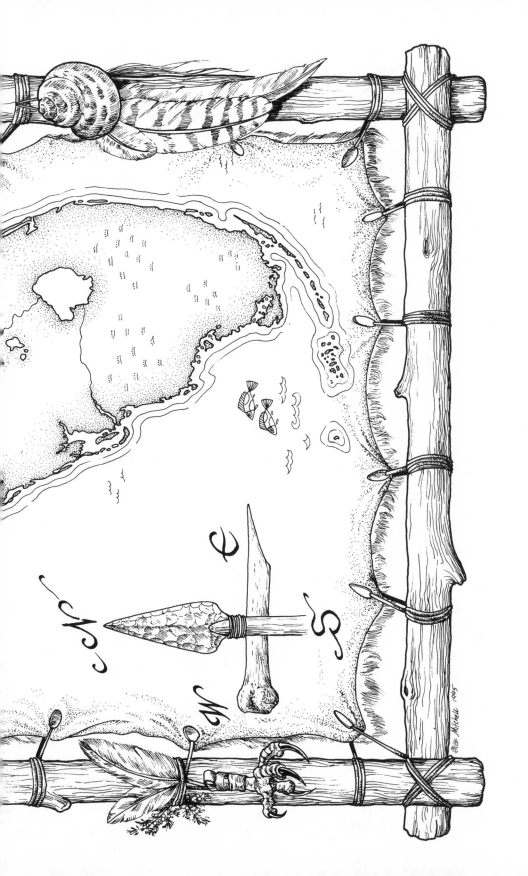

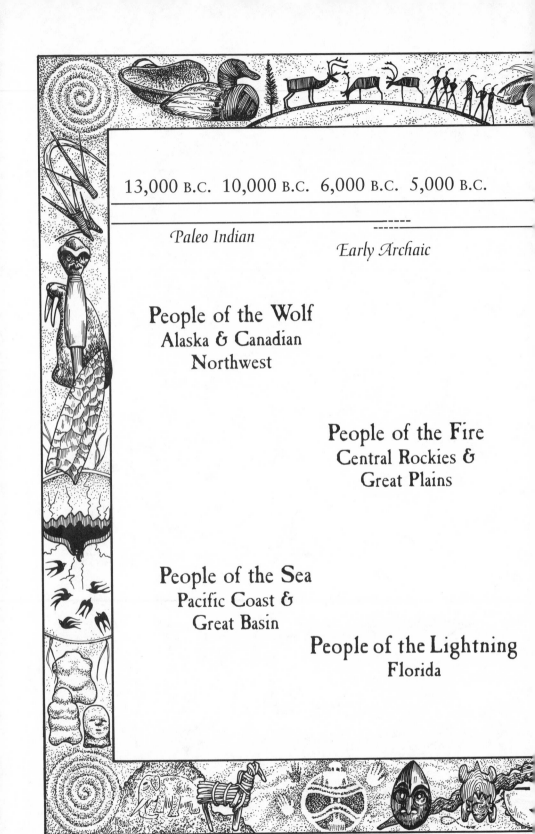

13,000 B.C. 10,000 B.C. 6,000 B.C. 5,000 B.C.

Paleo Indian

Early Archaic

People of the Wolf
Alaska & Canadian Northwest

People of the Fire
Central Rockies & Great Plains

People of the Sea
Pacific Coast & Great Basin

People of the Lightning
Florida

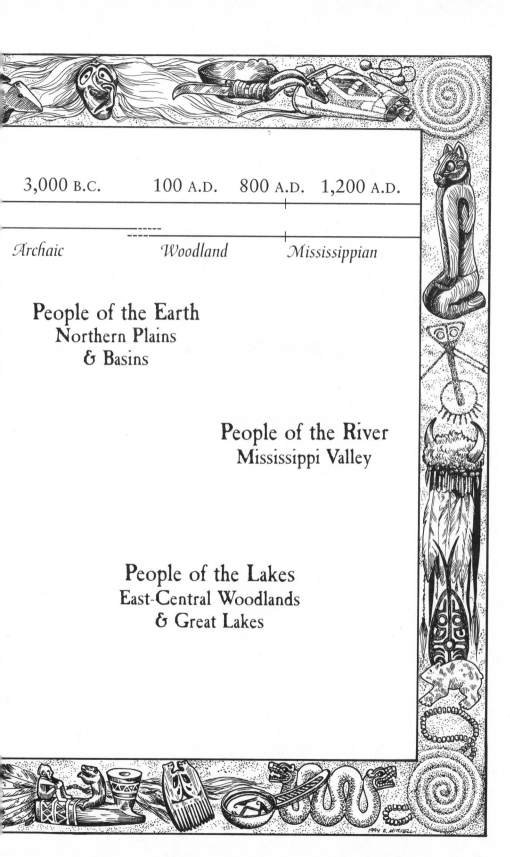

3,000 B.C.	100 A.D.	800 A.D.	1,200 A.D.

Archaic   *Woodland*   *Mississippian*

People of the Earth
Northern Plains
& Basins

People of the River
Mississippi Valley

People of the Lakes
East-Central Woodlands
& Great Lakes

1994 E. MITCHELL

Acknowledgments

We offer our sincere thanks to Dr. David Glenn Smith, Dr. Frederick W. Lorey, Dr. Becky K. Rolfs, and Dr. Glen Doran, for their careful work on Windover Pond, and a copy of their excellent unpublished paper entitled, "Serum Albumin Phenotypes for the Prehistoric Population of Windover Pond and Their Anthropological Significance," and to Dr. William Hauswirth for making the new science of molecular archaeology real and meaningful.

Dr. Cal Cummings and Dr. Linda Scott Cummings helped with Florida reference materials, and provided many wonderful insights into prehistoric lifeways. They are not only good friends, but two of the most conscientious scientists in America.

Steve Vanderjagt, the backhoe operator who stopped construction when he realized that what he'd hit were not rocks, but human skulls, deserves special note. Every archaeologist in America thanks you, Steve.

Sierra Adare, as always, held the world together while we were off researching, and writing.

Doug Nichols kept the buffalo on the ranch, and out of our neighbors' frying pans.

Harriet McDougal never lets us get away with anything, thank God.

Tom and Donna Espenshied, and Jim and Faye Naramore, turned an anticipated morning of fieldwork into a delightful day of conversation and laughter.

Thank you all.

Foreword

By 8,000 years ago, the huge glaciers that had once covered much of the North American continent had melted, and sea level stood at approximately its present-day level, though Florida's lakes had only just begun to fill. Oak and hardwood forests, interspersed with pines and palms, covered most of the state. At this time Archaic peoples lived throughout Florida, fishing, hunting, and gathering plant resources. These people made distinctive percussion-flaked stone tools, wove beautiful fabrics, and developed one of the most extraordinary mortuary cultures in the history of the world. An Archaic cemetery site was discovered near Titusville, Florida, in 1982. Called Windover Pond, the site dramatically changed our scientific understanding of Florida's prehistory.

Between 7,000 and 8,000 years ago, the Windover people buried their dead in ponds. We don't know why for certain, but the bodies were usually dressed in fine clothing, wrapped in blankets, and placed on their left sides with their heads to the west, and faces to the north. Grave goods accompanied some of the burials, particularly the children. The incredible preservation of the soft tissues of the bodies tell us that they were buried quickly, probably within forty-eight hours of death.

Ordinarily, human tissues, as well as fragile artifacts of wood, bone, or cloth, disintegrate in a few generations. But the anaerobic (oxygen-lacking) environment in Windover Pond, combined with relatively neutral pH levels, and a high concentration of calcium carbonate, resulted in incredible preservation. Fabrics were recovered which demonstrate seven different weaving or twining techniques. Incised bone and marine shell tools, wooden bowls, baskets, animal and plant remains were also found. Perhaps the most spectacular find of all was that of the 168 individuals buried in the pond, 91 brains had been preserved. Better yet, the actual DNA was intact.

The burials tell us many things. The average woman stood five feet, two inches tall, the average man five feet, seven inches. They were relatively healthy. Though many suffered from iron-deficiency anemia, some people lived to more than sixty-five years of age. Analyses of the DNA and the serum albumin—the most abundant blood protein—indicate that the Windover people *are not* closely related to any other Native American population.

Burial stakes were driven through the blankets wrapping the bodies to secure the dead to the bottom of the pond. These stakes were made from of a variety of woods: pine, oak, privet, persimmon, dogwood, ash, and buttonbrush. All of those trees, therefore, must have been growing fairly close to the pond.

The fabrics, blankets, cordage, baskets, and bags seem to have been woven from palm and palmetto fibers.

The stomach contents from several burials were analyzed and yielded grapes, persimmons, prickly pear fruit, maypop, elderberries, and black nightshade berries among many other things. Because these fruits mature between the months of June and December, we assume that Windover Pond was utilized only during those months, and that the Windover people moved to another camp or camps during the winter and spring. They probably had other burial ponds, as well.

One of the most fascinating discoveries relates to the unusual injuries suffered by the Windover people. Three adults and two children had cranial depression fractures—meaning they had been struck in the head by blunt objects. One adult male had a dart point embedded in his hip. Six men and five women had one or more fractured arms. One man, about age forty-seven, had a "parry" fracture of the left ulna, the lower arm. This injury is called a "parry" fracture because it is the kind of bone break that occurs when a person lifts his arm to block a blow. This same man had a puncture lesion in the floor of his eye socket caused when a sharp object entered the eye and penetrated the bone. Interpersonal violence, it seems, played a major role at Windover.

But the people also took very good care of their families. One fifteen-year-old boy suffered from spina bifida—a condition in which the vertebrae do not completely close around the spinal cord. This defect results in a number of pathologies: curvature of the spine, atrophy of the legs, disuse ulceration, and serious infections. At the time of this boy's death, he had lost his right foot, and the stump of his leg was infected and draining. The boy had probably been an invalid for at least three years. Yet, he lived. Someone fed him, cleaned him, carried him about, and did these things while the village was engaged in violent raiding, if not outright warfare. Someone clearly loved this boy very much.

Perhaps, in the end, they were not so very different from us.

Introduction

Janet Mabry-Catton looked at her watch for the tenth time, and sighed. She sat at the edge of the forest facing out across the white beach to the ocean. Sea gulls ran along in front of the waves, squawking and squealing in their hunt for food. Idly, she wondered if birds ever felt the kind of soul-draining disappointment that she did today.

She picked up a pine cone and lifted it to her nose to smell the sweet scent. Fifteen years in the archaeological field provided a person with a solid grounding in frustration and discouragement. Both were as inescapable as gravity. Over time natural processes like erosion and decomposition—even roots and burrowing animals—conspired to destroy bits and pieces of the archaeological record.

The urbanization of America added to the problem. Janet had done her share of mad scrambling while bulldozers roared and rumbled around her.

She turned slightly to look over her shoulder. The site in the cool forest shadows behind her was no different. Soon it would be a housing development, and she'd be running a desperate race to save just a tiny piece.

She had asked herself why many times. Part of it was that she felt certain there were people out there who really cared about America's magnificent past, people who longed to know more about the fascinating cultures that had thrived here.

Then she had days like today . . . days when she felt nobody really cared.

When she saw the ramshackle old truck coming down the beach, she took a deep breath, trying to prepare herself, and smoothed her clammy palms on her brown twill skirt.

Who would have ever thought it would come to this?

The truck squealed to a stop, and out came Johnny Grady, the tribe's cultural resources liaison, followed by a man in a blue suit. Janet scrutinized him. She didn't think she knew him. Grady held the door open, waiting.

After several moments, a very old man with long silver braids and a face like wind-scoured rock gingerly stepped to the ground. Hunched from age, he walked with a cane. Grady and the man in blue came toward her, but the elder hobbled out to the surf, his chin up as if enjoying the spray.

Grady cupped a hand to his mouth and called, "Dr. Mabry-Catton, I'm sorry we're late."

Janet got to her feet, brushed sand from her skirt, and tried to smile pleasantly.

Grady walked in an arrogant swinging stride. His tan shorts, sandals, and yellow tee-shirt all looked new. His Irish half showed in his lean, freckled face and tall, slender body. Two long black braids hung over his chest. He'd been the tribe's designate for only three months, but he had already wreaked havoc across Florida.

As the man in the blue suit drew closer, she was certain she did not know him. Perhaps forty-five, he stood about five ten and had short black hair.

Johnny gestured to the man in blue. "Dr. Mabry-Catton, this is Peter Samson, attorney for the tribe."

Samson studied Janet with a sparkle in his dark eyes.

"Good morning, Doctor." His slow baritone carried only the slightest hint of Indian accent. "How are you?" He extended his hand to her.

She shook it. "Oh . . . fine. I guess."

"Most of your work is in the southeast, isn't it? Florida, Georgia, and Alabama?"

"That's right." She looked him over, worried that he might be about to hang her for something she'd written ten years ago and could barely remember.

"I'm familiar with some of your work on the Calusa. I enjoyed it very much."

She arched an eyebrow. "Well . . . thanks."

Samson peered around her at the excavation unit in the forest—a standard two-by-two-meter square, a little over thirty centimeters deep. "Is that the site?"

"Part of it, yes. This was the first unit we opened and . . . well, you know the rest." Of course, he did. He was a lawyer. "Shall we get on with this? I'd like to explain—"

"No. We should not." Johnny Grady jerked his head toward the elder on the beach. "My great-grandfather needs time to contact the ghosts here. You'll start when *he's* ready."

Janet nodded. "Fine. That's fine."

Samson smiled. "I'm sure it won't take long. Mr. White Bear is a very great medicine elder. If there's something here, he'll know it soon."

Janet peered morosely out at the beach. The old man was skipping shells on the water. She could hear him chuckling. "How old is he? I've never worked with him before."

"Ninety-four," Johnny said. He pulled a small plastic box from the right pocket of his shorts and began tossing it into the air and catching it. His eyes glinted with hostility.

Janet didn't have to ask. She knew what the box contained.

She folded her arms, and forced herself to stay calm while they waited.

Charlie White Bear smiled at the lightning flashes dancing through the thunderheads far out over the vast sparkling ocean. On such a hot, humid day, he wished Thunderbird would bring the cool storm closer. Sweat ran down his wrinkled face as he hobbled toward the trees where three people stood. On sand, his cane wasn't really much help. Despite his poor hearing, his ears picked up Johnny's angry voice.

The woman must be Dr. Janet Mabry-Catton, the university archaeologist. She stood with her head down, arms folded, listening. But Johnny wasn't speaking to her, he talked to Peter Samson, the Indian lawyer. Charlie shook his head. Johnny had called him last night, saying he needed Charlie to "do his thing" with this archaeological site. Despite the fact that Charlie didn't really understand what that meant, he knew what Johnny needed.

Johnny turned and poked a finger in the archaeologist's face, and said something in a voice too low for Charlie to hear. Charlie worked to make his arthritic knees move faster. Johnny took after his Irish father in more ways than looks; he was a hothead.

As Charlie neared the group, he heard Johnny say, "*This hair represents the remains of one of our sacred ancestors!* Dr. Mabry-Catton admits she dug it up here. This is a burial site, for God's sake, Pete! We can't let the university keep desecrating the graves of our people!"

Samson frowned. "One hair is all they've found? No bones? Is that right, Dr. Mabry-Catton?"

She opened her mouth to answer, but Johnny cut her off.

"What difference does that make? This is a *human* hair. It came off somebody's head! Somebody who was buried here! Whose side are you on, Pete?"

Charlie walked up beside Johnny and sighed.

Johnny said, "Dr. Mabry-Catton this is Mr. Charles White Bear, one of our most revered elders."

Charlie smiled at her and stuck out his hand. She took it firmly and shook. She had a pretty oval face with green eyes and a pointed nose. Charlie guessed her age at forty. She didn't look angry. Her face showed more . . . despair.

Samson said, "Perhaps Mr. White Bear can help us. Sir, do you feel any-thing—"

"Tell them, Grandfather!" Johnny interrupted, putting a hand on Charlie's shoulder. The boy had been angry all his life, and had grown even worse after he got out of college. How sad. So few of the young knew how to live in harmony these days. "Tell them this *is* a burial ground and they have to stop digging it up! You can feel ghosts here, can't you, Grandfather?"

Dr. Mabry-Catton bowed her head. She seemed to be watching her twill skirt sway in the sea breeze. With slim fingers she pulled back a loose strand of straight, brown hair that had escaped her clasp-held ponytail.

"Grandfather!" Johnny said.

Charlie propped his cane and walked past his grandson into the forest to peer over the edge of the square pit. A gray stain filled with shiny flecks of charcoal marked the bottom. Charlie smiled. Just after the turn of the century, his grandfather had built fires like that, small, efficient, enough to warm and cook, but not wasteful. Charlie had been born Apache, far to the west, on the Fort Sill reservation in Oklahoma, but his father had been born in Florida. All his life, his father had talked about the trees and water in Florida—and with so much astonishment that the instant Charlie turned nineteen, he decided he had to come see for himself. He'd met people from dozens of different Florida tribes—he'd even married one: his beloved Sarah. Since her tribe was matrilineal, meaning they traced descent through the women, not only had Charlie become a relative, but all of Charlie's children, grandchildren, and great-grandchildren, including Johnny Grady, belonged to Sarah's tribe.

Johnny, the doctor, and the lawyer moved around him, taking up places on each side of the pit. Tree shadows mottled their concerned faces. It was very peaceful here, but his great-grandson could only manage to stay quiet for a few moments.

Johnny shoved the plastic box at Dr. Mabry-Catton. "The law's on our side now," he said. "The Native American Graves Protection and Repatriation Act says you have to stop digging if you find anything that might be from a burial. And this—"

"That's *why* I stopped and contacted you!" Dr. Mabry-Catton raised her head and for the first time fire lit her eyes. "I support NAGPRA," she said in a low shaking voice. "For God's sake, *I* helped draft the law! But NAGPRA was never meant to support idiocy like this! If you would only listen to me for one moment, I—"

"Listen? To what? More white academic bullshit about science? These are *my* ancestors!"

"Hold on!" Pete Samson said, extending his hands as if to keep the doctor and Johnny apart. His blue sleeves billowed in the pine-scented wind. "I know this is an emotional issue—"

"I'll say," Dr. Mabry-Catton murmured.

"Try to see it from our side," Samson said. "After five hundred years of war, disease, conquest, forced acculturation, and reservations, Indians feel like rats in a cage. Whites have done everything in their power to kill our cultures, stamp out our languages. The graves of our ancestors are one of our few ties to the past. They're very important to us."

"I understand that," Dr. Mabry-Catton said. "But NAGPRA was meant to protect legitimate burial sites, not a stray hair!"

Johnny stuck out his chin. "It came from the body of one of my sacred ancestors, and it must be returned for reburial and you must stop—"

"Please?" she pleaded, extending her hands to Johnny. "We don't know very much about this site, except that it dates to the Early Archaic, about eight thousand years ago. That's a very important time in Florida's prehistory. The whole world was changing. Don't you care who lived here? Don't you want to know what happened to them? What they made, or how they lived?" Her voice had gone tight. "If I have to close this excavation unit, and return that hair to you for reburial, then I will. But I'll never stop wondering what I might have discovered here. We know so little about early—"

"My people don't *need* archaeology," Johnny said. "We have our elders to tell us what happened thousands of years ago."

Everyone turned to Charlie.

He kept frowning down at the old fire pit. He was thinking about his grandfather; he'd been a great Apache chief, one of the few that fought alongside Geronimo until the bitter end, when the U.S. Army hunted them down, locked them in chains, and shipped them to Florida. Five hundred Apaches had been imprisoned in tiny Fort Marian at St. Augustine, but it had taken just a few months before they'd become such a huge tourist attraction, that Pensacolans lobbied to have the "painted demons" moved there. Charlie's father had been born at Fort Pickens on Santa Rosa Island in Pensacola Bay. While malaria and tuberculosis decimated the Apache, Pensacolans sold tickets. Whites came by the hundreds, day after day, to smile and watch the Apache die. Though they were moved soon after to Mt. Vernon, Alabama, by 1894 only three hundred remained, mostly children born in captivity. That year the federal government moved them one final time, to Fort Sill, Oklahoma. By then most of the old ones were dead, and few of the young people had ever spared the time to listen to their stories. They were warriors fighting for their lives! What did stories matter?

Charlie used his cane to prod at a pine cone. He remembered one day, oh, around the turn of the century, when his grandfather had put his head in his hands and cried because he couldn't recall part of a story his mother had told him. Charlie had been three or four at the time, and the sight had broken his heart.

"Isn't that right, Grandfather?" Johnny asked. "Our people don't need archaeology."

The boy sounded just like a white man, arrogant, stupid, only interested in showing what he could do with his newfound power. Power . . .

Charlie tipped his chin to a thin shaft of sunlight penetrating the branches. Power lived and breathed all around him—but not the kind his great-grandson knew. If Charlie strained his ears, he could hear the pines whispering to each other, and Sister Sea talking to Mother Earth as she gently washed her face. As long as Johnny clung to white man's "power" he would never know real Power . . . and he would never truly be able to help his people. And they needed help, badly. Despite the TV portrait of rich Indians earning millions from casinos, it was far from the truth. Most reservations didn't have casinos, and few of those that did were getting rich. Just last year Charlie had traveled back to Oklahoma to visit his sister and had stopped at reservations across the country. While most whites worried about how to buy a second car, most Indians worried about buying a second loaf of bread. Every day Indian children in America went hungry, and every night someone lay awake wondering how to pay the electric bill.

"Look," Pete Samson said to Dr. Mabry-Catton, jarring Charlie back to the present. "We want our heritage back. That's all. You're an archaeologist, right? How many archaeological reports have you written in your career?"

She waved a hand irritably. "Hundreds, I guess. Why?"

Samson's face hardened. "Did you send any to Indian tribes who might have had an interest, so they could learn, too?"

She blinked, her silence answer enough.

Samson looked smug. "I'll bet you wrote up your findings in obtuse language and sent them to some academic journal instead. Scholarship for scholars. Ever since the arrival of the Europeans, Indian studies have been largely the province of whites. I remember the anthropologists coming to the reservation every summer when I was a kid. They'd do their studies and disappear with their data. And for what? They wrote their dissertations, got their degrees, and made their careers. They got what they wanted from us, but what did we get from them?" He paused. "Nothing. We got nothing."

She sighed. "So you think that stopping all archaeological work now will change that? If you still care about your ancestors, let us—"

"I care!" Johnny shoved the plastic box in her face again. "I want you to leave my people alone! And if you don't—"

Charlie turned his back and walked away.

It was such a beautiful day. He gazed up at the swaying branches, seeing how the sunlight shone from their leaves. The heat had released the pine's sweetness and set it loose on the wind.

The angry voices stopped . . . and Charlie could hear something else now. Music. Beautiful music. Shishes, like rain falling, and booms of thunder. Images flashed through his mind, things he did not understand . . . being born in the belly of a cloud . . . plummeting through utter blackness . . . light so wondrous his human eyes ached for it.

He kept walking. Pine needles crunched beneath his feet. At the base of an old oak tree, something glimmered. He bent down, using a finger to pry it up. It looked like a turtle bone, pitted and scarred.

Very faintly, Charlie heard voices coming from the bone. He held it to his ear, and soft childish laughter echoed through his soul. . . .

"Mr. White Bear," Pete Samson said. "What is that? What are you doing?"

"Is there a ghost in there, Grandfather?" Johnny asked eagerly.

Charlie turned to face them. "No," he said softly, and shook his head. "No ghosts. Just memories." He used the bone to point at Dr. Mabry-Catton. "This is not a burial site, doctor. My people are sorry we troubled you. Go ahead with your dig."

"What?" Johnny's face reddened. "Grandfather! How can you say that when she found this hair here?" He shook the plastic box.

Charlie shrugged. "Maybe somebody combed his hair sitting there in front of that fire. I don't care. But I do care about this bone. *This* is important to our people."

Johnny scowled at the bone in disbelief. "Why?"

Dr. Mabry-Catton asked, "What is it? It looks like a turtle bone."

"Yes," Charlie answered. "A turtle bone with memories. Would you mind . . . would it be all right if I keep this? Take it back to the tribe? I think the other elders will wish to see it."

She stepped around Johnny, her skirt flapping with the breeze, and frowned at the bone. Charlie handed it to her, watching as she carefully looked it over. Two upright lines pinched the skin between her brows.

"Fossilized," she said. "But I don't see any markings on it." She knelt to study the hole Charlie had pried it from, brushed at the sand. "Surface find, not associated with the site." She looked over her shoulder at Charlie. "I don't think it's an artifact. Florida is covered with fossil shells and bones." She handed it back. "It's yours, Mr. White Bear."

Charlie pressed it to his heart.

His great-grandson shoved his fists into the pockets of his shorts and appeared to be sulking. Pete Samson didn't say a word; he just contemplated the sky.

"Come along, Great-Grandson," Charlie said. "I'm tired. Let's go home."

"Grandfather, wait a minute. Come over here." He tried to wave Charlie to the side. "Let me talk to you about this first. Listen to me—"

Charlie lifted the bone to his ear again and headed for the truck. Whispers filled his mind . . . an old man's frail voice, lilting, soft.

"Grandfather?"

"Don't interrupt," Charlie said as he walked out into the bright sunshine. "I'll miss part of the story."

Prologue

Ah, yes . . . Pondwader.

How strange that you should ask about him now. Over the past few days I, myself, have been wondering if he really lived or if I merely invented him, as I have invented so many people in my long life. That is what storytellers do, you know; they keep the old legends alive by spinning shining heroes where only frightened men and women existed, or lauding glorious wars where mere murder was the issue. But all for a purpose, my good child. You may call me the grandest of liars, if you wish, but remember that the view of every event depends upon which cloud you are riding at the time. The effect of Pondwader's death was just as powerful as if there had been a war, and so I . . .

Oh, don't let me do that, child! Didn't you notice that I almost told you the end of the story before I had begun it? Age is such a curse. Memories start to careen about like Brother Whirlwind. If you notice my thoughts wandering, shout to stop me, or you'll never hear the tale correctly. And you had best shout loudly, too, dear girl, or my ears won't realize you have spoken. I tell you what, try waving your hand when you shout. That ought to do it.

Now, let me see, why did I bore you with all that drivel about storytellers? Perhaps I only wished to warn you that I no longer know how much of what I remember about Pondwader is true, if any of it is, though Sun Mother will vouch that I lived most of it. And, well, even if it is not true, Pondwader had the gentlest, most forgiving soul I have ever been privileged to know. I doubt he would object to my version. I remember once, just before the baby Lightning Bird hatched in his chest, Pondwader had gone to the Sacred Pond. . . .

That's very rude, child. Why are you waving your hand like that?

. . . Oh. That's right.

Well, let me see. I need to get settled here on this cold ground. If you will throw more wood on the fire, I'll lean back against this old oak trunk and let the Shining People hanging in the dark sky above us stir my memory.

The story actually begins long before Pondwader's transformation. Many moons before. Raiders had taken to the forests, killing people, stealing women and children. No one felt safe. Musselwhite, the great woman warrior, had sent out a scouting party from Windy Cove Village to secure her clan's borders. That's when the real trouble began. . . .

One

Cottonmouth could not take his eyes from the young woman warrior who lay on her stomach before him. Feathers of long hair haloed her beautiful face, looking startlingly black against the white sand. Her short tunic, the color of dry grass, had been woven from the finest palm thread, and painted with the green images of bobcat, whale, and dolphin. In the past half a hand of time, so much blood had run from her wound that it had pooled, red and glistening, at her side. As his men moved among the dead, the amber gleam of their torches reflected in that pool like flashes of lightning.

Cottonmouth forced a shallow breath into his lungs. Every wet scent of the night smelled incredibly clear to him, as if it had soaked into his flesh and been carried through his veins like a powerful Spirit plant. The sweetness of the coastal pines mixed with the salty fragrances of fish and sea, and the earthiness of the rain storm that had washed the world just before the battle.

After his dart had pierced her back just below the shoulder blades, she had fallen, then weakly pushed up and tried to crawl away. When she could go no further, she had stiffened her trembling arms and legs, keeping herself upright so that she might turn and defiantly stare him in the eyes.

The shock of seeing that face had been like a hard fist in his stomach.

Blessed Sun Mother, how many times had he gazed into those eyes in his dreams? How many times had he tenderly touched that face?

Clenching his hands to nerve himself, he walked forward and knelt beside the young woman. Huge, amorphous shadows swayed through the trees as a few of his warriors lifted their torches momentarily to watch him, curious.

He had lost only two men in the battle. The remaining ten-and-eight moved through the camp, laughing and joking, kicking over the bodies, ripping Power bundles from around throats, plundering the dead for trinkets to take home to their wives and children. Against the wavering background of firelit palms, oaks, and pines, they seemed somehow unreal . . . more like scavenging ghosts floating over the sand than living men.

Cottonmouth broke off the dart shaft and flung it away. His heart had started to pound. He slipped his arms beneath the girl's knees and shoulders, and clutched her slender body against his bare chest. Blood leaked from her wound, running warmly down his muscular belly and legs, soaking his breechclout. His long, graying black hair fell over her face as he lifted her and rose to his feet.

Disapproving murmurs came from his warriors. The customs of their clan, the Standing Hollow Horn Clan, demanded that enemies killed in battle be left for scavengers. If their relatives did not find the dead within two days, their souls would justly be condemned to wander the earth forever.

Mulberry, a small skinny youth, stepped forward and lifted his torch so that it glared in Cottonmouth's eyes, forcing him to squint. The boy had coiled his black hair into a bun and fixed it with a manatee-bone pin. Blood spattered his legs. "Spirit Elder," he said sternly. "We must leave the dead." He cast a worried look over his shoulder. "The men expect it."

Cottonmouth stared at his warriors. They shifted uncomfortably.

Anger creased Mulberry's young face, hardening his jaw. Boldly, he stepped closer. "Elder, our men do not wish this filth to enter the afterworld and live among our relatives!"

Terse whispers passed back and forth.

"Have you searched the dead for Diver?" Cottonmouth asked. The very softness of his voice held threat. "Or did you allow him to escape?"

Mulberry tried to scowl, but his resolve quickly faltered and he wet his thin lips. "I . . . n-no. Not yet."

"He is about my age, four-tens-and-five or five tens of summers. I will return soon. When I do, I will wish to know where he is. *You* had better have an answer for me."

Cottonmouth walked away slowly, drowning in the sensation of her body pressed against his, the silken feel of her long black hair tumbling down his side. When he had first seen her, he'd stumbled and almost fallen. Only after moments of agony had he realized she must be Morning Glory, daughter of Musselwhite, and not Musselwhite herself—but she looked so much like her mother with those high cheekbones, that turned-up nose, and those fierce brown eyes, that he had been stunned and unable to take his gaze from her.

Cool wind blew across his face. Sister Moon shone so brightly tonight that every blade of grass threw a shadow. As he rounded the northern edge of a clearing, he could make out the gangly shape of a blue heron standing on one foot in the meadow, and a short distance further, a snowy egret.

On the western side of the clearing an ancient oak had fallen long ago, blocking the path. Great crooked branches held the heavy trunk off the ground. He would have to crawl through on his knees, then drag Morning Glory behind him.

Cottonmouth laid her on a soft pile of old leaves and slid under on his stomach. Powerful scents of wet bark and packrat dung stung his nose. He emerged on the opposite side and turned.

When he reached through the tangle to grasp her wrist, her fingers had stiffened, raking his arms like curled talons. He tugged. She moved, then stopped abruptly. He jerked harder and heard the sound of ripping fabric as her short tunic tore free from a snag. She came through on her stomach, her face in the dirt. The sight pained him. Blood trickled darkly from her back wound.

Cottonmouth sat down beside her and brushed the dirt from her smooth cheeks and forehead, but drew back his hand when he noticed that one of her eyes had opened. He did not want to look into those eyes again, though tens of times, in a dozen battles, he had lived only for that sight.

He gently spread her hair over her face, then picked her up and carried her on down the trail. When he reached the pond, he lowered her to the green grass, placing her in the same spot her mother had lain two tens and six summers before. Musselwhite had been laughing when they'd loved each other.

Since that day the world had changed. The forest had grown up around their secret places. Deadfall had accumulated, filling the spaces between the trees.

No lovers came here now.

It saddened Cottonmouth, for he could recall very clearly bright days when he and Musselwhite had walked here and felt Brother Earth's age like a warm cape upon their shoulders. This forest had held a stillness so great they could sense the wingbeats of the Spirit birds who flew around them. They had spent days listening to the trees sing. Each had its own distinct voice, and when they sang together, a harmony of extraordinary majesty filled the world.

Cottonmouth's sandals sank into the damp soil as he went in search of sticks to stake Morning Glory's body down. If she had been a member of his clan, he would have wrapped her in the finest blankets, showered her with rare shells and precious stone tools—but she was not, and he hadn't much time. Already his warriors would be growing restless, worrying about his odd behavior, ready to go home to their wives' beds.

Cottonmouth sifted through a pile of deadfall until he had selected nine sticks with sharp points. He tucked them into his belt, and went back to Morning Glory's side.

"I will Sing you to the afterworld," he murmured and began the Death Song in a low voice, just loud enough that the three strands of her braided soul could hear.

> *I have come with living waters,*
> *To give these healing ways of the Wolves,*

these healing ways of the living water Wolves.
Look northward now,
    down the pathway of living waters to the
Wolves in the Village of Wounded Souls.
Hear them call you?
    They are calling you,
        calling, calling.

Gripping her by the ankles, he walked into the pond. Cold water swirled around his knees. Her face sank below the dark surface, but her limp arms floated in a wealth of sinuous black hair. Through that half-open eye she watched him.

He rolled Morning Glory onto her left side, then turned her so that she faced north. "Look northward. Do you see the tunnel that leads to the Village of Wounded Souls? All ponds are openings to that distant afterworld, you know. You have a long way to swim, but there will be Spirit Helpers to guide you. Wait for Alligator, he'll show you the way."

With great care, he tucked her knees against her chest and drove one of his stakes through her sandal laces to keep her feet in place. The rest of the stakes he drove through the bloody fabric of her tunic, securing her to the bottom of the pond so she would not float free and lose sight of the tunnel. Black hair writhed in slow motion over Morning Glory's face, covering her open eye, but her perfect body lay calm and still beneath the glimmering veil of moonlit water.

She lay so quiet, like a woman dead for tens of tens of summers, rather than a single hand of time.

Cottonmouth waded out of the pond and piled logs around the edges of the grassy strip, blocking the gaps in the deadfall, making certain no animals could enter and drag her from her grave. Sister Moon's luminous face hung high above him. The Shining People had retreated to the far edges of her radiance, patiently waiting for her to sink into the Village of Wounded Souls so their own splendor could burst forth again.

Tomorrow Cottonmouth would order several warriors to return to the battle site and track down and capture each enemy who had escaped.

Two or three days from now, Musselwhite would start to panic, wondering what had happened to her husband and children, fearing the worst. It would not take long for her to mount a search party. She would do it over vehement protests from the Spirit Elders, who would warn her that if she left, the village would be almost defenseless.

But she would leave anyway.

Musselwhite would boldly face the rage of Sun Mother herself to keep her relatives from falling into Cottonmouth's hands. For two-tens-and-six summers his bitterness had been festering, eating him alive. She would rightly fear what tactics he might use to repay that old debt of honor.

He looked up to watch the bats flitting through the darkness, their wings flashing in the moonlight, and wondered what he would do when she came.

The ache in his chest grew overpowering. He dropped his head in his hands, and closed his eyes.

He knew only that he would be waiting for her.

Two

Gently, so that he made no sound, Diver gripped the palm frond blocking his path, and eased it forward. When he had stepped by, he returned the frond to its original position and released it. It barely swayed, tapping the dense tangle of grape vines on either side. He scanned the twilight forest, breathing hard, his legs shaking.

His thoughts had grown blurry, indistinct. For long hands of time, he could remember nothing, not his name, nor his clan, not even the direction which led home, then it would all come back in a terrifying rush and he would break out in a dead run.

A short length of dart shaft protruded from the lower left side of his back. It wouldn't stop bleeding. He pressed his hand over the wound, and tremors of pain possessed him. Every move he made caused the sharp chert point to slice deeper. He'd tried pulling out the shaft, but couldn't get a grip on it through the blood. He'd broken the shaft off . . . broken it . . . when?

Cottonmouth's warriors, he forced himself to think. *They attacked . . . the dart pierced my side. I fell. . . .*

He forced a swallow down his dry throat. Horrifying images of running men filled his souls.

He blinked at the tufts of fog that lay like cattail down in the thick vines looping the trees. As the evening cooled, the mist condensed and a constant patter of drops rained down upon the brown leaf mat of the forest floor, creating a faint drum-like cadence. Soaked to the bone, Diver shivered. Not even the hooded mid-thigh-length tunic he wore could shield him from the bitter wind. It sent probing fingers right through the fabric, taunting his skin.

Birds watched him with their feathers fluffed out for warmth, but few dared to chirp. The whole world had gone silent and glistening.

Only the mist moved.

Silver veils meandered around the broad bases of towering oaks, and climbed the trunks of pines to coil in their pointed tops.

Diver limped forward in ghostly silence. The single dart he carried had grown slick. He clutched it more tightly. He had tucked his atlatl, his dart thrower, into his belt. The weapon consisted of a piece of wood four hands long which had a shell hook in the end. When the butt of his dart was secured on the hook, the atlatl allowed him to cast his dart five times as far as he could have with his bare hand. Out on the sandy beaches, atlatls made lethal weapons, but in this dense forest he would be lucky to get a shot at all, let alone strike an enemy.

He pushed aside a curtain of hanging moss and saw a small pond ahead, crystal clear, ringed by lichen-covered logs. Mist haloed the surface. Desperately thirsty, Diver got down on his stomach and crawled toward it. Scents of wet leaves and grass filled his nostrils. He could not risk being out in the open for long . . . but he had to have water. He would die if he could not drink.

As he neared the pond, he saw the alligator that floated motionless in the center, covered entirely with green duckweed. Watching. Waiting. Diver's obsession with quiet, his shaking body, the scent of his fear, and blood, would tell the alligator all it needed to know about this hunt. The prey could not run much further. The desperate game Diver had been playing for two days would end soon. One way or another.

Diver's tunic whispered against the plants as he parted them, laid down his long dart, and stealthily dipped up a hand of the sweet cool water. He dipped another, and another, gulping the water, letting it run down his chin and throat, until he felt ill, then he sank into the grass and propped his chin on one hand. One of his souls, his reflection-in-water soul, stared at him from the calm surface of the pond. Knotted black hair framed his round face. That morning he had used charcoal from an old fire pit to paint his skin, but in the mist the designs had melted to gray smears which circled his brown eyes and flowed down around the corners of his wide mouth. A blood-caked lump the size of his fist protruded above his right temple. He stared at it, unable to recall being struck.

Blessed Spirits . . . what happened two days ago?

He had set out with a scouting party of eight to check the boundaries of their clan's territory. Stories had been filtering in on the lips of travelers that Cottonmouth planned to attack Windy Cove Village again, to steal food and women, and kill anyone who stood in his path. On the second day out, Diver's party had run headlong into two tens of Cottonmouth's warriors. He remembered the initial attack, being struck by the dart. . . .

He shook his head. But . . . what else? What else had happened?

Silver flashes of minnows darted through the water. Since the fight, he had eaten only what he could gather while moving, a few berries, some nuts. If he'd had the time, he could have woven a net from strips of palm fronds and netted these fish. But the snails inching along the dead logs would have to do. He plucked up several, corralled them with his left hand, then used his right hand to crush the shells, pull each snail out, and swallow it whole. His empty stomach cramped and squealed. He had slept little, allowing himself to doze for a few brief fingers of time before he rose and ran again. Trying to get home.

Old Man Fog thickened as darkness sheathed the forest, but Diver caught sight of some sort of berry, almost hidden in the leaves. Palm berries. He scratched the berries up and ate a handful. Pasty sweetness coated his tongue. Hallowed Spirits, what he would give for a single bite of Musselwhite's palm berry cakes. He had watched her make them tens of tens of times, mashing the palm berries, picking out the seeds, then mixing the gooey substance with pine nuts and pine sap. She spooned the concoction into big clamshells and let them cook slowly at the edges of the fire until they bubbled and steamed.

For just a moment, he granted himself the luxury of closing his eyes. Musselwhite's delicate oval face formed on the fabric of his souls. He smiled. Now that she was four tens and two summers old, silver strands mingled with her long black hair and lines grooved her forehead, but she had lost none of her beauty. Her full lips could still turn up in that ironic smile he loved so much, and her large black eyes still danced with mischief—though she let few people see those things. To most of the village she remained a hard-eyed leader: Musselwhite, the great warrior of the Windy Cove Clan, hero of the Pelican Isle Massacre. A woman to be revered, and feared.

With a trembling hand, Diver shoved his hood back and ran a hand through his wet hair. Exhaustion and pain so weighted him he could barely think, but his emotions soared and plunged like playing falcons.

Memories flashed . . . strange, mostly disconnected. He struggled to catch them, to piece them together. The night before the attack, he had been engaged in a violent argument with his son Blue Echo. Or . . . or had it been just moments before?

"*We are all going to die! Do you hear me, Father?*"

Blue Echo's voice crept from the depths of Diver's souls. A wavering image of his son's face formed, angry, the mouth hard, eyes glazed.

"*This scouting party was her idea, and she—*"

"And what would you have your mother do?" Diver had asked as he threw another stick of wood onto the fire. Sparks danced upward into the night sky. Trees canopied their camp, leaning over them, listening intently. His oldest son, Diamondback, and his daughter, Morning Glory, sat across the fire, staring unblinking into their gourd cups of tea. One by one, the other members of the scouting party left, politely seeking their blankets. Diver waited until they were gone. "Should your mother order our village to flee every time rumors of raiders fly? Or should she be prudent and try to verify their truth? That, my son, is our purpose."

Blue Echo's lips pursed unpleasantly. "Three of my friends died on the last scouting trip, Father. Three!"

"Death is part of a warrior's life. Your mother will assure that the murderers pay."

"Oh, yes." Blue Echo lurched to his feet. Against the shreds of mist, he seemed very tall for his ten-and-five summers, and on the verge of tears. He choked out, "And—and more of my friends will die this time. Maybe even my sister, brother, or my father. And why? Why, Father? Mother fights Cottonmouth at every turn! Why can't we just set our autumn camp further south, out of Cottonmouth's reach? It is *her* he's after, not us!"

Diver had massaged the back of his aching neck. Cottonmouth and Musselwhite had been lovers, as the boy perhaps knew; but Diver would not discuss it. Only Musselwhite had the right to tell her sons about her past.

"I cannot believe my ears," Diver said, and pinned Echo with his gaze. "My son asks why his clan cannot simply move their autumn camp. Just set it up elsewhere! Why not invite Cottonmouth into our camp and ask him to kick us about like mangy camp dogs? The humiliation would be the same."

Their clan moved three times each cycle. From winter solstice to spring equinox they lived far to the south, harvesting the plants and animals along the big shallow lakes. Then they packed up and journeyed northward to the inland rivers where they fished, stole birds' eggs, and collected tubers and roots. After Sun Mother's Celebration Day, they moved to their final camp near the ocean. Everyone loved this last camp most, because they could fish the fresh water rivers, collect nuts and berries, and dive for scallops, clams, and spiny lobsters off the coast.

"Echo," Diver added with a tired sigh, "the Windy Cove Clan has kept the same Autumn Camp for generations. Ten and two of your grandmothers are buried there. We can't just give it up because Cottonmouth wishes it."

"But why does he hate Mother so? Do you know, Father? It is almost as if she'd done something terrible to—"

"I will not listen to this," Diver warned in a low, hoarse voice. He gripped his gourd cup hard. "You are her son. Do not speculate about your mother's life before you were born. What she did and why is none of your concern. You—"

"You don't know, do you?" Blue Echo taunted. Firelight gilded his young face as he stepped closer to Diver. "Is that it? She has never told you? And you are her husband!"

Diver rose to his feet to face his son. "I know what she wishes me to know, and that is enough for me. I trust your mother."

"But, Father, surely you have heard the stories? People say—"

"*Stories?* You have been listening to *stories?* Did it give you pleasure to hear people saying bad things about your mother? Any of her other children would have killed the storyteller!"

"Father." Pain tinged the boy's voice. He extended his hands, pleading. "Will you tell me the truth? It is said that Mother and Cottonmouth used to be lovers. That she lived in his village. That she even bore him—"

Diver clenched both fists and shook them at the heavens. "Do not ask me these things!" he shouted. "Only your mother can answer such questions. If you had the courage to ask her, she might tell you. But no! You are too timid, too cowardly to face her with these, these, tales!"

For a sickening moment, images whirled . . . leaves blowing from the trees, spiraling across the ground. . . . Blue Echo's chest covered with blood, his eyes staring sightlessly at the tree boughs . . . leaves falling down, down . . . a dart thrusting up from Morning Glory's back . . . men running . . . screams . . . horrible screams.

Could his memory be correct? Had Cottonmouth's warriors attacked less than half a hand of time after Diver's shouting died away?

Diver opened his eyes. Darkness had flowed into the spaces between the trees, rousing the night insects. Hoppers churred in the grass while mosquitoes buzzed around his head.

Diver lowered a numb hand to pick up a golden leaf. Water droplets shimmered and twinkled in the gray twilight. Had any of his warriors escaped unhurt? Made it home? Was Musselwhite even now racing through the forests trying to find him?

"Oh, Musselwhite, forgive me."

Blessed Spirits, if he died, too, what would happen to her?

His gut twisted. She would take her children's deaths hard, but his death? Losing him would wound her very soul.

Diver plastered the cool leaf on the club wound, and tears filled his eyes.

"Oh, my wife, my wife. I have loved you so completely."

He dipped a handful of water to wash his face. The leaf came off. Blood smeared his fingers. His gaze focused on the red stain, but he did not really see it. Musselwhite's face smiled at him—from across a great distance. A time when they'd both been young, and filled with laughter and hope.

Diver had been her sole confidant for more than two-tens-and-five summers. She had shared her soul with him. Only Diver knew about the frightened little girl who lived inside Musselwhite's bones. Sometimes, at night, she wept in that child's pitiful voice, and he comforted her. Before every battle, every council meeting, every time the renowned warrior woman shouted, or negotiated, or displayed great courage, that little girl filled her dreams, and Diver could see the girl in her eyes, running, frantic, trying to find a place to hide.

A mournful smile moved Diver's lips. Long, long ago, he had built a shelter for that child in his heart—so she would always have a place to run to, a place where she would be safe. Would that little girl die without him as a refuge?

Heart pounding, Diver picked up his dart and dragged himself to his feet. Blood gushed from his wound. He bowed his head, gritting his teeth against the pain. For a time, he stood shaking. The alligator's eyes watched him. Quiet. Speculative. Probably wondering how much longer Diver could stay on his feet.

He forced his legs forward. As he entered the forest, Diver ducked low to clear a pine bough . . . and froze.

Cautious voices punctured the silence, coming toward him.

No. Oh, no.

Diver limped backward, then got down on his stomach and slid across the ground. The growing darkness might shield him if he could get far enough away from the trail. Pungent scents of rotting vegetation and moss rose as he scrambled for cover. Finally, he pulled himself behind a fallen log. Palmettos had grown up around it. Diver used his dart to push a frond to the left so he could see the deer trail.

Ahead, pale amber light suffused the mist, blushing color into the dark spreading limbs of a huge live oak. The light bounced, like a torch being carried, and tree shadows danced to the rhythm, painting the forest with odd stripes and elongated diamonds. Diver held his breath. In the shifting heart of that weave, men walked.

It took an eternity before the first warrior appeared.

Tall, no more than two tens of summers, he held the torch high. He walked so close Diver could smell his sweat. Two other men came behind the first, laughing softly at some private joke. They followed their leader around a curve and disappeared into the trees. Their voices faded. The bouncing golden halo marked their path as they veered away from him, heading north.

Were there others?

He listened.

Night hawks called across the twilight woods, and somewhere far away Diver heard the wail of a conch horn. Three short blasts. *Where are you?* Two long blares answered. *Here.* Then two short and one long. *We are making camp for the night.*

Hope turned his breathing shallow. He wet his chapped lips. It might be Musselwhite. If one of Diver's warriors had escaped the battle and run all the way home . . .

He fought his confusion. Was that possible? So soon? How far was home? He did not even know his position, let alone where Windy Cove Village sat. Diver struggled to think. Sun Mother had descended to his right, that meant south lay straight ahead. He drew a line on the fabric of his soul, trying to trace his winding course through the forest over the past two days. Windy Cove could not be more than half a day's run to the southeast. Could it? No, no, he—he felt certain of that.

It really *might* be Musselwhite.

Trembling, he drew himself to his knees, and inhaled a deep breath. . . .

The forest went quiet around him.

The impact of the dart sent Diver toppling backward, his feet flying from under him as he struck the forest floor.

A warrior erupted out of the swirling mist, and his shrill war cry shattered the night. The youth leaped the fallen log and stood over Diver with his dart poised to strike again. A wildly swinging torch light came up behind him, casting his shadow against the trees like a dancing giant.

"Old fool!" the warrior snarled. "Did you think we would not see the places in the trail where you dragged your left foot? We were just waiting for you to show yourself!"

Three

What's she doing out there?" Thorny Boy asked.

Seedpod patted his six-summers-old grandson's plump cheek, and his old eyes drifted to where Musselwhite stood, alone, on the beach. "She's waiting for your father."

As evening deepened, wavering translucent veils of rain swept in off the ocean, and the feathery shadows of live oaks and brush gradually pooled with the night. An unearthly silence took hold of the land, broken only by the whine of mosquitoes, the soft conversations of people cooking supper, and the gentle pattering of rain.

Seedpod handed Thorny Boy his supper bowl. The roasted catfish sent a tendril of steam up to tickle the boy's pug nose. Thorny Boy smiled. With his round face and light brown eyes, he looked very much like his father, Diver. He wore a tan, loose-fitting tunic that fell to just below his hips. A thin strip of fabric encircled his forehead to keep his unruly black hair out of his eyes.

"The fish is very hot, Thorny Boy," Seedpod said. "Test it before you put it in your mouth."

"I'll blow on it, Grandfather." Thorny Boy lifted his bowl and began blowing on his fish to cool it. "Isn't mother going to eat with us?"

"No, I—I don't think so."

Seedpod left his own bowl sitting on the floor mat to cool. Flickers of firelight danced over his shelter. Open-sided, three body-lengths across and four long, it consisted of four pine poles sunk into the earth, roofed with palm fronds. Coils of cordage and fishing nets draped from pegs on the poles, while fabric bags hung from the rafters. Seedpod wove his bags large and in two shapes, circular and globular. They bulged with smoked fish, hickory and pine nuts, armloads of fresh persimmons, gourds of differing sizes, and other belongings he wanted to keep from prowling animals. Raccoons proved the most pesky. Not a night went by that someone in the village didn't wake to the scritching sounds of a raccoon climbing the shelter poles to bat around the food bags.

Seedpod lived alone now. His wife had died two summers ago, and after her passing he had reluctantly begun arranging the shelters for his own convenience. Woven palmetto mats covered the floor to keep the ground's chill from leeching into his old bones. Along the shelter's northern side, a folded pile of blankets and clean tunics marked the location of his bed, and just above where his head rested at night, a small gourd pot hung from the pole, filled with a mixture of grease and marsh-flea bane. He rubbed the mixture on his skin to keep away biting insects. A small firepit lay in the middle of the floor, and along the southern side was everything else he owned. A big wooden bowl sitting beside the southeastern pole held an oak pestle, a flat stirring paddle, and several chert scrapers and choppers, all for preparing food. Two baskets, with lids, nestled alongside the bowl. One contained bone sewing awls, a spinning whorl to make thread, and an antler punch for holing leather. A chunk of dead coral, which he used as a hammerstone, lay on the floor in front of that basket. The other basket protected his jewelry: hairpins made from the leg bones of dogs and deer, drilled shark's teeth necklaces, and a variety of seashell pendants. Finally, a loom, just two wooden sticks really, leaned against the southwestern shelter post. Balls of fine palm thread filled his biggest circular bags, waiting to be woven into bright hoods, or blankets, or clothing.

His most precious possessions, three brightly painted Power bundles, hung on the northeastern pole. They had not talked in a long time, but

Seedpod knew they still lived. His heart could hear them breathing. When he'd been young and filled with life, the Spirits in the bundles had walked in his Dreams, guiding him, teaching him secrets no other human knew. The Spirit of the sea bundle had allowed him to ride on the cloudy back of Storm Girl once. . . . But the Spirits slept now.

Rain began to beat harder on Seedpod's roof. He gazed out at the village. Eight other shelters dotted the plaza. People sat around their fires, talking quietly. Many had pulled up their hoods to shield their faces from windblown rain drops, but it did little good when strong gusts pummeled the beach. On three sides, forest cradled Windy Cove Village; the fourth opened eastward, to endless ocean.

"I think mine's cool enough," Thorny Boy said. He reached pudgy hands into his bowl, gripped the small catfish, then stopped. "Grandfather, are you sure I shouldn't run and tell mother that supper is ready?"

"I don't think she's hungry, Grandson. Let us start without her. She'll be in soon. I'm sure of it."

Thorny Boy gave Seedpod a worried look as he stripped the skin from his fish and stuffed it into his mouth.

Musselwhite had been out there since sunrise, her long dart propped on the ground before her, face turned into the wind, peering up the trail that led north. Like all the people, she wore a hooded loose-fitting tunic, cut wide at the neck and belted at the waist with a cord. Black hair whipped around the edges of her hood. In the sky behind her, Lightning Birds rode the storm winds. Their jagged tail feathers slashed the sky as they leapt from their perches in the clouds and plunged downward, hunting the ocean for whales and dolphins.

Thorny Boy licked his lips. "Grandfather?" he asked. "Did Mother tell you about the bad dreams she had last night."

Seedpod frowned. "No, she didn't. What dreams?"

Thorny Boy swallowed his bite of fish. "She was moaning. It woke me up. She said she kept hearing my father call her name. Over and over, like he needed her. Once," he said and lowered his voice, "she even whispered Cottonmouth's name."

The wrinkles of Seedpod's gaunt face rearranged themselves. He could feel the mass of crisscrossing lines curve around his sharp nose and carve deep crevasses at the edges of his thin lips. The entire village had spent the night in wakefulness. At dusk, a thin directionless wind had begun to whimper through the shelters, shaking bags and clacking gourd bowls together, as if in warning.

He kissed the top of Thorny Boy's head. "Your father is only a day late. If they found suspicious markings in the forest, they would have had to track them out. Sometimes such things take a while. Your mother shouldn't be worried."

Thorny Boy flipped his catfish over and peeled the roasted skin from the other side. Tatters of firelight mottled his intent little face. "She is, though, and I don't think she wants a second husband, either."

Seedpod peered at him suddenly. "How do you know about that? Did your mother say something?"

Thorny Boy pulled off a long piece of white meat and put it in his mouth. While he chewed, he responded, "Mother said my father is enough for her."

"For two-tens-and-five summers I have respected that sentiment. But we live in a far more dangerous world now." Rain gusted into the shelter, and Seedpod grabbed for his hood, pulling it up to cover his white hair. The tiny top shells sewn to his sleeves tinkled as the wind thrashed about the shelter and ran away into the forest. "We need this alliance, Thorny Boy. Pondwader's clan has many warriors, five times as many as we do. Cottonmouth will think twice about attacking us if he knows he will be facing the combined forces of Windy Cove Clan and Heartwood Clan."

Thorny Boy rubbed his pug nose and grease smeared his face. It glimmered in the firelight. "But why does mother have to marry when she doesn't wish to? Why can't somebody else marry this Pondwader so we can get his warriors to help us?"

Seedpod pulled a piece of flesh from his own catfish and ate it. A swaying curtain of rain poured from the roof, momentarily obscuring Seedpod's view of Musselwhite.

"Because, Grandson, the matron of the Heartwood Clan, old Moonsnail, is cunning. This Pondwader is a very special young man. He's a Lightning Boy. Moonsnail would accept no woman from our little clan except the great Musselwhite."

Thorny Boy's dark eyes widened and his mouth opened, revealing a half-chewed piece of fish. "He's a Lightning Boy? I might have a Lightning Boy *living* with me?"

"We shall see."

Power nested in Lightning Boys like turtles in sand. When a bolt of lightning penetrated a woman's womb, the flash burned all the color from the child, and left it as pale as a comb jellyfish. The coloring varied, so that the last Lightning Boy in Windy Cove Clan, born more than ten tens of summers ago, had been called the Blue Lightning Boy. He'd had the characteristic white hair and pink skin, but his eyes had been the color of Brother Sky. Pondwader was called the White Lightning Boy. The fiery flash in his mother's womb had burned every shred of color from him, leaving even his eyes so translucent you could see the tiny blood vessels pulsing beneath.

Tens of legends revolved around Lightning Boys and their role in the creation and destruction of worlds. Pondwader, Seedpod had heard, was greatly feared by his clan.

"Did that nasty woman tell you about this Lightning Boy?" Thorny Boy asked.

"Yes. Her name is Dark Rain. That nasty woman was Pondwader's mother."

Thorny Boy blinked in surprise. "I hope Pondwader is nothing like Dark Rain. She was a mean woman. She slapped little Lizard Girl. Did you hear about that?"

Seedpod frowned. Dark Rain's reputation for wickedness and cunning spanned the world. She had been known to lure men into her lair, wring every bit of pleasure from them that she could, then, when she tired of them, slit their throats . . . or so the Traders said. Every summer they brought new and thrilling stories about her exploits.

"What did Lizard Girl do to deserve the slap?"

"Nothing!" Thorny Boy insisted. "She just crouched down beside Dark Rain during a dice game, and Dark Rain struck her right in the back of the head, and yelled at her to go away!" He plucked a bone out of his fish and dragged it to the side of his bowl. "I hope Pondwader isn't mean."

"Even if he is, he won't be for long. Not if he marries your mother. He wouldn't dare."

Summers ago Seedpod had given up on making an alliance with Heartwood Clan. They had too much wealth and power to be interested in any of the available women from Windy Cove. Then, two nights before, Dark Rain had abruptly appeared in Seedpod's shelter and made the offer: Pondwader had not yet taken a wife. Would Musselwhite be interested in him?

Seedpod could not believe his ears. Everyone for three tens of days distance had heard of Pondwader.

"Can you, an Outcast woman, accomplish this?" he'd asked.

Dark Rain had smiled. *"I can—for a price. You see, I have some gambling debts. . . ."*

More to himself than Thorny Boy, Seedpod murmured. "I wouldn't have to think about this marriage if Cottonmouth had any souls. But—"

"What?" Thorny Boy slid around to stare up at Seedpod. A bit of catfish skin hung from his nose. "Do you really think Cottonmouth has no souls?"

"Oh, he's soulless, all right. And as heartless as that dead fish in your bowl."

Thorny Boy looked into his bowl, then returned his gaze to Seedpod. "How long has he been soulless?"

"How long?"

"Yes. When did his souls fly away?"

The rain had slowed to a misty shower again, pattering on the roof, and drenching the palmetto floor mats when the wind gusted. Seedpod tucked the hem of his tunic around his hips for warmth.

"Well," Seedpod said, "your mother would tell you that Cottonmouth has never had any souls. But I think it happened two summers ago. Do you recall that Dream Cottonmouth had? No, maybe not. You were very young.

It happened just before Sun Mother's Celebration Day. Since then he's acted like a rabid panther, snapping at anything in sight. But I don't think his souls just up and flew away like sparrows. No, indeed."

Thorny Boy set down his bowl, stretched out on the mat, and put his head in Seedpod's lap. Sleep tugged at his eyelids. "Then what happened to them?"

Seedpod whispered, "I think the Lightning Birds soared down and blasted his souls clean out of his body."

"Why? As punishment?"

"Certainly. If you had created the world, what would you do to a puny human who claimed he knew the day it would end? It's like . . . well, claiming you have the Power of the Creators."

Thorny Boy yawned deeply, said, "I hate Cottonmouth," and leaned back against Seedpod's arm. Seedpod bent over to arrange the boy's hood around his face to shelter it from the chilling wind.

Cottonmouth's Dream . . . Traders had spread the story.

In the Time Before the World, only Hurricane Breather and the Lightning Birds existed. Then, one day, the female Lightning Bird laid a thunderegg in Hurricane Breather's eye, and sneaked away with her husband to the edge of the great winds to watch. When the thunderegg hatched, a blue world spun out, and it scared Hurricane Breather half to death. He was furious! He tried to dash the world to bits. Both of the Lightning Birds got together and talked it over, deciding whether they ought to try to save the world. The male didn't want to, but the female did. Finally, they created Four Shining Eagles, stationed them at the four corners of the sky, and ordered them to hold down Hurricane Breather's arms and legs, so he couldn't move. Now and then, Hurricane Breather would manage to sit up and a great hurricane would blast the coasts, snapping whole forests into kindling, and killing tens of people, but nothing like the devastation which would occur when the Eagles died.

A sad smile came to Seedpod's lips.

The Eagles had been faithfully holding back the winds of destruction ever since. But the great Soul Dancers, like crazy old Dogtooth, said the Eagles had grown old and frail.

That's why Cottonmouth's Dream had frightened everyone. He claimed that Sun Mother had promised to send him a Lightning Boy who would shoot down the Eagles. Then she had vowed to send the Lightning Birds to save Cottonmouth and anyone who would follow him. They would be carried up to a shining new world beyond the stars.

Thorny Boy started snoring softly.

Seedpod used his fingers to rake off one side of the catfish's flesh and ate it while he thought. Only fools believed such things. But followers had been flocking to Cottonmouth's village, hoping to be among the chosen who would survive.

Seedpod shook his head, wondering about Cottonmouth . . . and Pond-wader. How could anyone bear to think about that terrible day? When the last Eagle fell, Sister Moon would bury her face in the clouds and weep falling stars. Sun Mother's eye would slowly turn blacker and blacker until she could see only darkness, and then Hurricane Breather would suck up Sea Girl and Brother Earth and swallow them whole. . . . All would be as it had been in the beginning, Hurricane Breather blowing around and around, while the Lightning Birds danced in his eyes.

Seedpod whispered, "Yes, Cottonmouth deserved to die for saying such a thing. He's fortunate that the Lightning Birds took pity on him and just killed his souls. Though Sun Mother knows, a man without any souls has no eyes in his heart. He is blind to emotions. I can think of nothing more—"

"If I'd been Cottonmouth," Thorny Boy murmured sleepily, surprising Seedpod. "I would have asked the Lightning Birds to kill me and get it over with."

"Maybe the Lightning Birds are trying to teach him a lesson before they blast him."

Thorny Boy yawned again, wide and long. Golden light flickered over his plump cheeks as he turned his face toward the crackling fire. "Grandfather, what will happen to us if my mother doesn't want to marry Pondwader, and Cottonmouth attacks our village again?"

"Oh, let's not talk about it. It's too terrifying."

"Mother doesn't want Pondwader, you know she doesn't."

"Of course, I know. But it's necessary. If you were of age, I'd be looking for a powerful mate for you, too. A woman from a clan with many warriors and much wealth. Just like Pondwader's clan. Your mother will get used to the idea. And Pondwader . . . well, he'll be a good husband to her. I'm sure he will."

Thorny Boy thought about that, his little mouth moving. "And maybe she will even like him."

Seedpod looked out at Musselwhite. Rain had drenched her hood and tunic, making the fabric cling to her tall body like a second skin. Despite bearing twelve children, she remained as slender as a woman half her four tens and two summers. In the flashes of lightning, Seedpod could see water glistening on Musselwhite's beautiful face and long legs.

"Well," Seedpod said. "I hope she likes the boy. But I doubt she'll ever love him. She has room for only one man in her souls, and that's your father. May the Lightning Birds protect him. I don't know what your mother would do if something happened to Diver."

"Or me," Thorny Boy said. "I don't know what I would do if . . ." He couldn't finish.

Seedpod patted his grandson's leg. Thorny Boy knew death. Windy Cove Clan had been attacked three times since last winter's Celebration Day. The child had seen uncles and brothers killed, female cousins stolen. Thorny Boy's best friend, Coral, had been stolen by Cottonmouth eight moons ago. Coral and his mother, Glasswort. She had been a good woman, a valued member of their clan. Glasswort had tried to help everyone. They all missed her.

Thorny Boy thoughtfully picked at a loose thread in the skirt of his tunic, and watched the fires in the village going out. Hazes of windblown sand filled the air as people smothered their flames.

"Grandfather, may I sleep with you? Mother might stand in the rain all night."

"Of course, you may. Why don't you go crawl under my blanket. I'll be there soon. I want to drink one more cup of warm tea."

"Thank you, Grandfather." He got up, hugged Seedpod's neck, then trotted across the shelter and slipped beneath the red-striped blanket, leaving just the black top of his head showing.

Seedpod set his bowl in his lap and finished his cold fish. Indeed, Musselwhite might stand in the rain all night. Seedpod didn't blame her. He felt it, too, that sense of foreboding. Last night, every time Seedpod had closed his eyes, his memory painted dead men, dead animals, dead fish washing up on the shore, as if his soul writhed in some magical trap, and he could not escape.

In a gust of wind, the shelters creaked and moaned. The air smelled like washed stone, damp and earthy. Here and there the clouds had parted, and he could see the Shining People canoeing through the clean sky on their way to the Daybreak Land.

Seedpod exhaled a small breath. Thunderstorm, his wife, lived there, hunting and fishing, laughing. It pained him that he would probably never see her again. Only those who died peacefully left this world on the backs of the shooting stars and were carried up beyond the sky to join the Shining People. Those who died violently went to a different afterworld. They had to swim through a long dark tunnel to get to the Village of Wounded Souls, a place of snow and cold and constant battles. Just the thought of that cold made his bones ache.

The fabric bags tied to the rafters creaked in the wind. Seedpod listened to them, but his eyes focused on the forest. What were those shadowy figures? Sentries, probably. But they might be ghosts. Seedpod had been quite a warrior in his time. He had killed tens of men, old men, young men, boys barely beyond the manhood rituals, even a few women warriors. Some of those souls still prowled the darkness. They had remained on earth too long before their families found them to be able to leave. Seedpod knew each one. Their faces had been carved into his soul, some bathed in rays of slanting afternoon sun, others in the dim, gray light of dusk. Still other luminous faces stared at him, dyed lavender by the gleam of a long ago dawn.

Strange that he saw them as they had been moments before death, rather than after, their glazed eyes blinded by blood and dust.

They had been enemies then . . . but over the long summers, they had become friends, appearing to warn him of impending battle, or heartache.

For two nights, he'd thought he had seen them, stalking the forest, their transparent bodies awash in silver starlight. In his dreams, they whispered truths so monstrous that he could not, would not, let himself believe.

In the silent recesses of his souls, muted voices wailed, *"No, no, he can't be. Musselwhite will break into little pieces."*

For two-tens-and-five summers, Diver had stood like a rock wall between Musselwhite and the world, encouraging, supporting her. Only Diver and Seedpod knew the times Musselwhite had sobbed through the night after seeing friends die. Musselwhite believed that a War Leader had to be invincible before her warriors, that any frailties she showed weakened everyone around her. But it meant she could never be truly human—not in front of anyone. Except Diver. And, on occasion, Seedpod.

He let out a breath. Four sentries stood watch on the outskirts of the village. A short, stocky shadow moved through the northern oaks, and he knew Black Urchin manned that position. The sentries would shout an alarm if raiders appeared.

Thorny Boy started to snore softly.

Seedpod picked up his gourd cup of tea, hooked his atlatl on his belt, and grabbed three darts, then tiptoed out of the shelter into the misty rain. His bare feet sank into the wet sand as he headed for his daughter. The Shining People lit the beach brilliantly, shadowing every seashell and leaf, and spawning ominous shapes that seemed to dance through the coastal trees.

Pools of rainwater glistened in every hollow.

Seedpod stood by Musselwhite in silence for a moment, following his daughter's gaze up the shore into veils of rain.

"You have sentries posted, why don't you try to get some sleep?"

Musselwhite barely moved. "I won't sleep, father. I'll just lie in my bedding and stare at the rafters. I am of more use here."

"Any sign of raiders?"

"No."

"The village has been quiet, too. Other than a curious spotted skunk who wandered in about sunset and had everybody fleeing for their lives, it's been an uneventful night."

Seedpod's gaze drifted over the charcoal and silver landscape, checking every oddly shaped patch of starlight that penetrated the clouds, every waving palm frond, climbing the trees to look for enemy warriors hidden in the tangles of branches. "I brought my atlatl. I thought I'd stand guard with you for a while."

Musselwhite did not turn, but her eyes narrowed. Softly, she responded,

"I don't want you out here for long. This rain will eat straight to the marrow of your bones."

"Well," Seedpod said. "My marrow can stand it—for a while." He propped his darts in front of him and adjusted his hood, pulling it closed at his wrinkled throat. Already he could feel the warmth leaching from his muscles. "You shouldn't be so worried," he admonished. "Maybe they stopped to hunt a deer, or found a whale washed up on the beach and butchered some meat to bring home. They've only been out an extra day. That's nothing. Why, when I used to go on war walks, we would often—"

"Father." A deep breath expanded Musselwhite's lungs. She let it out slowly. "Diver would have sent a runner to tell us they were going to be late. Something . . ." her voice faded. "Something went wrong."

Seedpod looked down into his half-full cup of tea, and he could see the Shining People's souls. He wondered which one was Thunderstorm. Probably one of the stars in that cluster, she would want people around her. She loved to talk. Seedpod took a sip of the fruity tea and handed it to Musselwhite. "If you're going to be standing here all night, I'll bring you dinner. Thorny Boy and I roasted catfish. We put two fish in your bowl, and set it close to the fire to keep warm. Is there anything else you want me to bring you?"

"I'm not hungry, Father, I—"

A hoarse cry made them both freeze.

Someone shouted, *"Musselwhite! Musselwhite, where are you?"*

All over the village, people leaped from their bedding and raced toward the forest, where a confused din of voices erupted. Musselwhite ran. As she crossed the village, people surged toward her, tunics billowing in the wind, shouting questions. Musselwhite demanded, "What is it? What's happened?"

"In the forest!" someone answered. "Black Urchin called you! He found a wounded man—"

Musselwhite yelled, *"Diver?"* and Seedpod could hear the hope bursting her chest as she shoved through the crowd and vanished into the trees.

Seedpod hurried across the village as quickly as his aching legs would carry him, and took the path Musselwhite had taken. A knot of people had formed around Black Urchin and Musselwhite. They bent over someone, blocking the view of the man's face.

"Who is it?" Seedpod asked as he shouldered through the crowd. "Is it Diver?"

"No," Black Urchin said and straightened up. "It's Diamondback. He's hurt badly. I don't know how he made it this far." Black Urchin's round face tensed with fear.

Musselwhite knelt beside her son, and Seedpod crouched on the opposite side, surveying the youth's body for injuries. Crusted blood matted Diamondback's tunic to his thigh. The dart had gone clear through, leaving a clotted hole where he'd broken off the shaft and pulled it out. Sweat-soaked black hair stuck to his forehead and the high arches of his cheeks. He blinked up at Seedpod, smiled frailly, then turned to Musselwhite, his eyes drowsy.

"Mother—"

"What happened, my son?" She tenderly smoothed wet hair away from his face. "Where are the other members of the scouting party?" she asked.

Diamondback broke into dry sobs and Seedpod said, "The questions can wait. Diamondback needs to rest and eat. Black Urchin, carry him to my shelter. I—"

"No, Grandfather, please," Diamondback said feebly, and reached for Musselwhite; she gripped his hand tightly.

Gently, Musselwhite repeated, "Where are the other members of the scouting party?"

Diamondback swallowed and swallowed as if trying to wet a dust-dry throat. "Mother . . . dead. They're all dead." He drew her hand to his face and pressed it against his cheek. Sobs wracked his body. "Oh, Mother, it was terrible! Blue Echo was the first . . . darted through the heart . . . then Morning Glory. Father . . ."

Musselwhite clasped Diamondback's hand urgently, and her mouth tightened. "Your father?"

Diamondback looked up with huge eyes. "I saw him fall, Mother. Saw the dart, in his side . . . then a warrior clubbed him. . . ."

He kept talking, but Seedpod could tell that Musselwhite no longer heard. Her gaze focused on the darkness, as if her souls had left her body and floated somewhere high above.

"Dead?" someone behind Seedpod shouted. "Diver is dead? And all the others, too? Is that what Diamondback said?"

The words seemed to pierce Musselwhite like a well-aimed dart. She closed her eyes as the news traveled from mouth to mouth, *"Diver is dead. . . . Diver is dead. . . ."*

Musselwhite leaned over and kissed her son on the temple, whispering, "Rest now, my son. Your grandfather is right. We—"

"Oh, Mother," Diamondback wept, and clung desperately to her hand. "I couldn't do anything. You must believe me. They struck so fast, none of us even had time to nock our darts."

"Thank the Spirits that you escaped to warn us," Musselwhite said. "We will speak more of this in the morning. You're tired and sick. You must sleep, my son." She waved to Black Urchin. "Help him up."

Diamondback didn't want to release Musselwhite. She kissed his fingers and pulled her hand away, then got to her feet.

The crowd had gone silent. People stared at her as she walked past them, out into the trees, and disappeared among the shadows.

"Where's she going?" Black Urchin whispered to Seedpod. "It's dangerous out there, we don't know where they were attacked! Cottonmouth might be—"

"Close your mouth," Seedpod ordered. He felt weak, dazed. "I want half of this village standing watch tonight. Find every able-bodied person who can use an atlatl. It will be your duty, Black Urchin, to decide where to place them. Go now. Move. I will find two other men to carry Diamondback to my shelter."

He nodded obediently. "Yes, Spirit Elder. I—I will."

"What now, Grandfather?" Diamondback choked out the words. "What will we do? We just lost one third of our warriors! We are almost defenseless."

"Don't fret about it tonight, Grandson," he said gently and stroked his grandson's arm. "Tomorrow, the Spirit Elders will gather to discuss it. We'll figure out something."

Seedpod pointed to two young men in the crowd. "Ragged Wing. Shoal. Come. Carry Diamondback to my shelter."

The two youths trotted forward to obey, slipping their hands beneath Diamondback's knees and their arms around his back. They lifted him. Seedpod led the way back to the village with people following in a flood.

Seedpod's heart ached for Musselwhite. When Thunderstorm died, Seedpod had gone for a long walk down the beach. He had just wanted to feel the cool sea against his legs, and the spray coating his face—while he remembered little things, the way Thunderstorm's gray brows arched when she smiled, the feel of her arms around him, the sound of her voice in the darkness.

Old Ashleaf hobbled up beside Seedpod as he passed, his bushy white hair awry around his lean face. He carried a walking stick with him. "Seedpod?" he said softly. "Where is Musselwhite? We must call a meeting tonight to discuss this matter. We need her here."

Seedpod waved Shoal and Ragged Wing by him and stopped to peer into the old man's faded brown eyes. He had a deeply seamed brown face, like the flesh of an ancient palm berry. "Let us speak of this tomorrow, Ashleaf. Tonight, Musselwhite has a husband and two children to mourn. That is more than enough to occupy her."

Four

Kelp trotted through the forest behind her older brother, veering around dogwood and buttonbrush limbs until they found the white-tailed deer trail that led over the hill next to Bird Lake Marsh. Mist fluttered close to the ground. It hid the marsh, but she could hear ducks quaking, frogs croaking, and the splashes of diving turtles.

Pondwader, a summer older than Kelp, halted at a turn in the trail to listen. After a few moments, he motioned for Kelp to get down. Raiders had been sneaking through the forests, and they had to be very careful. She dropped to her stomach and lay flat on the dew-soaked red and gold leaves. Pungent scents of deer dung and pine needles filled her nose. What did Pondwader see? He cautiously walked ahead. The pale green color of his long robe melted into the forest background, but his waist-length white hair caught the diffused light like a torch, reflecting it back in rainbow waves.

Kelp followed him with her eyes. Everybody else in the village wore short tunics, but Pondwader's robe dragged the ground, had long sleeves, and an attached hood—to protect him from Sun Mother's wrath. Sun Mother didn't like Pondwader. She blistered his skin at every opportunity.

Pondwader glanced over his shoulder and signaled Kelp forward.

"Are you sure?" she called softly, wetting her lips. The closer they got to the Sacred Pond, the more her knees shook. They had been running since long before dawn to get here, and if they left this very moment, they wouldn't reach home before dark. Pondwader had to visit the Pond, he'd said, but Kelp didn't know why he had begged her to come along. "What if . . . what if there are alligators there?"

Pondwader turned to smile at her. He had a straight nose and odd eyes, pink, transparent as a fish scale. At the age of ten and five summers, he stood a head taller than any other boy in the village. The White Lightning Boy, her people called him, the first of his kind to be born in ten tens of summers.

"Of course there will be alligators, Kelp," Pondwader said. "They guard the souls of the dead. I would be very worried if there weren't any. It isn't much farther. Come on."

He ducked beneath a palmetto frond and headed up the hill.

Kelp frowned. His appearance still startled and awed her. Many people ran from him. Legends proclaimed that a Lightning Boy would shoot down the Four Shining Eagles who floated at the corners of the world, holding back the winds of destruction.

Kelp glanced up the hill. Her brother had craned his neck, studying something. Pondwader, shoot down an eagle? Not likely. He couldn't hit the ocean with a dart. He had to squint to see anything more than a few hands from his face. Before he'd be able to kill a sacred eagle, he'd have to sprout wings and fly close enough to use his dart as a spear, and even then, she doubted he could do it. Every time he caught a minnow, tears filled his eyes, and he had to Sing an apology over its soul before he could use it for fishing bait.

Kelp just couldn't believe he was truly a Lightning Boy. It didn't make sense. Lightning Boys happened when a bolt of lightning penetrated the womb of a very good woman—and, Hallowed Spirits knew, their mother rivaled Hurricane Breather for wickedness. Kelp *hated* her mother. Dark Rain had shamed their clan so many times Kelp had lost count. Only yesterday Pondwader had fought with his best friend, Dace, because he'd called their mother "a whore who would trade her souls for a clamshell necklace." Clamshells, of course, possessed no value because they could be found anywhere. Pondwader had lost the bout in less than ten heartbeats. He couldn't fight any better than he could use an atlatl. Grandmother Moonsnail said Pondwader would outgrow his awkwardness some day soon. Kelp prayed it happened before Pondwader had so many sharp knots on his head that he resembled an alligator or snapping turtle.

"Kelp?" Pondwader lifted a hand and motioned to her, then strode up the hill with his long robe flowing about him.

Sunlight permeated the tree branches, scattering fistfuls of golden diamonds across her path as she picked her way around a huge prickly-pear cactus, and followed him up the slope.

When Kelp crested the hill, she saw Pondwader lying on the top, examining the opposite side. He called, "Kelp? Are you sure this is the right trail?"

"Of course," she answered. "There's the old burned out tree over there, Pondwader."

"Huh?" He turned around. "Near that black splotch?"

"That splotch *is* the tree, Pondwader."

He blinked. "Oh."

She shook her head and trudged toward him. The understory had thinned out, and huge pine, hickory, and oak trees rose, their branches lacing together into a many-shaded mosaic over her head. Yellow leaves pirouetted out of the sky. Kelp slid the warclub hooked to her belt around to her back, and lay on the damp leaf mat beside Pondwader.

"If you stay very quiet," Pondwader murmured, "you can hear them from here." He tilted his head, listening, and his white hair dragged in the leaves.

Kelp concentrated. Sounds echoed from every part of the forest. Squirrels chittered in the branches around them, several different sorts of birds sang, frogs croaked. "Hear what?"

Pondwader squinted curiously. "You don't hear them?"

"I hear geese quacking, a jaybird chattering . . ." Her voice trailed away when an indigo snake slithered around the trunk of an oak and headed straight for her. She stiffened. Longer than both of their bodies laid end to end, it had a reddish jaw and almost black scales.

"It's not poisonous," Pondwader whispered.

"No, but . . . but it's so . . ." She swallowed hard. " . . . *big*. Look how big it is!"

Pondwader smiled at her and turned to the snake. "Hello, Grandfather," he said. The snake halted and coiled, as if the rabbit fur softness of Pondwader's voice soothed and fascinated it. "It's all right," Pondwader continued. "We are not hunting snakes today, just old Dogtooth. Have you seen him?"

"Dogtooth!" Kelp spun to glare. "What—"

Pondwader held up a hand to halt her words.

The snake's tongue licked out, then it slithered off in the direction of the Pond, tumbling acorns aside as it fled into the shadows.

Kelp grabbed the fabric over her pounding heart. "That was a warning, Pondwader! Did you see the look in its eyes? Snake Above sent it to tell us to go back to the village before it's too late!"

"Too late?" he inquired. "Too late for what?"

"I don't know! Those ghosts down there might not like us coming to see them! Maybe they'll wring our necks, or drown us or—"

"But, Kelp," Pondwader said gently, "don't you hear them calling to us, welcoming us? Besides, even if they wished to, Dogtooth wouldn't let them. He's meeting us and he's almost as Powerful as Sun Mother. Dogtooth wants us to speak with Aunt Fin. He says—"

"What are you talking about?" Kelp stared open-mouthed at her brother. "Aunt Fin died in Cottonmouth's raid half a moon ago!"

"Yes," he answered matter-of-factly, "but her voice is still alive." Pondwader grinned again, rose, and headed down the hill at a trot, with long white hair fluttering out behind him.

Kelp couldn't move.

Dead voices and Dogtooth. Both terrified her. But she thought maybe Dogtooth actually terrified her more. He'd been known to change humans he didn't like into loathsome things like sea slugs and pond slime.

On the last crescent moon, he'd wandered into their village, dressed in filthy rags, gathered up the Spirit Elders and told them he'd just returned from a long flight on the backs of the Lightning Birds. He said he'd visited the Four Shining Eagles. Then he had lowered his voice, and whispered that the Eagles were dying, that all their tail feathers had fallen out, and they struggled to fly on only one wing now. The Elders' ancient faces had twisted in horror. Since the first moments of Pondwader's birth people had feared the end of the world might be near. Now, they were certain.

When Pondwader noticed Kelp hadn't followed, he stopped and cupped a hand to his mouth, calling, "Are you coming?"

"I . . . Pondwader . . . have you heard Aunt Fin's voice since—since we buried her?"

He shook his head. "No, but Dogtooth says today is the day. He wants to show me how to talk to ghosts."

"Well, I don't think you should do it! He's an old madman. And . . . and he doesn't even like you!"

Pondwader sighed, and hiked back up the hill. Getting down on his knees, he stretched his tall body out on the leaves in front of her and gripped her hand. Faint glimmers of sunlight danced in his depthless eyes. "I must, Kelp, and I want you there with me."

"What for?"

Puffs of mist glided around them, trailing long tails over the ground, and painting the palmettos with a soft sheen of moisture. Pondwader ducked his head. He pulled a pine needle out of the leaf mat. "I—I'm a little afraid, Kelp, I—"

"So don't go!"

"But, Kelp . . ." His brow furrowed and he thoughtfully twirled the green needle in his fingers. "Dogtooth says Aunt Fin has been asking for me, and I loved Aunt Fin. Didn't you?"

"Yes, but why would she wish to speak with you? She was as old as the Lightning Birds. All of her friends and family died summers ago. She ought to have plenty of people to talk to in the Village of Wounded Souls. Why you, Pondwader?"

His long pale lashes cast gray crescents over his cheeks as he looked askance at Kelp. "I only know that she has asked for me. Please, come with me, Kelp. I won't be so scared if you are there." A lance of sunlight penetrated the trees and Pondwader quickly jerked up his hood to shield his face. The action sent thick white hair cascading over his eyes. He pushed it back and peered at her. "I need you, Kelp. I don't know what's going to happen, but I know that you are part of it. Please come."

"What do you mean I'm *part* of it?"

He placed the pine needle back on the leaves, exactly as he'd found it, and gently stroked it with his fingertip. Pondwader did that with everything, dogs, people, rocks. He touched them tenderly, as if in apology. Kelp had asked him about it once, and he'd replied that sometimes he sensed pain coming from things, and felt helpless and concerned. She'd told him it was stupid to sense pain from a rock, and he'd solemnly asked, *"Why? Rocks grow old. Bits of them fall away. They worry about dying, too, Kelp."*

"Is something wrong, Pondwader?"

He bit his lip. "I can't tell you, Kelp."

"But I'm your sister!"

"Yes, but . . . I—I haven't told anyone this. I've been too scared to." He closed his eyes a moment, as if gathering courage.

"What is it? Tell me."

He hesitated, then looked at her. "Promise you won't tell."

"You *know* I won't tell."

Pondwader tipped his head and sunlight splashed his face. His pink eyes glowed with an unearthly light, like a coral crab's claws at dawn. "For about a moon, Kelp," he began very softly. "I've been feeling strangely. As if something were being born inside me, like thunder waking up. A faint roaring starts in my chest and rumbles all the way out to my fingers and toes, growing louder and louder, until I—"

Kelp held up a hand and scanned the forest to make certain no one heard them. "Great Stars, Pondwader, don't ever repeat that! Especially not to old Dogtooth. He'll have the Spirit Elders darting you while you sleep! How long have you been feeling this?"

"Not long." His gaze met hers. He squinted slightly. "But sometimes, Kelp, in the middle of that roar, I hear your voice—no, don't look at me that way. It's not a dream, it's real. I know I should have told Grandmother Moonsnail about this, but I—I haven't."

"What do I say in the dream?" she asked.

"You are always yelling at me, but I can't make out your words because the roar is so loud. Still," he said and squeezed her hand. "I know you're trying to warn me."

"About what?"

"I don't know. But I need you, Kelp. I think I need you badly."

Kelp's gaze drifted over the forest while she thought. *A roar like thunder waking . . .*

"Pondwader," she murmured, "if you need me, I'll stick to you like boiled pine sap, but promise me that you will tell no one about this roar inside you. Not even Grandmother. She would feel obliged to call a council meeting of the Spirit Elders, and I . . . Well, just don't. It wouldn't be good, not after the things Dogtooth told them. The elders have been watching you like rabbits that see Hawk circling overhead. Do you promise?"

He hesitated, as if not certain he could do that. "I promise. Now, come on. I've delayed us, and I think that indigo snake was trying to tell me that old Dogtooth is already waiting at the Pond."

Turning around, he launched himself down the trail again, sliding on his stomach, like otter down a slick bank. When he'd piled too many leaves before him to keep going, he climbed over the mound and stood up.

Kelp got to her feet and walked down.

Pondwader waited for her in a copse of palmettos at the base of the hill. Black dirt and bits of forest duff clung to the front of his robe. He absently brushed at them as he watched her descend the hill. Standing there, he looked very tall and gangly. His long white hair streamed from within the loose frame of his hood, falling to his waist. Kelp shook her head. If only he'd had rich black hair, he might have been handsome—not that it mattered. Girls ran from him like schools of fish scattering at a thrown seashell. Kelp didn't really blame them, either. Pondwader's eyes affected people strangely. When Pondwader gazed intently at you, you felt as if you were being stripped naked inside, a layer peeled back here, one there, until all the layers you had so diligently woven to protect yourself had vanished—and your souls lay bare to him.

"I hear Dogtooth," Pondwader whispered when she strode up beside him. "He's Singing one of the Death Songs."

Morosely, she said, "Fine. Let us go find him so you can learn to talk to ghosts, and we can get home before dark."

Pondwader smiled. "Thank you for coming, Kelp."

A worn trail cut a swath between the palmettos fringing the Pond and the vine-shrouded trees of the forest. Kelp walked quietly behind Pondwader, her hand on her warclub.

"Do you still hear Dogtooth?" she asked.

"No, I don't. I . . ."

Pondwader stopped dead as they rounded the western curve of the trail. Kelp crowded close behind him and peered around his right arm.

"What's the matter?" she demanded. "Do you see him?"

Pondwader slowly lifted his arm and pointed.

Kelp's eyes widened. She swallowed hard. "Hallowed Brother Sky!"

In the black cavity of a lightning blasted oak, Dogtooth sat, his knobby old knees drawn up. He held a fire-sharpened wooden burial stake in his hands. Two white spots encircled his sparkling eyes, but the rest of his skinny body bore a thick coat of black paint. Antlers, covered with gray hair, curved up from his skull, as if the hair had been lifted by the antlers as they grew. He wore a deerhide breechclout and a polished palm seed necklace. Beneath the layer of paint deep wrinkles lined his thin face, old, so very old. He lifted his hooked nose and scented the breeze.

"Oh, you're here!" Dogtooth said. "I had begun to fear you wouldn't come."

"But I promised I would, Grandfather," Pondwader said.

"Well, yes, but promises are just words to most people. I'm glad you kept yours."

Dogtooth braced a hand on the trunk and rose on stringy legs. His black body blended so well with the charred background of the tree that he almost disappeared. "I see your sister came, too. I do not recall inviting her. I hope the ghosts let her live. What's her name?"

Kelp stepped from behind Pondwader as if walking on rattlesnake eggs. "Kelp. My name is Kelp."

"Yes, that's right." Dogtooth pointed at her with the burial stake. "Kelp. Daughter of Dark Rain and . . . did your mother ever tell you who your father was?"

"No," Kelp and Pondwader said in unison, and looked at each other. Neither of them knew the names of their fathers. They might have been the same man, or different men.

Dogtooth stepped into the sunlight and the white circles of his eyes blazed. He scanned the forest as if expecting intruders. "Well, that's not surprising. Dark Rain herself may not even know." He extended a black-painted hand to them. "Come along, the ghosts have grown weary of waiting."

"Weary? But, Grandfather," Pondwader defended as he fell in step behind Dogtooth, "I came at the time you said to. I—"

"That's not what I meant," Dogtooth replied with a negligent wave of his hand. "Some of the ghosts here have been waiting tens of summers to speak with a Lightning Boy. They knew you were coming. They just did not know when. So don't be surprised if they call you by name."

Kelp saw a mild shiver climb Pondwader's spine before he tightened his muscles to stop it. She knew how he felt. Dogtooth made her gut crawl. She thought it was mostly that demented tone of voice. As if to bolster his courage, Pondwader clenched his fists and asked, "You mean you told the ghosts my name, don't you?"

Dogtooth stopped so suddenly that Pondwader ran into him and knocked the old man backward two steps.

"Oh, forgive me, Dogtooth!" Pondwader apologized. "I didn't mean—"

"Why, no," Dogtooth answered, and cocked his head like a surprised cormorant. "What would give you that idea?" A tuft of mist floated before his eyes and he suddenly pulled his head back to examine it, then used both hands to brush it away as if irritated. "I didn't tell the ghosts your name! As a matter of fact, they told me . . . long before you were born, I might add."

Dogtooth gave Pondwader that bizarre smile, turned, and walked ahead.

Kelp grabbed Pondwader's arm and tugged him back. She whispered, "I thought Dogtooth told you one ghost, Aunt Fin, wanted to speak with you. Now it sounds like there are two tens of them. How many ghosts will you be talking to today?"

"I—I guess I . . . don't know. But I'd better go." He shrugged and sprinted to catch up with Dogtooth. Kelp cautiously followed.

On the far side of the pond, six body-lengths away, two alligators lay in the shallows with their mouths open. Water lilies floated around their long tails. Young animals, they had yellow crossbands on their bodies which would fade as they grew older. Given their small size, they probably would not attack, but Kelp kept her eye on them anyway.

Dogtooth pushed his way through a clump of palmettos and flopped down in the mud beside the Sacred Pond, waiting for them to join him. Against the green vegetation, his skeletal black body resembled a burned corpse.

A faint breeze stirred the forest, warm, carrying the brittle scent of autumn. As it moved through the trees, splinters of sunlight fell across the Pond, contrasting sharply with the dark brown forest floor, and flashing in the human eyes which peered up from beneath the green water. Effigy posts, with doves, pelicans, and other birds carved on the tops stood watch around the pond.

Pondwader nodded respectfully to the birds before he crouched beside Dogtooth. "I am here, Grandfather, and eager to learn whatever you would teach me."

Kelp stood behind Pondwader, gazing down into the Pond.

Some of the faces had been sheathed with silt so that they seemed to be wearing clay masks—others, the more recently dead, looked fully alive. Kelp's heart began to pound.

Because of the cold in the afterworld, her clan dressed the dead in warm clothing and wrapped them snugly in blankets. Then the Spirit Elders submerged the bodies in the water, and gently turned them onto their left sides, so that their heads pointed west and their faces looked north—down the long cold tunnel they would have to swim to reach the Village of Wounded Souls.

Kelp leaned over to look into Aunt Fin's eyes. She seemed . . . sad. A few of her precious belongings glinted in the sunlight, a shark's tooth necklace, an oak pestle, two long darts, and her favorite atlatl with the engraved deer-bone foreshaft.

To prevent their loved ones from being dragged from the portal by predators, the Spirit Elders drove an oval frame of fire-sharpened stakes through the blankets into the ground, pinning the bodies down. People dragged from the portal before they'd begun their journey might wander the earth forever, never finding a way to the Village of Wounded Souls. These souls would be so lonely, they might actually kill their relatives in revenge.

Dogtooth propped the point of his stake on the ground and peered seriously at Pondwader. "Come closer, Pondwader. Sit here beside me." He tilted his head to indicate the place and his antlers slipped to the left. "Oh, my," he said as the sharp points dipped toward his shoulder. He hastily righted the headdress and sighed.

Pondwader's sandals sank into the red-brown mud as he knelt beside Dogtooth. A smile came to his face when he looked into the Pond. "Hello, Aunt," he said tenderly. "I have missed you."

Dogtooth lifted his stake and aimed it at Pondwader's heart. Softly, he asked, "Can you hear them?"

"Yes," Pondwader answered with a frown, "but I can't understand them. It's as though they are very far away."

Dogtooth leaned forward and sunlight flashed across his black face. "That's odd," he said.

"What is?" Pondwader reluctantly sat down in the mud and grimaced when it oozed up around his hips.

"Hmm?" Dogtooth inquired.

Pondwader's pale eyebrows drew together over his pointed nose. "You said that it was odd that the voices sounded far away to me."

Dogtooth blinked. "Well, of course, it's odd," he answered indignantly. "Since the speakers are only four hand's breadth from your right kneecap."

Pondwader squinted at the old man for a moment, then nodded and smiled. "I see. Well, what was it you wished to teach me?"

Kelp scowled out across the forest. As shafts of sunlight penetrated the fog and warmed the ground, filaments of mist curled up, twining through the vines and nesting in the oak branches.

In a low hoarse voice, Dogtooth said, "Pondwader, do you know that humans have a braided soul?

"Yes, Grandfather. While living, the souls are spun tightly together, like the fine threads of our tunics, but at death, they separate."

"Good. Tell me where the three strands of your soul live?"

Pondwader answered, "One lives in my shadow, and . . . and that one is female . . . as Kelp's shadow-soul is male. Another soul lives in the image of my face reflected from water, and one lives in the pupils of my eyes."

"Yes, that's right," Dogtooth said.

Kelp's mouth dropped open. She didn't know that! How did Pondwader? Was this part of the secret knowledge passed on when a boy or girl came to adulthood? Which she had yet to. If so, would something terrible happen to a girl for hearing it? "Dogtooth," she said. "Should I . . . I mean, is it all right for me to listen to these things?"

"Of course not," he said ominously. "But you are here, and so are your ears." He turned back to Pondwader, leaving Kelp frowning. "Do you also know, Pondwader, that one of those souls, the one which resides in the pupils of the eyes, never leaves the body?"

A gust of wind flattened Pondwader's robe across his chest and fluttered long white hair around his pale face. He brushed it out of the way. "No, Grandfather. I did not."

"Yes, that soul clings to the bones forever. That's why if you listen to the Pond, you can hear souls talking and laughing, and sometimes weeping."

"I hear them, Grandfather." Pondwader's gaze drifted over the faces beneath the water. "But I can't understand them. I just know they are glad to see me."

"Of course," Dogtooth said and whispered, "They are glad because they know you will be joining them soon."

Pondwader shifted uneasily. "I don't understand. What do you mean?"

Dogtooth pressed the stake into Pondwader's chest, dimpling the pale green fabric. "When the last Eagle falls, Hurricane Breather will be unleashed. You know that. Everyone will die."

Pondwader nodded. "Yes, I know that, but you think it's going to happen soon?"

"Very soon."

Pondwader clearly did not know what to say. He glanced to Kelp for help and she just shook her head in disgust, giving her brother that *I told you the old man was a lunatic* look.

Dogtooth turned to point at the Pond and his antlers slid down over his right ear. Grumbling, he straightened them, and narrowed his eyes at Pondwader. "Do you deny that you are a Lightning Boy?"

"I don't know, Dogtooth," Pondwader answered. "I don't wish to be, but—"

"You *are* a Lightning Boy. I have seen it." Dogtooth grunted as he rose to his feet to loom over Pondwader. "You just don't know it yet. That is why I asked you here today."

"But, Dogtooth," Pondwader said. "Even if I am a Lightning Boy, that does not mean I will be *the* Lightning Boy, the one who shoots down the Eagles. I'm not very good with an atlatl. Maybe another is to come after me who—"

"It's time." Dogtooth bent over and propped his palms on his painted knees. "The ghosts are calling your name. Do you hear them? They have many things to discuss with you."

Pondwader's glance slid to the Pond. "I'm ready. I guess. Tell me how to speak with them, Grandfather."

Dogtooth grinned and handed Pondwader the stake. "Take this. I have Sung over it to bless it so the ghosts won't kill you. Go to the middle of the Pond, to the deepest part, which is only half your body length, and drive the stake into the bottom. Then hold onto it and keep your whole body under water for as long as you can—"

Kelp blurted, "With the alligators over there? That's suicide! Pondwader will be eaten alive!"

Dogtooth regarded her with the curiosity of a panther kitten. "Will he?"

"Well . . . he might!"

"Have you ever known the alligators who live in the Sacred Pond to disturb the dead? Have you ever heard of such a thing happening in the past?"

Kelp considered the alligators. They continued to lie serenely in the mud with their mouths open. "No," she answered, "but that does not mean—"

"My dear girl, the ghosts have already spoken with the alligators, and told them they wish to speak with Pondwader."

Dogtooth waded a short distance into the Pond, careful not to step in the burial frames, and motioned to Pondwader. "Don't be afraid. Come."

Pondwader's hand shook when he reached out to touch Kelp's arm. "I'll be all right," he said, then waded into the water with the stake clutched in his right hand.

"Go out into the middle." Dogtooth waggled his arm to indicate the place. "It's very shallow. The water will not even reach your hips, you'll see."

Pondwader gripped the stake like a knife as he neared the alligators, but the animals' silver eyes merely watched him. Water lilies crowded around Pondwader's robe.

"Drive the stake in," Dogtooth cupped a hand to his mouth to yell. "Then hold tight! Your whole body must be under water, just like the dead. Go on. Do it."

Suddenly frightened, Kelp ran to the edge of the water. "Pondwader? Wait."

He smiled. It was that incredibly charming smile that could make Wind Mother stop breathing. In a teasing voice, he said, "I'll be fine, Kelp. Really. Don't worry."

The wind gusted across the water, swirling the mist, and lifting Pondwader's white hair from his shoulders. His smile waned, and Kelp thought fear glinted in his eyes. Several deep breaths later, he dove under the water and colliding green rings bobbed out around him, heading for shore. Two tiny topminnows jumped. When they splashed down, one of the alligators closed its jaws.

Kelp unhooked her warclub and gripped it in both hands, just in case.

Dogtooth turned to Kelp, and a look of such utter silliness creased his ancient face, that Kelp snapped, "What are you looking at?"

Dogtooth's antlers glittered in the wavering sunlight as he shoved them toward the back of his head. "Now that I think about it, I'm glad you came today."

Suspicious, she asked, "Why?"

"Well, some member of his family should be present at his rebirth."

"Rebirth? What does that mean?"

Dogtooth leaned toward her and his white brows arched. "The Pond is a special Power place. It will take Pondwader's human souls and wash them right out of his body. Something new, wondrous, will be reborn in his chest. You see, everything that happens here is a consecration, an anointing. You will be amazed at the change he will undergo after his death. He—"

"Death!" Kelp shouted. "I thought you said he wasn't going to die! You said you'd prayed over that stake just so the ghosts—"

"Well, yes, but I was just speaking metaphorically. Naturally one must die to be reborn."

Kelp screamed and lunged into the Pond, shouting, "Pondwader! Pondwader! Where are you? *Where are you?"*

Her brother erupted from the surface, wet white hair sleeking down over his cheeks. "*What!* Kelp, what's wrong?"

Kelp stopped, pulse so loud in her ears that she felt sick. Her knees shook. Pondwader looked just the same. Very alive, with uprooted lilies dangling limply over his shoulders.

She whirled to Dogtooth. "You old madman!" she shouted. "Why did you tell me that?"

"Well," Dogtooth said, smiling, "you will need time to prepare yourself for your brother's transformation. And now, forgive me." He turned and thrashed past a palmetto. "I really have other things to do." Over his shoulder, he yelled, "I wish you well on your marriage, Pondwader!"

Kelp squinted after him until he disappeared into the gold and gray weave of the forest. "Marriage?" she said. "What's he talking about?"

Pondwader crawled out on the northern side of the Pond, and sat down heavily in a thicket of reeds. Green stems leaned at differing angles around him. A red stain appeared on his left side, and began growing, and growing.

"Are you hurt?" Kelp thrashed through the cattails to stand beside him.

"No. No, really. I don't think. There was a dart . . ." He appeared dazed as he reached down and probed his side. More blood stained the fabric, spreading in a bright red circle around his fingers.

"A dart?" Kelp threw down her warclub and bent over to survey the wound more closely. "Blessed Sun Mother, you're bleeding badly! Pondwader, what—"

He looked up. "It happened when I first dove down. The dart had been planted in the mud with the tip up. The cut isn't bad. The water just spreads the blood, makes it look like there's more than there is."

Kelp put her finger through the rip in the fabric to touch the wound. "How deep did it go, Pondwader?"

From somewhere out in the forest Dogtooth yelled, "He's dead! He's dead!"

"He is not!" Kelp shouted back. "He's sitting right here! You're a liar as well as a lunatic!"

"He may be alive now," Dogtooth's voice lilted on the wind. "But he'll be dead soon."

Pondwader's expression turned anguished. "Oh, Kelp, it's not my fault."

She pulled her gaze from the last place she'd seen Dogtooth and frowned at her brother. He looked absolutely terrified. "What, Pondwader? What isn't your fault?"

He held his stomach and rocked back and forth. "I'm dying. I'm dying, but I don't know why. I can *feel* my life seeping away." Wet white hair dragged the reeds around him, leaving trickles of water flowing down the stems. "What have I done to anger Sun Mother so much she would want me dead? I can't help what's happening to me. I didn't want the thunder to wake up. *It's not my fault!*"

Kelp crouched before him, breathing hard. Tears glistened on his colorless lashes. "Come on. I have to get you home," she said, and tugged on his hand until he stood up. He staggered. Kelp grabbed his arm and pulled it over her shoulders to steady him. "Pondwader? Can you walk?"

He rubbed a muddy hand over his forehead, and murmured. "Yes, I—I think so."

Five

I am certain of it, Spirit Elder!" The young warrior spoke quietly in the jumping firelight of the council shelter. "We tortured one of the runaways before we killed him. He said that Musselwhite's husband had escaped, too!"

"And you believe this man is Diver?"

Diver opened his eyes. His wounds, the one in his back and the more recent one in his left shoulder, throbbed so violently he could barely concentrate on their words. Though he knew they had tied his arms over his head and secured them to the main support beam of the shelter's roof, he could not feel them. His muscles neither ached nor tingled. They might have been severed from his body, except that he could see them, dripping sweat in the heat of the flames.

Two young warriors sat around the fire with gourd cups of tea in their hands. The other man stood with his back to Diver, a hand propped on the northeastern post, gazing out across the moonlit ocean where the white backs of floating gulls glimmered and vanished with the rolling waves. The man had braided his long, graying black hair and coiled it into a bun at the base of his skull, then secured it with a beautifully etched pelican bone hairpin. He wore only a breechclout, and all of his exposed skin shone with insect grease. A long white scar angled down his left shoulder. *Cottonmouth.* Diver had never seen him, but he knew that's who it must be. Musselwhite had described that deep, haunting voice tens of times. Though Diver had not suspected he would be so slender, or so tall.

A ripple of polished marginella shells flashed as the man slowly turned and his necklace caught the firelight. White shells, bleached by being roasted in hot sand. *Yes, Cottonmouth.* He had a reputation for being extremely handsome, though age had cut lines around his huge dark eyes, and turned the hair at his temples a solid silver. He had a perfect face, oval, the nose and full lips seemingly carved from stone.

Beneath that intent gaze, Diver straightened, getting his feet under him, and started shaking. Pain and fear blended to leave him pathetically weak.

Cottonmouth walked forward. "Are you?" he asked. "Are you my beloved Musselwhite's husband?"

The irony in Cottonmouth's voice sickened Diver. The man had said "beloved" like a curse. "I am Panther, of the Sea Turtle Clan."

"Indeed?" Cottonmouth replied. His bare feet whispered against the palmetto mats as he walked all the way around Diver. "And what would a man of the Sea Turtle Clan be doing on a war walk with Windy Cove warriors?" Cottonmouth smiled, but what filled his eyes bore no resemblance to amusement.

The young men around the fire had gone silent, clenching their cups of tea and watching with sweaty faces. The smaller of the men, who sat to Diver's right, keep swirling the liquid in his cup as if nervous that Cottonmouth's wrath might be turned upon him. Why? What had he done? Or not done?

"Answer me," Cottonmouth ordered.

Diver replied, "Many clans are banding together, Cottonmouth, to fight you. We must, or . . . or you will kill us all."

"Yes," Cottonmouth said softly. "I might."

Diver's legs gave way suddenly, and he staggered until he could brace them again. The young warriors laughed. Diver clamped his teeth and focused his gaze on the firelit shelters strewn like patches of sunlight through the dark forest behind the shelter. There had to be ten tens of them. Children played on the floors, men knapped out dart points, women sat before their looms, weaving. The faint strains of a flute carried on the damp air. Diver concentrated on it. If he could just stay conscious, and keep Cottonmouth talking, he might live to see another sunrise.

Diver twisted to look at Cottonmouth, who had walked to stand behind him, arms folded across his broad naked chest. "Why do you hate us so? Your raiding—"

"I raid," Cottonmouth said and tilted his head ever so slightly, "to fill my villages with new women and valuable trade items. I hate no one. Except your wife, Musselwhite. I mean to *kill* her."

Diver managed to wiggle his swollen fingers, and gripped the ropes above him to take some of the strain from his bound wrists. That simple movement made him wince and tremble again. His wounds had festered. He could feel the evil Spirits feeding on his flesh, eating his strength. "From what I have heard about Musselwhite," he said, "you had better be very very good with an atlatl, or she'll skewer your heart before you so much as see her."

Cottonmouth's expression seemed frozen, his eyes so cold that Diver suspected the man's gaze alone could make strong men quail.

Diver filled his lungs with precious air, and said through a long exhalation, "Is what people say about you true?"

"That depends. What do they say?"

"They say you have lost your souls. That the Lightning Birds soared down and killed them."

Cottonmouth appeared to be pondering that. "I think I will let my warriors use your miserable body for dart practice. Then I will have them carry you back and dump you in your wife's bedding."

"If you mean Musselwhite's bedding, that will not disturb my wife at all. She sleeps two days' walk to the north."

The small man by the fire lurched to his knees. "He *is* Diver! I swear it, Cottonmouth. I, myself, darted his son Blue Echo, and before the boy died, he reached out for this man and called, *'Father!'* Didn't he, Hanging Star?" he demanded of the warrior next to him, who nodded. "There is no doubt! He is the one you wished us to capture!"

Diver closed his eyes against the words. *Blue Echo called to me? I must have been so engaged in the battle. . . .* A deep dark chasm opened in his heart, making it pound and ache. Had Morning Glory called to him as well? Diamondback . . . ? Had they all died because Cottonmouth sought to trap Diver?

Cottonmouth took a step toward the small warrior, and the man eased back to the mat, as if he feared Cottonmouth so much he had to nerve himself to breathe in the man's presence.

Cottonmouth said, "You needn't worry, Mulberry. I know he's Diver."

"You . . . you do?" Mulberry asked, glancing at the warrior beside him. "How?"

Cottonmouth turned, and firelight slid along the smooth curve of his jaw. He peered deeply into Diver's eyes.

"Musselwhite is perfectly reflected in his soul," Cottonmouth said. "I recognize her because every time I look into a pool of water, I see her in my own eyes. Once she has shared her soul with a man, she lives forever inside him. And she has only shared her soul with two men in her life." Cottonmouth walked closer to Diver, and his tanned face contrasted sharply with the silver in his temples. "Do you see her in my eyes?"

Diver looked for her there, longing for a glimpse of her strength, or tenderness. Maybe a shred of her passionate loyalty . . . a lingering moment of her love.

"No," he answered with a tired sigh. "I do not. In fact, I see nothing in your eyes, Cottonmouth. You truly have lost your souls."

"Perhaps, Diver, but if so, it wasn't the Lightning Birds who killed them. It was Musselwhite." He examined Diver's torn and bloody tunic. "Did she tell you that she murdered my son before my eyes?"

Diver could not hide his shock. His face slackened before he could restrain the muscles. "W-why would she do that?"

The crowsfeet around Cottonmouth's eyes deepened. "Strange," he said softly. "I had imagined she would boast of that. Of how she brought the great Cottonmouth to his knees. And she does not? I'm surprised."

Musselwhite could no more kill one of her own sons than she could fly to Sister Moon. But . . . Diver had heard rumors that she'd borne a son to Cottonmouth, and on occasion he had wondered what had become of the boy.

"Did you never ask her about me?" Cottonmouth inquired.

Diver's legs shook severely now. Soon, he would have to shift his weight to his arms again, and the thought made him despair.

Cottonmouth's voice filled the silence like the distant roar of a waterfall, deep, silken. "I loved her very much. When she left me, I wanted to kill her—or kill myself." Then he smiled and quietly added, "You see that I managed neither."

Diver said nothing.

"Do you know why she left me?" Cottonmouth asked.

"I don't care why she left you."

"You really don't know?" Apparently he read the answer in Diver's eyes. "She has told you very little about herself."

The mats rasped as Cottonmouth walked to lean his shoulder against the southeastern post. He stood with his arms folded, watching the silver-edged clouds that drifted on the horizon. The flowery fragrance of his insect grease filled the shelter.

"I should start at the beginning, then," Cottonmouth said, "on the day she betrayed me."

Diver's jaw tightened.

Cottonmouth didn't deign to look at him, but he smiled sadly. "You trust her completely, don't you? So did I. I told her everything. On the eve of the most important war walk of my young life, I shared my plans with her. She was so good with war tactics, I—I wanted her opinion. Would this work? Should I station these warriors somewhere else?" His mouth pursed bitterly. "She told my enemies. Oh, yes, she did. She told them every detail of my plans. Of course, I lost."

"Was that the Pelican Isle Massacre? If I recall correctly, those were Musselwhite's own people you wanted to kill. No wonder—"

"No, no, Diver," he said as if objecting to another cup of tea, rather than an accusation of murder. "This was summers before Pelican Isle. Musselwhite was pregnant with my son at the time. I forgave her, naturally. She made up some excuse, and I wanted to believe her so desperately . . . I did."

Moonlight shining off the ocean outlined every muscle in Cottonmouth's slender body as he drew a deep breath, then let it out. "But you are correct," he continued. "Pelican Isle was the last time I saw her." His voice grew tight. "Just before the battle, she murdered my son, then she fled. Had I been able to get to her at Pelican Isle, I promise you I would have killed her then."

Diver silently thanked all the Spirits on earth that Musselwhite had escaped. "How long had you known her?"

"We became acquainted when she was ten-and-one summers, but we did not start loving each other until she was ten and three summers. We shared the same lodge for only three."

And Diver had loved her for two-tens-and-five. He had memorized every fold in her souls, and the cruelty that Cottonmouth described did not exist. If Musselwhite had betrayed the man she loved, she had been so desperate she could think of no other way out. Diver had seen her desperate . . . maybe even desperate enough to betray him if he'd tried to force her to carry out a course of action she found abhorrent, but he had never seen her desperate enough to murder one of her own sons.

"I must draw her into my trap, Diver," Cottonmouth murmured. "The Lightning Birds are coming for me soon. I must see Musselwhite first, or I will never see the shining new world my Dreams have promised."

"Why? What does she have to do with the Lightning Birds?"

Cottonmouth extended one hand, palm up, and held it motionless a long moment, then he closed his fingers. "She holds a Lightning Boy in the palm of her hand. *He* will free me. But only if Musselwhite tells him to."

Confused, Diver could only respond, "You'll never trap her."

Cottonmouth used his fist to gesture to Diver. "But I have the perfect bait."

"You're a fool! Do you think she would risk bringing a war party into this heavily guarded village just to rescue me? Never!"

Cottonmouth lowered his hand to his side. "I do not believe she would risk the lives of her warriors . . . just her own, and the Lightning Boy's." He nodded. "She'll be coming for you, Diver. I know her. She loves you. And she knows what I am capable of doing to you. Knows what I *will* do to you— once you are strong enough."

Cottonmouth turned to his warriors, and both men leaped to their feet, awaiting instructions. "Cut him down. Feed him. Call old woman Starfish. Inform her that I want Diver's wounds cared for. No matter what it takes, he must live. Do you understand?"

Mulberry said, "Yes, Spirit Elder. We will see to it."

Cottonmouth walked to the edge of the shelter and stopped. He appeared to be thinking. "Mulberry?"

"Yes?" the youth responded anxiously; his whole body had gone rigid at the sound of his name. "Is there something else?"

Firelight glittered from the silver strands in Cottonmouth's hair. "Send a messenger to Windy Cove Clan. Musselwhite may think her husband is dead. Tell her he is not."

Lightning flashes.

Blue veins cut across the black belly of Brother Sky. Shattering purple cracks follow, splitting the night. Every Lightning Bird in the world must have ridden the shoulders of Storm Girl to get here. They fly around me wildly, their brilliant tailfeathers slashing at the backs of my eyeballs.

I am afraid.

The rest of Heartwood village sleeps. After supper, Kelp and my grandmother moved their blankets close to the firepit for warmth. They are dark humps until the erratic flights of the Lightning Birds burn flickering trails across their faces. They do not wake. They do not even stir.

I lie on my sleeping mat shivering, clutching at my blankets. The tremors stretch all the way out to my toes and the tips of my fingers. I can't stop. Grandmother thinks I suffer from a fever. She has been feeding me broth. Washing my face and arms with a cool, wet cloth. But this is no fever. I know the truth.

The ghosts told me this would happen. They said that when the Sacred Pond cleanses away the braided souls, it unravels. The strands twist out through the mouth and slither into the air, abandoning the body. Then the flesh starts to shake apart, because there's nothing left to hold it together. Like rocks tumbling over a cliff in a landslide, legs, arms, stomach . . . they all plummet down, weightless in thin air, getting farther and farther away, until the distances swallow them.

That is how I feel. My heart still beats, my eyes still see. But that is all *I* am now. Heart and eyes. The rest of me is gone. Just a flash of lightning ago, my breathing stopped. My lungs tumbled out of my chest and fell, and fell.

I know it will not be long now. But I am . . .

The thundereggs hidden inside Storm Girl's soft, billowing body hatch, and a wall of water slams the ground. Lightning Birds slide out and burst into flight, striking so near, their flashes blind me. My eyelids have vanished, I cannot turn away. An eerie, luminescent web of purple spins over Heartwood Village. Thunder shakes the souls out of the world.

My eyes begin to clear, and something else takes shape. It leaps lightly across the bags that hang from the rafters, like a feather kept afloat on puffs of breath. But it is not a feather. No, I see it more clearly now. The hem of her faded tunic twirls as she Dances and spins. She is so whimsical, so unearthly, so beautiful. . . .

"What are you?"

"My name is Turtle Bone Doll."

I squint. "I can't see you very well. Can you come down closer?"

Turtle Bone Doll cartwheels across the rafters, then swoops down like a bird to hover just above my eyes. Still Dancing. Keeping time to music I cannot hear. Swaying. Bobbing.

She *is* a doll. Made from a turtle's leg bone, like a child's toy. Her face was once painted brightly, but over many summers, the colors have faded, so that I can barely see her brown eyes and red mouth. A few strands of black hair cling to her head, glued with pine pitch. The rest must have fallen out long ago. A master weaver created her tunic; the threads are fine and tight—but tens of tens of hands have left the fabric tattered. Threads stick out everywhere.

"You look more like a porcupine than a doll," I say.

"And you look more like a pair of pink eyes than a boy," she replies. *"Was that your heart that just flew by?"*

Panic grips me when I realize I no longer hear my heartbeat. Then I feel it, falling . . . falling. . . . It doesn't make a sound as it vanishes down those gaping jaws of darkness. "I wish you had thought to catch it," I say. "I could have used my heart."

"What for? Your body is almost gone. When did you lose your souls?"

"Three days ago. The Sacred Pond—"

"Ah. The Pond, yes." Turtle Bone Doll flips head over heels, then bounces around my eyes.

"You've been to the Pond?"

A magnificent flash of lightning turns the world blue, and I see a faint smile touch her faded red mouth. *"I should say so. That Pond was once a Hole-in-the-Ice. I crawled up it in the pocket of an old woman named Broken Branch. But that's not the first time I saw it. Hallowed Spirits, no. That Pond goes back to a time before the world. Of course it was much bigger then. Huge, in fact. It was the calm Eye of Hurricane Breather, the very spot where the first Thunderegg hatched and our blue world spun out."* Turtle Bone Doll cartwheels around me, flipping and laughing with childish delight. *"That's why I'm here tonight."*

"Why?"

"Blessed Shining People! Has no one taught you anything?"

"Well, I—I don't know. Like what?"

Turtle Bone Doll's frayed tunic billows as she leaps and skips about the shelter, Dancing over my grandmother and Kelp's heads before twirling her way back. She looks irritated. *"Maybe no one here knows. Well, I'll tell you.*

By entering the Pond, you entered the Eye. For a few heartbeats, you dwelled in the timeless moment before the world was born. That's why you lost your human souls. There weren't any back then. So obviously you couldn't have any."

"I don't understand. You said you were here tonight for a reason. Why?"

"To witness the conception."

"The conception of what?"

"The deliverer. I knew him once. He was a part of me, and I loved him very much. He will come from that timeless moment that still lives in your eyes."

"But . . . I'm dying."

"What difference does that make?"

My vision is suddenly cut in half and terror grips me. The rafters seem to plunge down while the floor rises up. A sickening blur of colors swirls, brown, green, black. The Doll is the only thing in the world that does not move. She is my still point. My anchor. I stare at her hard.

"Too bad," Turtle Bone Doll says. *"You lost an eye. There's not much of you left now."*

"W-what will happen," I ask fearfully, "when my last eye falls away?"

Her joyous laughter spills around me, sounding like a summer-old child's: free, innocent, as pure as dewdrops. Laughter that would sparkle in her eyes if she had any. *"The only thing Power asks of you, Pondwader, is that when the Lightning is within your reach, you extend your hand and take hold of it. That's simple enough, isn't it?"*

"No. I don't have hands anymore."

Turtle Bone Doll sighs, and the straggling hairs on her bony head begin, one by one, to stick straight up, pointing toward the sky. Sparks fly from the ends, like rubbed fox fur, and she goes still and quiet.

"What is it?" I ask. "What's the matter."

"Get ready," she warns.

I glance around, terrified, as if some monster is going to leap from the forest and devour me whole. Lightning lances across the sky in constant blinding streamers, and thunder roars so loudly the ground heaves and bucks beneath me. The whole village should be falling down! Why isn't it? Roofs should be collapsing, and people running for their lives! Grandmother and Kelp continue to sleep, their breathing deep, faces serene. Have they gone deaf?

"Here she comes," Turtle Bone Doll's voice is soft with reverence.

"Who?"

"First Mother."

Out over the ocean, an enormous Lightning Bird crackles from the black heart of the storm, and soars down, splitting clouds as she plummets toward earth. A stunning blue-white trail flares behind her. As she nears, the world becomes as broad daylight.

The last thing I see is liquid blue fire pouring down around me, splattering the floor mats and support poles, filling the shelter with frosty radiance.

The bolt pierces my one eye, and I am blind, plunging like Falcon through air that is molten ivory.

Turtle Bone Doll's sweet laughter penetrates the brilliance. She Sings, *"Pondwader's eye will bring life to the world! Just as Hurricane Breather's did! Life to the world . . . to the whole world!"*

Six

"Grandmother! Grandmother!"

Moonsnail briefly looked up to see Little Darter racing across the village toward her. Sand spurted beneath the girl's heels. Her voice sounded urgent, but at five summers, urgent might mean she'd found an odd fish washed up on the shore. Moonsnail continued mopping Pondwader's forehead. He lay beneath a mound of blankets, just his pale face and drenched white hair showing. His fever had raged for four days. Yesterday, during the lightning storm, there had been a terrifying moment when Moonsnail had feared she might lose him. She could sense Death, standing just at her grandson's shoulder, watching, waiting. . . . But Pondwader seemed better today. He breathed easier, and had even eaten a little.

Little Darter skidded to a stop, breathing hard. Sand coated her tunic and legs. *"Grandmother!"*

"Hush! Your cousin is ill." Moonsnail threw her rag into the gourd of cool water, and glowered menacingly at her granddaughter. In response, Little Darter's square face reddened. She put her hands behind her back and stood as if turned to stone. Only her dark eyes moved, trying not to look at Moonsnail. "All right. What is so important?"

Little Darter's tan tunic flared out as she swung around and pointed to the large shelter at the edge of the forest in the distance. "Dark Rain is back!

She grabbed me by the arm and tried to shake the liver out of me!" Little Darter held up her arm to display the red fingerprints. "See? Look what she did?"

"Dark Rain?" Moonsnail squinted at the woman standing in the council shelter, but could make out nothing more than a blur dressed in red. She reached for her walking stick and used it to steady herself while she got to her feet. "What does she want?"

"She ordered me to run and fetch you. She would not tell me why."

"You asked, eh?" Moonsnail chuckled. "No wonder she was after your liver. Probably wanted to eat it for such impudence." Little Darter twisted to look up, and Moonsnail put a gnarled old hand on the girl's head, patting it gently. "But you were right to ask. She has no business here. Now, go find Kelp. She may wish to see her mother before I cast Dark Rain out of the village again."

"Yes, Grandmother!"

Little Darter sped off toward the ocean with her dark hair flying. As she cut across the village a flock of laughing children and barking dogs fell in behind her, churning up a sandstorm with their feet as they angled out of sight toward the green water in the distance.

Moonsnail used the wet rag to push the straggling ends of gray hair out of her eyes. Dark Rain. Hallowed Shining People! The woman had more gall than a black bear. How many times did Moonsnail have to cast her out before it stuck? Moonsnail dropped the rag into the water again, picked up her walking stick, and touched Pondwader's pink cheek. "I'll return soon," she whispered. He did not awaken.

A golden veil of sunlight draped Moonsnail as she hobbled toward the council shelter. The cool pine-scented breeze played with her short hair, fluttering it around her face. She worked toward the shade of the trees which encircled the village on three sides, passing the shell midden—the mound where people dumped empty shells after eating the contents. Short beards of hanging moss draped the surrounding oak branches, swaying in the wind. The shade soothed Moonsnail. She had spent so much time tending her grandson in the last four days that she had managed scarce sleep. But she had been caring for members of her clan for six tens of summers. That's why the Heartwood Clan had grown large and strong.

Three tens of shelters filled the plaza.

Early that morning, the clan had gone into the woods to gather what they might for the day's meals. Wooden bowls overflowing with freshly picked elderberries and mushrooms sat on the palmetto-mat floors. Moonsnail's mouth watered. She loved nothing better than skewering a tree mushroom on a stick and roasting it slowly over the fire.

The council shelter sat with its back to the forest and its face to the open plaza. Six body-lengths wide and five long, it stretched three times the size of a family shelter. Rolled-up lengths of smoked fabric lay in long tubes against the roof. For privacy, or when night came and the Mosquito Nation sailed forth on another war walk, the clan would unroll the lengths of fabric to seal the shelter. Gourds of sea turtle oil mixed with powdered dogwood root hung from each pole for those who wished to rub their skin—an added protection against biting insects.

Moonsnail stabbed the point of her walking stick into the sandy soil at the northwestern corner of the council shelter and braced herself a moment while she caught her breath. Her oldest daughter, Dark Rain, stood on the opposite side of the shelter, leaning haughtily against one of the pine pole supports. Her left hand brimmed with black nightshade berries. She ate them leisurely, as though each were the last of its kind, and deserved her unwavering attention.

Moonsnail concentrated on the squeals of playing children, the barking of dogs, the hushed words of adults as they hurried from shelter to shelter, telling of Dark Rain's sudden appearance. Surprised gasps and a few curses laced the wind. Soon, they would begin gathering on the far side of the village, faces turned toward the council shelter. Everyone would want to know whether Dark Rain wished to petition the clan for readmittance.

Dark Rain picked another berry from her hand and tucked it into her prim mouth.

Moonsnail grimaced. Her daughter's every move possessed a cold, calculating elegance. She was very beautiful, with slanting eyes, a rich brown complexion, and long black hair as soft as a mink's fur. Moonsnail had often wished her daughter looked more like her, with a square face, eyes too small, and a bulbous nose. Perhaps then Dark Rain would have spent more time tending to the needs of her children and clan instead of traipsing about trying to sate her own . . . needs. But no, Sun Mother had seen to it that Dark Rain received the seductive face of a sea Spirit.

"Good afternoon, Mother. Are you happy to see me?"

"About as happy as I would be to see a poisonous toad in my bedding." Moonsnail brandished her walking stick at Dark Rain. "Whatever it is you wish to say, say it quickly and be gone, before you have the entire village in an uproar."

"Ah, my loving mother. You have not changed at all. I assure you, the matter I bring is crucial to our clan, or I would not be here."

"This is not your clan. You are Outcast. A clanless woman without relatives. And I like it that way. Keeps me from having to make excuses for you."

Moonsnail slumped down atop a thick pile of palmetto mats at the rear of the council shelter. The hem of her short, brown tunic spread around her thighs as she arranged herself so that her joints didn't ache so badly. In the past three summers the fire in her right hip had gone from a tiny flame to a raging blaze. She propped her walking stick and clutched the head with both hands. "Well, hurry it up. What do you want?"

Dark Rain angrily threw her berries on the floor and glared. "You *should* be proud of me. I have managed an alliance you could only dream of! Must you be so hostile?"

"I must."

Dark Rain propped slim brown hands on her shapely hips. The belt of her red tunic had been knotted tightly to accentuate her tiny waist. Before she had turned ten-and-five summers, Dark Rain knew a multitude of plants which would induce abortion: bay lavender, ground vanilla-tree bark, ripe fruit juice from the pink spine plant. Despite that fact, she had birthed two children, but Dark Rain had the maternal instincts of a horseshoe crab. She laid her eggs, and left them to the whims of nature—or rather to her mother. And Moonsnail admitted she felt grateful for that. She loved Pondwader and Kelp with all her heart.

"So," Moonsnail finally said. "I heard that you and—what was his name—that boy trader? I heard the two of you had gone to visit the northern clans, and yet here you are, back disgracing my shelter. What could possibly have drawn my daughter from the arms of her latest lover? I thought you were quite taken by that stout young man."

Dark Rain laughed in that low cruel way she had. "He was 'stout,' Mother. Unfortunately, the stiff manhood between his legs was all he had to give me. I left him."

Moonsnail did not smile. The silly boy had probably showered Dark Rain with valuable trinkets to secure her love, and once she'd stocked up enough, she'd left him for more interesting pursuits. Moonsnail had heard it all before. Her daughter's overwhelming passion for dice games had impoverished the Heartwood Clan three times. The clan bore the responsibility for its members' debts. Under normal circumstances, a person who had so shamed their clan would come crawling back, begging forgiveness and promising to repay every item which had been donated to cover such debts. But not Dark Rain. She had accepted the Outcast declaration with a laugh—and gone looking for a new fool to pay her debts.

"Mother," Dark Rain said. "I have news that I am sure you will appreciate. Do you wish to hear it, or not?"

Moonsnail clutched her walking stick more tightly. Beyond the council shelter four children chased a rolling willow hoop, seeing which of them could throw the most acorns through the circle before the hoop came to a stop. Their joyous voices filled the humid air. Moonsnail waited for them to move away, then spat, "What is this 'alliance'?"

Dark Rain flapped the cord which belted the waist of her short red tunic. Two small clamshells dangled at the ends of the cord, clicking together. "First, tell me about my children. The information is critical to our prospects for this 'alliance.' "

"Your daughter, Kelp, has turned into a terror. She's learned how to cast a dart better than any of the village boys, and has been racing around like a—"

"Oh," Dark Rain waved a hand dismissively, "I'm sure you are bringing her up as best you can. And what of Pondwader? Where is he? I looked for him the instant I arrived."

Moonsnail's suspicions roused. Rather than giving her daughter the truth, she said, "Probably out lying in the ocean weighted down by big pieces of coral. He likes to listen to passing fish. Says you can hear a school of croakers coming for a day's swim away." Which, if he had not been ill, would have been the truth.

"Blessed Sun Mother. Why do you allow him such freedoms? He's ten-and-five summers old. He should be married with a baby already planted in his wife's belly, and instead he's out running about like a wild dog."

Moonsnail stared at her. "At least he's not running about like a wild dog in *heat!* What is your interest in Pondwader?"

"He is my son. I am concerned about him."

"Are you? Well, then it might interest you to know that three days ago old Dogtooth tried to kill him. Made him swim to the bottom of the Sacred Pond and there was a dart—"

Dark Rain stepped forward, the color drained from her face. "Is—is he alive? Is he all right?"

"He's healing," Moonsnail answered and eyed her daughter severely. "I plastered a myrsine-bark poultice on his wound, and have been giving him willow-bark tea to keep his fever down."

"Thank the Blessed Shining People," Dark Rain breathed, and closed her eyes as if in relief. "Dogtooth has always been crazy. Why did you allow Pondwader to visit him?"

"I didn't allow it. He ran off with Kelp. You know how far the Pond is. They didn't get back until way after dark. I was worried sick."

"Hmm. Well, at least running off proves he's independent. Does he hunt? Has he killed his first bear? Or been on his first war walk? Is he . . . a man?"

Moonsnail frowned. Dark Rain took a good deal of time examining the berry stains on her fingers. "Of course, he is. *I* raised him. He killed his first bear last summer. Though, I admit, he has not yet been on a war walk, but I fear that will come soon enough, what with Cottonmouth's raiders out burning villages."

"He is not a warrior, then." Dark Rain's brow furrowed. "Well, perhaps no one will care."

Moonsnail shifted to her left hip, taking the weight off her aching right. What could this discussion be leading to? Dark Rain had never evinced an interest in her children. "What do you want, Dark Rain?"

Dark Rain ignored the question. "Is Pondwader at least tall?"

"He is, and muscular for a youth his age, though still on the skinny side.

If he did not have such pale skin and hair, his face would make a woman forget herself. . . . Do you plan on asking anything more about Kelp?"

Dark Rain seemed irritated at the change of subject. "Oh, tell me if you want."

Moonsnail's voice turned icy. "I see. The only one you are interested in is Pondwader. Why is that?"

Dark Rain gracefully sat down and leaned backward, bracing her palms on the mat. She looked like a glorious cat stretching in the sun. Her long hair caught the light and shimmered in blue-black waves. "On my way here, I passed Windy Cove Village. Old Seedpod cornered me, wanted to know if Pondwader had taken a wife yet. I said he had had many offers, but remained available for the right woman." A gloating smile twisted Dark Rain's lips.

How dare her daughter run home with such news when Moonsnail had only just begun to think of appropriate young women for Pondwader? Dark Rain knew nothing of such matters! The bride would have to be able to further the clan's goals, to strengthen their territorial claims, and promise support in times of war. Dark Rain cared nothing of these things. She cared only for herself. So . . . this marriage must offer some unknown advantage to her wayward daughter.

"Mother, are you not going to ask me about the intended bride?"

"I can think of no young woman in the Windy Cove Clan who is suitable. Our clan has much to offer. If such an alliance is—"

"Oh, Mother!" Dark Rain threw up her arms. "That is precisely the reason Seedpod is interested in Pondwader. That old man *knows* what our clan has to offer!"

"Does he?"

Dark Rain shifted to sit cross-legged. "You will not believe me, but I swear it's true. He wants to marry Pondwader to Musselwhite! Of course, Musselwhite is as old as a cypress tree and just as ugly. But she's still Musselwhite! The status of our clan will rise like a leaping dolphin!"

"*Musselwhite?*" Moonsnail whispered the name. It didn't seem possible. Musselwhite was a great hero. Two-tens-and-six summers before, in the midst of the Pelican Isle Massacre, when Cottonmouth's warriors were destroying the Windy Cove Clan, Musselwhite had appeared out of nowhere, and run through Cottonmouth's warriors like a hurricane through dry grass, bravely killing nine enemies with just her deerbone stiletto. Cottonmouth's warriors had been so terrified, many had thrown down their weapons and run. The woman was a legend. And at least four tens of summers old, maybe even more—plus she already had one husband.

Yes, Diver, if Moonsnail recalled correctly. Usually such a thing proved a minor factor in negotiations—the second husband would have to agree, for example, to perform all of the menial tasks which the first husband did not wish to, like digging tubers in the spring, or trimming the knots from dart shafts, or hunting mice or voles when no larger game presented itself—but if rumors could be believed, Musselwhite loved Diver with fanatical devotion. For tens of summers, Seedpod had been working to convince Musselwhite to take another husband, and Musselwhite had flatly refused. How, then, had Seedpod finally succeeded?

Moonsnail peered at Dark Rain. Her daughter had been right. Not in Moonsnail's wildest dreams would she have dared hope for this. Could it be true? Or another of Dark Rain's perverse amusements?

"Seedpod should have sent a runner to notify me, to ask for an audience and set up a time and place to discuss this matter. Why didn't he?"

Dark Rain clapped her hands and laughed with delight. "Mother, *I* am that runner. Seedpod asked me to deliver the proposal. Isn't it too good to be true? My Pondwader married to Musselwhite—for all that she's too old to give him children, or much else, I'll wager, except status. Our clan will be the envy of the—"

"Hush." Moonsnail sliced the air with her walking stick. "This demands a good deal of thought. The complex sort of which you are incapable. Why would the Windy Cove Clan decide to seek an alliance with us? There are other clans with more wealth, and more prestige."

"Yes, but they want us."

"So you say."

Through an exasperated exhalation, Dark Rain said, "All right, listen, mother. Three times since winter Celebration Day, Windy Cove has been raided. Twice at their Spring Camp far inland, and once since they arrived at Autumn Camp. It seems that Cottonmouth attacks his old lover no matter where she sets up her village. It must be an ancient vendetta between them. Musselwhite probably—"

"Your opinion is of no interest to me. What else did Seedpod say?"

Dark Rain ground her teeth. Stiffly, she answered, "He mentioned that Diver was gone on a war walk—but just to scout the clan's territory."

Moonsnail rubbed her aching hip while she considered this. Diver gone on a war walk? "Where was Musselwhite?"

"In the village. I saw her."

If Musselwhite had stayed at Windy Cove while Diver went out scouting, then Musselwhite must have believed Cottonmouth might strike the village again. And that meant that Heartwood could also be in danger.

"Mother, you should have been there. Musselwhite is even more ugly than I remember. Much too tall for a woman, and she walks like a stalking panther. No wonder men loathe her. I mean, she . . . ."

Moonsnail stopped listening. Musselwhite had always been stunning, not in Dark Rain's mysterious erotic way, but stunning like the Lightning Birds, with flashing eyes that could just as quickly entrance or bore a hole through an opponent's heart. And her voice . . . so rich and deep it seemed to thunder faintly in her listeners' souls.

Moonsnail turned cold eyes upon her daughter. "Now," she said, "let us discuss what you have to gain from this marriage."

Dark Rain's shoulders sagged. "Oh, Mother, do not insult me. I have nothing to gain. Except seeing my son happy. You know I have always loved him best. He—"

"Enough." Moonsnail pounded the floor with her walking stick. "You've never cared about any of your children—until today. Why?"

Dark Rain flipped the ends of her belt, delaying.

"*Why?*"

"Well, Mother. I wanted to tell you later, after we had warmed to each other, but since that may never happen . . . I am planning on petitioning for readmittance to the clan. I have nothing left but my children, and you." Dark Rain looked up at her from beneath long dark lashes and said in a contrite voice, "I won't announce my petition today. This is a grand day for our clan. I don't wish to spoil it, but perhaps tomorrow—"

Moonsnail lifted her stick and swung it with all her might, cracking her daughter across the knees.

Dark Rain cried out in shock, "Have you lost your souls! I am your daughter!"

"No," Moonsnail calmly replied. "You are not, and before I allow you to petition the clan for readmittance, you will tell me what you have to gain from this marriage. What really happened at Windy Cove? *Why* would Seedpod speak with an Outcast woman? Eh? How much do you owe his clan? Is that the core of this? More gambling debts? Did you think to trade your son to pay them off?"

Moonsnail rose on rickety knees and raised her walking stick over her head. Dark Rain scrambled backwards like a crab fleeing for its life. "*Mother!*"

"Tell me, blast you! Or as Sun Mother knows, I'll break every bone in your miserable body!"

Seven

Dripping wet, Kelp trotted through the sea-foam that scalloped the beach. Last night's storm had washed tens of tens of glittering shells up on the shore, as well as living creatures. Tiny crabs skittered across her path, forcing her to swerve to miss them. Salt-scented wind caressed her face. The group of children who had come to fetch her ran along far behind; she could hear their gay laughter as they played tag with the surf.

Kelp ran faster. Her mother . . . the very idea terrified her.

Before being Outcast, Dark Rain had returned to the clan only on Celebration Days, always with a new man, and always smiling as though she alone knew the secret of Sea Girl's rising tides. The sharp points of her teeth showed when she smiled that way, reminding Kelp of a shark's mouth. Her mother always laughed too much, and gave away bags full of jewelry: conch shell bracelets, strings of pearls, whelk whorl hairpins, and bleedingtooth shell necklaces. Items she had won gambling. But her mother spent less than a hand of time a day with her children—and if Pondwader or Kelp tried to hug her or touch her bright necklaces, Dark Rain would slap their hands and shove them away.

"Pondwader! Look what you did. You got sand down the front of my tunic! Mother, he will be a wild animal all his life if you don't teach him manners. Now, run away, Pondwader. Run far away. I do not wish to see you anymore. And you, too, Kelp. I am tired of you both."

As they'd grown older, Kelp and Pondwader had started running away the instant they saw her coming. They'd tried hiding in the forest, but someone always found them and dragged them back. Then they had discovered that if they plucked hollow reeds from the marshes to breathe through, and weighted themselves down with coral, they could lie invisible in any body of water. No one, not even their grandmother, could find them.

Kelp pounded up the path that led into the heart of the village. Shelters stood empty, food bags swinging in the wind, although dogs lay in the cool shade beneath the roofs. Children, and adults, crowded around the council shelter. They watched her approach with dark furtive eyes. Men whispered behind their hands, while women stared in silence.

Kelp slowed down and panted, "Where is my grandmother? She sent for me."

Her aunt, Polished Shells, a plump woman with bushy black eyebrows, shouldered through the crowd and guided Kelp a short distance away. She placed a hand on Kelp's shoulder, and the tiny shells of her bracelet glittered in the sunlight. "Moonsnail took your mother back to her shelter, so they could talk while she watched over Pondwader," she murmured. "Take great care, Kelp. Your mother is acting like Vulture with a moldy carcass in sight."

"She always acts that way, aunt," Kelp said, and gestured to the crowd. "Do my relatives believe I will take her side? Is that why they look at me with such indecision?"

"They do not know what to believe. We suspect Dark Rain wants readmittance to the clan."

Kelp lifted her chin. "Well, I, for one, will vote against her."

Polished Shells smiled wanly. "Yes, me too, even if she is my sister. She has shamed our clan too many times. But all this is for later. You had better go to your grandmother now, Kelp. I will handle things here."

"Are you certain you don't need my help?"

"No. I saw my sister's wicked face. I fear there is something very unpleasant awaiting you at your grandmother's shelter. Go now, and get it over with. Come speak with me tonight, at my shelter. I will tell you what passed here today."

"Thank you, aunt."

Frightened murmuring broke out as Kelp walked away. She knew how they felt, her belly hadn't stopped twisting in days. First Dogtooth's visit to the Four Shining Eagles, then Pondwader's brush with death, now her mother's return. The world might very well end.

The wind had picked up. Oak branches creaked and moaned in complaint, tossing the hanging moss as Kelp swung wide around the midden where last night's shells topped the pile, drying in the sun. A chaos of flapping gull wings moved over the pungent mound. The birds fought, hoping to discover a fragment of clam or oyster. Squawks serenaded the village all day long.

Her grandmother's shelter came into view. Kelp sucked in a deep breath to prepare herself.

Dark Rain lay draped over a pile of blankets on the northern end of the shelter, her eyes staring blandly up at the roof while Kelp's grandmother held a cup, probably water, to Pondwader's lips. He seemed to be drinking.

Kelp entered the shelter, ignoring her mother, and knelt at Pondwader's side. "You look better," she said. "How are you feeling?"

Pondwader reached out and weakly gripped Kelp's hand, then mouthed the words, *Be careful.*

Kelp nodded, and Pondwader smiled faintly.

Moonsnail noted the exchange. "Kelp," she said, "can you hold Pondwader up while I refill this cup with water?"

"Yes, Grandmother." She slipped an arm behind her brother's back to support him. Pondwader gazed at Kelp as if his spirit floated far away and he only half saw her, but knew the danger she faced and feared for her. She whispered, "Everything is fine. Don't worry."

He nodded.

Moonsnail turned to dip more water from the big gourd behind her, then tipped the gourd cup to Pondwader's lips again. He drank and drank. Rivulets ran down his cheeks and soaked Kelp's arm.

"There," Moonsnail said, "that's enough. I'll give you more later. I want you to rest now, Pondwader. Your fever's broken. Try to sleep some more."

Barely audible, Pondwader responded, "I'll try."

Kelp eased him down to the sleeping mat and pulled the blanket up over his pale throat.

Moonsnail sank back on the mat. "Kelp, your mother is back."

"Yes, I see that. Welcome, Mother."

Dark Rain laughed. "Great Vole, look at you. You've barely enough flesh on your bones to even attract a man's eye. How do you ever expect to get a decent husband?"

"I do not wish a husband, Mother."

"Not wish a husband! What kind of talk is that? Are you ill, or just stupid? Thank the Spirits that Pondwader has enough sense to realize it's time he took a wife."

A wife! The very word sent a shiver through Kelp's souls. Marriage . . . just as Dogtooth had said. And Kelp knew precisely the sort of woman her mother would find for Pondwader. Before she had been Outcast ten-and-four moons ago, she had taunted Pondwader with possibilities. One night just after winter Celebration Day, Dark Rain had stretched out on her stomach before her children and propped her chin in her hands. She had returned from a visit to the western shore and wanted to tell Pondwader a very funny story she'd heard, a story of a young man murdered by his own clan on his marriage day because he had taken one look at his intended bride and run away screaming. "She had the Madness, you see," Dark Rain had whispered, "and was staked to the ground so she could not tear his eyes out. She spread her legs for him, and he saw the oozing sores lining her thighs." When Pondwader had shuddered, Dark Rain had laughed wickedly. "Be a man, Pondwader. The clan must come first. Don't worry. I shall make the best match I can for you, and you will obey me and marry whatever wretch I choose. Even one so diseased she can barely walk." At her son's horrified face, Dark Rain had rolled onto her back and laughed until she'd choked. Kelp had dragged Pondwader away and they'd hid all night in the forest.

Kelp's brows lowered. "Have you asked Pondwader about this? Does he want the woman?"

"What he wants is of no importance. It is time. He is ten-and-five summers." Dark Rain showed her pointed teeth. "By the time I had reached his age you were already born, Kelp. Shall we allow your brother to romp about like a wolf-pup forever? It is his duty to put the puny manhood between his legs to work. And you, my daughter, are next. I want a man's penis in your hands by next summer Celebration Day."

Kelp could not explain the effect her mother's words had on her. She seemed to know exactly how to sink her talons into Kelp's braided souls and rip them apart.

"Dark Rain," Moonsnail said as she slammed down her gourd cup. "I will speak with Kelp and Pondwader alone. Leave us."

"Oh, Mother!" Dark Rain jumped to her feet. "I'm the one who managed the great feat. Why can't I tell them?"

Moonsnail slowly lifted her chin. Rage lit her old eyes. "If you do not leave this moment, I will kill you with my own hands, you bitch in heat."

Dark Rain's chin jutted out defiantly, then she whirled and stamped away.

Kelp fell back to the floor mats and shook her head. "Why does she always have to dart people with her tongue?"

"It is your mother's only talent, Kelp, so she practices it constantly." Moonsnail filled two cups with prickly pear tea, and handed one to Kelp. "Now, let us speak of more important things."

"Was she lying? About Pondwader marrying?"

Moonsnail grunted softly. "No. There is a woman who is interested in your brother."

Kelp squeezed her eyes closed. "Who?"

"The War Leader of Windy Cove Clan."

"Have I met her?"

"Yes, a few times. She was not War Leader then. I've forgotten what her title was. Her name is Musselwhite."

Kelp gasped and Pondwader's lips moved, but no words came out. He turned his head and opened his eyes. "*Musselwhite?*" he whispered. "She mentioned marriage, but I . . . I never dreamed . . ."

Moonsnail brushed soaked white hair from Pondwader's brow. "Are you strong enough to speak of this? It can wait. Your health is more important."

"I wish to speak of it," he answered weakly. "Kelp . . . could you bring some extra blankets . . . pile them so I can sit up?"

"Yes!" She ran to the opposite side of the shelter and gathered an armload, then came back, folded them until they seemed to be the right height. She lifted Pondwader and shoved them beneath his shoulders. "Is that all right?"

He nodded. "Thank you."

Kelp sat down again. The three blankets elevated Pondwader's torso just enough so that he could see over his feet to look at both of them. Kelp and Moonsnail moved to sit on either side of him. He seemed half dazed, his eyes moving erratically, as if he were dizzy, or had overindulged on fermented elderberries. Wet locks of white hair glued themselves to his cheeks, highlighting the arc of his cheekbones, and his straight nose. In the village behind him, a pack of new puppies romped in play, growling and nipping at each other as they loped around the shelters.

"Musselwhite," Pondwader breathed, sounding awed.

Kelp recalled their first meeting vividly, though she could not have been more than four summers. She and Pondwader had been playing, and they'd both run into the ceremonial shelter where the evening's feast lay on long mats—and could not be touched until Sun Mother slipped into the Village of Wounded Souls to sleep. Pit-roasted deer hindquarters, boiled clams, and other dishes—all delicious-smelling—had filled the shelter; just the sorts of things children longed to get their hands on. People packed the shelter, men laughing, talking, women holding crying babies, young couples preparing to be married, everyone sparkling in their shell-covered tunics and jewelry. Pondwader had attempted to follow Kelp through the tangle of grownup legs, and had run smack into Musselwhite before he'd seen her. Kelp had turned to find out where he was, and seen the warrior woman kneel before Pondwader, smiling. Musselwhite had asked, "Are you as hungry as I am, little Lightning Boy?" Speechless, Pondwader had only nodded, and the great Musselwhite had reached out, pulled off the leg of a roast quail, and smuggled it to him. "Here, this should keep your belly from grumbling until feast time."

Kelp knew that Pondwader had dreamed of Musselwhite's magnificent voice for years. He'd told her often enough.

"We need this marriage," Moonsnail said. "Being related to Musselwhite will give us Power we would not dream of now, and not just in war. Trade would benefit as well. But I would never wish you to be unhappy, Pondwader. I will not force—"

"Grandmother . . ." He tried to straighten himself against the blankets. "Why me?

"That's a good question," Kelp said. "Musselwhite could have any man she wished. Why skinny Pondwader?"

"I will not lie to either of you," Moonsnail said. "You deserve to know the circumstances of this arrangement. It seems your mother gambled away everything else she had, and when she had nothing left to pay her debts to Windy Cove Clan, she offered them her son."

Kelp's mouth dropped open in indignation, but Pondwader just smiled weakly.

"Have they accepted?"

"Not yet. If you agree to this, I will contact Seedpod, Patron of Windy Cove, and we will sit down and haggle about it."

"Musselwhite . . . does she even know my name?" His tone sounded wounded, as if he very much wanted her to know his name. "Or just that an alliance is being 'haggled' with Heartwood Clan?"

Moonsnail took his hand and squeezed tightly. "The Lightning Birds are flashing in your eyes, Grandson. Quiet them down. This is only a beginning." Moonsnail's face fell into a mass of wrinkles. "There is another reason I believe this would be good, Grandson. Dogtooth's Dream, and Cottonmouth's raids . . . well, people are frightened."

"I know." Pondwader looked down at the coarsely woven blanket covering him. Though his people dyed everything, the colors faded quickly, leaving vague red and yellow patterns. "I feel their fears growing. It will be better for everyone if I go away. I don't mind, Grandmother. In fact, I—"

"Well, I do!" Kelp blurted. "I don't want you to go away, Pondwader!"

A sandy gust of wind battered the shelter. Pondwader closed his eyes, waiting for it to pass, and Kelp ducked her head. It careened through the village, making children scream and dogs bark, and dissipated out over the ocean.

When he turned back, Pondwader murmured, "I will miss you, too, Kelp, but I must do this. Soon. Please, Grandmother. Make the arrangements. I . . . I need to be in Windy Cove Village by the beginning of the Moon of Mist."

Moonsnail's gaze slid from Pondwader's face to Kelp's, then she frowned down into her cup of tea, clearly searching the eyes of her soul. The Moon of Mist began in seven days. "Do you wish to tell me about this rush?"

Pondwader replied, "Forgive me, Grandmother. I can't. I promised." His eyes fell closed, and his head tilted to the left. In a few heartbeats he was fast asleep.

Kelp and Moonsnail sat quietly for a full finger of time. Then her grandmother leaned forward and whispered, "What was he talking about, Kelp? Who did he promise?"

She shook her head, thinking about the incident with old Dogtooth at the Sacred Pond. Her brother had been so sick by the time they'd gotten home that she had never been able to ask him what the ghosts had told him . . . but she suspected that's who he had promised. "I do not know, Grandmother."

Moonsnail scowled at Kelp as if she didn't believe her, but she let it go, and rose to her feet. "Well, come along, child. It's time we faced the clan. They will be worried that Dark Rain has caused some new calamity. Let's give them the good news. Quickly. Before they make any rash acts, like hanging your mother to stop the debate."

Seedpod sat with the other Spirit Elders of Windy Cove Clan in the council shelter around the dead coals of last night's fire. Old man Ashleaf's tunic had a red wolf painted on the skirt. As he leaned forward to whisper to Seedpod, short white hair blew over his eyes. He brushed it away. "I tell you, we must do something. Now! Before it's too late."

Dreamstone nodded as if in agreement. The woman's withered face changed expressions continually, going from terrified to amused in a heartbeat. She had left her long, gray hair loose to flutter in the wind. Both Dreamstone and Seedpod wore plain tan tunics belted with braided palm cord.

Seedpod concentrated on the feel of cool air moving in and out of his lungs while he studied his daughter.

Musselwhite sat cross-legged on a mat at the northeastern corner of the council shelter, her back against the support pole. She had bathed before dawn, washed her long silver-streaked black hair and braided it, then dressed in a clean tunic. Strings of oyster pearls chevroned the front. Not even their glistening beauty could lessen the frightening numbness that slackened her face. Every movement of her hands came sluggishly, as if a wall of black water had crashed down upon her while she slept, driving the air from her lungs, and no matter how hard she swam, trying to reach light and air, she could not. Ever.

Seedpod hurt for her. Musselwhite was undoubtedly realizing she would never again see the smiles of those she loved, feel their gentle touches, or hear the warmth in their voices.

"I tell you we cannot survive!" Ashleaf exclaimed and looked around the village to assure no one overheard. "We must go and beg another clan to take us in. It is our only choice!"

Seedpod wiped sweating hands on his hem and shook his head. "Our only choice is to give up our own clan and blend into another? Shall we allow our traditions, our special stories, to die, Ashleaf?"

The old man's pained eyes narrowed. "I do not wish it, Seedpod, but—"

"Then there must be another way!" Dreamstone said. "Let us consider every other possibility first. What if we move our village far to the south? What will Cottonmouth—"

"He will hunt us down and kill every one of us," Musselwhite answered softly, without taking her gaze from the hands folded in her lap. Scars crisscrossed the tanned skin. Many of the nails had been peeled to the quick. Diver used to grab her hands and hold them when he saw she was biting the nails so. When she tried to tug them back to peel them some more, he would refuse to let go and they would end up laughing and wrestling. . . . "Our only choice is to fight Cottonmouth."

"Musselwhite, we have eleven warriors left!" Dreamstone objected. "Cottonmouth has at least ten tens, and his numbers are growing daily. We can't fight him! There must be a place far away where we can run and he will not follow." She extended her hands in a pleading gesture to the other Spirit Elders. "Think! What about the islands far to the south?"

Ashleaf rubbed his wrinkled chin, and glanced at Seedpod. "It has been mentioned before, but none of us wanted to abandon the lands of our ancestors. But now . . ." he exhaled hard, "yes, it might work. Musselwhite? Has Cottonmouth ever visited those islands? Would he follow us so far?"

Musselwhite turned away, staring out at the white-edged ribbons of green water rolling into shore, leaving a many-colored blanket of twinkling seashells behind. Laughing gulls swaggered over them, pecking for food, squawking and fighting, fluttering up in defeat, then diving down again to join the foray.

"Musselwhite?" Ashleaf called. "Are you listening? Would Cottonmouth follow us to the southern islands?"

Reaching down, she picked up a golden leaf that had blown into the shelter, and sightlessly studied the pale green veins. All meaning seemed to have drained from her world. All joy. As if in punishment, Seedpod's memory displayed Diver and Musselwhite for him. . . . Diver giving Musselwhite that tender reproachful look, reminding her without words that she was being foolish, that she knew their children needed her. Their children and what remained of their clan.

Seedpod watched Musselwhite's eyes drift to his shelter, where Diamondback slept—watched over by little Thorny Boy, who kept a palmetto fan moving to cool his brother. Musselwhite crushed the leaf in her palm. Before they could hope to face Cottonmouth, she had to regain her composure. . . . But how could Seedpod help her do that?

Seedpod's white brows drew together as he peered at Musselwhite. "I believe we have another choice."

Ashleaf and Dreamstone followed Seedpod's gaze.

Musselwhite turned to face him, and her fists curled into claws as if in pain.

"Diver is gone," Seedpod said gently. "For the sake of the clan you must marry again. This boy from the Heartwood Clan—"

Musselwhite lurched to her feet, and shouted, "How can you ask such a thing so soon after . . ."

Diver's death. Go ahead, say it, my daughter. Say it! He's dead.

Musselwhite stood with her mouth open.

Dreamstone's eyes filled with sympathetic tears, while Ashleaf fiddled nervously with his sandal laces. Only Seedpod continued to look at his daughter, his heart torn with love.

Seedpod knew the other elders were waiting for Musselwhite to break into sobs, or run away. They would wait forever.

Musselwhite inhaled, visibly bracing herself, and sat down again. "T-tell me about this boy. Did you mention his name? I don't recall it if you did."

Seedpod murmured, "Pondwader. His name is Pondwader. His people know him as the White Lightning Boy."

"A Lightning Boy . . . Yes, I—I think I recall him. What does his clan have to offer us?"

Ashleaf said, "Six or seven tens of warriors. Added to ours, we might have a chance against Cottonmouth. What do you think, Musselwhite?"

All of the elders, including Seedpod, leaned forward, waiting for her reply.

For the first time, Seedpod noticed how intently the villagers were watching the council shelter. They had gathered in the middle of the village to talk. Men paced the sand, murmuring darkly, and women whispered amongst themselves. Children and even dogs lay quietly on sleeping mats, not daring to make a sound. All eyes were riveted on the council shelter.

Musselwhite's eyes again drifted to where Thorny Boy sat fanning Diamondback. Seedpod followed her gaze. Thorny Boy seemed to sense his mother's attention, or perhaps he'd been constantly glancing up. He waved his fan at Musselwhite and she lifted a hand in return. Thorny Boy smiled broadly.

"Musselwhite?" Ashleaf pressed. "Will eight tens of warriors be enough?"

An eerie sense of disaster to come filled Seedpod, as if one of the Four Shining Eagles had just fallen to earth and Hurricane Breather now stood on one foot.

"Perhaps," Musselwhite said tiredly. "Yes, we might have a chance." She looked up with numb weariness. Seedpod's heart ached. "Father, send word to Moonsnail. I will go with you when you meet to discuss the marriage. I will wish to speak with her War Leader, and I want to meet this Lightning Boy."

Seedpod got to his feet and walked over to put a hand on Musselwhite's shoulder. Pride filled his old chest. He patted her gently. "I will do it immediately."

Eight

Bah! Where did you hear that, child?

Hmm? Speak up! . . . Well, Red Bark is a fool. He always has been. Never listen to his stories. He makes most of them up, whereas *I* am telling you the truth.

. . . At least so far as I recall it.

When Pondwader dove into the Sacred Pond it really did wash away all his human souls, that's why he became so ill. For three days Pondwader lay on the verge of death. He would have died if the Lightning Bird had not flown down and laid a thunderegg in his chest to replace his souls. Oh, yes, he came very close. Poor Pondwader. That event was just the beginning. From the moment that baby bird began to peck holes in its fiery shell, his life changed forever. Every time a fragment of shell burned away, Pondwader began to shake and see flashes of light. . . .

Diver gritted his teeth while Starfish worked on his wounds, and fought back the urge to cry out. He lay on his belly on a soft yellow and blue blanket, his hands tied behind his back, his feet bound to the northeastern shelter pole. Wind swept the shelter, making it shudder and groan. Hatred animated the crone's touch. She hurt him whenever and however she could. That morning she had called four men to hold him down, then she had yanked the dart from his back, salved the gaping hole, and wrapped it in fine fabric, moving the roll of bandages brusquely around his back and pulling it under his stomach. Then she had roughly but thoroughly cleaned and salved the wound in his shoulder. That had been a hand of time ago and Diver still had not stopped shaking from shock.

He forced himself to gaze at the waves dashing the shore, throwing spume ten hands high. It helped take his mind off her cruelty. Starfish sat cross-legged beside him, gray wisps of hair blowing about her toothless sunken face. She dipped a cloth in a gourd of warm water and washed the club wound on Diver's head. The scent of leatherleaf soap encircled him. He winced when the rag deliberately rasped off a piece of his skin.

"Packrat Above!" he blurted in pain. "Can't you be a little more gentle?"

"I could. If I wished to." Her reedy voice betrayed no more emotion than a dead frog's. She dipped her rag again and scrubbed his wound even harder.

Diver clamped his jaw and squeezed his eyes closed. It felt as if she had poured boiling water into the bruised flesh! She seemed to enjoy his anguish. A vague smile curled her withered lips. He was concentrating so hard on his pain that he barely heard the soft steps on the sand.

"Starfish," Cottonmouth's haunting voice said. "Cut his hands loose. You have done enough for today. I wish to speak with Diver alone."

Diver peered at Cottonmouth. The man wore a rich golden-hued tunic. His long, graying black hair hung in a braid down his back. The style accentuated the silver in his temples, and made his dark eyes seem even larger, like gleaming black moons in the tanned oval of his face.

"Yes, Spirit Elder," Starfish replied and sawed through Diver's bonds with her hafted chert knife. His aching hands fell to his sides. It took great effort to flex his fingers. Starfish rose on wobbly legs. "Shall I return to finish my work later?"

"How is he?" Cottonmouth asked. Concern laced his words. "The wounds look clean."

"He is well enough," Starfish replied gruffly. "He'll live . . . I think."

"Make certain he does." Cottonmouth's soft tone left no room for failure. Starfish blanched. She jerked a nod. "Yes, I will."

"Go now. Return later to check on your patient."

The old woman threw Diver a hateful look, picked up her gourd of water, knife, and rag, and hobbled away through the center of the village, swatting at the dogs who loped playfully at her heels. The wind carried the scents of roasting fish, and Diver could see a group of women standing around a low fire, talking, laughing. Starfish headed toward them.

Cottonmouth scrutinized Diver's naked body. "I heard that you ate a good breakfast. Are you feeling stronger?"

Diver laughed, and squinted at the pounding surf. Water jetted upward, drops glittering against the sky's thin, gray clouds before they dropped to earth again. How could Cottonmouth always sound so sincere? Did he practice that tone at night when no one could overhear? Pelicans huddled together on the beach, their beaks tucked against their breasts.

"I brought you something, Diver."

Diver pulled his gaze back as Cottonmouth reached down and untied something from his belt. The man touched it reverently, then handed it to

Diver. It was a deerbone awl, the tip broken. Diver took it and turned it over in his hand. . . . His breath caught. On the opposite side the owner's personal identification mark had been etched into the bone, three chevrons, and a large X: Musselwhite's mark. If he concentrated, he could *feel* her there. Part of her still lived in the awl. She must have breathed Spirit into it when she'd made it. Diver's fingers closed around the tool and he clutched it to his chest.

"I thought it might ease your pain," Cottonmouth said.

"Why would you care?"

The small flamingo-tongue shells on Cottonmouth's belt jingled as he sat on the white sand and laced his fingers around one drawn-up knee. A long silver lock had come undone from his braid and whipped about his face. "Pain disturbs me. It always has."

Diver smoothed his thumb over Musselwhite's mark, cherishing the tool that she too had touched.

"Diver," Cottonmouth said. "I came to speak with you about . . . about a Dream I had. It was very strange."

"What dream?"

"Oh, I've had it many times, but I've never seen this part, so I did not know until last night that you would be at my side when the world ends."

"When the . . . the world ends?" Diver asked. Cottonmouth's voice was like mink's fur rubbed against the soul, soft and soothing, yet throwing sparks. "What are you talking about? Is this the same Dream you had two summers ago? About the Lightning Birds—"

"I don't know why you're there," Cottonmouth interrupted. "Do you? That is the curiosity. I think you must have joined me, become one of my followers, because you are wearing a tunic made here, at Standing Hollow Horn Village. It had a blue zigzag painted across the breast." He drew it on his own tunic, and in the sky behind him gulls swooped and soared on the fitful wind.

"I would never become one of your followers, Cottonmouth."

Cottonmouth tipped his head back and surveyed the swift-moving clouds above them. "The Dream . . . it begins just as today did. Blustery. Cool. We are standing over there." He pointed to a place at the edge of the trees where an old stump tilted at an angle, toward the sea. Cottonmouth's voice dropped to a pained murmur. "You and I . . . we see Hurricane Breather coming. He is ripping Sky Girl apart with his bare hands as he strides across the water. He's *huge,* Diver." Cottonmouth closed his eyes. "Rain pours down in unbroken blankets . . . whole trees snap and fly through the air around us . . . people are screaming, fleeing for their lives . . . *then I see them.*"

Caught in the captivating spell of his deep voice, Diver asked, "Who?"

"The Lightning Birds." Cottonmouth turned to peer due east. "They are coming for me, crackling through the clouds like blue-white flames." He extended a hand, as though reaching out to them now.

"And then?"

Cottonmouth pulled his hand back and rested his fist on his knee. "Then . . . then nothing. The world dies."

A prickle climbed Diver's spine. He raised the awl so that he could press Musselwhite's mark against his cheek. The bone felt smooth and warm. Cottonmouth's handsome face had slackened, his eyes gone wider, staring, unblinking.

"The death of the world is necessary, Diver," he said. "Evil has invaded every soul alive. Like a cancer, it has crept into the trees and animals. Even the tiny snails that crawl on the forest floor. Don't you see? Hurricane Breather is our savior. The destruction will be a cleansing—a necessary purging." In a slow, jerky motion, he filled his right hand with sand, and let the grains trickle through his fingers. They blew away.

Diver said, "Why do you wish to see the world die? The world is a beautiful place."

"I do not wish it, Diver. Not at all. Evil people have brought this about. Not me. People like Musselwhite."

Diver nuzzled the awl. "Musselwhite is not evil."

"Isn't she?"

"No."

Cottonmouth smiled that humorless smile. "Perhaps I shall send old man Barnacle over to tell you the story of his family, of how both his little children were murdered by Musselwhite in a raid. I was there, Diver. I saw what she did. Yes . . . Spirits Above, I did. I tried to stop her when she wanted to rob the babes of their jewelry before she—"

"Enough," Diver said. "I don't want to hear it! Your obsession with Musselwhite does not interest me!"

Cottonmouth did not move for a long time. Then he said, "Let us finish discussing my strange Dream. It interests me that you are there beside me at the end. Why do you think that is?"

"Perhaps I'm trying to murder you before the Lightning Birds can save you."

The lines around Cottonmouth's eyes deepened. "They'll save me anyway," he murmured. "In the Dream, I am looking frantically for Musselwhite or the Lightning Boy, but I see only you, Diver. You and I, and a village of shrieking people. I don't—"

"Do you truly believe that the Lightning Birds will save you from the wrath of Hurricane Breather? After the things you've done?"

"Everything and everyone will be cleansed—including me. What I have done makes no difference," Cottonmouth replied. "As Hurricane Breather cleanses the world, the Lightning Birds will cleanse the skies. They will burn away all the evil in the heavens and beyond. Once they have purged the clouds and birds, they will flash through the Daybreak Land, purging the Shining People." He turned empty eyes on Diver. Dark and Powerful, like the lull just before a monstrous tidal wave strikes the beach. "Even my own followers and I. We will be cleansed, too, Diver. We must be, before we can enter the shining new world that has been prepared for us. We . . ."

Diver shifted to bring his right arm up and rest his cheek upon it. The morning's ordeal, Starfish's cruelty, all had left him exhausted. He continued listening to Cottonmouth's Dream about the Lightning Birds' world beyond the Daybreak Land, but his eyelids drooped. He jerked them open again, and tried to force himself to concentrate.

Cottonmouth rose to his feet, standing tall and slender, peering down at Diver. "You are tired. When you are stronger, we will talk more of this."

As Cottonmouth walked away, Diver heard him say, "Mulberry, post four guards around the council shelter."

The order was followed by scurrying feet, darts clattering against each other, and a buzz of voices as men took their positions.

Nine

As Sun Mother sank below the western horizon, shafts of brilliant purple light shot across the sky and permeated the wall of fog rolling toward the beach. It sparkled and glimmered over the sea like a creeping rainbow until it twined with the tree branches and engulfed Heartwood Village. The children seemed to sense Old Man Fog's silent message that it was supper time. They stopped sculpting dolphins from piles of white sand, waved good-bye to each other, and headed for their own shelters with dogs trotting happily at their heels.

Beaverpaw, War Leader of the Heartwood Clan, watched them begin building cooking fires. Children laughed so much. It sent joy through his troubled souls. The things Musselwhite had told him had left him numb.

He stood beside her, a short distance away from Heartwood Clan's council shelter. Inside the council shelter, Seedpod and Moonsnail haggled over Musselwhite's marriage to Pondwader. Dark Rain leaned against the north-western shelter pole, listening. She kept casting Beaverpaw sultry glances, and smiling like a bobcat stretched before a mousehole. Every so often, Beaverpaw heard Seedpod's voice raise in outrage, and caught a few hot words, then Dark Rain's cold laugh would fill the pause, but for the most part the negotiations seemed to be proceeding smoothly—though Mussel-white did not seem to care at all.

Long, silvered locks of black hair hung over the front of her dark green tunic. Despite her age, she was still a magnificent woman, full-breasted, with a slim waist and long muscular legs. Her oval face with its high cheekbones and turned-up nose possessed a stony dignity. Fringes of sea-urchin spines adorned her collar and hem, and when the warm evening breeze gusted, they clicked melodiously.

Beaverpaw wore a plain tunic, unbelted, which hung to just below his narrow hips. A medium-sized man, he had trimmed his black hair even with his chin and tied a tan strip of cloth as a headband around his forehead. He had a tadpole's fat face, with small eyes and an even smaller mouth. He stood with his arms folded, nervously studying the great woman warrior before him.

A legend . . . the stories of her extraordinary deeds filled the world. Once, it was said, she had penetrated a heavily armed camp, and rushed ten-and-five enemy warriors to rescue one, *one*, of her own men. Beaverpaw had heard the story from the man himself: Rockroot. He'd said that after Mussel-white had cut his bonds, she had covered his retreat, darting four men while Rockroot, weary from torture, had fled into the forest, running with all his might. Musselwhite had found Rockroot later, hiding in a pile of deadfall. Taking his arm over her shoulder, she hauled him back to her camp and tended his wounds. . . . Rockroot swore that no dart could harm her.

Beaverpaw did not know what to believe. The only thing he could testify to with certainty was that her unnatural confidence and calmness wrested awe from a man.

"So you believe Cottonmouth may attack Heartwood?" he asked rever-ently. From the moment she had arrived, Musselwhite had treated him with great esteem, listening carefully to his words, regardless of the fact that he was no one compared to her. Oh, he had fought a number of battles, and had won most of them, but at the age of two-tens-and-nine summers, he had barely begun his career as a warrior, whereas she . . . she was what every warrior dreamed of being.

"It is a certainty, Beaverpaw. No village has been able to stand against him, and the repeated victories have made him overconfident. I wager he thinks he's invincible. Why shouldn't he attack every village on the coast? Think of the wealth and status he will gain."

Beaverpaw let his arms fall to his sides. "Then we must defend ourselves."

"What do you propose?"

Beaverpaw lifted a hand and gestured helplessly. "I do not know . . . not yet. Perhaps we should call upon our relatives in other villages to band together with us. If they agree, we might be able to—"

"How many total warriors would that give you?"

Beaverpaw's brows lowered. "Perhaps three tens more. Our related clans are very small. They haven't many warriors to offer."

"But if your relatives would provide three tens and Windy Cove added ten-and-one, together we would have a total of over ten tens of warriors. With such a force, we might be a match for Cottonmouth."

"So . . ." Beaverpaw paused to examine her. Wind whipped his short hair around his fat cheeks. The blanket of fog shimmered, but the color had drained away, leaving pale gray where only moments before a glittering pink cloud had existed. "You truly do plan to marry the Lightning Boy?"

"It remains to be negotiated," she answered honestly.

Beaverpaw shrugged. "Such things are often necessary, but he is an odd boy. Just agreeing to marry him proves your courage beyond any doubt. Have you met him?"

"No. I was told he is still ill, sleeping in his grandmother's shelter."

Beaverpaw swiveled his head to peer over his shoulder and frowned. "That's what Moonsnail said, eh?"

"Yes, why?" She tried to follow his gaze, but several shelters lay that way, and she clearly wasn't certain which he'd been staring at.

"Well, it's just that he is sitting up, speaking with his sister, Kelp, at this very instant. Moonsnail must want to delay your introduction. If I were you . . . no, never mind. I shouldn't have said anything."

"If you were me you would go over and introduce yourself? Is that what you were about to say?"

Beaverpaw gave her a lopsided grin. "If he is to be your husband, you should have the chance to see what you're getting into. Perhaps that's why Moonsnail told you he was sleeping. She doesn't wish to scare you away. I know she wants this marriage as much as your clan does."

Musselwhite scanned the village again. "Which shelter belongs to Moonsnail?"

Beaverpaw pointed to a shelter in the rear of the village, just beyond the shell midden.

"Thank you," Musselwhite said, "I would speak with you more later, Beaverpaw, if it will not interrupt your supper."

"I will be waiting for you. Just ask for directions to my shelter when you are ready."

Musselwhite nodded to him, and walked lithely away, heading toward Moonsnail's shelter. As she passed the intervening shelters, people stopped their supper preparations and stared. Excited whispers sounded. Children pointed, their eyes wide.

As Musselwhite neared the shelter, Pondwader watched Kelp rise from where she had been kneeling beside him. She wiped her palms on her tunic. "Blessed Spirits," Kelp whispered. "Here she comes."

Pondwader smiled. He could feel her approach, like an afternoon storm coming, but he could not see her, because he lay on his left side, facing the forest. Her footsteps shished in the sand.

"You must be Kelp," Musselwhite said in that deep, beautiful voice. "Beaverpaw has been telling me about your abilities with an atlatl. He says you can dart a field mouse in the head at five-and-ten paces. Is it true?"

Kelp's fear seemed to lessen. She smiled. "If Beaverpaw says so."

"Don't let her lie to you, Musselwhite," Pondwader said softly. "Kelp can dart a mosquito at ten tens of paces."

"I would like to see that," Musselwhite said and laughed.

"Yes," Kelp replied awkwardly, "so would I. And now, if you will excuse me, I think I will go and . . . and . . . find something to do. Drink all of your tea, Pondwader. I'll be back later." She nodded respectfully to Musselwhite. "Good evening, War Leader."

Kelp hurried out and trotted across the village toward the council shelter. With the sound of her retreating footsteps, Pondwader took a deep breath. Then, with great effort, he rolled onto his back to look up at Musselwhite. Great Shining People, she was even more lovely than he remembered. In the clear depths of those dark brown eyes, he saw kindness . . . and very tired souls.

"How are you feeling?" she asked.

"I'm fine." A smile moved his lips, and he used his chin to indicate the council shelter. "But much of my family isn't. It seems your boldness has disrupted the marriage negotiations."

Musselwhite looked over her shoulder. Dark Rain had walked out of the shelter with her fists clenched, while Moonsnail's old face had gone as pale as sea foam. Seedpod, on the contrary, smiled broadly. Musselwhite ignored them and sat down beside Pondwader. Her dark green tunic spread in a halo around her hips.

"They did not wish me to see you," she said. "They told me you were too ill to speak with anyone."

He nodded weakly. "I know. They fear that once you get to know me, you'll run as fast and as far as you can." He shivered lightly before he could suppress it. "Most people are terrified just by the sight of me."

Musselwhite reached up and pulled the blanket higher to cover his bare chest, then tucked the edges down around his sides. Her hands moved expertly, as if she had tucked many a boy into bed. Gratitude filled his souls. The faded red and yellow designs on his blanket highlighted the paleness of his skin. "You don't seem so frightening to me, Pondwader."

"Don't I?"

"No."

He smiled. "Then you are the only one here who feels so."

"Why do they fear you? The legends?"

"Yes . . . mostly." He winced suddenly and squeezed his eyes closed. The pains grew worse each hand of time, like icicles plunged into his heart.

"Are you all right?"

A swallow went down his throat. "It's just . . . I . . . I've been having sharp pains . . . in my chest."

"Fever does that. I'm sure they'll go away when you gain your strength back. Do you want me to leave you so that you may sleep? Perhaps I should have waited until—"

"No, please stay, Musselwhite," he said, and slowly opened his eyes and squinted at her. "I am so very glad you came to speak with me. There are things I wish to tell you, and I . . . I would like to say them to you now, while we are alone, and before I lose the courage." He glanced at the council shelter where his mother stood grimacing. He could feel her anger gnawing in the pit of his stomach. "Or someone comes over to stop me."

Musselwhite nodded. "Please. Go on."

"First," he said, rushing, "I—I am not a warrior. I know this will disappoint you. Kelp says I can't hit the ocean with a dart, and it's true. Because I am so inept with an atlatl, I am also a very bad hunter, but you must believe me when I tell you I have other—"

"But I heard that you killed a bear last summer. Beaverpaw said you darted the animal right through the heart."

"Yes, well," Pondwader kneaded his blanket with his hands, uncomfortable with the story. "That's true . . . as far as it goes. But I didn't hunt the bear. I hope they didn't tell you I did. Sometimes my family is overly eager to make me seem normal. Kelp and I were out picking berries and I accidentally walked between the sow and her cub. The sow attacked so quickly, I just defended myself, and managed to kill her in the process." His lips tightened into a white line. "I felt very bad about it. I'm sure the cub died, and all because I wasn't watching where I was walking. It was my fault."

Musselwhite tilted her head in understanding and Pondwader plunged on.

"Please believe me when I tell you I have other talents. Truly, I do. Things that will be useful to you. If you will only give me the chance to show you, I promise I will make you a good husband."

Pondwader bit his lip, waiting for her to respond. In essence, he had just told her he could neither protect nor provide food for their family—either of which would ordinarily result in the immediate termination of marriage negotiations. He lowered his eyes, frowning down at his hands, but from the corner of his eye he saw her smile. Had it occurred to her that his family had coached him on what to say to her and how to say it—and that his relatives would be stunned to discover what had come out of his mouth just now? From the expression on her face, she suspected it.

Musselwhite reached out and put her hand over his, stilling its restless movement. Her fingers felt slender and cool. "I would like to make a bargain with you, Pondwader. There are things I wish to say to you, as well, but I must ask that any words spoken between us tonight be ours and ours alone. Can you—"

"Oh, yes, yes, I do agree!" Relief slackened his face, and beneath her palm, he bravely turned his hand, so that he could clasp her fingers. She took his hand in a strong grip. "Thank you. If my mother ever found out what I just told you, she would certainly strangle me."

"You exaggerate, I'm sure."

"No, Musselwhite. Unfortunately, I do not. You see, I know that I am being offered as payment for my mother's gambling debts, and if this marriage should not occur, for whatever reason, she will think it is my fault, that I ruined it somehow. My relatives will surely find me dead—"

Musselwhite smiled, but he continued, afraid to stop now.

"—and I do not wish to ruin it. Please, if I offend you, or say something silly, tell me. I will find a way to make amends."

"I respect honesty, Pondwader. You will never offend me so long as you are telling me the truth. Now, please, go on. Finish what you wished to say to me earlier. About your talents."

He nodded obediently, but hesitated, squinting at her again. Two upright lines formed between his white brows. "My talents are . . . unusual. I often have Dreams—about the future. I—"

"You mean Spirit Dreams? That come true?"

Wetting his lips, he nodded. "Yes, that's what I mean. I have never told any of my relatives about them, because it would just frighten them more. But I knew, for example, that you would arrive at noon today, though the messenger said only your father, Seedpod, would be coming."

Musselwhite nodded. "You are a Lightning Boy, Pondwader. This is not unexpected. What else?"

He clutched her hand. "I also *sense* things, from animals, trees, people . . . even passing clouds."

"What do you mean? What kinds of things?"

"Well . . . I . . . don't know how to describe them. I sense 'intentions,' good or evil. Sometimes I know there are people in the forest, because I hear them half a day's walk away. I can do the same thing with a school of croakers. All I have to do is weight myself down with rocks and lie on the bottom of the ocean, listening."

"That could prove very valuable," she said. "It will allow us to throw our nets out early, and result in a bigger catch."

Eagerly, he said, "Yes. My own clan has never listened to me, but I promise I can improve your clan's catches. Just wait. You'll see. And—and I also know how to talk to ghosts. Crazy old Dogtooth taught me. He . . ."

Musselwhite looked away, suddenly, and Pondwader's belly knotted. *Ghosts.* She must be thinking of her husband. His death had probably torn a hole in her life which now gaped huge and black before her. She gently disentangled her fingers from Pondwader's and sat for a long while, quiet. When she looked back, Pondwader stared at her with all his souls in his eyes.

"I'm sorry," he said. "I'm so sorry. I had not thought—"

"Nor should you have, Pondwader. Forgive me. I'm being foolish. I—"

"Oh, no. No, you are not." His weak hand crept spiderlike across the blanket, reaching out to her again. "You have just lost two children and a husband, Musselwhite. Of course you are still bleeding inside."

"It is more than that, Pondwader," she said softly. "I am not myself just now. To tell you the truth, I don't know who I am. My strength has seeped away like water from a cracked bowl. All I see inside me is a weak old woman who can barely keep her knees from buckling as she walks through your village."

"I wish I could help. How can I? Please tell me."

She patted his hand. "The warmth in your voice has helped. Thank you."

He shifted against his pile of blankets, straightening up a little. That small effort left him breathing hard. He wilted back against the pile, and fought to make himself say what he knew he must. "There is one more thing I wish to say to you, Musselwhite. Please do not think me a child for saying it. I may never again have the opportunity to tell you . . . and I want you to know how very much I wish to marry you. I have idolized you since I was a small boy. Just the memory of your voice, your magnificent voice, has given me strength when I needed it most. Even if—"

"Pondwader, it is not proper—"

"Please, *please*, let me finish."

". . . Go on."

Pondwader's pink eyes widened. "Even if for some reason, we do not marry. Please know that I will always love you. . . ." his words trailed away. He fumbled with his blanket, crumpling it in pale fists. "If I had the power,

Musselwhite, I would ease all of your hurts. I know it is not proper to say such things this soon, but I wanted to tell you."

She ran her fingers over the weaving in the coarse floor mats, not looking at him. "I do not know what to say, Pondwader. It has been a long time since I have heard a young man make such a declaration. A very long time . . . On bright summer evenings long ago when Diver and I used to lie listening to the green rustlings and birdsong that filled the forest, he told me over and over how beautiful I was, how much he loved me, how many things he longed to give me. He vowed that he would fight the whole world to keep me safe. And he did. For two-tens-and-five wonderful summers. I want you to . . . to try to understand. It will take me a long time to grow accustomed to losing him. This marriage will not be easy for me. But my despair, my anger, has nothing to do with you. I like you very much. Do you understand?"

Musselwhite leaned forward and laid a gentle hand against Pondwader's cheek. His eyes shone. "Yes. I understand."

They looked at each other and, for a brief moment, they were close. "I regret that I must say goodnight," she said. "I promised Beaverpaw I would speak with him more tonight and I am already—"

"Will you come to see me tomorrow? Before you leave?"

"I'll try."

Pondwader reached up and took her hand, moving it to his lips so that he could kiss her palm. Her skin felt very soft. The tender, loverlike gesture made Musselwhite smile, and his heart soared.

"Good night, Pondwader." She drew her hand back. "Sleep well."

"And you also."

He watched her go. As she walked across the village, a young warrior named Bowfin stepped into her path. He wore a breechclout and headband, but carried no weapons. He said something too soft for Pondwader to hear, but he heard Musselwhite laugh. Smiling, Bowfin fell into a crouch, and began circling. Pondwader frowned. What was he doing? *Fighting!*

As if accepting the challenge, Musselwhite bent her knees and extended her arms, ready.

Bowfin let out a war cry, lunged, and Musselwhite struck—neat, fast, gauging Bowfin's speed perfectly. She spun, smashed him in the back of the head with her elbow, and when he stumbled, trying to regain his balance, she kicked his feet out from under him. Bowfin sprawled across the sand. He groaned.

Musselwhite chuckled and walked away.

Pondwader sank back against his sleeping mat . . . wondering.

When Musselwhite strode into the council shelter, long hair whipping about her shoulders, all conversation halted. Seedpod stifled a smile as Dark Rain's beautiful face tensed. Moonsnail peered at Musselwhite just as breathlessly. Her wrinkled old jaw had set.

"How was the fight?" Seedpod asked.

"Short."

"I saw that." Seedpod said. "And Pondwader?"

"He's a fine young man," Musselwhite said, alleviating Moonsnail's and Dark Rain's fears. She added, "Father, may I speak with you? It's important."

"Gladly. I could use a reprieve from Moonsnail's stubbornness. Let's go for a walk. It will do us both good."

"Bah!" Moonsnail growled. "You're the one who's stubborn. Go for your walk. I'll be here when you return."

Seedpod grinned, got to his feet, then linked his arm through Musselwhite's and allowed himself to be led through the village.

When they had gone beyond hearing range, Seedpod said, "What's the matter? Is the boy a blithering idiot?"

Musselwhite smiled. "No. Quite the opposite. He has one of the purest hearts I've ever seen. I found his innocence quite disarming."

"Hmph," Seedpod grunted. "He certainly didn't get it from the female side of his family, I can tell you that. Moonsnail and Dark Rain are both as sly and merciless as hunting panthers. What did you wish to speak with me about?"

"Nothing, really. I just needed to gaze into your stern old eyes again—to regain my balance. Pondwader left me floundering."

He gave Musselwhite a sidelong look. "That is . . . unexpected."

"I think he will be a loyal companion."

"That's something, especially since they're waging a real battle over this marriage. Because you can't give Pondwader any children, Moonsnail wants half of our nut harvest every autumn."

"Half!" Musselwhite shouted, stopping dead in her tracks. "That's outrageous! What did you say?"

Seedpod chuckled. "I told them I'd heard Pondwader couldn't even aim a dart, which meant he would be utterly useless to our clan. And especially to you, my dear daughter, since you would not even have a measly squirrel in your boiling bag to prove he was your husband. I promised them they wouldn't get a single nut! In fact, I demanded half their nut crop to pay for Pondwader's incompetence."

"So you are at a standoff?"

"Oh, no. As a matter of fact, the negotiations are going very well. I antic-ipate you'll be married tomorrow, after—"

"*Tomorrow!*" Musselwhite blurted.

"They are in a hurry. This is good, not bad."

"But it's so sudden."

Seedpod shrugged. "They are eager. And we are desperate, let's admit it. That's why I didn't object when Moonsnail suggested tomorrow afternoon. Now, tell me about Pondwader. What did you talk about?"

Musselwhite guided Seedpod around a pile of sand that earlier in the day had been a leaping dolphin, and now resembled a squashed gourd. "He wanted to tell me all of his failings. It was touching, really. He claims he has other talents which will benefit our clan."

"Of course he does," Seedpod replied matter-of-factly. "He's a Lightning Boy. All he has to do is sit beside me when a Trader arrives, and we'll get lower prices. Every Trader with a brain will be intimidated by Pondwader's presence. But don't tell Moonsnail. She hasn't been using Pondwader at all, and she's driving a hard enough bargain as it is." Then he added, "So, you liked the boy?"

Musselwhite sighed, "Yes. I did. Though I fear that being around me will kill his souls."

"You didn't kill Diver's."

Musselwhite gave Seedpod a tremulous smile. "Diver was a strong man. This boy is . . . a boy. When he looked at me his eyes held such longing. It made me sad, Father. No matter how many promises I make to myself not to hurt him, in the end, I will, and it will happen without the slightest effort on my part. His souls are too gentle, too frail, to withstand the rage and desperation that live in my heart. Yes, I'll hurt him. Repeatedly. In tens of small ways. A sharp glance. A harsh word. Like blood pumping from a sliced vein, that tender look in his eyes will gradually drain away until he does not care for me at all." She paused. "Even after our short acquaintance, I find that I do not like thinking of that time. I only hope that he will not come to hate me."

Seedpod squeezed Musselwhite's arm, and looked out toward the ocean. Sea Girl was teasing Brother Earth, sending big frothy waves toward shore, then pulling them quickly away. As Musselwhite and Seedpod neared the surf, a veil of sparkling water droplets glittered in the starlight, and fell cool upon their faces.

"Well," Seedpod said, "perhaps that means you can mold him to your liking. That's not all bad. Think of the possibilities."

He threw Musselwhite a sly glance, and Musselwhite smiled. "Tell me more about the negotiations, Father. I need you to distract me from all the dire thoughts I've been having."

Seedpod kicked at a sponge which rolled away down the beach, bouncing off a variety of large shells. "Oh, there's not much more to tell. Moonsnail is very eager to be related to you, though the old witch won't admit it."

Diver lay sleeping, dreaming of the warm, sunny days of his youth when he and Musselwhite had spent lazy days walking hand in hand through the forests, the scent of wildflowers all around them. Leaf shadows dappled Musselwhite's beautiful face as they passed blossoming berry briars and pushed huge garlands of hanging moss out of the way. She swung his hand and gave him a chiding look.

"That would not be wise," she said. "Not even as a joke. Brush may well kill you by accident."

"How could he? I'll be coming up from the south, striking his village from the densely forested side. We'll be under cover the entire time. He will never—"

She squeezed his hand. "That is the problem, Diver. Brush is no fool. Despite what you've heard, I'm sure he has warriors stationed in the forest all the time. The forest is his only weakness. He *knows* it."

"You give him credit for more brilliance than he deserves—and me less!"

She laughed, and the sound reminded him of shell bells tinkling in the wind. He cherished it, carving it into his memory to hear again and again when the stench of death and horror of war grew too much for him to bear. At the edges of his dream, scenes flitted, like moth wings flashing in the light of a flame . . . Morning Glory dead. Men shrieking, darts flying . . . Blue Echo . . . *Where is Musselwhite? Is she here? My wife! Have you seen my wife? Where . . .*

Faintly, he heard feet on sand. The palm mat beneath him shook. Diver fought against it, not wanting to wake. Voices crashed in.

"Get him up! Now."

Diver rolled to his back just as men's hands reached down for him, gripping his arms and dragging him to his feet. Four warriors encircled him, including the short man, Mulberry. Behind them, Cottonmouth stood. He wore a pale yellow tunic, and had twisted his long, graying black hair into a bun at the back of his head. The silver at his temples shone in the early morning light. His glazed expression sent a chill through Diver.

Diver blinked the sleep away and shifted his feet to get his balance. "What do you want?"

Cottonmouth silently walked forward. In his right hand, he carried something, and as he got closer, Diver saw that it was a child's doll, a turtle-bone doll with a frayed tan tunic and long black hair glued on with pine pitch. A face had once been painted on the toy, but it had faded long ago. Now, only pastel splotches remained. Cottonmouth's men glanced fearfully at the doll, and Mulberry clamped his jaw tight and glared at them, as if to signal them to keep quiet.

Diver glanced around, sensing their fear. "What is it? What's wrong?"

No one said a word. Cottonmouth entered the shelter, spread a blanket over the sandy mats, and stretched out on his side with the doll propped in front of him, staring into its long vanished eyes, an odd—almost loving—expression on his face.

"See?" he murmured intimately to the doll. "I told you he was here. Look at him with your own eyes." He turned the doll around and lifted it closer to Diver. "Do you believe me now?"

Mulberry's fingers sank into Diver's left arm, and Diver felt the youth shaking. His heart began to pound. Bracing his knees, Diver stiffened his muscles to keep standing erect. In bare whispers he heard two men behind him say, *"Crazy,"* and *"I hate it when he does this!"* then another man muttered, *"It's the doll. Every time he touches it . . . !"* Mulberry gave them stern warning glances.

Diver wet his chapped lips. "What—what's happening?"

Cottonmouth drew the doll back and held it to his heart, like a precious child. His eyes moved to Diver, cold, empty. "I have decided you are strong enough, Diver," he said.

"Strong enough? For what?"

Cottonmouth did not smile. His handsome face had gone as rigid as stone. "Mulberry? Stoke up the fire. We will need many coals."

"What are you going to do?" Diver said.

Cottonmouth propped his chin on the doll's head, and his eyes went unfocused. "Do you know, Diver, that all of my life I have struggled to understand the meaning of pain. I mean, why does it seem to be our constant companion throughout life? Why is it that the blood of innocents is so often spilled for no reason at all?"

Diver swallowed hard.

Cottonmouth said, "I am going to let you think on pain for a while. We shall see if it changes your understanding of life . . . as it has mine."

I rest against my pile of blankets and watch Kelp building up the fire in the middle of the shelter. She is carefully arranging small sticks over the old coals, and blowing on them. Her round face is tense with the need to ask me questions—but she hasn't yet, and I wonder what answers I will give her when she works up the courage. Flames lick through the new wood and sparks flit and sway, dancing toward the rafters where a black coating of creosote shines in the sudden flickering light. Kelp sits back on the floor mats and looks at me.

I smile. She is worried about me. I can sense it, like worms twisting in my belly. But she smiles back.

"Do you need more nickerbean tea?"

"Yes, thank you, Kelp."

Raw nickerbean seeds possess a strong poison, but when roasted and crushed they produce a deliciously bittersweet brew. Kelp refills my gourd cup from the gut bag that hangs on the tripod at the edge of the fire, keeping warm. She sets the cup down at my side and frowns at me.

"Are you all right?" she asks. "You've been acting strangely, I mean even worse than usual, and it's more than just the fact that you almost died." She slumps down beside me and extends her long legs. Her short pointed nose has a smudge of soot on the tip. "What's wrong, Pondwader?" Glistening black hair falls down her back. The front of her short tunic is sprinkled with grains of white sand, and she smells pleasantly of wood smoke.

I pick up my cup and stare down at my soul floating on the surface of the dark tea. It ripples in the wavering sea breeze. That's just how I feel, as if my whole being is rippling, going out of focus and coming back again, changing shapes, being born into something bright and new. . . . I swallow hard. "Kelp, I don't know how to explain it to you."

"Well, try, and do it fast before Grandmother or Mother come back. I need to know, Pondwader. Ever since crazy old Dogtooth said you were going to die, I've been worried sick."

"I know you have."

I bite my lower lip and squint at Kelp. How can I tell her that I did die, that I spent three days drifting in terrible darkness, watching each strand of my braided soul fray and come unraveled; each withered before my eyes . . . until only darkness remained. It will frighten her, and I can't bear the thought that my own sister, my best friend, might fear me the same way other people do.

"Do you still feel thunder waking up inside you?" she whispers hoarsely and leans closer.

"Oh, yes," I answer, glad to be on familiar ground. "I've even learned to tell his voice from—"

"What voice?" Her dark eyes narrow.

I take a sip of my tea so I won't have to say anything more. I had forgotten I hadn't told her that part. The truth is beginning to sink in, and I can see anxiety in Kelp's expression. Does she understand?

"The thunder is somebody's voice? But thunder is the voice of the Lightning Birds, how could you . . . ?" She grimaces, then her eyes flare. "Pondwader, do you mean there's a Lightning Bird living inside you?" She almost shouts the last and quickly whirls around to make certain no one overheard. Dropping her voice to a whisper, she says, "Is that what you're saying? Does it talk to you?"

"No. I just hear it roaring."

I swirl my tea in my cup, scattering my soul to the waves, and look away.

I didn't really lie. Sometimes that's all I do hear. Roars and rumbles. Often its voice is silent. But then there are other times . . . times when that voice calls out so loudly that it drowns my own relatives' voices. I marvel at this. Just this morning, a shudder began in the middle of my chest. I don't know what it is, but I have felt it, off and on, all day. Each time points of light have shot through me like tiny bolts of lightning. They hurt, but they are beautiful to watch.

Even though they frighten me.

I fear that soon all those little flashes of lightning may pull together to form one blinding bolt that splits the world asunder, and if that happens? What will become of me?

Will I exist at all?

Kelp says, "Tell me more about the Lightning Bird. What color is it?"

I lift a shoulder uncomfortably. "Could we talk of something else? This . . . it scares me."

"I can see why."

"Could we talk about Musselwhite?"

Kelp seems hesitant, obviously longing to discuss the Bird, but she asks, "What was she like? You talked for quite a while."

I lower my head so that my chin rests on my chest. The shudder is beginning again, building, threatening to tear me apart. The flashes of light . . . they're flying around inside me. I tug my blanket up to cover my chest, hoping Kelp will think I'm just cold. "I l-love her, Kelp. She—"

"What do you mean you love her? You just met her! Oh, are you cold, Pondwader? Let me get you another blanket." She runs to grab one.

I smile. "I love her, Kelp. I think I have always loved her. From the first moment I saw her, I—"

"All it takes is a quail leg, eh, big brother?" Kelp says irreverently and shakes her head as though disgusted. She spreads the new blanket over me. I smile more broadly. "Speaking of which. I had better start supper, or Grandmother will come back here and wring my neck. Keep talking while I work."

Kelp straightens and begins gathering up the necessary tools to make supper. A large wooden bowl of freshly picked mushrooms sits near the fire, our grandmother's favorite. Beside it are smaller bowls of hickory nutmeats and prickly pear fruits. Kelp uses a pestle to mash the fruits and nuts together, then begins forming them into patties to be fried into sweet cakes.

I watch her. There is a baby Lightning Bird thundering inside me. Soft and deep. Like a distant storm being born. I am terrified and ecstatic, as if something magnificent is about to happen.

And I don't know when, or where . . . or why.

Ten

Musselwhite sat bolt upright in her blankets in the council shelter, startling Seedpod from a sound sleep. He sat up, his pulse racing, and stared at his daughter. Sweat coursed down her beautiful face and darkened her thin, finely woven sleeping tunic. She was shaking. "What's wrong?" he asked.

She shook her head. Over the dark village, the Shining People twinkled. A cool salt-scented breeze ambled about, batting at the coils of cordage hanging on the shelter poles, and tugging on the blankets of sleeping people. Musselwhite reached for her atlatl and darts which lay on the floor at her side. Once she had them firmly in her grasp, she said, "I heard Diver. Calling to me."

Seedpod tenderly put a hand on her back. "It's all right. Calm yourself. Such things come from terrible grief."

"In my dream . . ." Musselwhite's voice broke. She took a deep breath. "Cottonmouth . . . Diver said Cottonmouth kept talking about a Lightning Boy."

"What about a Lightning Boy? You mean Pondwader?"

Musselwhite shook her head. "I—I don't know. But my fears, Father, they're so dark and throbbing. I'm too terrified I can't think straight. What's the matter with me?"

Seedpod pulled his blanket up around his shoulders and smiled gently into his daughter's starlit face. Black hair tangled about her cheeks. "The matter?" he said softly. "I think I can answer that question—having lost so many loved ones myself. You are searching everywhere for a safe place to hide, a place where you can lick your wounds and stand face-to-face with your losses, to really look at them. But—"

"But," she whispered and ran a hand through her long hair, "all the safe places in the world vanished with Diver. Oh, Father, I feel so empty. For the past few days I have gone through the motions of life like a sleepwalker, praying I never wake up."

"But you will, daughter," Seedpod assured her in a loving tone. "No matter what diversions you try to stop it. You will awaken."

Musselwhite shook her head. "Already I feel the tendrils of unbearable anguish filtering through my souls, and I know that soon that pain will grow to monstrous proportions and drive out every other concern. And there's this—this wild hope that rocks me, Father. Back and forth, two voices arguing inside me. One says 'He's dead,' the other insists, 'No, he's not.' If I had only seen Diver d-die . . . but I did not."

Seedpod kept silent. After all, not even Diamondback could say for certain that his father was dead.

Musselwhite threw her blanket off and rose to her feet. Starlight shimmered from her dark eyes and deepened the lines etching her forehead, making her seem tens of tens of summers old. "I need to walk. I'll be back soon."

Seedpod braced a hand on the floor mats. "Sounds like a good idea to me."

"You don't have to come, Father."

"I know that. But I'm awake. We can talk more."

He followed her out toward the surf. Her tunic whipped around her hips in the cool night wind. She hooked her atlatl on her belt and carried her darts in her right hand as she walked southward through a glittering field of seashells.

Seedpod walked beside her. "Are you all right?"

"He's dead. Isn't he, father? Diamondback saw him fall. This is just fear tormenting me. Fear and hope. Diver can't be alive . . . can he?"

"It is very unlikely. No matter how much it hurts to admit."

But a memory long buried rolled over and showed Seedpod its face. His nephew, Toad Slayer, had been alive. Two-tens-and-seven summers before, he had led his village against Cottonmouth's warriors and been wounded. Cottonmouth had kept him screaming for days before killing him. Those hideous cries still woke Musselwhite on occasion. She had told Seedpod the story over and over, like a litany used to drive out the evil spirits that possessed her souls. Cottonmouth had tied her in their shelter, so that she couldn't free her cousin, and so she could "stand witness" to what he did to his enemies. Every time Musselwhite had shouted or raged, Cottonmouth calmly returned to the shelter, knelt before her and slapped her until she stopped. She had been pregnant with his son at the time, and the child had kicked frantically throughout the episode, as if trying to escape. With each blow, Cottonmouth had tenderly murmured, "I love you, Musselwhite. Don't do this to me. . . . I love you, Musselwhite. This man is not *your* cousin. He is *our* enemy. Don't do this to me!"

Musselwhite crouched in the surf and picked up a small, perfectly-shaped conch shell that had washed up on shore. Foam encircled her ankles, coating them with bubbles which tickled when they burst. Seedpod stood beside her, looking down. Water filled the hollow of the shell, and in the starlight, her soul stared up at him.

"Maybe . . . maybe if I stare at my own watery soul," she whispered, "I'll be able to wash away my memories of Cottonmouth. Blessed Sea Girl, I still hear his voice, Father. Whispering, seeping from a crack in my souls that I thought I had buried beneath a huge mound of earth."

"What's he saying?"

"He's saying, *You are right, Musselwhite. You are right. . . .*"

"Right about what?"

She shook her head. "He's lying. He must be. He always lied to me." She clutched the shell more tightly.

Seedpod did not know the whole story of what had happened those long summers ago. He doubted anyone did. Musselwhite refused to talk about it, and Seedpod suspected that somewhere deep inside her she believed that by never speaking of those events, she could strip them from her past, or maybe just convince herself they had never happened.

She murmured, "No one is hurting Diver, are they, Father? Those were not his screams I hear in my dreams?"

"Diamondback saw him darted and clubbed, my daughter. To have survived that . . . well, it would take a miracle."

A sob lodged in her throat, but the renewed certainty of Diver's death seemed to ease her fear. She managed to nod. "I must force Cottonmouth's voice down and seal it in its hole again with all the other horrors in my life. Then . . . then I can go on."

"Were those times so bad, my daughter? Why do you never speak of them? It might help."

She placed the conch shell back on the sand and lifted her face to the silver wash of starlight. Long hair fluttered about her shoulders. The world smelled of fish and seaweed. Against the glossy black undercoat of night, the Shining People shone with unusual brilliance, like small blue, white, and yellow fires pushed this way and that by the winds of the Daybreak Land.

"Father . . . please, don't tell anyone about my dreams. They would just frighten people. And I—I must let the hope go, or I will never be able to hoard enough strength to do the things I must to safeguard our clan." She peered up at him. "Please, I could not bear to hear people talking about how Diver might be alive. It would make things . . . harder."

"Whatever you wish."

Rising to her feet, she hugged him. "Thank you, Father."

Seedpod lovingly stroked her back. "You do not need to thank me. I am on your side. I always have been."

She nodded against his hair and whispered, "I know. I thank Sun Mother every day for you."

Slowly, they began the journey back to the council shelter. Seedpod and Moonsnail had argued all afternoon and half the night, but they had not settled their negotiations. At dawn the entire Heartwood council of Spirit Elders would meet to discuss the marriage; it might be a very long day.

"Try to sleep," he said. "There is no telling what foolishness tomorrow might bring."

"I will . . . try," she answered tiredly. "But I make no guarantees."

Blessed . . . Spirits!" Beaverpaw gasped. He lay on his back in a soft pile of autumn leaves, staring up at the dark oak boughs that made a lacy filigree against the star-studded indigo sky. He clawed at the leaves at his sides. Dark Rain bent over him, her mouth working expertly, sucking his seed from his body. Her huge breasts dragged across his belly. He gasped again. Every time cascades of her shining hair fell over her face, obscuring her from his view, she carelessly tossed them back—wanting him to watch. Shameless. She had positioned herself so that all he had to do was turn his head to look directly between her open legs. What a glorious woman! Long legs turned into broad hips and narrowed to a tiny waist, then swelled into those magnificent breasts. "Brother . . . Earth!" he cried out and bucked against her mouth. She stayed with him, working him. When finally he fell back against the leaves, exhausted, she sat up and sensually used her fingers to comb long hair away from her beautiful face.

"Dark Rain," he whispered. "Where did you learn such things?"

"I have been many places, Beaverpaw," she replied tonelessly. "Fortunately I like adventurous men, and they like me." She ran her pink tongue over her lips, slowly. "They like me . . . very much."

"I understand why," he answered. His manhood actually ached. How many times had she nursed him to ecstasy this night, and without demanding anything in return? Though he had given her her share. What a strange, exotic creature she was. Almost . . . inhuman. She frightened him a little.

Dark Rain leaned forward and kissed him. "Tell me what Musselwhite said. About my son. About this marriage. Is she going to go through with it?"

Beaverpaw exhaled heavily. "Repeating things Musselwhite said is suicidal, Dark Rain. Besides, I have already told you everything important. She did not wish to speak to me about private matters. Her words were of war."

"War. Who cares about war?" Her mouth puckered into a pout. She rolled over on top of him and began moving in a rhythm as old as men and women.

"Dark Rain, forgive me. I am truly expended. I do not think I can—"

"But you will tell me, won't you? When Musselwhite speaks about this marriage. You'll come to me immediately and let me know what she says?"

Dark Rain slid forward, bringing her huge dark nipple to his mouth, moving it around his lips. To his surprise, he felt himself responding.

"Yes," he whispered, kissing her flesh. "Of course. Of course, I will."

Eleven

*A*re *you sleeping, eyeless boy?"*

I wake with a startled grunt and squint into the darkness. Turtle Bone Doll perches on the swaying fabric bag over my head. Every time the bag creaks and rocks, she leans the opposite direction.

"I'm not sleeping now," I say, and add, "what are you doing, leaning like that? Trying to keep your balance?"

"No, no. I've made myself part of the bag's Dance with the wind. Haven't you ever done that? Tried to be a part of another soul's Dance?"

"Well, no. It never occurred to me that I could. Though I'm not sure why I'd want to."

"You're not sure why you'd want to! Blessed ghosts." She just stares for a long time, then asks, " . . . *Do you know the story of the Catfish People?"*

"Which story?"

"In the beginning catfish were humans, but their brains were combed out by an evil witch, and they were forced to march north to live with First Catfish. Sealed in that cold land by a wall of snowstorms, First Catfish made the stupid catfish his slaves. Every time one of the stupid catfish did something wrong, First Catfish shoved the offender into the river, hoping he would drown. Finally, First Catfish had shoved all of his slaves in, but instead of drowning, Sun Mother gave them gills. They swam all over the earth and that's how they became food for humans and eagles."

"I've never heard that story before. Does it have a point?"

"I was just wondering if you'd met that same evil witch."

A gust shoves the bag and it starts swinging in little whining circles. Turtle Bone Doll leaps up every time the bag makes a complete turn, and when she lands she whines a different note in time with the bag's Song. Her ratty tunic flies about. Her hair, what little there is of it, appears freshly washed. It glints when she jumps.

"Why are you here?"

"That egg in your chest has been thundering so loudly the whole world is awake. I haven't slept in days."

"You sleep? I didn't know dolls had to sleep."

"You are amazing. Truly. At this very instant, the deliverer's heart and lungs are forming inside you, being constructed of pure light, and all you can think to ask me is if I have to sleep?"

I feel suddenly as stupid as the Catfish People with combed-out brains. Contrite, I say, "Is that why the egg has started to glow so brightly? Sometimes, it blinds me inside. And it gets hot. Very, very hot. As if I have a raging fire in my heart." I rub the sore spot on my chest.

"You do have. And you must learn to Dance with that soul, Pondwader. As quickly as you can."

"Why? What difference will it make?"

Turtle Bone Doll whines a new note in time with the bag's Song, this one so much lower it accents Sea Girl's deep voice. After several choruses, she stops, and turns to peer at me again. *"There is a great storm coming, Pondwader. The storm is Darkness itself. And Cold, like a freezing black abyss. If the world is to live, it will need all the light and warmth it can get. Every twinkle being born in that tiny thunderegg is a shout of joy, and a promise that Life will continue. Listen and remember. If you live . . . you must tell the story."*

"If I live?"

"I guarantee you will tell no stories if you refuse to Dance with that Lightning Bird's blinding soul."

"But how do I do that?"

"Firstly, give up your human feet. You are fighting very hard to keep them firmly planted on the ground. You must learn to soar and flash and thunder."

"And then what?"

A faint grimace twisted Turtle Bone Doll's painted face. *" . . . When you have accomplished all that, call me."*

The morning dawned cool, with the smell of distant rain scenting Sea Girl's breath. Diver inhaled deeply, enjoying the feel of his lungs moving. He lay on his stomach on the shelter floor, looking out at the ocean, his feet bound to the northeastern post, hands tied behind his back. The red welts of burns on his arms and legs hurt unbearably, and high fever roasted his body. Sweat poured from his face, stinging his eyes. Dirty strands of black hair fell over his left eye, but with his right he could see Sun Mother edging above the horizon, just a sliver of gold. Amber light flooded the water, twinkling and glimmering, dyeing the white caps yellow. Gauzy luminescent patches of cloud seemed to jump out from the deep blue background. *Such beauty.* He thanked Sun Mother that she had allowed him to live long enough to witness it.

There had been no honor in his torture! They were not trying to gain valuable information from him. Cottonmouth just wanted to see Diver in agony. Cottonmouth had stood by, clutching that doll to his bosom, calmly telling his warriors where to place the coals and how long to leave them. The man knew the human body too well. The ordeal had gone on until almost midnight. Diver swallowed down his raw throat. He had screamed. It shamed him . . . but he had.

Diver rubbed his cheek against the cool mat, trying to find a comfortable position, and heard footsteps approaching from behind him. Diver did not move. He didn't have to. He had been in Standing Hollow Horn Village for six days, and had memorized those soft, calculated steps. A tingle of antic- ipation went through him. To bolster his courage, he focused on the squeal- ing gulls strutting over the beach, searching for tiny animals stranded when the tide retreated. Their feathers gleamed with the palest of golds.

"I am surprised you're awake," Cottonmouth said.

He walked around and knelt on the sand before Diver, studying his pris- oner. He wore a green tunic painted with tiny scarlet images of barracuda, and belted at the waist by a red sash which he'd knotted on the left side. The ends of the sash fluttered in the breeze, and so did his hair, worn loosely today. He knelt for a long while, silent, as if brooding, then gracefully sat down cross-legged. Dawn's pearlescent gleam slid along the smooth curve of his jaw as he reached out to push Diver's hair from his face so he could look at him. Diver flinched, but his gaze never left Cottonmouth's handsome face.

"My runner has returned from Windy Cove Village," Cottonmouth said. Silhouetted against the radiance of sunrise, his long silvered hair blowing in the wind, he seemed . . . mythical. "Tell me what was happening in the village when you left."

"What? Why?" Diver's voice came so hoarsely, it didn't sound like his at all. "What difference could it possibly—"

Cottonmouth roughly gripped Diver by the chin and twisted his head around. Anger flickered in his cold eyes. "Because I want to know. That's why."

He released Diver's chin with a shove, and Diver gasped as the burns on his arms raked over the palm mat. Breathing hard, Diver rolled to his side and said, "Seedpod was weaving a new blanket. Pretty thing, made from four squares of different colored fabric. He'd made a strong dye from sea grapes that produce the vivid red color, and added nightshade berries—"

Cottonmouth's white teeth flashed. "I should kill you. I don't know why I let you live."

Diver sighed. "Why do you care what was going on in Windy Cove Village?"

Cottonmouth clasped his hands about his right knee and leaned back. Behind him, the molten ball of Sun Mother climbed slowly into the cloud-strewn azure sky. "When my runner arrived at Windy Cove, Musselwhite was gone."

Hope and fear twined through Diver. Was she coming for him? He suppressed the shiver that coursed through his fevered body, and said nothing.

Cottonmouth's huge dark eyes narrowed. "Did you know she was getting married again? Taking a second husband?"

"*Wh-what?*"

Cottonmouth studied Diver's startled expression, then continued, "Apparently, your son Diamondback made it home, only slightly wounded, and told your wife that you were dead. She acted very quickly after that."

"Seedpod acted quickly," Diver corrected. He stared sightlessly at the roof where slanting rays of sunlight glinted from the palm frond thatch, and globular bags of nuts swayed in the wind. At the thought of Musselwhite taking another husband, a sharp pain pierced his chest. Seedpod had been wrangling for this since the first day Diver and Musselwhite had married. And why shouldn't he? Musselwhite's reputation was the only truly great possession of their small clan, and therefore, the only thing Windy Cove could bargain with in times of travail—like now. Of course Seedpod had arranged a new alliance as fast as he could. It was practical, even necessary. But it still brought Diver pain. Their life together had been a miracle of warmth and love.

For more than two tens of summers they had raided and fought, and defended their clan . . . and lain twined in each other's arms at night. Ah, those were good times. Five strong sons born one right after another, then a daughter came like a life-giving spring rainstorm—a girl as beautiful as her mother. Then three more living sons. Three daughters had been born dead in between. They had lost other children, too, most before their second summers. Despite the grief, the sorrow they had shared, life had seemed so wondrous, as if every Spirit on earth and beyond the sky had smiled upon them. Then disaster had struck: four sons drowned when a waterspout ripped their dugout canoe in half and scattered the pieces of their bodies across the sea. Musselwhite's father had drifted away in his sleep. An eternal frost had settled over their family. Musselwhite had just begun to recover when, less than a summer later, Cottonmouth started raiding. Now, only Thorny Boy and Diamondback remained. Thank the Spirits that Diamondback had survived. Diver offered a solemn prayer to the Lightning Birds.

And now, after two-tens-and-five summers at his side and his alone, Musselwhite would remarry.

Diver twisted his tied hands, barely feeling the raw places the ropes had cut. *My poor Musselwhite* . . . She would be going through the motions, do-ing her duty, maintaining her appearance as the great warrior, and all the while her heart would be breaking. Diver hurt for her.

"I did not understand," Cottonmouth said, "until this morning."

"Understand? Understand what?"

"The Dream I had two summers ago. I knew that Musselwhite would bring me the Lightning Boy, but I did not know under what circumstances."

"What are you talking about?"

Cottonmouth wet his lips. "She is marrying a Lightning Boy, Diver. His name is Pondwader. He's from the Heartwood Clan."

"Yes . . . I recall him. He's very young, isn't he? Ten-and-four summers? Maybe ten and five?"

"Ten-and-five summers. His own clan is terrified of him. I have, of course, known about his existence from the day he was born, but I had no idea that he would be her husband when she brought him to me."

Diver shook his head, trying to clear away the fever. He felt as if he were floating on a hot steamy cloud. "You . . . you have Dreamed of this?"

Cottonmouth nodded. "Oh, yes. I know exactly how it will happen. I even know where. I just don't know when."

Diver forced himself to concentrate. "Tell me. What will happen?"

Cottonmouth stretched out on his side and braced himself on one elbow. He casually pointed to a large oak draped with hanging moss which sat on the northwest side of the village. Children played beneath it, laughing, squealing. "She will launch her attack from over there. Now, listen care-fully, because you play a very big part in this. You will call out to her, and she—"

"*I* will?" And at that moment Diver vowed he would never call out to her, not if the survival of the world depended upon it.

"Of course. Why do you think I had to capture you? It is only because of you that I am able to capture her. After you call out, she turns, startled, and then my warriors burst from their hiding places in the brush, and I walk forward. . . ."

Twelve

Moonsnail sat wearily on a pile of soft blankets in the rear of her shelter, watching Kelp scrub Pondwader's long white hair. The leatherleaf shampoo ran in foamy tufts down his pink temples and cheeks. He kept flinching and squirming. Too weak to do it on his own, he obviously felt indignant about having his sister do it. He had bathed earlier in the afternoon and now sat on a mat by the hearth, dressed in a breechclout and sandals. His marriage robe, long and dark blue, hung on the pole to Moonsnail's right. When the soft bodies of murex were extracted from their shells, dried and boiled, they yielded a magnificent yellow dye, which turned a rich bluish purple in the sunlight. The color suited Pondwader. Tens of baby lightning whelk shells scalloped the front of the robe and covered the sleeves, clicking and clacking as the garment swayed in the cool sea breeze. Storm Girl had pulled a thick blanket of blue-black clouds over Heartwood Village. No rain fell yet, but it would come before the day ended.

Kelp's face bespoke purpose. Her brows drew down over her short pointed nose, and her tongue stuck out the side of her mouth. She wore a plain tunic, dirty, splotched with water and soap bubbles, but her long black hair hung clean and glistening in a braid down her back. She stood on her knees behind her brother, vigorously scrubbing his hair. Around her lay wooden bowls, a fishbone comb, a brush made from the stiff inner bark of palm trees, and a large gourd filled with clean water.

"Pondwader," Kelp said. "Lean back. I'll hold you up. I need to rinse your hair."

"All right," he sighed, and leaned against her supporting arm.

Kelp used her other arm to position a wooden bowl beneath his head, then picked up the gourd of water and slowly poured it through his soapy hair. Lather streamed into the bowl, and splashed Kelp's legs. Pondwader had closed his eyes. A serene expression came over his young face, as though he enjoyed the sensation of clean water running over his scalp. He had been so ill, it probably did feel good.

Moonsnail waited until Kelp had emptied the bowl onto the sand and begun combing out her brother's long hair, then said, "Kelp, I left your clean tunic in Polished Shells' shelter. Why don't you go and get dressed? I wish to speak with Pondwader alone."

"But, Grandmother . . ." Kelp objected, the comb still clutched in her hand. "My mother is over there. I—"

"Go on, now! You can stand your mother for half a hand of time. Tell Polished Shells I said she was to loan you her top-shell necklace. I gave it to her, she ought to be able to loan it now and then. Now, get going."

Kelp lowered her eyes and laid the comb at Pondwader's side. He patted her hand and smiled his most charming smile. "This won't take long, Kelp," he whispered conspiratorially. "Grandmother wishes to tell me about my marital, uh, . . . 'duties.' " He turned and winked at Moonsnail, whose mouth puckered disdainfully.

Kelp's eyes widened as understanding dawned. "Oh. Well, good-bye, then. I'll see you later." She scrambled to her feet and ran.

Pondwader smiled as he watched her cross the village, weaving around shelters, and Moonsnail scowled at him. "How did you know what I wished to speak with you about?"

Pondwader suppressed his smile, picked up the comb and ran it through his wet hair. "Well, I will be married in less than two hands of time, and since my mother isn't going to—"

"She wanted to, let me tell you! It was the glee in her voice that made me refuse her the right. I had to order her out of the shelter, bellowing that it was *my* right, since I had raised you. No telling what she would have said. Knowing her, she would have terrified you so badly you wouldn't have had the strength to do anything."

"Grandmother," Pondwader said, "I barely have the strength to stand up by myself, let alone—"

"Well, you won't be standing up! At least I don't think so, and surely Musselwhite realizes your frail condition and will accommodate it, which means you'll be lying down. I know you've never been with a woman. Every girl you ever looked at twice ran away screaming, but—"

"Not *every* girl, Grandmother," Pondwader objected.

"—but surely you understand the general idea."

Pondwader sighed, "Experience isn't everything, I have observed dogs mating, and wolves and—"

"It's not the same," Moonsnail said. To give herself courage, she reached over for her walking stick, but didn't stand. She propped the stick on the floor in front of her and leaned against it, staring down at her grandson. Pondwader squinted his pink eyes at her. "Dogs and wolves do things . . .

Trust me. Musselwhite will expect more refinement. Do you understand what is required of you, or shall I describe it in detail?"

Pondwader flushed and bowed his head. "I understand, Grandmother."

"Good. Women like to be treated gently. Don't rush her. She's just lost her husband and if you jump on her like a panting dog, she's liable to dart you in your most vulnerable spot—which would certainly make the rest of this discussion pointless. In more ways than one."

"I wouldn't rush her, Grandmother!" Pondwader defended. "I love her."

Moonsnail eyed him severely. "Love is not so easily had, Pondwader, though I don't doubt your earnestness. But you must realize that despite what you feel it will take Musselwhite much longer to grow fond of you. In fact, she may never—"

"Yes she will!" he answered suddenly. "Oh, yes, she will love me, Grandmother. I can make her. I promise you. If she will let me."

The burl head of Moonsnail's walking stick felt cool beneath her gnarled old fingers. After summers of use she had worn it smooth, and the oils in her hands had turned the pine a deep dark brown that revealed the intricate swirls of the wood grain. She stared at the swirls now. The desperate longing and sincerity in Pondwader's voice made her heart ache, but what did he know of love or its difficulties—which were many, no matter how much two people cared for each other? He was a ten-and-five-summers-old boy who had never so much as kissed a girl. Not that she knew of, anyway, and since girls scattered at the sight of him, she figured she was probably right. How could he understand the complexities of love?

"Well, I hope it works out exactly that way, but sometimes it does not, Pondwader. No, don't interrupt me. Listen for a few moments. Musselwhite loved her husband very much. Old Seedpod, withered stick that he is, told me he feared Musselwhite might actually take her own life after Diver's death. That is how much she loved the man. She does not really want to live without him." Her voice softened, as she thought of her own dead husband. She had never stopped missing Sandbur. To this day, he filled her dreams, talking with her, loving her. "I understand. I felt the same terrible grief when your grandfather died. So, you must accept the fact that you are a poor replacement for a man Musselwhite lived with and loved for more than half her life. She *may* come to love you one day. But you should not expect it for a long time. It may take three or four summers before she lets herself think about loving you. Do you understand?"

"Yes, Grandmother," he said obediently, but he sounded unconvinced, and perhaps that was just as well. If he wanted to make her love him badly enough, he just might.

"One last thing," Moonsnail said.

Pondwader looked up at her from beneath pale lashes. "Yes?"

"Musselwhite is accustomed to being touched in certain ways. Lovers do that. They train each other. Ask her what she enjoys, and listen if she tells you she does not enjoy something." Moonsnail pointed her walking stick at him. "This will not be an easy thing for you to hear, but I feel it necessary to say. In all probability, my dear grandson, whenever her body is loving you, she will close her eyes and see Diver."

Pondwader's face slackened. "You mean she—"

"That is precisely what I mean. In her heart she will be loving Diver, not you." At his stricken expression, she said, "That will change, Pondwader. But you must be willing to give her time to mourn. Having you close will be a comfort to her in her grief. Treat her well. She is an honorable woman, and though she would never admit it, at this point in time she is vulnerable. The pain may force her to lash out at you without warning or reason. You must understand and forgive. She will come to love you if you are a loyal husband, and gentle with her."

"I will be, Grandmother. I want to be very much."

Moonsnail's old mouth trembled. She anxiously tapped the mats with her walking stick, poking here and there, stabbing a faded blue design, then a yellow one. Pondwader watched her curiously, as though he sensed her fears. He would be starting a new life, far away from Moonsnail, and she did not wish to let him go. For the past ten-and-five summers, she had been his protector, and now she would be turning that duty over to another woman. It worried her. She loved her grandson very much, and he was so delicate, always getting sunburned, and suffering headaches. Bright light hurt his eyes, and he could barely see more than two tens of hands away; after that, he said, the world became a many-colored blur. But Musselwhite would take good care of her grandson, Moonsnail had no doubt of that. It just . . . hurt. She sniffed and wiped her misty eyes on her arm.

"Are you all right, Grandmother?" Pondwader asked.

"No, I am not. I'm going to miss you. You have been a joy to me, Pondwader."

With effort, Pondwader rose to his feet and walked across the shelter to sit beside Moonsnail on the pile of blankets. He kissed her gray hair. "I love you, Grandmother. But I must go. Musselwhite needs me. She does not know it yet. But she does."

"What does she need you for?"

He smiled. "Everything."

"Is that so?" Moonsnail said, and for a time just enjoyed the boy's closeness. Then she pushed him away and noisily cleared her throat. "Let's get you dressed. After that, you had better rest for as long as you are able. With all the feasting and dancing tonight, you will be exhausted by the time you take Musselwhite's hand to go off to your marriage shelter in the forest. I do not want you to be too exhausted."

Kelp fingered the beautiful top shell necklace around her neck. The golden gleam of the shells set off the brown of her clean tunic. She frowned at Pondwader. He stood before their grandmother in his long, blue robe, letting Moonsnail straighten his sleeves and tie the golden sash around his waist. He looked very handsome, though skinny. He was smiling.

Already Kelp missed him. Who would she share her secrets with now? He was her best friend. Tears burned her eyes.

"Well, I do not care!" Dark Rain said.

"That doesn't surprise me," Polished Shells responded tersely.

Kelp didn't turn. Her mother and aunt had been locked in combat since she arrived. They had always hated each other, for as long as Kelp could remember. She suspected that Aunt Polished Shells would have loved to know how to weight herself down with coral so she could lie on the bottoms of ponds and escape her sister. Perhaps, later, Kelp would tell her how.

"It doesn't surprise me," Polished Shells continued, "because you've never cared about Kelp or Pondwader. The only person you care about—"

"That is not true," Dark Rain said in that cold voice. "Today I care very much about Pondwader. As soon as his pathetic penis is working inside Musselwhite, I am free. The bargain will be sealed, and my debts paid. I most certainly *do* care about that, sister of mine."

"You have the souls of a slug," Polished Shells replied angrily. "Get out of my shelter! I don't care what Mother says. I have endured you for as long as I can!"

"Gladly." Dark Rain glided by Kelp without a word, heading toward their grandmother's shelter. She had dressed in her red tunic again, and left her hair loose to hang down her back in a glossy wealth. Her hips swayed as she walked.

Pondwader tensed when he saw her coming. In the blink of an eye, he lay down on his sleeping mat and rolled to his side to sleep—or pretend sleep. Either way, Kelp wished him luck.

Polished Shells came up beside Kelp and put an affectionate arm around her shoulders. "I'm sorry you had to hear that," she apologized. "Your mother always makes me so mad that I—"

"I hate her," Kelp said.

Polished Shells stood silently, watching Dark Rain flop down beside Moonsnail on the pile of multicolored blankets. Her low laugh carried on the breeze. Polished Shells shook her head. "I don't know how Mother stands her—but I need to go see to the feast in the council shelter. Do you want to come?"

"Yes, thank you, Aunt. Anything to stay out of mother's way for another hand of time."

Polished Shells sighed. "Well, then, the council shelter is the only safe place. Your mother wouldn't think of entering it, because someone might suggest she do a little work. Come along, Kelp. I can use your help."

Cottonmouth lay on his side in his shelter, his blanket covering his legs, watching the heavy fruit bags tied to the rafters sway and groan. The sweet fragrance of ripe persimmons filled the air. He would have to eat those soon, before they spoiled. All around him, Standing Hollow Horn Village shimmered in the bluish gleam of predawn. A few snores rattled. Gulls squealed. The constant surf pounding the beach seemed to echo across the land. His shelter sat in the middle of the village, surrounded by the homes of the other Spirit Elders. In case of attack, they would be the most secure.

He tipped his head back to gaze out to the ocean. The water shone a soft gray, like dove's wings at dusk. Foam rode the waves, rushing up on shore, and leaving white ribbons curling across the sand when the water retreated.

Cottonmouth pulled his doll more tightly against his bare brown chest, trying to find in that small bony body some shred of the strong young man he had once been. He had spent many nights this way, staring sightlessly at the world outside while he fought desperately inside. He could find no safe place in his own body. Long ago all the secret, sacred spaces had been violated, and his souls had fled. Like frightened birds, for moons they had flown about, breathless, afraid to rest. No one had understood. People had whispered that he'd gone mad. Then, one lonely night, he had found the doll. It had been tucked in a basket in their shelter, covered with beautifully etched hairpins and necklaces. Things he had given her . . . He had dumped them all out, and picked up the doll. From that moment on his souls had lived in a glistening world of misty hills and firelit evenings, of eyes shining with moonlight, and loving hands offered and clasped. A world that no longer existed. Except in the doll.

When he took that doll out of the basket and held it against his heart, Cottonmouth could step into the body of a childhood self, young and brave, a self he had protected and nurtured for tens of summers. That young man's souls had not died. They were strong and vibrant, and for a time, a short time, he felt safe.

But it never lasted.

That bright world would suddenly fade into nothingness and he would find himself gazing out upon this world, cold and empty and lonely.

And he would be afraid.

Cottonmouth tucked the doll under his arm, keeping it warm, and pulled his blanket up to cover his shoulders. He should put the doll back into its basket, he knew, but he couldn't. Not yet. He needed to protect the doll, to be sure that no one could harm it. That was the way it had been for tens of summers. The doll could rely on him . . . but Cottonmouth had no one.

Thirteen

Polished Shells stood at the edge of the council shelter, wringing her hands. "The geese will never be done in time, I just know it. They were such huge birds. I don't know why Mother rushed this marriage! If she'd given me just two days' warning I could have prepared the feast carefully, but no! Pondwader had to be married mere hands of time after she'd finished the negotiations. This is crazy! Not only that, it's going to rain!"

Far out to sea, misty gray veils swayed across the calm surface of the ocean, heading for shore. Storm Girl had pulled a dense blanket of clouds over the world, and the distant rumble of thunder competed with the surf. Already Kelp could feel occasional drops on her face, cool and refreshing.

She looked at her aunt. More than ten tens of people filled the plaza around the shelter. Polished Shells kept glancing worriedly at them. She had dressed in her best light-green tunic, and arranged her hair in a bun, then pinned it with a sharpened dog ulna. Behind her, a large fire blazed, crackling and spitting in the breeze. Several women attended the boiling baskets, which contained turtle and mussel soups, thickened with pulverized bone. Chunks of bottle gourd floated on the surface, smelling sweet, and a wealth of different mushrooms bobbed around the edges. Roasted golden shiners and tiny killifish lay piled in a wooden bowl at the edge of the fire, keeping warm. Atop the coals, in huge clam shells, dozens of palm berry cakes steamed. And all around sat baskets, brimming with persimmons, hickory nuts, prickly pear fruits, elderberries, and pine nuts. The geese lay buried deep in the coals, simmering in their own juices.

"I don't know why you're worried, Aunt," Kelp said. "Even if the geese don't get done in time, there's plenty more to eat."

Polished Shells wiped her forehead. "How can you be so calm, Kelp? Your brother is about to be married."

"That's why I'm calm. Better him than me." Kelp saw her grandmother starting across the village with Pondwader on her arm. "Here they come."

"Who?" Polished Shells blurted and whirled around. "Oh, my, is it time? Are you hot, Kelp? I swear I've never been so hot in my life."

"Of course you're hot. You've been bending over cooking fires all day."

"I don't understand it, Kelp. You should be nervous. Your brother is going away forever, and you—"

"No, he's not," Kelp said.

Polished Shells frowned at her. "What are you talking about? Windy Cove is—"

"I overheard Grandmother speaking to my mother. She told Dark Rain that, as part of the final agreement, both villages decided to move together. For protection. We'll be moving north and they'll be moving south. I guess we'll meet somewhere in the middle."

"You heard that? Why didn't Mother tell me?"

"You were busy with the feast."

Polished Shells sighed gruffly. "That's true. What else did Mother say? Tell me quickly before the ritual begins."

Kelp shrugged. "Not very much. She said that Windy Cove agreed to give us one quarter of their nut crop in exchange for one quarter of our catfish catch. But I think that's silly, now that we've agreed to move together into one big village."

"It is silly. We'll just end up distributing everything equally, like we always do. What else?"

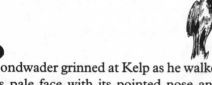

Pondwader grinned at Kelp as he walked closer. He looked very handsome. His pale face with its pointed nose and pink eyes seemed to glow in the frame of his dark blue hood. Long white hair hung down over the front of his robe. His hem dragged the ground, making him trip on occasion, but the scallops of baby lightning whelk shells on his breast and covering his sleeves distracted people's attention; they shimmered wildly. Her grandmother, short gray hair hanging over her eyes, wore a tan tunic covered with yellow cockle shells. Kelp wasn't certain which of them was supporting the other. Sometimes it seemed Pondwader held up Moonsnail, and other times it seemed her grandmother fought to keep Pondwader on his feet. It was truly amusing. Kelp glanced around the large gathering to see if anyone else thought so. Everybody was smiling, so it was hard to tell. People flooded in behind Pondwader and followed him out to the edge of the surf, where they would await the arrival of Musselwhite and Seedpod.

"Well, come along," Polished Shells said, wiping her hands on her tunic. "Let's join them. The ritual won't take long once we're all gathered, then I can worry more about the geese."

Kelp chuckled, and they walked out to the where the surf rushed up on shore, tumbling shells in its frothy wake, then scurried back to Sea Girl's bosom. Rain began to fall in a light misty shower.

Kelp sidled up next to Pondwader, and he beamed at her, but before Kelp could speak to him, an odd hush came over the crowd and people shoved each other until they opened a narrow lane. Dark Rain walked down it, smiling like a bobcat with a blue heron's neck in its jaws.

"Great Treefrog, she's *magnificent,*" Kelp heard Beaverpaw whisper to his squat wife, Waterbearer, who elbowed him in the gut in response. Once he'd caught his breath, he scowled at her.

Dark Rain wore red, her favorite, and seductively played with the cooter carapace necklace hanging between her breasts. She had left her long hair free and it fluttered elegantly about her face. When she stopped in front of Polished Shells, she whispered, "Go stand somewhere else. My place is beside my son."

Polished Shells smiled and replied, "I would strangle you with a cord, sister of mine, but I don't have one with me. *You* go stand somewhere else. You've never been a mother to your son."

Moonsnail hissed, "Stop it! Both of you!"

Pondwader lifted a hand to hide the smile that split his face, and Kelp leaned over to whisper, "Thank the Shining People that you'll soon have your own shelter and be able to escape this."

"You think so?"

"Of course, fool. Who would dare to torment Musselwhite's husband?"

Pondwader placed his hand on Kelp's shoulder. While smiling at the crowd, he asked from the corner of his mouth, "May I lean on you, Kelp? I think I'm going to fall over."

"Oh, Great Mouse!" She braced her legs, pulled his arm across her shoulders and helped him shift his weight to her. "You're trembling, Pondwader! You should be in bed."

"Grandmother promises me that will come later—if I can keep standing long enough to be married."

"Well, at least that means you'll get to lie down."

Pondwader leaned sideways to whisper, "I hope so. Grandmother suggested I may not, and it's been worrying me ever since."

"Huh?"

His blue hem whipped and crackled in a sudden gust of wind, and he gripped Kelp's shoulders more tightly to steady himself. "Never mind," he said. "I didn't understand it myself."

"You might not be lying down?" Possibilities wandered through her mind, and she blushed. "I'm glad you're the one getting married and not me, Pondwader. I'd faint."

For the first time in days, he laughed. A hearty laugh that came from his belly. It made Kelp laugh, too. They stood there, in front of everyone, holding each other and guffawing, though neither of them had the slightest idea what was so funny. But it felt good to laugh. Only when Moonsnail lifted a condemning brow did they stifle their amusement. Pondwader, however, kept breaking out in mirth intermittently, as though he had held it as long as he could.

Moonsnail hobbled forward and looked him in the eyes. "Quit that. People will think you're an idiot."

"I'm sorry, Grandmother," Pondwader said and attempted to look serious. "I know you'd just as soon Seedpod didn't find out until after I'm related to him."

Moonsnail pretended to be straightening Pondwader's hood as she whispered furiously, "Now, listen to me, Pondwader, this is a very solemn event, you are supposed to behave in a way befitting your station in life."

Pondwader blinked solemnly and nodded, like a good, obedient grandson should, but he pinched Kelp's shoulder and she almost choked swallowing her giggle. In a sober voice, Pondwader said, "I promise to conduct myself as you would wish, Grandmother."

"Good," Moonsnail whispered. "Now stand tall. Musselwhite is coming."

"She is?" Kelp asked breathlessly and craned her neck.

Pondwader sobered truly this time.

Seedpod led the way, emerging from the trees in the rear of the village with a folded blanket under his arm, his white head held high. He walked forward slowly. Musselwhite followed. She wore a cream-colored tunic with yellow splotches sprinkled irregularly over the fabric. It required careful work. Live sandstars had to be pressed against the fabric and left there long enough to leave their bright amber stain. It took one sandstar for every patch of yellow. Someone very patient had dyed that tunic. A polished sea-urchin-spine necklace encircled Musselwhite's throat. She had plaited her silver-streaked black hair into one long braid which lay over her right shoulder. As she approached, and met Pondwader's awed gaze, the lines around her eyes crinkled as she smiled.

Seedpod took his position alongside Moonsnail, and they turned in unison to face the crowd. A loud cheer went up, and ten-and-two warriors broke into a round dance, Singing the Warrior's Song in honor of Musselwhite.

Wrath has finished it,
Wrath has finished it,
   All our enemies are dead!
   They lie in pools of blood, like gutted
   mice.
Wrath has finished it!

Musselwhite walked up to Kelp and quietly asked, "Are you holding him up? It looks like it."

"Yes, I am. Your turn."

As Kelp stepped out from under Pondwader's arm, Musselwhite slipped beneath it and pulled his hand snugly over her shoulders.

Pondwader whispered, "I promise you won't have to hold me up my entire life."

"And I promise," Musselwhite whispered back, "that I will hold you up for as long as you need me to."

Deep emotion shone in Pondwader's eyes, and his pale fingers squeezed Musselwhite's shoulder. She slipped her arm around his waist, and hugged him.

Kelp stood beside Musselwhite and silently prayed the ritual would begin soon. Polished Shells and Dark Rain had lined up beside Pondwader; both were scowling, muttering insults to each other. Kelp caught only a few words, *shameless slut,* and . . . *you are jealous, my ugly sister* . . . as the members of Heartwood Clan formed a semicircle around them.

Seedpod raised a hand for silence and the crowd hushed. "I have come to your fine village, my friends, to witness the marriage between the greatest warrior in history, Musselwhite of the Windy Cove Clan, and Heartwood Clan's White Lightning Boy." He turned and gestured to Musselwhite and Pondwader, and the crowd went wild, hooting and clapping, stamping their feet. Children raced around in circles, shrieking their joy.

Over the din, Moonsnail shouted, "I beg the blessings of Sun Mother on this union. May it bring us all security and happiness!"

Kelp glanced at her mother. Her face was angry, but she was not looking at Moonsnail or Seedpod, or even Polished Shells. Her eyes were riveted on Beaverpaw, who was holding his squat wife's hand. When Beaverpaw caught her gaze, he hastily released his wife's hand and folded his arms. Kelp's brows lowered, wondering at that. She glanced back at her mother and found Dark Rain's pointed teeth gleaming in triumph.

Seedpod and Moonsnail walked toward Musselwhite and Pondwader. As they did so, Seedpod unfolded the marriage blanket and shook it out in the wind. It was dyed in the sacred colors, with alternating red, yellow, black, and blue strips. Moonsnail grabbed two corners, and together they draped the blanket around the couple's shoulders.

A roar of exultation went up from the crowd as Musselwhite and Pond-wader turned and waded out into the sea.

Pondwader clutched Musselwhite tightly as the backwash of water sought to trip him.

"Are you all right?" she asked softly.

"So far."

"Just hold on to me. I won't let you fall."

"I will. I—I like holding on to you," he answered timidly.

Musselwhite carefully led him out until the cool water came up to their breasts, then she turned to him, removed the wet blanket from around their shoulders, and cast it upward as high as she could. The wind caught it, whipped it around, and hurled it down into the water again. People on shore called congratulations to them, and began dancing, whirling and swinging each other around.

Musselwhite took Pondwader's face between both her hands, looked him in the eyes, and gently kissed his lips. Joy filled him. He longed to gaze into her eyes forever. The Lightning Bird in his chest thundered softly, sounding oddly like a child crying—suffocating tears that would not stop. Pondwader frowned and listened more closely. He could almost make out words. Rain began falling in earnest, stippling the water around them.

"We're supposed to swim back," Musselwhite said. "Can you?"

"I'm not much of a swimmer," he admitted. "When I'm in the water, I'm usually weighted down with chunks of coral and breathing through a hollow reed. But I'll try."

Her eyes examined him, moving from his hood to his long blue sleeves. "Maybe you shouldn't, after all. I tell you what: Gather up the hem of your robe in one hand, and hold tight to my belt with the other. If you can float, I'll get us to shore. No one will know the difference."

Pondwader reached out and stroked her arm affectionately. "You are so kind to me." Then he gathered up the hem of his robe, as she had instructed, and slipped his fingers into her belt.

"Ready?"

"Yes."

A strong swimmer, she took long, even strokes. The chilly water raised bumps on his skin. He noticed that Dark Rain had waded into the surf, watching. A writhing halo of black hair encircled her face.

Musselwhite said, "Your mother is very concerned about you."

"Yes, but not the way you think," he answered. "I'm sure she's worried I might drown and she'd have to find another way to pay her debts."

"Well, you won't drown. We're almost there," Musselwhite said and stood up in the water, which now reached the middle of her thighs. "Step down."

Pondwader did, and his knees hit bottom. Musselwhite gripped his arm and helped him to stand. His legs shook badly.

"Blessed Spirits," he said. "My wet robe feels as heavy as a dead whale."

"Put your arm over my shoulder again."

Musselwhite hauled him from the water and up onto the beach. People danced around them, slapping them on the backs, as they headed for the council shelter where the feast had been laid out. Pondwader breathed deeply. He was married. A boy no longer, but a man. He belonged to Musselwhite, the greatest warrior in memory, and she belonged to him. A giddy, light-headed feeling possessed him. He would have new responsibilities now. People would treat him differently, expect more from him. The thought thrilled him.

The marriage mat had been laid out along the northern side of the shelter. Musselwhite eased Pondwader down, then sat beside him. Rain pattered on the thatched roof and gusted into the shelter. Pondwader wrung out the hem of his robe and smiled. Outside, people dug up the geese buried in the coals and unwrapped the protective fabric layers before putting the big birds into broad shallow baskets. Steam rose and twisted away in the wind.

"Are you cold?" Musselwhite asked.

"Just a little."

She reached to the stack of folded blankets that always lay near the northwestern shelter pole, and draped one around Pondwader's shoulders. "Better?"

He held it closed near his throat, and did feel warmer. "Thank you." Boldly, he slipped his hand under the blanket and twined his fingers with Musselwhite's. She did not pull away, and happiness gladdened his heart. He squeezed her fingers.

Moonsnail used her walking stick to beat her way through the crowd into the shelter and slumped down at Pondwader's side. "Well, thank Brother Earth, the geese are done. I told Polished Shells they would be. As soon as the two of you are served, everyone else can eat. And they're ready, let me tell you. I had to post guards while you were out in the ocean. I feared there wouldn't be a scrap left by the time you returned."

Kelp shouldered in, carrying two bowls heaped with food, and Seedpod followed on her heels with two more. Kelp grinned at Pondwader as she set them before him. Steaming goose, roast catfish, and killifish were piled high in one, and the other brimmed with turtle and mussel soup. "How are you feeling?" she asked.

"Better now," he said.

Kelp grinned.

Seedpod set his bowls down next to Kelp's. A wealth of fruits and nuts filled them. Then he knelt beside his daughter and gently kissed Musselwhite on the cheek. "You are very beautiful, my daughter."

Musselwhite touched his white hair gently and smiled, and Pondwader could see for the first time that day the hollow, anguished look in her dark eyes. "Thank you for the lovely tunic, Father. You are the best weaver in the clan. It was the tunic that made me beautiful."

People clustered around the shelter, filling bowls with food, laughing, applauding, shoving each other, while out in the plaza a dance circle had already formed. Warriors with hunks of goose in their fists hopped from foot to foot, grabbing bites between shrieks and whoops.

Moonsnail leaned forward and urged, "*Eat,* Pondwader."

He reached for a piece of goose. "Trying to keep up my strength, Grandmother?"

"I am, indeed," she answered and slapped his knee. "I want you to stuff yourself. You're going to need it."

By dusk, Pondwader had eaten so much he felt as fat as an autumn bear, and very weary. He kept swallowing yawns, while trying to pay attention to the festivities. Kelp and the rest of his family stood near the ocean, talking with Seedpod. The fine tunics in the crowd showed food stains now, hair had been unbraided and set free to the wind, and here and there, Dancers had begun to stumble from exertion. Children raced between adult legs, faces gleaming with goose and catfish fat. Everyone seemed to be enjoying himself. The food bowls were down to scraps and heaps of fish bones. Already a few women had started cleaning up the mess, stacking bowls atop each other, carrying them out to the sea to wash. Musselwhite had Danced several dances with Heartwood's warriors, but now lay on her side beside Pondwader, her long muscular legs extended, her head propped on her hand. She looked exhausted, too.

"Musselwhite," Pondwader murmured and leaned toward her. "I'm very tired. Could we . . . I mean, are you ready to—I don't wish to interrupt your celebrating but—"

"Yes, Pondwader. I'm ready to go."

She rose to her feet and helped him to stand, then slipped her arm around his waist and supported him as they walked into the trees. No one even seemed to notice that they had gone. She took the deer trail that led to their marriage shelter.

Starlight fell around them in streaks and bars of pale silver. The smells of the forest, of pine and soaked autumn leaves carried on the night. Raindrops pattered on the branches, creating a soft hissing sound. Pondwader glanced sideways at her, around the edge of his blue hood. In the faint gleam of starlight that penetrated the clouds, he saw the sadness in her eyes. His chest constricted and a painful desire, a deep yearning, swelled inside him, the need to ease her hurts, as if he half-knew what their life together could be, and longed for that wholeness now . . . but could not have it. Would not, in all probability, for many summers.

"Did your mother speak with you about the marriage bed?" she asked quietly.

"No," he laughed. "Grandmother did. I think she had to beat Mother away with her walking stick, but it worked. Thank the Shining Ones. I'm not sure I could have borne it."

"You don't like your mother?"

In a melancholy voice, he said, "She—she seems to need to hurt people. As much as she can. Especially me and Kelp."

Musselwhite looked up at his anguished tone. "Are you all right?"

"Yes. Why? Didn't I sound like it?"

Musselwhite tightened her arm around his waist and hugged him. "One can be worn down, that's all. Constant cruelty leaves raw wounds on its victims' souls. Wounds that never really heal, Pondwader."

"What do you mean? Why wouldn't they heal, with time and—"

"Well, it's hard to explain," she replied, and exhaled a breath. "It's as if the evil person maintains a magical control over his victims, and forever, as long as that victim lives, all it takes is a single harsh word from the evil person and the wounds on the victim's souls bleed again. I don't really understand it myself. . . . Grown people should be able to overcome such things, shouldn't they?"

Pondwader thought about that. Musselwhite's face had tensed, the lines across her forehead deepening. "Does an evil person have that kind of magical control over your souls? As my mother does mine?"

For a time, she didn't answer. Then, in a hard bitter voice, she said, "I don't like to think so, but probably. I haven't seen him in a long time."

Pondwader blinked and watched the leaf-strewn trail passing beneath his sandaled feet. Did she mean Cottonmouth? For as long as Pondwader could remember, he'd heard people whisper about things that had happened summers before he'd been born, terrible things, brutal raiding, senseless murder— horrors he could not believe this kind honorable woman capable of, or perhaps it was that he *would not* believe them. Not until he had proof. Even then, he did not care what she had been. He cared only about who she was now.

They walked in silence the rest of the way, listening to the soft shishing of rain and the hooting of night owls that filtered through the wet forest.

The marriage shelter nestled in a copse of oaks half a hand of time from the village. Small, it spread barely large enough to shield them from the rain. Their bedding had been laid out over floor mats. To keep the blankets from blowing away in the wind, pieces of coral held down the corners. A small fire crackled at the southern end of the shelter, hissing at the raindrops that landed in the flames. Bowls of food made a circle around the fire, keeping warm, as if either of them could still be hungry. He couldn't see the contents, because other bowls had been turned upside-down over the tops, but the rich sweet scents of roast goose and persimmons filled the air.

Musselwhite left Pondwader standing and folded back the top blanket. A taut expression pinched her face, as though she dreaded the rest of the marriage ritual, or had to will herself to carry it out for the sake of duty. Pondwader thought about the things his grandmother had said, about

Musselwhite's grief, and how she had wanted to take her life after her husband's death, about how she would probably be dreaming of Diver while loving him . . .

"You don't have to, you know," he said quickly. "We can wait. I—I'm not very strong anyway, and I wouldn't mind. I mean, it would not bother me at all if you wished to wait for a better—"

"Pondwader," she said softly and sat on the bottom blanket, curling her long legs around her right side. "Come here. Sit by me."

He bit his lip and did as she said. He anxiously cradled his knees to his chest.

Musselwhite pushed his hood back to reveal his long white hair, then put her hand beneath his chin, and turned his face toward hers. "I thank you for that," she said. "You are right that my souls are hurting. I can't give you as much as I would like—but I owe you as much as I can give. Are you strong enough?"

He nodded. "I—I think so."

"Your grandmother says you are a virgin, but grandmothers aren't always aware of facts. Is it true?"

"Yes. It is. Most girls scream and run when they see me. I've never been fast enough to catch one. Or maybe it's that I don't see well enough. Once they get ten or two tens of hands away, all I see is a blur of color. And it's hard to tell one blur from another. I've always been afraid I might grab the wrong blur and get beaten half to death for it."

Musselwhite laughed and lessened some of Pondwader's fear. He smiled.

She reached out to take his hand. "I never expected humor from a bo— from a man your age. And it is so important. Other qualities fade over time, Pondwader, beauty goes, strength wanes, but so long as we can laugh, everything will be all right."

"I want it to be. So much."

She leaned forward and kissed him lightly on the lips. "Let's begin slowly. Can you stand up?"

He braced a hand and got to his feet. She stood beside him, untied her belt and slipped her tunic over her head. Pondwader could only stare. She was *beautiful*. Long, shapely legs spread to wide hips, then narrowed to a slim waist, and her breasts . . . they were perfect. When she began unbraiding her hair, his heart pounded—from fear and exhilaration. She fluffed her hair around her shoulders and reached for him.

"I would like to undress you, Pondwader. Is that all right?"

"Oh . . . yes!" He thrust his arms into the air.

Musselwhite smiled. She untied his belt and dropped it to the floor, then gathered the hem of his robe and lifted it over his head. He pulled his arms from his sleeves, and swallowed hard. He had never stood naked before a woman, not . . . not like this, with duties to perform.

Musselwhite got under the blankets and held them open for him. "Let me hold you, Pondwader."

He hurried to slide in beside her, laying on his back, and Musselwhite braced one elbow and leaned over him, her breasts pressed against his chest. A cascade of her hair fell around him. He could see starlight streaming through the wealth, glittering from the silver strands. He reached up and stroked it softly. It felt fine and silken, like shiny spiderwebs.

She touched his side and he jumped. "Did I startle you? I'm sorry."

"I wasn't . . . expecting . . ." He slipped his arms around her back, and said, "I want you to touch me, Musselwhite. I'm just a little nervous."

"My fingers are cold. I should have told you what I was doing. I am going to slide my hand down your side, Pondwader, like this, and across your stomach. . . ." As her hand moved slowly through the white hair below his navel, she kissed him on the lips and neck, sending a tingle up his spine. From somewhere deep inside him thunder rumbled as the baby Lightning Bird in his chest stretched, straining at the last bits of shell that bound it, knowing, like any other bird, that it had to break free of that shell or die. Flashes of brilliant light blinded Pondwader, and he gasped. Musselwhite took it for something else. . . .

"Now my hand is going to slide lower, Pondwader."

A fiery glow suffused his body, stretching out to the tips of his fingers and toes, filling his chest cavity like a flood of molten gold. Along with it came a strange wondrous joy, as if he'd drunk sunlight.

Despite his weariness, and the depths of his fear, his souls came alive.

Pondwader put a hand behind her neck and brought her face down to kiss her softly. He shivered, whispering, "Thank you for this, Musselwhite. Thank you for becoming my wife."

Distraught weeping wakes me.

I lift my head, frightened, and turn to Musselwhite. She is lying on her back, her beautiful face sheathed in starlight, sound asleep. The blanket has fallen away, revealing her breasts. Her eyelids jump with dreams. But her voice . . . it is not hers . . . not her voice *now*. It sounds like a little girl's.

I sit up and peer at her in confusion. Is she remembering her husband? Or lonely? Maybe suffering guilt for loving me when Diver's body has not yet been found? Her cries make me feel empty inside. I—I don't know what to do. Shall I wake her? I reach out . . . and my hand hovers over her shoulder. She is crying harder. Tears flood from the corners of her eyes. Sparkling dew drops stand upon the blanket, shimmering in the stargleam. I have never witnessed such wrenching tears. I suppose I thought a woman of her mettle, a great warrior, could not possibly possess such tears. But this is not a woman's voice . . . it is a child's. My souls twist. Did something terrible happen to her as a little girl? Is she there again, now?

"Musselwhite?" I call softly. When she does not answer, I place my hand on her forehead, and very lightly stroke her long hair. "Musselwhite," I murmur, "everything is all right. You are here in Heartwood Village. No one is going to hurt you. I promise, I—I won't let them. I am Pondwader, your husband," and with those words a joyous pride fills me. "I am your husband. I love you so very much. Please come back to me? Everything is all right."

I continue stroking her hair and finally she stops weeping and drifts into a deeper sleep. Her breathing slows. When she rolls to her side, facing me, I lie back down and pull the blanket up over her shoulders to shield her from the evening's chill. A calm, serene expression has come to her face.

Pain darts through me.

I clench my teeth against it. It has been happening all night. I quietly slide away from Musselwhite, so she will not know of my discomfort, then I turn onto my back, and dig my fingers into the blanket beneath me. The tiny Lightning Bird glowing in my chest is stretching, rumbling its joy at cracking the thunderegg. As the bird extends its new wings, a fiery fragment of broken shell falls away and dissolves in a brilliant eruption of light.

I can't breathe. My lungs hurt.

It is trying to bolt. I can feel the heat rising, then falling, and rising again. With each flare, more bits of shell tumble and blaze, and bizarre, eerie images flash before me. *Two men on a beach . . . a doll . . . a tornado . . .* The scenes are like mist in my fingers, slipping this way and that, never allowing me to get a good hold on them.

Thunder shakes me.

I stiffen my muscles, fighting to be still.

Through that roar, I hear a voice . . . soft, and low, calling my name.

For over two hands of time, Kelp had been standing at the edge of the water, watching silver-crested waves gently rolling toward her, washing around her feet, and politely listening to Seedpod, her grandmother, and another old warrior, Floating Stick, discuss Cottonmouth. They spoke in hushed tones about burned villages and killed babies, about the destruction of Windy Cove's scouting party and the certainty of widespread warfare.

"Yes, I do believe that," Seedpod said. The Shining People filled the sky with their twinkling splendor, peering down upon them, listening, watching. Seedpod exhaled hard. "Cottonmouth has lost all of his souls. I'm sure he's

mad. Completely mad. There have been rumors of strange behavior for summers, but—"

"It would frighten me far more," Moonsnail commented, "if he were
sane. Such crazy acts from a sane man would make me fear he had a plan."

"Plan?" Floating Stick asked. A tall, gangly old man, he had sparse gray
hair and a hooked nose. He had dressed in a dark brown tunic adorned with
fig shells. "What are you saying?"

"Just that he might not be acting from hatred or . . . or revenge," Moonsnail said. Her tone had grown ominous. "I cannot believe that Cottonmouth is either a fool, or mad—forgive me Seedpod. I mean no disrespect.
I just wonder if these random strikes at scattered villages aren't designed to
have a certain effect on us."

Seedpod rubbed his chin and his eyes narrowed. "You mean an effect like
forcing us to create alliances through marriage? To strengthen our defenses?"

"Maybe," Moonsnail replied. "Or maybe to force us to move our villages
together."

"But why would he want that?" Floating Stick asked. "What could he
gain—"

"He would have us all in one place, for one thing." Moonsnail said.

The breeze ruffled Seedpod's white hair over his forehead as he stared
unblinking at Moonsnail. "Blessed Sister Moon. You just terrified me. It
had never occurred to me that he might . . ."

The elders continued talking, but Kelp stopped listening. She didn't think
she could stomach another word about death and war. Gazing back at the
village, she watched the Dancers twirling and leaping in the orange light of
the bonfire's flames. The storm had broken, leaving patches of dark clouds
drifting westward. Children lay at the edges of the plaza, sleeping on wind-
tousled blankets. Old men and women had gathered near the council shelter
with their small square looms, weaving while the last revelers stubbornly
continued Dancing and Singing to celebrate the newly married couple.

Kelp had seen Musselwhite guide Pondwader down the deer trail that led
to their marriage shelter, and he had looked ill. Was he all right? Had he
been able to—to do what he needed to? Kelp blushed just thinking about it.
She had yet to grow accustomed to the notion that her brother had taken a
wife. An odd sort of mourning had overcome her. Never again would she
and Pondwader go adventuring in the forest, looking for ghosts or cagey
earth Spirits that lived in hollowed-out trees. Never again would they sit and
tell each other secrets buried deep in their hearts. Who would she talk to?
Who could she share her troubles with? No one knew her the way Pondwader
did.

Reaching up, she absently jingled her top shell necklace, and the elders
turned to peer at her. "I—I'm sorry. Grandmother, please excuse me, I
drank so much prickly pear tea, I need to make a trip into the forest."

Moonsnail gave her a suspicious look. Blast her. She always knew when Kelp was lying. Kelp fidgeted nervously. "Really, Grandmother. I need to go . . . *now*."

"Run along then," Moonsnail said. "When you have finished, see if your aunt needs any help with the final cleanup."

"I will, Grandmother. Good night, Spirit Elders."

Seedpod and Floating Stick nodded to her, and Kelp turned and walked slowly up the beach, heading for the large stand of pines just beyond the northernmost edge of the village. A few people in the plaza waved to her, and Kelp waved back. She saw Polished Shells kneeling outside the council shelter with two other women, scrubbing bowls with sand. Their low laughter carried to her. Everyone seemed to be having such a good time. Everyone but her.

Kelp folded her arms and hugged herself. She felt so lonely. What made it worse was that she didn't understand her upset. This was bound to happen. People married. Even her brother. It was the way of things. Though, Spirits knew, she never planned to. Not if she had to run away and join a pack of wolves. They would certainly be better company than any man her mother might find for her.

She walked straight ahead, her sandals dimpling the wet sand. Raindrops perched precariously on the pine needles. As wind swayed the boughs, the drops twinkled and glittered, pattering softly on the forest duff.

The trail that led northwest toward the pond where they got their fresh water took off just ahead. Kelp headed for it. Puddles stood in the path, shining so brightly that the dark branches reflected perfectly. Kelp studied them as she skirted the puddles, but she purposely avoided getting close enough to see her own soul. She didn't want to. It might appear as shattered as it felt, and she doubted she could handle the strain. Sighing, Kelp stepped off the path and ducked low to clear an oak branch . . . and heard laughter.

Through the weave of brush, she saw Beaverpaw standing over her mother, smiling. Dark Rain lay naked on the ground with another warrior half on and half off her. Kelp couldn't see his face because his back was to her, but she suspected it might be young Bowfin. He was Beaverpaw's best warrior.

"See?" Beaverpaw whispered. "What did I tell you? Isn't she magnificent?"

Her mother laughed and Beaverpaw knelt and bit her bare breast, then said, "Hurry up, Bowfin. I'm ready again."

Kelp hurriedly backed away, squarely into a palmetto. The fronds thrashed together.

Dark Rain gasped, "Beaverpaw! Go find out who that is!"

Kelp got up and ran with all her heart, swerving around puddles, leaping deadfall.

Beaverpaw chased her for a short distance, then gave up, laughed and yelled, "Go on! Get out of here!" Kelp hid behind a dense tangle of grape vines and watched him turn back, calling, "It's all right, Dark Rain. It was just a kid. I chased him off. Is Bowfin done yet? It's getting late! I have to get home to my wife soon!"

Fourteen

Sun Mother floated just above the horizon, streaming light into the shelter where Diver lay flat on his back, his fingers laced over his stomach. The fabric bags and baskets swinging from the rafters gleamed as though coated with liquid amber. The pathetic little man named Barnacle knelt at Diver's side, his skeletal face a mass of sagging wrinkles, his bald head splotched with age. He wore a faded blue tunic. Behind him, Cottonmouth stood with his arms folded, his shoulder braced against the pole. He had dressed in a black breechclout. No jewelry adorned his tall, slender body, and his graying black hair blew freely about his shoulders. He had his dark eyes fixed on Sea Girl, who shone a crystalline blue today. Three tens of hands away four guards sat playing dice with painted palm seeds. Their laughter struck Diver like bits of nightmare. After eight days of hearing it, he had each man's voice memorized. Even when they were halfway across the huge village, he could identify them.

Barnacle rocked back and forth, twisting his hands in his lap. "The Spirit Elder has asked that I speak with you. I do not wish to, the memories still bring me much pain, but because he asks, I will." He wet his thin lips. "This happened—"

"I do not wish to hear your story."

Barnacle glanced at Cottonmouth, but Cottonmouth did not turn. He did not even blink. It was as if he did not hear the conversation at all.

Barnacle swallowed nervously and continued, "This happened two-tens-and-eight summers ago, during the Moon of New Antlers. At the time, my family and I lived far inland, on the shores of a shallow lake. I had a wife . . ." his old voice shook, and it took him a moment to collect himself. "And three little children, two, five, and six summers old. They were beautiful babies. We were all out searching for tender spring tubers, laughing, working with our digging-sticks. I heard the warriors coming first. I yelled to my wife—"

"Go away!" Diver shouted. He sat up and roared in the old man's face, *"I don't care what happened to your family!"*

The guards swiveled to peer at him with gleaming eyes, and a pack of barking dogs raced toward the shelter. All over the village, people stood up from their daily tasks and looked in his direction. A hum of conversation broke out.

Barnacle sat back on his heels and turned to Cottonmouth again. Cottonmouth did not move for a long time, then he nodded his head once, the gesture so small a man might have missed it had he not been staring straight at Cottonmouth.

Desperately, Barnacle met Diver's hard eyes and gave him a pleading look, begging him to listen. He silently mouthed the word, *please.* Would the old man suffer for it later if Diver refused? Diver did not understand this village. Clearly, Cottonmouth terrified these people, but they also revered him as if he were one of the Shining People.

Barnacle wiped sweat from his bald head and let out a breath. "After I yelled to her, my wife, her name was Rose Stem, got to her feet and ran for the children, but Cottonmouth's warriors struck so quickly she couldn't reach them in time. The woman warrior, Musselwhite, struck Rose Stem in the head with her warclub, then ran toward my children. The babies shrieked in terror and scattered, trying to hide behind fallen logs, or in berry brambles. Musselwhite found each one. She . . ." Barnacle squeezed his laced fingers so tightly the knuckles went white. "Musselwhite dragged each of my children out and used her stiletto to puncture . . . their hearts. She whooped a triumphant war cry and . . . and began stripping my youngest daughter, two summers old . . . stripping off her bracelets, ripping the necklace from her little throat. Cottonmouth ran toward her when she leaned over my second child, a son of five, and gripped Musselwhite's hand, refusing to let her rob my boy. They fought." The old man used his sleeve to wipe sweat from his hollow cheek. "I have never seen two people on the same side fight so ferociously. She struck Cottonmouth on the shoulder with her chert-studded warclub, and I saw blood spurt . . ."

Diver could not help but look up at the jagged scar that marred Cottonmouth's left shoulder, running at an angle down his back. An old scar, healed into a pale shiny ridge of flesh.

"Cottonmouth," Barnacle went on, "threw her to the ground and wrestled the club away from her. She screamed and kicked—but he held her tightly." Barnacle dropped his gaze to the hands in his lap and pried the fingers apart. He winced and flexed them, as if they hurt, then placed them on his knees. "After that, I do not know what happened. I ran as fast as I could. I had nothing . . . no one . . . left to worry about, except me."

Barnacle held Diver's stony gaze, and Diver saw that his faded old eyes had tears in them.

When Diver said nothing, the old man rose to his feet and nodded respectfully to Cottonmouth before hobbling away across the village. People stopped him as he passed, speaking gently to him, asking him what had happened.

Diver said, "What did you hope to prove by that? Did you think his story would make me doubt my wife? A woman I have known for two tens and five summers?"

Cottonmouth continued staring at Sea Girl, but his mouth tightened.

Angry, Diver demanded, "How could he know the name of the woman who killed his children? Did you tell him it was Musselwhite? Is that why he thinks she did it?" Diver's breast had begun to heave with indignation and it caused pains to shoot up from his back and shoulder wounds and stab at his stomach. Nausea tormented him. He bent forward and braced a hand on the floor, waiting for it to pass. When he could, he eased back down to the floor mat, and concentrated on breathing deeply and evenly. The tangy scents of wood smoke and boiling clams soothed him. The nausea finally faded.

Out beyond the shelter a bald eagle hunted Sea Girl's shining surface, curving and soaring, then plunging like a lance into the water in search of fish. Her black wings flapped against the water. Diver watched her antics, set against the background of red rising sun and endless blue ocean, and some small amount of serenity seeped inside him.

"Who really killed that old man's children, Cottonmouth?" he asked. "You must know. Why don't you tell Barnacle the truth? He deserves to hear it. How can you live among these people and pretend to be righteous and good when you are a liar?"

Cottonmouth turned slowly, his huge dark eyes wide, and let his folded arms fall limply to his sides. "Sun Mother alone knows what is good, Diver," he answered softly. "I, of all people, would never claim goodness."

Pondwader crouched naked before the ashes of last night's fire, using a stick to separate out the hot coals, dragging them to the right side while he mounded the dead coals on the left. Morning sunlight slanted across the forest, shooting misty bands of gold through the trees over his head, and coaxing curls of fog from the wet forest floor. What a magnificent dawn.

The pleasant fragrance of damp bark mixed with the smell of woodsmoke. Somewhere in the distance an alligator roared, and Brother Earth went silent, then a riot of birdsong erupted again. The cackling of a purple gallinule carried above the others. Pondwader smiled. He could picture the beautiful bird walking across the lily pads in a nearby pond, its head and tail jerking while it hunted insects.

He plucked a handful of twigs from the wood pile stacked inside the shelter, then put them down again. Despite his relatives' great care, rain had soaked the sticks on top. He had to dig deeper to find dry twigs for kindling. When he had gathered enough, he placed them on the hot coals and blew gently. Yellow threads of flame licked up through the tinder, crackling and spitting. Pondwader gradually added more twigs, then larger pieces of wood.

His wife still slept and he . . . *my wife*, it felt so strange and wonderful to say those words. They made him want to shout his joy to the world, but he did not wish to wake her. She had tossed and turned most of the night. As had he.

. . . Even now he could see those strange images. They repeated, flashing across his souls each time the baby Lightning Bird beat its wings to dry them, or flopped its head about on the skinny stem of its neck. He wondered what they meant.

And how long do I have before that baby bird bursts through my chest and flashes across the sky?

He picked up the bowl closest to him and lifted the upside-down bowl covering it. Dark pieces of goose and large tree mushrooms nestled inside. Even cold, they smelled delicious. His stomach growled and squeaked. He recovered the bowl and set it close to the flames to warm, then methodically checked the other four bowls, finding persimmons, hulled hickory nuts, elderberries, and roasted catfish.

A sharp crack sounded in the forest and he glanced up to see a blur of white and brown—a white-tailed deer—grazing very nearby, where the tall trees let in enough light for long blades of grass to grow. The deer lifted its head cautiously, and he whispered, "It's all right, my sister. I will not harm you. Eat your fill. You are safe here today."

It stood utterly still, then flicked its tail, dropped it head. He heard blades of grass squeak as she plucked another mouthful.

Pondwader prodded his fire with a stick and studied Musselwhite. She lay on her left side, her head pillowed on one arm, the blanket pulled up so that it just covered her bare breasts. Hair tumbled down her back, and the silver strands glittered in the morning's glow. She looked so beautiful, so . . . vulnerable. A hot rush of blood came to Pondwader's face. She had made him feel very much like a man last night. Stronger. Older. He had not expected this—to be so radiantly happy with his new wife. But he loved her. Blessed Spirits, how he loved her. . . .

She stirred, almost as though she sensed his deep emotions. Pondwader whispered, "Sleep. Breakfast is not warm yet. I'm sure you're still tired."

Musselwhite raised herself on one elbow, yawned, and combed hair away from her face with her fingers. "You must be tired, too. Every time I moved in the night, you reached over to pat me. Why don't you come back and sleep with me, Pondwader? We could both use the rest, and no one will care if we don't appear in the village until this afternoon." Dark circles shone below her eyes. She appeared truly haggard.

"But what of our food?"

"It will keep," she replied and held out a hand to him.

Pondwader rose and walked over to slip beneath the warm blanket again, facing her. Musselwhite wrapped her arms around him, and pulled him closer. Tenderly, he ran his hand down her side and over the swell of her hip. Her chest expanded with a breath, and she smiled.

He continued stroking her side, because it soothed him. The texture of her skin was like cattail down, almost too soft to believe.

After a time, she whispered, "You're not sleeping, Pondwader."

"I'm sorry. I keep thinking about the Dream I had last night."

She mumbled, "Hmm? Dream?"

"Yes, it was . . . very curious."

"What was it about?"

Pondwader let himself drown for a long moment in the silken texture of her skin. "A turtle-bone doll."

"A doll?"

"Yes." He conjured it again on the fabric of his souls, seeing the ragged tunic and faded paint. "It's old, I think, dressed in a worn tunic, and has long black hair. It must have had a face painted on it once, because faint splotches of color—"

With lightning quickness, she threw off the blanket, revealing her naked torso, and gripped his hand hard, her eyes like black beads of obsidian. "Where did you see it?"

"What is it?" he asked, panicked. "What's wrong?"

"Tell me."

"In my Dream last night! It Danced in front of my eyes, the hem of its tunic whirling. Why? Who does it belong to?"

Her voice softened. "I'm not sure, but . . . maybe to my—my son."

"Your son? Do you mean Thorny Boy?"

She released his hand and sat up fully. Her breasts gleamed in the pale wash of sunlight. Perspiration had beaded on her turned-up nose and across the planes of her high cheekbones. She rubbed a hand over her face. "Forgive me, Pondwader. I didn't mean to frighten you. It's just that . . . that doll once meant something to me . . . if it's the same doll. Tell me what else you saw."

Anxiously, he stammered, "S-strange things. I saw a tornado and—"

"A tornado?"

"Yes." He could still see it, descending like a writhing black snake from the clouds out over the ocean. "It swayed drunkenly over a beach. I don't know where. I've never seen the place. But the whole time, while the tornado was ripping up trees and flinging them away, the doll Danced. Leaping and swirling, as if it was very happy." Pondwader swallowed past the knot that had grown in his throat. Bravely, he asked, "Musselwhite? Did you make the doll?"

The lines around her eyes deepened. "Why would you think that?"

"Well, it's just that, it *feels* like you. I can't explain it, but in the Dream, I thought it *was* you. I know that sounds silly, but—"

"No. It doesn't sound silly. If it's the same doll, I breathed my soul into it. I made it many summers ago. For my son. Just before he d-died."

The baby Lightning Bird in Pondwader's chest glowed to life suddenly. Dazzling flashes of light left blue-white tracks across his souls, and sheer terror possessed him.

"What is it?" Musselwhite asked.

"Nothing. I . . ." He could not tell her. Not yet. Not so soon after their marriage. "And there was a man, Musselwhite. Two men, really. But one had his arms open to the tornado, his head thrown back." Pondwader demonstrated the stance, gazing up into the pure light that had eaten his eyes. "All around the man falling stars struck the earth like rain and . . . at least I think they were falling stars . . . and I heard a voice, calling my name. Calling and calling, and—" he cocked his head—"and I never answer."

"Whose voice?"

"I don't know. Maybe my sister's. I think it's Kelp calling me. But I'm not sure . . . not anymore."

Musselwhite brushed her long hair behind her ears, and let out a breath. Against the background of yellowing vines twisting through the oak boughs, she looked very beautiful. "What did the man look like?"

Pondwader squinted, as if it would help clarify the image imprinted on his souls. "Cruel. Angry. I couldn't see him very well, but he was tall. He had black eyes and a scar on his back. About here. He was carrying a deerbone awl in one hand—"

Musselwhite made a soft pained sound. She squeezed her eyes closed and slowly lowered herself to the sleeping mat. Her knees came up as she curled into a ball in front of him, and started to shake.

"Musselwhite! What is it?"

"Hold me, Pondwader. Just hold me. I have no one . . . to help me through these bouts now . . . except you."

Stunned, he just stared. A flood of tenderness swept him, and he swiftly wrapped his arms around her and drew her against him, holding her as tightly as he could. "It's all right," he whispered, pressing her head to his heart. "Everything is all right."

Turtle Bone Doll comes to Dance in my dreams . . .

She spins, her skirt whirling. Sucking up the tendrils of mist that twine from the sun-splotched forest floor, she swirls them into glistening spirals around her bone body, and begins to dip from side to side. In a blink, she resembles a tiny tornado. Leaves leap from the ground and clothe her in autumn colors.

"He is not cruel, Pondwader."

"Who?"

"He is derelict. Desolate. A weightless shadow somersaulting underwater. The waves of his solitude drown him. But he can't let anyone see him flailing. He can never cry for help. It isn't that he wants to die. Can't you understand? He wants to be nothing."

"Who? Please tell me? I must know who the man is."

Turtle Bone Doll giggles. The sound is like crystal clear water falling on mossy rocks. She stops spinning and tips forward to peer directly into my eyes. Her faded face is sheathed with mist . . . or tears.

"For many summers, I slept with that awl across my heart. We made a perfect cross, the awl and I. That is what we are to him. Opposites crossed. The embodiment of everything he hates, and everything he loves. He longs to be rid of us— but cannot let us go. We are Light meeting Dark. The place where Death is Life. We are his only hope of salvation. . . . And he knows it."

"Turtle Bone Doll," I say, "you are so exasperating. I wish you would talk straightly. You are always posing riddles and I am lost before I begin."

"A human boy with a Lightning Bird in his chest condemns me for posing riddles," she says with an irritated switch of her skirt. *"No wonder the world is on the brink of catastrophe."*

A tiny cyclone of autumn leaves and mist, she spins upward into the glare of morning sunlight, until she pierces a tuft of cloud . . . and is gone.

Fifteen

Tendrils of fog, backlit by sunshine, crept through Heartwood Village, coiling around shelters and gently stroking people's happy faces. The joy of yesterday's celebration lingered. Laughter echoed, full and robust. Children shrilled as they raced along the edge of the forest, playing "chase" with their dogs. The remains of the feast had been evenly distributed to each shelter, and the scents of roasted gourds and warming palm berry cakes filled the air with sweetness. Sea Girl rocked in a slow, leisurely fashion, her voice soft amidst the squawking and squealing of gulls that sailed over the beach.

Moonsnail leaned back on a stack of blankets in her shelter and surveyed the morning's gathering. Kelp and Dark Rain sat to her right, dressed in plain tan tunics, and Seedpod, his short white hair blowing around his gaunt face, sat to her left. He was peering up at the bags of prickly pear fruit hanging from the ceiling. Floating Stick stretched out on his side next to Seedpod. Bars of ribs showed through the fine weave of his faded moss-colored tunic. He'd rubbed insect grease over his stringy legs and face, and the shine made his hooked nose seem all the more prominent. He had a ripe persimmon in one hand and a rabbit-scapula spoon in the other. He scooped out the ripe pulp and ate it with gusto. A variety of foods sat in wooden bowls before them: goose, roasted catfish, hickory nuts. Kelp had her head down. Dark hair hid most of her pretty face as she ran a finger over the sand on the bottom of her bare foot. She'd been silent all morning. Moping. She kept glancing at Pondwader's empty bedding, which Moonsnail had rolled up and placed along the southern side of the shelter. Was she missing her brother? Probably. That, or she was worried about him. Maybe both. Moonsnail sympathized. Those same tender emotions had been tormenting her. All morning, she'd kept watch on the deertrail, hoping to see Pondwader and Musselwhite walking into camp. Kelp looked up and Moonsnail winked supportively. Her granddaughter smiled, and a shared sense of loss and love passed between them.

From the moment Dark Rain had dumped the children in Moonsnail's lap, the three of them had grown together like greening vines in spring, twisting and twining around each other, protecting, loving, until it became difficult to imagine what life would be like with one of the strands cut. But, that was, after all, the way of human beings. Though Moonsnail didn't like thinking about it, some day soon, she would lose Kelp to marriage, too—the knowledge stabbed her to the heart.

"I don't know, Moonsnail," Seedpod said with a shake of his head. His cheeks seemed more hollow this morning, as if gouges had been carved in his leathery flesh, leaving his blunt chin jutting forward while his wise old eyes sank deeply into their sockets. "I cannot think of a single place which possesses all the things you demand. Fresh water, yes. There is a large pond on Manatee Lagoon, about halfway between Heartwood and Windy Cove villages, but will it be large enough? All ponds grow shallow this late in the season, and when we move together we will have over ten tens of people."

"And maybe more," Moonsnail said, "if we can convince related villages to join us. What about nut trees and berries?"

"Oh, that won't be a problem. There are many varieties," Seedpod answered. "Easily enough to sustain our combined villages for three or four moons. And Manatee Lagoon will provide plenty of shellfish, mussels, oysters, and clams. But there are not many deer, and few rabbits."

"Well," Moonsnail said as she rubbed her aching hip. "The large pond should provide other meat. Ducks and geese?"

Seedpod nodded. "Yes, and herons, grebes, and turtles. We will not starve, not if we use the resources wisely, and move the village when it's prudent."

Floating Stick finished his last bite of persimmon and threw the empty orange skin into the cold fire pit in the middle of the shelter. "I have another concern," he said and sat up. He wiped his mouth with his claw-like hand. "What about the Sacred Ponds of our clans? Will this new location allow us to reach our Ponds within two days' time, as is required to set our relatives on the path to the Village of Wounded Souls?"

Seedpod thought about that. A frown incised his forehead. "Yes, I believe so. Your Pond will be farther away than ours, but I'm fairly sure it is within two days' travel time."

Floating Stick rubbed his wrinkled chin. "And what of plants for making fabrics? Does this new site have enough palms for thread?"

Seedpod gestured uncertainly. "I honestly do not recall. Before we move either of our villages, we should send someone to check for all of these things. Just to make sure this spot will serve our needs."

"Who?" Floating Stick asked. "Did you have someone in mind?"

"No." Seedpod shook his head. "But it should be someone who understands defensive needs as well as domestic ones. Perhaps your War Leader? What's his name?"

Dark Rain smiled seductively and said, "Beaverpaw. His name is Beaverpaw." Her voice came out like silken fibers pulled over polished shell.

Kelp's mouth puckered as though she wanted to spit, and Moonsnail almost shouted a reprimand . . . but didn't, because it was not like Kelp to malign a person of status and reputation for no reason at all. So. What did Kelp know about Beaverpaw that Moonsnail did not? Later, after this discussion ended, Moonsnail would wring the truth out of the girl.

Moonsnail turned back to Seedpod. He watched her with sharp old eyes. Obviously he'd seen her scrutiny of Kelp, and wondered about it. He was perceptive, all right. She could see his sudden doubts about Beaverpaw. "Let us leave the decision about who we should send for another time. I—"

"Why?" Floating Stick inquired. "I think Beaverpaw is a fine choice. He—"

"I do, too," Dark Rain added, giving the old man that shark's tooth smile.

Seedpod's gaze rested on Kelp, and finally shifted to Moonsnail. A knowing glint shone in those brown depths. "That decision can wait. Instead, let us speak of when we should plan to move."

Floating Stick said, "How long will it take Windy Cove to pack up?"

Seedpod's expression turned grim. "After four attacks by Cottonmouth, three upon our village and one upon our scouting party, we have little left, people or possessions. We could be ready within three days. What about Heartwood?"

Floating Stick bent forward and laced his fingers together in his lap. Sparse white hair fluttered around his wrinkled face. Only ten summers ago he'd had thick lustrous hair, but since then it had fallen out in handfuls, leaving a wispy covering for his freckled scalp. The nostrils of his hooked nose flared. He said, "I should think we could be ready in five or six days' time. After, that is, the runner returns to tell us if the site is right for us. What do you think, Moonsnail?"

She nodded. "I believe that is reasonable. Which means we can be ready to leave in, let me see—if we send a runner tomorrow morning—two days for him to get there, two days back, then five days to pack. We could be ready in, say, nine or ten days. But it may take us three or four days to get there, carrying our belongings and shepherding the children."

"In total, then," Seedpod said, "we could expect you at the new village site in about ten-and-three days."

"Yes."

"Good." Seedpod nodded. "By the time your runner returns here, Musselwhite, Pondwader, and I should be at Windy Cove. If the site has proven out, we will leave Windy Cove five days later. That way we can all start for the new site at about the same time."

"And arrive at roughly the same time," Floating Stick added. "This will be helpful. We can organize our clans and aid each other with setting up shelters, then hunting and gathering food. It will be a good way for new relatives to become acquainted."

Floating Stick smiled and Seedpod nodded approvingly.

"It is settled then," Moonsnail said.

"Yes." Seedpod slapped his hands on his knees. "And, if you have nothing more to discuss with me, Moonsnail, I will begin packing for my trip home."

Moonsnail nodded. "Will you be staying this night will us? Or do you plan to leave later today?"

"I'll need to consult with Musselwhite. I don't—"

Floating Stick sniggered, then leaned backward and laughed aloud. Seedpod turned to peer at him curiously, and Floating Stick said, "That may depend on whether or not your new son-in-law keeps your daughter busy in the blankets all day! Eh, Moonsnail? What do you think? Will Pondwader let his wife up long enough to get packed for the journey to Windy Cove? Or will he keep her pinned to the floor mats?"

Moonsnail chuckled. "We shall see."

Seedpod's white brows arched. With a smile, he said, "If Pondwader is still alive after trying to pin Musselwhite to the mats, we had all best help him get packed—because he'll need to run fast."

Floating Stick roared and clapped appreciatively while Moonsnail chuckled. Dark Rain smiled. Only Kelp seemed unaffected by the joke. In fact, she seemed dejected by the entire discussion. She had begun following the edge of her big toe with her thumb.

Moonsnail waved a hand at Seedpod. "Go prepare your things! I will be over later with food and water for your journey."

Seedpod bowed. "My daughter and I thank you." Then, as an afterthought, he smiled and amended, "My daughter, *son-in-law,* and I thank you." He turned and walked across the village toward the council shelter.

Floating Stick rose on rickety knees, still snickering. His stringy old muscles quivered. "Call if you need me, Moonsnail. I'm going to go and nap. All this talk of coupling has sapped my strength."

"You old fool," Moonsnail said affectionately. "Go on. Go home to your wife. I will let you know if anything of importance occurs."

Floating Stick nodded and headed toward his own shelter on the southern end of the village. Sunlight sparkled in his wispy hair as he bent over to talk to a crowd of children playing in the sand. Bright giggles erupted, and two little boys rose and clung to his hands as he continued on his way.

Moonsnail smiled. What an old fool he was. She had known him for five-tens-and-five summers, and had enjoyed every moment. He'd been quite a prankster as a youth. One of his favorite tricks had been to hide in the blankets of newly married couples and leap up just before they found him. *If* they found him. He claimed he'd witnessed the conception of half a dozen babies because the couples had not discovered him until too late—and, knowing him, it was probably true.

Dark Rain got to her feet and stretched her arms over her head in that lazy sensual manner that made her breasts strain against her tunic. "Mother, I'm very tired. I think I'll go take a nap, too."

"Please do."

Dark Rain hesitated, then eyed her askance. "Why? Are you planning on talking about me when I'm gone?"

"You may be absolutely certain, daughter of mine, that I will save anything unpleasant to say to your face. Now, go. I wish to speak with my grand-daughter."

Kelp seemed to wake. She jerked and looked up. "What? What did you say, Grandmother?"

"I said I wish to speak with you."

Kelp blanched and peered fearfully at her mother. Dark Rain's eyes narrowed, as if she sensed something amiss, but didn't know what.

"Leave, Dark Rain," Moonsnail ordered. When Dark Rain opened her mouth to say something else, Moonsnail cut her off with, *"Do I have to find my walking stick to beat you?"*

Unwittingly, Kelp said, "I know where it is, Grandmother. Shall I fetch it for you?"

She had meant to be helpful, and when it dawned on her what she'd said, Kelp let out a sharp yip. "Oh! I didn't mean—"

Dark Rain exploded, "Yes, you did, you little—!"

"Do fetch it, Kelp." Moonsnail smiled grimly.

As Kelp leaped up to find Moonsnail's walking stick, Dark Rain glowered. "I'm leaving."

"I thought you would."

Dark Rain lifted her chin and stalked away.

Kelp ran back with Moonsnail's walking stick and handed it to her. "Grandmother, really, I didn't mean anything by what I said."

"Do you think it would bother me if you had? Sit down, girl. Let us talk for a time."

Kelp knelt on the mats at Moonsnail's feet, and began fussing with the hem of her tunic, creasing it with her fingernails. "What? Have I done something bad?"

Moonsnail braced her walking stick before her and propped her hands on the polished knob. "Well, that remains to be seen. Tell me what you know about Beaverpaw?"

Kelp's head came up like a startled stork's. "I—I don't know anything."

"Oh, yes, you do. Did you think I'd miss that sour expression on your face when Seedpod suggested Beaverpaw go to survey the new village location? Well, I didn't. So, tell me what you know."

"Grandmother . . ." Kelp twisted her hands, looking miserable. "Really, I don't—"

"Don't lie to me!" Moonsnail batted her in the shoulder with her walking stick. Kelp flinched. "Does it have something to do with your mother? I noticed that when you frowned Dark Rain grinned like a coyote digging into a burrow filled with newborn rabbits. Are she and Beaverpaw consorting?"

Kelp deflated with relief. "Thank the Spirits you already know."

"Tell me about it."

"Well, I—I saw them, in the forest last night. Mother was . . . lying on the ground . . . and Beaverpaw . . ." Red climbed her cheeks.

Moonsnail's gray brows plunged down over her bulbous nose, and she gripped her stick more firmly. Anger rose in her breast, fit to burst her ribs. "I must be getting old not to have suspected as much."

"But Grandmother," Kelp whispered and leaned forward confidentially. "I thought you knew!"

"The only thing I knew was that *you* knew something."

"Oh, Grandmother, I'm scared. Beaverpaw has a wife and seven children! If mother ever found out that I'd . . . she would think I'd been spying on her and . . ." Kelp closed her eyes tightly. "Blessed Spirits, I just went out into the forest to relieve my bladder. I never wanted this."

"You should thank your bladder, girl. It's fortunate for the clan that you discovered this."

"But, Grandmother, how could Mother even think about—"

"She doesn't think, child. Not ever. If she can't feel it in her private places, it doesn't interest her." Moonsnail grunted, disgusted with herself. She used to have the sharpest eyes in the village where such things were concerned. Had age blinded her woman's sensibilities? Now there was a truly horrifying thought. "You know, I have seen your mother giving Beaverpaw the eye once or twice. But, Blessed Forest Spirits! Tadpole-faced Beaverpaw, and the beautiful Dark Rain? Who would have thought! Your mother must have found a way to use him to her advantage. Though I can't imagine what. I suppose I should feel sorry for him."

Kelp reached out and squeezed Moonsnail's hands where they rested on the walking stick. Her young fingers felt warm and strong. "What will happen, Grandmother?"

"Well, your mother is already an Outcast. There's nothing more we can do to her. Besides, she is an unmarried woman and it is acceptable for her to flit around like a bee searching for nectar. I used to wonder if that was why she always refused to marry. She knew it would curtail her 'flitting.' . . . Beaverpaw is another matter. The punishments for adultery are severe."

"Will . . . will he be killed?"

Moonsnail shrugged. "It will be up to the council of Spirit Elders. If Waterbearer still wants him, the punishment will be light, but if Waterbearer gets mad and decides to take revenge for his unfaithful ways . . . Well, Beaverpaw will have fathered his last child—and be lucky not to bleed to death." She sighed. "Then again, maybe we'll just cast him out. I can't say."

"I'm sure it's Mother's fault, Grandmother. You know how wicked she is! Why can't we just—" She looked up suddenly. "They're here!" A smile came to her lips as she leaped to her feet.

Moonsnail swiveled around to see Pondwader and Musselwhite walking into the village hand in hand. They wore their marriage garb, Pondwader his blue robe, with the hood pulled up, and Musselwhite her yellow sandstar-print tunic. Pondwader's hair hung down over his chest, very white against the deep blue of his robe. Musselwhite had plaited her hair into a single long braid. Both looked very tired. Moonsnail grinned. When Pondwader got close enough to see them, he smiled and waved.

Kelp ran out and threw her arms around his neck to hug him. Brother and sister laughed, then Kelp bowed respectfully to Musselwhite, and followed them into Moonsnail's shelter.

"Good Morning, Grandmother," Pondwader said as he bent down to kiss her on the forehead. He smelled of woodsmoke and persimmons. "You look lovely this morning."

"Bah!" Moonsnail said. "I couldn't sleep for worrying about you, how much strength you had. Now, sit down. Kelp and I were discussing something important."

Pondwader glanced at Kelp's suddenly downcast face, and said, "What's wrong?"

"It's mother," Kelp responded as she sank to the mats beside Moonsnail's walking stick.

"What's she done this time?" Pondwader asked.

Musselwhite said, "Shall I leave? I could help my father pack—"

"No, stay. This is your family now. You have a right to know our debility." Moonsnail lifted her stick and pointed at Dark Rain, who stood in the plaza with young Bowfin. "And there it is."

Musselwhite turned and frowned. "Your daughter?"

"Only by blood. She's been Outcast for ten-and-four moons, and the clan has refused her petition for readmission."

Pondwader knelt on the floor mats beside Kelp and shoved his blue hood back, revealing his long white hair. His pink skin had a curious glow today. Musselwhite leaned against the shelter pole to Moonsnail's left, and folded her arms. Against the background of sky, she looked very tall and slender.

Pondwader grimaced. "Tell me, what did she do? Offend one of the Spirit Elders? Gamble away Kelp's life? What?"

The idea pulled a laugh from Kelp. She playfully slapped her brother on the shoulder. "No. Not yet. That will probably come next moon. But she may have threatened Beaverpaw's."

"Beaverpaw?" Musselwhite said with a frown. "What does he have to do with this?"

Moonsnail sighed, "Apparently he and Dark Rain are lovers."

"Ah," Musselwhite said and bowed her head. Lines etched her brow. "I'm sorry to hear that. He seemed a capable War Leader. I will miss his knowledge."

"What do you mean?" Pondwader asked.

Musselwhite glanced at him gently, and turned to Moonsnail. "I assume he will be stripped of his title immediately."

Moonsnail nodded. "I'm sure of it. Then the Elders will convene to discuss other punishments."

"Who will be War Leader, then?" Musselwhite shifted, and her long braid fell over her shoulder. In the plaza behind her, Bowfin's high-pitched laugh rang out, followed by Dark Rain's seductive murmuring.

Moonsnail responded, "Hard to say. Perhaps Bowfin. Maybe young Tailfeather. His reputation is growing."

"Yes," Musselwhite said and nodded firmly. "I've heard of Tailfeather. He is much respected. From what I know, he would be a good choice, though I realize it is not my place to recommend."

Under her breath, Kelp said, "Much better than Bowfin."

Moonsnail yanked her neck around. "What's wrong with Bowfin? Do you know something else?" And her gaze went back to the plaza. Dark Rain sidled up next to Bowfin to whisper something. Bowfin's smile broadened. Moonsnail might not know much, but she knew what that grin meant. "Great Mouse. I *am* getting old." She swatted the floor with her walking stick.

Kelp whispered, "I shouldn't have said anything. He's not married. So, I guess it doesn't matter what he and my mother do together."

"Oh, yes, it does!" Moonsnail snapped. "She is Outcast from our clan. He shouldn't be consorting with her at all!"

Moonsnail sank back against her blankets, and mopped her forehead with her sleeve. "Great Shining People. I don't know how Dark Rain does it. Adultery and clan infighting, all in a matter of days."

Pondwader shook his head. "My mother can be truly exasperating."

Musselwhite suppressed a smile at the gross understatement, and Kelp clamped both hands over her mouth to muffle her laughter.

Moonsnail gave him an irritated look. "Enough of this. Let's talk of other things. Musselwhite, I tried to talk your father into staying for another night, but he didn't seem inclined to do it. Will you speak with him? It would be our honor if you two—"

"You are very kind, Moonsnail, but I fear he's right. We should be heading home. Our village has been in danger every moment we've been gone. He is probably as worried about Windy Cove as I am."

Moonsnail nodded. "Well, I understand. If things work out, we will see you soon anyway, but I'll let Seedpod explain that to you. Now, let me see . . . Kelp, if you will fetch me a bag, I will put together some food for your brother and his new family to take on their journey. And get me one of those big narrow-necked gourds, too. They'll need fresh water."

Beaverpaw stood in a circle with Dark Rain and Bowfin, his gut twisting as he looked up at the giant oaks around them, their gnarled branches silhouetted darkly against the pink sunset sky. Owls perched in the tops. With the coming of evening, crickets and grasshoppers had come alive in the grass. They chirped and churred.

"I cannot believe it!" Beaverpaw said. "We've been very careful. How could anyone have found out?"

Dark Rain thrust out her chin. She looked glorious when she did that. Starlight sheathed her beautiful face, and her full lips pursed, as though longing to be kissed. "I don't know! But I overheard my mother hissing the story to Floating Stick, so someone did! Believe me, Beaverpaw, *they know.*"

He flapped his arms against his sides. "Well, what should we do?"

"We must all leave," Dark Rain said.

"But what of my wife and children? Who will take care of them? I can't just—"

"Forget them! Unless you wish to go around for the rest of your life with your penis in a basket by your bed! And that is the least of what they will do to you!"

Beaverpaw stared at her magnificent face and felt sick. He loved his children . . . and his wife. He had never planned on leaving them. The very idea tore his souls to shreds. He had only wanted to have a little fun with this strange, erotic creature. Now, it did not seem like such fun. The faces of each of his young children floated before his eyes, smiling at him, touching him gently, loving him. How could he live without his children? Little Manatee Flipper had only begun to learn how to cast a dart—and his son had been so joyous when Beaverpaw had first started teaching him. Who would teach him now? It would break the boy's heart if Beaverpaw left. And despite Waterbearer's ugly face, she had always stood by him—even when he'd been wrong. She had been the sharp blade that had protected him from criticism and prodded him to greater achievements. . . . Beaverpaw owed her everything.

"I don't think the village elders will recommend such harsh punishment," Beaverpaw said. "I'm sure Waterbearer will take me back, and if she does—"

"She may not have a choice!" Dark Rain spat. "Do you remember ten summers ago when Dry Cloud was found dipping his manhood into young Bog? His wife screamed for his release! But the village elders ordered his death! How could you have forgotten?"

Blood drained from Beaverpaw's head. How *had* he forgotten. Dark Rain was right. Dry Cloud had been tied to a tree and every warrior in the village had darted him. But that had been a unique circumstance. Bog was only ten. Not even close to a woman yet. The village elders had been certain she'd been forced. Still . . . Dry Cloud's wife had begged for his life. And wept and pleaded and done everything possible to save Dry Cloud. But he'd been killed anyway. For the sake of the clan.

A tingle of terror climbed Beaverpaw's back. "Blessed Brother Sky," he whispered, and massaged his forehead. "How did I ever get here?"

But he knew how. He fancied himself in love with Dark Rain. Every time she smiled at him, his souls soared and his manhood hardened. No woman had ever affected him so powerfully. The lightest of her touches left him quivering.

Bowfin laughed, a low laugh that made Beaverpaw's blood turn to ice. A grin spread across his long face and his deep-set eyes glinted. He reached out, grabbed Dark Rain by the arm, and kissed her hard. She pretended to struggle, but kissed him back. "I'll tell you how you got here," Bowfin said. "This woman has a body like Sun Mother's, so hot and bright you must reach for it, or go mad." Dark Rain rubbed herself against him, smiling and making those soft sensual sounds that could, indeed, drive a man crazy with longing.

Beaverpaw reached out and dragged her away, back to his side. Dark Rain slipped her arms around his waist, clinging to him, but he ignored her. His gaze fixed on Bowfin. "And you, my young warrior, what will you do? You have been consorting with a woman Outcast by our clan. The elders will certainly cast you out, too."

Bowfin gestured nonchalantly. "What do I care? I have nothing here to hold me. No wife. No children. I don't even *like* my family. Both of my cowardly brothers hate me for the great warrior I have become. Running away does not sound so bad to me. Perhaps I may find another clan that will appreciate my talents."

Beaverpaw let his head fall forward, and stared blindly at the dew drops on the oak leaves covering the ground. "How could they have found out? It just doesn't make sense! We never even touched in the village and we—"

"Perhaps that child you chased off told his parents what he'd seen. Who cares?" Dark Rain said as she stood on her tiptoes and bit Beaverpaw's chin. "Come on. It will be fun." Her hand slid down to his crotch. "If you run away with me, I guarantee I will take good care of *this.* "

Sixteen

You're a thoughtful child. I could have refilled my cup myself, but I appreciate your help. My hands aren't near as steady as they used to be. This bone-stiffening disease gets worse every— Yes, that's full. Thank you—every summer. Some day you will understand that the only things that matter in life are a cup of warm tea, a blanket on a cold night, and the touch of someone you love. All else is just clutter. Umm, that's good tea. Where did you find the mint in this season? Well, it's quite good, even if it is from dried leaves.

Now, let me see, where was I?

Hmm? . . . Oh, yes, Diver . . .

Things were not going well for him. Despite Diver's efforts, being in Standing Hollow Horn Village was beginning to take a toll. Doubts had entered Diver's mind. He could no longer be certain that the woman he loved with all his heart was innocent of the crimes Cottonmouth claimed. And just the possibility that Musselwhite might have been able to hide such a cruel streak from him for two-tens-and-five summers had upended his world.

What? Talk louder! I can't hear a word you're saying.

. . . Well, think about it. When people fall in love, child, they fall and break their necks. They walk around wounded for moons after that, and the only way to ease the pain is to learn how to crawl into your lover's heart and make a home there. Love involves an intimacy which is closer and more precious than anything in the world. In a very real sense, lovers *live* inside each other all the time, even when they are far apart.

So Diver was suffering the anguish of uncertainty. The possibility that his wife might have kept something from him—and not just that she would, but that she *could* keep something from him—had left him empty and aching.

Hmm?

Oh, no. It was just uncertainty. Diver loved her too much to be angry. Besides, he had saved all his rage for his captor. And Cottonmouth was obsessed with Diver, like a man who has just had one of the Shining People fall through the roof of his shelter, and has the chance to speak with a god. . . .

Leave me alone!" Diver shouted, and threw his rabbit-scapula spoon into his bowl of fish soup. Warm liquid splashed out on his hand. "Won't you even let me eat in peace?"

Cottonmouth waved his guards back, and waited until they had walked two tens of paces away, out of hearing range, before he dipped his hand into the insect grease gourd hanging from the northwestern shelter pole and rubbed it on his arms and chest as he slowly walked around the shelter to sit down with his back braced against the southeastern shelter pole, facing Diver. He had pulled his long hair away from his face and twisted it into a bun. The fires of sunset turned his silver temples a pale pink hue.

Sun Mother had sent out crimson light to blanket Sea Girl and transform her whitecaps into frothy carnelian. A short distance from shore, dolphins fished the shallows, their dorsal fins weaving through the water. Frightened mullets leaped before them, breaking the surface to sail in the air for a few glorious moments, before diving down again.

Diver looked at his own food. Clams, seaweed, and chunks of sunfish floated in the broth. It smelled wonderful. The sight of Cottonmouth had made him lose his appetite, but he ate ravenously anyway, using his scapula spoon to lift out the chunks of fish. They fed him once a day, if he was lucky, and this soup tasted delicious. When he ate, they usually untied his hands and feet, and for a short time the numbness and pain went away. Not to mention the fact that he could slap mosquitoes; the pesky insects drove him mad when he was tied up. No one, it seemed, wanted to waste insect grease on him, so red welts covered Diver's whole body, including the sensitive areas beneath his breechclout. Cottonmouth had ordered the old hag Starfish to provide him with the breechclout yesterday, for which Diver was very grateful, though the wrap of cloth did little to protect the rest of his body. He itched feverishly.

As Diver chewed his clams, he gazed down at Musselwhite's deerbone awl, which lay next to him on the floor mat. Just looking at it comforted him. He'd been dreaming of her constantly, wondering if she had married yet, worrying about the guilt she must be feeling. She would blame herself for her children's deaths and his capture. It was her way. She would be suffering from the mistaken belief that if she had been there, she could have saved them. And perhaps her presence *could* have saved her children . . . by preventing his argument with Blue Echo. Grief cramped his stomach. He lifted his bowl, drained it dry, and set it to the side.

"Are you ready to talk?" Cottonmouth asked. The lines around his eyes looked as deep as canyons.

"I have nothing to say to you. I want to be left alone."

"There is no such thing as 'alone,' Diver," Cottonmouth responded softly. "To be is to be related. To the white-tailed deer, the dolphins, the clouds floating on the horizon. Separateness is an illusion we create to justify our wrongdoings—that way we don't feel responsible for breaking the world's heart. But we do, you know. We break the heart of the world every moment of our lives. Even when we—"

"You're crazy."

Cottonmouth drew up one knee and cradled it in the circle of his arms. "Maybe. Doesn't matter. Pain is pain. Truth is Truth."

"What would you know of *truth?*" Diver spat the word. "Or pain? Y-you who cannot even breathe without hurting someone!"

"That, Diver," he said in a haunting voice, "is precisely what I have been trying to tell you. No one can. It is the lot of humans, and the single most important thing we must understand before we can save ourselves. To live is to inflict pain. To live in pain. We cannot help it. But we *can* learn to live with that Truth without killing our souls over it." Waning sunlight shone purplish on his tanned cheeks. "Do you wish to save yourself? If you do, I will teach you."

Diver laughed derisively. "Is that the sort of trash you tell these people to convince them to follow you? To believe in your ridiculous Dreams?"

Cottonmouth looked away. "When Hurricane Breather stalks the land again, you will long to escape to the shining new world that awaits my followers beyond the stars. The things you must learn are simple. If you will listen, they will take only a little—"

"There is *nothing* I wish to learn from you."

Cottonmouth inclined his head agreeably. "As you wish."

Pelicans hunted the darkening ocean, sailing low over the water, twisting and splashing down. Cottonmouth turned his head to watch them with narrowed eyes.

Diver clutched the deerbone awl and slid across the mats until he could brace his back against the northeastern pole. The guards had begun gambling, tossing sticks, but they still paid attention to his every move. Diver let his head fall back against the pole and exhaled. The evening wind tousled his disheveled hair and cooled his hot face. He had begun living from day to day, expecting nothing, praying for everything. And he'd found that such an outlook allowed him to find pleasure in the smallest of things: a gull squabble on the beach could make him laugh for a full hand of time; a husband touching his wife gently brought forth feelings of stunning tenderness; a child tripping over his dog's tail filled him with unimaginable joy.

Cottonmouth lightly turned over a fragment of clamshell buried in the sand, and examined the faded purple ridges. "I *do* believe in that other world promised in my Dreams, Diver. I realize that you think I am lying to gain followers, but that is not the case."

"Isn't it?"

Cottonmouth shook his head. "Don't you see, Diver, a person who sees nothing before him but a straight line to burial lives a futile life, a life of ever-increasing care and bitterness, and I cannot bear—"

"I do not know anyone who believes that! All of my relatives know that the Daybreak Land and the Village of Wounded Souls exist. None of them sees life as a straight line to the grave."

Cottonmouth lowered a hand to draw spirals into the sand at his side. "Well, I did. For many, many summers. I thought humans just lived hard and died, and there was nothing after that."

"That's absurd. All the great Soul Dancers have visited the afterworlds. How could you not believe?"

Cottonmouth shrugged. "The fact is, I didn't. I didn't believe in an afterlife, or Sun Mother, or any other Spirit. And because I didn't, I tried to pack ten lives into my one, to enjoy as much as I could, hate as much as I could, kill and save as many as I could." He laughed grimly. "The only thing I believed in was the world."

"But you believe the world is evil. I've heard you say it."

"Yes. The world is filled with pain and suffering. I have always believed that. That is why those years without Sun Mother were so terrible. If the world is all you believe in . . . well, you are destined to an infinity of suffering yourself. Indeed, I was so devoured by cares, I could barely live at all. I felt dead, and hopeless inside myself."

Diver tipped his bowl to finish the last few drops of his broth, and set it aside. He closed his eyes, preferring the red-tinged backs of his eyelids to Cottonmouth's curiously reverent face. "And that is when the Dream of a shining new world came to you?"

"Yes, two summers ago."

"So, tell me, what happens to all those people who do not follow you? Who think your Dream is just foolishness?"

Diver opened his eyes when Cottonmouth got to his feet. The man folded his arms tightly across his bare breast and came to stand over Diver. Silver wisps of hair blew around his cheeks. His eyes looked . . . odd, glistening. As though the empty wells of his souls had been overturned and all of the dark hollowness had flooded out like black water.

Diver clutched Musselwhite's deerbone awl in his right hand, and glanced toward the guards. They had ceased watching, totally engrossed in their gambling. Curses and shouts of triumph rang out from their circle. The rest of the villagers had retired to their shelters, lit their cook fires, and begun preparing supper.

A burst of adrenaline pumped through Diver's veins. *What if . . . ?* Could the broken awl go deep enough to puncture a lung? If it did, could he escape in the commotion? Darkness fell quickly these autumn days. If he could just get into the forest, he might be able to hide. His back wound still ached constantly, but his shoulder wound had begun to heal, and some of his strength had returned.

"Those who do not believe in my Dream," Cottonmouth said, "will be crushed beneath the heel of Hurricane Breather and their souls cast to the winds of destruction."

"Hurricane Breather will kill their souls in punishment? For refusing to follow *you?*"

"Oh, yes, I've seen it."

"*Seen* it?" Diver's pulse raced so fast he felt light-headed. "What do you mean? How could you see souls dying?"

Cottonmouth crouched beside Diver to stare him in the eyes, no more than eight hands away. His voice took on that ghostly quality. "It was like watching fires being smothered, Diver. Little by little, all the light went out of the universe until only darkness remained."

"What about the Lightning Birds?"

"Oh, he killed them, too. Hurricane Breather devoured all the light."

That bizarre look in his eyes intensified, reminding Diver of a dead animal's sightless gaze. There was nothing human there. Nothing at all.

For an eternity, their gazes held, then the lines of Cottonmouth's perfect face sagged and he sat back on the sand. He said, "Forgive me, sometimes I fall back into that Dream when—"

Diver struck, launching himself from his seated position with the awl gripped like a knife and aimed at Cottonmouth's chest. Cottonmouth gasped, threw up his arm to deflect the blow and dove out of the way. Diver landed face-first in the sand, and scrambled up just in time to see Cottonmouth lunging for the awl in Diver's fist. He knocked Diver backward, and the pain in Diver's wounded kidney sent such a white hot flash through him that it wrung a cry from his throat. Instantly feet pounded the sand, and guards encircled them, holding their long darts like spears, shouting and cursing.

Cottonmouth lay on top of Diver, nose to nose, breathing hard. In one quick movement, he jerked the awl from Diver's hand and held it up before Diver's eyes. The bone shone a gray-white in the twilight.

"That's how *she* did it," Cottonmouth whispered to him. "She took the awl and plunged it into my little son's chest and punctured his heart." He looked straight into Diver's eyes. "The boy didn't die right away, Diver. You know how stab wounds are. It took a while for his blood to run out. I held him. Rocked him in my arms. I Sang to Sun Mother, praying for his life." His gaze shifted to the awl again. "But I had abandoned her, shunned her for most of my life, so Sun Mother refused to hear me."

"How did the awl get broken?" Mulberry asked from behind Cottonmouth. The young warrior had a fearful, fascinated expression on his face. He was such a small man, and so skinny, he seemed nothing more than a grim-faced boy.

"I broke it," Cottonmouth murmured, "withdrawing it from my son's dying body."

Mulberry glanced at the other horrified guards and cried, "You should have killed her!"

Cottonmouth stared hollowly into Diver's eyes a moment longer, and Diver saw insanity flicker there, then Cottonmouth got up, leaving Diver panting from pain and exertion. Cottonmouth stood quietly, his head cocked, as if listening to voices no one else could hear. Then a small smile twisted his lips. "Musselwhite is not home yet," he said softly. "Perhaps I should have a 'gift' waiting for her when she arrives."

"A . . . a gift?" Mulberry asked, and took a confused step forward. He propped the butt of his long dart on the ground. The yellow goldfinch feathers which fletched the shaft gleamed in the red sunset.

"Yes. At dawn I want a war party headed south for Windy Cove Village. Thirty warriors should be enough. Take no captives this time. Do you understand? I wish no one to—"

"*No!*" Diver shouted. "No, Cottonmouth! For the sake of Sun Mother, do not do this! *Please!*" he pleaded. "They are innocent people. They have never hurt you!"

Cottonmouth looked down, his face a blank mask. "Did I not tell you, Diver, that it is the nature of human beings to inflict pain? Innocence or guilt makes no difference." He turned back to Mulberry, awaiting the young warrior's answer.

Mulberry's thin lips pressed together. "Yes, Elder. I understand."

Cottonmouth walked slowly through the darkening village, holding the awl lightly in his right hand and listening to the soft footsteps of the children who trotted around him on their ways to their own shelters. His shoulders ached from the struggle with Diver. He rotated them and winced. Flute music, high and sweet, lilted over the village. Few people dared look at him when he passed. Most huddled together over supper, speaking in low tones, firelight flickering from their worried faces. The sweet, tangy scent of turtles cooking in their juices filled the air. Cottonmouth could see them, upside down, their shells resting on the hot coals at the edges of fires. A strange eerie stillness had possessed the village. Could his people sense it, too? That somber sensation that the end of the world was at hand?

. . . Just a few days. That's all. Then I will be released from this—we *will be released.*

Sun Mother herself had promised to send Cottonmouth a Lightning Boy who would shoot down the Four Shining Eagles and unleash the wrath of Hurricane Breather. But . . . why hadn't she told him that the Boy would be married to the only woman he had ever loved?

He entered his shelter and sank down onto his bedding along the northern side. Cool wind penetrated the shelter, meandering around his cold firepit, stirring up the ashes and sending them flitting through the air. He turned the awl in his hand, studying every indentation in the bone, running his finger over her mark. It had gained a polished sheen that reflected the firelight coming from the other shelters. He ought to light his own fire. The evening's chill deepened by the moment. But he just pulled his yellow and blue blanket up and swung it over his shoulders.

Oh, how Cottonmouth had missed Musselwhite after she'd gone. Despite all the terrible things she'd done to him . . . he had missed her. She had an ironic way of analyzing things that put troubles in their proper place, and often left him rolling with laughter. His laughter had pleased her, probably because he did it so rarely, and so she had made an art of the ability. And he had loved her for it.

She had done the same thing with their son. Cottonmouth would never forget the day he'd walked into their shelter and found Musselwhite hiding behind a stack of baskets, throwing strange objects over the top at their ten-and-eight-moons-old son. A pile of curiosities lay around Glade, tiny shells, feathers, spring flowers. When an acorn landed at Glade's little feet, he shrieked with surprised delight and reached down to pick it up, then a big sponge bounced off his back and his eyes went wide. The acorn forgotten, Glade stamped his feet and giggled uproariously, waiting for the next item to come flying over the baskets. Instead, Musselwhite had leaped up, grabbed the boy in her arms, and began kissing him all over the face and neck. Glade had laughed until tears streamed down his beautiful round face.

And so had Cottonmouth.

When she had put the boy down for a nap before supper, she had laid the turtle-bone doll beside him, and Glade had immediately picked it up and clutched it to his chest with a soft satisfied sigh. Glade had slept with that doll every night of his life. . . .

Even now the joy of the time they had spent together kept Cottonmouth company in his loneliness. He had memorized every tender touch, every shared secret, and when he retired alone at night, he would take those memories out and look at them again—and remember how wonderful those summers had been.

Cottonmouth stretched out on top of his blanket and peered upward at the soot-coated roof which seemed to have sprouted fur in the past three moons of rising ash and smoke. Musselwhite's smile, Glade's happy face, drifted across his souls, and a powerful, familiar ache beat in his chest.

. . . Blessed Sun Mother, after what she had done to him, how could he still love her so deeply?

Seventeen

On the second day of their journey home, they reached Manatee Lagoon. Here the coastline took a smooth westward swing inland, and the silent green blanket of the land retreated from the shore, leaving a wide white beach to sparkle and glitter in the lavender gleam of sunset.

Seedpod paused to shift the circular bag draped over his left shoulder. With old Moonsnail's help, the bag had grown twice as heavy, weighing down his shoulders like a sack of stones. Pondwader and Musselwhite walked a short distance in front of him, hand in hand. Every now and again, Musselwhite had been apologizing to Pondwader, then disentangling her fingers from his to shift her three long darts to her other hand. When she did, Pondwader would trot around so that he might grip her newly freed hand. The young man had a perpetual smile on his oval face. The sight brought joy to Seedpod's old breast. How wondrous to know that young love still existed. In the purpling veils of light that fell with silken quiet over the land, the couple seemed truly radiant. Or at least his new son-in-law did.

"Pondwader!" Seedpod called. He smiled when the tall, skinny youth turned, his face pink in the frame of his tan hood. "Your grandmother is a master at torture. She gave us enough food to keep us fat for half a moon— and to prove to me I still have every blasted muscle that I recall from my youth."

Pondwader's mouth opened and he ran back. "Oh, Seedpod, I'm sorry. Please, allow me to carry that for you. I—" He reached out his hands.

"No, no," Seedpod said. "I'm fine. Really. You have your own pack to carry. I just wished you to know you are obliged to lighten my load by eating heartily tonight."

"Gladly," Pondwader agreed, and confidentially whispered, "And the sooner the better. I'm so hungry I could eat a whale by myself."

Musselwhite had been pushing them hard, demanding they keep up a brisk pace from before sunrise until after sunset. The same worry that tormented Seedpod had turned to desperation in her. They had been gone too long. They both knew it. He would swear that over the past nine days, since they left Windy Cove Village, another handful of silver strands had emerged in her lustrous black hair.

Musselwhite halted and looked back at the two men. She had plaited her hair into a single long braid, which hung down to the middle of her back, and wore a plain tan tunic, belted with a strip of leather. Though she appeared calm, Seedpod knew differently. Fear lay in the very set of her face. She ran a hand up and down the shafts of her darts, like a woman terrified they might have grown wet in the rain, too waterlogged to fly straight.

"And how are you, my beautiful daughter?" he called.

She surveyed the golden underbellies of the clouds that drifted lazily across the blue-gray background of coming night. Gulls squawked and wheeled in the skies above them. "We haven't much light left. Why don't we make camp early tonight? It's been a long walk."

Seedpod patted Pondwader on the back, and said, "Both of the men in your life are grateful!"

As they started forward, Pondwader said, "Please, Seedpod, let me carry that."

"No, no, really. I'm fine."

"But I am much younger than you. *Please* let me have it," he said as he lifted the bag from Seedpod's shoulders and swung it over his own.

Seedpod smiled. "I suppose I won't feel guilty letting you carry it this short distance," he said. "Thank you, Pondwader."

They followed Musselwhite around the shimmering lagoon, toward the trees that created a dark green wall along the beach ahead.

Fragrances of fish and salt grew heavier as night closed around them, making Seedpod's belly squeak with hunger. "I think I'm even hungrier than you," he murmured to Pondwader. "It seems the great Musselwhite is conniving to keep both of us so weak from hunger that we can't argue with her about this murderous pace."

"I think she's scared, Seedpod," Pondwader said softly. "She's been waking several times each night and lunging for her darts and atlatl—as though she expects an attack. I don't really understand it. I've been trying to make her feel safe."

Seedpod gazed into those depthless pink eyes and smiled gently. "She has been a warrior most of her life, Son-in-law. She knows that the only safety in life comes from her own hand, her own abilities. Old habits do not die just because you are newly married. We should thank the Spirits for her vigilance."

Pondwader nodded solemnly. "I do, I just . . . I love her so much, Seedpod. I want her to be happy."

"That will come. You just keep loving her." Seedpod placed a hand on his son-in-law's shoulder and squeezed.

They continued on in companionable silence, skirting the waves that swept in and out over the sand. Several large conch shells had washed up on shore. Their brilliant pink interiors gleamed in the dusk.

As they neared the trees, Seedpod saw Musselwhite crouch and slip her atlatl from her belt, and his fingers sank into Pondwader's shoulder to pull him back hard.

"What's—"

"*Shh!*" Seedpod hissed. Musselwhite had nocked a dart, lifted her atlatl, and moved into the mottled shadows at the edge of the treeline. Very quietly, Seedpod pulled his deerbone stiletto from his belt and edged forward. Pondwader stayed close on his heels.

"There's a fire," Seedpod whispered. "Burning just inside the trees. I can see the orange flicker."

"A fire?"

"Yes. Let's hope it belongs to some innocent traveler like ourselves, and not to an enemy warrior."

Seedpod's eyes narrowed when Musselwhite stood up from the brush where she'd been hidden and said something in a calm tone. Then she laughed, and he saw her walk into the light of the fire.

"It's all right," he told Pondwader as he slipped his stiletto into his belt again. "The camp belongs to a friend."

"How do you know?" Pondwader's white brows had pulled down over his pointed nose.

"Your wife hasn't killed anyone yet, that's how."

"Oh, I—I see."

"Come along, let us greet the people that Sun Mother has thrown in our path this night."

Seedpod stalked forward with Pondwader bringing up the rear. As they entered the small clearing, Seedpod saw Musselwhite crouched across the fire from scraggly old Dogtooth. Great Mouse, he looked ancient! Amber firelight fluttered over his thin hooked nose and gray hair, and accentuated every stringy muscle in his skinny body. He wore only a breechclout, and sat on a blanket before the flames, roasting a redfish he'd skewered on a long stick. The fish's fat dripped onto the coals where it steamed and sizzled.

"Come in, come in!" Dogtooth greeted, and waved them forward. "Sit down and share my fire!"

Pondwader's head came up. "Dogtooth?" he asked. "Is that old Dogtooth? It sounds like his voice."

"Yes, he's—" Seedpod began.

"Yes, of course, it's me, young Lightning Boy!" Dogtooth broke in. "Come over here. I have many things to discuss with you. I see your chest hasn't been blasted open yet. How are you otherwise?"

Seedpod turned to see his son-in-law's transparent eyes go as round and wide as an owl's. Seedpod walked back and linked his arm with Pondwader's, then guided the youth into camp. The boy came, reluctantly, placing each foot unsteadily. Perhaps Pondwader couldn't see well in the dark? Which made sense. He could barely see in bright daylight.

Seedpod sank down on the cool sand beside Musselwhite and said, "Great Forest Spirits! Dogtooth, you look as old as I feel. I thought you'd be dead by now."

"Oh, no, I'm very much alive." Dogtooth spun his fish on his stick, letting the other side roast. More fat dripped, and brilliant flares of fire leaped and crackled, sending shadows dancing over the smoke-colored trunks of the oak trees. "Pondwader, sit down! If you keep standing like that with your mouth open, you'll catch so many mosquitoes, you won't be hungry for supper— and Seedpod will be angry with you for not eating some of that roast goose he's been hauling around."

Seedpod sat forward. "How do you know about our goose?"

With a chuckle, Dogtooth answered, "You didn't think I made this camp here out of chance, did you? No, no. I've been waiting here for two days. You're late! What took you so long?"

Seedpod stretched his cramped legs out and sighed. "The marriage negotiations took longer than we'd expected. Moonsnail is shrewd. She wrung everything out of me that she could." He hesitated, watching Pondwader. The boy looked as if Grandfather Bear had stepped out of the brush and reared on his hind legs with his teeth bared. Pondwader dropped both packs by the fire, and weakly slumped to the sand.

"So, Dogtooth," Seedpod said, drawing his gaze back to the old Soul Dancer. "You've been waiting for us. How did you know we'd come this way? If we hadn't been in such a hurry we would have stuck to the forest trails—where it's safer."

"Yes, but I knew you'd be in a hurry." Dogtooth moved his redfish away from the flames, and slid it off the cooking stick into a wooden bowl, where it steamed and sizzled.

"How could you have known we'd be in a hurry?" Musselwhite asked warily.

"Pondwader's brilliant new soul told me." Dogtooth winked at the boy, who looked even paler, if that were possible. "It blinded one of my Dreams, and rumbled, 'Go to the seashore at Manatee Lagoon if you wish to speak with Pondwader before he gets toasted like a hickory nut.' " Dogtooth grinned. "So, I did."

Seedpod exchanged a glance with Musselwhite, and they both shifted to peer at Pondwader. The boy seemed to have turned to stone; he stared unblinking at Dogtooth. In the fluttering orange light of the flames, he looked a little queasy. It was just like Dogtooth to show up unexpectedly and open the conversation with something completely discomfiting.

"Well," Seedpod said with a smile as he rubbed his hands together, "let's eat!"

He grabbed up the food bag, doled out goose-legs to Musselwhite and Pondwader, and offered one to Dogtooth, who shook his head in refusal. The old Soul Dancer had begun stripping succulent flesh from his fish and eating it. Pondwader lifted his goose leg to his mouth, but didn't take a bite. He just stared unblinking over the roasted skin at Dogtooth. What had happened to his hunger? Had the boy gone into some sort of trance? Musselwhite, on the other hand, had already made a big dent in hers, but she was watching Dogtooth just as alertly—which Seedpod didn't understand. The old man was odd, but not dangerous. Despite the bizarre effect he had on his new son-in-law.

"Pondwader," Seedpod said. "What's the matter? You look like the Lightning Birds just darted the earth at your feet."

The youth opened his mouth as if to speak, but no words came out.

Seedpod leaned over and elbowed Pondwader in the belly, bringing forth a grunt. Pondwader scrambled to straighten, as if he'd awakened from a very vivid nightmare. "Eat!" Seedpod ordered. "Your wife will have us up long before Sun Mother rises, and you will need every bit of strength you can muster."

Pondwader glanced sheepishly at Musselwhite and obediently bit into his goose leg. Seedpod launched into his as well. The goose tasted so sweet and rich, it made him sigh with contentment.

"Where did you get the goose?" Dogtooth asked as he flipped over his redfish and began tearing flesh from the other side.

"You mean Pondwader's brilliant new soul didn't tell you? That was inconsiderate."

"Oh, not at all," Dogtooth responded. "Spirits only reveal what is necessary for humans to survive—and sometimes not even that much. They're greedy that way. Was the goose left over from the marriage feast?"

"Yes. You should have seen it, Dogtooth. Heartwood Clan cooked five geese, and tens of tens of killifish and ducks, and turtles. There were dozens of baskets mounded high with berries, nuts, and fruits. It was truly delightful."

"Well, Moonsnail is a smart woman," Dogtooth said affectionately. "She knows how to celebrate a great day for her clan." He lifted a gnarled finger and pointed at Musselwhite. "Being related to the great Musselwhite will bring Heartwood more honor than it could ever have dreamed of before." He swallowed a large mouthful of fish. "I suppose it was a good thing that Dark Rain gambled away every item that young Trader gave her. Of course," Dogtooth added thoughtfully, "he didn't think so. I'm sure he went off and committed suicide, though naturally no one noticed."

"What do you mean no one noticed?" Musselwhite asked with a lifted brow. Firelight flickered over her disgusted expression. She finished her goose leg and tossed the bones into the fire where they sent up a black tendril of smoke. "Somebody must have noticed."

"Not necessarily, my dear child. . . . Pondwader, you understand what I mean, don't you?" He reached out to touch the youth's sleeve, but stopped when Pondwader stiffened as if he'd been struck. Dogtooth squinted at him, then drew his hand back. "No, I suppose not. Well, what I meant is that if a man chooses to go out into the forest and slit his own throat in a makeshift shelter, it's hardly likely that nearby villagers will discover his dead body for . . . oh, maybe summers. And maybe never if the wolves and coyotes get to him first." Dogtooth filled his mouth with more fish and chewed noisily. "So, Pondwader," he said around the food, "tell us about your death. How was it?"

"Death?" Seedpod blurted. "What are you talking about? Look at him! He's sitting there looking very healthy—for Pondwader."

Dogtooth loudly whispered, "You mean you haven't told your wife and father-in-law about what happened to you at the Sacred Pond? You could have at least repeated what the ghosts said about her. She . . ."

Musselwhite gruffly rose to her feet. "Please excuse me. If we rise early tomorrow we might be able to make it back to Windy Cove by sundown. Good night." She grabbed up her pack and walked into the forest, where she untied her blanket from the pack's straps and threw it out across the ground. Close enough to watch the campfire, but far enough away to dart someone if necessary.

Seedpod squelched his smile. "The idea of ghosts has always disturbed her. She—"

"That's true," Pondwader said and nodded vigorously. "When I told her I could talk to ghosts, she almost fainted."

"Fainted?" Seedpod scoffed with a chuckle. "More likely she was contemplating murdering you."

"Th-thank you for telling me."

"You're welcome. And now," he added, "I think I'll join my daughter. But it's been truly *interesting* seeing you again, Dogtooth. I will leave you to speak with Pondwader, as you'd planned. Good night."

"Good night, Seedpod," Dogtooth said with real cordiality. "Sleep well. We will be safe here tonight. I have seen it in a Dream."

"You won't take offense if I sleep with my stiletto anyway, will you?"

"Not a bit."

Seedpod nodded politely, picked up his pack, and headed into the forest near Musselwhite.

Pondwader could hear them murmuring to each other, then Seedpod laughed softly, and Pondwader saw him throw out his blanket. Pondwader looked down at his goose leg and took another half-hearted bite. Despite the sweetness of the meat, his appetite had vanished.

"All right, Dogtooth," he said feebly, and threw the rest of the leg out into the forest for scavenging animals to find. "Tell me."

Dogtooth swiveled around on his blanket and whispered, "Don't sound so worried. You can talk to me." His faded old eyes had an eerie glow.

"About what?"

Dogtooth reached out with lightning quickness and seized Pondwader's right wrist in a death grip. Pondwader let out a small yip of surprise, and Dogtooth asked, "You aren't afraid of me, are you?"

"No." Pondwader jerked his arm away irritably. "What do you mean?"

Dogtooth leaned closer and his disconcerting brown eyes flared. To the left of his firelit face, Pondwader saw a black blur move out in the forest— and watched as Musselwhite sat up in her blanket and drew it about her shoulders . . . he knew it was she because he'd memorized all the surrounding blurs of trees so he could find his way to her later. After the long hard day they'd had, she should be sleeping. What was she doing? Keeping watch over him? Yes, she must be. It would be just like her. A loving smile tugged at the corners of his mouth.

Dogtooth said, "You love her very much, don't you?"

"Oh, yes. She means everything to me." And she did. He would do anything for her.

The breeze penetrated this clearing capriciously, sometimes assaulting the fire, other times leaving the flames to stretch long fingers toward the sheltering oak boughs. Pondwader focused on them, hoping their dance would ease his discomfort.

"That's good," Dogtooth said. "Because she is extremely unhappy and it will require all of your love to help her through it."

"I know." Pondwader shoved back his hood, relieved at the new topic, and let out the breath he'd unwittingly been holding. Feathers of white hair danced around his face. "I've been trying so hard to make her feel better, Dogtooth, but she—she so often seems beyond my reach."

"Of course, she does. Because she is."

"But I am her husband, Dogtooth. She needs me. I must gain enough of her trust that she will let me reach her."

"That will be very difficult, Pondwader."

"I know. But I must. I just don't know a quick way to gain her trust. Is there one? I want so much—"

"Oh, I shouldn't think so," Dogtooth replied. "No, those barriers were erected long ago, and have stood the test of time. I doubt that even Diver could penetrate them."

Pondwader squinted at the mosquitoes swaying and dipping in the firelight. If Diver couldn't penetrate them, then what hope did Pondwader have? "Why would she find it necessary to have such shields?"

"Why would anyone?" Dogtooth watched him with gleaming eyes.

"I guess I don't know, Dogtooth. I myself have never felt that need."

Dogtooth rolled to his side and propped his head in his left palm. "You are special, Pondwader. Because you are a Lightning Boy, you have been protected and petted your whole life. Musselwhite has not. No," he murmured, "far from it. Some day soon you must ask Seedpod to tell you what Cottonmouth did to Musselwhite when she was a little girl—ten-and-one summers, if I recall correctly. So . . . unfortunate."

"What?" Pondwader asked sharply. "What did he do to her?"

"It is not my place to tell you such things. I do not even know whether she remembers—or whether Seedpod would reveal the secret to another living soul. He covered it up as quick as a ferret snatching a mouse, to protect her, of course. But you must get him to tell you. It's important that you know."

The ominous tone of Dogtooth's voice frightened Pondwader. What could have been so terrible that Seedpod had chosen to hide the truth from everyone, including his clan? Seedpod had obviously felt that having the truth widely known would damage Musselwhite. But there were few crimes which would warrant punishing a child. Had he been protecting Cottonmouth? And how could Musselwhite herself have "forgotten" what had happened?

Pondwader said, "Is that why you came here? You wanted me to ask Seedpod about this event? Why? What difference will it make?"

A squirrel chittered out in the forest—probably being hunted by a night bird. Pondwader brought his gaze back to Dogtooth and found the old man's eyes glinting.

In a hoarse whisper, Dogtooth said, "It just may save your life—and hers. Very soon, you and Musselwhite will be going on a dangerous journey. You *must* know who she is—what made her who she is—before you leave."

"What journey? Where will we be going?"

Dogtooth broke into that lopsided grin again. "Tell me, what did it feel like when the baby bird pecked through its shell? Did the flash of light blind you? I've always wondered."

Pondwader's mouth gaped. "How did you know?"

"Well every Lightning Boy goes through—"

"*Every Lightning Boy!*" Pondwader yelled, and then forced his voice lower. "You mean others have gone through this before me?"

"What? Of course! The Blue Lightning Boy had a far worse time of it than you. He was deathly afraid of water, and his clan had to bind him up like a netted turkey and throw him in the Pond weighted down by rocks." Dogtooth tugged at his earlobe and grimaced. "Well, legends say that when the Blue Lightning Boy got to the surface, gasping and spitting, he was so terrified that the chick had already hatched."

Pondwader's hands knotted in his robe. "I—I don't . . . Are you trying to tell me that fear has something to do with the Bird's growth?"

"Everything is connected, Pondwader. You know that. How many people do you know who hide their heads every time a bad lightning storm comes? Many, I'll bet."

"What in the world does that have to do with the Lightning Bird glowing in my chest?"

"Why, it has everything to do with the Bird in your chest." Dogtooth blinked. "Think about it."

Pondwader did. "Do you mean that people's fears draw the storm? Or make it worse? Does fear *feed* the Bird? I thought Lightning Birds ate whales and dolphins, and other sea creatures."

"Yes."

"Yes to *what?*" Pondwader shook his fists at the darkness. "The Bird feeds on fear?" He peered solemnly into the old lunatic's eyes, and Dogtooth gazed back with unnerving intentness.

"Pondwader, don't you care why your brilliant new soul came to see me?"

Pondwader lowered his fists to his lap. "Yes, I—I care. But . . . I don't understand why it would fly off to talk to you when it hasn't spoken to me at all."

"It *hasn't?* Dogtooth's mouth dropped open in astonishment. "Not even one word?"

"No!"

"Well"—he waved a hand—"it will. When the time is right. And after it does you'll be able to do all sorts of wondrous things, like calling rain from a clear sky, and—"

"Dogtooth." Pondwader's gaze darted around uncomfortably. "What did it say to you?"

"You didn't even realize it had flown away, did you?"

"No," Pondwader whispered in awe. "How could it do that without my knowing it?"

"It's quite common. Souls do that all the time. They fly here and there while you're sleeping. That's why souls know so many things that people don't—they are explorers. And you have a rather rambunctious Bird inside you. He darted me right out of a dead sleep." Dogtooth scratched his backside, as if it were still sore. "Wanted to talk about that Dream I had. Do you recall my Dream?"

"About the Four Shining Eagles?"

"Yes, that's the one. That baby Bird—"

"How could I forget it?" Pondwader inquired sharply. "I was half afraid my own clan might murder me in my sleep!"

"Well, I must admit, I thought about it myself," Dogtooth replied. "The Eagles are so old and frail, flying on only one wing. They're pathetic sights, desperately tired, fighting to stay in the air. Their day is almost done, Pondwader. If—"

"Dogtooth . . ." Pondwader breathed, knowing what came next—the fears, the accusations. . . . All his life he'd heard them. "I *promise* you I will not kill the Eagles. I—I wouldn't even know how! And I do not wish the world to end! I have just married the most wonderful woman in the world. I want our life together to last—"

"Let me finish." Dogtooth held up a hand. It cast an eerie, swaying shadow over the trees, like a warrior Dancing with a warclub. "If the Lightning Birds had not soared down and blasted some sense into me, I'm sure I would have killed you. But they did blast me. That's why I called you to the Sacred Pond—so that you might be reborn in the Lightning. And that's why that blindingly beautiful baby bird inside you came to see me. To tell me about your progress."

Pondwader shifted uncomfortably. "I don't understand."

"You will. And soon. That chick is growing very quickly. It will not be long before she slices through your ribs and goes hunting. Then everything will be clear to you."

The blue-white glow inside Pondwader expanded, trickling out to warm his fingers and toes. "Hunting?"

"Yes. *Hunting.* Power is about to ask many things of you, Pondwader. It's all right to be afraid. Just do what you must."

Pondwader tentatively lifted his hand and placed his fingers over his heart; the skin beneath his robe felt unnaturally hot; as if fevered. He could feel two heartbeats, one slamming against his ribs, the other like a faint faraway rumble. "I promise I will try to do whatever Power asks of me, Dogtooth," he said, and added more softly, "whatever this baby Lightning Bird asks of me."

Pondwader wet his lips, and braced himself to ask Dogtooth the question that kept him awake at nights—the question that had been tormenting him for days. The old man seemed to sense it, his brows pulled together in anticipation.

"Dogtooth," he said. "You are a great Soul Dancer. Please, tell me. I can face the truth—if I just know what it is. . . . When the baby bird soars free, will I die?"

Dogtooth grinned suddenly. "You have died once already. Did it hurt?"

"Well . . ." His hand went to the place on his side where the dart had punctured. "Only a little."

"So what are you afraid of?"

Pondwader inhaled a shaky breath. "That means 'yes,' doesn't it?"

Dogtooth gasped. A big wolf spider dropped on its dragline from one of the oak branches, and dangled before his old eyes. Dogtooth squinted at the insect. As the strand of web twisted around, firelight glinted from the spider's bulbous brownish-yellow body, and threw its shadow like a huge amorphous monster on the trees near Seedpod.

"Hmm?" Dogtooth asked softly. He cocked an ear toward the spider. "But why should I tell him when he already knows the important part . . . ? Bah! The details will just get him in more trouble. And, as you well know, he's in quite enough as it is. When he's standing face-to-face with Cottonmouth, he'll know what to do. I'm sure of it."

"*Cottonmouth?*" Pondwader mouthed the name, then more loudly, demanded, "What are you talking about? Is that where Musselwhite and I will be going on our journey? *Tell me!*"

As though the discussion had ended, the spider began climbing up its invisible strand. Dogtooth watched, his gray head leaning further and further back, until the insect disappeared into the swaying shadows overhead, then Dogtooth sighed, and said, "Spiders are so pushy." He shook his head, and rolled up in his blanket. "Good night, young Lightning Boy."

"*Dogtooth!* How can you expect me to—to do anything if you won't tell me what sort of trouble I'm facing?"

Dogtooth yawned. "You already know you're going to die. Isn't that enough?"

The breath in Pondwader's lungs stilled. Until this very moment, he hadn't believed it. He sat quietly. When the wind blew the flames, the wolf spider's shadow danced over the firelit trees again, twisting and bouncing, swinging like a pebble on a string. Deep inside him, a voice kept whispering, *But I'm afraid of dying. I'm barely ten and five summers! I want to live!*

"Dogtooth?" Pondwader whispered. "Dogtooth . . . ?"

The old man didn't move a muscle. He appeared to be sound asleep.

When Dogtooth started snoring, Pondwader rose and walked out through the darkness, veering around black blurs of trees and piles of deadfall, to where Musselwhite waited. She had thrown out their bedding beneath the spreading limbs of a large pine. As he neared, she held the top blanket open and slid over, making him room. Seedpod lay a short distance away, snoring. Pondwader slipped off his sandals, crawled in beside Musselwhite, and hugged her fiercely. It comforted him to feel her body against his, to hear her steady breathing.

"Are you all right?" she asked softly, as if she sensed his fear.

Pondwader buried his face in the wealth of her hair. It smelled sweetly of pine needles. "So long as you are safe, I will be content. You are all that matters, my wife."

But he couldn't keep the quaver from his voice.

Musselwhite stroked his back long into the night, until he fell asleep in her arms.

Eighteen

Diamondback lay in his grandfather's shelter, his back supported by a pile of blankets, playing cat's cradle with Thorny Boy. The six-summers-old child sat cross-legged at Diamondback's side, his face a mask of concentration as he studied the complicated lacing of strings that Diamondback held before him.

"I don't know which ones to pull," Thorny Boy said plaintively. "Tell me." His brown headband did not keep the unruly tangle of black locks from falling over his eyes. With a quick swipe of the hand, he shoved them back.

Diamondback smiled. He extended the cradle and waggled his thumb. "First, you'll want to grab this one. Then—"

Thorny Boy lunged for the crossed strings and Diamondback jerked the cradle away, which drew a frustrated whine from his little brother. Thorny Boy slammed his fists into the floor mat. "Why did you *do* that?"

"Because," Diamondback said, "you make the same mistake every time we play this game. Now, listen!"

Thorny Boy's mouth puckered into a pout. "Hurry."

Diamondback smiled. "You have to pull both crosses out at the same time, then up and away. After that, you have to pull the crosses over the edge of the cradle and take them under the bottom, bringing your fingers up here . . . and here . . . or the whole weave will fall apart. Remember? That's what you did wrong last time. That's why we can't get any further in the game. If you don't go slow, Thorny Boy, you'll never learn to finish this series of patterns and you'll never be good enough to go on to the game of Precocious Cat's Cradle—which is much harder. You'll be stuck here, at the beginning, for the rest of your life."

Thorny Boy groaned, "I know, I know. You tell me this every time!"

"I'm trying to get you to *think*."

"I *am* thinking!" Thorny Boy sucked his bottom lip in and clamped his teeth down on it, while he attempted the feat. He pinched the two patches of string, pulled—stopped momentarily to frown—then pulled the crosses over the edge of the cradle and brought his fingers up through the bottom. Diamondback let him take the string, and as Thorny Boy pulled it out, the next beautiful pattern in the game emerged: four interlocking squares, filled by diamonds.

Thorny Boy shrieked in glee. "I *did* it! Look!"

Diamondback laughed. "I told you. You just had to think about what you were doing."

"Mother is going to be so proud of me when she returns!"

"Yes," Diamondback said as he playfully punched his brother in the shoulder. Thorny Boy fell backward, laughing, and had to take quick action to keep the string on his fingers. Diamondback added, "She will be proud of you, and so will her new husband—I hope."

Thorny Boy grinned as he studied the pattern he'd created, and Diamondback let his gaze drift over the village, seeing all the familiar faces of his clan, hearing their warm voices as they spoke to each other, and wondered how a Lightning Boy would fit into this tightly woven group. The scent of cooking mussels and maypop rose on the evening breeze. Adults murmured and children giggled as they gathered around their evening fires. Windy Cove Clan possessed more knots and twisted strands than a game of Precocious Cat's Cradle. Diamondback hoped the Lightning Boy would be happy here—though, Diamondback admitted, ever since his mother told him she might marry again, he himself had been undergoing fits of depression and anger . . . and then when the news came that his father still lived, those feelings had just grown worse.

He had begged Ashleaf to send a messenger to Heartwood Village so his mother could stop the marriage—but the elder had refused, saying they had too few people left as it was. They could spare no one. And, besides, they *needed* this alliance.

Since then, Diamondback's resentment had been festering, and he'd been playing a guessing game with himself. What would his mother do first? Would she waste a day divorcing her new husband? Or just take off at a dead run for Standing Hollow Horn Village? It hurt that he would not be able to go with her. She needed him. His father needed him. And he could help neither of them.

Diamondback prodded his injured leg. Healing fast, it still hurt when he tried to stay on his feet for long. If he used a walking stick he could make it around the village pretty well, but he felt as weak as a newborn kit afterward. He kept his atlatl and darts close at hand, but he knew he would be almost useless in a fight, and just the thought of running to Cottonmouth's village on a war walk made him break out in a sweat.

Guards had been posted around the perimeter of the village, and Ragged Wing, Shoal, and Black Urchin sat in a circle in the middle of the shelters, waiting their turns to stand guard. They had been keeping night watch, and had awakened only a short time ago. Their atlatls lay at their sides while they yawned and gambled. They were playing Stick, called so because the gaming pieces consisted of five decorated lengths of reedgrass which were cast across the ground. Their different positions determined how many points each throw totaled. Sticks which pointed directly north and south earned two points, east-west sticks earned one. Anything lying at an angle scored no points. Diamondback could see the pile wagered on Black Urchin's next throw: A large conch horn, a lightning whelk necklace, and a chert knife. The last was the most valuable. The stone had to be traded from the north and cost a great deal. Black Urchin cast, and frustrated howls went up from Ragged Wing and Shoal. Black Urchin chuckled and gathered up his winnings.

Diamondback stared hollowly at the eastern horizon. The mauve glow on Sea Girl's face had begun to die. As the white caps turned gray, the shells seemed to melt into the background of sand. Even the constant roar of Sea Girl's voice softened with nightfall.

Diamondback lowered his gaze to the polished circlets of conch shell on his belt. Was Cottonmouth torturing his father? Hatred welled so powerfully in Diamondback's belly that he had to clench his fists.

Thorny Boy whispered, "What's wrong?"

Diamondback forced a feeble smile. "Nothing. I was just thinking."

"About the Lightning Boy?" His eyes widened.

". . . Yes."

Thorny Boy tipped his fingers down and let the string fall to the floor. The tangled strands resembled a bird's innards—white and stringy. "He worries me. When father gets home, if . . . if we rescue him. Will the Lightning Boy still be married to mother? Will both of them sleep under the same blanket with her?"

Diamondback had been wondering that himself. He understood the necessities of being related to Heartwood Clan, but somehow the idea of their mother lying with another man grated deep down. His parents, though both warriors, had always refused to take other spouses. Everyone knew it was because they loved each other so very much. What would happen to that love with an intruder in their bed? "Many warriors have more than one spouse, Thorny Boy."

"Yes, I know but—but they are not my mother." Dread filled the boy's dark eyes. "How will father feel about sharing our mother with the Lightning Boy?"

Diamondback gently tugged a lock of Thorny Boy's hair. In a low confidential voice, he said, "I think that should be between Mother and Father and the Lightning Boy. I don't think you or I need to worry about it."

Thorny Boy picked up the wad of string, and began shaking out the tangles. "I can't help worrying, Diamondback. I mean, what if Father doesn't like sharing Mother? Will he fight with the Lightning Boy? I've heard that Lightning Boys are very Powerful, that they can call the Lightning Birds from the sky and tell them to blast people!" Thorny Boy examined Diamondback's face. "How could our father fight something like that?"

"I don't know." Diamondback sighed, "I guess we'd have to make sure that didn't happen."

Thorny Boy crawled forward to peer deeply into Diamondback's eyes. He whispered, "Yes, maybe we ought to kill the Lightning Boy in his sleep right off. As soon as he gets here. He couldn't tell the Lightning Birds to blast us if he was asleep—could he?"

Diamondback suppressed his smile and ruffled Thorny Boy's dark hair. "To tell you the truth, Little Brother, I haven't the slightest idea. But I suggest we ask Mother before we do that. She might actually like her new husband."

"But not better than our father!"

"No," Diamondback agreed. "Not better than our father. But you know what?"

"What?"

Diamondback leaned sideways and whispered, "If the Lightning Boy even thought about hurting Father, I bet Mother would dart the Lightning Boy before we even had a chance to kill him in his sleep."

Thorny Boy grinned. "Yes, she would, wouldn't she?"

"I expect so. I even . . ." He saw old Dreamstone suddenly stand up in her shelter at the far edge of the village. Long white hair fluttered around her bony shoulders as she stepped forward to peer out into the forest, as though she had spotted movement, then stumbled backward, lifting one arm as if to point. . . .

The dart came out her back.

Stunned, Diamondback watched her crumple to the sand as silently as a brittle autumn leaf.

Her daughter leaped up and ran toward Dreamstone. Her hoarse scream split the dusk, growing louder until the very fabric of twilight quaked with its terror. *"Warriors!"* she shouted. *"Warriors!"*

An instant later war cries drowned her screams, riding the breeze like soaring falcons. Hideously painted warriors burst from the trees with their atlatls raised. How many . . . ? Two tens? Three tens?

Black Urchin was on his feet in an instant, his atlatl in his hand. *"Run!"* he screamed. *"Hurry! Into the forest! We can't fight this many!"* Ragged Wing and Shoal leaped up and ran forward with their atlatls poised to defend the village. *"Go! Now!"*

Stunned people grabbed for their children, shrieking and shouting, and scattered in every direction. The amber halos of the cooking fires threw their shadows over the sand like swaying black giants. There were so many enemy warriors! They raced through the village, casting darts, swinging warclubs, using their stilettos on women, children, and men alike. Bodies sprawled across the sand.

Diamondback dove for Thorny Boy, clamped a hand over his little brother's mouth, and shoved him into the pile of blankets which had been supporting his back. *"Don't move!"* he ordered. "Stay there until I've drawn their attention, then run for the trees and hide! Don't try to outrun them. Understand? Hide yourself until they've gone. Then head south. Mother is down there somewhere! Do you understand me?"

Thorny Boy cried, "Yes!"

Diamondback grabbed his atlatl and four darts and managed to get his injured leg beneath him, then he limped away from the shelter, and out into the crowd of running, shrieking people.

Old Ashleaf hunched in the middle of the village, a dart protruding from his stomach, one hand braced on the ground, the other raised pleadingly. *"Stop this! I beg you. Don't kill us! What do you want? We will give you whatever we have! Don't kill us!"*

A big, burly warrior lifted his warclub over Ashleaf, and Diamondback yipped a war cry, nocked his own atlatl, and drove the dart all the way through the warrior's chest. The man toppled backward, and as Diamondback nocked another dart, he saw Thorny Boy throw off his blankets, leap up, and run with all his might, racing away through the palmettos into the wavering firelit shadows of the forest.

Two warriors spotted the boy, pointed, and one charged in pursuit. An incoherent cry broke Diamondback's lips as he spun, and cast his dart in one smooth motion. The dart caught the warrior in the lower back, and he flopped forward. The force of the impact drove the dart part way out of his back again.

The other warrior swung around to face Diamondback. He shrieked a war cry and, lifting his warclub, dashed forward. Diamondback recognized this man . . . he had been in the war party that had attacked their camp the night Blue Echo and Morning Glory died!

Diamondback had just managed to nock his last dart and began drawing back his atlatl when the whistling warclub struck his arm and sent his atlatl tumbling across the sand. Diamondback lunged for it, and the warrior kicked it out of the way. He stood over Diamondback laughing, his heavy chert-studded warclub gripped in both hands.

"I remember you," the man shouted. "This time you die, filth!"

Diamondback rolled and threw up his arms to block the blow. . . .

A *hiss* sounded. Followed by a meaty *splat!*

The warrior grunted, stumbled, and peered down at the dart that protruded from just below his left nipple. Blood coursed down his muscular belly. As the man sank to his knees, Diamondback's mother exploded from the forest, her atlatl in her hand, her black eyes gleaming. When she threw back her head and let out her bloodcurdling war cry, Diamondback's heart almost stopped. Every enemy in camp froze. Clubs and stilettos hovered over intended victims. *They didn't expect my mother to be here.* . . .

Musselwhite gave them no time to recover. She cast three darts on the run, nocking, aiming, and letting fly. Two men fell immediately, the third kept standing, but his mouth dropped open in shock as he gripped the shaft piercing his belly and ran his fingers over the fine eagle-feather fletching. Warriors raced around him, barely noticing when he collapsed to stare sightlessly at the night sky.

Diamondback grabbed his attacker's warclub, hoisted himself to his feet, and swung hard at a charging warrior. He caught the man in the stomach, hurling him over the club and sending him sprawling across the sand with his belly ripped open. The pungent reek of torn intestines filled the air. Diamondback quickly turned, took aim at the man's dazed face, and brought his club down at an angle, crushing the nose, driving splinters of bone upward through the eye sockets and into the brain.

A hail of responding darts flew, and Diamondback hit the ground and dragged himself forward on his stomach to take shelter behind the dead man. His mother stayed on her feet, dodging between the shelters, using them as cover, picking up miscast darts, and flinging them back with deadly accuracy. Two more men lay in her wake, blood draining from their wounds to pool on the white sand.

A warrior charged from Musselwhite's left, and Diamondback screamed, *"Mother! On your left!"*

The man swung his warclub, but she ducked with the fleetness of a weasel, grabbed her stiletto from her belt, pivoted, and drove the sharpened deer-bone between the man's ribs. As she withdrew the weapon, the victim gripped her hand and stumbled into her. His weight made Musselwhite stagger backward, and two enemy warriors leaped on her from behind, grabbing her arms.

"We have her!" one of the men shouted, jumping up and down like an excited boy. "We'll take her dead body back to Cottonmouth and live in glory for the rest of our lives!"

Despite his terror, Diamondback got to his feet, his warclub in his hands, and hobbled forward. His injured leg throbbed sickeningly. The tall thin warrior holding Musselwhite's right arm laughed at Diamondback and ordered, "Kill him. Quickly! So we can hunt down the survivors and go home!"

Before the warrior could lift his atlatl, another dart hissed, and Diamondback saw the chert point glint in the firelight as it sailed across the village. The impact flung the young warrior forward in a shambling trot, and Musselwhite threw all of her weight into breaking the other warrior's grip. The action sent both of them sprawling across the ground. The warrior rolled, got his knees under him, and prepared to leap on her. In mid-jump, his mother thrust her deerbone stiletto into the man's vulnerable throat. Then she was on her feet again, racing forward, the man on the ground not even dead yet, though he would be—soon enough.

Stunned gasps came from Cottonmouth's remaining warriors. One of them, small and skinny, pointed and shouted, *"Look!"*

Diamondback jerked around.

A hooded figure emerged from the trees. His long sleeves hung down over his hands, and the hem of his tan robe dragged the ground, but in the frame of that hood white hair streamed around a ghostly pale face. As he walked forward, he was so graceful he seemed to float over the sand, and his eyes— Blessed Spirits!—they burned with a pink glittering light. He spread his arms. . . .

"It's the Lightning Boy!"

The cry spread through the enemy warriors like wildfire.

"Look! There he is!"

"It's Cottonmouth's Lightning Boy!"

And Musselwhite used every moment of their gaping fear to kill them. She had plucked up a warclub somewhere and swung it with lethal expertise. The hollow *smack!* of a skull-crushing blow was followed by startled yell, and another *smack!* Cottonmouth's warriors stumbled over each other, whispering darkly. Then they broke and ran.

Musselwhite followed them into the forest.

Diamondback whirled around again and saw the Lightning Boy lower his outstretched arms. As if suddenly weak, the youth slumped to the ground, and clutched the fabric over his heart. "Blessed Sun Mother," the boy panted.

Seedpod trotted out of the forest with his atlatl raised. *"Pondwader,"* he shouted, *"stand up!* I want them to see you!"

The youth did it, but barely. White hair fluttered around his taut face as he pushed back his hood, braced his legs, and stood shaking like a blade of grass in a gale.

Seedpod strode by the Lightning Boy, his eyes scanning the forest as he made his way to Diamondback.

"Grandfather," Diamondback said in relief as they embraced. "Thank the Spirits you got here when you did, or we'd all be dead."

"You mean thank the Spirits your mother got here. She sensed something was wrong about half a hand of time ago. She threw her pack at us and ran with all her strength. Pondwader and I came along as quickly as we could—but we only just arrived. I got to the edge of the trees in time to see the two warriors grab your mother. That was my dart that skewered the one on her right."

Diamondback proudly clamped a hand on his grandfather's shoulder. "Bless the Spirits."

Seedpod's gaunt old face slackened as he saw the dead sprawled around the village. Ragged Wing lay not far from Shoal, both young warriors dead. Pain tightened Seedpod's eyes when he saw Ashleaf—the elder had managed to stay alive long enough to pick up a miscast dart. He lay on his side with that dart clutched in his outstretched hand.

Seedpod said, "Where are the others?"

"People ran into the forest, but many of Cottonmouth's warriors followed. I think Black Urchin ran out to defend our women and children. We can only hope that some of them . . ." Diamondback shook his head.

Seedpod nodded. "Where is your brother? I don't see him." Fear and anguish laced his old voice. His gaze searched the dead, landing on tiny bodies.

"I told him to run and hide in the forest." Diamondback cupped a hand to his mouth and called, "Thorny Boy? Thorny Boy!"

Palmettos thrashed in the forest and the little boy came running from the shadows, his face and arms scratched, old leaves stuck in his black hair. His eyes had gone the size of small moons.

Seedpod knelt and scooped up Thorny Boy, then hugged him tightly. "I was worried," he said.

"I hid in a badger hole, Grandfather, and pulled old branches over the top! Warriors ran all around me!"

Seedpod fiercely kissed the boy's forehead. "You were very smart. You will be a great warrior one day."

Diamondback patted his brother's back and limped over to the Lightning Boy. Pondwader was a good hand taller than Diamondback, but he had yet to fill out in the shoulders, and so looked very skinny in that long robe. He still shook badly, and he was breathing hard, as though he'd run all the way from Heartwood Village to halt the slaughter. As Diamondback drew closer, the Boy squinted and two upright lines etched the pink flesh between his thin white brows.

"I am Diamondback," he said, "Musselwhite's son. . . . You were very brave to face those men without an atlatl in your hand."

Pondwader looked up, wet his pale lips, and replied, "No, not—not really.

I couldn't see any of them. Now and then—" he gestured uncertainly—"I caught a blur moving across the village, but I wasn't even sure it was human. It could have been a big bear for all I knew."

Diamondback gazed up into those eerie pink eyes and said, "You can't see?"

"Only up close. I can see you pretty well."

Seedpod joined them, carrying Thorny Boy on his hip. When Thorny Boy got close to the Lightning Boy, he stared unblinking. Seedpod said, "Thorny Boy, this is Pondwader. He is your mother's new husband."

Thorny Boy brought up a finger and tucked it into his open mouth. Around it, he slurred, "I saw you scare away those warriors, so I don't wish to kill you anymore. It might be good to have you around."

Pondwader frowned at Seedpod. "Your grandson wanted to kill me?"

Seedpod's white brows lifted. "That's what he said, but I don't—"

"Wait." Diamondback raised a hand. Seedpod turned to him, waiting, and in a soft, tired voice, Diamondback said, "Cottonmouth sent a runner ten-and-one days ago. Father is alive. He's a prisoner in Standing Hollow Horn Village."

Seedpod bowed his head. He didn't say anything for a time, then he whispered, "Let me tell your mother."

"Yes, Grandfather." Diamondback glanced at the Lightning Boy.

Pondwader bit his lip and closed his eyes. In a heartfelt voice, he said, "Thank the Spirits."

But I wish to help, Seedpod."

"No, Pondwader. This is not your concern. You are new here. I fear that your presence will just cause more turmoil. Please. You are still trembling. Go to Musselwhite's shelter. Let us tend our dead by ourselves."

Pondwader nodded and turned.

It had taken more than a hand of time for people to begin wandering back into Windy Cove Village. A few men came first, followed by women and children.

Pondwader entered Musselwhite's shelter and knelt by the cold firepit, listening to the grief of his new relatives as they moved among the bodies, cracking off dart shafts, carrying their loved ones to the southern side of the village to await burial. A variety of beautiful colored blankets had been spread over the dead. Tomorrow they would be washed and dressed and prepared for burial. Pondwader would be an outsider, relegated to observing. He did not mind, but he felt . . . alone. He was a stranger here. Out of place. No one, except Musselwhite's immediate family, had so much as looked him in the eyes. And Musselwhite had not yet returned. His heart cried out for her. Was she alive? Or had Cottonmouth's warriors killed her and left her in some dark place in the forest? He feared they might do that, just so he couldn't find her and she would be condemned to wander the earth forever.

Pondwader pulled up his hood to block the chilly night wind. He *would* find her. No matter what it took. Even if he had to ask the instrument of his own death, the baby Lightning Bird glowing in the cage of his chest. The creature never slept. It kept darting about his ribs, making him flinch and wince, as if it were desperate to strengthen its blue-white wings so it could soar away. The moment Pondwader had stepped out of the trees and spread his arms to the enemy warriors, a rumble of thunder had begun racing through his veins—and had not stopped. His whole body continued to quake from it.

He whispered, "Baby Bird, I wish you would stop that."

The rumble continued, and Pondwader sighed and gazed out at the ocean. To his poor eyes, Sister Moon seemed a huge silver smear that filled half the night sky, and the moonlight upon the water resembled the beach in bright daylight, white and glimmering. Once, when they'd been very young, Kelp had tried to teach him what things really looked like. Since he could see things up close, she had taken a clam shell, cut it into a circle about the size of Sister Moon as she really appeared in the sky, and laid it in Pondwader's palm. He'd been amazed at how small she was! What? A circle of silver only a little larger than his childish palm? Impossible! After his grandmother had assured him Kelp was telling the truth, he'd never again looked at the night sky the same way. If Sister Moon were that small, what about the huge glorious Shining People? Were they nothing more than thorn pricks of light? It had all been very confusing. He thanked Sun Mother that he'd had Kelp to help him learn these lessons.

Pondwader lowered his head and studied the old leaves that had blown onto the coarsely woven floor mats. He missed Kelp. And his grandmother. He missed all of Heartwood Village. No matter how much he wanted to be here with Musselwhite—or how much he knew he *had* to be here—he couldn't seem to comfort his souls. He . . .

Musselwhite walked out of the forest no more than forty hands away. A stocky warrior emerged behind her, and Pondwader lurched to his feet, pulse racing. The entire village looked up.

Thorny Boy yelled, "Mother! Mother!" and sprinted for her with his little chest thrown out. Seedpod and Diamondback followed close on the boy's heels.

Musselwhite knelt and Thorny Boy rushed into her arms. She hugged him tightly and reached out a hand to Diamondback. Her older son gripped her fingers and smiled.

Seedpod slapped the warrior on the shoulder. "Black Urchin," he said. "It is good to see you. All the children are Singing your honor and telling the story of how you fought four enemy warriors to save them."

Black Urchin made a light gesture. A short, stocky man, he had so much muscle packed on his bones he resembled a small bear. "I saved a handful—but so many more died, Seedpod."

"Yes," Seedpod replied softly. "I know. It's all right. Tomorrow, after we have buried our dead, we will pack up and head south. We will be joining Heartwood Clan at Manatee Lagoon."

Black Urchin nodded. "I cannot tell you how glad I am to hear that. Have you told the others yet?"

"No, not yet."

"May I?" He held a hand out to the people roaming the village like lost souls. "I think it will ease some of their terror."

"Yes, of course. Go ahead."

Their voices sounded so warm, loving, that Pondwader longed to walk over and join them, but he did not wish to interfere in their reunion. As Black Urchin walked away, Seedpod clenched his hands into fists and stood waiting. When Thorny Boy let go of Musselwhite and she rose, Seedpod placed both hands on her shoulders and stared directly into her eyes.

"What is it?" she asked, as if knowing something dreadful had happened just from his wrinkled face. Her eyes had gone hard, blazing.

"Diver is alive. He—"

"*Alive?*" Musselwhite said in disbelief. "Where? Where is he? *Where is my husband?*" Her eyes searched the village. She shoved off Seedpod's hands, but he grabbed her shoulders again before she could run, his grip so tight his fingers dimpled the fabric of her blood-splotched tunic.

"He's not here," Seedpod said. "He's being held captive in Standing Hollow Horn Village. Cottonmouth—"

For a moment, she seemed to sway under the impact of those words. Seedpod's arm went around her waist to steady her. "He's all right, Musselwhite."

"Yes, Mother. He is," Diamondback rushed to add. "Cottonmouth sent a messenger to tell us. He—"

"Yes," she murmured. "Of course, he did." The buried rage in her voice made it shake. "He could not stand it that I might think Diver dead. What else did the messenger say?"

"Nothing, Mother," Diamondback answered, frowning. "He ran in, delivered his news, and was gone."

Musselwhite closed her eyes a moment, as if gathering strength, then she walked away so swiftly Seedpod stumbled as she tore free from him. Thorny Boy stood, watching his grandfather and brother, his little face puckered, as if he might cry.

Musselwhite strode into the shelter and passed Pondwader without a word. She reached up, unhooked three small fabric bags from the rafters, then spread them on the floor before her. One bag was empty, the others contained dried meat, fish, and mushrooms. She began stuffing food into the empty bag.

Pondwader said, "You're going to Cottonmouth's village, aren't you?"

"Yes."

He went to pick up his own pack, larger than hers, three hands wide and four hands tall. He walked back and crouched before her. She did not even seem to notice as he started filling it with food. "When are we leaving?"

"*I* am leaving at dawn. I must sleep to rebuild my strength, then I'll go. If I run all the way, I can be there in three or four days."

"I'm going with you."

"I'm going alone."

"No!" Pondwader shouted. "Please, Musselwhite. You *need* me! I—"

Her blazing eyes bored into him. Throwing down her pack, she reached out, gripped his shoulders, and shook him hard. "If you never listen to anything else I tell you, Pondwader, listen to me now. I need *no* one. You will be a burden to me on this war walk. One I cannot afford."

"But . . . !"

"Your helplessness will doom us both! And if I die, Diver dies. I will not let that happen."

She stalked across the shelter and picked a fresh tunic from a pile which lay neatly folded near her bedding along the north side. In a flash, she had pulled her soiled tunic over her head and thrown it on the floor mats. He barely noticed the beauty of her nakedness before she'd slipped the clean tunic on, reached down to remove the old belt from her soiled tunic, and tied it around her slender waist again. Then she dug beneath her blankets, pulled out three darts which had been hidden there—did she always sleep with darts under her bedding?—and pulled a new atlatl from a peg on the shelter pole. She placed all of these items on the floor, lifted her blanket, and crawled into her bedding.

"Musselwhite?" he called. "Let me talk with you more."

She rolled to her back and closed her eyes. Within moments her breathing had deepened to the rhythms of slumber. Pondwader's brows drew together as her beautiful face slackened. Did all warriors know how to do that? To fall into a deep sleep instantly? He had heard of such a talent, but he had never witnessed it. . . . Or was she just pretending sleep? Avoiding him?

Pondwader went over and sat by her side. He drew her weapons onto his lap, holding them in case her enemies returned and came close enough for him to dart them. For a full hand of time, he watched the villagers. Diamondback and Thorny Boy returned to Seedpod's shelter and seemed to be heating up supper, making tea.

Seedpod joined those carrying away the dead. Because of his age, he was relegated to childrens' bodies. Tears streamed down his leathery cheeks. He whispered softly to each dead baby, and often he would bend down and kiss a forehead, or stroke blood-matted hair away from a cheek. Choking sobs filled the night.

Finally, people returned to their shelters and built warming fires, then sat around holding each other, weeping softly and talking, trying to eat a little supper.

Pondwader frowned when Thorny Boy trotted out of Seedpod's shelter. The child ran across the village and stopped a short distance away from Pondwader, breathing hard. His black hair hung in a mass of tangles around his plump cheeks.

"What is it, Thorny Boy?" Pondwader asked softly.

The boy braced his hands on knees and leaned forward—so Pondwader could hear him, but also so Thorny Boy did not have to get too close. "Please come. Grandfather said to tell you supper is ready, and he wishes to speak with you."

Nineteen

Seedpod stretched out on his side in front of the fire, idly prodding the flames with a long stick. Orange sparks winked and spun upward in the mild salt-scented breeze. The horror had numbed his senses, left him feeling as hollow as a torn old basket. Diamondback sat across from him. He had already finished one bowl of roasted goose and had begun a second. He glanced up from the rich, dark meat, and wiped the back of his hand over his mouth.

"When he arrives, do you wish me to leave?" Diamondback asked.

Seedpod sighed, "Yes, I think that's wise. He will not like hearing what I have to say to him, and it's best that he hears it alone. That way he will not be embarrassed."

Diamondback nodded. "Hand me one of those darts you gathered up, will you, Grandfather? I'll use it to brace myself as I cross the village."

Seedpod turned, picked up one of the darts and handed it across to Diamondback. The youth placed it at his side, and continued stuffing goose into his mouth and swallowing it as quickly as he could. Fat smeared his face and hands. "That must have been a fine feast," he commented.

Seedpod smiled. His heart throbbed. "Oh, yes, it was. Heartwood Clan spared no expense. Baskets and bowls were heaped with food. It was a grand wedding."

"I wish I had been there."

"I do, too. It would have made your mother happy."

Diamondback set his bowl down and braced the butt of the dart on the mat to help him rise. Pain tensed his face, but he smiled at Pondwader when the young Lightning Boy followed Thorny Boy into the shelter, standing uneasily in his long robe with his white hair blowing about the edges of his hood. He had his arms hanging at his sides, and his sleeves covered his hands.

Diamondback said, "I'll guard Mother while you are here, Pondwader, if that's all right."

"Oh, yes, Diamondback." Pondwader tried a smile, but it vanished before it had even begun. "Thank you."

Diamondback patted Thorny Boy on the head. "Come along, little brother. You can help me guard Mother."

"But I wish to stay here," Thorny Boy said, craning his neck to look up. Obviously, he wanted to stare at the Lightning Boy some more—in the protective presence of his grandfather and brother.

"No, you don't," Diamondback corrected. "Grandfather wishes to speak with Pondwader alone. You and I are not welcome. Let's go." Diamondback hobbled across the village with a reluctant Thorny Boy at his side. Thorny Boy kept peering at Pondwader over his shoulder.

Seedpod gestured to the floor mats. "Sit down, Pondwader. Help yourself to some food. You must be starving."

"I—I haven't even thought about food."

"Well, you must eat. Sit down."

In that fluid way of his, Pondwader sat on the floor and pulled a thick piece of goose from the wooden bowl by the fire. He looked upset, vulnerable. His eyes glistened with pain. Seedpod sat quietly, waiting until he had finished his first piece of meat and was well into his second. The youth needed something in his stomach before Seedpod began this discussion. Pondwader, he had discovered, possessed an extremely tender heart, and Seedpod did not wish to hurt him anymore than Musselwhite already had— and would, over the next few hands of time. But there were things that must be said, no matter how unpleasant.

When Pondwader had finished, and began wiping his greasy hands on the hem of his tan robe, Seedpod poured himself another cup of hanging-moss tea. The delicate tartness had healing Powers and soothed raw nerves. He filled a gourd cup for Pondwader too, and handed it to the boy.

"Thank you," Pondwader said as he took it. He sipped the tea and frowned. "She is intent on going, Seedpod. Alone. She wouldn't even listen to me."

He nodded. "I know. That's what I wished to speak with you about. I'm sure she must have wounded you tonight. When she is frantic she grows blunt, sometimes even cruel. It isn't because she wants to hurt you, Pondwader. It's just that she hasn't the time right now to explain herself. She—"

"I'm going with her."

Seedpod paused, startled, then took another drink of his tea. Quietly, he asked, "And will she allow this?"

"She doesn't wish me to, but I—I don't care. I'm going," Pondwader said stubbornly. "I won't allow her to go alone. It's too dangerous."

Seedpod turned his cup in his hands, and Pondwader watched him expectantly, his pink face flushed. "Did it occur to you, Pondwader, that your presence might actually make it more dangerous for her?"

"She told me I would be a burden, but I—"

"You would. Don't you see, with you there she will have to worry about your safety. She cares about you, Pondwader. You will distract her. She will not be able to concentrate on the forest, on anomalies of color or shape— all of which might allow her to see an enemy warrior before he sees her. No, instead she will be worrying about whether or not you can see that poisonous snake in the grass, or see her signal you to stand still and be quiet, because there is movement ahead. And what if you don't, Pondwader, and it turns out to be one of Cottonmouth's war parties? Your poor vision might kill both of you."

"But I *have* to be there, Seedpod!" he said. "You don't understand! It's not because I wish to go! The very idea scares me to death. I must be with her. It's . . ." He pushed awkwardly at his long sleeves. More softly, he finished, "It's what the ghosts told me."

"The ghosts?"

Pondwader swallowed hard. He seemed to be struggling with himself, trying to decide what to say, and what not to. "I can't explain it, Seedpod. I promised I wouldn't tell anyone—except Musselwhite—and I haven't had a chance to tell her yet, but I *must* go with her on this journey!"

Seedpod ran his thumb down the side of his cup. "Is this what the ghosts told you at the Sacred Pond? I recall crazy old Dogtooth mentioning something about that."

Pondwader nodded.

"Well," Seedpod said. "I take such things very seriously, but I want you to consider your wife's safety first. Ghosts don't know everything. At least I don't think they do. It might be better for everyone concerned if you stayed here with us to help us pack and move down to join Heartwood Village. We could use you, Pondwader." Seedpod's eyes drifted to the line of dead bodies on the outskirts of the village. The colored blankets covering them billowed in the wind, and occasionally Seedpod caught sight of a loved friend's face frozen in terror. Mourning cries still filtered from the shelters. A rawhide band seemed to tighten around his heart, making it feel as if it were about to burst. "We need every able-bodied person we can get."

Pondwader peered into the wavering flames, and the orange gleam sheathed his face. His pink flesh mixed oddly with the fire's glow, creating a color as startlingly beautiful as it was eerie. He felt as if he might have dived to the bottom of a reef and found a face sculpted into the coral there.

When he didn't answer, Seedpod said, "And what will you do if your wife is killed? You will be truly alone and in the midst of hostile strangers. Be honest with yourself, Pondwader. The dumbest warrior in the world could sneak up behind you and cut your throat, and you know it. I do not wish that to happen, and neither does your wife."

The boy looked up with clear eyes. As though he hadn't heard, he said, "Seedpod, before we leave there is something I must ask you. Dogtooth told me to."

"Dogtooth told you to? Hallowed Spirits, that's frightening. What could it be?"

Pondwader's white brows pulled together. "It's about what Cottonmouth did to Musselwhite when she was ten-and-one summers old. Dogtooth said knowing about it would be very important to me on this journey."

Seedpod felt that a huge hand had gripped his souls and shaken them. "Dogtooth . . . told you to ask me?"

Pondwader nodded. "Yes."

Seedpod's hands had grown unsteady. He clasped them together to hide his discomfort. "What difference would it make if you knew?"

"I asked Dogtooth that same question." Pondwader answered. "These were his words. He said, 'It just may save your life, and hers. Very soon, you and Musselwhite will be going on a difficult journey. You *must* know who she is—what made her who she is—before you leave.' " Pondwader peered at Seedpod from beneath his colorless lashes. "I don't know why he said that. But he thought it very important that I ask you about it. He told me it would be difficult for me. But please tell me, Seedpod. I vow never to tell anyone else."

It had happened so long ago . . . but not long enough that Seedpod had forgotten the rage, the hatred he'd felt. The past three tens of summers had not even dimmed the strength of those emotions. . . . And now his daughter's life might depend upon his talking about those events?

Seedpod set his gourd cup down. Pondwader watched him, his boyish face taut, pink eyes wide with hope . . . and a little afraid. Mosquitoes flitted about his face, but he didn't seem to notice.

Seedpod took a breath, and held it. Dogtooth was crazy, but he had never known the great Soul Dancer to lie. If he said Musselwhite's life depended upon it—then well it might. Still, it took a moment for Seedpod to convince himself to speak.

"Cottonmouth . . . had a—a strange Power over Musselwhite," he began softly. "I think it grew worse after they married."

"She was married to Cottonmouth? No one ever told me that," Pondwader whispered.

"I doubt many people know. They underwent the ceremony alone. There were no witnesses. No feast. No celebration of their joining."

"But why not?"

Seedpod pushed his gourd cup around with his index finger. "Because that's the way Cottonmouth wanted it. He feared that if people knew she was his wife, they would find a way to use her against him. But if his relatives thought he and Musselwhite were merely sharing the same shelter, they would think it was a casual mating and no one would suspect the depth of his love for her."

Pondwader sat back. "But why would she accept such an arrangement?"

"Because he asked her to. She loved him, Pondwader. Very much."

Pondwader mulled that over. His gaze flickered over the shelter, lingering on the Power bundles hanging from the pole to Seedpod's left. Strangely, for the first time in summers, Seedpod thought he could hear their voices. Soft. Worried. Like the mewing of newborn bobcat kittens.

Without taking his eyes from the Sea bundle, Pondwader asked, "Why did Cottonmouth fear that his relatives would use the marriage against him? Are they bad people?"

"No, no, Pondwader," Seedpod replied. "Cottonmouth is the most terrified man alive. He fears everything and everyone. His relatives were no exceptions. The only person I think he has ever trusted was Musselwhite."

In the depths of his souls, Seedpod could still see the look of utter adoration that had filled Cottonmouth's eyes when he gazed at Musselwhite. Like a man gazing upon paradise, and not quite able to believe it.

"I didn't think anything frightened Cottonmouth," Pondwader said. He drew up his knees and cradled them in his long arms. "He has so much Power, he—"

"He does have Power, you are right about that. The Power he had over Musselwhite was . . . unnerving."

Wind gusted through the shelter, rustling in the thatched roof, and Pondwader clutched his hood closed at his throat. "What do you mean?"

Seedpod picked up his stick again and poked at the fire. A log broke and the crimson flash lit Pondwader's rapt face. For an instant, his pink, translucent eyes seemed to be floating in a wavering pool of blood. "Cottonmouth used to 'call' her. I don't know any other way of describing it. She knew when he wanted her, and no matter the time of night, she would rise from her bed and go to him."

Pondwader stopped lifting his tea cup to his lips; it hovered beneath his chin. "What do you mean 'call' her? You mean like a witch's summons?"

"I don't know anything about witches, but Dogtooth told me it might have been something like that." Seedpod quelled the shiver that prickled his spine. Witches . . . He had met only four in his life, and each had left him terrified for moons. Their souls could fly, and kill with a word, or the touch of an invisible hand. They used Power the way fine fabric artists used thread—to weave patterns. Often those patterns were not pretty to look at. Witches tended to have cruel streaks. Great Soul Dancers whispered that witches could suck souls out a living man's body, and shoot them into the dead to bring them back to life. They . . .

"Go on," Pondwader urged. "Please. Tell me everything you can."

Seedpod sighed. He said, "It began the instant Cottonmouth laid eyes on Musselwhite. She was such a beauty. Even at her age a man could see it. But she was so young, not even a woman yet. My wife and I forbade Musselwhite to see him. Thunderstorm, Musselwhite's mother, hated Cottonmouth. I never knew why, though he was an arrogant, odd youth—which was reason enough. He was ten-and-seven summers, and already much feared as a warrior. We forbade Musselwhite to see him, and . . ." Seedpod's souls seemed to drift up out of his body, leaving him light as a feather. "And that's when Cottonmouth began calling her."

"What happened?"

Memories filled Seedpod. The fragrances of new leaves, and warm mist. Amid the images of tens of shelters, he could hear men snoring, and infants whimpering. Windy Cove Clan had been so much larger then, five times the size it was now. They had been camped on the big inland lake, fishing the shallow waters, and hunting water fowl.

"I remember one warm spring night," Seedpod said. "I saw her rise soundlessly from her blankets and walk across the village. Her steps were . . . strange . . . too clumsy for her. She was always extremely graceful, even as a little girl. I followed, for I thought she might be sleepwalking and could harm herself. At the edge of the forest, I spoke to her, but she stared at me with glassy eyes. When she walked by me, I trailed her, walking far behind so I wouldn't frighten her if she woke suddenly."

Pondwader stretched out on his side, facing Seedpod, and placed his bare feet closer to the fire. Seedpod kept his voice low. Despite the cold, he could feel sweat on his face. He wet his lips and absently ran his fingers over the mat before him, like a blind man searching for something he'd lost. And perhaps he had. He had never been the same since that night. Had some bit of his souls slipped away?

"What happened then?" Pondwader pressed. Wind rippled his hood.

"I saw Cottonmouth. I watched Musselwhite walk up to him. He murmured something I couldn't hear, but I saw my little girl reach for him, and he bent down to kiss her. It made a sickening sight. This tall muscular man leaning over this . . . *this child!*" Seedpod turned horrified eyes on his new son-in-law. "Then I heard a sound I will never forget if I live to be tens of tens of summers old. It made my blood turn to ice. My daughter, ten-and-one summers, laughed like a woman. Do you understand, Pondwader? It was a soft, seductive laugh, but in a child's voice. When Cottonmouth's hand reached for her barely budded breast, I burst from my hiding place and shouted, 'Stay away from my daughter! Or I will kill you!' Cottonmouth immediately jumped back from Musselwhite . . . then I heard him murmur, 'Go home. Your mother is calling you,' and she turned, stumbled clumsily past me with that dazed expression on her face, and headed back into the village." Seedpod gripped the air as if to wring the life from it. "I wanted to strangle him."

"Why didn't you? He deserved to be punished for what he had done! Why didn't you tell the council of Spirit Elders?"

The rage and shock on Pondwader's young face shamed Seedpod. He had often wondered that himself.

"It was not so easy, Pondwader." He lowered his hands to the floor mat. "I am a fair man—probably fair to a fault. I relived that night over and over in my souls, and after much thought I was no longer certain that what I had witnessed was witchcraft. More likely it was just youthful indiscretion. Witchery is such a heinous crime, for the witch and his victim. I knew that if anyone discovered Musselwhite *had* been witched, they would fear her as much as him. Indeed, they might kill her to protect themselves."

Pondwader said, "You mean, because a person who is witched can bring the evil into the village?"

Seedpod nodded. "Yes."

"Did you confront Cottonmouth about it?"

"Of course," he sighed. "I accused him of witching my daughter, and he vehemently denied it, shouting that he loved her. But he promised never to see her again until she became a woman. A promise he kept, incidentally."

"He did?"

"Oh, yes. In fact, I never saw him at all for the next two summers. Though he appeared at our spring village site the moment she began her first bleeding. I recall it very clearly."

His thoughts wandered, seeing it again. Another spring day. Childish giggles came from the three newly made women in the menstrual hut. Thunderstorm was so proud she could barely contain it. She had been cooking for days, preparing a great feast.

"When Musselwhite emerged from the sacred hut, Cottonmouth was there. Waiting for her." Seedpod's face fell into a mass of crisscrossing wrinkles. He fumbled with his gourd cup, drained it dry.

Pondwader gazed intently at Seedpod. "And Musselwhite remembers none of this?"

The fire flared, and its glow spread through the shelter, picking out the delicate designs painted on the globular bags swaying over Pondwader's head. Seedpod had woven those bags last summer, just after Sun Mother's Celebration Day. He had to touch up the paint, though; it faded so quickly in the bright sunlight. He took a breath, and answered, "Dogtooth must have told you that."

"Yes. He said he didn't think she recalled what had happened."

"Well," Seedpod sighed. "I don't really know. We have never spoken of it. She begged to marry Cottonmouth. We refused. So she ran away to be with him. It tore her mother's heart. . . . And mine. For a long time, I was very angry." He toyed with a palm thread that had frayed from the floor mat. "I refused to see her."

"But, Seedpod," Pondwader said, "didn't you ever wonder whether she had run away of her own choice? If he hadn't witched her again?"

"Of course. I watched her very closely. But she acted perfectly normal. Stubborn, headstrong, but normal. I had no reason to accuse Cottonmouth a second time."

But moons later, for a flickering instant, I wondered. . . .

Seedpod had passed by Standing Hollow Horn Village and stopped to see her, just for a moment, he'd proclaimed, but the moment had lasted five days. Musselwhite had seemed so happy. Almost *too* happy. But Cottonmouth seemed just as unnaturally blissful. His eyes never left Musselwhite. She was all he talked about—all he appeared to care about.

"It would have made as much sense for me to accuse my daughter of witching Cottonmouth, as the reverse. They were both mindlessly happy, Pondwader. Moons after she'd left Windy Cove, she told me, in strictest confidence, that they had secretly married—and that she carried his baby."

Pondwader propped his head in his palm. "What happened to the child?"

Grief swelled Seedpod's heart. He whispered, "I don't really know. He was a beautiful boy. I only saw him twice before he died. I know he caught a fever. I assume that's what killed him. Musselwhite has never spoken of the boy's death. Not one word, Pondwader." He lifted a warning finger. "And I would not ask her about him, if I were you."

Pondwader blinked. "Why not?"

"I have only known one person who dared to. That was Dogtooth, and had I not been there to pull my daughter off him, that old Soul Dancer would be dead. She leaped across the fire and grabbed him around the throat so quickly, I barely had time to react."

"She tried to kill *Dogtooth!*"

"Yes, and almost succeeded."

"What did Dogtooth do?"

Seedpod shook his head. "He's such an odd character. While I was wrestling with Musselwhite, shouting at her to stop fighting, Dogtooth began whirling around like a demented bird, squawking, 'Musselwhite saved one of Glade's souls! She changed it into Lightning! Look at Glade soar!"

"*Glade?*" Pondwader's face went slack. "The boy's name was Glade?"

"Yes. Why?"

Pondwader had gone extremely pale. His expression resembled that of a man running for his life and suddenly finding himself trapped, and too alarmed to think straight.

Seedpod frowned. "What's wrong?"

"Nothing, I . . . I'm sorry. Did—did you ever figure out what Dogtooth meant?"

"No, but Musselwhite seemed to understand immediately. The words soothed her. I remember how she relaxed in my arms, and tears filled her eyes."

Pondwader's jaw trembled. He tipped his head to peer at her shelter. Musselwhite had not moved. Wind whipped lose strands of her silver-streaked black hair about her face. Thorny Boy and Diamondback had rolled up in blankets and both fallen asleep near the firepit.

Seedpod said, "I'm glad Diamondback is sleeping. I feared he might try to stay awake all night to stand guard, and he is still ill from his wound. He needs rest. . . . As you do, Pondwader. Why don't you stay here tonight? There's no room for you in Musselwhite's shelter now, and I won't be here anyway. I promised Black Urchin I would stand night watch with him."

Pondwader whispered, "But I should be with my wife. She needs me."

"She has her sons. And I will post myself near her shelter. If you plan to go with her, you had better sleep all you can." Seedpod reached over to the folded pile of blankets and tossed one at Pondwader. "If you think she pushed us hard on the way home, you have a grave surprise in store for you tomorrow."

Pondwader unfolded the blanket and held it in his lap. "Let me stand watch with you, Seedpod. I would like to be useful. I—I don't think I can sleep now anyway."

"Try. You will be of far more use to all of us if you sleep." Seedpod picked up his atlatl and darts and rose to his feet. White hair fluttered before his eyes. "I'll sleep tomorrow. You will not have another opportunity for two, or maybe three, days. You will certainly kill my daughter if you are weaving on your feet when the time comes to sneak into Cottonmouth's village. You see what I mean, Pondwader?"

"Yes," he whispered.

Seedpod trotted away toward the place in the forest where he had promised to meet Black Urchin. Just before he entered the grove of tall pines, he looked back, and saw Pondwader wrap up in the blanket and stretch out on his back beside the fire. But the boy didn't close his eyes. He tilted his head to frown curiously at the Power bundles. Could he hear them? Were they speaking to him?

Seedpod strained his ears, and a frail sweet voice came to him . . . the Sea Bundle? Or just the wind? He prayed the bundles had opened their eternal eyes, seen the troubled Lightning Boy and wanted to help him. Pondwader could use their guidance.

If, by some miracle, Musselwhite allowed the boy to go, the journey would be difficult and deadly. Musselwhite would be no friend to him. She would expect him to act like a warrior. And if he did not . . . Seedpod didn't even want to contemplate the possibilities. Sun Mother knew she had it in her to kill him and let him lie, while she went on to do what she must. He knew his daughter as well as himself. Already her souls would be weaving the strategy and tactics necessary to rescue Diver, and bring them both out safely.

Musselwhite could not spare a single precious moment for sentimentality. Not even for her new husband.

Twenty

• • • *Not meant to hurt you . . . your life . . . too precious to risk . . .* "

Soft words. They floated about Pondwader's dreams like sunlight, rising and falling, chasing away the images of Heartwood Village. . . .

Pale blue light bathed his face. He rolled to his side and groggily opened his eyes. Already the Shining People had vanished from the eastern horizon, leaving an unmarred gleaming blue halo over the ocean. Sea Girl's voice carried on the cool morning breeze, a soothing whisper, as if she, too, had just awakened. Pondwader's gaze followed the dark blue arc of Brother Sky's belly, then dropped to the trees where he could hear birds chirping. He stretched his long legs and groaned himself awake.

On the beach, pelicans strutted, no doubt watching gulls wheel in the sky above them, though Pondwader saw only blue. Windy Cove Village lay still and quiet. No breakfast fires burned yet.

Pondwader sat up. He could still see three blurry humps of blankets in Musselwhite's shelter. Good. She needed her rest. Pondwader would wake her at dawn. By then he would have filled gourds with fresh water, finished loading their packs for the journey, and have breakfast cooking. They could eat and leave at sunup—as she had planned. He had not figured out how to convince her to allow him to go yet, but he would. Because he had to. Surely this morning, after a good night's rest, she would be more reasonable.

A faint morning breeze tousled his white hair as he stood and folded his blanket, then returned it to the pile where Seedpod had found it last night. Darkness cloaked the forest. Pondwader saw no sign of either Black Urchin or Seedpod. When would they be coming in? Dawn? Pondwader would make enough breakfast to feed five, just in case.

He combed out his hair with his fingers and went about gathering cooking tools. Two gut bags hung on tripods by the cold fire pit. One of them, he knew, held hanging moss tea from last night. The other was empty. Next to the bags sat a large gourd filled with water. Covered wooden bowls made a semicircle around the gourd. Pondwader knelt and removed the top bowl of each to survey the contents: smoked frogs' legs, prickly-pear fruits, black nightshade berries, small bottle gourds. They must have finished off the wedding feast at supper last night.

Pondwader looked around. Along the southern side of the shelter a big wooden bowl held chert blades and scrapers, an oak pestle and stirring paddle. Beside it nestled two squat baskets. He went and knelt beside the bowl, selecting the tools he would need: a blade and the stirring paddle. Then he returned to the fire pit. With the long chert blade, Pondwader cut up five bottle gourds, quartered several prickly-pear fruits, and dropped all of them into the boiling basket, along with the entire bowl of frogs' legs. Then he lifted the large gourd of water and poured in enough to cover the contents. It should cook down nicely. The prickly-pear fruits would add a delightful tang to the smoky flavor of the frogs' legs, while the gourds would give the stew sweetness. For good measure, he added water to the hanging moss tea bag. It might be weak, but it would be warm.

As he knelt by the fire and began digging through the ashes with a stick, separating out the hot coals, the village awoke. A baby started whimpering, and a mother hushed the child by singing a soft lullaby. An old woman sat up nearby and threw off her blankets. He could see her, silhouetted darkly against the dawn, her gray hair blowing. A man said something and a woman answered.

From the wood pile, Pondwader pulled small sticks and placed them atop the hot coals, then blew gently. When yellow tongues of flame licked up around the tinder, he added larger sticks. The chunks of dead coral circling the firepit still held warmth from last night, but not enough to boil his stew. Pondwader shoved several into the flames to heat up. He took three warm chunks and dropped them into the hanging moss tea bag. They sizzled as they sank, sending up tendrils of steam. He continued adding larger pieces of wood to the fire until he had a good blaze going. Then he moved the stew basket over the flames. The water in the boiling basket kept it from catching fire, but the bottom always charred, which meant such baskets generally had a short life.

Pondwader backed away. In another two or three fingers of time, the stew would be ready to eat, and he could hardly wait. He was starving this morning. But first things first. . . .

He rose and walked out into the forest.

Ducking beneath a curtain of grape vines, he skirted a dense growth of palmettos and stopped with one foot in mid-air. A copperhead lay coiled in the hollowed-out trunk of the fallen oak tree at his feet. The alternating dark and light brown bands blended almost perfectly with the weathered patterns of the wood. Pondwader slowly backed away, then turned, lifted his long robe, and let his night water spill out onto the ground. The entire time, he looked over his shoulder, watching the snake. The copperhead never moved . . . but something else did, amid the pines to Pondwader's right. He let his robe fall and squinted. A smear of tan about the size of a man came toward him. Pondwader crouched, ready to run.

"It's all right, Pondwader. It's me," Seedpod said.

"Oh! Good morning, Seedpod. Is your watch over?"

"Yes, thank the Spirits. I'm so tired I've lost my prudence."

Seedpod shoved aside a palm frond and came close enough for Pondwader to see him. Puffy patches of dark blue skin lay beneath his eyes, and his old face seemed gaunt, as if just barely enough flesh covered his cheekbones to keep them from protruding through his skin. He smiled.

"Did you rest well, son-in-law?"

Pondwader replied, "Yes," though dreams had haunted his sleep. The Lightning Bird in his chest had kept him awake, rumbling all night long, and in the midst of that thunder Pondwader kept hearing Seedpod's frightened voice describing the way Cottonmouth used to "call" Musselwhite. His souls shuddered. It had to be witchery. Pondwader felt certain of that.

Seedpod came alongside him and put a hand on Pondwader's shoulder. "Come. Let us return to my shelter and I'll make us breakfast. I said good-bye—"

"I already have a frogs' legs stew going, Seedpod. It should be ready shortly. But the tea is already warm."

Seedpod clamped his shoulder affectionately. "Thank you. I tried to convince your wife to stay for breakfast, but she refused. She—"

Pondwader spun around breathlessly. "What? What are you talking about?"

Seedpod frowned and stepped back. "You didn't know? But she said she'd—"

"*Know what?*"

"Musselwhite is gone, Pondwader. She left half a hand of time ago. She stopped to say good-bye to me only because I happened to be standing in her path, but she said she'd spoken to you before she left. So naturally I assumed—"

"I . . . I did hear . . . something. But I hear so many voices in my dreams, it didn't occur to me . . ."

Pondwader broke into a run, flying around deadfall and brush, slapping grape vines out of his way. He charged across the village with his robe whipping around his legs. People watched him in silence, then murmured as he passed. Diamondback and Thorny Boy sat in Seedpod's shelter, sipping gourd cups of tea. Diamondback lifted a hand as Pondwader raced by. But Pondwader did not respond. His long legs stretched out as he crossed the plaza and burst into Musselwhite's empty shelter. She'd rolled up her blanket. That's why he'd thought she still slept.

"She's gone! She's really gone. She left me!"

Lunging forward, he grabbed his pack from where he'd left it last night, took her rolled-up blanket, and tied it to the bottom. She did not understand! It wasn't that he wanted to be a burden to her! He had to be with her! *Or she might die. . . .*

"Pondwader?" Seedpod said as he trotted into the shelter, breathing hard. "Forget this madness. Come and eat breakfast with us."

"I can't. I must find her."

Seedpod's wrinkled face tensed with sympathy. All over the village, people stood up and looked in their direction, murmuring. "How will you do that? You can barely see well enough to avoid stepping off cliffs, let alone to track the finest warrior in generations."

Pondwader slung his pack over his shoulder and stood up. "I *will* find her. I—I don't know how. But I must."

Seedpod gripped Pondwader's arm. "Listen to me," he said in a pained voice. "I know you love her and wish to help her, but from the instant she left here she ceased being your wife, and became Musselwhite the warrior. *Believe me*, not even *I* could track her. She—"

"Maybe I won't have to track her, not if I leave right now and run up the trail as fast as I—"

"She won't set foot on a trail, Pondwader. She'll be moving through the densest heart of the forest, walking on fallen logs, and through any pond she can find, climbing trees to gain a vantage over her surroundings. You will never see her, Pondwader. You will not even see one of her sandalprints!"

Worriedly, Seedpod pleaded, "Stop this nonsense. Come and join us for breakfast. After that, you can help me—".

"Seedpod." Pondwader finished stuffing things into his pack, and picked up a gourd a fresh water. "When you see my grandmother and Kelp please tell them where I've gone. I thank you for your kindness. You've been very good to me, Seedpod. I truly hope I see you again. Good-bye."

Pondwader ran out, his long stride eating at the white sand on the beach.

"Pondwader? Pondwader! Don't do this!" Seedpod shouted after him, but he did not turn.

A flock of pelicans took wing as he sprinted toward them, their heavy brown bodies lifting out over the dark water.

Standing Hollow Horn Village lay on the coast in the north. That much, he knew. If he ran hard, he might beat Musselwhite there. Yes. That made sense. After all, if she were moving through the forest, he could certainly travel more quickly out in the open. When he arrived, he would hide in the forest and wait for her. Perhaps *she* would find *him*.

The curve of the shore took him inland just as Sun Mother slipped above the horizon, and dusty sunlight shafted across Sea Girl's dark face, turning it into a waving luminous blanket. The wings of gulls flashed golden as they soared and dove.

A faint roar began in Pondwader's chest. He placed a hand over his heart and forced himself to breathe deeply. "Not now, baby bird. *Please.* I can't afford any weakness."

Every time his sandals struck the ground, the roar grew louder, rolling through him like peals of thunder, until even the blood in his veins trembled with the coming storm. . . .

Moonsnail sat on a blanket in her shelter, tying a band of green cloth around her short gray hair. She knotted it on the side, so it would be easier to reach later. The wind had been stiff all day, shrieking and moaning through the shelters like an angry soul. The earthy promise of afternoon rain scented the world.

Kelp stood in front of Moonsnail, using a forked stick to lift bags from their pegs on the rafters. A pile of cordage, blankets, and baskets already lay piled outside the shelter, waiting to be packed on the dog travois and hauled to the new village site. Moonsnail sighed. Despite the fact that she knew the move was necessary, she hated to leave this place. Of all their camps, this had been her favorite. Heartwood Clan had been coming here for five tens of summers. As Moonsnail looked out across the village, she remembered every death, every birth, every marriage. Life had been good here. Four of

Sandbur's sons had been born here—and died here, all within days of each other, during a terrible fever. How long ago had that been? Oh, a very long time, almost forty summers.

Kelp retrieved a small bag containing pine nuts and let it fall to the sand with a soft thud. The rich scent of pine sap filled the air, bringing Moonsnail from her reverie.

"I'll miss this place," Moonsnail said softly.

Kelp glanced over at her. She had tied her long hair back, and her face, with its short, pointed nose and big, black eyes looked even more than usual like a raccoon's. She wore a tan tunic; faded yellow geometric designs shone around the hem and neckline.

"I don't understand why we're packing," Kelp said. "Tailfeather hasn't even returned yet to tell us whether the Manatee Lagoon site will suit our needs."

Moonsnail rocked back on her bony hips. Puffs of pure white clouds sailed westward, but far out on the eastern horizon was a solid wall of deep blue. Already, thunderheads reached long arms across the sky. A lot of water lived in that storm. "No, but he will. Old Seedpod is knowledgeable. He wouldn't have mentioned the site if he hadn't believed it was a good place. It will prove out. You'll see."

Kelp stood on her tiptoes and hooked her forked stick under the handle of a dried palm berry bag. As she brought it down, she fished in the bag for a handful, plopped several berries in her mouth, and chewed them thoughtfully. Hesitantly, Kelp asked, "Do you think we'll ever see Mother again?"

Moonsnail's mouth pursed in disgust. "Of course. My worthless daughter can't stay away for long. The instant she runs out of men she'll be back."

Kelp sat down cross-legged and ate another berry. "What about Beaverpaw and Bowfin? Bowfin could come back if he wanted to, couldn't he?"

"If he were willing to accept the clan's punishment for consorting with an Outcast woman, yes."

"Would the punishment be harsh?"

Moonsnail lifted a shoulder, and reached down to straighten the hem of her pale green tunic. "I doubt it. I suspect the council would take your mother's wickedness into consideration and let him go with some minor penance, like shaving off the knots on all the dart shafts for a moon or two." She spread her brown hands wide. "Then again, the council might vote to cast him out, too. A good deal would depend upon how contrite he was about his crime. If he crawled into camp on his hands and knees begging forgiveness, it would go a long way."

Kelp bit her lower lip and pushed the berries around her palm with her index finger. "And Beaverpaw? Is he gone forever?"

Moonsnail's eyes lifted to the place where Waterbearer knelt on the beach with her children, using sand to scrub out the breakfast bowls. Little Manatee Flipper had been crying off and on for five days straight. From the first morning the boy had awakened and found his father gone, he'd been wandering around the village like a homeless ghost. Waterbearer seemed just as miserable. Poor woman, she had loved Beaverpaw with a loyalty almost unknown these days. When the council had summoned her and told her about her husband's adultery, she had flown into a rage, shouting his innocence to the entire village, maintaining that he had just gone off hunting and would be back soon. Then, as the truth became apparent, she had dragged her children from one elder's shelter to the next, declaring that she did not care what he had done, she loved Beaverpaw and wanted him back. Her children had stood at her side, screaming for their father. Waterbearer's devotion had touched everyone.

"I honestly cannot say," Moonsnail replied. "If he manages to extricate himself from Dark Rain's clutches, I'm sure Waterbearer would be happy to see him. And I suspect the council would be lenient with him—just because his family loves him so much."

"I hope he comes home." Kelp frowned.

Moonsnail studied her. "If you're feeling guilty, stop it. It was your duty as a member of this clan to inform the elders before his behavior became a scandal and reflected on all of us." Moonsnail put a hand on top of Kelp's head. "If you hadn't told me what you'd seen, I would have beaten you bloody with a green willow switch."

Kelp smiled, disbelieving, and looked so much like her grandfather that it warmed Moonsnail's heart. "Grandmother," Kelp said, "the closest you've ever come to beating me was a good whack on the shin with your walking stick."

"Poor judgment on my part. I've always been too merciful where my children were concerned. If I'd taken a willow switch to Dark Rain she might have turned out to be a decent human being. Just look at the trouble my indulgence brought our clan."

Dark Rain had asked everything of her, every possession, every shred of love in her heart; over and over again she'd begged Moonsnail to intercede with the clan on her behalf. Yet she'd repeatedly defiled the clan's honor, and then casually turned her back on all of them. Moonsnail shook her head.

"You loved her, Grandmother," Kelp said. "It isn't your fault that she turned her back on us."

"If I'd whacked her shins more often, it might have helped."

Kelp shifted, pulling her knees up and propping her elbows on them. "Grandmother, you can't even beat one of the dogs when you find it lapping stew right out of your supper bowl."

"Well, I *ought* to," Moonsnail responded tartly, "Softness is my greatest failing."

Kelp jumped up and kissed her wrinkled cheek. "I love you, Grandmother."

Moonsnail grinned. What would she do if anything happened to Kelp?

Pondwader's absence had left a bigger hole in her own life than she had feared. She longed to see him squinting curiously at something, or stroking rocks and trees in that gentle apologetic manner, as if soothing their hurts. Kelp was all she had left.

Moonsnail bent forward and said, "I love you, too, Granddaughter. Now finish your palm berries. I promised Floating Stick we would come by his shelter and help him. . . ."

She looked up when a flock of children raced down the beach, waving their arms, calling, *"Tailfeather! It's Tailfeather!"*

Moonsnail gestured to Kelp. "Hand me my walking stick, girl. Let's go see what our new War Leader has to say."

Tailfeather trotted into the village surrounded by children, who clung to the hem of his tunic and pestered him with tens of questions. Adults abandoned whatever tasks they worked at and stood up. A crowd slowly developed.

"Give me your arm, Kelp," Moonsnail said. "I'm awfully unsteady on my feet today."

"Yes, Grandmother." Kelp ran up and held out her elbow for Moonsnail to grip.

Holding tight to that strong, young arm, Moonsnail hobbled out of the shelter and into the bright sunshine. Kelp took slow steps, giving Moonsnail time to plant her walking stick and carefully place each foot. By the time they reached Tailfeather, the crowd had him surrounded.

When he spied Moonsnail, Tailfeather disengaged himself, and shouldered forward toward her. A tall youth, two-tens-and-one summers old, he had a triangular face with a broad flat nose and ears that stuck out through his shoulder-length black hair. He wore his atlatl hooked to his breechclout and carried three darts in his left hand. A sheen of sweat covered his muscular body.

"Greetings, Spirit Elder," he said as he stopped before Moonsnail.

"You made good time," she responded. "What did you find? Is the site suitable?"

Floating Stick came up beside Moonsnail, his sparse white hair awry, as if he'd just risen from his morning nap. His faded blue tunic bore ten tens of wrinkles; he must have slept in it. Through a wide yawn, he asked, "Well, is it a good place?"

Tailfeather nodded and propped his darts on the ground at his side. "Yes. It will work very well, I think. Manatee Lagoon contains many varieties of shellfish, clams, oysters, mussels, and conchs. Not only that, the freshwater pond that Seedpod spoke of is large, though shallow, and I saw many palmettos and palms. We should have no trouble spinning thread for our fabrics. I also—"

"What about defense?" Moonsnail asked pointedly. A cacophony of speculative voices rose, people relaying every word to those behind them. "Can we defend the site if we're attacked?"

Tailfeather inhaled a breath and let it out slowly. "I believe so. It is not the perfect location. The forest is very dense. It will provide cover for anyone who wishes to sneak up on us. But if we set our village between the pond and the lagoon—" he knelt and drew in the sand "—the ocean curves around like this, and the pond sits here. We will have water on three sides. We should be able to defend ourselves, if we need to."

"What about deer?" Floating Stick asked. "Did you see any?"

"None, Elder. Though I did see some tracks. But I suspect that what Seedpod told us is true—there aren't many deer at that location."

Moonsnail nodded. "We expected as much. The sooner we get packed up, the better."

"There is one more thing, Elders." He looked back and forth between Moonsnail and Floating Stick.

"What is it?" Moonsnail asked.

Tailfeather shifted uncomfortably, moving his darts to his right hand. "Dogtooth is there. I spoke with him. He said he plans on living with us, and he also said—"

Kelp let out a yip, at the same time that Floating Stick blurted, "Hallowed Spirits! What for?"

"I didn't think it appropriate to ask," Tailfeather answered. "His other news—"

"But Great Muskrat Above!" Floating Stick shouted. "He'll have us—"

"Hush!" Moonsnail said and gave Floating Stick a disgruntled look. "If Dogtooth wishes to live with us, we should be honored."

"He'll have us darting each other in our sleep!" Floating Stick said. "You know how he is. Always wandering around saying bizarre things to people."

Indeed, Moonsnail did know. Dogtooth had not lived in a community for tens of summers. He'd always been a loner, off Soul Dancing somewhere, and the isolation had seriously affected him. Every time he opened his mouth, he offended someone, and just his demented smile could send people fleeing for their lives.

"What do you want me to do?" Moonsnail asked and scowled at Floating Stick. "Tell him 'no'?"

Floating Stick grunted. "Angering a Soul Dancer is the best way I know of making sure you don't suffer a lingering death."

"No, it'd be quick, all right. But I'm not that anxious to see my relatives in the Village of Wounded Souls. Are you?"

"Not in the form of a sea slug or pond slime, I'm not. None of my relatives would recognize me."

Moonsnail nodded. "That's what I thought you'd say."

She lifted her walking stick and waved it at the crowd to quiet their muttering. People shushed their children and looked up expectantly. "Tailfeather says Manatee Lagoon is a good site! If we begin packing and cutting poles to make travois, we should be ready to leave in a few days. Our new relatives will probably be there when we arrive. Let us not keep them waiting!"

The crowd began to disperse, but Tailfeather kept standing before her.

"What is it?" Moonsnail asked. "Was there something else?"

Tailfeather nodded. "Yes, Elder. Dogtooth told me that he had had a Dream. He said that in the Dream, he saw warriors attacking Windy Cove Village."

Floating Stick edged closer, his old face gone serious. "Cottonmouth's warriors?"

"He did not say. I don't think he knew."

Moonsnail and Floating Stick exchanged worried glances. "Blessed Sun Mother," Moonsnail whispered. "Come back to my shelter with me, Tailfeather. And you, too, Floating Stick. We need to speak more of this."

"I think," Floating Stick said, "that it might be best for all of us if we sent warriors on ahead while we finish packing up the village. Our new relatives at Windy Cove may need them."

Moonsnail gripped Kelp's elbow to steady herself so she could turn and head back to her shelter. Floating Stick and Tailfeather followed behind, talking quietly.

Kelp gave Moonsnail a sidelong look. "Do you think Pondwader was there when the warriors attacked?"

Moonsnail's wrinkled mouth tightened. "There is no way to know."

Kelp nodded. She returned her gaze to the sand, and Moonsnail placed her walking stick with great care. Her legs had suddenly grown very unsteady.

Twenty-one

As evening approached, Pondwader shoved back his hood and let his long white hair blow free in the cool wind. Gulls floated in the air in front of him, squawking and circling over his head. He had been skirting the edge of the water, letting Sea Girl wash his feet as he hurried up the curving shore. The sand glittered with a purplish hue as Sun Mother dropped below the western horizon, and the sky changed from bright turquoise to blue-gray. Clams had burrowed into the sand. He could see their blow holes, which reminded him how hungry he was. He had eaten nothing today, preferring to maintain his distance-eating pace. Soon, however, he would have to stop and make camp for the night.

The passing hands of time had not diminished his fear. It had become a constant, like his heartbeat, the one thing he could depend upon. Not once in his life had he gone off alone like this. Just knowing that enemy warriors might be lurking in the black blur of trees to his left kept him so anxious, he could barely think straight.

"It doesn't matter," he murmured to himself. "I must find her. She needs me."

He'd left Windy Cove Village so quickly that he had not thought to grab a weapon, and the sensation of impending doom weighed him down more with every step, like a tree trunk across his chest. Not even a stiletto hung from his belt, let alone an atlatl or warclub. What a fool he was! If Kelp saw him now, she would threaten to kill him for his stupidity. She had been his guide through the blurry world, and his best friend. He prayed he would live to see her again.

Pondwader broke into a trot again, his sandals leaving a trail of indentations on the darkening beach. The air felt crisp on his flushed cheeks and smelled of seaweed and shellfish. Mole crabs tumbled up the beach with the incoming waves, forcing him to leap over them. He inhaled deeply and let the scents cleanse his souls.

The baby Lightning Bird had been strangely quiet for the past few hands of time, as though resting, or perhaps it merely perched patiently on his heart, waiting its chance to crackle through his ribs and soar into the heavens. It had not even rumbled since just after he'd left Windy Cove.

But the Bird knew, just as Pondwader did, that they had finally taken destiny into their own hands. The right path lay before them. They had but to follow it, and do as the ghosts had said.

Still, Pondwader could not help wondering . . . about his death. How long did he have? Days? A moon? He let his gaze drop to his chest. Sweat stained the front of his robe. "Do you know, baby Bird . . . ? When will you leave your nest in my heart? Soon?"

Not even a faint rumble answered him.

The Lightning Bird had gone deathly silent.

Pondwader's thoughts wandered as he ran. Maybe the Bird was not even in there. Had it gone soul flying again? To see old Dogtooth?

Ahead, the eastward curve of the beach formed a small cove surrounded by pines and palms. The dark, shiny, green palm fronds sheltered heavy clusters of berries which drooped down to within his reach. He could not imagine a better place to camp. His long robe billowed around his legs as he sprinted forward, and entered the trees breathing hard.

He reached up and plucked a hanging cluster of berries. Pine cones littered the needle-covered ground. If the squirrels had not gotten to them before him, he might find pine nuts to go along with the rest of his supper.

Removing his pack, Pondwader knelt beneath the waving boughs, laid his berries aside, and untied his blanket. He spread it out over the ground and sank tiredly atop the blue and black geometric designs. His whole body ached. Wind soughed through the forest around him, whispering and whimpering. As he extended his legs, he winced. Dogtooth had been right. Because he was a Lightning Boy he had been petted and protected, never allowed to risk himself. No warrior would be suffering as he was from a single day's run up the beach. Warriors conditioned their muscles so they could run for days if necessary. It shamed Pondwader that he hadn't more strength. Especially now, when he needed it so badly.

He sat down and opened his pack. How good it felt to be off his feet. His arches ached. Drawing out his gourd of fresh water and a bag of smoked fish, he set them beside the palm berries, then reached out and took one of the pine cones that made a lump under the corner of his blanket. Every nut had been eaten. Pondwader tossed the cone into the shadows.

"Just my luck. The fish and berries will have to do, since I haven't the energy to get up and hunt for anything else."

He took a bite of the fish and followed it up with several palm berries.

The combination of smoky and sweet flavors tasted so good he sighed with contentment and rolled to his back to stare up at the swaying branches over his head. Through the splotches of pine needles he could see the first Shining People emerging like blazing fires across the night sky. Their different colored tunics shimmered brilliantly. He had told Kelp once how striking the reds looked against the pale blues, and she had frowned at him, and said she could see the colors if she really looked hard, but they weren't nearly as obvious to her as to him. Perhaps his poor vision magnified the shades. Whatever the reason, each of the Shining People looked distinctly unique to him. Near the pointed top of the pine, a golden Shining Person sparkled next to a pure silver one. A delighted smile curled his lips. Poor vision had some rewards.

He ate more fish and berries, stuffing himself until he felt sleepy, then rolled up in his blanket, facing Sea Girl, and watched the starlight flood the water. Wind whipped hair around his eyes. Pondwader yawned and before he realized it, slumber had overtaken him.

• • • The scent of insect grease, tangy with smoke, startles me.

My lungs want to pant, and when I try to suppress the urge I feel as if I might explode. But if this person wanted to kill me, wouldn't I already be dead? Cautiously, I slit one eye.

Against the silver-splotched bowl of the night sky, Turtle Bone Doll flies. She rides the wind currents down, soaring and dipping, and hovers just over the tip of my pointed nose. Her tattered tunic looks even more ragged—as if a cruel stranger has twisted her in his hands, trying to tear her apart. A wide rip slashes her skirt.

"Are you all right?" I whisper. "You look like someone nearly rubbed your face off."

Turtle Bone Doll flips, and pirouettes above my head. *"Nothing in the world is all right. One of the Shining Eagles died. I came to tell you."*

Terror grips me. I shove up on one elbow. "Hallowed Spirits! And I had nothing to do with it! What about the other Eagles? Can they hold Hurricane Breather?"

Turtle Bone Doll swoops about like Falcon with her wings tucked, swerving through branches, and over palmettos. Her dark hair whips in the wind. *"For the moment."*

"But why tell me about it? There's nothing I can do to help them."

"Isn't there?"

"No! I mean, I don't think so. . . . Is there?"

Turtle Bone Doll stops. *"Humans fascinate me. Cottonmouth is always telling me what he can do, and you're always telling me what you can't do."*

My chin jerks up, and I stare into her faded brown eyes. "You know Cottonmouth?"

"Oh, yes. Very well."

"Why have you never told me this! I have so many questions about him! I wish you'd—"

"I will allow you to ask one. But just one, Pondwader. Be careful which you choose."

"Just one?" Pondwader frowned. "Why? Why can't I ask as many as I need to?"

"Ask me one. And do it quickly, I haven't much time."

My hood has fallen down, leaving my long white hair tangled around my face. I gather it up with one hand and hold it at the back of my neck while I consider this. Which question is the most important? What do I need to know most of all?

"All right," I say, and heave a breath. "Is Cottonmouth a witch, or just mad?"

"He has a rage for pain which gives him exquisite clarity. Darkness unobstructed by light. In that place, all questions go quiet, and he can be with himself as a stranger. He can live a moment without their past. Are you too young to understand this? To know what it is to clutch the agony of regret to your bosom like a precious child? To be willing to die to protect it?"

I rake my fingers through the cool sand. Bits of shell shimmer. "What I really wanted to know is if he is a witch?"

Turtle Bone Doll sighs. *"I just told you everything you need to know about Cottonmouth, and you complain."*

"You . . . you did?" I blush. "But I didn't understand it! Why would anyone want to die to protect agony?"

In that innocent little girl voice, Turtle Bone Doll whispers, *"When the agony is all you have left, Pondwader, you dare not give it up. Because then you will have nothing at all."*

Turtle Bone Doll launches herself into the air, and flies away toward the stars. An almost imperceptible trail glitters in her path, loops upon loops, circles within circles . . .

Mulberry huddled in the forest with another warrior, Loonfoot, watching the sleeping Lightning Boy. His white face shone so in the darkness it seemed to glow, and his hair . . . the strands that haloed his head had surely come from Sister Moon herself. They seemed made of moonlit mist.

"Should we capture him?" Loonfoot asked softly. Tall and lean, he had a square chin and small black eyes. He'd braided his hair and coiled it into a bun at the base of his skull. He wore only a breechclout.

Mulberry released the palm frond he'd been holding aside and sat back on the sandy forest floor. He had stood witness to the murder of at least two tens of his warriors. All he really wanted now was to return to his wife and infant daughter. The attack had been madness in the first place. What was Cottonmouth trying to prove? That he could wipe out every other village on the coast? For what purpose? If, indeed, the end of the world was at hand, what did it matter if these paltry clans lived out their remaining days in peace?

"What happened to Batfish and Spotted Paw?" Mulberry asked, evading Loonfoot's question, while he scanned the trees. "Did you see where they went?"

"Batfish said he had to find some cobwebs to stop the blood from Spotted Paw's wound. I didn't see what direction they headed, but they'll return soon. There are cobwebs under every fallen log."

"Yes," Mulberry whispered and frowned.

Two summers ago, Mulberry had believed Cottonmouth's Dream with all his heart, but now doubts consumed him. The Spirit Elder simply seemed to have gone mad. Mulberry had the urge to sneak into Standing Hollow Horn Village, secretly pack up his family, and escape into the night before Cottonmouth got him killed.

He turned to Loonfoot. "Have you ever wondered . . . I mean, if we killed the Lightning Boy, it might assure that Cottonmouth's Dream didn't come true. Maybe the world wouldn't end if there was no Lightning Boy to shoot down the Four Shining Eagles."

A nervous swallow went down Loonfoot's throat. "Yes . . . I—I have wondered about that."

They stared at each other. A goose honked out in the trees, and then a flurry of startled wings erupted as the flock burst into the night sky, honking and quacking at whatever had disturbed them.

Loonfoot whispered, "I don't wish the world to end."

"Neither do I."

They both turned back and peered at the Lightning Boy. The youth lay completely vulnerable. One could come up behind the boy, while the other stood in front of him. Even if he woke, they would have surprise on their side.

"Shh! What's that? Did you hear it?" Loonfoot asked.

"What?"

Loonfoot suddenly peered over Mulberry's shoulder. He half rose, his mouth open to speak, but the dart pierced his right eye and sliced through his brain. As silent as a feather, he toppled to the sand. Mulberry ripped his stiletto from his belt and whirled to meet his assailant.

The hard arm that closed over his throat yanked his feet off the ground. "Drop your stiletto," her voice hissed. "*Now.*"

He threw all of his weight into swiftly turning, his stiletto lifted. . . .

She shoved him away so hard that he stumbled. In the instant it took him to regain his balance, he saw her warclub slicing the darkness, the chert studs glinting in the starlight. Instinctively, he lunged for her, but the club's impact against his head slammed him face-first into the soft sand. Dazed, he pushed himself up, and nausea overwhelmed him. He vomited repeatedly. Footsteps brushed the sand, but he couldn't focus his eyes. A gray haze fluttered around him, like tens of bat wings. He worked his stiff fingers into the sand, grasping, trying to hold onto consciousness, but his muscles betrayed him. He fell.

The hollow smack of the warclub bashing his head again was the last sound Mulberry ever heard.

Twenty-two

Oh, no, child. The Turtle Bone Doll really existed. I saw her once. No one would let me touch her because she was so Powerful and I was just a boy, but I looked upon her with these very eyes.

Hmm?

Well, let me see, it was shortly after old Snailtoes' death. He had been the Keeper of the Sacred Doll for three or four tens of summers by then. I was present at the Transfer Ritual, where the Doll was placed into a new Keeper's hands. Her name was Cloud-Walking-Over-the-Earth. I recall very clearly the terror and reverence with which she touched it. She took that doll, wrapped it in a swaddling cloth, and rocked it in her arms like a baby.

Then, we all Sang to the Doll.

Cloud-Walking-Over-the-Earth told me later that the instant she laid hands on the Turtle Bone Doll, she heard echoes of the things the Doll had said to Pondwader.

. . . What?

Yes, she did. She cleaned the Doll, and made a new tunic for her. Cloud-Walking-Over-the-Earth swore that Musselwhite's mark was still visible on the bone of the Doll's back. I never saw that. Though I would have liked to. I think the sight would have eased my sorrow. I had a hard time of it after Musselwhite's death. I remember her burial. There were tens of tens of people present. They had come from all over just to . . .

What's wrong?

Oh.

Yes, of course I saw you waving your hand, child. That's why I stopped! Did you shout at me before that?

Well, I warned you. My ears have minds of their own.

All right, where was I?

. . . Yes, that's right. Pondwader and Musselwhite on the sacred journey to Standing Hollow Horn Village.

Pondwader was no warrior, you'll recall. In fact, he had trouble convincing himself to swat mosquitoes. He loved everything alive, and worried about it, too, but he knew so little about the world . . .

O range flickers danced on the backs of Pondwader's eyelids. For a long time, he saw them in the context of his dream; he was sitting in his grandmother's shelter at Heartwood Village, laughing and talking with Kelp, discussing where they would go to hunt mushrooms that morning. . . . Then the sound of a log snapping in the fire brought him straight out of his sleep. He lay still, listening in terror to the crackling flames. *I'm not at Heartwood. . . . Where am I?* Sea Girl's voice sounded different, deeper and stronger, dashing the shore. *I left Windy Cove this morning. Yes, I left Windy Cove and went searching for Musselwhite.* He'd camped on the beach beneath a tall pine tree. But he hadn't lit a fire. Had he? Wind whistled through the trees, slapping a few pine cones from the branches and sending them thudding down against the sand. The scent of wood smoke mixed with sea salt.

Cautiously, he slitted one eye. She crouched on the opposite side of the fire, staring at him, her eyes dark and brooding. Against the night, her face might have been carved from stone. Her long braid hung over her shoulder and, in the windblown weave of flame and shadow, gleamed like silver-streaked weasel fur.

"Musselwhite!" he said and sat up in his blanket. "I—"

"I should kill you for following me."

He lowered his eyes and pushed his blanket down around his waist. Her voice brooked no disagreement. "I had to find you. I—"

"You've found me. Now go home."

He met her harsh gaze. Something akin to hatred creased her face. Did she despise him so much? "I can't, Musselwhite. The ghosts at the Sacred Pond told me I must be with you when you face Cottonmouth."

"I have no intention of facing him," she answered. "My goal is to get in, rescue Diver, and get out alive. That is all. Someday I will face him, but not this time. This time I—"

"You may not wish to," he interrupted in a strained voice, "but that is the way it will happen." He pulled his hood up to block the night wind. The Shining People glittered wildly above them. "Please, my wife. There are many things I must tell you. We have been together for such a short time that I haven't had the chance until now. Before you try to force me to go home, let me speak with you. Please?"

She ground her teeth for a moment, then added more wood to the fire. "No." She stood up.

"But, you do not understand! I must protect you. That's why—"

"Protect me? You are not a warrior. You are not even a *man*. You are a boy, and a puny one at that. I have nothing more to say to you. I will keep watch over you for the rest of the night, and at dawn you will go home."

Pondwader bowed his head in pain. He had never seen her like this, so distant, and filled with venom. In a trembling voice, he said, "Th—the Sacred Pond . . . I went there because . . . because Dogtooth told me the ghosts wished to speak with me." He glanced up to see if his words about ghosts made her uneasy. She glared at him. "The water washed away my souls, Musselwhite. For three days I lay near death. Then a new soul was reborn in my body."

A glint of horror lit her eyes. Her face slackened. "What soul? A dead man's?"

Pondwader swallowed. His throat was dry. "It's the soul of a baby Lightning Bird, Musselwhite."

"A Lightning Bird?"

"Yes." He put a hand over his heart. "It glows all the time. Blue-white. And . . . Musselwhite? My soul has a name. The ghosts told me. I don't wish you to be afraid, though. Promise me you will stay calm. I didn't understand why the baby Bird's name was important until a—a short time ago. And that's only if it's the same . . . person. I don't know because I—"

"I promise I'll be calm," she said, slightly exasperated. Then she exhaled, and seemed to be deliberately working to defuse her anger. "I didn't know Lightning Birds had names," she said in a normal voice.

Pondwader smiled broadly. "Yes, well, I didn't either. But this one does." He held her gaze. "Its name is Glade, Musselwhite."

She did not move.

"Don't be frightened, please. The ghosts wanted me to tell you that Glade has come back to help you. In the same way you helped him."

For a long while, she just stared at him, then she sank to the ground, as if her legs would no longer hold her, and squeezed her eyes closed.

"Musselwhite!" Pondwader threw off his blanket and went to her. Touching her hair gently, he said, "Let me make some tea. Then we'll talk. You mustn't be worried. Everything is all right."

Beyond camp, the breakers had grown violent, crashing upon the dark shore in shining white smears, roaring like hungry lions. Pondwader returned his gaze to Musselwhite. She sat with her back to the chill wind, and peered down into her gourd cup of pine needle tea. The firelit shadows played over her beautiful, troubled face, and cast a flickering weave of gray and orange across the pines behind her. He'd hung his boiling basket on a tripod constructed of three branches tied together at the top with a cord. Then he'd moved it over the heat of the flames to warm while he'd gathered pine needles. The tea tasted of pine sap, sweet and tangy.

"What else, Pondwader?" Musselwhite asked as she lifted her eyes. "What else did the ghosts tell you?"

The lines around her eyes deepened. Wispy silver-streaked locks had escaped her braid and fluttered about her face. Only now, in the light of the flames, could he see the starburst of fresh blood that stained the hem of her tan tunic. Had she engaged enemy warriors? Nearby? And he hadn't heard a thing?

Pondwader propped his gourd cup on his knee.

He took a long drink, letting the flavor soothe him. "They asked me to tell you something even more curious," he answered.

She gave him a sharp glance. "What?"

He hesitated, turning his warm cup in his hands, watching the green liquid shimmer in the firelight. After the things Seedpod and Dogtooth had told him about Musselwhite, he felt great fear. If she had dared to leap upon a renowned Soul Dancer and try to choke him to death . . . well, Pondwader's chances didn't look so good.

"First," he said softly. "They asked me to tell you that Glade would protect you from Cottonmouth. So you see, it isn't actually me who has to be with you, just . . . just my body. That . . ." he said, sighing, ". . . is why I must go with you, my wife."

She frowned at Pondwader's chest, as if longing to slice it open and see if her dead son truly lived in there. "How could Glade protect me?"

"The ghosts didn't explain. I wish they had. I didn't understand half of what they said to me. They also told me . . . how did they put it?" He tried to recall the exact words. "They said, 'Tell Musselwhite that when Glade's soul hatches, and he sprouts wings of light, Cottonmouth will never be able to hunt her again. Glade won't let him.' " Pondwader peered at her. "Does that make sense to you?"

Musselwhite stared at him unblinking. She looked thin and haunted, her beautiful face worn down to its elegant bones. In her eyes, he saw old pain, and hatred grown keen, honed over time to a fine deadly edge. Beside her, three darts thrust up from the sand like spears, their chert points glinting. As if for security, she pulled them up, then laid them across her lap.

"Yes," she answered softly. "I do understand."

"What did they mean? Please tell me. Perhaps if I understand one part I can make sense of the rest."

She shifted uneasily, and he could see her shoulder blades under the thin fabric of her tunic. Had she lost so much weight recently? From mourning her loved ones? Or from the constant, gnawing fear?

She waved a hand, and irritated, said, "It is difficult to explain, Pond-wader. I would have to start at the beginning and I'm not sure you could grasp the—"

"I know I am very young," he admitted, embarrassed. "But please try to explain it, Musselwhite. I must know. This is very important." The Light-ning Bird had begun rumbling again, its voice low, distant, but rolling toward him, growing louder. "What did they mean about Cottonmouth not being able to hunt you?"

"Cottonmouth . . ." she said, and halted, as though just uttering his name gave her pain. A swallow went down her throat. Then words poured out in a fast flood, as if she wanted this over with. "He has a curious ability to win the hearts of those he wants, and after he has made them love him, their loyalty is unquestioning, almost fanatical. I wasn't the first girl he had . . . hunted."

Pondwader searched her bitter face. "There had been others before you?"

"At least one. Her name was Reef. Just before he told me he wanted me, he cast her aside. But she kept coming back, pleading with him, crawling on her hands and knees, begging him to take her back. It was . . ." She lowered her eyes and peer into her tea. ". . . difficult to watch."

"What happened to her?"

Musselwhite shrugged. "I heard that she committed suicide. I never knew whether it was true or not, but probably it was."

In the golden gleam of the fire, he saw the curve of her mouth tighten.

Pondwader blinked thoughtfully and looked away. Swarms of glittering mosquitoes and gnats had been buzzing around him since dusk. He waved away one that landed on his big toe and tucked his bare feet securely beneath his long robe. Musselwhite had been smart enough to coat her exposed flesh with insect grease. She smelled like pine smudge. Pleasant. Pondwader took another sip of his tea, and wondered about Reef, and this strange Power of Cottonmouth's to make people love him. Witchery. *It must be.*

"Is he mad?" Pondwader asked, and prayed for a straight answer.

"Everyone says so. But I never saw it."

"Not ever?"

"No. I saw him insane from grief. Worried sick. Desperate. But not mad. He was always fickle, volatile, like a man clinging to a log in a rough ocean, soaring up one instant and plunging down the next. And, believe me, when he was on the bottom of that trough, no one wanted to be close to him. He could kill without a second thought. I used to try to soothe him then. To make him laugh." Tenderness flickered in her eyes for a brief moment, then it was gone, locked behind that shield again. She clutched her cup hard.

"How curious," Pondwader said.

"Hmm?" she asked, as though awakening. "What?"

"This is the first time I have ever heard anyone speak of Cottonmouth with fondness. Did you love him?"

For a time the silence stretched, unbroken except for the surge of waves and whimpering of wind. She set her cup on the ground, and gripped her darts tightly again.

"Did I love Cottonmouth?" she repeated in a faint, curious voice. "No one has ever asked me that. Not once in my whole life. From the time I turned ten-and-three summers, people just assumed we were in love. It was so obvious. Painfully so. Whenever we were close to each other, we were always touching gently. I was so drawn to him, Pondwader, that whenever we were apart, I was frantic. Desperate for him, ready to kill to see him again. There was nothing I would not have done for him, or given him— except my souls. And for a time, I would even have given them up, if he'd asked me to."

The fingers around her darts knotted to fists as she closed her eyes, blocking out the firelight and flickering stars, sealing herself from Pondwader's gaze. Her eyelids fluttered, as if memories danced across her souls, and from the hard set of her jaw, she must not have liked what she saw.

Softly, Pondwader asked, "Is that what made you stop loving him? His dark side?"

She turned her head to regard him seriously. "I never stopped loving him."

"B-but you ran away from him!"

She leaned her head back, and wavering shadows cloaked her beautiful face, above a square of light that lit her throat. She seemed to be peering intently at the Shining People. "Yes," she answered softly. "I ran away."

"If you still loved him, how could you?"

A ghostly smile touched her lips, but her eyes were not amused; they brimmed with bitterness. "Is the world so simple for you, Pondwader?"

He suddenly felt very small inside himself. He lowered his gaze. "Could you answer me? I really need to know. Why did you run away if you loved him?"

"Because I had to."

"Why?"

"I do not wish to speak of these things, Pondwader!" she snapped. "Can't you understand that I—"

"I understand that these things bring you pain," he answered gently. "And I don't want to hurt you, but this is very important, Musselwhite. Please. Help me. I must—"

She shouted, *"Cottonmouth told me if I did not let him take Glade with him on his next war walk, he was going to attack Windy Cove's village site on Pelican Isle, and kill everyone that I loved! . . . Just as . . . as I would be killing Glade."*

"You? Killing Glade? What did he mean?"

She bowed her head. "Glade had been in a coma for two-tens-and-two days. He'd had such a high fever . . . I had been giving him spoons of water, dribbling them down his throat, and he would swallow the water, but I couldn't get him to eat anything. He kept losing weight, until only a tiny bundle of bones remained. He was so little. He felt like a feather in my arms when I rocked him."

As if those haunted words had painted pictures across Pondwader's souls, he glimpsed that little boy lying limply in his mother's arms while she rocked him, and wept, and tore herself apart. Like a cactus thorn hidden in a sandal, he felt the unexpected stab of her grief.

"I think . . . I think it was even harder on Cottonmouth than me," she continued sadly. "He could not let Glade go. He tried force-feeding him, and when the food just lodged in Glade's throat, Cottonmouth would shriek and slam our son on the back to dislodge it. Then he would sink to the floor of our shelter and sob."

"But if Glade was so ill, why would Cottonmouth have wished to take him on a war walk?"

Musselwhite ran her fingers up and down her dart shafts, as if concentrating on the texture of the wood, feeling every place a knot had been shaved off. Her beautiful firelit face contrasted sharply with the silver frosted trees at her back, which swayed and moaned in the night wind.

Tightly, she answered, "He . . . Cottonmouth believed that if he could wound a man, then lay Glade on his chest, so that Glade's eyes were looking directly into the wounded man's when Cottonmouth killed the man . . . He thought the man's souls would seep into Glade's body and bring him to life again."

Wind flicked Pondwader's white hair and it brushed coldly across his cheeks. White light flashed inside him, followed by a rumble that shook his ribs. Pondwader shivered and whispered, "I have heard of such things, though people do not speak of them often. Did Cottonmouth possess such great Power? Was he a witch?"

Musselwhite moved her head slightly. Pondwader could not discern whether it was a nod or a shake, and from the confusion on her face, he didn't think she knew either. "I cannot say, Pondwader. Just after Glade slipped into the coma, he began talking of the old witch who lived over by Slender Grass Village. I think the man's name was Bright Feather." Her forehead furrowed. "For a brief time, Cottonmouth was gone. A night and half a day. I remember thinking he probably just needed time alone, to mourn."

"So . . ." Pondwader nervously smoothed his sleeves. The thought of standing face-to-face with a witch horrified him. "Cottonmouth might have gone to learn things from Bright Feather?"

"It's possible. But I think I would have known, Pondwader. I don't think he could have hidden that from me." She seemed to drift away from him, eyes going vacant, seeing something on the fabric of her souls. "We were very close."

Pondwader tucked his robe back around his leg where the wind had worried it loose. "Have you never hidden something from someone you love, like Diver?" he asked innocently, just wondering, and so her response left him stunned.

In a lightning-quick move, she was on her knees, leaning over him with a deadly glare. "Do not *ever* ask me such a thing again!"

He nodded, too numb to say anything for a several moments. Then, he mustered his courage and said, "I'm sorry. I did not mean to pry. It's just . . . I asked because people do that. Everyone has secrets." Slowly, she eased back to the sand, but her fierce expression remained. He continued gingerly, "And, Musselwhite, I asked because I have heard that the best witches never reveal the truth to anyone. They leave people fearing, and guessing. Was that illness caused by an evil Spirit, or a witch? Did those men die in a bad storm, or did a witch make their canoe overturn? That sort of thing. If people can't definitely lay blame, then the witch is liable to work for many summers before being discovered."

Her hard warrior's face had returned, jaw clamped, eyes narrowed. "Well, whether Cottonmouth was or was not a witch doesn't matter. The possibility horrified me so terribly, that I killed my own son . . . so Glade would not have to go through that." A flicker of agony etched her face. "And so I would not have to, Pondwader. How could I ever look into my son's eyes again, knowing someone else's soul lived there? A man my husband had murdered?"

He gently stroked her arm. "Grandmother Moonsnail used to whisper about the terrible things the murdered souls did to their new body . . . madness, mutilation . . . horrors too awful to imagine."

As though from a stabbing ache in her heart, she bent forward, and suddenly she looked very old and very tired. "Cottonmouth said that sometimes the souls actually learn to accept their new bodies. He wanted Glade to live so much that he was willing to take the chance. He hoped that if we were good and kind to those new souls, they would not hurt Glade. I . . ." She bowed her head. "I could not bear the thought."

Pondwader longed to wrap his arms around her and hold her tightly, but he sensed she would not like that, so he folded his arms and hugged himself instead, to lessen the need. "The Pelican Isle Massacre occurred after that?"

"Yes." She nodded. "Immediately afterward. Glade's death almost killed Cottonmouth. He leaped upon me, screaming, and tried to tear me to pieces with his bare hands. I ran away, to Pelican Isle, to warn my family, but he and his warriors beat me there." The flames had died, though every so often, tiny yellow tongues would lick up around the red eyes of coals, and shine in her fierce eyes. "He never made a promise he didn't keep. Had I not been at Pelican Isle, he would have killed everyone I loved."

"I'm glad you escaped him, my wife," he said softly, squeezing her arm.

She lightly worked her thumb along the sharp edge of her dart point, using the nail to follow each indentation in the red stone. "I never escaped him, Pondwader. Not really. From the instant I left him, he has hunted me in my dreams. I hear him calling me in that strange haunting voice of his, and I am a child again. Terrified. Wanting him with all my heart, and at the same time running as hard and as fast as I can to get away from him."

Was that what was happening when she cried in that little girl's voice at night? He was "calling" her? Trying to coax her into coming to him again? Could it be possible that after all these years, after all the horrors they had inflicted upon each other, Cottonmouth still wanted her? And more terrifying, Pondwader heard an undertone of want in her own voice. But he could not ask her about that—would not—because he feared her answer too much.

"I wonder if that's what the ghosts meant," he said.

"What?"

"When they said Cottonmouth would not be able to hunt you anymore. Do you think they meant in your dreams? Has he hunted you recently?"

Despite the cold, a drip of sweat ran along the smooth curve of her jaw. "Let me think. . . ." She frowned and her eyes darted about for several moments.

"The ghosts said that Glade would protect you, as soon as he hatched and sprouted wings of light. That happened the night of our marriage. The blue-white flash was so brilliant, it blinded me. I floated in an ocean of light for hands of time."

She regarded Pondwader from the corner of her eye. "I have not heard Cottonmouth's voice in my dreams since just after we loved each other for the first time, Pondwader."

The coals flared when the wind gusted suddenly, scattering ash, carrying it up through the tree boughs in a swaying, whirling pillar of white. They both turned to shield their faces, and the amber flare caught in the bloody starburst on her tunic, turning it a soft coral.

When Musselwhite turned back, she had closed her eyes, appearing very weary. Pondwader's heart went out to her. It had to be around midnight.

She had not slept since before dawn, and somewhere along the way she had killed, probably in a fight for her life. How had she stayed awake this long?

"Please, my wife," he said. "Try to sleep. We will need our strength. I'll stay awake and keep watch."

She shook her head. "I cannot. You aren't a reliable guard, Pondwader."

He rose, walked to the opposite side of the fire, took up his blanket, and returned. Tenderly, he draped it around her shoulders, and knelt beside her on the sand, peering seriously into her dark eyes. "I know it, but I will do the best I can. You must rest, Musselwhite. You will never be able to save Diver if you are too exhausted to think straight."

She scrutinized him, then rested her hand on his shoulder. "Just for a short while," she said. "If you hear *anything*, wake me immediately. Do you understand?"

"Yes. I will."

She scanned the forest carefully, then pulled the blanket close and curled on her side on the sand. Pondwader slid over, gently lifted her head and placed it in his lap.

"Is this all right?" he whispered.

"I am comfortable, yes. Good night, Pondwader."

"Good night, my wife."

Pondwader let his hand slide down her throat and arm until he could twine his fingers with hers. She did not clasp his hand back, but she didn't pull it away either. He was contented.

The Shining People cast a silver glow over the forest and ocean, illuminating an owl that sailed silently over the tree tops, little more than a gray blur to Pondwader. His gaze drifted, searching the world for movement. He might not be able to see clearly, but motion usually caught his eye. Now he made it a matter of pride. Against the silvered water, gulls walked, their dark heads bobbing as they hunted the beach. Down the shore a single cormorant flapped its wings to dry them.

Pondwader lifted a hand to his chest. The rumble had drowned out his heartbeat, low, but constant. Reverently, he rubbed the space over his heart. It felt hot. Why would Musselwhite's dead son choose to be reborn inside him? Why not a warrior, or a great Soul Dancer? Why "puny" Pondwader? The word hurt. But he could face that truth. He was not a warrior, she had been right about that. But he *was* a man. Truly, he was. He just needed more time to show her his strengths.

He prayed that he had that time.

Nothing made sense anymore.

Despite his aching confusion, Pondwader knew the pain of hope. Perhaps Glade could help the Shining Eagles where Pondwader could not? Is that why Turtle Bone Doll called him the "deliverer"?

He struggled to fit this new thought into the framework of his Dreams.

They had been bizarre, filled with tornadoes, and strange men, and Turtle Bone Doll, all dancing and spinning, seeming so joyous.

And rain.

Rain that fell and fell from a bruised sky. Rain that went on forever.

Twenty-three

Beaverpaw stood in the shadows, his back to an oak trunk, watching Dark Rain and Bowfin gambling. They sat in a circle with ten other men, tossing Bones. Three bones, from a man's index finger, were shaken, then thrown out, and points counted depending upon how many joints lined up in their correct anatomical positions. The gamblers had been throwing the dried pods of beach pea onto the fire all evening, then leaning over and sniffing the smoke, growing crazier by the instant, laughing louder, shoving each other hard. Soul Dancers used beach pea to obtain visions. Beaverpaw had never known anyone to treat the pods the way these people did, like a strip of sweet bark, or a palm berry cake. The Spirit of the beach pea often killed those who took her Power lightly. Secretly, Beaverpaw half hoped the Spirit would take her revenge tonight. It would serve these despicable men right.

The wind blew, causing their fire to spit and flare. Patchy shadows danced over the clearing where the gamblers sat, mottling their triumphant faces. Blessed Sun Mother, the things he had witnessed over the past few days . . . ! After they'd run from Heartwood Village, Dark Rain had led them along forest trails so dark and narrow, Beaverpaw had feared every moment for their lives. He had sweated in spite of the chill breezes, and kept a dart nocked in his atlatl at all times. Dark Rain seemed to know exactly where she wanted to go, so he and Bowfin had obligingly brought up the rear. They had hunted the food, searched out the fresh water, made the camps. Dark

Rain had done nothing—except taken turns servicing them each night. The woman was insatiable. She would crawl from Beaverpaw to Bowfin and back again. Her needs were . . . inhuman.

Then tonight, at dusk, the sound of laughter had drifted through the trees, and Dark Rain had whooped and broken into a run. Bowfin had followed on her heels, like an excited stag during mating season. Beaverpaw had lagged behind, proceeding with care. Not only did he not know the people ahead, he did not even really know where he was. Far to the north of Heartwood, and inland about a half day's walk—more than that he could not say.

As he'd neared the clearing, the stink of human wastes, of rot, accosted his nose. Skin crawling, he had sneaked off the trail and come up behind the men who, by then, were passing Dark Rain amongst them, kissing and caressing her. Bowfin had stood looking on, confusion on his young face. The clearing had brimmed with filthy men who shouted crude comments at Dark Rain, and kept their weapons very close at hand. Dirt filled the creases on their necks, arms, and legs. Every one had greasy, unkempt hair that looked as if it hadn't been brushed in moons. They wore filthy breechclouts, black with grime. Did none of them ever bathe or wash their clothing? And they all coveted his Dark Rain. . . .

When Beaverpaw entered the clearing, the men had whirled, and lifted their atlatls in a single practiced motion.

"He's mine!" Dark Rain had yelled. "Leave him be."

After four hands of time sniffing beach-pea smoke and gambling, Beaverpaw barely recognized her. Her beautiful face had flushed, her eyes had gone glassy and cruel. Each time she lost a throw, she lunged at the winner, trying to claw his eyes out. These men knew her. Knew what to expect. They fended her off with a slap, or a fist, and then they all laughed and called her a whore. She did not seem to mind at all—but the word grated on Beaverpaw, deep down, like a burning brand thrust into his belly. He *loved* her. If she was a whore, and everyone here knew it, what did that make him? A whoremaster, or a whore's dupe? His anger simmered and soured—and beneath it homesickness ate at him.

He had not even hugged Waterbearer or his children good-bye before he'd left. Why hadn't he? He owed them at least that much. He certainly owed them some kind of explanation. He knew now that he should have just confessed and thrown himself on his wife's mercy, rather than letting Dark Rain talk him into taking the coward's way out. Running away. Him! War Leader of Heartwood Clan! For the rest of his miserable days, he would bear that shame. And little Manatee Flipper would be forced to live with it, too, and all of Beaverpaw's other children. He could hear the taunts already, boys shrieking, "Your father was a coward! He consorted with an Outcast woman, and ran away when we needed him most!" He . . .

Beaverpaw's stomach heaved. He turned and vomited into the autumn leaves that carpeted the forest. The gamblers jeered and called him names, but he did not care. No matter what his body did to try and cleanse itself, he could not rid his souls of the foul taste of failure. Or the knowledge that this futility, this desperate regret, had been born in his erect manhood. The moment he had allowed it to shout down his heart, he had doomed himself. And his family.

All because he had fancied himself in love with the perverse, ruthless shrew before him.

As though she'd heard his thoughts, she turned and ordered, "Give me your stiletto."

"What?" he asked, wiping his mouth with the back of his hand. Dark Rain did not seem to notice his discomfort—or perhaps she just didn't care. "What for?"

"I am out of goods to bet with. I'll win it back, don't worry. Give it to me! It's my throw. I need it now!" She imperiously stretched out her hand.

Beaverpaw untied it from his belt, studied the designs he had so carefully etched into the bone, and walked forward to place it in her hand.

The big man sitting across the fire from her grinned, showing his rotten yellow teeth. He had a chest like the thick trunk of a hickory tree, and stringy black hair that hung down to his waist. "Oh, Dark Rain," he said. "I see you have found another generous lover. Is he as good as that boy trader? What was his name? Seashore, wasn't it?"

Dark Rain ignored him, closing her eyes while she shook the bones in her cupped hands, then threw them out across the ground. She shrieked angrily and the men erupted in a cacophony of laughter and clapping.

The big man picked up Beaverpaw's beloved stiletto and smoothed his dirty hands over the sharp point. "You lost your new lover's stiletto, Dark Rain. What will he think of you now?"

"Beaverpaw is a *man*, Westwind," she challenged. "Not a weakling like you. Beaverpaw can *take* his stiletto back if he wishes it."

"Can he?" Westwind smiled and turned to glare at Beaverpaw. He had chilling eyes, and he stood a good hand taller than Beaverpaw. "Do you wish this back?" he asked, holding up the stiletto.

Beaverpaw shook his head. "You won it fairly. Keep it."

Westwind laughed. "It would seem that your latest victim is not as enamored with you as your last. Seashore would have leaped on me like a dog if I had challenged him."

Dark Rain shifted, kneeling to watch her opponent shake up the bones and prepare to throw them out. "Seashore was a stupid fool," she replied.

"Perhaps you are right," Westwind said. "I heard that when you gambled away his last conch shell, then had the audacity to leave him, he went out into the forest and slit his own throat. Only an imbecile would give up his life for a woman." He thrust out a hand. "And *such* a woman!"

The circle roared with laughter at the joke, men throwing their heads back and slapping their thighs. Bowfin, who sat to Dark Rain's left, clamped his jaw and stared sightlessly at the ground. He had that look. Beaverpaw had seen it many times before. That look as if he were about to jump up and drive his dart through the closest man, just to relieve his own shame.

Dark Rain's opponent tossed the bones. When all three landed in the correct positions, she shrilled and lunged for his throat, managing to claw gashes in his right cheek before he savagely shoved her back into Bowfin's arms.

"Do that again, woman!" he said, wiping at the blood running down his chin. "And I will drag you out into the forest and take my payment out of your pretty hide!"

Smiling seductively, she leaned toward him, her mouth puckered into a pout, and cooed, "Will you give me two chert dart points if I let you inside me? I work a man so well, you will think I have a third hand. You'll never find a better bargain. Ask any of these men. They will tell you that I—"

"*Dark Rain!*" Beaverpaw shouted as he stepped out of the shadows. "Get up this instant! We are leaving here. Now!"

She did not even look at him. She scooped up the bones and said, "You may leave if you wish. I am not finished gambling." With the flick of her hand, she added, "You are beginning to bore me, Beaverpaw. You are getting more and more morose. Why don't you go out and find your blankets? I will be along later." Then she turned to Bowfin, rubbed a hand along the line of his young jaw, and said, "Didn't I see you using a stone scraper yesterday? Where is it? I want it."

Dutifully, Bowfin rose, walked passed Beaverpaw, and went out into the forest. He picked up his pack, and brought the scraper back. Dark Rain kissed him as a reward, and Bowfin eagerly dropped at her side again. Beaverpaw's gut wrenched. She began shaking up the bones.

Westwind's gaze moved from Bowfin to Beaverpaw and his dislike showed in the set of his mouth. Clearly, he thought them both fools. "So," he said, looking at Beaverpaw, "Dark Rain told me you were the War Leader for Heartwood Clan. Do you know Musselwhite? Have you heard of Cottonmouth's latest attack?"

Beaverpaw went cold. As his childrens' faces flashed before his eyes, he stepped forward. "What attack? On Heartwood?"

"No. On Musselwhite's village. Windy Cove. A warrior, fleeing for his life, ran through here yesterday. He said that Cottonmouth had sent two tens of warriors to wipe out Windy Cove once and for all. He had promised them that Musselwhite would not be there, but when they arrived, they found out different. She ran through them like a dart through bear grease." Westwind's eyes gleamed his admiration. "That warrior claimed she killed eight men by herself."

"*Eight?*"

"So he said, and he had no reason to lie. The greater the number, the more it would shame him and Standing Hollow Horn Clan. Because of that,

I imagine the number may have even been higher. Musselwhite may have killed nine or ten."

Beaverpaw clenched his fists. "Blessed Spirits. And what of the Lightning Boy? Did he survive?"

Westwind lifted a shoulder, and returned his gaze to Dark Rain's intent face. "The warrior did not stay around long enough to find out. He said he saw the Lightning Boy step out of the trees, and that was enough for him. The warrior ran like a scared badger."

Pondwader had no fighting skills. He rarely even carried weapons because he didn't know how to use them. If he had walked out of the trees into a swarm of Cottonmouth's warriors . . .

Beaverpaw turned to peer at Dark Rain. She had lost again and sat with her eyes narrowed, her jaw stuck out in rage. "Your son, Pondwader, may be dead, Dark Rain," he said. "Don't you care?"

Her eyes remained glued to her opponent's hands. "Care? Why should I? When he married Musselwhite, he paid off all my debts. He served his usefulness. I don't need him anymore."

That cold voice made Beaverpaw feel as if he stood face-to-face with the darker side of himself. Had he not abandoned his own family just as casually? Used them and left them without even a good-bye? How easy it was for a man to lose himself in a woman's flesh. To forget obligations and kindnesses when he felt that wanton warmth wrap around him. He longed to run away, far away. *Home. Home. . . .* The word called to him. He would bury himself in his childrens' arms and hide. Their laughter and love would make him forget the stink of this place, the filth of these men . . . and the fierce glow in Dark Rain's eyes.

For the first time in many summers, he felt tears burn his eyes. Tears he would not shed. Could not. So they would fill up his body and drown his souls. And he deserved it.

Beaverpaw turned and strode out into the forest. Dark Rain was right. He was morose. It was time he found his blankets.

Diver awakened to the sound of many footsteps, and scrambled up to a sitting position, trying to blink himself awake. It was not even dawn. The brightest Shining People still canoed across the Daybreak Land. Cool wind blew in off the quiet ocean and tousled his long hair around his bare shoulders. Diver felt cold to the bone. He shivered, and turned, as best he could, given his bound hands and feet. Cottonmouth stood on the west side of the shelter, at the forefront of a group of warriors, all dragging coils of rope or . . . vines. They looked like vines. Shriveled leaves dotted the lengths.

"What are we up to this morning, Cottonmouth?" he asked.

"A lesson."

Graying black hair hung loose about his shoulders, fluttering in the wind. Cottonmouth stepped forward, and Diver almost cried out when he saw the turtle-bone doll tucked into Cottonmouth's belt. Instinctively, Diver slid away, to the far eastern edge of the mats. His pulse began to race.

"A lesson about what?"

"Woundedness."

". . . What?" Diver asked in confusion.

Cottonmouth waved his warriors forward. "Tie him. Do it quickly before the others arrive." Then he turned and walked away.

Hard hands gripped Diver's arms and dragged him to his feet. The warriors laughed as they hauled him to the middle of the shelter and pulled down the rope tied to the central rafter pole.

"Hold up your arms," the tall, skinny man said. "Littlehorn, secure his bound hands to the rope."

"Yes, Woodduck," a young warrior, barely more than ten-and-six summers, said, as he hurried forward to obey. He wore only a breechclout and had his black hair cropped short, so that it hung at chin level. A coarsely woven headband kept it out of his eyes.

Diver soon found himself once again strung up to the rafters with his hands bound over his head. His shoulder and back wounds ached from the strain. How long would they leave him this time? Just hands of time? Or days?

Littlehorn backed away and wet his lips anxiously. "Now what?" he asked. "Woodduck, should we—"

"Yes. Bring the vines."

Diver swiveled his head to watch the warriors run out of the shelter, chuckling and whispering about how crazy Cottonmouth was, and carefully gather up the coils of thorned vines.

"What are you doing?" Diver asked in alarm. "What is this?"

Woodduck stepped back to let his men crowd around Diver. "Littlehorn, you and Cloudfish, wrap him tightly from head to toe, just as the Spirit Elder said."

"What? Why?" Diver demanded to know.

"I do not question my orders, filth. I follow them," Woodduck replied and crossed his arms authoritatively.

Littlehorn came forward holding up a vine with long, thick thorns. He whispered, "Hold still. It will not hurt so much."

The youth lifted the end of the vine toward Diver's face and Diver stumbled back, trying to get away. "No!"

"Gullwing, hold the coward's feet!" Woodduck commanded and sneered at Diver.

Another warrior ran forward, dropped to the mats, and grabbed Diver around the legs, holding him while Littlehorn and Cloudfish tied him. They wrapped him round and round. . . .

"Pull them tight!" Woodduck shouted. "This man is our enemy!"

"Yes . . . all right," Littlehorn murmured and gritted his teeth, then he jerked the vines hard, raking gashes in Diver's body, breaking embedded thorns off at skin level, and wrapping him so tightly Diver could barely breathe.

Diver shuddered. The long thorns penetrated his flesh deeply. Blood flowed down his face so fast he could not blink quickly enough to keep it out of his eyes. He saw his tormentors through a pale crimson veil. Hot streams flooded over his chest. He should have been grateful that the men avoided his eyes and genitals, but he felt only hatred and loathing. When they had finished and stood musing about their work, Diver bent his head forward as far as he could without crying out in agony. Blood misted his entire body and trickled around his feet.

"Hallowed Sun Mother," Littlehorn said hoarsely, backing away with his eyes narrowed. "What is Cottonmouth's purpose in this? I can't see—"

"Move!" Woodduck shouted. "The Spirit Elders are coming. Let us go. Cottonmouth said that when we had finished, we were to leave immediately. We will keep guard from a short distance away."

The men trotted out, Littlehorn muttering darkly while Woodduck laughed. Diver saw several gray-haired men and women walking in his direction. Not one—not one of them!—looked at him as they threw down their mats, and sat down inside the shelter. They wrapped blankets around their bony elderly shoulders, and continued speaking in soft, genial voices . . . as if Diver did not exist.

His muscles quaked. What madness was this? For ten-and-four days Cottonmouth had kept him isolated. If a villager strayed close to Diver's shelter, the guards drove him or her off with their atlatls. As a result, the only members of Standing Hollow Horn Clan that Diver had seen up close were Cottonmouth, a variety of taciturn guards, and the old woman Starfish. And now this?

Diver scanned the twelve Spirit Elders. They had arranged their mats in a distinct order. Two elders, one man and one woman, sat in front, facing Sea Girl, and the others sat in a semicircle behind them. Against the pale golden halo that had just colored the horizon, their silver heads gleamed.

"Shh!" the old woman in front hissed and held up a hand.

Every head turned, looking right through Diver to something in the village behind him.

Cottonmouth made a quiet entrance, walking slowly, his head down. He had changed clothes, and wore a green tunic with sea-urchin spines sewn around the hem. They clicked and clacked as he walked. The turtle-bone doll no longer stared at Diver from Cottonmouth's belt. Had he left it in his shelter? Rounding the group, Cottonmouth went to stand in front of them, facing Diver. But when he looked at Diver, a strange expression slackened his face.

"Spirit Elders," he said softly in that deep voice. "Today I would speak with you about suffering."

People nodded and smiled.

"I am eager to hear your words," the old woman in front said.

"Thank you, Alder. And you, Basketmaker?" he looked at the old man in front. "Is this topic acceptable to you as well?"

"Oh, yes. Proceed." Reverence tinged that reedy voice. The old man's eyes shone.

Cottonmouth nodded. "I will not speak for long." He clasped his hands in front of him and breathed deeply for a time, staring at the sand. Then he lifted his head to look directly at Diver.

Diver tasted blood in his mouth. Salty and slightly earthy. He swallowed, and peered out at the horizon. Thick clouds had eaten the blue, leaving a sullen gray blanket in its place. Storm Girl's scent rode the wind. For half a moon, Diver had been in Standing Hollow Horn Village, but had yet to understand it. The average person feared Cottonmouth, often looking at the man as if he were a loathsome creature just emerged from the ocean's darkest reaches. But the elders, here and now, hung on his every word. That's what gave Cottonmouth his Power. The elders considered him on a par with Brother Earth or Sister Moon, and their families and friends would never dishonor the elders by suggesting otherwise. But how had Cottonmouth so completely fooled these wise old men and women?

Diver glanced through the group. Cottonmouth had called the two in front by name. The man with long hair hanging over his shoulders like frost-killed weeds was Basketmaker. The ancient woman seated next to him, the one with the short silver braid and bulbous nose, was Alder.

"We are all wounded," Cottonmouth began, his deep voice lilting over the gathering. Against the slate-colored sky, he looked very tall and muscular. He had pulled his hair back into a bun, making his silver temples more prominent. "That *woundedness* is the heart of what it means to be human. Agony is what draws us together. Not joy."

"Yes, yes it is," Alder agreed with a fervent nod.

Diver's brows lowered. What did that mean? Oddly, it had a ring of truth. Another person's wounds drew Diver far more powerfully than physical appearance, sense of humor, or happiness. In fact, beautiful, funny women, with constant smiles, did not interest him at all. And never had. But a beautiful woman with pain in her eyes . . . that was a different story.

"The eyes of other people are the heart of our woundedness. They are like clamshell mirrors. We see our own pain and suffering reflected, and it draws us like the mating scent. Powerful. Irresistible. That shared woundedness is what we call love. If we would only close our eyes long enough—" and he closed his and tipped his chin to the cloudy heavens "—we could separate ourselves from that entrancing reflection and finally be healed. Only when we are at rest in lonely darkness is salvation possible."

As though his words had stirred tears from heaven, a fine misty rain began to fall, the drops standing like pearls on Cottonmouth's graying black hair. Wind swept in off the sea and the elders pulled their blankets up over their heads. A hum of conversation broke out.

Alder and Basketmaker leaned sideways to whisper to each other, then they smiled and returned their gazes to Cottonmouth. He looked down upon them with such adoration, it seemed to charge the cool air. The hair on Diver's arms stood out. All of the other elders smiled and murmured approvingly.

"Yes," Cottonmouth added, "we spend our entire lives searching for salvation in the eyes of others. But it cannot be found there. We must willingly cast off the reflection we see in our lovers' eyes, and seek rest in the very heart of our own woundedness. Then the Lightning Birds will find us."

Basketmaker whispered, "We must be brave enough to go alone into that terrible darkness—or those wounds will never be cauterized by the Lightning."

Cottonmouth nodded. "That's it. We must seek out the loneliness and the darkness. Seek them without fear, because one day soon the Lightning Birds will come looking for us. We must be ready. When they soar down, we must each be standing in the midst of our own woundedness, in that lonely darkness—waiting for them." He lifted his hands to the rainy heavens.

When he lowered his hands and bowed his head, the elders seemed to take it as a familiar signal. They rose, quietly gathered up their mats, and walked away, murmuring in awe to each other. Alder and Basketmaker waited until the others had gone, then they went forward and spoke softly to Cottonmouth, touching him gently on the shoulders, praising him. The awe in their voices sickened Diver. Finally, they, too, left.

Diver watched them go, their colored blankets whipping about them in the wind. The further they went from Cottonmouth, the more animated their voices became, brimming with excitement, longing for the Lightning Birds to soar down and carry them away from this wicked world to a better one beyond the stars.

Fools. Every one of them.

Cottonmouth took a deep breath and slowly returned to Diver's shelter. He knelt by the southeastern pole and braced his forearms on his thighs. His eyes were downcast, frowning thoughtfully at the white sand which blew around his sandals. The grains shished across the mats, mixing with the clicking anemone spines on Cottonmouth's tunic, the rush of waves and the whistling wind to create a soft music.

"Why are you doing this to me?"

Cottonmouth looked up. "The end of the world is close, Diver. A matter of days. That's all." He narrowed his eyes at the sky. "This storm is the beginning. Storm Girl is cleansing the world for the arrival of Hurricane Breather. She is preparing the way."

Diver just closed his eyes.

"The Lightning Birds are coming. They will rescue you, too, if you will only—"

"I thought you said that Hurricane Breather destroyed all the light, including the Lightning Birds?"

"He does. But only after my followers have been safely delivered to the new world. Then Hurricane Breather completely consumes this old world."

"I see." Diver opened his eyes. Cottonmouth stared up at him. "But I do not wish to enter a new world with you and your followers, Cottonmouth. I can imagine nothing more horrifying than spending eternity with such fools."

Cottonmouth slowly rose to his feet and came to stand a hand's breadth from Diver. His eyes resembled winter lakes in the far north, cold and glazed. He seemed to be studying the blood trails on Diver's cheeks. No expression moved his face. Then his mouth widened a little, but it could not really be called a smile.

Cottonmouth reached up and touched the vine across Diver's forehead. Diver flinched—the thorns had bitten deeply—but his gaze never left Cottonmouth.

Dawn's translucent gleam sheathed Cottonmouth's hands as he raised them and placed them on either side of Diver's head, gripping it tightly, driving the thorns deeper. Diver clamped his jaw to stifle the cry in his throat.

"Yes," Cottonmouth whispered, as he probed Diver's eyes. "She is coming."

"Who?"

"Our lover. I can see her soul moving through the forests in your eyes." Cottonmouth straightened up. "And she has the Lightning Boy with her. Just as I knew she would."

He dropped his hands, and walked away.

Diver shouted, "Wait! Cottonmouth, cut me down! What purpose does this serve? *Cottonmouth!*"

But the man's steps never faltered, never veered from their straight course across the village.

Diver saw Cottonmouth enter his shelter and pick up the turtle bone doll. Its white body glowed in the soft rays of morning.

Twenty-four

Lavender light penetrated the heavy fog, announcing the arrival of dawn, but Moonsnail paid it little attention. She and the other members of the Council of Spirit Elders had been up and engaged in debate for more than a hand of time already. Floating Stick sat to her left, his gnarled old hands extended to the warmth of the crackling fire. His hooked nose and sparse white hair glimmered with mist. Directly across the fire from Moonsnail, Tailfeather sat beside Kelp. The War Leader's triangular face with its flat nose could have been carved from wood, so little emotion did it show—despite the desperate topic of discussion. Kelp sat next to Tailfeather, her head down, as was appropriate. She was present only because she slept here. She was not, however, allowed to speak. To Moonsnail's right, Rivercobble huddled under a blanket with her twin sister, Sun Hawk. Because of their extreme old ages, eight tens of summers, Moonsnail rarely called them to meet, unless the situation required the full council's attention. The twins resembled skeletons more than living humans. They had no teeth, and only a few wisps of gray hair dotted their ancient heads. Their muscles had vanished long ago, leaving nearly transparent skin clinging to their bones. Their arms and legs looked like knobby sticks, and their faces were as gaunt as a corpse's. Huge black eyes stared out from sunken eye sockets.

Moonsnail added another branch to the fire. Flames leaped and spat out sparks which wafted leisurely for the rafters. The fog had grown so thick she could not see to the next shelter thirty hands away, though sounds carried—people cooking breakfast, children speaking softly, a dog growling—and so did the delicious odors of roasting opossum and bottle gourds.

Floating Stick lowered his hands to grip his knees and turned to Tailfeather. "Did Dogtooth say how many people were killed at Windy Cove?"

The nostrils of Tailfeather's flat nose flared. "No. Though he described the scene he saw in his Dream. He said that dead scattered the entire village, mostly mothers, children, and the elderly. But he said he saw several warriors, too."

Floating Stick shook his head. "I recall Seedpod telling me they only had ten-and-one warriors left. If even a few were killed in the attack . . ." His mouth hung open, not wishing to finish the statement.

Rivercobble did it for him. "They are defenseless. We must assume that."

Sun Hawk's head shook in a frail nod. "Yes. Our new relatives need our help. We must decide what to do."

Moonsnail saw Kelp squeeze her eyes closed and bite her lip, undoubtedly worrying about her brother. She had tied her long black hair with a cord, but strands had escaped and hung damply around her cheeks. The blanket snugged over her narrow shoulders had belonged to Pondwader. In fact, he had designed the red and blue geometric pattern. Kelp clutched the blanket as if it represented her last link with her best friend. Moonsnail felt sorry for her. She herself had been unable to sleep last night for worrying about Pondwader. Moonsnail knew as well as Kelp that he would have been almost helpless in a battle with skilled warriors, and feared the worst.

"Did Dogtooth say anything about Musselwhite, Seedpod, or Pondwader?" Moonsnail asked.

Tailfeather hesitated, and Moonsnail's jaw clenched, anticipating his answer. His hesitation could only be because he feared their responses, and had been carefully laying the foundation for his news.

"Well?" Floating Stick demanded. "Did he?"

Tailfeather grimaced. "Yes, but it did not make much sense to me, Spirit Elders. Dogtooth can be . . . exasperating."

Rivercobble chuckled, sounding like a branch creaking in a gale. Her toothless mouth spread in a smile. "We all know this to be true," she said. "After all, we have known Dogtooth for five tens of summers. Now, what did he say? Perhaps we will understand. We have had much more practice at deciphering his confusing babble than you, War Leader."

"Yes, Elder," Tailfeather said with a nod. "Well, it was a curious situation. We were sitting around his fire, eating clams, when he suddenly turned to me and blurted, 'Did I tell you about Musselwhite?' I said 'no,' and his eyes widened. He leaned toward me and whispered, in that . . . bizarre . . . manner he has"—Tailfeather's mouth puckered distastefully—"he whispered, 'Musselwhite streaked through those warriors like a Lightning Bird, but not like the one inside Pondwader, that one is too young yet to streak about at all.' " Tailfeather gestured his irritation. Moonsnail caught Kelp's startled expression before her granddaughter glanced up, saw Moonsnail watching, and forced her face to go blank. Moonsnail lifted a brow, but let it go . . . for now. Tailfeather continued, "I took the first part to mean that Musselwhite was there, and that she had fought bravely in the battle . . . but I did not know what to think of the rest." Tailfeather glanced from elder to elder, hoping one of them understood. Curtains of mist wavered behind him, resembling tiptoeing ghosts. Drops had condensed on the rafters and began to drip. The fire hissed in protest.

Sun Hawk said, "I assume you are correct about Musselwhite's actions, but as for the rest, I have no idea what Dogtooth meant. Do you, Moonsnail?"

All eyes turned to peer inquisitively at Moonsnail. She shrugged. "None. Dogtooth's words about Pondwader are completely meaningless to me—" she paused briefly to watch the red creeping up Kelp's cheeks "—but if Musselwhite was present at the battle, she killed as many as she could. Of that, we may be certain. If Cottonmouth sent those warriors, he will be even more angry when he hears of his losses. He is sure to hunt down Musselwhite, and any of her relatives—"

"If she survived," Floating Stick said softly. He had fixed his gaze on his sandals, perhaps not wishing to see their expressions when he uttered the words.

Rivercobble and Sun Hawk leaned their heads together and whispered softly, worriedly. No one who knew Musselwhite, or her reputation, would find such a thing easy to believe. She had worked so many miracles in the past, gotten out of so many impossible situations, how could she fail now? *Just because she is over four tens of summers, has borne twelve children, and has just suffered devastating losses which certainly must have left her weak and lost inside . . .* Moonsnail's souls went cold.

"Yes," Tailfeather agreed. "If she did. As I mentioned, Dogtooth said that there were so many enemy warriors he could not count them. If Musselwhite ran head-to-head with three or four tens of warriors, survival would be unlikely."

"Hallowed Shining People," Moonsnail whispered.

If Musselwhite had been killed, Pondwader's chances dropped to almost zero. Moonsnail's souls recited the litany of possibilities: Perhaps Seedpod had been able to protect her grandson; maybe Musselwhite had ordered Pondwader to hide in the forest; maybe those warriors had fled at the sight of a Lightning Boy and left him unharmed; and maybe Pondwader was dead, along with everybody else at Windy Cove.

The sudden thought jarred her. "Tailfeather," Moonsnail asked, "did Dogtooth see any survivors? Anyone at all? How did his Dream end?"

Floating Stick turned anxiously. "Yes, you haven't said. What was the rest of Dogtooth's Dream?"

Kelp seemed to be holding her breath. Her dark eyes fastened on Tailfeather's triangular face. Rivercobble and Sun Hawk had drawn their blanket tightly closed over their frail old chests, and listened quietly. Perhaps at their ages, it required too much energy to get upset—or maybe, after what they had witnessed in their long lives, little could surprise them.

"Again," Tailfeather said, gesturing awkwardly with his hand. "His words were meaningless to me. He spoke about 'a little boy turning into Badger and hiding in a badger hole,' and said that 'people became spiders and crept through the forest hidden in the shadows.' Things like that. I am sorry that I can't recall more of his words, but they bewildered me so much that I—"

"We know," Floating Stick said with a sigh, "Dogtooth bewilders everyone. He always has." Then he turned to peer at Moonsnail. "But I think all of his talk about 'hiding' means that people did escape. That some of the villagers managed to run into the forest and conceal themselves from the enemy warriors. What do you think?"

Moonsnail frowned. "It sounds reasonable. Rivercobble? Sun Hawk?"

Both old women nodded. Sun Hawk sucked thoughtfully on her lower lip for a time, then said, "Someone almost always survives. We would be shirking our duties to our new relatives if we just assume no one could have."

"Yes," Rivercobble added. "We would, and it would be unforgivable. Even if only one child survived, that baby is frightened, and hungry, and needs us badly right now."

Moonsnail turned when Floating Stick exhaled hard. The old man had hunched forward, resting his chin on his drawn-up knees. He appeared disheartened, but determined. Moonsnail said, "What are you thinking, Floating Stick?"

He replied, "I was wondering how many warriors we should send ahead. Four tens? Or more?"

Moonsnail's lips tightened into a bloodless line. She held her comments, waiting to see if anyone would object. When no one did, she asked, "Are we agreed, then? That we should dispatch a war party to seek out survivors and escort them to the new village site?"

Nods went all the way around the circle.

Tailfeather lifted a hand. His jaw moved as he ground his teeth. "May I suggest that we keep at least half our warriors to protect our own clan? Walking with loaded packs and shepherding children is hard enough. Our people should not also have to worry about being vulnerable to enemy raiders."

Sun Hawk lifted her head, and the sagging wrinkles on her skinny neck refolded themselves. Her gray hair bore a shimmering net of mist. "This is wise. Shouldn't two tens of warriors be adequate to protect survivors? Windy Cove did not have many members left before the attack. After it, they will be lucky to have two tens total, and most will probably be women and children."

"Let us send three tens," Floating Stick said. His face had gone grim. "At least three tens. That will leave half of our warriors with Heartwood for the journey north, as Tailfeather recommends. We should be safe, and they might need—"

"Three tens is too many," Rivercobble argued. "Even if two tens survived the attack at Windy Cove, which seems high given their previous numbers, they will not need so many of our warriors as escorts."

"But I really think—!" Floating Stick began.

Moonsnail cut him off. "Let us compromise. Can we all agree that two-tens-and-five should be sufficient?"

"I could agree with that," Rivercobble said.

"I also," Sun Hawk added.

Moonsnail turned to Floating Stick. He looked sullen, as though worried enough to go on the war walk himself, despite the constant ache in his joints. "And you, Floating Stick?" she pressed. "What do you say?"

A somber nod moved his head. "Very well. I wish it could be more, but two-tens-and-five will have to do. We should make certain that our warriors carry enough extra food and fresh water to help our relatives if any of them are injured—which is likely, given the things Dogtooth said."

"We cannot carry much extra," Tailfeather cautioned, "or we will be too burdened to fight if—"

"A little extra will not hurt you or your warriors!" Floating Stick snapped.

The anguish in his tone made Moonsnail's stomach muscles contract. Floating Stick had been on enough war walks in his life to know the desperation of survivors, the terror, the running, and the hiding, the inability to hunt or fish for fear of being seen by pursuers. She could almost see the painful memories reflected on his eyes' soul. His fists had clenched.

Tailfeather bowed his head respectfully. "Yes, Spirit Elder. We will carry whatever amount you believe is necessary."

Floating Stick gripped Tailfeather by the arm. "Forgive me, War Leader. Your warriors must be free to fight. That is their first duty. But just a little food and water. That's all. For the sake of the children. They are sure to be hungry."

Rivercobble said, "Floating Stick is right. For the children. Take extra supplies."

Sun Hawk nodded and looked to Moonsnail for the final vote. "What do you say, Moonsnail?"

"Yes, yes, of course," she replied. "Now, when should the warriors leave?"

"Now!" Floating Stick blurted. "As soon as they can be ready! The survivors will be desperate."

Moonsnail saw Rivercobble and Sun Hawk nod in assent, and she said, "Tailfeather, assemble your warriors. Be prepared to leave immediately."

"Yes, Elder." He rose, bowed to each of the elders, and left at a trot, disappearing into the waving veils of fog. As Sun Mother climbed higher in the sky, a pale yellow glow was beginning to permeate them.

Floating Stick rose to help Rivercobble and Sun Hawk to their feet. They stood in a small circle gazing seriously at each other, no one saying a word, until Sun Hawk observed, "It may not be wise for us to move our village. Not now. Not after what happened to Windy Cove. We must think more of this."

Moonsnail nodded. "Yes. If only a few people survived the attack, there is no point in combining villages, since they have none. It might be more prudent to just adopt their survivors into our own clan."

"The problem," Floating Stick noted, "is that we have no way of knowing the number of survivors until we see them—and we promised Seedpod we would meet him at Manatee Lagoon. I think we should keep our promise."

Sun Hawk's wrinkled face rearranged into distressed lines. "Yes, I must agree with Floating Stick. We promised. Either our word is good, or it is not."

Moonsnail and Rivercobble exchanged looks, reading the other's expression. They both nodded at the same time.

Moonsnail said, "Very well. Let us get on with the move then."

The other Spirit Elders left and made their way through the mist toward their own shelters. Moonsnail could hear their soft conversations for some time after they had gone. Fog swirled in their wakes, twisting and turning as if Dancing.

Kelp rose to her feet and stood stiffly, her chin up.

"What?" Moonsnail asked.

Kelp stepped forward, walking wide around the fire and coming to a halt in front of Moonsnail. Her young face wore a resolute expression.

"Grandmother," she said. "I wish to accompany our warriors on the war walk. I am—"

"I need you here!"

Kelp took Moonsnail's hand and held it tightly. "There are many other people to help you, Grandmother, and I am good with an atlatl. You know I am. I must do this. Please don't tell me 'no.' Pondwader . . ." Tears filled her eyes, but she sternly blinked them back and looked at Moonsnail again. "The day we went to the Sacred Pond to meet Dogtooth, Pondwader told me something, in secret. I promised not to tell anyone, but I don't think he would mind now."

A queasy flutter invaded Moonsnail's chest. "What? Tell me."

Fog had slicked wet black hair down Kelp's cheeks, framing her short pointed nose and large eyes. She smelled of the palm-berry cakes she had made for the council meeting. She said, "Pondwader told me that for about a moon he had been feeling strangely, as if something were being born inside him. The way he put it was 'like thunder waking up.' He . . ." She hesitated.

Moonsnail squeezed Kelp's hand hard. "Go on."

"He said that a faint roaring had started in his chest, and that sometimes, in the middle of that roar, he heard my voice. Mine, Grandmother. Pondwader said he knew I was trying to warn him."

"Warn him about what?" Moonsnail shook Kelp's hands, urging her to hurry.

"He didn't know, Grandmother. But he said, 'I need you, Kelp. I think I need you very badly.' I didn't understand then. But I do now. I believe he needs me there with him *now*."

They gazed deeply into each other's eyes, and Moonsnail saw Kelp's fear and her utter devotion to her brother. "What else?" Moonsnail said. "You are holding something back. I can feel it. Tell me!"

Kelp wet her lips. "Grandmother . . . Dogtooth's Dream? Those crazy things he said about Pondwader?"

"What about them?"

Kelp gently pulled her hands back and wiped her moist palms on the skirt of her tunic. Fog rolled through the shelter, cold, borne on a chilling breath of wind, and the thatched roof shished and thumped. Moonsnail rubbed her arms briskly to warm them.

In a low voice, Kelp said, "Pondwader told me that he heard a voice inside him, and I thought . . . that is, he didn't really say so, but I took it to mean that it was the voice of a Lightning Bird."

Moonsnail just stared.

Kelp rushed to add, "Don't ask me what it means, Grandmother, because I don't know. Pondwader got married and was gone so quickly, I never had a chance to ask him to explain."

Moonsnail irritably waved the words away, struggling to think. She had heard many strange things in her time, and most of them had come from Dogtooth's mouth, but this . . . Thunder waking up? A Lightning Bird inside Pondwader? How did these things fit with the legends about a Lightning Boy shooting down the Shining Eagles and unleashing the end of the world? She shook her head. If they fit at all, she did not see how. Moonsnail felt the sudden urge to run all the way to Manatee Lagoon and hold Dogtooth at dart point until he told her. Providing he knew. Often, his Dreams came in fragments, a bit now, and another bit later. His Dreams had frustrated the Council of Spirit Elders for tens of summers. Often it took moons to piece together the old lunatic's Dreams, so they could make sense out of them.

Kelp reached out and touched Moonsnail's shoulder. "Grandmother? Please. Pondwader needs me. I don't know why. But he does. I must go on this war walk with Tailfeather."

"Kelp, you are a child! You are not even a woman yet! How can I send you out into the world? And on war walk! If I do that to my granddaughter, when I get to the Daybreak Land the ancestors will flay me and feed my souls to the dogs!"

Kelp's face fell. She tried to smile. Her hand slowly slid down Moonsnail's arm, in a loving, forgiving gesture, and it broke Moonsnail's heart.

Kelp turned away and went to stand over the fire. She shivered. Softly, she said, "If he dies, Grandmother, I'll never be able to look at my soul again."

Moonsnail closed her eyes, fighting with herself. So much danger lay ahead. None of them knew what tomorrow might bring. And her grand-daughter, the last and most precious thing left to her, wanted to run away with her brother.

Moonsnail opened her eyes.

Kelp had not moved. She looked forlorn.

"Go, Kelp. Go on."

Kelp jerked her head up and hope filled her eyes. "You mean it? I can go?"

"Hurry. Get your things together, and join Tailfeather. Go quickly . . . ! Before I think about how much I love you and come to my senses!"

Kelp bounded across the floor, hugged Moonsnail so hard it drove the air from her lungs, then ran for her pack and began stuffing it full.

Moonsnail's old mouth trembled. She watched Kelp through blurry eyes.

Swaying tree shadows dappled Seedpod's face as he waded into the cool water of the Sacred Pond and stood with his hands folded, watching Black Urchin carry Ashleaf's frail old body. The warrior took slow, reverent steps. The people made a path for him as he passed. Out of respect, they had waited until the last to bury Ashleaf. For more than six-tens-and-three summers, he had guided, supported, and loved the clan. Ashleaf's death hurt Seedpod more than all the others. He and Ashleaf had grown up together, played as boys, fought over the same women as young men, and guarded each other's backs as warriors. The war walks had turned them into fast friends. Then, after they had been elected to the Council of Spirit Elders, they had worked, and thought, and prayed together to keep Windy Cove strong.

. . . And failed. They had failed.

The pitiful remnants of Windy Cove stood on the bank: four women, seven children, and six men. Everyone had dressed in their brightest tunics. Brilliant scarlets, dark greens, and magnificent blues shone in the pale lances of sunlight that streamed down through the thin layer of clouds. The pungent scents of peat and damp forest floor filled his nose. Seedpod inhaled deeply to help steady himself. All morning long, he'd been living in the fabric of his souls, hearing Ashleaf's laughter, feeling his friend's affectionate hand on his shoulder, and seeing the old man's sparkling eyes. He could not imagine what the world would be like without Ashleaf's warmth and humor. Except that it would be a much colder place. . . .

Diamondback and Thorny Boy stood to his far right, in a thick pile of autumn leaves. The gnarled branches of an ancient oak tree twisted above their heads. Both had worn red, the color of life, and Diamondback stood braced on a walking stick. Sweat dotted his forehead—an indication of his pain—and the fresh bandage around his leg had gone crimson with blood.

He should not have come. The walk to the Pond, though short, had left him weak and trembling, and he would need every bit of his strength for the journey to Manatee Lagoon. But the youth had pleaded to come. These were his beloved relatives, too, he said. He wanted to be present when they entered the portal to the afterworld. Reluctantly, Seedpod had given in.

Black Urchin stepped into the water, and waded toward Seedpod, taking great care to step around the other burial frames they had lain that morning. Before dawn, they had dressed Ashleaf in his finest tunic and favorite hood, then placed his most precious possessions around him, things he would need in the Village of Wounded Souls—his atlatl with the antler-tine hook, two clamshell scrapers, a wolf tooth glued onto a haft with pine pitch, for holing leather, a hairbrush made from palm bark tied in a bundle with cord and evened off by burning, and two dog-ulna awls. After his possessions had been carefully arranged, the clan had flexed his knees, then wrapped him in three warm blankets. Still, the bundle Black Urchin carried looked small and light.

Black Urchin knelt in the water and gently laid Ashleaf's blanket-wrapped body down, then Seedpod unslung the bag of fire-sharpened stakes from his shoulder and knelt on the opposite side from Black Urchin.

"Let us immerse him," Seedpod murmured, and together he and Black Urchin placed their hands on Ashleaf and sank his body beneath the pale green water, making certain he lay on his left side with his head pointed west and his face looking northward, down the tunnel he would have to swim to reach the Village of Wounded Souls. People moved closer, to the very edge of the Sacred Pond, peering down with tears in their eyes. Two women wept openly, and several children whimpered.

Seedpod opened his bag and removed about two tens of stakes. He handed half of them to Black Urchin, and said, "I will do the south half if you will lay the north half."

"Yes, Elder," the short, stocky warrior replied. His dark brows knitted as he began the process of staking Ashleaf down.

It required little effort. The bottom of the Pond was so soft, and the stakes so sharp, that all Seedpod had to do was work his stake through the edge of the outermost blanket, then drive it into the sticky peat. When he and Black Urchin had finished, a rough circle of stakes framed Ashleaf's body.

Seedpod stood and faced north, toward the crowd. "Let us Sing him to the afterworld," Seedpod said quietly and lifted his voice in the Death Song:

> *I have come with living waters,*
> *To give these healing ways of the Wolves,*
>   *these healing ways of the living water Wolves.*
> *Look northward now, Ashleaf,*
>   *down the pathway of living waters to the*

Wolves in the Village of Wounded Souls.
Hear them call you?
  They are calling you, Ashleaf.
  calling, calling.
Your Spirit Helper was Otter,
  Wait for Otter,
  He will show you the way.
  Wait for Otter,
  Wait for Otter,
He will show you the way
  through the living waters
  to the village of living water Wolves.

One last time, Seedpod bent down and placed his hand on his good friend's shoulder, then he rose and waded out of the Sacred Pond. The soaked hem of his tunic felt as heavy as stone.

People followed him down the curving trail that led back to Windy Cove through the palmettos. Fronds slashed at his legs as he hurried past, and when an eagle cried, Seedpod looked up to watch it circling against the background of wispy clouds, its white head and tail shimmering like polished shell in the sunlight. When he broke from the trees and headed out across the white sandy beach toward the shelters, his steps faltered.

On the eastern horizon, thunderheads billowed high into the sky, and stretched long black arms northward. A huge flock of Lightning Birds soared through the clouds, burning them pale blue, then bright white. Very faintly, Seedpod could hear their thundering voices echoing over the soft roar of the surf.

Black Urchin stopped beside him and his brows plunged down. "Blessed Spirits," he whispered. "Storm Girl looks angry."

"Yes," Seedpod murmured.

"Perhaps we should stay in our shelters here until the weather clears, then head south to Manatee Lagoon?"

A curious tingling grew in Seedpod's belly, and he felt suddenly frantic, wanting to be away from here now, this instant. He couldn't explain it. But the longer he gazed upon those clouds, the more urgent the feeling became.

Thorny Boy trotted up and hugged Seedpod's leg. Distractedly, he lowered a hand to smooth the boy's tangled black hair. They all frowned out at the building storm.

"No," Seedpod said. "No, I think we should head south this afternoon. As soon as we can."

Twenty-five

Cottonmouth tossed and turned, shoving at his sweat-drenched blanket, reaching for a woman who was not there, who had not been there for two-tens-and-six summers. The dream hurled itself at him from the darkness of the past, and he saw her as clearly as he had that day so long ago. Beautiful, heartbreakingly young, crying.

"*Musselwhite!*" he shouted, as he ran through the forest behind her. His voice echoed from the palms and oaks. "Musselwhite, please. Don't do this! Stop!"

Distorted, monstrous images flared and died. He fought them, but still they came. . . .

He ran wildly, slapping fronds and vines out of his way. She was so fast. On the flats, he could outrun her, but in the forest, her long legs and her greater agility combined to make her almost impossible to catch. White fragrant dogwood petals fluttered around him as he burst through a copse of saplings, leaped a fallen log, and headed on down the deer trail. He caught sight of her, hugging Glade tightly against her breast, as she veered off to the left. He ran harder, his lungs panting.

"*Musselwhite!*" he screamed. "Musselwhite, listen to me! Stop this madness!"

She shouted, "Leave me alone, Cottonmouth. Leave me alone! I must . . ." Her voice faded as she disappeared into the spring leaves and newly budded brush. Limbs clattered in her wake.

Terror had held them both by the throats for days as Glade grew weaker and weaker. But she had been frantic, and so desperate he feared what she might do to herself in punishment. She blamed herself for Glade's fever. She had taken their son with her when she'd gone to tend a sick friend. Though Cottonmouth had asked her not to, she'd done it anyway. Then, three days later, the evil spirits had hatched in his chest. Musselwhite had been insane with worry, cursing herself, rocking Glade in her arms. Glade's fever had soared, and on the fourth day Glade had smiled at her, his little mouth moving feebly as he blinked his fever-bright eyes. He had reached out, murmured, *Mother,* and Musselwhite had clutched him to her as if she would never let go, promising, "Don't worry, baby. Everything will be all right. I love you, Glade. I love you so much."

Cottonmouth's souls wrenched. That had been ten-and-eight days ago. For some time after Glade had fallen into the coma, Cottonmouth had been too angry with Musselwhite, and too frightened to do anything but wallow in his own grief. He had been so absorbed remembering Glade's joyous laughter, and the love in his son's eyes, that it had never occurred to Cottonmouth that she, too, might be remembering, and with despair as great as his own.

He veered left, and pounded down the same palmetto-choked trail she'd taken. Fronds slashed at his bare legs. He burst out of the forest into a clearing where a small pond glinted green in the afternoon sunlight. The shadows of swaying oak boughs mottled the surface, and tender shoots of reed and water lily ringed the edges. Musselwhite stood in the middle of the pond, crying against Glade's chest. Soft, pitiable cries. His little head fell limply over her arm, his mouth ajar. The turtle bone doll lay tucked into the collar of Glade's tunic.

Cottonmouth halted, breathing hard. When she turned, her hollow eyes gazed upon Cottonmouth as if he were a stranger. He walked forward slowly, his sandals silent in the wet grass. "Musselwhite? Come home. Bring Glade home."

She rubbed her cheek against Glade's. "No. I must bury him."

Cottonmouth moved to the edge of the water. "In a pond? But Glade should go to the Daybreak Land, not—"

"I'll be going to the Village of Wounded Souls, Cottonmouth! So will you. I want Glade to . . . to be there when I arrive. I must see him again. I *must.*"

His heart ached. "He's not gone, Musselwhite. Not yet. *Please,* bring our son home. We will find a way to wake him up. I promise you. I promise you, we will find a way."

"He *is* gone," she'd choked out. "His body may be alive, but his souls have come unbraided. We must bury him before his souls flee and get lost! I don't want our son wandering the earth forever! Alone." She began sobbing again and clutched Glade's limp body against her. "He needs us to help him. To . . . to leave this world."

"Listen to me, please," Cottonmouth said softly as he waded into the cool water. It came up to his knees. Each of his steps sent out bobbing silver rings. Gently, he wrapped his arms around Musselwhite and pulled her close. She leaned her head against his shoulder, and her long hair fell down his side like a curtain of midnight-colored silk.

"I'm sorry," she wept. "I'm so sorry."

The sound of her tortured voice made every muscle in his body go stiff. He held her tightly, with Glade's thin body pressed between them. "It wasn't your fault. Don't blame yourself. Many other children in the village are ill. The evil Spirits would have entered Glade anyway. We must find a way of casting them out. Let's take Glade home," he whispered. "We will find a way of driving the evil Spirits out and weaving Glade's souls together again."

"How? How can we?"

He kissed her hair, and said, "I don't know. But I'll find a way. *I will.*"

The dream shifted.

Images swirled, filled with faces, terrifying, like being caught in a huge whirlpool, and sucked down, down. . . .

Sunrise. He'd been running all night. The pearlescent rays of dawn streamed through the trees, glimmering from the shallow water before him. A chill moss-scented breeze snaked about the swamp. Bright Feather hobbled about his shelter, shaking his bony fist and bellowing angrily. Little more than skin and rags and bulging eyes, he appeared to be ten tens of summers old. His freckled scalp held only a few wisps of white hair, and his lips sank inward over toothless gums.

Cottonmouth glanced around to see what offended the old man, but saw only swamp bays filled with birds, and three small alligators sunning themselves on the opposite bank.

"Fly away! Go on!" the old man yelled at the empty air. "How many times do I have to chase you off?"

His face was a sagging mass of wrinkles, but when he turned, his black eyes glinted with an inhuman light. He scratched his side and squinted at Cottonmouth as he hobbled to a folded pile of blankets on the south side of his shelter, and slumped down. Waving a hand he said, "Come in. The Spirit hawks won't bother you. They're after me! Besides, they are all cowards. They come soaring down like they own the world, and drive humans crazy with their constant squealing and swooping." Sharply, he ordered, "I told you to come in! Now do it! What do you wish this time, Cottonmouth? Another love charm? Or something else?"

Cottonmouth warily advanced and knelt in the grass just outside the shelter, studying the sky for any sign of the Spirit hawks. He feared this ancient witch, and felt no shame at showing it. "No, Bright Feather. This time I need more. Much more. I am willing to pay you anything you wish."

"Anything?" the old man said as he groaned himself into a more comfortable position, his stick-like legs extended. "Well, this must be important to you, then. Tell me about it."

"My son is dying. . . ."

Memories tumbled, coming close and fading away. Fragments of scenes, of dialogue, flashed. Colors spun a sickening rainbow of shades. . . .

"*I have breathed special Spirit Power into this awl,*" the old man said as he leaned forward to peer into Cottonmouth's eyes. "Take it. Give it to your wife. Do not tell her what it is for. It must have time to absorb part of her souls, too. Yours, hers, and the boy's. Then, after you have captured your victim, and laid your sick son on his chest, use this awl to kill the man. His souls will seep up through the awl and flow into your little son."

"The awl will give my son life again?"

Bright Feather's gaze impaled him; it made Cottonmouth squirm, like a lance embedded in his stomach and twisted slowly.

In a hoarse whisper, the old man said, "This awl came from the most dreaded Power Bundle in the world. The Raven Bundle. It was handed down from Soul Dancer to Soul Dancer over tens of tens of tens of summers. Many people gave their very lives to protect it." He turned the awl in his hands and wonder slackened his wrinkled face. "Sometimes, it Sings to me. Songs about ice walls and Monster Children fighting in the sky. It Sings in a voice so beautiful and fierce, it is unimaginable."

Cottonmouth sat staring at the awl. It bore a brown patina from the tens of hands that had held it. "If it's so precious, how did you get it?" he bravely asked.

Bright Feather smiled toothlessly. "I killed the man who owned it." He held out the awl.

"If you wanted it so badly then, why would you be willing to give it to me now? What is your price?"

"Nothing. Take it."

"W-why?"

That toothless smile metamorphosed into a terrifying grimace. His eyes bulged until Cottonmouth feared they might pop from their sockets. Bright Feather glanced around, then whispered, "It's driving me mad. The awl hates me. It told me so. Take it. Take it, I say!"

Cottonmouth's fear rose so strongly, he almost woke. With a shaking hand, he reached for the awl . . . and knocked over the gourd of water he kept by his bedding. The splash of cold across his arm roused him with a start. He sucked in a breath and stared wide-eyed at the night. Pitch blackness met his searching eyes. Not a shred of light illumined the world. Clouds must have moved in.

Cottonmouth sat up and rubbed his throbbing temples. The basket with the turtle bone doll and awl sat near the foot of his bed. He could just make out its squat shape, blacker than the darkness.

He'd given the awl to Musselwhite as a gift. She'd etched her mark into it. The next day he'd told her of his plan, hoping it would ease the pain in her eyes. Instead, a wild animal-like terror had filled her. She hated Spirit Power. It terrified her. They had argued violently. To stop him from trying to bring Glade to life again, she had plunged the awl into their little son's heart.

And in that single instant, all his dreams, all his hopes had died.

He'd gone mad . . . tried to kill his wife . . . then her family.

He'd wanted to die himself.

He had succeeded only in destroying his own precious world.

Cottonmouth inhaled deeply of the wet scents of the night. Tired to the bone, he clumsily reached down for the basket and drew out the turtle bone doll. The doll had always comforted him . . . he felt certain that she had wanted Glade to live again, too.

Clutching the doll to his chest, Cottonmouth stretched out on his back and stared sightlessly at the creosote-covered rafters.

Kelp crouched on the outskirts of the warriors' camp, her hands extended to her fire. She had darted a fat squirrel just before sunset, cleaned it, skinned it, and skewered it on a stick. It now roasted over the low flames, smelling sweet and succulent. The other warriors stood four tens of hands away, around a larger fire, laughing, talking, their tall muscular bodies silhouetted against the backdrop of star-spotted sky and frothy gray ocean. The blaze's orange gleam flickered over their faces.

Kelp turned her stick so her squirrel would roast on the other side, and juices dripped down and sizzled on the coals. They had run all day. She had kept up, but every muscle in her body ached from the effort. Their legs were twice as long as hers. Would she be able to match their pace tomorrow? She had to. If things worked as Tailfeather expected, they might find the survivors of Windy Cove Clan by nightfall, and she would see Pondwader. The thought brought a smile to her lips. A brief one. The terrible possibility that he might have been killed had been plaguing her. Perhaps that's when he had needed her—during the raid. Had the fact that she had been sitting safely at home in Heartwood Village doomed her brother?

Kelp untied her blanket from her pack and knotted it around her shoulders against the night's deepening chill. She stared out at the shoreline. Dark waves washed the starlit white sand. A gull fluttered up, squawked, then sailed sideways and vanished out over the water. They had camped on the south side of a small inlet, which meant they had ocean on two sides and open sand behind them. Trees formed a solid black wall to the west. Despite their relatively safe location, Tailfeather had posted six guards to watch over every conceivable route of attack.

Kelp dug into her pack and took out her wooden bowl, then she slid her squirrel off its roasting stick. It plopped into the bowl sizzling. It would be cool soon, though, the cold wind would assure that. She set the bowl before her and sank back on the sand to extend her legs. Her calves hurt. Strands of long black hair blew around her face.

Loneliness taunted her. These men were her people. She had grown up with them, played with them. Yet out here, on this war walk, she sensed resentment. She had never given the other warriors any hint that she might, one day, want to join them. As a result, none took her seriously. They considered her a burden to be ignored. She couldn't go home. Wouldn't go. If Pondwader were alive, he needed her desperately, and nobody in the world could force her to abandon her duty to her brother. . . . Not even if her own clanspeople treated her like an invisible ghost.

The silver shimmer of starlight danced across the sea for as far as she could see.

Someone broke away from the group of warriors and walked toward her. Tall and lean, he'd braided his long hair. It hung over his left shoulder. He wore only a breechclout. Kelp bit her lip as Black Dace crouched on the opposite side of the fire. She hadn't seen him since that day he'd called their mother "a whore who would trade her souls for a clamshell necklace," and fought with Pondwader. Actually, Dace had fought, Pondwader had sort of hunched and swung when he had an opening—and that had not been often. At the age of ten-and-five summers, Dace's broad shoulders bulged with muscles. He'd been one of Pondwader's best friends less than a summer ago. But as they grew older, they seemed to grow apart. Pondwader turned inward, cutting himself off from friends, searching for spiritual things that Kelp didn't really understand, and Dace turned outward, seeking his souls among his peers. Not many moons ago, Kelp had loved Dace almost as much as Pondwader—mostly because Dace had treated her as much like his own little sister as Pondwader's. In the past summer, Dace had blossomed into an extremely handsome boy, with a strong jaw, pointed chin, and a straight nose.

"Good evening, Kelp," he said, a little nervous. "Are you all right?"

"Yes," she answered, surprised. "Why do you ask?"

He shrugged awkwardly. "It was a hard day. My muscles are all aching, and I thought if mine were, you must be in agony."

Kelp reached for her bowl and set it in her lap. "I'll be all right."

Dace studied her as she pulled off one of the squirrel's legs, and lifted it to her mouth. She hesitated, then handed the leg to Dace. "Help me eat this, will you, Dace? It's too much for me."

A smile split his young face. "Gladly." He sat down across the fire and bit into the succulent squirrel. "Um, it's delicious. I didn't see you go hunting. When did you dart this squirrel?"

Kelp tore off another leg and sank her teeth into it. It did taste good. Grease smeared her fingers. "Just before dark. He was standing on his hind legs on a branch, chittering at me. He made too good a target to turn down."

"He must have been fat," Dace said as he wiped his hand in the sand. "This meat is as greasy as an opossum."

Kelp nodded, and wondered why Dace, of all people, would come to join her. They were of the same clan. There could be nothing more than friendship between them. Besides, she wasn't sure she liked him anymore.

Dace saw her discomfort and his smile waned. He finished his squirrel leg and tossed the bones into the fire where they sputtered and charred. He looked up at her from beneath his lashes. "Are you still angry with me?" he asked.

"Angry?"

"For saying what I did about your mother? I'm sorry, Kelp. I should not have called her names." His brows lowered, and he squinted at the flickering red coals.

Kelp tore off one of the squirrel's forelegs and handed it to him. He took it hesitantly, as though wanting to make certain she meant it.

"Does this mean you're not mad at me anymore?"

"Not for calling my mother a whore," she said. She adjusted the blanket around her shoulders where the wind had flipped it back, and tore the last leg from her squirrel. As she bit into it, she said, "My mother is a whore. I was angry with you for beating up my brother."

Dace tilted his head. "Pondwader is not a fighter. I took advantage, and I shouldn't have. I would ask that you forgive me for that, as well. Sometimes I do not think. I just act. I always regret it later."

Kelp peered at him with wide eyes. "Why are you telling me these things, Dace? What difference would it make if I forgave you?"

"I . . ." His mouth hung open. He took another bite of his squirrel and chewed it thoughtfully. Firelight glimmered in the folds of his black braid. "I have always enjoyed your company, Kelp, and now that we are both out on our first war walk together I would like us to be friends again."

Straightforwardly, she said, "Dace, why are you being so nice to me? We are both Heartwood Clan. Related. If you are hoping to—"

"No!" he blurted, eyes wide. "Blessed Brother Sky, no, Kelp. I would never do such a thing. It would be *incest.* I just . . . I am lonely here. None of these men take me seriously. I have no friends—except you. If you wish to be my friend again."

Kelp nodded. "That would be fine with me, I guess."

For a time, they ate in silence, glancing at each other across the fire. Kelp would hand him a piece of the squirrel. He would take it, smiling uncertainly, as if fearing she might suddenly change her mind and jerk it back. This behavior intrigued Kelp. For as long as she could remember, Dace had been Heartwood's most feared bully, perhaps because he had been forced to defend Pondwader so often—and her. Dace had jumped into the middle of Kelp's fights more than once. Not that Dace found that difficult. Even as a little boy, he'd been bigger than everyone else, and seemed to enjoy fighting. Whatever he had wanted, he had taken. He was not a man yet, though he had killed his first bear two summers ago. But this war walk might change that.

That made her think of Pondwader. He was a man by virtue of his marriage—but Kelp wondered if he had been forced to kill during the raid. She hoped not. It would have broken Pondwader's heart.

"Are you scared, Kelp?"

"Scared?" She wiped her greasy hand in the sand. "Of what?"

"Of being on a war walk? I mean, we may run into Cottonmouth's warriors." His eyes tightened when he looked at her, and she could see that fear gnawed at him, though he didn't wish to say so. His dark brows slanted down over his straight nose.

"Oh," she said with a laugh, "that possibility terrifies me. I'm pretty good with an atlatl, but the idea of casting at a man makes me feel queasy inside."

"But we are warriors," he said so softly that the rhythm of the sea almost drowned out his words. His hands tightened on his piece of squirrel. "We aren't supposed to be afraid. Are we?"

Kelp finished her last bite and tossed the rib cage into the fire. Flames licked up around the bones and black smoke spiraled away in the wind. He had called her a warrior. Included her. Pride tingled in her chest. "I've heard warriors speak of being very much afraid in battles. How could they not be? When an enemy aims his dart at your chest, you are going to be afraid, I don't care how courageous you are."

Dace appeared to be considering that. Finally, he nodded. "Yes, I suppose."

"Are you scared, Dace?"

A thin smile graced his full lips. He whispered, "Petrified, little sister. And there's not a single enemy warrior in sight."

Kelp smiled. "You are on your first war walk. Did you expect to feel safe?"

"Well," he said and cocked his head, "no. But I expected to feel . . . brave. Didn't you?"

Kelp smiled wistfully. "I guess I'm too desperate to worry about being brave."

"Desperate?" he asked. "Why are you desperate?"

Men began to drift away from the central fire, seeking their beds, and the sound of their conversations died. Kelp watched several warriors roll up in their blankets and shove their packs beneath their heads. But Dace remained sitting on the other side of the fire, his eyes fastened on Kelp's face.

"Can't you tell me?" he pressed. "If you can't, I would understand. Some things are not to be shared. I just thought you might—"

"I would like to tell you, Dace," she answered. "But it's late. Everyone is seeking their blankets. We should be sleeping, too. I suspect tomorrow will be even harder on us than today."

Dace got to his feet and awkwardly wiped the sand from his legs. "Would you . . . would you mind if I brought my blanket over here and slept by your fire?" He hastily added, "If you don't wish me to, please say so. I will not feel offended. I realize that I—"

"I would like that, Dace. I've been feeling lonely all day. Having a friend close would make me feel safer."

He smiled broadly. "Thank you. I'll go get my things."

Kelp watched him trot away. His pack, atlatl and darts, nestled beside the dwindling flames of the warriors' fire. Dace had to step around bodies rolled in blankets to get to his belongings. A few men grumbled and rolled over as he tiptoed passed. One man spoke to him, and Kelp heard the gruff words.

"What are doing with that girl?" the man asked. "She will be the death of all of us! Slowing us down, forcing us to watch out for her. Just because she is Moonsnail's granddaughter does not mean we should have to risk our own lives to—"

Dace answered in a curt voice. "What I do is none of your business, Cord. Kelp is . . . is like my sister. It is my concern, not yours."

The man flopped over and covered his head with his blanket.

Dace slung his pack over his left shoulder, gathered his weapons, and headed back toward Kelp.

. . . So that's why he had come over. He'd heard the things the other men were saying about her, and had taken it upon himself to be her friend— despite the fact that they would probably isolate him because of it.

When he knelt on the opposite side of the fire, he smiled, and the firelight gleamed on his straight white teeth.

"Good night, Kelp," he said.

"Good night, Dace. . . . Dace?"

"Yes?"

"Thanks."

"For what, little sister?"

"For . . . for treating me like you used to."

He frowned and began working at the laces on his pack. "I'm just sorry it took me so long, Kelp. I should have apologized long ago. I have missed you. And Pondwader."

Kelp unknotted her blanket, shook it out, and wrapped up in it. As she curled on her side before the fire, she saw Dace lay his atlatl and darts on the sand. He untied his blanket from his pack, and rolled up in it, facing her. His handsome features wavered in the orange glow of the coals.

"Kelp?" he said.

"Hmm?"

"What did you mean about being desperate?"

She pulled her blanket up around her throat. "I'm worried about Pond- wader," she answered. "If Musselwhite was at Windy Cove when it was attacked, Pondwader must have been, too."

Dace's voice came out soft. "I've been worried about him, too."

Twenty-six

Afternoon sunlight slanted through the trees in streaks of pure gold, glaring in Pondwader's eyes as he struggled to follow Musselwhite across the dew-slippery fallen tree trunk that bridged the shallow stream. Birds chirped in the overhanging hickory branches, hopping about to watch them as they passed. His pack kept shifting, which forced Pondwader to scramble to keep from splashing into the water. Musselwhite, however, moved like a stalking cat, her steps sure and silent. She carried her atlatl and darts crossways before her, using them to help her balance. Every time she lowered her foot to the trunk, her gaze cut across the encircling trees, searching.

Pondwader's foot slipped, and he gasped.

Musselwhite whirled, observed his flailing arms, and pinned him with a lethal glare.

Once Pondwader had regained his footing, he whispered, "Sorry."

Her eyes narrowed. For some time, she frowned at the mottled green and gray forest shadows, as if something had disturbed her, but she could not discern what. Finally, she turned around and continued down the trunk at a faster pace. When she reached the end, she quietly stepped off to the swampy ground, and brusquely waved Pondwader toward her.

He slipped and skidded his way until he could jump down beside Musselwhite, breathing hard. "What's wrong?" he whispered.

Only a blur of shadows met his probing gaze. But he did *sense* something, like a predator, sneaking about, observing them. He opened his mouth to mention this to Musselwhite, but she stilled him with an upraised hand.

Barely audible, she said, "Stay here. Hide in that hole made when the tree uprooted itself. Do not make a sound." More harshly, she demanded, "Do you understand? Not one sound."

"Yes, I—I understand."

The hood of his long robe flapped against his back as he trotted around the end and leaped into the scooped-out hollow. When the ancient oak toppled, it had ripped a cavity large enough to hold Pondwader's entire body. He snuggled down, just his eyes showing over the horizon of black dirt, and watched Musselwhite creeping through a tangled weave of hanging moss and grapevines. The yellow leaves on the vines stood out against the darker background of moss and branches.

Pondwader lost sight of Musselwhite and he settled back into his damp hole. She had led them around like the lead doe in a herd of frightened deer, doubling back on their tracks, changing direction frequently, stretching out on their stomachs to watch their backtrail from a different perspective. When he had asked her about this behavior, she had explained that often you could not see a pursuer from a standing position, because trackers deliberately worked to hide their upper bodies, but when you got down on your belly, you could see their feet moving.

They had been on the trail since long before dawn this morning, and exhaustion weighted Pondwader like a cape of stone. His body ached for sleep and food. Worse, guilt ate him. He was slowing her down, and she continually let him know it—a sharp glance, an irritated wave of her hand, a deep-throated growl when he stumbled or stopped to dip up a handful of water. But he understood. She *had* to reach Standing Hollow Horn Village in time to save Diver. Which meant she had to get there quickly. Of course Pondwader's presence upset her. He couldn't walk more than three paces without tripping over the hem of his robe. Though he had been trying so very hard. . . .

As he leaned back against the muddy wall, the familiar ache began, like tens of thorns pricking his calves. He grimaced and rubbed his legs.

"Blessed Spirits, I'm tired," he murmured to himself.

The baby Lightning Bird made a new sound now, not the old rumbles and roars. Pondwader couldn't quite define it, but it resembled the high-pitched crackle of lightning flashing right overhead, except that the crackle whispered to him—almost words—but no matter how hard he concentrated, he could not understand. And with every crackle, Pondwader sensed something crawling in his veins, like . . . like swarms of tiny biting ants.

Above him, to his left, Pondwader heard the splashing of turtles as they dove into the shallow stream, followed by a sparrow's indignant chirp.

He stopped breathing.

He listened.

What had frightened the animals? It might have been anything. The shadow of a passing hawk, an alligator . . .

Something groaned.

The first time he heard it, he told himself it could not be a heavy foot placed hastily in the deadfall.

The second time, he decided it had to be wind in the trees, and squinted at the swaying branches.

The third time, he sank into his hole, panting.

"Lightning Boy?"

Pondwader's insides shriveled. He did not recognize that hushed voice. Another groan, closer.

Sweat soaked the robe beneath Pondwader's arms, and beaded on his pointed nose. He'd started breathing like a hunted fox.

"I'm not going to hurt you," the man said. *"I heard you talking to yourself, and came to see you. You can come out."*

If he had been able to, Pondwader would have turned himself into dirt and melted into the ground. The panicked urge to run filled him. He silently squirmed into a crouch, preparing to bolt.

"Come out!" the man ordered, still in a hoarse whisper. *"If you don't stand up, by the Shining People, I'll—"*

"All right," Pondwader answered. "D-don't hurt me!"

It took a few moments to convince his shaking legs to hold him, but when he'd done it, he slowly rose to his feet. Just as his eyes cleared the hole, he saw the warrior, crouching much closer than Pondwader had expected, a stiletto in his left hand. His right arm had been injured. Filthy, blood-encrusted rags wrapped the wound. The man's eyes widened when he saw Pondwader. He stood up.

"Please!" Pondwader pleaded. "Don't—"

At the sound of Pondwader's voice, the forest seemed to explode. Musselwhite lunged from the trees, her atlatl raised.

"No!" the unknown man cried and dove, trying to escape as she cast her dart, but it caught him low in the back, flinging him to the ground with a dull thud. Blood splashed the trunk of the pine beside him. The man managed to grab onto the tree and pull himself to his knees, shuddering, his stiletto up to defend himself. Musselwhite stealthily approached him, another dart nocked in her atlatl.

Pondwader stood staring, stunned. The entire battle had lasted only a few instants, barely enough for him to grasp what was happening. Musselwhite knelt beside the wounded man, and Pondwader saw a blot move behind her. The scream tore from his throat as he scrambled out of his hole, *"Musselwhite!"*

She pivoted, but too late. The warclub slammed into her skull, and she sprawled across the ground, then struggled to get on her knees, but her strength failed. She wilted, her tall slender body falling into the brittle autumn leaves.

Her attacker threw his head back and shrieked a hideous war cry, then laughed joyously. "I killed Musselwhite! The great Musselwhite! People will Sing my honor for tens of summers!"

"No!" Pondwader shouted as he ran. "She's not dead! My wife can't be dead!"

The man gripped his warclub in both hands, smiling. He stood about the same height as Pondwader, but his shoulders spread twice as wide, and rippled with muscle. Without taking his eyes from Pondwader, he asked the wounded man, "How badly are you hurt, Batfish?"

"Bad," the man croaked as he struggled to sit up. "I can't feel my legs! My legs are numb! Give me a hand, Spotted Paw. Help me up!"

"In a moment," Spotted Paw responded, and shouted, "Stop, Lightning Boy! Do not come any closer! I don't wish to kill you. You are much more valuable alive, but I will kill you, if necessary."

Pondwader halted, trembling, staring in terror at Musselwhite. She lay on her stomach, her face hidden in the leaves, blood matting her black hair to the back of her head. Had the blow crushed her skull?

"Let me go to my wife," he begged. "Please. I need to—"

"She's dead," Spotted Paw declared proudly. "Forget her. Come over here!" He pointed to his friend, who was still writhing on the ground, tugging pitifully at the dart in his back. "Pull that dart from Batfish's back."

Pondwader walked forward, and knelt between Batfish and Musselwhite, close enough to touch her. But he didn't. Instead, his gaze glanced over the dart that had fallen from her atlatl. It rested no more than ten hands away. Then he scrutinized Batfish's wound.

"The dart," Pondwader said, "is embedded in your friend's spine. If I pull it out, it may slice all the way through."

Batfish gaped in horror. "I'd be paralyzed for the rest of my life! Great Shining People, no. Not that!" He reached out to Spotted Paw. "Get me to Bright Feather! You're my wife's brother! Help me! If you can get me to Bright Feather, he might be able to—"

"I don't have time for that!" Spotted Paw shouted. "I have to get back to tell Cottonmouth what happened at Windy Cove! And boast of how I killed his greatest enemy! The woman he could never catch!"

"You can't just leave me here!" Batfish shrieked and reached pleadingly to Spotted Paw. "The lions and wolves will find me long before you can return! You must take me—"

"Lightning Boy," Spotted Paw ordered, "pick up that dart over there. Kill Batfish. Make it quick. I do not wish my brother-in-law to suffer."

Pondwader's knees quaked. "Kill . . . kill him?"

"That's what I said. Do it! Hurry!"

"You can't!" Batfish shrieked. "You're my relative. How will you ever face my sister?"

"Why don't you do it?" Pondwader shouted. "Why do I have to?"

Spotted Paw lifted his warclub and waved it threateningly. "Do it, Boy! Do it *now.*"

Pondwader turned, forced himself to walk by Musselwhite and pick up the dart, then he walked back and stood over Batfish. The man's fat, ugly face was drenched with sweat. As Pondwader lifted the dart, Batfish screamed, and threw himself at Spotted Paw's legs, trying to grab hold of his brother-in-law.

Surprised, Spotted Paw stumbled sideways, and Pondwader reacted without thinking. He swung around, the dart in his right hand, and drove the chert point deep into Spotted Paw's chest.

Spotted Paw gasped, blinked disbelievingly. His warclub clattered to the ground and he gripped the dart with both hands. He ran his fingers down the smooth wooden shaft in an almost loving gesture. "Look what you've done to me!" Spotted Paw raged as he staggered, fighting to stay on his feet. He collapsed in a clawing heap beside Batfish.

Pondwader backed away. Dazed, in shock.

Batfish dragged himself forward, examining the dart in his relative's heart, then lunged for the club.

Pondwader leaped forward, jerked it from his hands, and stood there holding the club, though he barely realized it.

Batfish roared in rage, yanked the dart from Spotted Paw's chest, then reared back and aimed it at Pondwader. Pondwader's arms swung without any conscious awareness. The club whistled as it sliced the air and connected with Batfish's temple. A loud *crack!* pierced the afternoon. Batfish smashed into the pine, then sank to the ground.

Pondwader froze.

The—the blood!

He could not believe how much blood there was . . .

The warclub fell from his nerveless hands.

He stumbled backward, tripped over a stone, and crashed to the ground. Rolling over, he crawled on all fours to Musselwhite's side. His hand shook so badly, he had trouble guiding it to her bloody head. Red coated his fingers.

"Oh, my wife," he whimpered.

Pondwader sat down and gathered her into his arms, kissing her face, pulling leaves from her long hair. "I did this, didn't I? This is my fault. *My fault!*"

Awareness came, slow and gray, seeping through a throbbing sea of pain, and she glimpsed starlight falling through trees she had never seen before. She blinked. She dared not try to move for fear her head would rupture into a glittering mass of bone fragments. The place, the trees, the smells of swamp and darkness were unfamiliar, but the hooded robe, she knew. And the boyish face within it, white as moonlight. Tears glittered on his cheeks.

He shifted, whispered, "Musselwhite?" and lowered a cold hand to her shoulder. "Are you awake?"

"How . . . long?"

"How long?" he repeated as if uncertain what she meant, then he blurted, "Just a few hands of time! Maybe four. Five at most."

She might make it, then. If they could stay hidden. If Pondwader could hunt food. If Cottonmouth did not come looking for them. *But Diver . . . oh, Diver . . . forgive me . . .*

Musselwhite longed to lie in his arms and weep for all the mistakes she had made. Diver would know how to comfort her. She needed him, his gentleness, and strength, the irony in his voice that always teased her out of terror. If she could just look into his eyes, feel his warm touch . . .

But she could not.

And after today she might never again.

In her worry over Pondwader, she had been careless, failing to watch her back. She could not blame the boy. He was doing the best he could, and she knew that. She had only herself to blame. The burden grew heavier with every breath that entered her lungs. Diver would be waiting for her, knowing she would come—just as she would have known, were the situation reversed, that Diver was hunting for her.

"Water?" she croaked. "Is there water?"

"Yes, let me get it!"

Pondwader rose and ran a short distance, then returned with the gourd he carried in his pack. Very gently, he slipped an arm beneath her neck and lifted her head. The agony of the movement left her trembling all over, but the position allowed her to see the two dead men. Relief went through her.

"Try to drink," Pondwader said as he tipped the gourd to her lips.

Musselwhite took four swallows. "Enough. . . ." She had seen too many head blows not to realize what might happen if she drank her fill.

When Pondwader lowered her to the grass again, the world spun, stars becoming silver streaks, branches smearing into black waves. The bitter taste of bile rose into the back of her throat.

Pondwader set the gourd aside and leaned over her, his face frantic. "Better?" he asked.

After a time, she managed to say, "Pondwader?"

"Yes, my wife?"

"Are you all right?"

His gaze searched her face, and he seemed to understand what she meant without forcing her to expend more of her strength on words. "You must think me a weak fool," he murmured. "But I—I have never killed before." He wiped his palms on his robe, as though to rid them of blood. "I don't know how it happened. My hands seemed to act before I knew what they were doing."

"And?"

"I feel sick."

Musselwhite filled her lungs with air, letting the cool night take some of the searing heat from her body. "You should. If you did not feel sick . . . I would think you liked killing. And I would have to . . . whack you over the head, and leave you for the bears." She smiled feebly.

Pondwader frowned. "But I thought warriors—"

"No." She closed her eyes. The waves of nausea had begun. She fought them, trying to keep the water down. "No warrior enjoys killing. It is just necessary. . . . And when it is necessary, warriors do not think. They do what they must to survive. If you had stopped to think about your actions, you would be dead . . . and so would I."

"But *two* men," he said in a strained voice. "I killed two men."

"Would you rather have them alive? And us dead?"

His head fell forward and his long white hair draped around his face. "I would rather that all of us were alive."

"Did you have a choice?"

"I—I don't think so."

It took great effort, but she slid her hand across the ground and touched his knee. He gripped her fingers and held them tightly.

"Oh, my wife, I feel so empty."

"I know, but I am proud of you, Pondwader. Today, you were a warrior. I owe you my life."

He kissed her fingers, his lips like ice, and tears coursed down his pale cheeks and fell on her forehead, cool, soothing. She could feel the silent sobs shaking him. Like a lost child, he clung to her hand as though his world might crumble if he let go.

"I thank you, my husband, for my life."

She tried to squeeze his hand, to ease his fears, and the attempt brought on crashing waves of pain. The agony sucked her into a hot black sea where the winds of nothingness blew her around and around. Utter loneliness and terror lived there, cloaked in the bodies of huge amorphous monsters. They lunged at her, biting and snarling, trying to tear her apart. Faces formed in that blackness, then melted into scenes . . . villages burned as thatched roofs leaped with flames; an old man she had darted fell, his skeletal body landing face-first in the sand . . . the corpses of people she loved lay stacked on the beach after Pelican Isle . . . women grabbed children and ran . . . raccoons and gulls swarmed over the bodies of five women warriors she had killed for not obeying quickly enough when she ordered them to lay down their weapons. Where . . . where had that happened? Which village? The screams of a child spun from the blackness, interrupting her search. A little boy. Four summers. Maybe five. He'd sneaked up behind her when she'd been killing his father and plunged his pitiful dart into her shoulder. She'd swung around without thinking, knife in her hand. . . .

Through the horror, she could hear Diver calling her. Calling and calling, but she could not find the strength to answer. Monsters were chasing her and she had to run . . . runrunrun . . .

I lie on my side before my small fire, shivering, watching the ruby-eyed coals blink in the cold breeze blowing across the swamp. It smells of peat and reeds. My heart aches. I tucked my blanket around Musselwhite to keep her warm, and came over here to sleep. The Shining People shimmer in the indigo spaces between the dark overarching branches. My eyelids are very heavy.

I spent a full hand of time dragging away the men I murdered. I carried them into the swamp and buried them beneath the pale green water, facing north. I did not know what Songs their clans might have Sung for them, or who their Spirit Helpers might have been, so I Sang Heartwood's death Song, and asked Alligator to guide them on their long journey. I pray with all my heart that they find their ways to the Village of Wounded Souls. I still cannot bear to look at the places where they fell—clots of blood cover the forest floor, shining in the starlight.

In a very soft voice, I start to Sing, begging Sun Mother to help Musselwhite. She has been thrashing weakly and moaning in her sleep. I do not know what else I can do for her. I am very frightened. When I grow too tired, I Sing the words in my dreams. . . .

"She's dying. And you, stupid boy, are lying there like a brainless catfish doing nothing."

I gasp and flop to my back. Turtle Bone Doll perches on the twisted oak branch over my head. Her tunic is even more tattered than last time; it clings to her bone body like a rotting tangle of threads. Almost all of her hair has been ripped off. Four or five strands glint in the starlight. That is all.

I leap up, stumbling through the darkness. Terror has gripped me. "What do you mean she's dying? She can't be dying!"

But when I kneel, and peer down at Musselwhite's starlit face, my own good sense will not permit me to believe anything else. Her skin is pasty and pale against the blanket. I grab up her wrist and feel the weak flutter of her heartbeat. My voice is quaking. "Blessed Spirits," I whisper. "What can I do? Tell me how to save her!"

Turtle Bone Doll does not move. *"I already have."*

"What . . . ? When? Was I asleep?"

"I have come to the conclusion that you are always sleeping when I am revealing great truths, boy. I told you that you had to learn to Dance with the Lightning Bird's soul. But have you even tried? No! So, naturally, she's dying."

I jump up with my fists clenched to stand directly beneath the oak limb. I can barely breathe. Turtle Bone Doll tilts to look down on me. "But you never taught me *how* to Dance with the Lightning Bird's soul! How can I do it if you won't teach me? You can't expect me to just know things by myself!"

Turtle Bone Doll lifts lightly off the branch and floats toward me like a dandelion seed borne on a warm updraft. She settles on my left shoulder.

"Not only are you brainless, your memory is going. I taught you everything you need to know about the Dance. Give up your human feet, I said. Learn to soar and flash and thunder."

I feel frantic; my eyes are swimming with tears. "How?" I plead. "Please. Tell me how to give up my human feet?"

"Leap into the air, Pondwader. And keep leaping, don't stop for an instant, until your feet forget what the ground feels like. You have to let go of earth and air and water. Then, the next time that baby Lightning Bird flashes, you'll be able to grab hold of his blinding tailfeathers and soar away in a deafening roar."

"Keep leaping? Into the air?"

"That's right."

"But how will 'leaping' allow me to save Musselwhite? This is all gibberish! I don't understand!" I shout. "I haven't much time and you're spouting gibberish!"

Turtle Bone Doll somersaults from my shoulder and lazily floats upward, going higher and higher until she seems one of the Shining People. *"You are right about one thing,"* her little girl voice calls, *"You haven't much time."*

"Come back here!" I shout. "You can't leave me! Not now. I need you!"

She vanishes, trailing glimmers of stardust behind her.

Lonely and frightened, I look at my wife. Her breathing has dropped to swift shallow gasps. I feel as if a huge, gaping hole has replaced my chest. There is nothing there. Nothing! No Lightning Bird. No thunder. No hope. I long to smash my fists into something!

I stalk to my fire. The coals cast a crimson gleam over the tree trunks. I wish . . . I wish Musselwhite could speak to me. I would not be so afraid.

But she can't.

I am alone. And she needs me.

My first steps are tentative. I jump a finger's breadth off the ground. Nothing happens. I jump again. Finally, like a fool, I start leaping. High into the air. Leaping up, and coming down. Landing softly on the thick forest duff. Leaping up. Coming down. Leaping and leaping . . .

Sobs shake my chest.

Here I am, hopping like a madman while my wife dies before my eyes. Why am I so helpless? I have always relied on other people to protect me, to overlook my weaknesses. And look where my helplessness has gotten me?

Hot tears flood my face.

Leaping . . . leaping! Leaping!

To keep my balance, I focus my eyes on the blurry bed of red coals. They shift and waver in the breeze. Scenes form, from Heartwood and Windy

Cove—my marriage, the battle—then they flicker away in the next gust of wind.

I have failed, not just at the things Grandmother Moonsnail wanted me to do, like hunting and fighting, but at things I wanted to do myself—like making Musselwhite love me, helping her to free Diver. I was willing to die to give this baby Lightning Bird life—and I haven't even done that! Can't I do anything right? Am I completely useless?

I stare down at the coals. An angry red glare seeps up as if fed by wind. Tendrils of light stretch long fingers out. They reach for me. I am leaping almost unconsciously now, spending most of my time in the air. The red tendrils swirl together, and a tiny tornado is born above the coals. Fascinated, I cannot take my eyes from it. The heat grows as the tornado spins upward, and it begins to scorch my face. I keep leaping!

In the eye of the tornado a white hot blaze forms. The red glare whirls around it, gaining speed. Fiery crimson filaments spiral out from the glare to feed the white core. It glows brighter and brighter.

"Come, Lightning Boy," a soft voice says, but it is not Turtle Bone Doll. The voice is male. *"Dance with me. Come and Dance away the darkness. You have only to reach out . . . just extend a hand to me, Lightning Boy."*

Like a waterspout made of liquid silver, the core suddenly shoots up, crackling past my face on its way to the starlit heavens. In terror, I jump back, shielding my face. Then, when understanding dawns, I scream . . . and leap. With both hands, I grab for its blinding tail. . . .

P̲ondwader's own incoherent cry woke him. He sat bolt upright from where he had curled around the fire and panted into the darkness. The coals had burned down to white ashes. Not even a pale, red glow could be seen in the firepit. The sky had begun to blue with the coming of dawn. Sweat coursed down his face and chest.

From Musselwhite's bedding a faint voice said, "Pondwader? You . . . cried out. Are you . . . all right?"

"Yes, I—I am, my wife."

"Dream?"

He nodded. "Yes. Just a dream. But it seemed so real."

He looked over, and saw her sitting up, braced on one elbow. She had managed to grip a dart in her hand, and held it aimed in his direction. Shaking, she eased back down to her bedding, lowered the dart and laid it across her stomach. Her eyes fell closed instantly, her head rolling to the side in sleep—or unconsciousness. Pain etched her face. She must have wakened, feared he was in trouble, and forced herself to rise to protect him. And Pondwader suspected that if he really had been in trouble, she'd have dragged herself to her feet somehow, and made certain he did not have to fight his attackers alone.

He rose and went to kneel at her side. Tenderly, he brushed hair from her face, and flinched as pain lanced him. Bright. Fiery. Uncomprehending, he turned his palms up to the starlight.

Blisters . . . my hands are covered with blisters!

Only after a long time of staring, did Pondwader lift his gaze to the brightening sky. The Shining People had gone. A purplish hue dyed the drifting clouds. Not a single Lightning Bird Danced up there.

When he dared to remember the feel of those blinding white-hot tailfeathers, a faint crackle flowed out of his heart with his blood, and pumped through his veins, filtering through every part of him until his whole body seemed to *be* thunder.

He did not know why, or how, but he knew what he had to do. He reached out and gently placed his hands on either side of Musselwhite's injured head. It took no effort at all on his part, he just let the thunder flow through his hands into his wife.

Her dark eyes fluttered open. In a barely audible voice, she said, "Thank you. Feels . . . good." Then her eyes fell closed again. She went limp.

After the thunder had crackled into silence, Pondwader slumped weakly back on the ground, wrapped his arms around his chest, and hugged himself. Was that what Turtle Bone Doll meant by learning to thunder?

His hands ached unbearably.

He looked back at Musselwhite. Her beautiful face had relaxed. She seemed to be breathing easier.

In a whisper, he Sang a lilting prayer to the Lightning Birds, begging them to give him the courage he would need to reach out to them again.

Twenty-seven

Beaverpaw sat in a meadow of dry grass, knapping out stone tools, and talking with a stranger named Hanging Star. They had met last night when Dark Rain had led them to this new camp, but had barely spoken until this morning. At dawn, Dark Rain and Bowfin had trotted off to gamble, and Hanging Star and Beaverpaw had walked to this meadow to sit in the pale sunlight filtering through a haze of high clouds. A chill wind blew, carrying the damp scents of moss and rich earth, shaking the palmettos that encircled the meadow. Shiny spiderwebs glittered across the fronds. With each gust webs shook loose and floated over Beaverpaw's head.

"You mean you actually believe you're in love with her? With the infamous Dark Rain! How could that be? You seemed like such a smart fellow earlier."

Hanging Star flopped back on the dead grass and laughed. Two-tens-and-six summers old, the man had an ugly, square face and blunt jaw. Tens of pock marks dented his cheeks and forehead, which made his bulbous nose seem even uglier. His tunic had once been blue, but had faded to tan with pale azure streaks.

Beaverpaw flushed. He glanced at Dark Rain. Fifty hands away, she and Bowfin played dice with two other men. The game had been going since dawn, and while the men had taken the time to cook breakfast and eat, Dark Rain's attention had not left the dice. She watched the two hickory nuts, painted red on one side, as if her very life depended upon them.

"I do love her," Beaverpaw said, but he sounded unconvincing, even to himself.

To hide his discomfort, he rearranged his tools, laying his chunks of chert between his quartzite hammerstone and antler-tine baton, then tossed his hand-sized piece of leather on top of his antler tine. Chert had to be worked correctly, or it would not produce the long thin slices of stone, called flakes, that made usable tools. The secret lay in knowing how to use the hammerstone. Direction of blow was critical. If you slammed your hammerstone directly down on a piece of chert it would not create a flake, it would create a circular cone, a little pointed mound of virtually useless stone. You had to strike at an angle.

Beaverpaw reached for a rectangular piece of chert, about as long as his hand, and four finger-widths across. He first surveyed it for surface imperfections that must be avoided. When he found none, he picked up his hammerstone—a round cobble of hard quartzite that fit into his right palm. In his mind he imagined the point of the cone sitting on the upper tip of the rock. The stone would naturally break on a straight line through the center of the cone, so if he wished to drive off a good flake, he had to strike the chert at just the right angle. Long thin flakes made excellent blades for cutting up meat, while thick flakes could be fashioned into scrapers or choppers for processing plants.

Beaverpaw turned his rectangular piece of chert on its side, laid it out lengthwise before him, and picked the place on the stone to strike, near the right edge. The strike point was called the platform. Since he wanted a thin blade, he brought his hammerstone down at an acute angle. The blade cracked off perfectly, about as long as his index finger and one third of the width.

Hanging Star scrutinized Beaverpaw. "I'm sorry. I should not have laughed. I believe you love her. Just as I have believed *all* of her men. Her affect on men is . . . unnatural."

Beaverpaw's bushy brows pulled down. He had not had the opportunity to wash his chin-length black hair, and it draped in dirty strands around his fat tadpole face. Angrily, Beaverpaw said, "What do you know of Dark Rain?"

Hanging Star stifled his merriment. "Ah, well, that could be a very long story. Where would you like me to begin?" One last irrepressible chuckle bubbled up his throat. He shook his head and watched the puffs of cloud sailing through the blue sky. Sun Mother stood straight overhead, forcing him to squint.

Beaverpaw sat sternly silent. He changed the angle of his hammerstone and knocked off a thicker flake. It would be a scraper once he'd finished sharpening the edge. To do that, he spread his piece of leather over his left palm, placed the thick flake on top, then used his thumb to fold the edge of the leather over so he could grip the left side of the flake. He picked up his antler-tine baton, and carefully rapped small flakes off around the circumference, rounding the flake, and giving it a scalloped cutting edge.

Hanging Star eyed Beaverpaw. "You don't really care what I have to say, do you?"

"I'm listening. Tell your story."

Hanging Star smiled. "You are sure? You won't be angry? The last one of her lovers that I tried to forewarn offered to slit my throat for me."

"I am not like her other lovers."

"Aren't you?" Hanging Star peered at Beaverpaw speculatively.

Beaverpaw looked up. "Perhaps I will slit your throat—but not because of your silly stories."

Hanging Star guffawed and slapped the ground. "Oh, I like you, Beaverpaw. Very well, then. I shall tell you one of my 'silly' stories." He braced himself on one elbow. "I met Dark Rain ten summers ago, in Standing Hollow Horn Clan's spring village. She was trying to catch Cottonmouth's attention, but he would have nothing to do with her. I, on the other hand, appreciate beauty. And since she offered herself for such a small price, two conch shell horns, I accepted."

Hanging Star plucked a stem of grass and put in his mouth, and appeared to be thinking about those days. The lechery showed on his face.

Beaverpaw sat so still that his gray chert scraper caught the gleam of sunlight and held it like a clamshell mirror. Only the faded fabric over his broad chest moved with the rise and fall of his angry breathing.

Beaverpaw put his scraper down. He said, "I don't know much about her, except she is of my wife's clan, but I do not care what she's done—"

"Your wife!" Hanging Star roared, slapping his thigh. "So you are her adulterous lover! This gets better and better! Go on!"

Beaverpaw lowered his gaze to his growing pile of stone tools. His jaw set. "I have been married to Waterbearer for ten-and-five summers, and in all that time, I rarely saw Dark Rain. She spent most of her life out wandering about. When she did return, she always stirred controversy. I never knew what to think of her—except that she was exciting."

"Well, I won't deny that," Hanging Star agreed. "How many children do you have?"

"Seven."

Hanging Star chuckled again, this time low and disparagingly. "No wonder she wanted you so badly. What a prize! War Leader, *and* married with children. I do not think she has ever won a lover like you, Beaverpaw. Most of her 'friends' are worthless scavengers unfit for decent company. But you! Ha! She must feel as Powerful as Sister Moon!" Hanging Star moved his head closer to Beaverpaw, and whispered, "Tell me. How did she do it?"

"Do what?"

"How did she convince you to give up everything for her? You are a smart man, and were much respected by your people. It had to be more than her delicious body. What did she do? Eh? You can tell me."

Beaverpaw's jaw hardened. He wouldn't repeat the conversation he had had with Dark Rain on the night of Pondwader's marriage to Musselwhite. Hanging Star would not understand Heartwood Clan's history . . . and Beaverpaw could not forget it. No, he still believed Dark Rain had been correct about that. The elders would have punished him severely—just as they had Dry Cloud.

Hanging Star's eyes glinted. He seemed to be waiting for Beaverpaw's response.

Beaverpaw decided to change the subject. "You mentioned Standing Hollow Horn Village. Have you been there recently?"

Hanging Star stretched out on the grass and laced his hands beneath his head. The stem in his mouth switched from one side to the other. His square face with its blunt chin looked very brown against the dead grass. "Of course. It is my clan."

"Your clan?" Beaverpaw asked. "Standing Hollow Horn is your clan? Then you must know about the recent attack on Windy Cove Village! I have heard—"

"Know about it?" Hanging Star replied. "I was there! I killed more than my share of their pitiful warriors."

Haughty amusement twisted the man's mouth, and anger lit a fire in Beaverpaw's veins. Obviously, Hanging Star did not realize he had just admitted to murdering Beaverpaw's new relatives. Or perhaps he did, and did not care that the admission gave Beaverpaw the right to cut out his liver on the spot.

"I heard that Musselwhite was there," Beaverpaw said calmly.

"Yes," Hanging Star laughed. "Indeed! She was *magnificent.* She moved like a dart in flight, striking down anything in her path. It was glorious to watch."

"Even though she was murdering your relatives?"

"Certainly!" Hanging Star shouted. "I didn't say I liked it. I tried to kill her myself. It doesn't lessen my admiration for her skill as a warrior." He smiled. "I cannot wait to see what happens when she reaches Standing Hollow Horn Village."

Beaverpaw frowned. "Why would she go there?"

"What? You haven't heard?" Hanging Star jerked the grass stem from his mouth to gape at Beaverpaw. "Cottonmouth captured her husband, Diver! I, myself, delivered the message to Windy Cove. I—"

"Diver is *alive?*"

"Oh, yes, at least he was the last time I saw him. Though, I admit, he did not look so well." Hanging Star grinned. "But he was alive enough to still draw his wife like a fly to fresh blood. I'm sure Musselwhite must already be on her way—and Cottonmouth is waiting for her."

A bright hot fire raced through Beaverpaw's veins. "Waiting for her? What do you mean?"

Hanging Star tucked the stem in his mouth again and chewed on it. "I mean he knows she's coming. He had a Spirit Dream about it. That's why he sent us out to capture Diver."

"I thought you had just accidentally run into Diver's scouting party?"

"No, no. Cottonmouth knew just where the Windy Cove scouting party would be camped, and he knew that Diver would be there. It was very strange. Diver escaped. We had to hunt him down. But we found him."

"Great Ancestors," Beaverpaw murmured. Sun Mother emerged from the film of clouds and glared down. The chert tools sparkled wildly.

Beaverpaw remembered Musselwhite's pain. Grief had tightened every line in her beautiful face. Discovering that her husband had been taken prisoner must have been a terrible shock.

"So," he said, "Musselwhite would have heard the truth after your attack on Windy Cove. From the survivors?"

Hanging Star waved a hand, as if shooing away insects. "Yes, I suppose. What does it matter?"

It mattered a great deal. If she were headed toward Standing Hollow Horn Village, she needed help. And badly. She had asked Beaverpaw for help once, and he had promised to provide it.

Casually, Beaverpaw asked, "How many Windy Cove warriors do you think she could gather to go with her?"

Hanging Star used his tongue to move the grass stem around his wide mouth. "None! We killed as many as we could. But, more important—" Hanging Star lifted a finger "—if Cottonmouth's Dream was correct, and I'm not saying it was, mind you. But if it was, she will bring only the Lightning Boy with her. She will have no war party."

". . . No war party?" Beaverpaw whispered in disbelief. "But how could she hope to rescue Diver without—"

"She won't rescue him," Hanging Star interrupted with a chuckle. "She will be captured herself. That is what Cottonmouth Dreamed anyway. But, who knows? I am on my way back there now, just because I am curious about how it will all turn out."

"You don't believe Cottonmouth's Dream?"

Hanging Star heaved a disgruntled sigh. "What do I know of Soul Dancers? Cottonmouth is scary, I will say that for him. But a man with Spirit Dreams? I have never been convinced of that."

"But what if he is a Soul Dancer?"

Hanging Star rubbed his blunt jaw, and glanced sideways at Beaverpaw. "That's a frightening prospect. And he does seem to know things that others—even the Spirit Elders of Standing Hollow Horn Clan—do not know."

"On the other hand, he may just be insane."

Hanging Star nodded. "Oh, yes, I believe that. I do. Cottonmouth truly *believes* these murders are helping to prepare the way for the Lightning Birds to soar down and carry him and his followers to a new world beyond the stars." He laughed derisively. "You should come back with me. See for yourself. Even if he is insane, Cottonmouth can be very entertaining."

Beaverpaw's belly prickled, but he smiled, picked up his newly completed scraper, and gestured with it. "Perhaps I will. If I can convince my companions to come."

"That will not take much!" Hanging Star said. "Convince Dark Rain and you will have convinced Bowfin. He follows her around like a lost wolf pup.

It's really embarrassing. Does he realize how foolish he appears? Well, anyway, you'll have no trouble talking Dark Rain into going. Just tell her the truth. Once every moon there is a *big* shell game at Standing Hollow Horn Village. People come from all the surrounding villages to gamble on the players." He pulled the grass stem from his mouth and tossed it away. "Tell Dark Rain that, and she will beat you there."

Beaverpaw's eyes drifted back to Dark Rain. For the first time in days, he knew where his path led. Her obsession would give him the perfect cover. Long hair flowed around the curves of her flawless body, accentuating her broad hips and full breasts. She had been winning steadily. He knew because of her almost erotic shrieks of pleasure. She treated dice like a lover. Her face lit whenever she touched them, and her lips pursed into that sensual pout.

He gripped his chunk of chert, set it up before him, and used his hammerstone to prepare a new platform, lightly tapping to chip away enough stone to form just the right striking surface; then he gave it a good *whack!* and drove off a flat, moderately thick, but even piece. This one would be a dart point. He prepared a new platform, struck again, and again.

If he were going to Standing Hollow Horn, he would need many good dart points.

Twenty-eight

For a long time after she woke, Musselwhite lay among the mottled forest shadows with the soft pearlescent light of early morning falling around her, wondering where she was. She recognized nothing. Not the black gum or bay trees, nor the crystalline blue sky. The swamp to her right seemed vaguely familiar, but she did not know why. Had she . . . had she crossed it? Vague memories laced with fear surfaced. Turtles sunned themselves on the deadfall at the edge of the water, and a snake slithered through the grass two tens of hands away.

Head wound. That part was not hard to guess. Clots of old blood clung to the grass, and throbbing pain kept her sick to her stomach. *Or is it the fear? Knowing that if trouble comes looking, you are helpless to defend yourself?* She could neither fight, nor run. She did not even have the strength to hide herself.

Two packs nestled on the dark forest duff to her left. One belonged to her. The other she could not identify. But it meant she had a companion. . . . Who? Someone had covered her with blankets, tucked them in around her sides, and left a gourd of water within reach.

Thirst struck her with a vengeance. She felt as though she hadn't drunk anything in days. She tried to sit up, and her headache swelled to a bone-deep assault that left her trembling. She eased back down, breathing hard, and the moist air tasted sweet on her tongue. If only she could lie here in the soft folds of her blankets and get her fill from the fragrant air . . .

Where am I?

Her father had told her they would be moving Windy Cove Village to join with Heartwood Clan. Is that where she was? At the new village site? But why didn't she hear voices? Dogs barking? Children laughing? The smack of stone axes chopping trees for shelter poles?

No. She could not be at Manatee Lagoon. *Fool. There is no sound of surf here. No scent of the sea. No cry of gulls. You are not on the ocean . . . but far inland.* Where? Why couldn't she recall?

Musselwhite feebly shoved her blanket off her chest and blinked at the swaying tree boughs. How long had she been sleeping? Days? Half a moon? She had no way of knowing. She recalled very little of the past few days.

Slowly, concentrating, she took her hand and again reached for the gourd of water. She had just managed to hook her fingers over the edge of the cup, when her heart thundered and her souls careened, flitting from one memory to another. Diver smiled at her . . . Thorny Boy crawled into her lap . . . Morning Glory laughed . . . then the comforting images swirled and faded, changing. Cottonmouth's handsome face appeared.

She could not help but gaze into those black eyes. They stared straight past all of her disguises, all the lies she told herself, and looked directly at her souls.

He always had.

Even long after she'd left him, his eyes found her. She could recall many times when she had been talking with Diver, smiling, and those eyes had suddenly appeared on the fabric of her souls—staring at her. Reminding her.

The strength of the emotions caught her offguard. Before she realized it, black shadows had seeped from deep inside her, and wailed through her heart: sounds of wrenching sobs, the feel of his hands desperately clutching her arm in the darkness, his warm tears drenching her hair. *"Blessed Spirits, what can we do? How can we save him?"* I don't know. . . . I don't know. *"I'll find a way. I promise you. I will!"*

She wiped a trembling hand over her sweaty forehead, and struggled to force the sounds and sights away. A secret cage of memories existed inside her, blacker than black, filled with writhing unthinkable things. Long ago, she had trapped those memories and imprisoned them there, so that she knew where they were, and they could not sneak up on her when she least expected it. One of her souls guarded that cage at all times, vigilantly, making certain that the horrors within never escaped.

Only Cottonmouth's eyes remained loose. . . . The one memory she had never been able to capture and control.

A faint rustle sounded. Palmetto fronds brushed fabric. Musselwhite stilled her breathing. Sandals crunched twigs.

Without a sound, she extended a hand and patted the ground to her left. Empty. She used her other hand to search the space to her right. Still nothing. Almost as an afterthought, she slipped her hand beneath the blanket where she lay—and found her atlatl and darts. Just where she kept them at home in her own shelter. Her companion understood her needs.

Her souls tumbled again, memories soaring down, flashing, then slipping away. For a horrifying instant she could not recall what she had been doing. . . . Her hand . . . what was . . . smooth wood? *Yes.* She eased out one of the darts and propped it across her stomach. The movements nearly incapacitated her with pain. Her breathing came in agonizing gasps.

More thrashing. Arms shoving grapevines aside. The loops slapped against each other when they fell free, creating an erratic percussion symphony. Musselwhite waited.

Pondwader stepped out of the forest. He carried a dripping net of fish in one hand, and a small basket of sundew leaves in the other. Veering around a clump of palmettos, he quietly walked to his firepit to deposit his net and basket, then shook his long white hair away from his face, and used his sleeve to soak up the sweat that coated his pointed nose and beaded across the high planes of his cheekbones. From the corner of his eye, he saw Musselwhite move. She let out a breath.

Pondwader bounded over to her. "Are you awake? How are you feeling?"

Musselwhite swallowed, and squinted, as if her head rebelled at even that small chore. Silver-streaked black hair stuck to her cheeks in wisps, framing her turned-up nose and accentuating the deep lines in her forehead.

"Better," she whispered.

Pondwader reached over her head, wrung out the cloth waiting there in the gourd of fresh water, and washed her face. She seemed to enjoy the cool dampness. He kept his touch especially gentle, as light as sea spray, fearing that he might hurt her.

"Are you strong enough to eat?" he asked. "I wove a net from strips of palm fronds, and caught four fish."

"Yes. I'd . . . better. To . . . to build my strength."

She tried to roll to her side, and a faint moan escaped her lips. She sank onto her back again.

Pondwader stroked her hair soothingly. Perspiration had soaked the strands, leaving it feeling like a river otter's fur, softer than soft. "I have some mint tea left in the boiling bag hanging from the tripod. I'll make a fire and get it warm, then cook the fish," he said. "After we've eaten, I'll tend your wound again."

"Again?"

"Yes, I cleaned it early this morning."

"What did it . . . what does the wound look like?"

He hesitated, not certain he wished to tell her. The scalp had been sliced down to the skull. Once he had washed away all the clotted blood, he'd seen the bare bone gleaming.

She sensed his reluctance and glared at him. "Tell me. *Now.*"

"The—the warclub cut your scalp. A small portion of the skull can be seen."

"How small?"

He gestured uncomfortably. "The size of my thumb."

She nodded and closed her eyes. "Thank you, Pondwader . . . for taking care of me."

"You needed me to, and I wished to," he answered. Then he added, "I'll get the fire going. You've lost a lot of blood. You must be very thirsty."

His long robe rustled as he set about gathering dry twigs from the camp site. Yes, she had lost a lot of blood. Her hair had been matted with it. It had taken him over a hand of time combing and rinsing it with water to clean it. Wind stirred the tree branches, bringing him the musty scents of swamp and moss. He walked back and dumped the wood by the firepit.

"Pondwader?" Musselwhite called weakly.

"Yes?" He looked up.

"Did my father live through the attack on Windy Cove? I—I can't remember."

"Oh, yes, Musselwhite. I spoke with Seedpod just before I left. He was very well. Just . . . sad."

"And my sons? What happened to Diamondback and Thorny Boy?"

"They both survived." He swiveled around to frown at her. He had heard that people who endured severe head blows lost their memories for a short time. "Thorny Boy hid in a badger hole in the forest and covered himself with branches. He said Cottonmouth's warriors ran all around him. Diamondback fought at your side during the battle. Don't you recall any of this?"

Musselwhite lifted a hand to her forehead and pulled damp strands away. "Some. Pieces of the fight. I remember you bravely walking out . . . spreading your arms to our enemies. Despite . . . despite the fact that I told you not to enter the village . . . until everything was secure."

"I know, but you needed me. You just didn't realize it."

"Yes," she agreed with a faint nod. "I know that now. . . . I also remember, Pondwader, that I was . . . unkind . . . to you when I returned to camp . . . after the battle. Sorry. I must have . . . hurt you."

He smiled his forgiveness. "You were worried sick about Diver. I knew that, Musselwhite."

The warm stir of wind brought him the distant switching of an alligator's tail as it hunted the swamps. A crane let out a sharp shriek. Flurries of wings and more desperate shrieks followed, then died away abruptly.

Pondwader scooped ashes out of the firepit, laid a small bed of dry pine needles and twigs in the hole, then reached for his fire drill and fire board. The board, a flat piece of pine about three hands long, and a finger wide, had two drill holes in it already. He selected a new spot. The drill consisted of a sharpened cattail stem, and stretched as long as his arm. Pondwader stood his drill on the board and grabbed it up high. As he rapidly spun the drill, he applied a constant downward pressure, so his hands descended the stem as he worked. When he reached the bottom, he had to move his hands to the top again and start spinning all over.

In less than ten tens of heartbeats, a thin gray spiral of smoke rose from the fireboard and Pondwader carefully lifted the board, dumped the hot drill dust onto his kindling, and blew gently. The pine needles caught almost immediately. Sparks crackled and spat as tiny tongues of yellow licked up around the twigs. Pondwader kept blowing as he added larger branches, until he had a good fire going. Then he skewered the fish on long sticks and propped three of them up to roast. The fourth fish, he laid to the side.

"Saving . . . one?" Musselwhite asked.

Pondwader grinned. He felt somehow different this morning. Happy. Strangely confident. Older. "No," he answered and reached for his pack which lay near the firepit. He pulled out a chert blade and held it up. "As soon as I've stripped out the fish fat, I'm going to melt it with the sundew leaves and plaster the mixture on your head."

"I've never . . . heard of that."

"Oh, it's very good for open wounds," he assured her. "Grandmother Moonsnail has used it on me tens of times. Injuries always heal faster with a sundew poultice."

Pondwader used his blade to split the fish open all the way, then laid the halves back and carefully scraped the fat into a wooden bowl. After dumping in the wilted sundew leaves, he stirred the mixture, and set the bowl at the edge of the fire to warm, and skewered the fish on a stick. He propped it over the fire alongside the others. He'd started humming to himself, a beautiful lilting lullaby that he remembered from his earliest childhood. A song about warriors and honor. His grandmother had sung it to him. He missed her very much.

"Pondwader," Musselwhite said. "You seem . . . different today. Is there a reason?"

He stopped humming and shifted uncomfortably. His long white hair fell around his young face, highlighting his pink skin and white brows. How could she be so perceptive? She seemed to sense his every thought. He tucked his skinned fish into the empty basket that had held the sundew leaves, and scooped up some of the fat to rub on his hands. It felt cool and soothing.

"I—I feel well today," he answered cryptically.

"You don't have to talk . . . about it," she said. "I was just wondering. That's all."

When he turned to look at her, he found her watching him. "I do wish to speak with you about it. I am just not sure . . . that the time is right. You are hurt. We are vulnerable out here alone in the forest. Perhaps it would be better if I waited until a time when—"

"You may tell me . . . whenever you wish, Pondwader. Now. Later. Or never. I will understand."

"No, I will tell you," he assured her. "You are my wife. I must tell you."

Musselwhite shifted her shoulders to take some of the ache out of her back. "No," she murmured. "Tell me only if you wish to. There are many things, Pondwader . . . that I—I will never share with you. Not because I don't trust you. But because remembering them hurts me . . . too much. I don't expect you to share everything with me. . . . Just the things you wish to."

He flipped their fish so they would roast on the opposite side. The sweet scent filled the air, along with the faintly pungent odor of steeping sundew leaves. He added more branches to the fire. Just thinking about last night left him nervous. He tossed on another piece of wood. Flames leaped up, crackling.

"Pondwader," Musselwhite gently pointed out. "Not too much wood . . . please. The smoke will rise and be visible . . . for a great distance. We don't want—"

"Oh!" he yipped. "Great Dolphin!" He lurched to his feet and began kicking dirt over the fire. A haze of dust rose and wafted upward through the tree branches. "I can't believe I am so stupid!"

"You are not stupid. You just don't . . . don't know any better. I wager you will not make that mistake again."

"I promise, I won't." He crouched, peered sharply at their fish, and whirled to Musselwhite. Exasperated, he said, "I got dirt on our fish! I'm sorry! I didn't even think—"

"Pondwader," she whispered. "We'll peel off the skin. The meat will be fine. . . . Do you think the tea is warm, yet? I am so thirsty . . . I could drink Sister Sea."

"Forgive me. I should have brought it to you before." He hastily rummaged in his pack, pulled out a gourd cup, and dipped it into the boiling bag. As he carried it to her, he said, "I'm not thinking very well this morning. I'm sorry."

The weary lines around her eyes deepened. "Your souls are wrestling . . . with other thoughts. I can see that. Could you . . . would you sit down for a moment? May we speak frankly to each other?"

Pondwader set the new cup down by the empty one, then knelt and bit his lip, peering at her from beneath his pale lashes. His breathing quickened, as though he feared what she might ask him. Did she recall last night?

"Today, Pondwader . . . you are more than my husband. You are my best friend. And I need to . . . to speak with a friend."

He jerked his head up. "Why? What's wrong?"

A shaft of pallid sunlight penetrated the trees and outlined her beautiful taut face in gold. She squinted her eyes rather than chancing the pain movement would have caused. "Tomorrow . . . I must be on my feet. Headed for Standing Hollow Horn Village again. No, don't . . . don't object," she said when his mouth fell open. "I must do this. But I will have to go slowly . . . letting myself heal on the way. That means we must take great care . . . not to draw attention to ourselves. I don't think I will be . . . able to fight . . . for days."

"I understand. I promise you I will be very cautious."

Musselwhite feebly reached for his hand, and Pondwader took her fingers gently. She murmured, "I know . . . you will. But . . . regardless . . . the journey will not be easy. Once Cottonmouth . . . discovers . . . what happened at Windy Cove, there may be war parties . . . out combing the forests for us."

"Why? Why would they?"

"He knows I am on my way. And he—"

"How could he know that?"

She squeezed Pondwader's hand. The look on her face made him afraid to breathe. She stared straight ahead, her face blank with a kind of shock, or perhaps just uncanny certainty. When she returned her gaze to Pondwader again, she frowned.

"Everything he's done, from the attack . . . on my raiding party . . . to capturing Diver . . . sending a messenger to tell me he was alive . . . then attacking Windy Cove. Everything, Pondwader, has been designed to force me to come to him."

Fear slackened Pondwader's face. "Why?"

She shook her head faintly. "He needs me. I do not know why. But I know how he thinks. He must need me very badly . . . or he would not have gone to all this trouble."

Musselwhite's eyes filled with a strange luminosity, and Pondwader's souls shriveled. Bravely, he asked. "Do you want to go to him?"

"There is nothing in the world I want less, Pondwader."

"But I do not understand, my wife. You said you never stopped loving him. And if he needs you—"

"Pondwader," she said through a shaky exhalation, "there are many more things in the world than love and need."

Pondwader lowered himself to sit down cross-legged beside her. As he always did when he wanted to try and say exactly what he meant, Pondwader spoke softly. "I would very much like to know about those things. I think I *need* to understand more about the world . . . about Cottonmouth."

The slanting light moved, and gray shadows once again covered her face. She sighed, and her whole body shook when she forced herself to roll to her side and reach for her gourd cup of tea. The liquid sloshed as she lifted it to her lips.

"Oh, let me help you!" Pondwader said and lunged for her cup.

"No." She shook her head. "I must do this . . . myself. But thank you."

Her hand shook so badly that tea ran down her chin and splashed on her blanket, but she managed to empty the cup. Slowly, she eased back to her bedding, and set the cup aside. She closed her eyes, and grimaced, as if waiting for the sickness to pass.

Pondwader watched her intently. "What else is there, other than love and need? Which emotion is the most . . ." He thought about it. "Powerful?"

She closed her eyes. "Hatred," she replied softly.

"Hatred? Hatred of what, Musselwhite?"

She made a movement that he thought might be a shrug, and Pondwader frowned. He drew up his legs, wrapped his arms around them, and propped his chin atop his knees. "Why would anyone let hatred—"

"Because he has nothing else left."

A frown incised his forehead, thinking of what Turtle Bone Doll had said about agony. *When the agony is all you have left, Pondwader, you dare not give it up. Because then you will have nothing at all.*

Pondwader picked up Musselwhite's hand, and tenderly held it to his cool cheek. "Are you all right?"

"So far," she said, and smiled. "My stomach seems to have settled. But I make no . . . guarantees. You might wish to—to be ready to move quickly. Just in case I need that space where you're sitting."

His worry dissolved into amusement. He beamed down at her and kissed her fingers. "I'm very fast when I have to be, don't worry."

"Despite my nausea and headache . . . I really do feel better today, Pondwader. Much better. And that's a good sign." She sighed. "You must have used some Spirit Power on me last night that I don't remember."

The breeze carried a stench of burning to Pondwader's nose.

He put her hand down and leapt to his feet, shouted, "I forgot our fish! They're probably burning!" and ran across the camp with his long robe flying about his legs.

He grabbed the sticks and pulled them away from the fire, then used a small branch to slide them off into their wooden bowls. They looked terrible. He glanced back at Musselwhite. Had she sensed the Power flowing out of him and into her? Would she ask about it . . . ? What would he tell her? She had not spoken with him about the things he had told her that night on the beach. And he feared it might be because she had decided she didn't believe him. That, or the very idea that her dead son had been reborn inside him terrified her into silence.

Rising, he carefully started back, endeavoring not to trip over his hem.

Her eyes narrowed as he knelt, carefully set one bowl at her side, then sank back, crossed his legs, and balanced his bowl on his left knee.

"They didn't burn," Pondwader said, "but I hope they're not as dry as ancient bones. The skins seared."

Musselwhite looked down at the curlicues of brown skin and replied, "Only on one side, Pondwader."

He grinned sheepishly. "Here," he said, reaching for one of her fish. "Let me strip out the bones. It will make it easier for you."

He touched the skin to peel it back, and charred flakes covered his hand. He wiped them on his knee and glanced at her, hoping she hadn't noticed. When he did manage to get a good hold, the dry meat clung to the skin as he stripped it back. "Oh, Musselwhite," he said ominously. "This doesn't look good. It is as dry as a bone."

"Try the other side."

He gently pulled out the bone and tossed it into the forest, then prodded the meat. "You're right, this looks better. At least, it's edible. I think."

As Sun Mother climbed higher into the sky, the tops of the trees shimmered with golden sunshine. The autumn-touched leaves on the grapevines shone a dazzling yellow, framed by loops of brown vine. He could hear frogs croaking in the swamp, and the occasional splash of a diving turtle. Flutters of wings and birdsong filled the fragrant morning.

Pondwader lifted her bowl and held it near her face. "How do you wish to eat, Musselwhite? May I help you?"

"Just set the bowl at my side, Pondwader. I'll manage." He did, and she said, "Thank you."

Reaching across with her shaking left hand, she pulled out a piece of fish and ate it. When she swallowed, her stomach squealed, and she winced, as if experiencing cramps. After several moments, she commented, "Well, that was quite a battle, but I think I won."

Pondwader, starving, gobbled his fish, eating them as fast as he could clean them of bones. Around a mouthful, he said, "Good. Please eat some more. It will help you to heal."

She ate, but cautiously. She had barely finished half of her first fish when Pondwader set his empty bowl aside, propped his elbows on his knees, and settled in to watch her with wide, glowing eyes. A gentle breeze blew across the swamp, penetrating the trees, and flicking his long white hair about his shoulders.

"Why don't you talk for a while, Pondwader?" she said as she picked at her fish.

"About what?"

"Anything. What was it you wished to tell me earlier?"

Uncertainly, he said, "Let me get you another cup of tea first. You might—"

He started to lurch to his feet, and she caught his hand. "No. Thank you. It's kind of you to offer, but I would rather that you sat down. Good. Now, please go on."

He bowed his head and frowned at the wavering shadows on the dark forest duff. "M-musselwhite?"

"Yes, Pondwader."

"Do you remember when I asked you about Turtle Bone Doll?"

"I do."

Pondwader braced himself, watching her carefully work her shaking hand to carry the piece of fish to her mouth. It took great effort, but she managed.

Quietly, he said, "She—she comes to me."

"Who?"

"Turtle Bone Doll."

Musselwhite had picked up another piece, but slowly lowered it, and placed it back in her bowl. "What do you mean she comes to you?"

"I think . . ." he said softly and touched the robe over his heart. The space felt unusually warm. "I think she really comes to see Glade. To find out how he is doing. Sometimes, I swear I hear them talking to each other, though I can't make out any of their words."

"But, Pondwader, I never breathed Power into that doll. I breathed my souls into it. I loved it when I fashioned it. But I would never have attempted to do more. I will grant that the bone from which she is made is curious. It looks like bone, but it is stone. And very old. It was handed down to me by my grandmother, who claimed she received it from her grandmother. But none of them were Soul Dancers. Just weavers of beautiful fabrics." Musselwhite's eyes narrowed. "How could the doll have gained such Spirit Power? Where did it come from?"

"I don't know. She never said. Still . . . she comes, and she talks to me. She—she tells me the strangest things."

"What does she tell you?"

He twined his fingers in his robe, clutching it tightly. "Well, she . . . she told me there was a great storm coming, that it was darkness itself, and that if the world is to live, it will need all the light and warmth it can get. She said that every twinkle being born inside me was a shout of joy . . . a promise that life will continue. Turtle Bone Doll calls Glade the 'deliverer.' I don't know what she means by that, but that's what she calls him." He blinked contemplatively. "Do you know, Musselwhite?"

"No."

Pondwader looked away. He wet his dry lips. "And she says things about people. Like Cottonmouth. But I didn't really understand—"

"What did she say?"

"She said he wasn't cruel. That Cottonmouth is . . . how did she put it . . . ? 'Derelict. Desolate. A weightless shadow somersaulting underwater.' She also said that the waves of his solitude drown him, but that he can never cry for help. And that it isn't that he wants to die. She said he . . . he wants to be nothing."

Musselwhite went deathly pale. "I'm sure he does." She toyed with the corner of her blanket, crumpling it, then smoothing it flat. In a faint voice, she asked, "Has the doll said anything about me?"

"Oh, yes." Pondwader nodded. "Last night. She came to tell me you were dying—"

"Dying?"

"Yes, and Turtle Bone Doll said that it was my fault, because I refused to learn to Dance with the Lightning Bird's soul. She told me that if I didn't learn to soar and flash and thunder, that you would die!" He stopped with his mouth open. ". . . So I did."

"Did what?"

"I learned to thunder."

She forced herself to roll to her side, facing him. Her brows drew together. "What does that mean? How did you do that?"

Pondwader repeatedly threw his hand up. "I leaped."

"You . . . you what?"

He got to his feet and jumped up and down a few times to demonstrate. Dry exhalations of dust puffed beneath his sandals, forcing Musselwhite to squint in defense. "I leaped. The doll said I had to give up my human feet, and to do that I had to keep leaping until I forgot what the ground felt like, so I spent all night leaping up and down, and finally—"

"Your legs went numb?"

"No, no," he corrected with a shake of his head. Had she asked the question in earnest or not? She watched him expectantly. He knelt by her side again. "I was standing right there, beside the firepit, looking down into the coals, when this red tornado spun up from the ashes and grew a white hot core—like one of the Shining People fallen to earth. And I . . . I . . . ."

"Go on."

He coolly reached down and cleaned the sand from between his toes, while he said, "A white lance of light soared by my face, and I leaped up and grabbed its tail with both hands." He reached into the air, his hands clasping the invisible tail.

Musselwhite did not even blink. "Then?"

"I woke up."

"You woke?"

"Yes. Just like that. I bolted straight up. Breathing like a hunted wolf."

"So it was a dream?"

He brought his hands down and stared at them, then turned the palms out for her to see. She took his right hand and pulled it close for inspection. Tiny blisters bubbled over the skin.

Her face slackened. In a hoarse whisper, she asked, "How did this happen? Did you fall into the fire?"

"No, my wife, I—"

"Then what caused this?" she demanded fiercely.

"The—the Lightning Bird. His tailfeathers were burning hot." He tugged, trying to get his hand back. She refused to release it. She kept frowning at the blisters. Pondwader pulled harder, and, finally, she let go.

He cupped his fingers over his knees. "My wife, do you remember last night when I put my hands on your head?"

She frowned. ". . . Wait. Yes, I do. It felt good. Like cool water flowing through my body."

"Yes, but it . . . it was thunder. *I* became thunder, Musselwhite. And when I touched you? The roar spilled out of me and ran into you." Awe strained his voice. "I could not believe it, but it happened just as Turtle Bone Doll said it would."

She did not reply.

Pondwader bit his lip. "You don't look like you believe me, my wife."

"Pondwader, I . . ."

What did he expect? He had told her so many bizarre things—and now this. "Turtle Bone Doll told me something else, too, Musselwhite. Something you must know."

"What?"

"She said that one of the Shining Eagles died."

Musselwhite moved a hand down to her stomach, pressing, as though to probe a pain. "Then why is there no wind? Hurricane Breather—"

"I—I don't know."

She examined him gently for a few moments, then eased onto her back again, and stared sightlessly at the sky.

Pondwader waited for more questions, or comments, or . . . anything. But when nothing came, he got to his feet. "It really happened, Musselwhite."

"I know you think it did, Pondwader. I know, too, that you are not lying. I just . . . I need more time to consider your words. Try to understand. I have known some very great Soul Dancers, and heard them tell some curious . . . tales . . . about the Spirit World. But I—"

"Didn't believe them?"

"Not always, I admit. Power frightens me, Pondwader," she said honestly. "Very much. I try to believe as little of it as possible."

He nodded, feeling hollow, not knowing what to say. "Let me get the sundew-leaf salve. It will help to ease your pain."

As he walked away, she said, "Pondwader?"

He stopped and turned.

Sunlight glinted from the sweat on her face. "I do not doubt your word. I want you to know that."

He continued on his way, kicking at pine cones, wondering about Turtle Bone Doll and the mystery of her Spirit Power. How *could* she have come to life? Spirit Power could not just be imbued by a word. Rituals had to be performed, sacred Songs Sung. And by someone who knew those things. Musselwhite did not. Did Cottonmouth? If he were a witch, he would. Or . . . could someone else have performed the rituals? Who would Cottonmouth have trusted enough to let them touch that precious object?

Bright Feather?

A shudder ran through him. Could that be the secret? Had Cottonmouth taken Turtle Bone Doll to the old witch and asked him to breathe life into it? But that would mean that the Doll was evil, possessed by dark Spirit Power.

Pondwader floundered, filled with horror and wonder.

She didn't *feel* evil. Could she have deceived Pondwader?

The next time Turtle Bone Doll appeared, he would ask her all of these questions.

Twenty-nine

W̲ho are they?"

Kelp looked up. "I don't know, Dace."

"Do you think it's Windy Cove Clan? What's left of it?"

". . . Maybe."

Anxiety swelled in Kelp's chest. Too far away to tell, she nonetheless searched the small group of people for Pondwader's tall, skinny form.

The milky gleam of dusk descended upon the beach like a gossamer veil, falling lightly, slowly turning the white sand a sparkling glacial blue. Birds quieted with the coming of night. Only the constant pounding of surf serenaded the evening. Kelp ran alongside Dace, at the rear of the war party. The other men trotted far ahead of them, clustered in a tight knot. The long, gray pool of Manatee Lagoon stretched to the east. They had been running since before dawn, and Kelp prayed they would stop soon. Every time her foot struck the sand, her leg muscles cramped and cried in agony. Dace appeared just as miserable. His face had tightened, fighting the strain. But she feared she might be holding him back.

"You do not have to wait for me, Dace," she said. "Run ahead, if you wish. See who that is. I will catch up."

"Run ahead?" he asked. "I couldn't run ahead if I wanted to. I'm ready to collapse as it is."

Kelp smiled and forced herself to disregard the pain as she quickened her steps. Dace gave her a knowing glance and grinned, keeping up with her. As they neared the rear of the warriors' group, she saw an old, white-haired man break away from the people and run headlong for Tailfeather. Shouts of joy sounded.

"Is that Seedpod, Kelp? I can't tell."

Breathlessly, she answered. "Yes, it is. Do you see, Pondwader?"

Dace craned his neck, and searched the crowd. Warriors mingled with the survivors of Windy Cove Clan, creating one running, talking swirl of activity. Children dashed forward, shrieking and tugging on the warriors' hands, while dogs, hauling travois piled high with belongings, wagged their tails.

"No," Dace replied. "I do not see Pondwader."

Kelp's heart clutched up. "I have to speak with Seedpod," she said. "I must speak with him *now*."

"I'm coming with you."

They both headed for Seedpod. The old man wore a tattered tunic. His gaunt face with its leathery cheeks and blunt chin appeared haggard, though he smiled as he took Tailfeather's hands in greeting.

"Did Moonsnail send you?" Seedpod asked.

"The entire Council of Spirit Elders sent us," Tailfeather responded, and patted Seedpod's hands. His ears stuck out, sunburned and peeling, through his shoulder-length black hair. His flat nose bore a streak of dirt across the bridge. "Dogtooth told me about the battle, and I ran home to Heartwood as fast as I could to—"

"Dogtooth?" Seedpod asked. He whirled to look around. "Is he still here?"

"I do not know," Tailfeather responded uneasily. "He was three days ago. That's when I spoke with him last."

"Well . . . let us talk first. Then we will look for the old lunatic."

Seedpod gripped Tailfeather's arm and started to lead him through the gathering out toward the lonely beach. Kelp boldly stepped in front of Seedpod, swallowing hard.

"Forgive me, Elder," she said. "I am—"

"Kelp!" Seedpod replied and wrapped his stick-like old arms around her. "Blessed Spirits, I'm glad to see you again. Your brother gave me a message for you."

Kelp's knees shook. "Is . . . is Pondwader all right? Is he alive?"

Seedpod's wrinkled face tensed. "Oh, my dear child. I'm sorry. I did not think . . . Yes. Yes, Kelp. He survived the battle at Windy Cove. And thereby hangs a tale. Please," he said and gestured to the beach. "Come. Join Tailfeather and me. I will tell you all about it."

Relief left Kelp feeling weak. "Thank you, Elder. I would like to do that."

Seedpod and Tailfeather led the way across the sand, and Dace waited until they had gone a short distance ahead to put a hand on Kelp's narrow shoulder. Grinning, he whispered, "Can you walk? Or should I carry you?"

Kelp laughed and slapped his hand. "I'm fine. Just shaky."

"Then come on. I can't wait to hear about the battle."

They trotted forward.

Seedpod and Tailfeather sat down near the surf, where the noise would cover their voices. Kelp frowned at that, and exchanged a worried look with Dace. They both understood what it meant. Seedpod's news would frighten the others. What the old man had to say would be told in private first, then slowly disseminated through the rest of the Heartwood–Windy Cove clanspeople.

Kelp dropped silently to her knees beside Seedpod and unslung her pack, placing it on the sand in front of her. The old man put a gentle hand on her shoulder. "Kelp, could I ask you a favor?"

"Yes, of course."

"Would you and . . . and your friend gather wood for a fire? It will be getting cold soon. I promise not to say anything important until you return."

"Of course, Seedpod."

As she and Dace trotted down the beach picking up driftwood, Kelp heard Seedpod mention Cottonmouth, and saw Tailfeather's face fall. The two leaned close together to talk. Kelp broke into a run, gathering wood as quickly as she could. It didn't take long. When they had armloads, they ran back and dumped it in a pile. Without a word, they hastily reseated themselves.

"Yes," Tailfeather said, and the nostrils of his flat nose flared. He worked to make fire, spinning his drill on his fireboard, no small task on the windy beach. "Dogtooth said that there were so many warriors in his Dream that he could not count them—"

"Two or three tens," Seedpod said. "By the time we arrived, many had fled into the forest, hunting down our people. I'm not even certain how many were there. What else did Dogtooth say?"

Tailfeather moved his hands to the top of his drill again, and continued spinning. "He said Musselwhite streaked through those warriors like a Lightning Bird."

Seedpod nodded. "She did indeed. Without her, we would all be dead." The he turned and smiled at Kelp. "Thank you for the wood, Kelp and . . . and what is your name, young warrior?"

"Dace, Spirit Elder. I am Black Dace. A friend of Pondwader's." He straightened, throwing out his chest proudly.

"And mine," Kelp added.

Seedpod was digging a hole in the sand with a large clamshell. When he'd scooped out enough, he said, "Could you select a small stick for me, Kelp?"

"Yes." She rummaged around in the pile, pulled one out, and handed it to him.

"Thank you," Seedpod settled back, removed a hafted chert knife from his pack, and began whittling on the stick, letting the thin strips of wood fall into the hole in the sand. Gusts played with them as they fell, tumbling and spiraling the strips around before they landed.

"I'm ready," Tailfeather said.

The War Leader laid down his drill, cupped his hand around the glowing dust in the hole on his fireboard, and carefully moved it to the firepit, where he dumped the contents on top of Seedpod's whittling. Seedpod sliced more strips of wood on top of the dust. Tailfeather shielded the kindling with both hands, and blew gently. Flames crackled and whipped in the wind. Seedpod pulled larger sticks from the pile and fed the flames until they had a good blaze going.

Kelp shivered when the warmth struck her. She had been sweating all day, and her damp tunic stuck to her body in clammy folds. Soon, she would be bitterly cold. She slid forward, snuggling up to the firepit with her hands extended.

"And then what happened?" Tailfeather asked.

Seedpod untied his blanket from his pack and swung it around his elderly shoulders. Wind fluttered the ends. He gathered them up and held them, sighing. "Let me start at the beginning," Seedpod said. "Three days out from Heartwood, Musselwhite felt something terrible had happened at Windy Cove. She decided to run on ahead, but before she left us, she gave Pondwader strict orders to hide in the forest until she had made certain everything at Windy Cove was all right."

"Which he didn't," Kelp said, knowing her brother.

"That's right," Seedpod smiled. "Before we even arrived, we heard the screams and cries. We raced forward as quickly as we could. I told Pondwader to do as his wife had said, and he crouched down behind a scrub oak. Musselwhite was in trouble, though. Surrounded. It looked very bad. I nocked my atlatl and cast, killing one of the men who threatened her. Then . . ."

A tall youth walked across the sand, and Seedpod stopped and looked up. "Ah, Diamondback," he said. "Come, join us."

"I didn't wish to disturb you, Grandfather," Diamondback said, and glanced at Kelp. "I just wanted to tell you that I found Dogtooth. I set up our camp near his."

"Good. Thank you, Grandson. And Thorny Boy?"

"I fed him supper and put him to bed. He was asleep in my arms before he finished his dried redfish. He was a very tired boy."

Diamondback smiled and Kelp saw the bandage tied around his leg. He'd been wounded, though he seemed to be walking pretty well—just stiffly. She scrutinized his face in the firelight. What a handsome young man. He looked very much like Musselwhite, with an oval face and turned-up nose. He had long, black hair; it hung down his back in a braid. Diamondback saw her looking at him and smiled. Kelp blushed and looked away.

Seedpod caught the exchange. "Sit down, Grandson," he said. "You have already met War Leader Tailfeather. Let me introduce you to Pondwader's sister, Kelp, and her friend, Dace."

Diamondback took Dace's hand in a strong grip, saying, "Dace, thank you for coming to help us."

Dace nodded. "I am glad to help in any way I can."

Then Diamondback leaned over and reached for Kelp's hand. As he did, his shaggy eyebrows drew down over his nose, a little worried, but his full lips tipped in another smile. "Kelp, thank you, as well. I did not know your brother for long, but I considered him to be a friend. I hope we will be friends, too."

She took his hand and his fingers felt warm and strong in her grip. "I hope so, too, Diamondback," she answered.

He eased down next to Dace, making certain his hurt leg extended straight out.

"Anyway," Seedpod said to Tailfeather, who listened intently. "I killed one of the men attacking my daughter, but then Pondwader, *Pondwader*, rose from his hiding place, spread his arms, and walked out into the midst of the battle!"

Tailfeather's mouth gaped. "Pondwader? Is this the same White Lightning Boy I know? The one who is afraid of his own souls smiling up at him from a conchshell mirror?"

Kelp scowled and she saw Diamondback bow his head to smother a smile. Dace glanced back and forth between them. His brow furrowed.

"Oh, yes, indeed," Seedpod continued. White hair flipped around his cheeks, teased by the sea breeze. "And when Pondwader walked out, I tell you, Cottonmouth's warriors screamed and ran like a pack of spooked coyotes. Truly, I would never have imagined Pondwader could do such a brave thing. He—"

"Pondwader is very courageous," Kelp said softly. "People just don't know it because he is also very gentle. Isn't that right, Dace?"

Dace nodded. "Absolutely."

Seedpod reached out and patted Kelp's hair. "I did not mean to sound as if I were dishonoring your brother. Pondwader saved the lives of many people that day, Kelp. All of Windy Cove Clan is grateful for Pondwader's bravery." He smiled at Tailfeather. "Anyway, after Cottonmouth's warriors fled, Musselwhite chased them into the forest, and I went around . . ."

Kelp peered at Diamondback. He kept glancing at her. One instant he looked frightened, and the next he seemed to be admiring her. He seemed almost as worried about his interest as she did. She guessed his age at ten-and-six or ten-and-seven summers. Old enough to be married. Was he?

Dace leaned over to whisper, "Now that I know Pondwader is safe, I'm going to go set up camp and cook supper. I'm starved. Do you want to come?"

She whispered back, "I'll be along soon."

Dace shifted. He cupped a hand to her ear to ask, "Will you be all right?" then he subtly jerked his head toward Diamondback.

Surprised, she lifted her brows, silently questioning what in the world he meant.

Dace shrugged, but he still looked concerned. Politely, he rose and bowed to Seedpod, then Tailfeather, neither of whom seemed to notice he'd risen at all. Seedpod continued with his lively story about surveying the damage after the battle, and Tailfeather kept adding wood to the fire. Dace strode away across the sand, his broad back swaying. He turned once, walked backward a short distance, looking at Kelp, then shook his head and broke into a trot toward the warriors gathered near the trees. She saw his black silhouette blend into those standing around the fire.

"Kelp?" Seedpod halted his story. "We are almost out of wood. Would you mind—"

"Oh, no, of course not!"

She rose to her feet, and Diamondback got up. "I'll help you, Kelp."

"All right."

They walked out across the moist sand at the edge of the surf, and Kelp noticed that he kept sneaking glances at her. Two hands taller than she, with long legs, he matched his stride to hers. When he gazed out at the waves rolling across Sea Girl's face, the starglow accentuated the lines of his handsome face and gleamed from the muscles in his bare chest. The sight affected Kelp strangely, making her heart pound.

She bent, tossed a big shell out of the way, and picked up a piece of driftwood. "Diamondback? Why don't I collect the wood, and hand it to you? That way you won't have to bend down so much."

"Oh, I can bend down, Kelp. Really, I—"

"You are hurt. I can see that. Besides, you can carry more than I can anyway. This way, we will be sharing the work."

He nodded, smiled obligingly, and said, "All right."

Kelp smiled back, but it almost scared her to death to do it. She handed him the wood. He took it and put it in the crook of his arm. As they wandered down the beach, Kelp asked, "How were you wounded? Was it a dart or—"

"Yes, a dart," he answered, and the curve of his mouth tightened. He lowered his gaze and watched his feet as they walked. "Though my leg is almost healed. It's just stiff."

"It must have been scary." As she bent and handed him another piece of wood, he nodded.

"It was, yes. Very scary. But I was not wounded at the Windy Cove battle, Kelp. I was wounded ten days before that, while out with my father's scouting party. It happened north of Windy Cove."

Their gazes met and held. Blessed Sun Mother, he had eyes with a pull like the ocean, powerful, constant. A deep ache shone in those dark depths.

"Cottonmouth's warriors?" she asked.

"Yes. They came out of nowhere. We did not even have time to nock our atlatls."

Kelp knelt to retrieve more wood, and tried to imagine what it would be like to be trapped that way, caught completely without warning. The terror must have been beyond imagining. "You had family killed at that battle, didn't you?"

"Yes, I did. I miss them . . . very much."

She could barely hear him. The beach, with its jumble of shells and sponges, and the moonlight glinting brilliantly from the waves, all worked together to muffle sound. That, and his voice had come softly. Kelp looked up, considering him. Insect grease smeared his body. It seemed to snare the moonglow and hold it in a glistening sheen across the high planes of his cheekbones, and in the wells of his deeply set eyes, and on the muscles of his left arm, where he carried the bundle of driftwood.

"How old are you, Diamondback?"

"Ten-and-six summers."

Kelp thought about that. "Yet you are still living in your grandfather's lodge?"

"Yes."

"Why have you not married?"

"Oh . . . You ask hard questions, Kelp." He let his head fall forward and squinted at the glimmering shells strewn along the shore. "I was to be married last summer. But she"—he inhaled and let the breath out in a rush—"she was killed in Cottonmouth's raid during the Moon of Flowering Yucca."

"I'm sorry," Kelp said. "I'm so sorry."

The sadness went from his eyes and he smiled again. "You remind me of her," he said. "Her name was Torchwood. She was very beautiful, too."

Kelp took a deep breath, hoping to slow her pulse. No one had ever called her beautiful, though on occasion her grandmother had told her she looked pretty. "That's very nice of you to say, but—"

"I mean it."

"You do?"

He nodded. "Yes." After a pause, he continued, "I watched you this evening, Kelp, as you were coming up the beach. You ran so hard. I knew you had to be tired, but you never showed it. You ran like a warrior. The slanting rays of sunlight were in your face, your hair blowing free in the wind. I swear, you looked . . . magnificent.''

An embarrassed smile tugged her mouth, though she tried to squelch it. She stood up and handed him more driftwood. Diamondback smiled, too. Against the background of stars and sky, he looked very tall. Boldly, he reached out and took her hand. His breathing had gone shallow, as if the act scared him half to death. "Do you . . . mind?" he asked.

"No, I don't mind."

"I think we have enough wood. Shall we head back?"

"All right."

As they walked down the beach, his fingers twined warmly with hers, the sounds of the night became incredibly clear to Kelp. Waves splashed the shore. Wind soughed through the oaks. Men and women laughed. No one seemed to care in the slightest that a girl, not yet a woman, and an honored warrior, walked down the beach together.

Fear tickled her stomach. She stole a glance at Diamondback and found him watching her from the corner of his eye.

"You have no idea," he said through a tight exhalation, "how much courage it took for me to get up and come with you to collect wood tonight. I almost fainted just thinking about it."

"Why?"

"Well, I did not wish to offend Dace, and I wasn't certain—"

"Dace is of my clan, Diamondback. He is . . . he is my best friend. Other than my brother, Pondwader, I mean."

Diamondback squeezed her fingers. "Good."

A light-headed sensation possessed Kelp, like nothing she had ever known. She could have been walking on air. "I'm glad you came to collect wood, Diamondback."

His grip tightened. "I am, too."

They walked back, their sandals squishing in the wet sand. Dark wisps of cloud scudded by overhead. Several jellyfish had washed ashore, and they had to take care to walk around them. Now and then, she spied a shiny cowrie shell. If it had been light, she would have collected them all and strung them together for a necklace.

"Diamondback," she asked, "where are Pondwader and Musselwhite? I know your father said they were all right, but why aren't they here? Are they coming?"

Diamondback stopped dead in his tracks. "Oh, Kelp. I'm sorry. No one has told you?"

Her souls went numb. She had to force herself to breathe. "Told me what?"

Diamondback looked at her. "This is a long story. My—"

"Hurry, please."

"Yes. Forgive me. My father, Diver, is alive. Cottonmouth is holding him captive. Mother did not find out until after the battle and when she did, she . . . well, I think she went a little crazy. She packed up and left for Standing Hollow Horn Village before dawn of the next day. And—"

"Pondwader went with her?"

Diamondback shook his head. "No. Mother went alone. She did not wish Pondwader to go with her. I think she cares about him too much, Kelp, and she knew how difficult the journey would be."

"So, where is Pondwader?"

"He ran after Mother. My father tried to stop him, to convince Pondwader to come here, to Manatee Lagoon with us . . . but Pondwader refused."

Kelp felt that her heart might pound through her ribs. "Yes, he would have. It's just like him. So, by now, they're together?"

Diamondback didn't look eager to answer that. "Yes, I'm sure they are. They must be."

"And they are headed for Standing Hollow Horn Village to rescue your father, is that right?"

He nodded. "Yes."

Kelp resumed walking, heading back toward the fire where Seedpod and Tailfeather sat in animated conversation. Seedpod's arms waved expressively. A sick sensation had started prickling in her stomach. Pondwader knew he'd be going on this journey. That's why he'd wanted to marry Musselwhite so quickly. It had to be. Is that what the ghosts had told him?

"What are you thinking, Kelp?" Diamondback asked as he limped at her side.

"How far is Standing Hollow Horn Village, Diamondback? Do you know?"

"From here? Let me see. At a warrior's trot, you could make it in five days. Four, if you could run straight through."

"*If* you could?"

"Well, yes. Cottonmouth has war parties everywhere. It would be suicide to try to run straight up the beach. You would certainly be spotted and killed."

"So, I'll have to sneak through the trees, you mean?"

Diamondback stopped, and pulled hard on her hand to jerk her around to face him. "What are we discussing?"

"Nothing, I just—"

"It's too dangerous. I have thought of it myself. And dismissed the notion. You will be killed before you get halfway there."

Kelp gazed up blankly, but he seemed to see straight through her, because his brows lowered. She said, "You must think I am very stupid, Diamond-back."

He gave her a sidelong look. "No," he answered. "I just fear you may share many of my mother's characteristics, young warrior woman."

Kelp proudly lifted her chin. "Like what?"

Diamondback released her hand and ran his fingertips down the side of her face. When he reached her chin, he held it in his palm, and bent down to stare at her, nose-to-nose. Moonlight glinted from his dark eyes. "For one, the longing to do crazy things when someone you love is in danger. For another, the arrogance to feel you can do them alone. I think the last is the worst."

Kelp smiled at him. "And you do not share any of your mother's characteristics?"

Diamondback released her chin. With a sour tone, he replied, "Unfortunately, I share all of them."

"That's probably why I like you."

A slow smile came to his face. "Do you like me?"

"Yes, but I would like you even better if you said you'd come with me. No, listen! It won't take long. If we leave before dawn, and—"

"Great Mouse! You didn't hear a word I said!"

"Oh, yes, I did." Kelp took a step closer to him, standing with her fists clenched. "You said you'd been many days' walk to the north of Windy Cove, which means you know the forest trails almost all the way to Standing Hollow Horn Village. You also said—"

"*Why* am I always attracted to warrior women?" Diamondback groaned. "It will be the death of me!"

"Well, you want that death to be meaningful, don't you? *Come with me, Diamondback.* You can help your mother! And I can help Pondwader. He needs me. He really does. And I'll bet . . ." she hesitated, lowering her voice. "I'll bet your mother needs you, too."

"Ah!" He lifted a finger and shook it. "Now the guilt comes. Are all women good at that? At making men feel guilty?"

Kelp smiled and linked her arm with his, hugging it warmly. "I knew you had a conscience," she said. "How long will it take you to get ready? And what about your leg? Will you be able to run?"

"I never said I was going!"

Kelp frowned contemplatively. "Of course, if we follow the forest trails, we won't be able to run very often. How much longer do you think the journey will take if we—"

"Kelp . . ." Diamondback wilted, his shoulders hunching forward. A quizzical expression creased his handsome face. "Let us take this wood back before my father comes to get it—then we'll talk more. All right?"

She patted his arm tenderly. "Thank you, Diamondback. I would like that very much."

Dace crouched beside his fire, watching Kelp talking with Diamondback. They'd been out there for more than a hand of time, sitting together by the surf. She hadn't eaten, or drunk any water—and after a day of hard running! Seedpod and Tailfeather had risen long ago and come in to eat. What was wrong with that Windy Cove warrior? Was he just dim-witted? He must be, or he wouldn't be keeping Kelp out there so long. Didn't he understand how tired and thirsty she must be? What kind of a man would do that?

The strips of fat raccoon that Dace had darted, roasted, and saved for Kelp lay stone cold in a bowl on the other side of the fire. Wind-blown ashes had settled on the strips, giving them a white crusty appearance. The meat had tasted so sweet!

Angrily, Dace slammed more wood into his firepit and winced when the bottom log cracked and sputtered, shooting sparks out all around him. More flitted upward, winking, as they sailed away in the wind. One of the warriors, sleeping three tens of hands away, grumbled, jerked his blanket up over his head, and flopped to his other side.

Dace unlaced his pack and pulled out a pale green tunic. He slipped it over his head. As he smoothed it down around his hips, he watched Sister Moon wander like a polished shell through a sea of puffy charcoal clouds. She scattered sparkling handfuls of silver light across the ocean and forest.

He ought to go get Kelp. Yes, get her, drag her back here, and give her a good talking to! That's exactly what he ought to do. For her own sake. She did not understand Diamondback's intentions, but Dace did. He'd given many women the same look that Diamondback had been giving Kelp—but Dace's quarry had been *women!* Not little girls. Kelp had no one here but Dace to protect her. To tell her things about life. And men. He gritted his teeth. Yes, she needed him, and here he sat! Smoldering. Doing nothing!

I swear on my ancestors' graves, that if that Windy Cove warrior hurts her, I will strangle him to death with my bare hands. After that, I'll drag his body off so no one will ever find it!

Reflexively, Dace worked his fingers, exercising them for the task ahead. When he realized it, he looked down, felt like an idiot, and gruffly folded his arms across his chest.

In a whisper, he reminded himself, "She is a smart girl. She will know when to tell him 'no.' . . . Won't she?"

The question made his gut roil.

Kelp had been like a sister to him his entire life. The sister he'd never known, and he loved her. More than once she'd talked sense into him when his temper had burned his sense to soot. And that seemed to be quite often in the past few summers. He could not count the times Kelp had soothed his vanity after he'd made a fool of himself. She had always been there for him—until a short while ago.

The past seven moons had left Dace hollow and hurting. Both his parents had died from a fever, and Dace had gone to live with his aunt. She was a good woman, but he'd felt so lost and scared, he'd started acting desperate, picking fights, growing as surly as a mating alligator. Pondwader, his best friend, had drifted away. How had that happened? The change had been gradual. Pondwader just seemed to want to spend more time alone. Or talking with his sister. Kelp, too, had grown distant. Her friendship had shifted from Dace to other girls. And Dace had suddenly found himself alone. Oh, he'd had cousins, aunts and uncles, and second and third cousins—but they weren't friends. They were relatives.

The wind changed and smoke billowed over him, forcing him to squint. The sweet smell of pine sap bathed him. He could see it, boiling up from a crack in a log, sizzling away into nothingness.

Out on the beach, Kelp and Diamondback rose. Dace jumped to his feet and stood with the wind flapping his braid against his back. They were holding hands! His blood surged feverishly.

They parted. Kelp headed toward Dace, and Diamondback angled up the beach. The warrior walked contemplatively, as if lost in thought.

Dace slipped into the darkness of the forest, following a winding deer trail that led north. He paralleled Diamondback's course. Stepping lightly over deadfall and around brush, he didn't make a sound. The rhythmic roar of Sea Girl helped. Even when his sandals snapped a twig hidden in the shadows, the surf swallowed the noise.

Dace slowed when he heard voices up ahead. Through the tangled weave of branches, he spied a fire's glow. Someone laughed softly, then a blanket whipped in the wind, as if being spread out for sleeping.

Diamondback entered the woods just ahead of him and started down the trail toward the fire.

Dace ran on his tiptoes. Just as he prepared to leap and grab the man around the shoulders, his leg brushed a palm frond, and Diamondback whirled, leveling a kick before he even saw who followed him. The blow took Dace in the stomach and knocked him flat on his back on the deer trail. Dace grunted, started to scramble up, but Diamondback fell upon him, bashing him to the ground again. Dace glimpsed the stiletto in Diamondback's hand, and saw the deadly intent on his face.

"Don't kill me!" he yelled.

It took a few moments for Diamondback's face to change. The stiletto hovered. *"Dace?"* he said. "What are you doing out here?"

"Get off me! And I'll tell you!"

Diamondback slid off and slumped to the ground, breathing hard. Even in the wavering moonlight, Dace could see the flush that rouged his cheeks.

Dace rolled over and slammed a fist into the forest floor. Gray puffs twirled up. "I am so stupid! I could be dead now!" he whispered harshly. "How could I have thought . . . You've been in many battles. This is my first war walk!" He slammed his fist down several more times to relieve his humiliation. "I can't believe I tried it! You are a *real* warrior!"

Diamondback slipped his stiletto back into his belt, and braced his elbow on the ground, propping himself up. "That may be . . ." he panted. "But you are . . . lucky to still be dry. I came out here to empty my bladder."

Dace looked up, chuckled, then broke into a roar of laughter.

Diamondback laughed, too. When their mirth began to die down, Diamondback wiped tears from his eyes and said, "You took a grave risk, Dace. So, tell me. What were you doing sneaking up on me?"

Dace sat up and heaved a heavy sigh. "I was going to kill you."

"Why? What did I do?"

"Probably nothing." Dace shrugged, rubbing his aching stomach.

"I don't understand."

Dace sucked in a lung full of air and bent forward. "Do you have a sister, Diamondback?"

The warrior's eyes tightened. "I used to. She's dead. Why?"

Dace brushed at a root that snaked across the trail. "None of my brothers or sisters lived past the age of five summers. Kelp has been very special to me. She is like my little sister, and I . . ." He waved a hand helplessly. "I was worried that you might not realize how precious she is."

Diamondback smiled. "I think I do," he said. "Anyway, I would never hurt her, if that is what was worrying you. I like her very much."

Dace glanced up. "I could tell. I saw the way you were looking at her early and I *knew* what you were thinking."

"Of course I was. What's wrong with that?"

Dace's eyes narrowed. "What's wrong with that?" he blurted. "She is not a woman yet! That's what!"

Diamondback's jaw slackened as his eyes widened. A swallow went down his throat. "She didn't tell me that."

"Well, no, of course not! Did you ask?"

"No." He shook his head. "That makes this even worse."

"Makes what worse?"

Diamondback peered unblinking at Dace. "Do you know she's planning on following Pondwader?"

"What are you talking about?"

"Pondwader is heading for Standing Hollow Horn Village, right into Cottonmouth's lair, and—"

Dace shouted, *"Why?"*

Diamondback held up a hand, and cautiously surveyed the area near the fire's glow. The voices had stopped. Shadows moved across the trees. "Shh," he whispered. "I don't want my grandfather to hear about this until I tell him."

Dace crawled closer to Diamondback and sat down again, whispering, "Why would Pondwader—"

"He is with my mother," Diamondback said, then wet his lips uncertainly. "At least I hope he is. My mother left to go and rescue my father, who is being held prisoner by Cottonmouth. Pondwader ran off to follow her."

"Oh, no." Dace dropped his head into his hands. The pain in his stomach intensified. "Pondwader can't even muster the nerve to throw a snail into boiling water. This is terrible."

"I know." Diamondback nodded. "So the question is this: Should we go and help them, or not?"

Dace filled his cheeks with air and blew it out in a gush. "Well, I can tell you this. If Kelp thinks Pondwader is in trouble, nothing will stop her. With or without us, she's going to go after him."

Diamondback put a friendly hand on Dace's shoulder. "Thank you for affirming my greatest fear. Is Kelp good with an atlatl?"

"Better than good," Dace replied. "She can dart a dragonfly in the head at ten tens of paces."

Diamondback's brows lifted appreciatively. "Well, then," he said. "We had better start making plans."

"But what about your leg?" Dace asked, staring at the thick bandage. "Can you—"

"I must. I'm the only one of us who knows the forest trails that far north." Diamondback massaged his leg as if to reassure himself. Pain lined his face. "Now, Dace, go back to your camp. Let Kelp talk you into going. She practiced every word on me." He smiled and shook his head. "She can be very convincing—and charming."

"For a *girl*."

Diamondback sighed, then got to his feet, lifted his tunic, and began urinating onto the dry leaves. "I haven't forgotten, my friend."

Dace rose to his feet. "Nor will you. I plan on reminding you. Often."

Sister Moon peered down at Cottonmouth through a milky film of clouds. Her gleam floundered through his shelter, groping at him tentatively, then jerking back as if afraid. He sat on his bedding, a piece of sandstone before him, the awl in his hand. The barest of breezes rocked the fabric bags hanging from the rafters. They creaked softly.

As he bent forward to continue sharpening the awl, his long, silvered black hair fell over his bare chest. Expertly, he pulled the broken tip back and forth across the piece of sandstone. The rhythmic *zizzing* sound felt like cool balm on a fevered wound.

Glade's turtle bone doll sat propped in the midst of his rumpled blankets, watching. Her faded eyes shone unusually bright in the moonlight. But, then, she had been there at the end, tucked into the collar of Glade's tunic. She would understand this only too well.

Very softly, Cottonmouth asked, "Why has it never occurred to me before? Hmm? Do you think it's because the thought still frightens me?"

A tremor like an earthquake worked its way up his spine. Cottonmouth held his breath a moment, willing it away.

. . . Then he went back to sharpening the awl, honing it to a fine deadly point.

Thirty

What? Why, that's rubbish, child! Cottonmouth would have never tried to skewer the Turtle Bone Doll with the Awl! Blessed Spirits, just the thought unsettles me. Who told you that?

. . . Well, I must say that makes me want to break things. I didn't even realize that Star-that-Never-Moves knew these stories.

Ha! Yes, that's a good observation, child. Obviously, she doesn't.

Well, anyway, the very idea is ridiculous. Why would Cottonmouth have wasted the Awl's Power on such a . . . Hmm?

She told you *that*!

Great Worm. Yes, of course, Turtle Bone Doll was alive, but why would Cottonmouth have wanted the Doll's souls inside him? That's not merely ridiculous, it's moronic.

No, no, dear. Listen to me. Cottonmouth was much too smart to use the sacred Awl's Power for such foolishness. He had far more important plans.

Yes, indeed, terrifying plans . . .

Sun Mother's Winter Celebration Day was almost upon them, and everyone at Standing Hollow Horn Village was occupied with preparations. There would be a great feast, Dancing from dawn until dusk, and ritual games where tremendous wagers would be bet. . . .

The day had dawned hot and sweltering, much to Pondwader's dismay. His worry about Musselwhite had grown to panicked proportions. Perspiration dripped down her cheeks as she walked along the deer trail behind him, her beautiful face pale and drawn. He kept turning to check on her. The pain in her head forced her to go slowly. Today, things like upturned shells and twigs crunched beneath her carefully placed sandals. Pondwader suspected that ordinarily she would have cursed herself for producing such noise, but this morning she could only keep her gaze focused on the ground and pray she could make it to the next tree, where she would brace her shoulder and catch her breath. Dressed in a lightweight tunic, belted at the waist with a yucca cord, she looked miserable. A headband, knotted on the left side, kept her long hair out of her eyes, and held her sundew-salve poultice in place.

Around them, oaks and hickory and hackberry trees had sunk their roots in the dark mat of soil. Branches thrust up into the clear blue sky, as if reaching for Sun Mother's blessing. Palmettos sprouted everywhere. Pondwader winced when the serrated leaves of one plant tugged at Musselwhite's tunic, threatening to topple her. She tried to push them out of the way, but just didn't have the strength. She turned sideways and edged by.

No wind penetrated the forest. Even the birds seemed daunted by the smothering heat. They sat glumly on the branches—songless.

"I'd give anything," Musselwhite said softly, "for a cool breeze to ease the burning in my head."

"I know. Autumn weather is so fickle. One day freezing, the next roasting." Pondwader led the way around a curve in the trail, his long robe dragging across the duff, and entered a well of forest shadows. "It's better up here, Musselwhite. A little cooler."

An old oak stood on the bend of the trail. When Musselwhite reached it, she sank against the thick trunk and breathed in the fragrance of warm bark. Pondwader ached for her. His long white hair clung wetly to his skull, and formed little curls on his forehead. He shook them away. His own sweat-drenched robe felt like a cape of stone. And if the heat sapped his strength, she must be suffering greatly.

"Are you all right?" Pondwader asked. "Do you need to rest again?"

"Just . . . just for a moment. Then we can be on our way." She leaned her aching head against the trunk.

If only she'd let him, Pondwader could have searched out a patch of willow, boiled down the stems, and made an effective headache powder. Maypop roots would have worked, too, though not as well. But she had told him no, that they had to keep moving. Perhaps tomorrow, before she woke, he would find the time.

With a shaking hand, she massaged the base of her skull, then lowered her hand to her stomach. . . .

Pondwader walked back to her. "Are you feeling nauseated again?"

Musselwhite smiled feebly. "My stomach has tied itself in knots trying not to throw up."

Gently, he laid a cool hand on her cheek. "Would you like some water?"

"Yes, that might help. Thank you."

He unslung his pack from his shoulder, drew out the gourd of water, and removed the stem-lid. As he handed it to her, he shivered suddenly and squeezed his eyes closed.

Musselwhite sipped the water. "What's wrong?"

Pondwader peered at her with glistening eyes. "It's—it's the Lightning Bird. He's rumbling."

Her brows pulled together. She took a long drink from the gourd. "If that Bird is so eager to talk, ask him to call out to Storm Girl. We could use some rain to cool off the day."

"Rain?" Pondwader said. He studied the cloudless sky, and his smooth forehead puckered.

"Yes," Musselwhite answered. "I've known several Soul Dancers who claimed to have the souls of birds. They could call storms."

"Dogtooth mentioned something about that."

She handed him the gourd and wiped the sweat from her chin with the back of her hand, then leaned more heavily against the oak. "Dogtooth ought to know. Why don't you try? After all, Lightning Birds are related to Storm Girl. And I would very much enjoy a few cool drops of rain."

Pondwader blinked worriedly. "But maybe this Lightning Bird can't call Storm Girl."

"Well," she said. "We will have wasted only a little time."

Nervous, Pondwader flapped his long arms against his sides. "If you are ready, let's . . . let's keep walking down the deer trail. I'll speak to the Lightning Bird while we're moving. That might be easier. I won't feel so much pressure if we're walking."

Musselwhite nodded, and smiled. "Go ahead. I'll follow you."

Pondwader walked forward, his head down, biting his lip.

Musselwhite resumed her own pace, one step at a time. She had to use caution. A single fall might confine her to her bedding again. It couldn't be risked. An eerie whisper seeped through the trees . . . then it vanished. She frowned.

In the branches overhead, a squirrel leaped and ran, trying to keep up with Pondwader. Chittering and jumping, the tiny animal ran down a hickory trunk and bounded into the deer trail in front of Pondwader. Pondwader halted. The squirrel stood up on its hind legs, chest puffing in and out quickly, and cocked its head.

"What is it, little one?" Pondwader whispered. "You want it to rain, too?"

Musselwhite stopped. The way the trail curved, she could see Pondwader from a side view. He had his chin up, frowning at the blue sky visible through the tangle of branches. The squirrel twisted around to peer up, too. Both stood, quiet, completely still, expectant.

Musselwhite braced a hand against a hackberry tree to keep herself standing. Her knees had started to shake. High in the sky above them, a few wisps of cloud sailed. A smile touched her lips. The squirrel cheeped, and dropped on all fours—but it didn't run.

Pondwader closed his eyes. A gentle breeze rustled the leaves, blowing cool up the trail, fluttering Pondwader's white hair. Sunlight flooded the damp strands, adding pink glints.

Musselwhite turned her face into the breeze. Oh, it felt good.

The squirrel cheeped again, and its soft brown eyes widened as it looked upward.

Musselwhite followed its gaze. The wisps of cloud had woven themselves together, forming a puff. As she watched, more puffs sailed in, coming from every direction, and melded with the first.

She glanced back at Pondwader. He'd lifted a hand to his chest, placing two fingers over his heart. The faint rumble of thunder echoed. Fascinated, Musselwhite searched the sky for the Lightning Birds. But she saw only the constant movement of clouds, rolling in to crowd the sky.

Scattered drops of rain fell, soft on her upturned face.

The squirrel let out a high-pitched chur and bounded into the brush, bending blades of grass in its wake. Just as the animal scrambled into a hole in a rotten tree trunk, lightning flashed. A thunderclap split the day.

Musselwhite jumped, breathing hard, her head throbbing.

It began to rain harder, big drops cascading down, batting at tree leaves and palmetto fronds, splatting on deadfall. She stared at Pondwader. He had not moved. Where anxiety had furrowed his brow, now serenity shone on his young face.

A huge Lightning Bird swooped from the clouds and crackled downward in a blue-white arc, blasting a tree a short distance away. Musselwhite dodged behind a hackberry and cupped hands to her ears to block the roar.

"Pondwader!" she called.

Rain poured down in blinding sheets, drenching the world.

Another Lightning Bird flashed through the sky, the glare so brilliant that Musselwhite jerked her eyes away. An explosion rocked the ground, and wood splinters showered her. The lightning-blasted air sizzled with the scent of destruction. Blue afterimages seared her gaze when she pulled her eyes open, and fought to get a good look at the riven tree. It lay, split down the middle, each half lying on either side of Pondwader.

Musselwhite ran forward, sick to her stomach, and placed a hand on the top of his white head while she watched the sky. Rain had soaked her through. "Pondwader," she said. "That's enough. I believe. Do you hear me? I believe you!"

"What?" he murmured. He tipped his head to examine her, and water slid from his cheeks as if poured from a basket. "What did you say? Oh! Look, my wife! It's raining!" He lurched to his feet and shouted, "I did it! It's raining, Musselwhite!" He jumped up and down excitedly. "I did it! Look!"

"You certainly *did* do it. Now, stop it, will you?"

Another Lightning Bird soared right over their heads, roaring so loud Musselwhite cried out. She threw up an arm, and Pondwader hit the ground on his stomach, his face in the mud.

"Pondwader!"

"I'm trying!"

He rolled to his back and squinted upward into the deluge of rain. The flood washed his long hair away from his face, and sent tendrils slithering onto the trail like a fleeing swarm of white snakes.

Musselwhite gaped as the clouds parted. Lances of golden sunlight shot through the misty forest. Before her heart could pound ten times, the storm had dissolved into a clean bright blue bowl which arched into infinity above them.

Pondwader sat up, covered from head to toe with mud, his hair dark with it. He whirled to gaze in astonishment at Musselwhite. "I can't believe it worked!"

She just stared at him, mouth open.

He scrambled to his feet, then hesitantly edged toward her. "Did I scare you?"

"How did you do that?"

Pondwader flashed a wide grin. "I just asked the baby Lightning Bird if he would please give us some rain to cool the day. Of course, I had to concentrate, to make sure that Gl—the Bird heard me. But that was all, Musselwhite. And it worked!"

Her gaze landed on the charred halves of the tree. The spot where Pondwader had sat still dimpled the wet ground.

She wiped the rain from her face. Her heartbeat felt like hammerstone blows to her skull. As she skirted the smoldering trunk and angled onto the trail again, she struggled to slow her pulse. Small, shimmering ponds filled every depression. She stepped wide around them.

Pondwader ran up behind her, walking so close she could feel his heavy breathing on the back of her neck.

"My wife?" he asked. He speeded up to walk alongside her. "Are you all right?"

"Well, you've spoiled it."

"Spoiled w-what?"

Musselwhite stopped and scowled at him. "I always thought it was coincidence. I never actually believed those Soul Dancers called the rain. I thought it was all"—she made an airy gesture—"trickery."

Pondwader chewed his lip anxiously. "Did you wish to keep believing that?"

"It was singularly comforting, Pondwader."

"But, my wife, then why did you ask me to call the rain?"

"Probably because I didn't believe you could."

Pondwader shifted his weight to his opposite foot. "That's all right. I didn't either."

Musselwhite glanced at the forest. Despite the drenching downpour, tiny spirals of smoke twisted up from the charred trees. With a sigh, she replied, "So much for logic and common sense," and started down the trail again.

"Are you sorry I did it?" he asked as he followed.

She shook her head. "No, Pondwader."

"Then, you're all right?"

"No, of course not! I feel much sicker now, and it isn't just my body that's queasy."

"But I did it for you. Because you asked me to. I wanted you to—"

"I know that, Pondwader." She put a hand on his shoulder. "Come along. Now that it's so much cooler, we should be able to reach Marshtail Lagoon by dusk."

A sudden smile graced his face. "Yes, my wife."

He thrashed through the brush at her side to get in front of her, so he could hold palmettos and branches out of the way for her to pass.

"You don't have to do that, Pondwader."

"No, but it helps you, doesn't it? It makes it easier for you?" He looked at her through wide, anxious eyes.

She smiled. "Yes, it does. Thank you. Just . . . will you try to be quiet while you help me?"

"Oh, yes, I'm sorry! I will."

Thirty-one

With the hot weather, all the ruthless insects that dwelt beneath blades of grass or in rotting wood emerged. The mosquito, ant, spider, and biting fly nations had taken to the land and sky on war walks again. Dark Rain's hands stayed in constant motion, slapping anything that buzzed, whined, or dared to crawl on her, but her red tunic felt as if it possessed a squirming life of its own.

She mashed a spider, then brushed ants from her blanket, and stretched out on her side before the fire, watching Beaverpaw finish his supper of froglegs, elderberries, and prickly-pear fruits. They had walked hard today, and made camp late. Everyone needed rest. Bowfin sat beside Dark Rain, yawning and half asleep, but staring contemplatively into the flames. The flat planes of his young face reflected the firelight like a water-mirror. Hanging Star crouched on the other side of the fire, near Beaverpaw, making pemmican—a mixture of dried venison, plums, and fat.

"How far are we from Standing Hollow Horn Village, Hanging Star?" Beaverpaw asked.

Hanging Star shrugged. "If we can keep Dark Rain from entering every game we pass . . . maybe two . . . three days."

Dark Rain smiled, but she was not amused. She had known Hanging Star for many summers, and he lacked even the basic qualities of manhood. He was a coward, a thief, and a liar—worse, his lovemaking method consisted of "jump, ride, and run."

What a mistake that had been. She had never stopped regretting it—or the fact that she now found herself in his revolting company again. Beaverpaw would pay for that. The instant he had mentioned traveling with Hanging Star, she had objected, but Beaverpaw had invited the man along anyway, "to show them the fastest trails," he'd said. Surely she would want to get to the big game as soon as possible? Dark Rain suspected Beaverpaw had other motives, but she had not learned them yet. Poor Beaverpaw, he missed his family. It showed in every sagging line of his tadpole face. That and the fact that he talked about his children all the time. "Little Manatee Flipper learned to make dart points at the age of three summers. . . ." and "If you think that's impressive, my son Manatee Flipper hit a dove on the wing the first time he cast a dart. No, really, I swear it!"

She turned to glare at Bowfin. Another mistake, a huge one. The youth had proven the ultimate bore. No conversation, no entertainment, and he had even less stamina between the blankets than Hanging Star. It would take true genius to imagine a more worthless man. Dark Rain had come to despise Bowfin. If she could just figure a way of ridding herself . . .

"We are that close?" Beaverpaw asked. "I hadn't realized."

"Oh, it's not far if you have a good guide," Hanging Star answered.

A frown incised Beaverpaw's forehead. Like all the other men around the fire, he wore only a breechclout. Sweat poured down his muscular chest and dripped from his fat face. He'd washed his black chin-length hair with yucca soap. It glistened in the flameglow. Dark Rain sighed, waved away a biting fly, and grimaced. The hairstyle did not suit Beaverpaw. She would have to tell him about that. It made his small eyes and tiny circle of a mouth seem dainty.

"And this battle with Musselwhite?" Beaverpaw asked. "When is it supposed to take place?"

"Who knows?" Hanging Star replied. "As soon as she arrives. Which should be about the time we do."

Beaverpaw's eyes took on a curious gleam. "What do you know of Cottonmouth's Dreams, Hanging Star?" he asked. "You never speak about them. Do you fear he'll—"

"Oh," Hanging Star said and laughed in that yipping manner of his, "no, it isn't that I fear Cottonmouth's revenge. I just don't know very much about his Dreams. I never cared to. They are truly bizarre." As if he couldn't resist, he winked at Dark Rain. "Eh, Dark Rain? As bizarre as the visions of a woman who's been chewing moon-vine seeds all day."

She lifted an elegant brow.

Beaverpaw finished his frog leg and tossed the bones into the fire, then reached for a handful of elderberries. But as he did so, he glanced at her and his brows lowered, obviously wondering if that explained her aloofness today. Blind fool. Though she had not eaten any seeds since noon, the exhilarating effects continued, and Hanging Star knew the signs.

When he saw her threatening look, Hanging Star's mouth twisted into a contemptuous grin. He'd plaited his hair into two braids that framed his ugly square face. With a chuckle, he returned to his pemmican.

He had rinsed and cleaned several lengths of deer intestine, then hung them on the palmetto stems to his left. After that, he'd laid out a rectangular piece of limestone, spread long, thin pieces of jerked venison on top, and used a round river cobble to pound the meat to powder. He'd just begun adding the plums, pounding and grinding them into the meat, seeds and all. A gooey concoction resulted. She sniffed the aroma. It smelled delicious, rich with the smoked scent of deer, and pleasantly sour from the plums. Despite the fact that Dark Rain had just eaten, her mouth watered.

Beaverpaw made a light gesture. "Has Cottonmouth ever said how the battle begins? What time of day is it, or—"

"Oh, yes," Hanging Star answered, not bothering to look up from his work. "He boasts about such details. He never tells us anything truly meaningful, but he's very free with lots of little things. The battle is supposed to begin at dusk."

Beaverpaw slapped a mosquito on his forehead. Several more whined around his ears, their transparent wings glinting in the firelight. "That's when Musselwhite enters Standing Hollow Horn Village?"

"So he says. Musselwhite and the Lightning Boy."

Hanging Star leaned forward to check the wooden bowl filled with deer fat which sat on the sandy ground in front of him. He had melted it earlier, and it had just begun to cool and congeal. Pemmican had to be made with a "sturdy" tallow, usually the fat from deer. If made from softer fats, like those of raccoon or bear, it would spoil. Or if the fat were too hot when added to the meat, it would go rancid. It had to be just the right texture and temperature. But pemmican made correctly would last for many summers.

Dark Rain shook long hair away from her face, and said, "So my son will be with her. Poor Musselwhite. She does not deserve such a handicap. She will, no doubt, die because of him."

Pondwader had been a curse to her from the day he'd been born. He couldn't hunt, couldn't fight, couldn't see well enough to weave or make stone tools. He scared the souls out of everyone who saw him. In fact, so far as Dark Rain knew, Pondwader couldn't do anything. The only productive thing the boy had ever accomplished—and that by accident—was to pay off her gambling debts.

Beaverpaw had a hurt expression on his face. He shook his head. "Pondwader is a good, kind boy, Dark Rain. You never got to know him very well. He—"

"I did not care to, Beaverpaw," she answered tersely. "Thank Sister Moon that my mother wanted him. When I first saw him after his birth, I seriously thought about leaving him in the forest for the big cats to find."

At Beaverpaw's horrified look, Hanging Star said, "Perhaps she's been witched, eh? What do you think, Beaverpaw? Dark Rain's human souls were drained away and replaced with the souls of a rattlesnake or crocodile. Don't her bloodless souls remind you of those beasts?"

Dark Rain smiled broadly—and in it, she knew, Hanging Star would see the promise of her revenge.

Beaverpaw glanced at Bowfin, who endeavored not to hear a word anyone else said, then bowed his head. "And what of the end of the battle, Hanging Star?" Beaverpaw asked. "Does Musselwhite die? Or Pondwader?"

"Cottonmouth never says how the battle will end—except that the Lightning Birds will soar out of the clouds and carry him and his loyal followers to a glorious new world beyond the stars." Hanging Star pounded another plum into his venison mush. The sharp clacking carried on the still night. "I don't think Cottonmouth knows how the battle will end."

"Then he's no Soul Dancer. He's a fraud. I have always suspected it," Dark Rain said, and leaned back, bracing her hands behind her and extending her long, beautiful legs to the glimmers of firelight.

The men, naturally, could not help but stare. Just her posture aroused them. Her full breasts pressed at her tunic, while she had her legs positioned just right to give them glimpses of the glories beneath her skirt. Bowfin grinned like a fool, while Hanging Star studied her with a raised brow. Beaverpaw, through obvious effort, managed to look away.

Hanging Star reached for a length of clean intestine and, in a mocking voice, said, "Oh, yes, I'm sure Cottonmouth must be a fraud. The sublime Dark Rain, after all, knows a great deal about Soul Dancers."

She leaned forward. "I could tell you things about their masculine prowess you would not believe—or be able to duplicate, I might add, Hanging Star."

Hanging Star sneered his response. Gruffly, he tied a knot in the one end of the length of intestine and began scooping up the venison mush and loosely stuffing it inside. If stuffed too tight, the warm fat would not completely coat the meat mixture and evil spirits would grow, making the man who ate the pemmican very ill. Once he'd stuffed the intestine half full, he handed it to Beaverpaw. "Here, hold this for me while I pour, will you?"

"Yes, gladly." Beaverpaw held the end open.

Hanging Star brought the bowl over and carefully poured the warm tallow down the opening. Not too much, though. Just enough to coat the meat-plum mix.

"Very good, my friend," Hanging Star said as he set the bowl down. "Thank you."

Beaverpaw handed the finished pemmican back and watched Hanging Star tie a knot into the top end. After that, he massaged the intestine, working the fat thoroughly through the meat mixture—making certain every morsel had been coated.

"You do not wish me to tell you about Soul Dancers, Hanging Star?" she taunted. "Jealous?"

"Dark Rain," he responded, "there is nothing you know that I wish to know." He finished working his pemmican and turned to drape it over the palmetto again. Then he pulled down another length, and stuffed it with the remaining mush. He handed it to Beaverpaw to hold again while he poured in the rendered fat.

Beaverpaw, trying to divert hostilities, asked, "Why do you think Cottonmouth has never seen the end of the battle? That's very odd. Every Soul Dancer I've ever known—"

"Which is very few," Dark Rain scoffed. "I have known many more than you have, Beaverpaw, and they are all fakes."

Bowfin laughed and slapped his knee, but Beaverpaw did not even look her way. He exchanged a knowing glance with Hanging Star, and concentrated on keeping the intestine open. Rage smoldered in her chest. When the fat covered the meat, Hanging Star took it back and knotted the end.

Beaverpaw persisted. "If Cottonmouth really is a Soul Dancer, his Spirit Helper should have shown him the end of the battle. Why would his Spirit Helper keep that from him?"

Hanging Star draped the pemmican over the palmetto and rubbed his hands in the sand to clean them. "Perhaps his Spirit Helper wishes him to fail. If I were Cottonmouth's Spirit Helper I would do everything in my power to see that he suffered for all the suffering he has forced others to endure."

"Justice, eh?" Bowfin called. He crawled to sit beside Dark Rain. His young face had a hot glow as he slipped an arm around her shoulders, and began sensually caressing her skin.

Beaverpaw's eyes tightened. She had not shared his blankets last night, and he knew why. She had been trying vainly to teach Bowfin how to arouse a woman. Beaverpaw had been forced to listen to their desperate coupling for half the night. Her neglect had almost driven him mad. She smiled across the fire at him. He'd been so enraged last night that he'd lurched to his feet, grabbed his blanket, and stamped away from camp. But he would be back tonight. She had no doubts. Yes, he'd come crawling to her, touching her gently, pleading for her favors. Dark Rain had not yet decided how she would respond. At least Beaverpaw could be counted upon to provide her with ecstasy, whereas Bowfin only succeeded in whetting her appetite before he went limp and started snoring in her hair.

"Of course it would be justice," Hanging Star said. "Cottonmouth is a monster. You have no idea, my young friend. He has never attacked your village. Yet."

Beaverpaw sat up. "Does he have plans to attack Heartwood?"

"He has plans to attack every village in striking range—whether or not he succeeds depends upon his battle with Musselwhite. If she dies, no coastal village will be safe."

Beaverpaw looked at Hanging Star. "Has Cottonmouth spoken about how it happens? The battle at Standing Hollow Horn, I mean."

Hanging Star stretched out on his side, used a finger to scoop the remains from his grinding stone, and tucked it into his mouth. He chewed slowly, as if relishing the flavor. "There is a tree, an old oak, covered with hanging moss, which stands on the northwest corner of the village. Cottonmouth says Musselwhite will launch her attack from there."

Beaverpaw nodded, eager. "And then?"

Hanging Star flicked a hand, as if shooing away biting flies. "And then he captures her. He claims—"

"Not now!" Dark Rain hissed to Bowfin who had started to grope her breasts.

"But why?" he asked in confusion. "You have never objected to my caresses before."

"Well, I do tonight!" she said. Roughly, she shoved away from him, rose, and walked to stand near the fire, warming her hands.

Hanging Star watched her approach through gleaming eyes. His desires had been growing over the past several days, until now he could barely contain himself. Dark Rain let her gaze linger on the swell in his breechclout— and smiled at him. He smiled back.

This might work to her benefit, after all.

She knelt beside him and kissed him on the lips. In a violent move, Hanging Star gripped her by the shoulders, threw her to the ground and crawled on top of her, kissing her hungrily in return.

"Hanging Star! For Sun Mother's sake! Have you no skill at all?" She bit him hard, and laughed when blood welled.

"You whore! You filthy whore!" Hanging Star shouted, grasped her arms roughly, and used one hand to pin them over her head. With his other hand, he pulled his engorged manhood from his breechclout.

Dark Rain glanced at Bowfin's gaping face. He looked frightened, eager to come to her aid. She half-heartedly struggled against Hanging Star. "Release me!" she ordered.

"You wish it!" Hanging Star responded. "You have always preferred lust to love."

Dark Rain cried out, "Stop it! Hanging Star let me go! Bowfin . . . ? Bowfin, help me! He's hurting me!"

Hanging Star used his knee to force her legs open and thrust himself inside her. She kicked and screamed . . . and Bowfin rose to his feet, his eyes wide.

Beaverpaw ordered, "Bowfin! Sit down! She's not in danger, she's—"

"Shut up!" Bowfin yelled as he watched her struggling.

Tears streamed down her cheeks, and horror lined Bowfin's young face. She wept, "Bowfin . . . Oh, please, *please,* I beg you!"

"Stop it!" Bowfin shouted. "Hanging Star! Let her go!" He drew his stiletto, from his belt and stalked forward.

"No!" Beaverpaw shouted. He jumped to his feet. "Hanging Star, he's armed! He—"

As Bowfin gripped Hanging Star's shoulder and jerked him off Dark Rain, Hanging Star rolled, came up with his own stiletto, and plunged it into Bowfin.

Beaverpaw shouted, "No!"

Bowfin staggered backwards, staring open-mouthed at the weapon embedded in his lungs. Blood bubbled on his lips. He coughed, choked, and stumbled over an exposed tree root. The stiletto fell from his fingers as he toppled to the ground and scrambled aimlessly on his hands and knees.

"Oh, Brother Earth, no," Beaverpaw murmured as he shoved past Hanging Star and knelt beside Bowfin.

The young warrior's strength failed him. He sagged to the ground, his fingers clawing at the sand as blood ran from his lips. His eyes had gone huge. He stared up at Beaverpaw in terror. Lungs filled with blood, he could not speak. He lay suffocating, his gaze riveted to Beaverpaw.

Dark Rain watched in fascination. This male ritual of death had always attracted her.

"Forgive me," Beaverpaw whispered. "Oh, Bowfin. This is my fault! If not for me, you would have never become involved . . . and this . . . this . . ."

The youth stared sightlessly out at the dark silhouettes of trees, unable to hear Beaverpaw now. Beaverpaw hung his head and closed his eyes.

Dark Rain said, "Hanging Star, come back. I *need* you inside me."

And she saw hatred, powerful, heady, rush through Beaverpaw. He glared pure loathing at her. Dark Rain smiled as Hanging Star laid down on top of her again, kissing her fiercely.

Beaverpaw sat unmoving.

Thinking about his future . . .

Musselwhite did not realize the trap that awaited her. Someone needed to warn her, and then fight at her side. That person would gain a great deal of status.

Once he'd finished his work at Standing Hollow Horn Village, Beaverpaw planned to run home as fast as his legs would carry him. He would beg Waterbearer for mercy. If she took him back, the Council might also. Having fought on the side of the great Musselwhite would go a long ways toward convincing the Spirit Elders of his worthiness for readmission to the clan. Perhaps he could even convince Musselwhite herself to speak for him.

Behind him, Hanging Star gasped and started to groan.

Beaverpaw gently slipped his arms beneath Bowfin's body and lifted him. A small pond nestled in the woods half a hand of time away. He would send this young warrior to the Village of Wounded Souls by himself. No one should be condemned to wander the earth alone.

As he walked down the trail toward the pond, moonlight sprinkled his path. In each flicker, he glimpsed the smiling faces of his children, holding out their hands to him, pleading with him to come home. The raw wound in his heart ached.

He hurried down the trail.

Thirty-two

"Cut him down," Cottonmouth ordered softly. "Tie his hands. I will speak with him after supper." To Diver he added, "I'll be bringing along an old friend of yours."

"What friend?"

Diver struggled to get his feet under him, twisting his head to watch Cottonmouth walk across the twilit village. Racing children and barking dogs filled the plaza. Men and women spoke gently to each other where they crouched in their shelters piling wood to feed the nightly fires. The succulent smell of turtles simmering in their own juices wafted on the sea breeze. Diver had not eaten in three days. He felt lightheaded. The tens of thorn wounds in his body burned and ached, but he could ignore them. This hunger, however, stalked him like a bear with a wounded doe in sight.

Woodduck came forward, grinning maliciously, and used a hafted knife to saw through the vines; he pulled them off, and tossed them out of the shelter. Then he cut Diver's bonds, and as his numb arms slapped his sides, he fell to his knees on the floor mats. His shoulder and back wounds lanced him with staggering pain, and he leaned forward to retch, but no liquid came up, only dry heaves, over and over.

Woodduck bent down, grabbed Diver's unfeeling hands, and tied them with a rawhide cord. He whispered, "Don't worry. This will all be over soon. Cottonmouth says we're going to kill you tomorrow."

At Diver's horrified look, the warrior roared with laughter, turned on his heel, and tramped away, waving his other warriors to follow him. They took up their guard stations thirty hands away.

Diver's dry heaves lasted until his body simply no longer had the strength, then he toppled onto his side and blinked wearily out at Sea Girl. Big waves tormented the beach tonight, crashing upon the shore in a constant deep-throated growl. Purple twinkles of light danced on the water, and in his foggy sight they resembled scatters of dogwood petals.

Dogwood . . . blooming . . . so sweetly scented . . .

Diver drifted into an exhausted sleep.

And in his dreams, he heard singing, the voice so pure, the notes so deep and resonant, that Diver feared the woman might not be human. Many forest Spirits wandered these scrub oak woods, playing pranks on passersby, and there would be angry ghosts out here too, seeking to take revenge on living humans for the fact that they still walked the earth. Diver tiptoed forward carefully, his atlatl nocked, breathing shallow.

Dogwood flowers dangled from the branches overhanging the trail, filling the air with sweetness. He carefully pushed the lavender clusters out of his way as he ducked beneath the limbs.

He stopped when he heard voices coming from up ahead, followed by the erratic scratching of a bone straightener being worked down the length of a dart shaft.

People! He had seen no one in days!

He broke into a trot. Young again, vibrant and strong, he was dressed in his warrior's tunic, the front painted with the black image of Whale. Gulls floated through the halo of sunshine over his head. The warm spring breeze flapped the hem of his tunic, and fluttered long black hair before his eyes. Serenity filled him. For the first time in moons, his burdens and fears had vanished. Through the maze of tree trunks, he saw a small palmetto-choked hill. Hickory and oak trees grew densely on the crest, and gray wisps of smoke twisted away in the wind.

The sound of the bone straightener working wood came so clearly now that Diver could almost feel it working up the lengths of his own long bones. He slowly ambled up the hill, holding aside palm fronds and ducking beneath oak boughs.

A boy, perhaps ten-and-four summers, leaned against the base of a huge hickory tree making cordage from the neck skin of a sea tortoise. When cut into very thin strips, then stretched and two strands twisted together, it made a very strong cord. A big dog lay on his side beside the boy. The animal studied Diver with kind brown eyes, and wagged its tail. The boy lifted his chin in greeting. Diver nodded, then continued along the trail.

He entered a section of dark shadows. and from somewhere far away . . . memories struggled to surface . . . horrifying . . . his sons dying one by one . . . his beautiful daughter screaming . . .

He fought to meld with the calm heart of the dream again, concentrating on the oak trees towering above him. On the crooked branches, thick with gray-green beards of hanging moss. On the air, redolent with dogwood blossoms. They swayed in the breeze, swirling the air like a fan. Diver lifted his sweating face, and let the blossoms breathe fragrant coolness over him.

The delicious odors of burning hickory logs and hot grease met his nostrils, as well. He inhaled deeply, and grew frantic to reach that food. . . .

He ran headlong down the winding trail. Breaking out of the tall trees, he burst into a grassy clearing filled with people.

Men and women sat in the shade at the edges of the clearing, some laughing, others talking in low tones. Baskets of food nestled around them. In the center of the clearing, a fire burned. A broad bed of glowing coals filled the pit that had been scooped out in the sand. On the far side of the fire, in a patch of wavering shadows, a woman worked the bone straightener—a femur bone split in half with a hole drilled in one end—down the length of her dart shaft. A neat line of tools lay to her right side: chert flakes and knives, a wooden bowl of bear grease, two blocks of grooved wood filled with sand, a pile of owl tailfeathers. And last, a roasted section of deer ribs. Another warrior, a young man, sat beside her.

Diver glanced at the woman as he wandered through the gathering, his stomach cramping painfully, listening to fragments of conversation, enjoying the warm breeze that danced over the clearing.

He stopped at the edge of the firepit to watch her crafting her dart. She smiled at him when she noticed his attention. The man next to her nudged her with his elbow and gestured at Diver. She laughed gaily and looked up. She was tall, with a beautiful oval face, and a blue-black wealth of hair, and her obsidian eyes shone warmly. A gust of wind flattened her tunic against her chest, accentuating the swell of her breasts and the narrowness of her waist.

Diver smiled, and started to back away, but the woman said, "Please, share our fire. You are unknown to us. Where do you come from?"

Eagerly, he seated himself. The man whispered something to her, then nodded politely to Diver, and wandered over to a small group of warriors. Their laughter greeted him.

The woman said, "You must have traveled a long way. Help yourself to the deer ribs."

"You are very kind. Thank you." Diver reached over, pulled off a section of two ribs, and immediately sank his teeth into the succulent meat. Eating ravenously, he chewed, smiled at her, and watched her work.

The woman used a hafted chert knife to scrape her dart shaft free of knots. Turning the shaft constantly, she could maintain even scrapes, keeping the shaft round. After she had shaved off the irregularities, she dipped her fingers into the bear grease bowl and rubbed the newly scraped section down, then held the shaft over the coals. She had to keep it moving constantly, or the shaft would scorch and break on impact. Heating the hickory made it as pliable as freshly cut green wood, so it could be bent straight, but it also strengthened the wood. The grease helped to keep it from overheating and scorching.

"I am Diver," he said through a mouthful of food, "of the Wasp Nest Clan."

She kept rotating her dart shaft. "I'm Musselwhite, of the Windy Cove Clan." Her eyes shone as she smiled.

At that moment, he thought her the most beautiful woman in the world. Joy spread wings in his chest. And his stomach. Finally, the cramps of hunger abated, and Diver let out a slow, soothing breath.

The woman smiled, but with a frown on her beautiful face. "You must not have eaten in a while."

"I haven't," he answered, and when memories of pain and torture started to rise, he hastily added, "But I'm fine now. You work those dart shafts like an expert. Have you made many?"

"Yes."

She pulled her shaft back, lifted her straightener, and slid the shaft through the hole drilled in the end of the straightener. As she moved it down the heated section of the shaft, bending where the dart needed it, the bone straightener scritched and scratched. She held the dart out to the side and sighted down the length, checking its alignment, then greased a new section, about the length of her hand, and extended it to the heat.

"And what, Diver of the Wasp Nest Clan, are you doing starving to death so far from home?"

He shrugged. "I am an explorer. I love nothing better than running just to see what's there. And I do some Trading while I'm out."

She flashed him that wonderful smile again, and he couldn't help but smile back. "I see. You are irresponsible. An unwed youth, with no war to fight, and so many brothers that your family can afford to let you act deranged."

Diver's face fell, then he blinked, and burst out laughing. "Guilty! I admit it. On every charge. My grandfather has always accused me of laziness. So I guess that means I am a lazy-irresponsible-deranged youth. But a very good Trader!"

"You said you did 'some' Trading."

"Yes, that's right."

"When you choose to?"

"Well, yes," he said and shrugged. "Trading is not always a delight. Most people think it's their duty to cheat you over every rare good you've obtained. And not one of them considers what it has cost you. All the traveling and haggling is really tiresome. As a result, now I only Trade when I wish to."

She ran the straightener down the entire length of her dart shaft while she sighted along it again. As she moved her two wooden blocks in front of her, she said, "You mean you only Trade when it looks as if you can swindle your buyer."

"Uh . . . well . . ."

"A lazy-irresponsible-deranged *swindler.*"

Diver grinned broadly. She gave him a coy look from the corner of her eye, then concentrated on her craft again. Lightly, she sprinkled the grooves in the blocks with fine sand, placed her shaft in the groove on the bottom block, covered it with the top block, and pulled the shaft through the sanded hole, back and forth, smoothing it to perfection. When too much sand had been pushed out the ends, she removed the shaft, added more sand, then smoothed a new section of her dart.

"Do you really think I'm a swindler?" Diver asked.

She shifted to look at him, and her eyes gleamed softly. Strange. Those eyes drew him powerfully. When he gazed into them, he felt as if gale force winds buffeted his souls. He could sense despair just beneath the surface, barely hidden in those deep dark wells, and something inside him longed to soothe that hurt. How easy it would be to love this beautiful woman . . .

"It sounds like you're a swindler."

"Is that the reason you invited me to share your fire? So you could insult me?"

Musselwhite finished smoothing her dart, and removed it from the wooden blocks. Picking up a piece of fabric, she wiped off the clinging sand. "No," she finally answered. "To feed you. You were staring at my deer ribs as if you might steal them if I didn't invite you to eat."

"You were right. I might have." He grinned. "I don't know why I'm so hungry, but I . . ." *Footsteps on sand. Voices from far far away . . .*

"I think I like you," she said.

"Because I look like a swindler?" The bantering had made the world come alive. The sky looked incredibly blue. Birdsong lilted, so loud it almost hurt his ears.

She smiled, lay down her dart, and reached out to touch his hand. The warmth of her skin, the tenderness of her touch made him turn up his palm and clasp her fingers tightly. For a long moment, he let himself drown in the feel of her flesh against his.

Without thinking, he kissed her and she . . .

"Wake him up," a harsh voice ordered.

Diver started, his eyes jerking open as hard hands pulled him to a sitting position. His festered thorn wounds felt as if they were on fire. His whole body burned. Panting, he blinked, trying to figure out where he was. Scenes and feelings from the dream would not let him go. But Musselwhite had vanished; she no longer sat beside him. Wrenching despair brought tears to his eyes. If he'd had the strength, he would have wept.

"Leave us," Cottonmouth said.

The warriors retreated to their former guard positions, and, strangely, Cottonmouth walked several paces away, folded his arms over his bare chest, and fixed his gaze upon the crashing waves. Though he wore only a breechclout, a beautiful periwinkle shell necklace draped his neck. The silver hair at his temples glittered in the flutters of firelight coming from around the village.

Diver hunched forward, his bound hands in his lap. A sob had lodged in his throat. He peered sightlessly at the coarse weave of the floor mat. He longed for Musselwhite so desperately that he felt certain he would die if he could not see her soon. See her, touch her, hear her loving voice. . . .

"Diver?" a woman called.

His head snapped up. He watched breathlessly as she entered the shelter and knelt before him. Kindness and worry filled her eyes when she gazed upon his hideous wounds. Infection oozed from the punctures and drained down his chest and arms. She carried a folded piece of fabric in her hands, which she set aside, and softly touched Diver's face.

"Diver? Do you remember me? I'm—"

"*Glasswort*," he whispered in astonishment. She had the same round pretty face, with delicately arched eyebrows and a thin beak of a nose. She'd cut her hair short, in mourning. "Is it really you?"

"Yes." She embraced Diver, heedless of his foul body. "It's me. I've been trying to get permission to see you for days."

"Glasswort," he repeated, trying to convince himself. She and her son, Coral, had been captured in Cottonmouth's raid last summer. "Blessed Sun Mother, it's so good to see you. We had feared you might be dead."

She pushed back and touched the festering thorns still buried in his forehead. "No, no, I'm fine."

"And Coral? Thorny Boy cried for a full moon after his best friend was—"

"My son is dead, Diver," she said softly. But tears did not fill her eyes. Hatred did. Fiery. Passionate. She checked to see how far away Cottonmouth stood—a good two-tens of hands. Still, she kept her voice low, barely audible. "The Standing Hollow Horn warriors pushed us so hard getting here that many of the old people and children could not keep up. When they fell behind, the warriors killed them. Then they drove the rest of us just that much harder to make up the lost time."

With his bound hands, Diver reached out to grip her wrist. "I'm glad you made it, Glasswort. People will be so happy to hear . . ." She motioned for him to keep talking, and Diver said, "that you are alive and well"—she reached into her sandal and pulled a small stiletto out—"Do you have a family here?"—then tucked it beneath his right knee—"A husband or children?"

"Yes," she answered. "My husband's name is Woodduck. You've met him, I think. I carry his child." As if to push it from her body, she put both hands on her belly and pressed hard. Sick rage contorted her face. "He is a renowned warrior, but I am his third wife, so I do all of the things the other wives do not wish to. They treat me badly. It is not a good life, Diver, and I . . . I miss my family very much. How is Black Urchin?" Anguish tightened her eyes.

"Your husband is well. He still loves you. After you were captured, I thought he would go mad. He—"

"No." She squeezed Diver's hands hard. "Do not tell me. I couldn't bear to hear it, Diver. But—but please tell him, when you get home, that my souls live because of him. He fills my thoughts and dreams. Every day. If I thought I—"

"It's time, Glasswort," Cottonmouth said as he turned. Wind whipped strands of his silvered black hair around his handsome face. "Your family is waiting for you. But before you go, please show Diver what you made for him. I wish him to know it came from your hands, not mine."

Glasswort frowned, and hesitated, then reached over and shook the folds from the tunic. "I made this for you, Diver. It eased my homesickness. I begged the Spirit Elder to allow me to give it to you and, after he saw it, he agreed. But—" she glanced at Cottonmouth—"but only so long as I brought it to you myself."

Diver could not speak. He just stared. The wind flapped the garment, making the blue lightning bolt painted across the breast seem to flash and soar. From the depths of his memories, Cottonmouth's voice seeped. . . . *I did not know until last night that you would be there at my side when the world ends. . . . I don't know why you're there. . . . I think you must have joined me, become one of my followers, because you are wearing a tunic made here, at Standing Hollow Horn. It had a blue zigzag. . . .*

"Thank you, Glasswort," Diver choked out hoarsely. "It's beautiful."

"I wanted you to be warm." Her voice broke. She hugged Diver tightly one last time, then rose to her feet. "Good-bye." Quickly, she walked across the shelter and trotted into the village.

Diver ran his index finger along the blue zigzag, tracing the bolt's path across the tunic. His mouth had gone dry.

Cottonmouth leaned against the shelter pole in front of Diver, arms folded across his muscular chest, watching. His eyes gleamed like huge black moons. That gaze alone made Diver tremble; it brimmed with terrifying faith. The firelight from the village struck his face at an angle, throwing the right side into shadow, but the rest . . . his nose and full lips might have been sculpted from the purest amber.

Cottonmouth's deep voice filled the world, as silken as spun cobwebs. "Why isn't she here, Diver?"

". . . Who?"

"She should have been here yesterday. With the White Lightning Boy. Two of my own warriors straggled in last night. They told me about the battle. If they could get here . . . she should have been able to as well."

"I told you she wouldn't come. Not to rescue me. It would be foolish when Windy Cove needs her so badly. And, no matter what you may think of her, she is *not* a fool, Cottonmouth." Diver glared.

"Something must have happened." Cottonmouth shook his head. "But I don't understand why my Dreams haven't warned me about the delay."

"I've noticed that everyone seems to be readying themselves. I didn't know whether for Sun Mother's Winter Celebration Day, or their journey to this shining new world you've promised them."

"They will happen at the same time, Diver." The crowsfeet around his eyes deepened. He shoved away from the pole and dropped his hands to his sides. "But I thought I would have some time with her first. I need—"

"What do you mean they will happen at the same time? Winter solstice . . . I—I've lost track of time. Isn't solstice in just a few days?"

Cottonmouth nodded. "And the Lightning Birds will come for me at dusk. If she does not arrive soon, I won't have the time with her that I need!"

Diver's eyes narrowed. Fear knotted his belly, threatening to wring more dry heaves from him. "I thought you said you only needed her to bring you the Lightning Boy. So he could free you. Why do you need time with Musselwhite?"

A shudder went through Cottonmouth, but his eyes never left Diver. He clenched his hands into fists, and hesitated a long time before replying, his face tense with struggle. "There are questions I must ask her."

"About what?"

"Things of which you know nothing."

"But I thought you wanted to kill her? To punish her for murdering your son? For betraying you to your enemies?"

Cottonmouth bowed his head.

In the long silence that followed, Diver heard raucous laughter rising from his guards, and the sharp smacking of a warclub striking a palm. The muscles of Cottonmouth's jaw tightened. Finally, he answered, "I must ask her about things that happened two-tens-and-six summers ago. After Pelican Isle."

"But she was gone by then. How would she know?"

He looked up and held Diver's gaze. "She may not. But I must ask just the same. You see, Diver, I came home the next day to bury my son. But all the Soul Dancers, including crazy old Dogtooth, told me there was no reason to."

"I don't understand."

"Don't you?" Cottonmouth asked so low Diver could barely hear him. "That's good."

"Why would they tell you something so terrible? Soul Dancers know better than anyone—"

"They had their reasons." Cottonmouth's full lips pressed into a bloodless line. "Though, I admit, I defied them and buried my son anyway. By myself.

After what the Soul Dancers said, people were frightened. No one wanted to touch him." In a small voice, he continued, "I had to bury my son."

"But why . . ."

Cottonmouth walked away, out onto the beach. He hung very close to the raging breakers, as if the roar might drown out the rest of the world. Spray coated his hair and nearly naked body, and Diver saw him shivering. But he did not come back to the warmth of the village. He continued south, until Diver lost sight of him.

Very cautiously, Diver reached beneath his knee and slipped out the stiletto. Small, the length of Glasswort's foot, it had been honed to a lethal point. He could not risk using it until he truly had a chance to escape, but where could he hide it in the meantime? He looked around. If he moved, it would draw the attention of the guards.

Two floor mats abutted each other six hands in front of him. He had to chance it. Diver stretched out on his side, as if to sleep, pulled up one edge of the mat, and drove the stiletto point into the sand, then let the mat down again.

By the time Woodduck strode around the shelter and stood over him, Diver had closed his eyes. He didn't need to fake exhaustion.

Woodduck stood for a short while, his feet kneading the sand, then he left.

Thank you, Sun Mother. Thank you Forest Spirits and homeless ghosts. . . .

Before he could finish the litany, Diver had fallen into a deep sleep.

. . . He dreamed of a little boy lying dead in his father's arms, and no one there to help the man bury his son.

Thirty-three

W hat's wrong, Moonsnail? Are you worrying about Pondwader and Kelp?" Seedpod asked.

Morning campfires trailed gray streamers of smoke over the forests surrounding Manatee Lagoon. Sun Mother had been up for four hands of time, but her gleam through the high clouds was a pale reflection of itself, pallid, washed out, glinting dully from the vast blue ocean. A few towering thunderheads drifted toward the shore. Burning hickory and oak scented the air.

Moonsnail nodded as she carefully poked her walking stick into the sand. "Yes, I'd like to wring both their necks. I just pray I have the chance."

The freshly built council shelter stood near the trees on the southern side of the village site, separated from the other shelters by a small copse of palms. Moonsnail could see that Dogtooth and Floating Stick had already seated themselves in the soothing shade cast by the thatched roof. Floating Stick's arms waved over his head.

"Do you think they're getting along any better today?" Seedpod asked. He walked slowly at her side, waiting for her to prop her walking stick. He had his hands clasped behind his back, his white hair blowing in the hot breeze. His gaunt face looked particularly leathery today.

"Well, it would be a miracle if they are," she answered. "Considering that they've never gotten along."

Seedpod chuckled. "And I thought it was just the heat."

Late autumn rarely saw this kind of hot weather, and it seemed to shorten tempers. All around them, people grumbled as they worked, chopping saplings for shelter poles, gathering berries and prickly-pear fruits, erecting shelters, and thatching roofs. No one looked happy.

Moonsnail sighed. From the moment Heartwood Clan arrived last night, nothing had gone well. Arguments had broken out between the clans, disputes over choice shelter locations, warriors testing each other, children screeching like little animals as they chased around the village, pulling hair and wrestling, vicious dog fights. The worst news, of course, had come from Seedpod, when he'd informed Moonsnail that neither Kelp nor Pondwader were here. Both had run off to commit suicide in Standing Hollow Horn Village.

"I shouldn't talk about Floating Stick and Dogtooth. I'm in just as bad a mood," Moonsnail said. "But it isn't the heat. It's my stomach."

"I know how you feel. I've been worried sick about Diamondback. His leg has not even fully healed, and he's off on another war walk. I only hope . . ." A gust of wind moved across the shore, throwing sand in people's eyes, and bringing forth strings of curses, before thrashing through the trees. Seedpod turned his face away until it passed, then he continued. "I only hope Diamondback can help Kelp and Dace to survive. He insisted on going because he feared they would be lost without him."

Moonsnail gripped the polished head of her walking stick more tightly. "I'm certain he was right. I thank Sun Mother for Diamondback's courage."

"He's a fine young warrior," Seedpod said, his voice tinged with sad pride. "Diamondback is very good with trails. Once he's run a path, he knows everything about it, where it connects with other trails, where the best camps are, and how each branch winds through the forest. I'm sure he will lead Kelp and Dace safely to Musselwhite and Pondwader. But after that . . . well, who can say."

"I wish they were all here where we could guard and protect them. But Diamondback was right, Kelp and Dace would have gone on alone—no matter what anyone said. I'm deeply grateful to you, Seedpod, for allowing Diamondback to accompany them."

Seedpod smiled sadly. "My son left me no choice, Moonsnail. Clearly, his presence was vital."

Moonsnail lifted her walking stick and poked it into the sand again, thinking. Cottonmouth's expertise with torture was widely known, and greatly feared. The thought that he might capture one of her precious grandchildren and . . . She dared not think about it. If she let the frightened rage get out of control, she would surely dispatch a war party to burn Standing Hollow Horn Village to the ground. That oozing wound needed cauterizing, and badly. But not yet. She couldn't risk it for quite some time.

A wry twist pulled at Seedpod's mouth. "From the look on your face," he said, "you're contemplating murder."

"Unfortunately, my good sense tells me it would be a grave error. We need our warriors here. After the attack on Windy Cove, we must all be vigilant."

Seedpod's white brows drew down. Sweat ran from the deep furrows in his forehead to the hollows of his cheeks. "Yes, we must."

"I wish we knew more about Cottonmouth. It would help us to defend ourselves. Did you know him well?"

"No," Seedpod shook his head. "I've seen him maybe five or six times, usually for just a few hands of time, once for several days."

Moonsnail wondered about that, since everyone knew that Musselwhite and Cottonmouth had shared a shelter for several summers. Had Seedpod despised his daughter's lover so much?

Silent fears tormented her again. It took force of will to shove the pictures from her mind. . . . Kelp and Pondwader strung up . . . warriors surrounding them . . .

She asked, "Is Cottonmouth as cruel as people say? As his attacks make him seem?"

Seedpod massaged the sore muscles in his right arm. "I do not know, Moonsnail. When I saw him, he was never cruel. Quite the opposite, in fact. Though he was always an insecure young man, scared to death of what other people thought of him."

"I would say, then, that he has changed. He doesn't seem to care what anyone thinks now."

Seedpod softly answered, "Perhaps."

As they neared the council shelter, Floating Stick turned and waved them onward. "Thank Sun Mother!" he yelled. "I feared you would never get here. I was on the verge of slicing that big artery that runs down the inside of my leg."

Moonsnail called, "Why, what's wrong?"

"You'll see."

"That sounds like a threat," she replied.

"Would you think it a threat if I told you Sun Mother was going to vanish tonight?" Floating Stick asked as he lounged on his side on the floor mats.

Moonsnail lifted a brow, wondering what Dogtooth had done. The Soul Dancer appeared to have fallen asleep with a half-finished fishing net clutched in his hands. He lay flat on his back, the net over his stomach, eyes closed. Both old men wore breechclouts, and sweat glistened on their skinny bodies.

Moonsnail hobbled to sit on a pile of mats near Floating Stick, while Seedpod sat down cross-legged near Dogtooth. She carefully shifted to take the strain from her hip. The joint ached with a fiery intensity today. Setting her walking stick aside, she surveyed the shelter. Stark. Little more than four poles and a roof. People had just begun unpacking travoises and packs. Not a single basket or bag adorned the shelter. Moonsnail let out a breath. She should be happy someone had thrown down floor mats—probably Polished Shells. Her daughter would have wanted Moonsnail to be as comfortable as possible during the village's construction. Gratitude filled her heart. At least she still had Polished Shells.

"Look!" Floating Stick shouted, and pointed. "There it is again! It told you it would be back." His eyes looked past the billowing blue-rimmed thunderheads, and sought the wall of deepest black that stretched like a monstrous snake on the horizon. "It comes and goes. We've been watching it for days. Dogtooth? Was that bank of clouds here before we arrived?"

"Not that I noticed."

"Then when did it first blow up?"

Dogtooth scratched his hooked nose. Sweat had glued gray hair to his cheeks. "Well," he said thoughtfully, "if I recall correctly, the clouds began massing the day before Pondwader became a man."

Moonsnail frowned. She looked at Floating Stick, then back to Dogtooth. "What do you mean? The day he married Musselwhite?"

"No, no, the day he killed his first man."

Seedpod and Moonsnail exchanged curious glances, and Floating Stick gave them both an "I told you so" look.

Seedpod said, "Pondwader didn't kill anyone at the Windy Cove battle, Dogtooth."

Dogtooth yawned loud and long, clawed at a bead of sweat trickling down his side, then closed his eyes again. "I know that."

Floating Stick leaned closer to Moonsnail to whisper, "See? I told you you'd understand pretty quick. He's having one of his 'demented' days."

"Great Raccoon," Moonsnail murmured. Sometimes Dogtooth could be completely lucid—but every now and then he talked like an idiot. "Well, let's try to work out what he's saying."

"It's impossible," Floating Stick promised. He brushed his sparse white hair out of his eyes. "Watch this. Dogtooth?" he said gruffly. ". . . Dogtooth, listen to me! Answer the question! Is it just a bad storm?"

Dogtooth opened his eyes, blinked. "What?"

"What do you mean, 'what?' That black wall of clouds!"

Dogtooth sat up and squinted out to sea. "Oh, yes, that's a black wall of clouds, all right." He lay down again, and straightened the net over his stomach like a blanket. "I'll bet the Lightning Birds are soaring everywhere. The whales and dolphins had better look out." He yawned again. "And Pondwader, too."

Moonsnail bent sideways to whisper to Floating Stick, "How long has he been like this?"

"From the instant I sat down in the council shelter! Let me tell you, the past hand of time has been worse than having your skin slowly peeled off with a sharp flake."

Seedpod's mouth tucked in a repressed smile.

Floating Stick turned back to Dogtooth. Sharply, he said, "Listen, Dogtooth. This is important! If that really is a bad storm, we'd better stop building and go hide in the forest somewhere until it's over. Can you tell us—"

"*What?*" Dogtooth twisted to his left side and peered angrily at Floating Stick. "What are you talking about? Are we moving the villages again? Why didn't anyone tell me!"

Floating Stick closed his open mouth, and shoved to his feet. "Seedpod, Moonsnail, I hope to see both of you over supper." He left.

Dogtooth watched Floating Stick walk into the forest, then gazed at Moonsnail. "He really doesn't like me, does he?" He flopped onto his back again and sighed.

"Dogtooth?" Moonsnail asked. "This really is important. Have you had Dreams? Will that storm be bad enough that we should seek shelter in the forest?"

"We probably should, yes, and soon, before . . ." His eyes riveted on a passing cloud. He braced himself up on his elbow to study it intently.

Moonsnail glanced at the puff. "Before what?"

Dogtooth jerked around. "What?"

"You said we should probably seek shelter in the forest before . . . something? *What?*"

"Oh!" Dogtooth blurted as if coming to himself. "I'm sorry. Sometimes I get distracted." He sat up and gazed apologetically into Moonsnail's eyes. "Before Kelp becomes a woman, because after that it will be much too late."

Moonsnail just stared.

Seedpod ran a hand through his white hair. "Let me try," he said. ". . . Too late for what, Dogtooth?"

Dogtooth peered at him inquiringly. "Why, to escape, of course. What's the matter with you, Seedpod? You haven't heard a word I've said, have you?"

Seedpod's mouth hung open. "Moonsnail. Your turn."

The corners of her mouth turned down at the thought. "I wouldn't know where to begin."

"Ah!" Dogtooth said and shook a finger in the air. "Yes, I understand. I was there at the time, you'll recall. I didn't know where to begin either."

Seedpod lifted a brow. Cleverly, he said, "Were you?"

"Oh, yes. Standing Hollow Horn Village was in an uproar after Cottonmouth returned from Pelican Isle. I was lucky to get out alive. He threatened to kill me. Did you know that?"

Moonsnail said nothing, but watched closely.

"No," Seedpod answered. "Why did he do that?"

"I think he believed the Soul Dancers in Standing Hollow Horn—there were four of us—he believed we were responsible, though I don't see how he could have accused us of such a heinous crime. Do you recall Snailtoes? It broke his heart. He was very young then, but already an accomplished Soul Dancer. We had spent days with that dead boy, trying to figure out what had happened. But we never did. Not completely anyway. It was truly horrifying."

Seedpod's face darkened. "Do you mean Glade?"

"Why, yes, of course," Dogtooth replied irritably. "Who else would I mean?"

Moonsnail sat back. The name pricked her memories, but she couldn't place it. Glade . . . a boy . . . in Standing Hollow Horn, who died around the time of the Pelican Isle Massacre.

"What was horrifying?" Seedpod pressed.

Dogtooth glanced about fearfully, rose to his feet, and came to sit close beside Moonsnail. If she'd had the luxury, she would have moved. Instead, she gripped her knees hard. Insanity sparkled in Dogtooth's eyes.

The Soul Dancer whispered, "The fact that the boy had only one soul left—the soul that stays with the body forever. His other souls were gone."

"Dear Brother Earth," Seedpod whispered. "You mean his body had been left for more than two days? Why would—"

"No, no," Dogtooth said softly, and craned his neck to make certain no one else could overhear their conversation. "The boy had been dead for less than a day, Seedpod. *That* was the horror."

Seedpod's eyes tightened. "But how could that be? What happened to his other souls?" Suddenly, Seedpod's eyes flared. He braced his palm on the floor mat and leaned toward Dogtooth. "Didn't you say one of them had been changed into lightning?"

"Oh, yes, First Mother took his reflection-in-water soul back. We knew that. But what happened to his shadow soul, Seedpod? That was the great mystery. I suppose that if Cottonmouth knew the answer to that he could kill Musselwhite the instant she sets foot in his village. Fortunately, he does not. Which gives her a chance." Dogtooth turned to frown sympathetically at Moonsnail. "And the others, too, of course. I didn't mean to frighten you." He reached out and patted Moonsnail's hand gently. "Not that Musselwhite has any answers, of course, but—"

Moonsnail jerked her hand away. "Dogtooth, do you realize how infuriating—"

"Yes, I do," Dogtooth said. "And here he comes again, so, if you don't mind, I think I'll be going." He briskly got to his feet, and trotted away.

"What was that all about?" she asked.

Seedpod pointed and Moonsnail turned to see Floating Stick walking out of the forest. She shook her head. "Well, I can't say I'm sorry to see Dogtooth go. Did you understand any of that? What was all that talk about missing souls?"

Seedpod frowned at the dead coals in the firepit. "I have no idea. But he did tell us a few important things." He looked up and pinned Moonsnail's eyes with his own. "First, apparently that storm out there is a threat. I think it might be wise if we moved inland for a few days. And, second, Musselwhite has not yet arrived at Standing Hollow Horn Village . . . and she should have, Moonsnail. She and Pondwader should have been there days ago."

Moonsnail's throat tightened with emotion. "Do you think they're in trouble?"

He shook his head, said, "I don't know," and let out a gruff breath. "Dog-tooth wasn't much help, was he?"

Seedpod's gaze narrowed to watch the Soul Dancer. Dogtooth waved to people as he crossed the village, calling greetings. A flock of children formed and ran along behind him. Dogs followed the children, nipping playfully at their heels, barking and growling. Dogtooth didn't even seem to notice the parade he'd begun.

Floating Stick waited until certain Dogtooth had left for good, then he came back to the council shelter and seated himself beside Seedpod. Sweat dripped from the end of his hooked nose. He wiped at it, and his glance took in first Moonsnail's expression, then Seedpod's. Without a word, he pulled a hafted knife from his belt and handed it to Seedpod. "Here. That big artery runs right down the inside of the thigh."

Thirty-four

The barks and whines of foxes carried on the warm night wind. Pondwader drew his blanket up to his throat and listened. They had prey in sight. He could tell because the female kept signaling the pack, demanding to know the locations of each hunter, calling them in closer, closer, so they could make their kill. It required only a finger of time. A rabbit let out a terrified cry—followed by a few sharp fox yips, then utter silence.

He breathed in the night air and looked up at the persimmon branches that created a black filigree over his head. They had made camp in the woods at the edge of a grassy clearing. High, stringy clouds sheathed the sky. When Sister Moon found an opening, her gleam fluttered across the meadow like a dropped scarf of glistening spider silk.

Pondwader turned his head to the side. Musselwhite lay beside him, wrapped in blankets, sound asleep. She had fallen three times today. Once, she had tripped over an exposed root. The other times, he had heard her gasp, then turned to see her reel, and collapse. She'd told him that she had tripped again. . . . But he feared it was more. After each event, the mere effort of standing had left her panting. She had braced a hand upon Pondwader's shoulder and breathed deeply, her nostrils flaring as she struggled to stay on her feet.

Pondwader did not know what to do. If only she . . .

He winced. The Lightning Bird shifted inside him. He could *feel* its life, like a restless fetus grown huge and eager to be free of its mother's body. Each time it moved, Pondwader heard faint strains of music. Deep-throated drum rolls and booms, overlain with a cracking like someone playing dried bones, the constant shishing of a palm brush moved over leather, sounding like raindrops . . . Thunder music. Every part of Pondwader's body filled with this unutterably beautiful Song; and sometimes he thought he caught words—about billowing clouds, and infinite blue sky, and soaring euphorically across endless expanses of darkness. It filled Pondwader with such longing, he could scarcely endure it. Like a lover's arms, the Song promised things he dared not believe possible. Light shimmering along his limbs, plummeting through unearthly silence. . . . The thunder music seeped into the marrow of his bones and made him ache for that blinding flight. If only he could—

You have but to reach out your hand, Lightning Boy, a soft voice said. *And you, too, can soar.*

Pondwader stiffened with fear. He whispered, "Who are you?"

He hadn't heard that voice since the night when he'd grabbed hold of the Lightning Bird's burning tailfeathers. His breathing grew rapid and shallow, hissing through his nostrils. He waited for the voice to speak again.

"Pondwader?" Musselwhite murmured.

"Y-yes, my wife?" He turned to look at her.

"What's wrong?"

"Nothing. Go back to sleep. You must rest."

She rolled to her side to face him. Silvered hair fell over her shoulder in the wavering moonlight. "You jumped as if bitten by something."

"I had a dream."

"A dream?" she softly pressed. "Or a Spirit Dream?"

Pondwader sat up and his blanket coiled around his waist in bluish folds. He briskly rubbed his cheeks. "I don't know how to tell the difference any longer."

"You're shaking," she said.

"Am I?" He looked down at himself in bewilderment and discovered she was right. "I don't know when it started."

"*Why* did it start? What happened in the dream?"

"It's not important."

Musselwhite lifted a hand to him. "Come, Pondwader. Lie down next to me."

Her voice sounded so strong and sure, it comforted him. Pulling his blanket over his shoulders again, he slid against her, his face no more than a hand's breadth from hers. She put her arm around him and stroked his back tenderly. Pondwader sighed as relief stole through him.

"You're all right," she whispered. "We're all right. Try to sleep."

Pondwader tucked his head in the hollow of her shoulder, and she smoothed his long white hair, as if enjoying the softness.

"I love you, Musselwhite. Thank you."

"For what?"

"For taking care of me."

He felt her smile against his hair. She patted his back. "You've been taking care of me, too."

"Not very well. Though I've been trying hard. I just don't seem to be able—"

"I've been very grateful to have you on this journey. You bandaged my injury, made me willow bark tea, hunted, and caught fish. What would I have done without you?"

Pondwader pushed back and lifted his head, his whole aching heart in his eyes. "Thank you for saying that, I know you don't mean a word of it. I haven't caught very many animals." He thought about his inept efforts at hunting. "Though my last snare worked pretty well, didn't it?"

"You laid it in the game trail perfectly. When the raccoon stepped into it, he didn't know what hit him."

"Yes," Pondwader smiled. "I found him dangling by his foot from the tree branch where I had secured my snare." His smile faded, and he frowned down at his blanket. It had been a baby raccoon. When the little animal saw Pondwader coming through the trees, it had cried out in fear, and the sound had pierced Pondwader clean to the souls. The hardest part had been the killing. He'd used his knife to saw through the raccoon's windpipe. The whole time the animal was suffocating, he watched Pondwader with wide forgiving eyes. Animals understood death better than humans. . . .

"What are you thinking about?" Musselwhite asked.

"The little raccoon—what happened after I killed him."

Gently, she asked, "And what was that?"

Pondwader could not look at her. He fumbled with the corner of his blanket. "I couldn't help it, Musselwhite. I sat down in the middle of the trail and cried. I know we needed the meat, especially you, to rebuild your strength, and I didn't regret killing the raccoon, I just . . ."

"You just hurt." Musselwhite reached over and tipped his chin up to peer into his eyes. "Why couldn't you look at me when you told me that?"

He hesitated. "I was afraid you might be ashamed of me."

"For weeping over his death? For caring deeply about other creatures?

How could I be ashamed that you understand the preciousness of life?" She smiled wearily. "Pondwader, that is your greatest strength."

He reached for her hand and held it. "You always know how to soothe my hurts. Thank you . . . and now go to sleep, my wife. You need it very badly. I'm sorry I've kept you awake this long."

Musselwhite patted the blanket beside her, and Pondwader snuggled against her again, listening to the steady rhythm of her heartbeat, drowning in the comforting rise and fall of her breathing.

Musselwhite lightly kissed his forehead. "I do need sleep, Pondwader, but more than that, I need you to tell me about your dream."

"Really, it wasn't important."

"Are you afraid I won't believe you? I will. I must, Pondwader."

He frowned. "You must?"

She nodded against his hair. "Yes. I can't afford to dismiss anything now. We are too close to Standing Hollow Horn Village, and in too much danger. I need every scrap of information I can get. I wish you would trust me."

"Oh, but I do trust you!" he blurted. "I trust you with all my heart, Musselwhite! It's just that . . . well, I'm not sure that the things I've been feeling have anything to do with—"

"Pondwader," she said through a tired exhalation. "Just tell me. Please."

He nodded against her shoulder. "The Lightning Bird has been moving. Inside me."

"Moving? Like an unborn child, you mean?"

"Yes."

As if thinking, she stroked his hair for several moments. "So the Bird is growing?"

He nodded again, wishing he could see her expression, but afraid to. "And there's music."

Musselwhite's hand hovered over his shoulder. "Music?"

"Yes, it's curious. And very, very beautiful. Almost too beautiful to bear. Shishes and booms, and crackles, and beneath them all a deep constant drum roll. Thunder music. That's what I call it, anyway."

Pondwader felt Musselwhite cock her head. "How strange," she whispered.

"What?"

"Just before each of my children were born, I thought I could sense fear from them, fear and uncertainty about being born. It might have been my own emotions I was feeling, but I thought it came from my children. So I used to sing to them in my womb. It seemed to soothe them. To ease their fears." Moonlight filled the forest, and momentarily sheathed the trees and grass with glitters of silver. Musselwhite kept silent for a time, then said, "If that is Glade inside you, perhaps . . . perhaps he's trying to soothe you, Pondwader. As I once did him."

"To ease my fears . . . about his being born?"

"Yes. Are you frightened, Pondwader?"

Pondwader put his arm around her waist and hugged her tightly. His voice came out hoarse. "Very much, my wife."

Musselwhite nuzzled her cheek against the top of his head. "I wish I knew what to say to help you, Pondwader. But I've spent so much of my life trying to avoid Spirit Power, that now . . . well, I'm not—"

"It's all right, my wife. Just hearing your voice eases me."

She combed his white hair with her fingers. "I wish Dogtooth were here. He would know what to tell you. Pondwader . . ." she said, as if the thought had just occurred to her. "When we met Dogtooth at Manatee Lagoon, he said he'd come specifically to speak with you. He even mentioned something about the Lightning Bird. Did you discuss this with him?"

He curled into a tighter ball, burying his face against her tunic. "Yes."

"What did he tell you? Did he . . . did he say anything about what would happen when the Lightning Bird was born?"

"Yes."

"Pondwader!" She raised herself on one arm, and pushed him over onto his back to glare down at him. "What did Dogtooth say?"

He forced himself to meet her gaze, though the look in her eyes made his heart pound. "He said the—the chick was growing very fast, and that it would not be long before it sliced through my ribs and went hunting."

"Hunting? Hunting for what?"

Pondwader gestured helplessly. "Dogtooth was talking to a pushy wolf spider at the time and didn't seem to want to answer any of my questions— except one."

Her eyes narrowed. "Which one?"

"I asked him what would happen when the baby Lightning Bird soared free."

Musselwhite waited, searching his eyes. As the clouds shifted, moonlight coated the forest, and the black shadows of tangled branches interlaced like war paint over her face. "And? What did he say?"

"He said . . ." Pondwader's hand shook as he reached up and put his palm on her smooth cheek. "He said that I would die."

He felt her muscles go rigid. But she said nothing. Her gaze darted over the clearing, surveyed the dark trees, then returned to Pondwader.

"Did he say anything else about this death?" she asked cryptically.

"What do you mean?"

"Tell me everything he said about your dying that night."

"Well . . . let me see. I started by asking him if I would die when the baby bird soared free, and he said, 'You have died once already. Did it hurt?' I answered—"

"Did he mean you had died when you went into the Sacred Pond?"

"Yes. That's what he was talking about, having my souls washed away in the Pond. Anyway, I answered that it had hurt only a little when I died the first time, and Dogtooth said, 'So what are you afraid of?'" Pondwader ran his hand down her arm. ". . . I wasn't quite sure how he could put it so casually."

Musselwhite smiled broadly. "Pondwader, don't you see? Dogtooth speaks in riddles all the time. You can't be sure that he meant you would actually die. He might have meant you would die as you did in the Pond—meaning your souls would undergo another transformation of some kind." Her mouth quirked. "Knowing Dogtooth, he could have meant one of your toenails was going to die. There's just no telling. So . . ." She tipped her forehead to rest on Pondwader's and he grinned at her, staring up into her warm eyes. "Stop worrying. You may well live another eight tens of summers."

"Do you think so? Really?"

"It's very possible."

Relief flooded through Pondwader. Musselwhite would not lie to him, and if she thought Dogtooth might have been posing a riddle—then perhaps his fears had been for nothing. He would have to think about this.

"Did it ever occur to you," Musselwhite whispered, "that maybe that's what the baby Lightning Bird is trying to tell you? 'Don't be afraid, Pondwader. Everything is going to be all right?' "

Pondwader put a hand over his heart and rubbed lightly. "No, I—I never thought of it that way. But his sounds are so majestic and entrancing, they do take my mind off my fears."

"Well, I suspect that Lightning Birds know more than Dogtooth does. If that baby Bird is struggling to ease your fears, then it doesn't want you to be afraid. And, maybe—just maybe—that's because you have nothing to fear."

Pondwader murmured, "I love you so much." He longed to hear her tell him that she loved him, too, but he realized that might be especially hard for her now—while running a trail that led to Diver. Pondwader could wait. Someday Musselwhite would say those words to him. "Sleep now," he whispered. "Please, Musselwhite. You must have your strength back by the time we get to Standing Hollow Horn Village. To do that, you must sleep, my wife."

"I will, if you will."

"I'll try."

After she had pulled the blanket up over his shoulders and scanned the forest to assure their safety, she enfolded Pondwader in her arms and closed her eyes.

Pondwader did not sleep for a time. He thought about the things she'd said. And about the Lightning Bird's Song that filled him with such magnificent and unearthly longings.

You've been calling me, eyeless boy. I'm here. What do you want?"

My eyes jerk open and I pant in terror, scanning the pale blue dawn. The twisting branches have thrown off the cloak of night, and absorbed the first faint rays of Sun Mother's glory. Leaves shine and flutter in the whisper of pine-scented wind. It is cool, and feels good after yesterday's heat.

I turn my head, and see her.

Turtle Bone Doll sits in the middle of a palmetto frond over my head, her shabby tunic and white body framed perfectly in the dark green fan.

"What took you so long?" I whisper. "I've been calling you for days!"

"And you expect me to come, just because you call? I have many other things to worry about than you, stupid boy."

"Why do you call me stupid?" I ask angrily. "I learned to thunder, didn't I?"

Wind rustles through the forest, and the frond where Turtle Bone Doll sits bobs up and down, making her frayed skirt billow. *"Just because I forced you to learn one simple skill, you think it means you're no longer related to those catfish with combed-out brains?"*

I stretch my back muscles. "I've learned other things, too. The Lightning Bird has been Singing to me. Did you know that? He's been telling me the most dazzling things—what it feels like to leap from the soft belly of clouds and plunge through the sky—"

"I don't suppose it occurred to you that perhaps the Bird was trying to get you to SOAR . . . did it, brainless boy? Maybe the Bird has also been showing you sights of such wondrous light that your human eyes cannot conceive the beauty?"

Astonished, I whisper, "How did you know?"

Turtle Bone Doll vents an exasperated sigh. *"Could it be that the Bird is tantalizing you, making you long so for the Light, that eventually, when you have the time, providing you live long enough, you will want to learn to FLASH?"*

I frown. Turtle Bone Doll has leaned forward on the palm frond, so that she is perched over my face. One of her eyes is gone, apparently rubbed off. A sly grin comes to my face.

"I guess you can't call me an 'eyeless' boy anymore, since you only have one left."

"You missed your own point. And mine too, it seems."

My thoughts flounder, trying to decipher that comment. "Oh," I say, "you mean you're not eyeless because you still have one left, and—"

"And you are as blind as a mud mole. Listen to me, will you, Pondwader? The Lightning Bird is working as hard as he can to make you want to become part of his Dance, before it's too late, and you find out the hard way."

"What is that supposed to mean?"

Turtle Bone Doll slides down to the very tip of the frond's serrated leaf, little more than a hand's breadth away, and whispers, *"Have you really been screaming my name in your dreams, just to ask me these sorts of questions?"*

I stare into her faded face. Her mouth has been smeared into a gray smudge. "Uh . . . no. I've been calling you because I want to know how you came to life. Musselwhite said she didn't breathe life into you, and if she didn't—"

"Finally! An important question . . . Did Musselwhite ever tell you about the time four of her sons died in a single day when a waterspout spun out of the sky and ripped their canoe in half?"

My mouth drops open. "No," I say softly.

"She swam out at dawn to dive in the warm water, searching for their bodies. The storm had churned up the ocean so badly she couldn't see anything. She had to pat her hands over the bottom, feeling for them. All day, she swam and searched. At dusk, on the brink of exhaustion, her right hand touched something cold and smooth. Her fingertips recognized the mouth and nose. It took all her strength to pull the boy from beneath the sand, and when she did, she dragged him to the surface, put her mouth over his and tried to breathe life back into him . . . but she couldn't, Pondwader. Do you know why?"

I reach up, grab the tip of the frond and pull her down closer. Turtle Bone Doll tilts forward to oblige me, staring expressionlessly into my face. "What does that have to do with how you came to life?"

"How does anything come to life, Pondwader?"

"It gets a soul, or souls." I release the frond and Turtle Bone Doll floats with its bobbing motion.

"How did you get one when your souls had been washed away in the Pond?"

"You were there. You don't need me to—"

"Think about this, brainless boy. Even you are smart enough to figure it out."

She shoots upward, like a perfectly cast dart, flying straight and true, heading northeast.

The frond bounces above me, fanning me with cool morning air.

Thirty-five

Dark Rain trotted down the game trail between Beaverpaw, who led the way, and Hanging Star, who brought up the rear. Palms lined their path, fronds swaying in the wind. Heavy clusters of berries draped within her reach. If she'd only had time, she would have stopped and collected several handfuls to eat along the way. But she didn't. Hanging Star said that they would reach Standing Hollow Horn Village tonight, or at the latest tomorrow morning, so she had dressed in her best red tunic, belted tightly at the waist with a braided rabbit-fur cord. Her freshly washed black hair hung in a glossy wealth over her shoulders, blowing freely in the wind. The small pack on her back jingled with riches. She had won many valuable stone tools, necklaces, hafted wolfteeth punches, for holing leather, even a few fire-sharpened burial stakes enlaced with brightly dyed cord. In the big game ahead, she would need them. Huge sums would be wagered, and she planned to be in the hottest games.

"Blast!" Hanging Star growled behind her.

Dark Rain looked over her shoulder. "What's wrong with you?"

He raised his sweating arm to wipe his ugly square face. He wore a breech-clout and a tawdry whelkshell necklace. "I was thinking about other things and ran through a cluster of ripe palm berries!"

Dark Rain laughed. "Well, pay attention." She turned back and trotted faster, catching up with Beaverpaw.

While she doubted the wisdom of thrashing through the forest this way, Hanging Star had promised that the only possible threat would be from Cottonmouth's warriors and, after all, most of them were his relatives. During a nasty disagreement, Hanging Star had absolutely assured Beaverpaw that his presence alone would guarantee their safety. Dark Rain smirked to herself. Beaverpaw had believed him! Even after Hanging Star had insisted on bringing up the rear. If the man felt such certainty, why wasn't he running in the lead? Why hadn't Beaverpaw *demanded* that Hanging Star take the lead?

Not that it mattered to her. Beaverpaw's position meant he would probably be the first to stop a dart, and that would suit Dark Rain just fine. He'd been deliberately ignoring her. Last night, after she'd tired of Hanging Star, which hadn't taken long, she'd crawled under Beaverpaw's blankets and embraced him passionately—and he'd pretended to sleep! She could not rouse him, despite doing things with her mouth that would have driven any ordinary man to take her on the spot, no matter what his better judgment suggested.

Dark Rain glowered at his broad back. Did Beaverpaw really think he could go home, that his spurned wife might take him back and he could live just exactly as he had before he'd met Dark Rain? What a fool. Even if that squat toad of a wife did take him back, nothing would be the same. The clan would remind him of his adultery tens of tens of times a day, in a look, a twist of the mouth, just someone folding his arms at the wrong moment. And worse. His children would plague him with questions. "Father, where were you?" "Why did you go away?" "Did you stop loving us?" "Did you really leave us for that repulsive Outcast woman?" "How could you do that, Father?" "We love you so much. We needed you."

And when the children grew old enough to truly understand Beaverpaw's crime, they would look at him with different eyes, suspicious, filled with scorn. It would kill his souls—but he did not see that. Not now. Not with the possibility of going home so new.

Dark Rain had seen it all before. If she'd wished to keep him, she would have expended the effort to point these things out—but Beaverpaw had lost his gleam. As most men did. The creature that ran in front of her, his muscular shoulders shining with sweat, counted for no more now than a broken shell necklace. Not only that, he had given her every precious item he owned, except his weapons, and not even she could convince a true warrior to relinquish those. Beaverpaw's usefulness had run out.

Dark Rain needed a new lover. Another Trader would be perfect, one with many fine possessions, and preferably more pleasant to look at than this tadpole-faced War Leader. With all the gambling that would be going on at Standing Hollow Horn, she could surely find someone. Just thinking about the hunt thrilled her. No man could resist once she had—

Beaverpaw crouched down in the trail, and Dark Rain came to a halt abruptly. He waved her back with his hand, his eyes narrowing to slits, then nocked a dart in his atlatl and lifted it into throwing position.

Hanging Star eased up behind her, whispering, "What is it? What does he see?"

"How would I know? I haven't talked to him!"

"Not in days, I think." Hanging Star bit her neck, hard.

Dark Rain shoved him away. "Why aren't you up there helping Beaverpaw? These are probably your relatives, isn't that right?"

Hanging Star grinned. "Probably."

Dark Rain smiled, too. "You have souls worthy of a water moccasin, Hanging Star. Or is it that your relatives might dart you on sight?"

Hanging Star glanced at her, then craned his neck to watch Beaverpaw, who had stood up and lowered his atlatl. "Come. It looks as if we're safe." He put a hand on Dark Rain's arm.

She jerked it away. "No thanks to you," she said and stalked forward.

When she rounded the curve in the trail, she stopped dead in her tracks. Beaverpaw stood with Musselwhite and Pondwader! Blessed Brother Sky! Could she never get rid of that boy? Musselwhite wore a thick bandage around her head, but she stood tall, her eyes gleaming with deadly intent— as usual. When Pondwader saw Dark Rain, he went even paler than normal. He'd pulled his long white hair back and plaited it into a single braid, which accentuated the lines of his oval face and pointed nose. His long tan robe bore streaks of dirt and sweat stains. He didn't look as if he'd bathed in days.

Musselwhite did not so much as glance at Dark Rain. Her gaze remained riveted to Beaverpaw, as she listened intently to him murmur, "Thank the Spirits we found you. I have things I must tell you."

Dark Rain smiled and walked to stand beside Beaverpaw. He instantly stopped talking.

Musselwhite said, "Hello, Dark Rain. I hope you are well."

"I am. But you look poorly. Is that a head wound?"

Musselwhite's face showed no more emotion than a wooden statue's. To Beaverpaw, she said, "Come. Let us speak in private." Then, to the others added, "We will return soon."

Musselwhite led Beaverpaw five tens of hands away and they crouched together beneath an old oak's hanging beard of moss. Both had grim expressions.

Dark Rain turned to Pondwader, who seemed to wilt. "Well, well," she said. "Come and sit down with me. Tell what has been happening with you."

"Perhaps I should go sit with my wife, she might need—"

Dark Rain grabbed his arm. "She needs no help from you, Pondwader. She and Beaverpaw are probably talking about warfare or raiding—things you know nothing about. I need you more than Musselwhite does." She dragged him to the spotty shade of a spindly dogwood tree. "Sit down."

Pondwader knelt, but appeared as nervous as a fox with its hind foot in a snare. Hanging Star flopped on the ground beside him, and Pondwader frowned.

"So *this* is the White Lightning Boy," Hanging Star said in wonder.

"Yes, this is my son, Pondwader. Pondwader, this is Hanging Star," Dark Rain said glumly. "He's from Standing Hollow Horn Clan."

Pondwader just squinted.

Hanging Star said, "Shot down any Shining Eagles lately, Lightning Boy?"

When Pondwader didn't answer, Hanging Star lifted his brows and asked Dark Rain, "Does it have a voice? Or is it just white hair and pink eyes?"

Dark Rain ordered, "Pondwader, say something."

Her son shifted uncomfortably. In a pathetic whisper, he asked, "What?"

Hanging Star chuckled. "Well, it has a voice, but not much of one. Tell me, Dark Rain, how did you convince the illustrious Musselwhite to marry the likes of . . . this?"

Dark Rain stared at him coldly. "Go find something to do, Hanging Star. I wish to speak with my son alone."

From the corner of her eye, she saw Pondwader close his eyes as if in pain, but just for an instant, then he jerked them wide again, and stared at Dark Rain as if expecting punishment.

Hanging Star surveyed the two of them, then laughed out loud. "Oh, yes, Dark Rain. I can see the boy is very eager to speak with his loving mother. I'm not going anywhere. This could be the most entertainment I've had in half a moon," he said, insulting her lovemaking on purpose. When her lips pressed into a hard line, he gave Dark Rain the full benefit of his rotting teeth.

Pondwader glanced back and forth between them, red rising in his cheeks.

"Ah," Hanging Star said, "your son knows you, Dark Rain. But then, how could he not? You've scandalized your clan . . . how many times? Three, or is it four?"

"F-four," Pondwader stammered.

Dark Rain smiled elegantly, and stretched out on her side between the men, crossing her long beautiful legs. "So my association with Beaverpaw makes it four, eh? What is your grandmother saying? She must be livid."

Pondwader creased the hem of his robe with his fingernails.

Hanging Star commented, "I had no idea that a human face could get that color. But then, it's not fully human, is it? How did you come to be, boy? Tell me the story again."

Pondwader seemed to be debating whether or not to answer.

Dark Rain said, "Tell him, Pondwader. It's not an act. He really is an ignoramus."

Wearily, Pondwader began, "Lighting Boys are created when a bolt of lightning penetrates a woman's womb and—"

"Well, I wouldn't doubt that," Hanging Star said. "In fact, a bolt of lightning might be the only thing that would surprise your mother. I'd wager she lay out in every lightning storm with her legs spread, hoping—"

"Are you jealous, Hanging Star? Pay him no attention, Pondwader. A blade of grass would make him jealous. Now tell me—"

"Not jealous, Dark Rain," Hanging Star replied with a sly smile. "Bored. Utterly and completely. And that's the last thing you'd want to be, isn't it?"

She longed to slap that smile off his ugly face. Later, she promised herself. She would find a way of avenging that comment. She turned to her son. "How is your marriage, Pondwader? Are you happy?"

The boy seemed short of breath. He could barely force enough out to make words. "Yes, Mother."

"And Musselwhite? How was she injured?"

Pondwader prodded at an oak twig on the ground at his side. "We were attacked."

"And she was struck in the head?"

Pondwader nodded.

"But why isn't she wrapped in a blanket sleeping? She should be—"

"Because, my beauty," Hanging Star answered for Pondwader. "She is Musselwhite. It would take more than a glancing blow to the head to keep her down, especially when she knows that her husband Diver is still alive and in Cottonmouth's hands. Speaking of which," he said and eyed Pondwader a little fearfully, "the only reason Cottonmouth seeks to trap Musselwhite is because of you, Lightning Boy. I wonder why that is?"

"*Me?*"

"Oh, yes. Cottonmouth wants you very badly."

Dark Rain stiffened at the name. "I never liked Cottonmouth."

"He didn't like you, either, precious." Hanging Star's eyes glinted. "I recall the time you tried to grope him at Sun Mother's Winter Celebration and he—"

Pondwader stumbled to his feet. "My wife needs me . . ."

Hanging Star laughed, watching Pondwader blunder into an oak tree, trip over a palmetto, and run for Musselwhite with his robe flying about his legs. When he knelt at her side, Musselwhite tenderly put an arm around him. Pondwader sat as close to her as he could without getting into her lap.

Disdainfully, Dark Rain said, "He never was the man he ought to have been."

"That must be the only reason you didn't drag your own son into your blankets."

"Don't be ridiculous. My mother would have slit my throat."

Hanging Star rubbed his jaw. "I'm amazed she didn't anyway."

Beaverpaw examined Pondwader. The youth looked ill. He held to Musselwhite's hand as if it were a tree trunk in a hurricane. Beaverpaw felt sorry for him, wondering what Dark Rain must have said to sicken her own son.

"Go on," Musselwhite urged.

Beaverpaw nodded. Despite her injury, Musselwhite radiated a strength that bolstered even Beaverpaw. He leaned forward, keeping his voice low. "Hanging Star says that Cottonmouth has Dreamed your arrival in the village. He knows you are coming. And the rest is just as bad."

"Tell me."

Beaverpaw laced his fingers and rubbed his palms together. "In his Dream, you had no war party; just you and the Lightning Boy would be coming to rescue Diver. He has set up a trap to capture you."

Her jaw tightened. "What sort of trap?"

Beaverpaw wet his lips, and glanced at Dark Rain and Hanging Star, just to make certain they hadn't moved. Then his eyes met Musselwhite's again. "You are supposed to enter the village at dusk. There is an old oak, covered with hanging moss, at the northwest corner of the village—"

"Yes. I know that tree."

"Cottonmouth has Dreamed that you and Pondwader launch your attack from there. He will have warriors stationed and waiting to capture you when you do."

Musselwhite's nostrils flared, but Beaverpaw could not tell whether in anger or frustration. She drew back the arm she'd had around Pondwader and laced her hands in her lap. "Then I assure you, I won't do that." She glared at her whitening knuckles. "Has Hanging Star said where Diver is being held? Tens of years ago, he would have been in the council shelter near the water . . . but now, I don't know."

"Hanging Star hasn't said," Beaverpaw replied. "But I'll find out for you."

Dark Rain's seductive laughter rose into the air, and Beaverpaw's gut clenched. He spat to clean his mouth of the foul taste of it.

Musselwhite asked, "What is it?"

He shook his head. Inhaling a deep breath, he glanced sympathetically at Pondwader's pale face, then said, "You will not be fighting alone when you enter Standing Hollow Horn Village, Musselwhite. I don't know what good it will do, but I—"

"Beaverpaw, let me be honest with you. If we are forced to fight, we will lose. Cottonmouth has too many warriors. We must find a way of sneaking into the village, locating Diver, and getting out. Otherwise, none of us will live to enjoy our triumphs. Do you understand? We can't fight Cottonmouth."

Beaverpaw nodded. "I do understand. Perhaps, then, I could create a diversion for you, to give you time to get to Diver."

Musselwhite reached out and placed a hand on his shoulder. "I would be very grateful for your help, War Leader."

Shame welled powerfully inside him. "I do not deserve that title, Musselwhite, though I thank you for—"

"But . . ." Pondwader blurted, and turned to Musselwhite as if asking approval before he continued.

Musselwhite's gaze went over his face. Gently, she said, "What did you wish to say, Pondwader?"

He reached for her hand again, as if her touch reassured him. Pondwader murmured, "Well, just that . . . I'm sure . . . I mean, if we succeed at Standing Hollow Horn, Beaverpaw, I'm sure my grandmother will speak to the Council on your behalf. And . . . Beaverpaw? Waterbearer never stopped loving you. She wants you back very much."

Beaverpaw bowed his head to keep his heartache hidden. In a constricted voice, he said, "I hope so, Pondwader. I cannot tell you how hard I am praying for exactly that."

Thirty-six

Diamondback leaned against the gnarled trunk of a scrub oak, massaging his aching leg, and watching the tiny flames leap through the kindling he'd piled in the firepit. Mornings always brought him the most pain. His leg stiffened up overnight, so that he hobbled like an old man gathering wood and lighting the breakfast fires. They had divided the duties. Diamondback found the trails, selected the campsites and built the fires, while Dace and Kelp hunted, fished, located freshwater and filled their water gourds.

They had been making good time. So far, the only obstacle they had encountered was a fat, belligerent bear that wanted to walk the same trail they did. Dace suggested they dart it, but Kelp pointed out that they didn't have the time to clean and butcher the animal, and wasting such fine meat and hide would have been unforgivable. Diamondback had backtracked and taken a parallel trail.

He scratched his back on the tree. Twisted branches hung down around him, suspended like Eagle Above's talons ready to clutch him up and carry him off to eat in the Daybreak Land. He smiled at the thought. Milky morning sunlight shimmered from the wind-blown leaves on the branches. A half a hand past dawn, Sun Mother rose through a black curtain of clouds and hung, huge and crimson, in a clear blue sky. Sea Girl's green face shimmered with flecks of deep scarlet.

Diamondback threw two large pieces of wood on the fire, arranging them so they wouldn't smother his modest blaze, then prodded the coals with a long stick. Sparks leaped and whirled upward, winking as they tumbled away in the breeze. The sweet scent of burning pine sap encircled him.

Just as he had settled back against the tree trunk again, he saw Dace break out of the trees and trot toward him. He looked frightened. Diamondback shoved to his feet, and hobbled stiff-legged out across the sand to meet him.

"What's wrong?" Diamondback asked.

Dace came to a halt, breathing hard, his pointed chin and straight nose coated with perspiration. His atlatl and stiletto hung from the belt of his breechclout. He said. "Come and see for yourself. I don't know what to make of this."

Dace led the way back down a section of trail lined by head-high prickly-pear cactus. Red fruits dotted the end of most pads, and gave off a faintly tangy scent. Diamondback frequently had to turn sideways to avoid the long thorns. Ahead, he saw Dace kneel behind a thicket of palmettos, and then the stench hit Diamondback: decomposing flesh. . . . And fear swelled his chest until he could scarcely think. *Not my mother! Please, Brother Earth . . .*

Dace stood up.

Diamondback called, "Who is it? Tell me!"

Dace shook his head. "I don't know. Two men."

"You're sure?" Diamondback asked as he came to a halt beside Dace.

"Yes. They are both barechested, dressed in breechclouts."

Diamondback had to hold his breath to keep from retching. He backed up a few paces, examining the swollen, rotting bodies. One man had been darted through the right eye. The other's skull had been crushed by two powerful blows from a warclub.

Diamondback's eyes widened. "Blessed Spirits, Dace," he said. "I know that man on the left, the one with the crushed skull. He used to be Cottonmouth's War Leader! I've seen him five times since last summer. Every time Windy Cove Village was attacked, and again when he led his warriors against our scouting party."

"And the man on the right?"

Diamondback shook his head. "I don't think I recog—" His brows pulled together suddenly. "Wait." He edged forward three paces to study the fletching on the dart. "Dace! My mother killed these men! This is her dart. I would swear to it!"

"So she came this way."

"Yes, certainly." Diamondback bent over and began scanning the ground. "Look around, Dace. Do you see any tracks? Was Pondwader with her when she was attacked?"

Dace began looking, but he said, "It has rained since these men died, Diamondback. Even if Pondwader was with her, we may never find evidence of it."

Diamondback pushed aside a palm frond and gazed at the sheltered spot beneath the stems. Nothing. "I know, Dace. I just hoped we could give Kelp some good news."

In a soft voice, Dace asked, "Are you still worried that Pondwader may not have found Musselwhite?"

"The only thing we know for sure is that Cottonmouth's warriors scattered through the forest after they attacked Windy Cove Village, and that my mother encountered and killed two of them. As for Pondwader . . ."

Dace knelt and scrutinized an indentation in a patch of old leaves. It might have been a sandalprint, but it wasn't. "You mean he might have met some of those warriors, too—but before he could reach Musselwhite."

Diamondback heard the hurt and fear in Dace's voice. He said, "Don't worry yet. Pondwader may be fine. I just wish we had some way of knowing that he'd met up with my mother. I would feel better."

"So would I. I . . ." Dace fell to his knees. "Diamondback?"

"What? What did you find?" He hobbled over and braced his hands on his knees.

In the sand beneath a dense cluster of palmettos, Dace pointed to a clump of leaves, then looked up at Diamondback. "That looks like a bloody sandalprint to me," he said.

"Can you pick it up, Dace? Let me take a closer look."

Dace gathered the leaves and handed them to Diamondback. Four oak leaves with several pine needles. Clotted together with old blood. And the blood had a distinct pattern, from the woven sole of a sandal. "She must have stepped in her victim's blood and tracked it in this direction. See if you can find another one, Dace!"

Dace crawled forward on his hands and knees, looking in every sheltered location. "Diamondback? Look at this. . . . And this! Here's another one!"

Ropes of thick vines draped an oak's branch. Dace held them aside and pointed. The crescent shapes of two right sandalprints pressed into the soil. Diamondback slapped Dace on the back, then surveyed the route they had come, from the bodies, to the bloody leaves, to these prints.

Ominously, Diamondback said, "Mother was in a hurry, Dace. She was running. See the length of her stride here? And she was running in a straight line. That's not like her. Not when she's on a war walk. She must have been very worried about something."

Dace straightened up and frowned, drawing the line in his imagination. "About something on the beach? Out there?" He gestured with his chin to a grove of mixed palms and pines.

"Let's go see."

They sprinted forward, shoving through blossoming knots of wild alamanda vines. Petals fluttered around them. Some landed in the sweat on their bare shoulders and stuck there like a mottled yellow cape, others crushed beneath their feet, releasing a rich sweet fragrance.

When they reached the grove, Diamondback looked around and said, "Let's spread out. We can cover the beach more quickly."

"Good idea."

The sand here shone brilliantly white in the slanting morning sunlight. As Diamondback searched the area beneath some hanging clusters of palm berries, he spied something black.

"Dace?" he called. "I found charcoal! Someone built a fire here."

Dace trotted over and they both bent down, surveying the black specks. Diamondback unbelted his hafted knife and dug a small hole through the layer of wind-deposited sand. The deeper he went, the more charcoal he found. Large chunks filled the old firepit.

"This can't be more than five or six days old."

Dace lifted his head. "But who built it? Those dead warriors back there? Musselwhite?"

Diamondback straightened up and tied his knife to his belt again. From here Sea Girl's waves sounded loud, crashing against the shore of the small cove. "No, Dace," he answered. "No warrior would choose this place to camp. It's too exposed. Look around. Your enemies could sneak up on you from three sides, and the sound of the waves would cover their approach. You'd be dead before you knew it."

Hope lit Dace's young face. "You think it was Pondwader?"

"That would explain my mother's hurry after she killed those warriors. She may have been worried that they had reached Pondwader before she'd seen them."

Dace craned his neck, seeking the place in the trees where the dead men lay. "But . . . she could have seen this camp from there . . . I think. If she could see Pondwader—"

"Maybe it was night, Dace. He could have been rolled up in his blanket sleeping, and she didn't know whether he was alive or dead."

"Maybe."

A smile curled Diamondback's lips. "I think she found him, Dace. I think she found him and they're together right now."

Dace closed his eyes and exhaled an elated breath. "If so, they should already be at Standing Hollow Horn Village. How long will it take us to get there?"

"If we can keep up this pace, two days." Unconsciously, Diamondback lowered his hand to massage his aching leg. It always felt better after he'd walked the stiffness out, the pain not quite so fiery. "And we can, I think."

Wind flapped Dace's braid against his back. "We may be too late to help them. In two days, they could have rescued your father and already be on their way home."

". . . Or they may have been captured."

The thought had been running through Diamondback's souls, though he had not, until this moment, mentioned it aloud. Mostly because he did not wish to contemplate the possibilities. He watched Dace's eyes narrow.

"Then we had better hurry," Dace said. "Cottonmouth is not known for treating captives kindly."

"No," Diamondback murmured, staring down at the old firepit again.

"Let's find Kelp," Dace said. "She was netting killifish in that small pond due west of where we camped. The sooner we eat and start up the trail, the sooner we will reach Standing Hollow Horn Village."

Dace started to turn, and Diamondback gripped him by the arm. "Let's not mention the possibility to Kelp that they might have been captured. Let's just tell her that we've found good evidence that Pondwader is safe with my mother."

Dace smiled. "I wager, my friend, that she considered the possibility of their capture long ago—but, yes, I agree. If she doesn't mention it, I won't."

Diamondback nodded his gratitude. "I don't know why I keep trying to protect her when I know she's a very smart woman—"

"*Girl*," Dace said and punched Diamondback in the arm so hard he staggered sideways. "She's a very smart girl."

Diamondback smiled. "Keep reminding me."

In a small pool surrounded by palmettos, water sparkled, smooth and transparent. Moss cushioned Moonsnail's feet as she used her walking stick to pry open a path through the dense fronds. She knelt by the pond. Fragments of shells and old leaves coated the bottom. A young watersnake swam along the edge on the far side, sending out glimmering silver waves. She dipped up a handful of the crystalline liquid and drank. It went down cool and earthy.

People filed by her, heading on down the game trail. Men scouted the lead, their atlatls nocked and ready, while women carried heavy packs and shepherded dogs hauling travoises. A few held infants on their hips. Polished Shells walked in the middle of a crowd of laughing, skipping children. Thorny Boy trotted at her side. He'd become fast friends with Polished Shells' youngest daughter, Little Darter. Old people brought up the rear, walking as fast as they could, but not nearly quick enough to keep pace with the younger clan members. More than a dozen tribal elders straggled along at the end of the line. Seedpod stopped and waved to Moonsnail. She waved back. He seemed to be waiting for her. He'd backed up to lean against the trunk of a tall pine, resting, watching her.

For two days, cougars and wolves had been paralleling their path, slinking through the trees, just beyond dart range, growling softly, threateningly. No healthy animal would attack a group so large, but they might leap upon a straying child, or attack a lone elder. Is that what worried Seedpod? That she might get eaten? At night, around the cooking fires, people muttered curses and retold stories about close calls. Not a single rain cloud had darkened the sky since they'd left Manatee Lagoon, and Moonsnail had heard more than one person whisper bitterly that they ought to turn around and go back. Mutters traveled through the ranks, people saying that Dogtooth was an old fool—and so was anyone who listened to him.

Moonsnail couldn't condemn them. They'd stowed the bulk of their belongings in the trees near Manatee Lagoon. Men and women missed their special possessions, the everyday things that made their lives easier, like extra blankets, heavy wooden cooking bowls, large baskets filled with palm thread, cordage, and ropes, while children cried for missing toys. After consulting with the other clan elders, Moonsnail and Seedpod had ordained that only lightweight belongings could be taken, since this would be a short trip, lasting a few days at most. Yet with all the raiding, people understandably feared their possessions might be stolen, or destroyed in the interim.

She dipped another handful of cool, earthy water, as Dogtooth thrashed through the palmettos beside her. Sweat matted his gray hair to his cheeks and made his hooked nose seem all the more prominent. He wore a breechclout and a cowrie shell necklace. Narrow bars of ribs lined his chest. His skinny body looked very old and frail. Using a small wooden cup he dipped up a drink, and swallowed the contents in three gulps, his throat working. Stringy muscles bulged in his calves as he rose to his feet again, and peered down at her. His eyes glinted.

Irreverently, Moonsnail said, "You look sane today." She cocked her head. "Are you? If so, I'd like to have a talk. If not, I wouldn't."

Dogtooth scratched his withered cheek. "I've never known how to tell," he answered.

Moonsnail braced her walking stick, and grunted as she stood up. With her tunic sleeve, she wiped perspiration from her forehead. Dogtooth gave her that enigmatic grin.

"What's there to smile about?" she demanded. "It's as hot as boiling stones, we're being stalked by hungry animals, and people openly accuse me of being demented for forcing them to go on this inland journey."

"You're not demented," Dogtooth said. "You are simply cautious. And they should thank the Shining Ones you are."

"Why?"

"For one thing, Kelp, Diamondback, and Dace are still alive."

Moonsnail leaned on her stick and eyed him carefully, wondering whether to press him on how he knew that. Behind Dogtooth, swallows dived through the oaks and palms. She couldn't help herself. She asked, "Are you certain? Have they found Pondwader and Musselwhite yet?"

"No, but Beaverpaw and Dark Rain have. Beaverpaw had a long talk with Musselwhite about Standing Hollow Horn Village. They laid out a very good strategy for freeing Diver."

"So . . . Beaverpaw is going to Standing Hollow Horn Village, too? Along with Dark Rain?"

"Oh, yes," Dogtooth said, and shook a finger emphatically, "and thereby hangs a tale. They weren't going there originally, but they met a runaway warrior named Hanging Star—he's the man who killed Dreamstone during the Windy Cove battle—and later Hanging Star killed Bowfin, he—"

"Bowfin is dead?" Moonsnail blurted. "Are you sure?"

"Oh, yes, he's quite dead."

Moonsnail's heart squeezed tight. He'd been so young, and a fine warrior, if wild. His mother, Plainweave, had spoken of nothing else since he'd gone. She'd narrated every event in her son's life, every prank he'd pulled, all of which had led to his defection—and blamed herself for each. Bowfin's brothers had wandered about, defending him to anyone who cared to listen. Moonsnail shook her head. The youth might have been flighty, but he didn't deserve to die. "Why did this Hanging Star kill him?"

Dogtooth exchanged a knowing glance with her, and Moonsnail nodded. "Over my worthless daughter, eh? Great Whale. I wish you'd told me to bash out her brains when she was born, Dogtooth. A lot of good people would be alive today if I had."

"And a lot of good people would be dead, too," he countered, "or rather, never have been born, like Pondwader and Kelp."

Moonsnail shifted the small pack on her back and made her way through the palmettos onto the trail again. Dogtooth followed her. When they stood facing each other, Moonsnail said, "Yes, you're right about that. I could never regret the births of my grandchildren. I wish Sandbur had lived to see them grown up."

They walked side by side, until they reached Seedpod. As Seedpod smiled, his blunt chin jutted out from his gaunt leathery face. White hair lay flat against his head. His breechclout had been dyed bright red, but had faded to a pale pink shade.

"How are you two this afternoon?" Seedpod asked, looking first at her, then at Dogtooth.

"Better now," Moonsnail answered. "A drink and a short rest helps restore strength. Not only that, Dogtooth just told me that Kelp, Diamondback, and Dace are alive."

Seedpod stepped closer. "What about Musselwhite and Pondwader? Have you Dreamed about them, Dogtooth? Are they all right?"

Moonsnail turned to Dogtooth, who appeared to be considering the question. She had assumed from his words about Beaverpaw and Musselwhite's plan to rescue Diver that they must be safe—but Dogtooth's hesitation made her heart pound. Could something terrible have happened after that event? She waited, scrutinizing every wrinkle in the old Soul Dancer's face. "Well?" she demanded. "Are they all right?"

Dogtooth rubbed the toe of his sandal over the pine needles in the trail. "Fine."

"Fine? If they're fine, why did it take you so long to answer?" Moonsnail asked.

Dogtooth folded his arms across his chest, and considered his reply carefully for several moments, before saying, "Puzzles are the heart of Spirit Dreams."

"What puzzles?" she asked.

Seedpod added, "What could be puzzling about that question? Either they're fine, or they're not."

"Well . . ." Dogtooth said, and his face softened as he heard the desperation in their voices. "Yes and no."

"Blessed Spirits," Moonsnail groaned, "and you looked so sane."

Seedpod spread his legs to brace himself for a lengthy and difficult discussion. "What puzzle relates to Pondwader and Musselwhite? Where are they now?"

"Let's walk and talk," Dogtooth suggested. "We'd better catch up with the rest of the clans soon, or people will fear that the big cat in the woods over there is gnawing our bones." He gestured with his chin.

Moonsnail whirled around and saw the two yellow eyes glinting beyond a tangle of vines. The cougar's long tail stretched along the branch where it lay, like a golden snake against the brown bark. Every so often, the tail switched back and forth, as if to shoo flies, then went still again.

Seedpod's hand lowered to his belted stiletto. "I agree," he said. "Let's walk."

Seedpod led the way, and Dogtooth fell in behind Moonsnail, humming to himself.

"Dogtooth," Seedpod called over his shoulder. "Please finish what you were saying. What was the puzzle about Pondwader and Musselwhite?"

"Oh! Last night, I Dreamed that Kelp, Diamondback, and Dace were following Musselwhite's trail across a fallen log which bridged a small pond, and Musselwhite and Pondwader were watching them."

Moonsnail said, "What's so mysterious about that? It sounds like they finally found each other."

"Well," Dogtooth replied, "not exactly. You see, Pondwader and Musselwhite were watching them from beneath the water. I saw their faces on the bottom of the pond."

Seedpod halted so fast that Moonsnail ran into him, and stumbled backwards. She had to take quick action, bracing her walking stick, to keep from falling.

Seedpod clenched his fists at his sides. "You mean . . . they were dead? Buried in the pond?"

Dogtooth peered at Seedpod. "No, no. I mean, I don't think so. But how curious that such a possibility never occurred to me. I suppose it's conceivable. I hadn't—"

"That makes no sense," Moonsnail said. "If they were dead and buried in that pond, how could Diamondback be following their trail across the log?"

"And Cottonmouth's warriors," Seedpod added, "would never have buried them. They would have left both to rot."

Dogtooth rubbed a hand over his chin. "There is that," he agreed.

Moonsnail exchanged a worried glance with Seedpod. The three walked in silence for a time, weaving around a hillock and entering a shadowed section of the trail floored with fallen acorns. Dogtooth's "puzzle" had made Moonsnail's knees go weak. She had to slow down to make sure she did not turn an ankle on the acorns. Seedpod gripped her arm to steady her. In the distance, they saw people standing in small groups, talking, waiting for them. Children had taken the opportunity to play. They chased each other through the trees with sweet childish laughter. Polished Shells had walked several paces back down the trail, and stood in a well of mottled sunlight, a hand up to shield her eyes as she looked for Moonsnail. Little Darter and Thorny Boy raced around her legs.

Moonsnail lifted a hand to her daughter, and Polished Shells waved and smiled her relief. When Thorny Boy saw Seedpod, he ran forward, his little legs pumping, and grabbed his grandfather around the leg. Seedpod smoothed the boy's black tangled hair.

"Are you having fun, Thorny Boy?" Seedpod asked.

Thorny Boy looked up at him. Dirt splotched his pug nose and streaked his plump cheeks. The headband which kept his tangled hair out of his eyes sat at an angle. "Yes, Grandfather. I like Little Darter. She—"

"No," Dogwood sighed, interrupting everyone. The old man shook his head, then nodded, as if he'd changed his mind about something. "I'm certain that Pondwader and Musselwhite are safe. They must be . . . or we are all doomed."

Both Seedpod and Moonsnail started. They turned to face him, and Thorny Boy peered up inquisitively.

"What do you mean by that?" Moonsnail asked.

Dogtooth shouldered between them, and walked past. He answered, "I'm just frightened. Power can be so fickle sometimes."

Thirty-seven

Diamondback paced around the campsite, trying to work out the story. The gray gleam of dusk made the task more difficult. He shoved palmetto foliage aside to peer beneath the broad sheltering fronds, searching for more footprints. The widely spaced, toe-first prints must have been Pondwader's, and the shuffling, stumbling tracks certainly belonged to his mother. He had followed her many times on war walks, and had memorized the size and distinct patterns she wove into her sandal bottoms.

His brows lowered. To himself, he whispered, "Those two dead men we found hurt you, didn't they, Mother? They hurt you badly."

From the moment they had arrived at the campsite in late afternoon, his gut had been crawling. Now, he knew why. The blood had been his mother's.

Turning, he frowned back at the fallen log that traversed the expanse of water. Cranes hunted the shallows, watched by a huge alligator that lay camouflaged in the reeds. They'd seen the bodies peering up at them from beneath the calm surface as they crossed the log. Someone, probably Pondwader, had dragged the dead men into the pool, turned them onto their left sides, and made certain they faced north, toward the Village of Wounded Souls. An array of weapons and stone tools glinted beside them. Yes, it must have been Pondwader who buried them. No one else would have treated his enemies so gently.

Wind breathed through the soughing branches, filling the air with the scents of the marsh and brittle mustiness of autumn. Diamondback inhaled deeply. Most of the oaks bore pale curtains of hanging moss that touched the ground. He'd found long strands of gray and black hair tangled with the moss two tens of paces from where Pondwader had been hiding—in the hole made when the toppling tree's roots had ripped from the earth. Pondwader's tracks, his handprints, and bits of thread torn from his long robe marked that irregular depression.

Diamondback returned to the place where his mother had lain. He knelt. The imprint of her tall body still remained visible. From the location of the old blood that clung to the forest duff, it looked as if she had suffered a head wound. He could not be certain of the severity. Scalp wounds bled profusely, even when minor. But it would have taken a hard blow to force her to lie down, even for a short time, while on a journey to rescue his father.

"If she'd been capable of putting one foot in front of the other, she would have kept walking." His fingers moved tenderly over the depression, and his stomach muscles clenched. "You couldn't even stand up, could you, Mother?"

Diamondback straightened. Kelp and Dace had spread out, searching for more signs while he finished scrutinizing the camp. Worry gnawed at him. Darkness fell quickly in these dense inland forests, and with the cloud cover, it would not be long until pitch blackness enveloped them.

The air cooled, and a shiver climbed his spine. He walked to the old fire pit where he had dropped his pack, opened it, and pulled out his tunic. He slipped it over his head. A strange quiet descended with the twilight. The trills and chirps of the birds gave way to the calls of the night predators . . . owls hooted, bats squeaked. The faint roar of a distant alligator wafted on the wind, and the alligator in the marsh a few paces away roared back. Diamondback turned to watch the big animal crawl up onto shore and hide in the tall grasses. Its eyes glowed red. Scattered through the reeds nearby, the yellow eyes of bullfrogs and large water spiders reflected the pale dusky gleam. Tens of frogs began croaking. Diamondback smiled.

He crouched before the old fire pit and pulled twigs from the wood pile stacked to his right. A big wood pile. Pondwader had collected a good supply, and had been unable to use it. Because his mother had risen and demanded they leave? Probably. Diamondback drew his knife, fireboard, and drill, from his pack and began shaving slivers of wood into the pit. When he had a small mound of shavings, he arranged the kindling over it, and started spinning his drill into his fireboard. Sparks crackled in the pit just as darkness closed in around him. He bent down to blow gently on the tiny tongues of flame, and firelight leapt and wavered, gilding the ghostly charcoal landscape with luminescent orange. He added more wood, but kept the blaze small. Just enough to warm them and their food.

When he felt certain the fire would not die, he dug more deeply into his pack, took out a small boiling basket, charred on the bottom, and rose to his feet. As he walked to the marsh to fill it with water for tea, he heard voices. Dace's soft, pleading. Kelp's angry. Diamondback listened. He couldn't distinguish any of their words. In a few moments, he saw a black shadow slipping through the trees on the western side of the marsh. But just one shadow.

Diamondback wondered about that. Had they argued? Dropping to his knees, he filled his boiling basket with water. By the time he'd risen again, Dace had walked into the firelight. The youth's mouth had twisted into a confused pout. He'd put on his tunic, and wore his dark hair in a single braid. Throwing his pack down by the fire, Dace slumped and extended his hands to the warmth of the blaze.

Diamondback returned and knelt across the fire from Dace. "Do you have a cord handy, Dace?" he asked.

"What?" Dace demanded.

"A cord. Do you have one? I need to make a tripod for my basket."

Dace's tight expression relaxed. "Oh, I'm sorry. Yes. Here." He drew a small coil from his pack and handed it across to Diamondback.

Diamondback took three sticks from the wood pile, tied them together at the top, then looped the cord through the holes in the rim of his basket and suspended it from the tripod. As he moved the basket closer to the flames, he said, "Did you and Kelp find anything out there?"

Dace glared into the fire. "No. Nothing important. More tracks."

"What about a trail? Did you find the path my mother and Pondwader took for Standing Hollow Horn Village?"

Dace blinked, seemed to come out of his inner world, and said, "Hallowed Spirits, yes, we did. Forgive me, Diamondback. I . . . I'm preoccupied." He turned and pointed toward the place where Musselwhite had lain. "The trail starts near the clots of blood, and winds through the trees, heading just about straight northeast."

"Is it a good trail? Can we follow it tomorrow?"

Dace nodded. "It's as clear as if a herd of deer had gone through. Tracks are everywhere. Broken fronds line the path. I don't understand their lack of caution. They must have been very confident of their safety, or—"

"No." Diamondback laced his fingers before him. "I doubt that. Such carelessness can only mean my mother was very ill. That she was fighting every step of the way just to stay on her feet."

"Blessed Spirits. That makes sense."

Diamondback removed a small pouch of red blossoms from his pack, and dropped them into his boiling basket. Flowers from the horn tree produced a delicious tangy tea, and bloomed almost constantly. The rich fragrance wafted up to him.

Gingerly, Diamondback said, "I heard your voice earlier. Did you and Kelp have a disagreement?"

Dace scowled. "I have no idea," he answered. "I heard her crying and nearly broke my neck running through the trees to find her. When I did, she shouted at me to go away."

"Why was she crying?"

Dace spread his hands. "How do I know? She wouldn't tell me!"

Diamondback frowned. "Did you offend her in some manner? Maybe—"

"No!" Dace objected. His young face tensed. "I didn't do anything! I swear it! I hadn't even been with her for a hand of time. We'd gone separate directions, searching for tracks or other evidence of Pondwader's and Musselwhite's activities here. Then I heard her crying. That was all that happened!"

Diamondback picked up a stick and scooped some of the coals out and under his basket, taking care not to get them too close to the legs of his tripod. "Where was she?"

Dace pointed toward the southern end of the marsh. "Near that stand of cattail down there."

Diamondback nodded. "Could you start supper?"

"Yes, but there's no use in going after her, Diamondback. I've known her all my life. When she gets like this, you can't talk to her. You just have to let her sort out whatever's bothering her and eventually she'll return to her senses."

Diamondback smiled. "I believe you, but I have to try. I'll be back soon."

Dace grumbled, roughly lifted his pack, and dumped the contents on the ground, then began separating out distinctively colored fabric bags. Dace, Diamondback had discovered, had an obsession with organization. The red bag contained dried meat, the green held an assortment of nuts, and the black was stuffed with long ropes of pemmican. He never put anything else in those bags—as if the act might bring him bad luck. Every warrior Diamondback had ever known had at least one superstitious habit. Black Urchin, for example, always insisted upon knotting a belt made from his wife's hair around his waist before he would even consider leaving the village, and Diamondback's own mother always wore a sandstar necklace beneath her warrior's tunic. He had never seen her without it. Not on a war walk.

Diamondback silently followed the narrow game trail that skirted the western edge of the marsh. Bullfrogs serenaded him as he passed, but the turtles splashed into the water and paddled away. He could just make out the black humps of their shells gliding through widening firelit rings. The night smelled sweetly of moss and burning hickory.

As he curved around the southern end of the marsh, he saw Kelp standing almost hidden in the head-high cattails, and he could hear her soft weeping.

"Kelp?" he called. "It's Diamondback. Are you—"

"*Go away!*" she commanded with a vehemence he would have never imagined possible.

Diamondback paused, then continued forward. She turned her back to him. He stopped three paces away and folded his arms. Her long black hair draped her back, falling almost to the hem of her tunic. In the faint gleam of the firelight the wealth of it glimmered. "I can't go away," he answered. "Not when I can see that you are sad. What's wrong, Kelp?"

"Diamondback, just go away, please. I don't wish to speak of this to—to anyone. Especially not you."

Shame tinged her voice. She sniffed at her clogged nose, and Diamondback cocked his head. "What is it, Kelp? You can tell me."

She peered at him over her shoulder, and sobbed, "No, I can't. I—I don't know why this happened now! Sun Mother must be punishing me for coming on a war walk without my grandmother's permission! That must be it, Diamondback!" She whirled around, and shook her fists at him. Tufts of cattail down stuck out between her fingers. "Grandmother Moonsnail was expecting to see me at Manatee Lagoon. She must be worried sick, and it's all my fault, and Sun Mother is taking out her anger—"

"Kelp . . ."

Her face puckered as she met and held his gaze. In the bare veneer of firelight, she looked heartbreakingly beautiful. Her eyes swam with tears. He looked again at the thick tufts of cattail down, and nodded to himself. Impulsively, Diamondback reached out and gave her right fist a quick, comforting squeeze, then tightly refolded his arms across his broad chest.

Trying to appear nonchalant, he tipped his chin and examined the pitch black sky. He said, "Let me see, have I been on ten-and-one war walks with women warriors, or is it ten-and-two? The curious thing about war walks is that warriors keep few secrets. Not because they all like each other necessarily, but because the intimacy is just so natural it rarely occurs to anyone to try to hide something. That means that I have—"

"Oh, Diamondback," she choked out, "this is not a thing of men! If I were home—"

"Yes," he said gently, "if you were home there would be a great celebration. Your grandmother and aunts and female cousins would be washing and combing your hair, weaving magnificent new clothes for you, cooking a feast . . ." He stopped when he saw her eyes go wide with understanding.

She turned away from him and covered her face with her cattail-filled fists. The tears shook her shoulders, but she didn't make a sound.

Diamondback shifted his weight from one foot to the other, clenched his fists, and when he could no longer stand it, threw propriety to the sky, walked forward, and wrapped his arms around her. Without a word, Kelp buried her face against the tunic over his shoulder. He could feel the wetness of her tears soaking through, warming his skin. He longed to laugh. If his mother had been here, she would have taken Kelp aside, as she had done many women warriors before her, Sung a Song of joy, hugged her tightly, and told her to get back to camp before she darted her for stupidity. . . . But Diamondback could not find it in himself to be so brusque.

He stroked Kelp's long hair. "Hush. Hush now, my dear young woman. You should be proud. Sun Mother isn't punishing you. She's given you the ability to bring children to your clan. There is no greater gift. I'll admit her timing could have been better, but gods aren't always considerate."

Kelp said nothing, and Diamondback bit his lip. He didn't know what to do except hold her more tightly. Nuzzling his cheek against her hair, he softly said, "May I help you collect more cattail down? The other women warriors I've known have always filled their packs when they had the chance, fearing that circumstances might prevent it later on."

"You—you would help me?"

"Of course. Did you think I wouldn't?"

Kelp disentangled herself from his arms and wiped her cheeks on the backs of her hands. When she lifted her head, she looked up at him with gratitude in her eyes. "Thank you," she said. "F-for everything. I know I have probably disgraced myself in your eyes. I am n-not a warrior today, and I realize that, but I—"

"No one is a warrior every day, Kelp. Not even the great Musselwhite. And I thank Sister Moon for that."

He draped a friendly arm around Kelp's shoulders and guided her back to the thick stand of cattails. The heads had all fluffed out. Seeds detached themselves in each slight breath of wind and lilted over the marsh, glittering like sparks in the flickers of firelight.

Kelp retrieved her pack from where she'd dropped it earlier and tucked the fistfuls of down inside. Then she hesitated, standing beside him with her head bowed, not wanting to look at Diamondback now. Despite the darkness, he could see the blush that mottled her face. He couldn't help but smile. Standing there red-cheeked, with her hair tumbling over her shoulders, she looked very innocent and very charming. She could not possibly realize how deeply her mortification touched him.

Diamondback stripped two handfuls of fluff from the closest stem and tucked them into her pack. As he reached for two more, he said, "Do you have enough strips of fabric to wrap these in? I brought an extra tunic and if you would like to tear it—"

"Oh, Great Mouse!" she said in a strangled voice. "Let's not talk about it."

Diamondback continued as though he hadn't heard. "Father always told me I had no shame. I guess it's true. I remember when I was little I used to want to crawl into the menstrual hut to find out what the women did in there. Naturally no one would let me, but I often sneaked away at night to sit outside the hut and listen to the women's laughter. Being in the hut always sounded like fun."

"Fun . . . ! *Fun!*"

"Yes. Didn't you ever think so?"

"Hallowed Spirits, no! When they're in the hut women can't eat any meat, or drink anything except pure water. They're not allowed to touch their looms or other tools. All they get to do is sit in there and talk!"

"Well, that doesn't sound so bad to me." He stuffed another handful of down into her pack. "They don't have to take care of screaming children or coddle demanding husbands. They don't have to cook or clean—"

"I hate the idea of the menstrual hut!"

The tears had vanished from her eyes, replaced by something akin to fury. Diamondback smiled. It wouldn't take long at this rate until she were her old self again.

"Well," he said, "then you chose wisely when you decided to be a warrior, since women warriors are endowed with a special Power, and it frees them from such responsibilities."

"Yes, well," she added, "I've always suspected that's why women become warriors. Being killed in battle is preferable to enduring the menstrual hut."

Diamondback squelched his grin. "Whatever the reason, I like it. On war walks men are allowed to look women warriors in the eyes, and treat them like normal humans, no matter what time of the moon it happens to be."

Kelp managed to inhale a deep steady breath. She reached out and roughly raked a handful of fluff from a stem. A fuzzy halo of seeds floated around them. She stuffed the down in her pack.

Diamondback added his own. "Kelp?" he said.

"What?"

Weak glimmers of firelight shaded the upper half her face, accentuating her round eyes and short, pointed nose. Diamondback laid his palm on her cheek. "I feel joyous that you've become a woman."

"You do?"

"Yes. Don't you?"

She gave him a rueful smile. "Off and on all day, I've found myself wishing I were a little girl again, not because it was easy, it wasn't, but because I knew what was expected of me, what I could and could not do. Now, I don't know anything. I just feel . . . overwhelmed. And lonely, Diamondback. I miss my family." Her voice constricted. She hastily tied her pack and slung it over her shoulder, then gazed across the marsh to the tiny campfire. "My grandmother," Kelp whispered, "I miss her most of all. And Pondwader."

"We will see Pondwader soon, Kelp. They can't be more than a day ahead of us, and my mother is injured. They will be moving slowly."

She jerked around to peer at him. "Your mother . . . that's where the blood—"

"Yes. I think she suffered a head wound."

Kelp reached out and grasped his hand. "Oh, Diamondback, do you think she's all right?"

"She is well enough to walk. More than that, I can't tell."

Their gazes held, and for a time it seemed as if neither of them breathed. Sparkles of firelight reflected from the marsh, and shone in her dark eyes. The scents of damp grass and wet earth enveloped him, mixed with the faint fragrance of her yucca shampoo. Diamondback stood unmoving for so long that he felt as if he floated above the ground.

"Kelp?" He took a deep breath, and closed his eyes a moment, conscious the entire time that her gaze had not left him. His emotions soared and dove like playing kestrels, and they appalled him. They possessed a strength he had never known. He told himself it had to be the drama of the day, finding the camp site, working out the battle, realizing his mother had been wounded, then Dace coming into camp upset. And, finally, discovering that Kelp had become a woman. The past few hands of time had been nothing but soaring emotions. Perhaps . . . perhaps he should wait to speak to her of this? Until he had settled down, and could think straight? He felt certain his mother would counsel him to wait.

As though his souls feared he might do just that, his mouth rushed to say, "Kelp, if we live through this, I would like to ask your grandmother if I may court you. I—I . . ." He couldn't force himself to finish.

Kelp stood quietly, as if in shock, then she leaped forward and flung her arms around his neck with such force that he stumbled backward, and almost fell into the water.

They were both laughing when she said, "Oh, Diamondback, I would like that very much."

Thirty-eight

Beaverpaw stepped lightly through the shadowed forest around Standing Hollow Horn Village. Shelters dotted the land for as far as he could see, and ten tens of people bustled about, cooking, laughing, gambling. So many fires lit the village that Sister Moon's almost full face barely penetrated the orange gleam, though a gauzy silver sheen coated the sea and reflected with blinding intensity from the frothy crests of waves. Breakers crashed on the beach. Amid the rush and retreat of water, swallows dove. The weather had been so warm that a haze of glittering insect wings filled the air. Their whine added to the village's din.

Beaverpaw veered wide around an old lightning-blasted stump and watched the dogs that padded the trails between the shelters, wagging their tails at anyone who paid attention to them. This had to be the largest village ever assembled. People from many different clans had flocked here to be close to Cottonmouth when the end came, praying he could save them. The crowd astounded Beaverpaw. How many fools existed in the world? Too many, it seemed.

Salt-scented gusts of wind blew his chin-length hair over his face. He tucked it behind his ears and narrowed his small eyes as a huge bonfire blazed to life in the central plaza. Sparks flitted and tumbled over the heads of the people gathered there. He heard Dark Rain's low laugh, followed by a whoop from Hanging Star, and an unknown man's curse.

They had arrived three hands of time ago, set up camp, and immediately gone their separate ways, Beaverpaw studying the lay of the village, his companions seeking the biggest game they could find. It sounded as though they had achieved their goal. The distinctive rattle of bones being thrown carried above the crackling of the flames. Beaverpaw sincerely hoped Dark Rain was winning. When she lost, she grew hostile and unmanageable. Generally, she stalked back to camp, packed her things, and ordered him to hurry it up, declaring she wanted to leave as quickly as possible.

. . . He needed her to be happy here. If necessary, he would sell his cherished weapons to provide her with more goods to wager. So long as she could gamble, he had a cover for his wanderings through the village.

Homesickness gnawed him. If everything went well, he would be back in Waterbearer's arms in five days, maybe six. He longed so to hug his children, to hear their laughter, that he could barely endure the waiting. The only thing that kept him sane was the certain knowledge that he must succeed . . . or his clan would not take him back. No matter the cost, Beaverpaw *must* see to it that Musselwhite succeeded in rescuing Diver.

He had already scouted the southern and western boundaries of Standing Hollow Horn. The placement of shelters had at first appeared random, but as Beaverpaw continued his quiet scout, he saw that that assessment could not have been more untrue. Shelters stood around the plaza in a series of ever widening semicircles, like shells nested inside one another. Along the outside crescent, shelters sat next to large trees, and beside each one two men stood guard. The organization stunned him. No one, not even Musselwhite, could have created a more frightening stronghold. Every possible point of attack had been anticipated and sealed. It would take tens of tens of warriors to break through these defenses, and the battle would cost many lives. Indeed, Beaverpaw doubted that any enemy force now in existence could overrun Standing Hollow Horn.

Shaking his head, he marveled at Musselwhite's grasp of the situation. She had not been here in tens of summers, yet she knew that they could not hope to fight Cottonmouth. How right she had been. Only a small group could ever penetrate this fortress. . . . But once inside, how would they ever get out?

He continued along the northern edge of the village. He took his time, walking slowly, avoiding brush and vines, ducking under low-hanging branches, making as little sound as possible. And thinking about the plan he and Musselwhite had agreed to. *It just might work!* He offered a silent prayer to every Spirit he could name. All Beaverpaw had to do was create a diversion at exactly the right moment . . . and manage to live through the aftermath. He did not know what the diversion would be yet; perhaps, just to soothe his souls, he would start a brawl with Hanging Star. Warriors would flock from everywhere to watch. Undoubtedly bets would be laid. His task when it had ended would be to convince Cottonmouth that his fight had had nothing to do with Musselwhite's attempt to free her husband . . . that she had merely taken advantage of it, and acted.

He stopped at a gnarled old oak draped with hanging moss. It grew at the northwest corner of the village. As he scanned the surroundings, he knew this must be the tree Cottonmouth had seen in his Dream. The tree where he first expected to see Musselwhite. Two shelters sat just behind the tree, but . . .

No guards.

Beaverpaw's gaze took in the arc of the crescent created by the outer shelters. This gap represented the only vulnerability. The only possible point of unobserved entry into the village. His lip curled down. Did Cottonmouth really believe Musselwhite such a simpleton? That all he had to do was leave her an opening and she would walk right into his arms? If he'd had the luxury, Beaverpaw would have spat his contempt.

But he continued on around the perimeter, until he could see the glitter of Sea Girl through the trees. A great blue heron stood on the shore, its long neck stretched out, watching a pelican gobble down a fish a few wingbeats away. When the pelican finished, it gave its feathers a good shake and strutted up the beach. Disappointed that not a scrap remained, the heron folded its neck and tucked its bill under its wing to go to sleep again.

Beaverpaw wished he had his atlatl with him. The heron made an easy target. But when they'd entered the village, guards had stopped them, told them to make camp in the forest beyond the perimeter, and leave their weapons there. Cottonmouth had decreed that outsiders could not carry weapons into the village.

Beaverpaw went on. The last shelter, a very large one, sat on the beach, backed by scrub oaks on the north side. *The council shelter.*

He crept forward silently, and knelt behind a tangle of brush. A man lay on the floormats in the center of the shelter, his hands and feet bound. He had long black hair, a round face, and wide mouth. Though he wore a beautiful tunic with a blue bolt of lightning painted across the breast, Beaverpaw could see that festering puncture wounds covered the man's exposed flesh.

Diver?

It must be.

Musselwhite had been right about where her husband would be held.

And Beaverpaw suddenly wondered if Cottonmouth knew that. Did Cottonmouth understand the workings of Musselwhite's mind as well as she understood his?

As he backed away, a horrifying thought occurred to Beaverpaw. Hallowed Spirits . . . no. But . . . could it be possible? Had Cottonmouth laid his trap even more cunningly than either Beaverpaw or Musselwhite suspected? Perhaps all the stories of his "Dreams," which he told everyone, represented part of the deception. Had Cottonmouth actually intended for those stories to reach Musselwhite's ears? Was he, in fact, depending upon it?

Anxiety flooded Beaverpaw's veins. He held a loop of grapevine aside and eased past, his eyes scanning the guards clotted around the council shelter. More had secreted themselves in the limbs of the tallest pines, scrutinizing the beach, and still more guards wandered the plaza where Dark Rain and

Hanging Star gambled. Each carried an atlatl and three darts clutched in his right hand.

Beaverpaw swung wide around the perimeter, and boldly entered the village from the gap by the old oak tree. Not a man stopped him. He walked straight through the opening, down a trail between four lodges, and out into the teeming plaza.

Fear crowded his rationality. He'd started breathing like a hunted rabbit, his chest puffing in and out in rapid shallow gasps.

He had to warn Musselwhite before she entered this village. . . .

Woodduck knelt beside Hanging Star in the gambling circle around the plaza bonfire. Four groups of people crowded the area, playing different games: Dice, Bones, Sticks, and the Shell game, where the opponent had to guess which clamshell hid the plum pit. Out on the beach, men charged along the shore, their feet throwing up sand. Many stood watching, placing bets on the races.

"I have told you many things," Hanging Star whispered. "I wish to see my payment. What have you brought me?"

Woodduck turned back and glowered. Hanging Star grinned with rotting yellow teeth. His tunic bore a thick coating of soot and grease and he smelled as if he hadn't bathed in a moon. Woodduck longed to knock those rotting teeth down his throat.

But he said, "Stay close. I may not be finished with you yet," and surreptitiously tucked a fine chert scraper into Hanging Star's grimy hand.

Hanging Star vented a low laugh, and said, "I'll be here. Next time, bring dart points and fine blankets, I—"

"I wouldn't raise my price too high, if I were you," Woodduck whispered tersely as his eyes scanned the tens of people around them. "Cottonmouth might decide to slice the information from your hide a piece at a time, rather than buying it."

Hanging Star's ugly square face drooped. "Uh . . . tell the Spirit Elder I will be happy to help him in any way I can. At no charge."

Woodduck smiled. "You are wiser than I remember, Hanging Star."

Woodduck rose from the gambling circle and walked slowly toward Cottonmouth's shelter. Sister Moon hung like a silver shell above him, her gleaming face wavering through a thin layer of clouds. Autumn leaves tore loose from the trees and swirled upward into the moonlight like ash blown from a huge fire. Woodduck's gaze clung to Cottonmouth.

The Spirit Elder stood with his shoulder braced against the southeastern pole of his shelter. The horrible turtle bone doll hung from a cord on his belt. Cottonmouth had plaited his long graying black hair and left the braid hanging over his right shoulder. He wore a black breechclout and a marginella shell necklace. The shells looked very white against the deeply tanned background of his skin. His huge dark eyes gleamed in the frame of his oval face. But they did not watch Woodduck, rather they seemed glued to the stout warrior who prowled the edges of the plaza.

Woodduck stopped in front of Cottonmouth and waited until the Elder looked down at him. Nothing filled those eyes. Absolutely nothing. No emotion. No warmth. Emptiness. That's all Woodduck saw there. "You were right, Elder," Woodduck said. "Hanging Star told me *many* things."

Cottonmouth's deep voice sounded even more haunting tonight as he softly said, "Did you ask him about our inquisitive guest? The man has scouted our defenses thoroughly."

"I did ask," Woodduck answered.

"And?"

Woodduck's hand dropped to the stiletto on his belt. "Hanging Star says his name is Beaverpaw. He is the former War Leader of Heartwood Clan."

"Former?"

"Yes." Woodduck snorted derisively. "He committed adultery with the woman shaking up the bones over there. She—"

"Dark Rain," Cottonmouth said.

"Yes." Woodduck turned to look at the woman. Every time he did so, her extraordinary beauty stunned him. She wore a brilliant red tunic which accentuated her tiny waist and full breasts. Lustrous black hair fell over her shoulders. "Do you know her?" Woodduck asked.

Cottonmouth nodded. "Beaverpaw committed adultery and was Outcast by his clan?"

"Yes, that's what Hanging Star says. He also told me," Woodduck lowered his voice, "that Beaverpaw met Musselwhite in the forest and had a long talk with her. She—"

Cottonmouth did not move a muscle, but his eyes were suddenly on Woodduck's face. *"When?"*

"This morning. No more than half a day's walk to the southwest. I suspect, Spirit Elder, that Beaverpaw is a spy for Musselwhite."

"Perhaps," Cottonmouth said calmly.

Woodduck spread his feet, bracing himself. Despite the cool wind, he'd started to sweat. Looking into Cottonmouth's face always affected him this way, making him wish he were anywhere but here—especially when Cottonmouth carried the turtle bone doll. He could go crazy at any moment, for no reason.

"What do you wish me to do?" Woodduck asked. "Shall I kill this Beaverpaw? It would be a simple matter. His camp is fifty paces west of the village. My warriors can have him surrounded before he suspects we are there."

Cottonmouth did not answer for a while, then he used his chin to indicate Dark Rain. "How is her game going?"

"Badly." Woodduck's mouth pursed in disgust. "She is no gambler. She's been losing steadily. Already she is covering her bets with her body, promising men she can bring them more pleasure than they have ever imagined. In one hand of time, I expect she will be forced to leave the game to pay off her debts—and it will take her all night. I doubt anyone will let her enter a game tomorrow."

"Is her son, the White Lightning Boy, with Musselwhite? Did Hanging Star tell you?"

"Yes. The boy is coming, just as you Dreamed, Spirit Elder."

Cottonmouth's shoulder whispered against the pole as he shoved away. "But no one else?"

"No. Musselwhite brings only the Lightning Boy."

Cottonmouth's face seemed frozen, his gaze so cold it made Woodduck long to run. Woodduck concentrated on breathing slowly, lest he appear as alarmed as he felt. Every time Cottonmouth carried the doll, he did something truly terrible. Woodduck hated to contemplate what it might be this time. Sun Mother's Winter Celebration loomed only three days away. A really crazy act could . . .

Very quietly, Cottonmouth said, "I think I shall go and say hello to my old friend, Dark Rain." He started out of the shelter, then stopped. Over his shoulder, he said, "Gather a small group of warriors. Have them ready."

"For what, Elder?"

Cottonmouth returned his gaze to Dark Rain, and his eyes narrowed. "For whatever is necessary," he answered.

Woodduck grimaced as Cottonmouth walked out across the plaza. People glanced at the doll tied to his belt, halted in mid-stride, and backed up, clearing a path for him. Cottonmouth did not seem to notice.

Thirty-nine

You greedy whore! Throw the dice!" One Hunt, a long-nosed young man, shouted at Dark Rain.

She ignored him, held the hickory-nut dice up to her mouth, and breathed her Spirit into them, concentrating, praying the souls of the dice would feel their kinship with her and help her on her next throw. The six men in the circle around her leered, and yelled crude taunts, but she closed her mind to them, focusing on the dice, *the dice.*

She had won the last three throws. A dogbone hairpin, three shell necklaces, and one poorly made gray chert dart point lay before her. If she could just touch the dice's souls again, they would continue to help her. Like a lover, she whispered to the dice, telling them she knew she could count on them, promising she would care for them, smoke them, and rub them with hickory oil, if only they would let her win. *Let me win, let me win. . . .*

People milled around the village. They'd been arriving in droves all night, pitching their camps on the outskirts of the village, then coming to the plaza, looking for entertainment. She suspected the village had doubled its size since this morning. The rich smells of roasting venison, rabbits, geese, and boiling clams encircled her, along with the tart fragrances of pine-needle tea and prickly-pear fruits. Dark Rain loved the sights and scents of ceremonial gatherings. Men and women wore a variety of gleaming shell necklaces, and tunics dyed in dazzling geometric designs. Brilliant reds, deep blues, greens, and yellows flashed as people walked by.

"Dark Rain, for the sake of Brother Sky, throw the dice!" Hanging Star shouted. His repulsive, square face shone with insect grease. Pools of it had formed in his pock marks, and accentuated the size of his bulbous nose. He had been eating roasted duck and wiping his hands on his breechclout, which now bore a grimy coating of fat.

. . . Oh, how she detested him.

The six men in her group pounded their fists into the white sand, urging her to hurry. Three other groups of gamblers sat around the bonfire, engaged in their own games. When anyone shouted, men and women would crane their necks to see what had caused the disturbance. Three tens of people frowned in Dark Rain's direction at this very instant.

"Dark Rain!" Hanging Star shoved her sideways. "Play!"

"All right!" she shouted back. "If you will shut up, I'll throw!"

Men's faces went serious. Black painted one side of the die, and white the other. A player scored when the same color came up on both dice. Black scored one point. White scored two points. If each nut showed different colors, the player lost his or her turn. Her current opponent, One Hunt, had earned a total of six points on his last turn. He'd had four lucky throws. His gleaming eyes appraised her now, filled with fear and loathing.

Dark Rain smiled. "What do you bet, One Hunt? Eh? How much do you wish to lose?"

One Hunt's lip curled disdainfully. His long black hair blew around his young face. He had to be around ten-and-eight summers, and as arrogant as a mating bear. His breechclout bore a beautiful red geometric design. Before the night ended, Dark Rain planned to win even that from him. The haughty youth deserved to go home naked and destitute.

One Hunt surveyed his booty, and selected a beautifully crafted deerbone dart point. He tossed it into the center of the circle. "That will cost you all three of your shell necklaces, Dark Rain."

"All three!" she blurted. "For one miserable bone point? I'll wager two necklaces. That will match—"

"No, it won't!" One Hunt glared at her. "Your necklaces are made of common shells. My point came from old man Whistling Bird himself!"

Murmurs broke out in the group, the name passing from man to man. Awe tinged their voices.

Hanging Star leaned sideways and whispered, "Careful. Whistling Bird's dart points are renowned for their Power. He is a very great Soul Dancer. One Hunt could demand far more than your three—"

"If Whistling Bird is so great, why have I never heard of him?"

Hanging Star made an airy gesture with his dirty hand. "Perhaps, despite the illustrious Dark Rain's extensive travels, she has never been to the far northern forests . . . *where Whistling Bird lives.*"

She surveyed the gamblers again. They had yet to stop muttering about that measly bone point, which meant it really must have value. Yet, she would have precious little left if she wagered three necklaces and lost.

But I'm not going to lose! Am I, dice? No, you'll help me, won't you?

"Are you playing, *whore?*" One Hunt bellowed.

She picked up the pretty necklaces and casually threw them atop his dart point. Wagers exchanged hands around the circle. Even Hanging Star, she noticed, bet against her. When she gave him her most hateful look, he grinned and puckered his lips, as if to kiss her. Men rolled with laughter.

"Go ahead, beauty," Hanging Star said. "Throw the dice, so I can collect my winnings."

Dark Rain breathed her Spirit into the nuts one more time, then closed her eyes, shook them in her hands, and threw them out.

A roar went up. She jerked her eyes open, and saw two white dice staring up at her. "Two points!" she shrilled in delight.

One Hunt closed his eyes for a long moment, then he smiled and nodded. "Go on, Dark Rain. Throw. But know this, the souls of the dice have shifted. They are *mine* now. You will not score again, not against me. So . . ."

He reached into his pile and drew out a magnificently carved wooden bowl, which he set beside her necklaces. "If you wish to keep playing, it will cost you that ugly chert point."

She picked it up, held it over the pile for a moment, then dropped it on top.

"Oh, brave woman!" Hanging Star said. "I wager an oak pestle against Dark Rain! Who will challenge me?"

She ignored the flurry of conversation. Holding the dice to her lips, she breathed more Spirit into them. As if smelling the foul stench rising from a dead animal, she could sense that something had changed. Anxiety gnawed her stomach. One Hunt really had affected the dice. Their souls had turned against her!

Calm down, she mouthed to herself. *I can win their souls back again. Of course I can. I must!*

Sensually, she ran her tongue around the rim of each hickory nut, all the while breathing her Spirit back into them, forcing One Hunt's vile Spirit out.

"Come on, Dark Rain!" Hanging Star demanded. "We don't wish to spend all night on your turn!"

Dark Rain shook the dice up. They felt warm in her hands. As she threw them out, raucous laughter rose.

One black. One white.

Shrieking in rage, she slammed her fists into the sand.

One Hunt chuckled, raked in his winnings, and collected the dice. He smiled at her lone dogbone hairpin. "That pathetic adornment is all you have left to gamble with?"

"No," she responded, and straightened up so that her breasts pressed again the fabric of her tunic. Men "oohed" and laughed. "I will give you the same ecstasy that I have promised these other men. But it will cost you. I want—"

"I have no desire for your polluted body, woman. I want trade goods. If you have nothing left but that hairpin, you are out of the game."

Hanging Star hoarsely whispered, "Oh, friend, you have no concept of how wondrous Dark Rain can be. She does things . . ." His voice faded as he saw Cottonmouth walk up to stand behind One Hunt.

The entire circle went deathly quiet. Eyes widened. Each man looked as if staring his doom in the face. Dark Rain examined Cottonmouth. She had not seen him in seven summers. Since that time, the hair at his temples had gone a solid silver that highlighted his black deeply set eyes and tanned skin. Though a few lines etched the flesh at the corners of mouth, he looked like a man of three tens of summers, not a man nearly five tens of summers old. His tall, slender body and extremely handsome face brought a smile to her lips.

Cottonmouth gazed at Dark Rain as though entranced. His black breech-clout had been freshly washed, and a strange toy hung from his belt. Dark Rain glanced at the doll. It seemed to be made of a turtle's leg bone. Someone had dressed the toy in a frayed tunic, and glued on long strands of black hair with pine pitch. Very faintly, she could make out a painted face.

Cottonmouth slowly walked around the circle and knelt on her left side. He smelled fragrant, as if he'd bathed in a pool filled with water lilies. In a deep voice, he murmured, "Are you winning?"

"No, I'm losing, and this—" she gestured offensively at One Hunt, "this skinny *boy* refuses to allow me to play."

Cottonmouth's gaze lifted to One Hunt. Orange firelight fluttered over his expressionless face, reflecting like molten flame in his eyes. "Play, One Hunt," he softly commanded. "I will cover Dark Rain's bet."

"You?" Dark Rain blurted. *"You* will?"

Cottonmouth's penetrating gaze remained on One Hunt, but his head dipped once in affirmation.

One Hunt wet his lips. He glanced around the circle, as if silently seeking guidance from the other men. No one so much as blinked. Dark Rain knew why. Cottonmouth never participated in games of chance. He might compete in a race or at dart casting, activities which relied upon his own skills, but nothing so unpredictable as outright gambling.

"Very well, Spirit Elder," One Hunt replied with a stern nod, "what do you wish to wager?"

Cottonmouth replied, "I wager ten-and-five red chert dart points against all of your goods." He pointed to One Hunt's pile of winnings.

"Ten-and-five chert dart points!" Hanging Star yelled in shock. "You could buy One Hunt's wife for that! And without even—"

One Hunt backhanded Hanging Star so hard it sent the man sprawling across the sand. Dark Rain laughed. Blood poured from Hanging Star's cut lip, but he smiled, a vengeful smile. As he sat up and wiped his mouth, Hanging Star said, "I will settle with you, later, young warrior."

"If you have the courage," One Hunt said in a low, threatening voice, then turned to peer at Cottonmouth. "Were your words in earnest, Elder? You wish to wager so much? On this woman's behalf?"

"I do."

One Hunt shook his head disbelievingly. "Very well. What rules will we play by?"

"One throw. If you score, you win. If you don't, you lose."

Dark Rain sat up straighter. She gave Cottonmouth a surprised look, but he no longer gazed at her. His eyes were riveted on One Hunt. Dark Rain's veins throbbed as she watched One Hunt squirm. She adored high-stakes games, and rarely had a chance to play them. Usually her poverty relegated her to watching from afar while more skillful players wagered everything they owned on the fall of a handful of bones or sticks.

One Hunt took a deep breath. "I accept your challenge, Elder."

Cottonmouth gestured to the dice. "Good. Your turn."

The circle leaned inward. Every man held his breath as he watched One Hunt shake up the dice. Hanging Star's eyes seemed ready to pop from his skull. The sounds of the village, which Dark Rain had barely noticed before, became suddenly deafening. Dogs barked. Surf splashed. Fires roared and crackled in the gusting wind. Men whooped and women laughed.

Cottonmouth gazed unblinking at One Hunt. Sweat broke out across the youth's cheeks. He bowed his head and begin Singing a soft prayer to Sun Mother. Then his young face tensed.

One black. One white.

Silence.

Everyone turned to stare at Cottonmouth. Fear glistened in their eyes: surely he had witched the dice. One Hunt closed his eyes, shoved his pile over in front of Dark Rain, and got to his feet. "Good night," he said, and left.

Dark Rain turned all the way around to watch his skinny form trot for the closest trail which would take him out of the village. He vanished into the wavering firelit shadows of the forest.

"It seems you won," Cottonmouth said to Dark Rain.

She looked at him askance, wondering what his help would cost her. She gave Cottonmouth her most alluring smile. "Yes," she said. "How shall I repay you for your help?"

Cottonmouth toyed with the beautiful deerbone dart point in the middle of the pile, smoothing it reverently with his fingers. "Play dice with me."

"That's all?"

Cottonmouth's gaze seemed to impale her. "That will be adequate."

She dared not refuse. Besides, she had a lot of goods to wager with. No matter what happened the game would be glorious.

"I didn't think you liked gambling," she said.

"Like has never had anything to do with it. No one wants to gamble with me." He looked around the circle, meeting each man's gaze. "I suspect people fear my Spirit Helpers."

The four men on Cottonmouth's left swallowed convulsively, and rose so quickly, they tripped over each other's feet. Hostile murmurs broke out, laced with curses. Then the men bowed respectfully to Cottonmouth—and excused themselves.

Only Hanging Star remained, seated to her right, his ugly face congealed in sheer terror. Dark Rain lifted an elegant brow. It could not be bravery that kept him here. Why did he stay? He had a reputation for curiosity. Was that it? He *had* to know how the night would end?

Cottonmouth stretched out on his side on the sand and propped his head on his fist. "Proceed," he said.

Dark Rain picked up the dice. An eerie chill climbed her spine. She swiftly handed them to Cottonmouth. "Why don't you throw first?"

"If you wish." He held the dice in his right palm, gently, as though they were a bird's fragile eggs. "That means it's my wager, doesn't it?"

"Yes."

Hanging Star slid around, repositioning himself to get a better view. Sweat trickled down his jaw.

Dark Rain studied Cottonmouth. What sort of game would he play? The man could wager any sum and his village would cover it. And Standing Hollow Horn possessed great wealth. One had only to look around to see furs, rare stone tools, magnificently woven blankets and baskets. . . .

An almost orgasmic thrill taunted her. If she ran the stakes up . . . and won! Hallowed Sister Moon. Luckily, she had never truly believed in Cottonmouth's "powers." To Dark Rain, he represented just another man . . . one inexperienced in the finer points of gambling.

"Let me see," Cottonmouth said. "I wager one red and blue striped blanket—made by the finest weaver in the village. Do you wish to see it before I throw?"

"That's not necessary," Dark Rain said. "I trust you, Cottonmouth."

"Do you?"

"Yes, of course."

A smile touched his face, but his eyes remained as cold as frozen lakes.

Dark Rain picked up the bone dart point and tossed it on the sand in front of him. He looked down, and waited. Grudgingly, she added the chert point. "Is that sufficient?"

"Throw in the bowl, too," he responded.

Angry, she did.

His gaze held hers as he threw out the dice. Two white. Dark Rain paled.

Hanging Star leaned closer. "Cottonmouth has earned two points. Are you scared, Dark Rain?"

"Certainly not," she said and forced a smile. "It's still your turn, Cottonmouth. Do you wish to up your wager?"

Cottonmouth used one finger to push the dice around the sand. They left curving trails. "I think I will throw in another two blankets."

Dark Rain looked down at her pile, knowing that her pitiful array of necklaces, bowls, and hairpins would not match his wager. "What will you take to cover me?"

"I don't wish anything you have in front of you, Dark Rain."

"You mean you came over here just to force me out of the game?" she said indignantly. "One Hunt was doing that all by himself, you needn't have troubled—"

"Let's discuss other 'goods.'"

Dark Rain sat back. Could he mean it the way it sounded? Cottonmouth had spurned her advances so many times it seemed unlikely. Still, perhaps he'd come to his senses. And what a rare pleasure it would be to bed this powerful holy man. Just the thought sent a sexual tingle through her.

She stretched out on her side next to him, her face no more than four hands from Cottonmouth's, and asked, "What other 'goods' did you have in mind?"

He picked up the dice, and shook them. A silver lock had come loose from his braid, and danced beside his handsome face. "Tell me about your son."

"My son?"

"Yes. Pondwader is his name, isn't that right? As a Lightning Boy he must have special talents."

Dark Rain snorted. "If he does, I've never noticed them."

"Never?"

"No. Pondwader can't do anything, Cottonmouth. He's half blind. He can't hunt, or fight, or fish. He's a weakling, a puny, worthless human being."

Cottonmouth tilted his head. "You've covered your bet," he said, and threw out the dice.

Two black.

Dark Rain clenched her fists. She growled, "That's three points. It's still your turn."

Cottonmouth braced himself up on his elbow. "I'll add two chert scrapers, if you will tell me everything you have noticed about Musselwhite." When he said her name, tenderness tinged his voice. "What she was wearing. What she looked like. The—"

"That's easy," she said. "Musselwhite wore a torn and bloody tunic and had a bandage around her head. Holding in her brains, I think. One of your warriors tried to split her skull with his warclub."

Cottonmouth stared at her unblinking. "She was hurt?"

"Badly."

His eyes tightened. "What else?"

Dark Rain shrugged. "Nothing. That was all I noticed."

Cottonmouth threw out the dice.

Two white.

Dark Rain shrieked, "I don't believe it! Are you cheating me?"

"This time," Cottonmouth said softly. "I wager my ten-and-five red chert dart points, plus four of Standing Hollow Horn's finest blankets."

Blood pounded in Dark Rain's temples. "And what do you wish in return? More information?" If she won, she could live in luxury for summers, and he knew it. She eagerly awaited his next question.

A fiery light glowed in his black eyes. "Just one thing," he said.

"Anything. What is it you wish?"

Hanging Star had gone rigid, waiting. Dark Rain could smell his foul sweat.

"Anything?" Cottonmouth asked.

Dark Rain smiled. "Yes," she answered seductively. *"Anything."*

"Will you wager your own life?"

He had said it casually, as though asking for another cup of tea, but the question struck Dark Rain like a fist in the stomach.

She jerked to sit up. "Don't be ridiculous! There's nothing you could offer me—"

"Are you sure?" Cottonmouth's fist closed around the dice.

"Yes. I'm sure! To buy a life would take more than you have, Cottonmouth. You or Standing Hollow Horn Village!"

"Really? What if I offered to match your weight with the finest stone tools that can be found."

The very idea left her speechless. When she found her voice, she replied, "Not enough."

"What if I match your weight with stone tools, and throw in ten tens of the most exquisite blankets ever made?"

"Ten tens?" Dark Rain laughed. He must be joking. That amount of wealth would make her the richest woman on the coast. But how could she enjoy it if she were dead?

"Ten tens," he answered. "Would that buy a life?"

"Not mine," she answered flippantly. "But—"

"But?"

They stared at each other. Cottonmouth smiled.

Hanging Star glanced back and forth between them, leaped to his feet, hastily bowed to Cottonmouth, and said, "I must be going. Good night."

Dark Rain noticed only that he'd gone—she could not take her gaze from Cottonmouth's. A strange, erotic warmth had filled his eyes. She felt its impact all over her body, like a Spirit Plant seeping through her veins.

Cottonmouth held up the dice. "If you won't wager your own life, will you wager Beaverpaw's?"

Dark Rain laughed. "Beaverpaw's? He's as worthless as my son. Why do you care about—"

"For your weight in stone tools and ten tens of the most exquisite blankets ever made. That's the bet. Will you play with me, Dark Rain? Do you have the courage?"

"Well, I—I don't—"

"One throw," he said, and held out the dice. *"Yours."*

Cottonmouth reached out, gripped her hand, and put the dice in it. It seemed impossible that the only point of contact between them was his hand holding hers. Euphoria possessed her, similar to the moment just before orgasm, painful and wonderful. If just his touch could do this to her . . .

"I want one more thing," she boldly said.

His eyes narrowed. "What is it?"

"If I win, I want to share your bed. One night. That's all. I assure you, you will not regret it. I can turn a man inside out, make him writhe in ecstasy, and beg me for—"

Cottonmouth held up a hand to halt her words. "I accept your terms."

Swaying tree shadows danced over Beaverpaw's closed eyes. In his dreams, he walked the paths between the shelters at Heartwood Village. His children hung onto his hands, laughing. Little Manatee Flipper played with his newly made dart, nocking his atlatl and casting as far as he could, then running to retrieve the dart, and doing it all over again.

"Watch me, Father!" the boy shouted. "Did you see how good I am?"

Waterbearer walked beside Beaverpaw. She smiled up at him the way she used to, with her souls in her eyes, as if giving them to him for safekeeping, because she trusted him.

"Waterbearer," Beaverpaw said. "Forgive me. I missed you very much. I don't know how I could have been so foolish. I—"

She put a hand to his lips. "Let's not speak of it. I forgave you long ago, my husband. I love you. Our children love you. That is all that matters now."

Beaverpaw reached out to touch her dark hair. . . .

The warclub made a dull sickening thump when it struck his head, sounding like a gourd dropped from a tall tree. At first, Beaverpaw did not understand what had happened. He rolled to his stomach and struggled to get his hands under him so he could push up. The night swam in blurred colors. He—

The club came down again, and again, pounding him face-first into the pine-scented forest duff.

In a last desperate act, he got his knees under him, and lunged for his attacker's legs. . . .

The hoarse guttural scream woke Diver from a sound sleep. His eyes jerked open, but he lay completely still, staring up at the thatched roof, listening.

Muttering broke out in the village. Several babies started crying simultaneously. Diver turned his head. In the gleam of moonlight, people ran, blankets flapping around their shoulders. Shouts rose from the forest. Woodduck's hostile voice ordered, "Go back to your shelters! Get away! This is none of your concern!"

"But what happened?" a woman demanded. "Who screamed?"

"Get away from here before I do the same to you! Go on! You heard me!"

More people woke. Men with weapons trotted across the plaza.

Diver filled his lungs with the cool night air. The smell of burning pine wafted on the wind. Diver worked his bound hands, and winced. His raw, rope-burned wrists ached with fiery intensity, as if every frayed rope fiber had been dipped in the lethal poison of coast spurge. Gingerly, he rolled over, facing the plaza.

The entire village appeared to be in motion, arms waving, legs pumping. The three guards around Diver's shelter turned as one, in Woodduck's direction. They muttered to each other, voices harsh, speculative.

Gullwing hissed, "Littlehorn, why don't you and Cloudfish go and see what's happening? I'll stay here."

"Yes, Gullwing." Littlehorn trotted off with Cloudfish on his heels.

They ran through the plaza, passing a lone woman who stood frozen, long black hair fluttering around her beautiful face. Her gaze had fixed on the point in the forest from which the scream had come.

After a few moments, the woman turned her back, and walked away.

Forty

Musselwhite knelt at the edge of the fire pit, staring at the red eyes of coals that winked when the wind blew. She felt sick to her stomach and cold, despite the warm gusts that rustled through the blossoming golden creeper shrubs which surrounded their camp. The small white flowers flashed with moonlight. Their sweetness perfumed the wind, blending with the tang of pines.

She shivered and looked over at Pondwader to make certain the blanket still covered him. He lay on his back, white hair arrayed like a glistening halo around his head, the blanket under his chin.

She rubbed the back of her neck. All night long she had been lost in a haunted forest of memories. Unable to sleep. The fact angered her. She had learned long ago that on a war walk sleep was more precious than food or water. Without it, a warrior would certainly die. Yet she had spent the past three hands of time in desperate nightmares, twisting away from cast darts, rolling to avoid club blows, running . . . running with every shred of her strength, but she did not know from what, or to where.

She knew only to whom.

The sandstar pendant moved between her breasts. She tugged on the leather thong and drew it out. Her flesh had warmed the shell. As she tipped it to study the petal-like designs, the surface caught and held the crimson gleam of the dying fire. Such a perilous thing. The past thirty summers had been filled with so many partings, so much death and suffering—this small pendant, too. Why, then, did it bring her such joy?

"Oh, Glade," she whispered.

A moon before her son's death, Musselwhite had been sitting on the beach, weaving a basket, when she'd heard Glade's bubbly giggle. She had turned in time to see the little boy trotting up the shore with the perfect sandstar clutched in his pudgy hands. He'd dropped to his knees, beaming up at her, and lifted the shell.

"For you, Mother. I love you."

Musselwhite pressed the pendant against her cheek. When Glade had taken sick, madness had possessed her. Every instant of that tragic Moon of Falling Leaves, each flicker of sunlight, each of Cottonmouth's rages, every touch shared in pain had been woven into the fabric of her souls.

Strange, that those three brief summers seemed more real to her than anything in the past two-tens-and-six summers. Not because she loved them better—she didn't—but because everything she was today, and everything she would ever become, had been forged there . . . with Cottonmouth.

She closed her eyes, and tried not to think. Not to imagine how it would be. If all went well, she would glimpse him only from afar. She could stand that. Surely she could. They would not speak. They would not gaze into each other's eyes. He would never even know she had stood in his village. Not if she could help it. She would get in and out quickly, for both their sakes.

Deliberately, she forced her thoughts to Diver, and a scarcely endurable longing grew in her chest. *Diver . . . my Diver.* Her mind drifted back through the long summers to the hot, muggy day when she had given birth to their first son. Diver had knelt at her side through the agony, gripping her hand to transfer his strength into her body. She remembered that she had thought, "Look at those burning eyes. How powerful he is. How composed." And when their son finally slid out onto the soft blanket, Diver had released her hand, walked several paces away, and broken down into wrenching tears.

Yes, though his own souls were ripping apart, he had been there that day, his love encircling her like a stone fortress. He had always been there, loving her, protecting her with passionate loyalty, battling enemies, his clan, even their own children . . . anyone who dared to criticize her knew the depths of his wrath.

She opened her eyes, and gazed blindly at a tiny flame that sputtered on the far side of the firepit.

Diver is the only dream I ever had that lived and breathed, and walked at my side.

She had been trying to prepare herself for what she would find. Cottonmouth had certainly tortured him. But how badly would Diver be hurt? Could he run? Would she have to carry him? She would, if necessary. If necessary, she would die to see that he lived. And do it without a second thought, knowing how much their children needed and loved him. . . . How much she loved him. Her souls kept throwing taunts at her, Diver without any feet or hands. Diver with both of his eyes gone.

The only possibility she could not contemplate was that he might be dead.

Her head fell forward. No matter what . . .

Pondwader's pained voice broke her thoughts.

"No," he whispered. "Oh, no. Please. I—I can't . . ."

Musselwhite rose and went to crouch at his side. His fingers weakly dug into the soft forest duff, as if he fought to escape some terror. Sweat gleamed like raindrops on his pale moonlit cheeks.

"Pondwader," she whispered. "It's all right. Everything is all right."

He moaned and clutched at his blanket.

Musselwhite smoothed the drenched white hair away from his face. What a precious young man. And how much he had come to mean to her. Given the dangers they would face tomorrow night, it was no wonder nightmares tormented him. He knew nothing of war. He must be terrified.

Musselwhite leaned down and gently kissed his forehead. "Pondwader?" she whispered. "I'm here. You don't need to be afraid. I'm right here beside you."

A tear welled at the corner of his left eye and ran down his temple. In a faint voice, he said, "My wife?"

"Yes. Are you all right?"

Pondwader sat up in his blanket and peered at her. His wide pink eyes had a silvered cast. Wet white hair framed his face, making him look ghostly.

"Oh, Musselwhite," he said. "I have been talking with Turtle Bone Doll. Did you see her? She was just here! She flew down and stood right in the middle of my chest."

"No, I didn't see her. I'm sorry." She stroked his arm, trying to soothe him.

Pondwader let out a halting breath. "She—she rushed here from Standing Hollow Horn Village. I've never seen her in such a panic! She is usually overbearing and confident, but tonight she was talking so fast that I—"

"What did she want?"

Pondwader's mouth trembled. "She said to tell you that your plans will not work."

A prickle ran the length of Musselwhite's arms. It took monumental effort not to shiver. "Why not? Has something gone wrong?"

Pondwader shook his head. "I don't know. She told me only that she knew another way we might be able to penetrate Cottonmouth's defenses. She couldn't guarantee it, but—"

"Tell me." Musselwhite sat down cross-legged beside Pondwader, drew his hand into her lap and held it tightly. "I want to know every word."

I lie here, gazing up at the starry heavens, saturated with dread. The Shining People have driven Sister Moon into the Village of Wounded Souls for the rest of the night, and reclaimed the Daybreak Land. Fuzzy twinkles and spurts of yellow and pale blue light the heavens. I watch them fly about. Terror has become a living thing inside me. I have never been this afraid in my life.

I turn to peer at the sandstar pendant. After we wore ourselves out talking, Musselwhite curled beside me under the blanket, and rested her cheek on the pendant. Just the edge of the shell sticks out.

The Lightning Bird inside me has been crying. Whimpering soft and low, like distant storm winds. I don't know why. But it has to do with the sandstar—and Turtle Bone Doll. The weeping began at the very instant Turtle Bone Doll appeared in the sky above me, spiraling down, leaving a brilliant golden trail. But the crying didn't stop when she flew away. It grew louder when Musselwhite rolled to her side and the sandstar fell from the front of her tunic.

I can feel the baby Bird reaching out to touch that sandstar, yearning desperately to hold the shell.

And there is nothing I can do to help. I feel so anxious and confused, I . . .

My fingers creep across the blanket and touch the shell.

A warm flood of contentment filters through my body, so sweet and quiet. The crying stops.

Sleep, Lightning Boy, a voice whispers. *Sleep now.*

As if my eyes are not my own, the lids grow heavier and heavier, until they fall closed.

From nowhere, everywhere at once, come soft shishes and booms, and a faint drum beat rumbles through my body, stretching all the way to my fingers and toes. The thunder music soothes my fears, smoothing them away like a silky weasel-fur brush. Images flash and flit, and I feel myself soaring through the sky, high above the rainy world, bathed in roaring light. My heart aches with wonder. My frail human body feels that it may burst from the magnificent joy welling in my chest. And I know that if it does, molten radiance will spill out of me and drench the sky with fiery blue raindrops.

. . . If only this flight could last forever.

Forty-one

As the full moon slipped above the eastern horizon, ghostly silver light frosted the sky, and gilded the drifting thunderheads with a pale sheen. The howls of wolves carried on the warm wind that swept the shore. Musselwhite let her souls drift with that mournful serenade as she tied another piece of dead coral to her length of cordage. Pondwader stood before her, dressed in a breechclout, breathing hard. He'd started shaking a short time ago, and the tremor seemed to be getting worse. Moonlight penetrating the oak branches threw dark streaks of shadow across his white body. He looked at her with huge eyes.

Pondwader picked up another piece of dead coral, dropped it, picked it up again, and tried his best to wrap the cord around the irregular chunk. He couldn't seem to make his fingers work. "M-musselwhite?"

"Here, Pondwader, let me do that. Why don't you try to find a dry spot to stow our packs and your long robe. When we're running south tomorrow, you'll need your robe desperately."

"A-all right." He handed his cord to her and walked toward the trees with face downcast.

They had been forced to rip a wide strip of fabric from the foot of his robe to make his breechclout, knowing he could not survive the swim with the long robe tangling around his legs. But in the bright sunlight tomorrow afternoon, he would need that robe again, very badly. When the time came, she would use the breechclout to construct leggings for him.

When the time came. When she and Diver and Pondwader were all together, heading south toward Manatee Lagoon.

Longing rended her heart. She watched Pondwader gather up their packs and his folded robe, and wander into the dark forest. Moonlight reflected so from his pale flesh that she could follow his progress through the trees. It felt eerie, like observing a homeless soul going about its curious nightly duties. Except Pondwader made far more noise. Twigs snapped beneath his stumbling feet. Branches cracked when he butted into them. Very faintly, Musselwhite heard him heave an exasperated sigh.

"Blessed Sun Mother," she said in a low reverent voice. "Let him live through this. He has so much ahead of him. So many wonderful adventures."

She adjusted the bandage on her head. Her pain had eased to a dull constant headache. Annoying, but she could stand it. She tied three more large chunks of dead coral to Pondwader's cord, and hefted it to determine its weight. The ocean lay as smooth as chalcedony, Sea Girl's voice a bare murmur of waves. They would make it. This plan would work. It surprised her that she had not thought of it herself.

Musselwhite wore a pale green tunic. She had tied her stiletto and atlatl to her belt. On the ground at her feet lay two turtle-shell facemasks. That afternoon they'd drilled eyeholes in each, so they could see when they had to emerge from the water. Hopefully the masks would make them look like nothing more than floating turtles. She might not need it; her skin had been tanned to a deep brown, and would blend with the night, but Pondwader certainly would. She tied her mask on her belt. The atlatl would probably be useless, since she could not carry darts with her—but she wanted it in the event that she could retrieve an opponent's miscast dart. Though, if she needed to, it would mean they had been discovered, and were probably dead anyway.

Pondwader emerged from the trees, his face taut. Both of them had braided and coiled their hair into buns at the backs of their heads. The style accented the oval shape of his young face. In the flood of silver light, he looked very tall and skinny for a ten-and-five-summers-old youth. Most warriors his age had packed their legs and shoulders with muscle from constant running and dart throwing. But Pondwader had had other priorities. His pink eyes gleamed with an unearthly light, as if he perceived a far more insubstantial world than she.

"I think I found a good place," he said as he came up to stand beside her. He crossed his arms over his bare chest. "A rotten log with a hole in the center. I stuffed them in there."

Musselwhite said, "Thank you, Pondwader." And she prayed it didn't rain, because if it did, the water would run in streams into that hollow log and pool around their packs. "It's time, Pondwader. I promised Beaverpaw we would be there exactly one hand of time after moonrise. Are you ready?"

"Yes." His throat worked as he swallowed.

He bent down to pick up his belt of coral. "It's heavy," he said. His hands had started shaking again.

"Do you think it's heavy enough? You've done this before, I haven't."

"Oh, yes. It will be fine. We just need enough to keep us underwater."

She smiled. "Good. Here, let me tie it on you."

He handed her the weighted cord. "Thank you. I don't know why I'm so nervous."

"You have every right to be nervous," she said. "Don't worry. You'll calm down once we get into the water."

"Are you s-sure?"

"Yes," she said as she knotted the cord around his slim waist. Pondwader lifted his arms to give her room. "I'm going to tie the cord into a bow knot, so you can get out of it quickly if the need arises."

"I always do, too, whenever I lie on the bottom of the lagoon to listen to the fishes. You never know when a shark might come along and you have to leave quickly."

Musselwhite tied the face mask on Pondwader's cord, then put on her own weighted belt, and peered into his anxious face. His white brows had pulled together over his pointed nose. "Has that ever happened to you?"

He shook his head. "No. The sharks and I are friends. We've never bothered each other."

"I'm glad to hear that," she replied. "Talk to them tonight, will you? Tell them we mean them no harm, and would appreciate the same courtesy."

"Yes, I will, though . . ." He cocked his head to the sounds of the ocean, waves lapping the shore, gulls squealing and fluttering. "I don't hear any sharks out there, at least no big ones. No, there are some croakers, and a few dolphins . . . but no sharks."

He appeared so earnest, Musselwhite could not tease him about his extraordinary comment. Besides, she wasn't altogether certain he couldn't hear what he claimed to. And, more than that, she frankly didn't feel up to teasing anyone. Every nerve in her body hummed.

She took a deep breath and smiled at Pondwader. "Let's get started. Do you have the hollow reeds?"

Pondwader pulled three from his belt and handed her two of them. Each had a length of cord attached. "Just be sure not to breathe through your nose," he advised. "It's a very frightening feeling."

"I'm sure that's true. We won't need these until the very last anyway. At least I hope not. However, be sure to tuck yours in a convenient place. If warriors appear on the shore, duck your head underwater as fast as you can. When we get close enough to survey the village, we'll use our turtle-shell facemasks."

Musselwhite securely tied both reeds to her belt beside her stiletto, and strode for the water. Pondwader followed quietly behind her.

She waded in a short distance, then leaned forward, as if to swim, testing to see if she could touch the silt bottom. The coral belt tugged at her waist more forcefully than she had anticipated. Her knees thumped the bottom. But she found that if she braced her palms on the bottom, too, she could keep her head above the water, and the belt assured that the rest of her body stayed submerged.

The bank curved inward, and Musselwhite crawled along on hands and knees. Pondwader eased up beside her, his hair gleaming like sea foam. From a distance, his white head might also be mistaken for a floating gull, and when they neared the beach the mask would conceal him. *Good.* She had worried about that, that his face and hair would give them away to their enemies. It wouldn't, she felt almost certain now. Still, if anyone found them out, Pondwader's head would provide a clear target for darts.

Water swirled blackly around them, lapping at their throats, and a sudden wave splashed Musselwhite's face. She closed her eyes, then blinked away the saltwater. Swallows wheeled overhead, swooping low to examine them, then sailing away.

Pondwader whispered, "How much f-further?"

His teeth had started chattering, but she knew it had little to do with the cold water. "Not far. Do you see that point of land jutting into the water ahead?"

He squinted. "No."

"Trust me, it's there. As soon as we swim around that point we should see Standing Hollow Horn Village. It sits right on the water."

"Then what will we do?" His eyes glinted silver when he turned to face her.

"We swim past the village, all the way to the far northern boundary. I think that's where Diver is being held. That's where the council shelter used to sit, and I pray it still does."

They swam in silence for a while, bobbing along side-by-side. Pondwader's eyes looked like huge silver moons. "What if . . . if it doesn't? What if Diver is being held in the center of the village, or—"

"Then we'll scout the village until we find him. Don't worry, Pondwader, everything is going to be all right. *You* are going to be all right."

"I love you, my wife. Please, always remember that, no matter what happens."

He closed his mouth, but Musselwhite could still hear his teeth clicking together. He bowed his head and focused his eyes on the moonlight dancing on the water.

"Stop worrying, we—"

"I can't, my wife."

A large piece of driftwood floated in front of her. She pushed it aside. "You're not thinking about what Dogtooth said, are you?"

"Yes," he whispered.

"Pondwader, please trust me. I have known Dogtooth for nearly three times as long as you have. I'm certain he did not mean you were really going to die. Besides, I have always found that a warrior who believes he's going to die, will—and I would appreciate it if you didn't."

A fleeting smile graced his face. "Thank you. I'll try not to, my wife."

The shore began its outward swing near a treeless sandy spit that jutted into the water. As Musselwhite swam forward, she caught movement, just a waver of shadow against the white sand. She gripped Pondwader's shoulder and pulled him back.

"What's wrong?" he asked, looking around frantically.

"Movement," she whispered, scrutinizing the shadows that now swayed in the moonlight. "Guards. On the bank at the tip of the point. I should have guessed as much."

Pondwader squinted. "I can't see anything. How many are there?"

"Too many." Fear soured her belly. "Five or six."

"Maybe they're just people out fishing, or enjoying the moonlight. Sun Mother's Winter Celebration Day is tomorrow, and many people will be in Standing Hollow Horn for the—"

"They move like warriors, Pondwader," she said. "But why are they out here on the shore? Does Cottonmouth fear he may be attacked from the sea? By people in canoes . . . or . . . No. Blessed Spirits."

"What?"

Her thoughts raced. "Does he know we're coming by water? But that doesn't make any sense. Not if what Hanging Star told Beaverpaw is correct—that Cottonmouth's Dreams have assured him I bring no war party, that I'll be entering the village from the northwestern corner. Why would he waste so many guards out here?"

"Do you think Hanging Star lied to Beaverpaw?" Pondwader asked. The vein in his white temple throbbed. "Or—or that Beaverpaw lied to you?"

"Not Beaverpaw, no." She shook her head. "And perhaps not even Hanging Star. Cottonmouth may just be creating a solid wall of guards as a precaution." But another possibility increased her dread. What if Cottonmouth had had a new Dream? That every time she changed her plans . . . Musselwhite dared not finish that thought.

"I must find out, Pondwader."

"How?"

She turned. "I need to go and scout the village, which means I must alter our plans."

"What? *Now?*"

"Yes. I want you to wait here for me. I'll go on ahead, and—"

"No! Musselwhite, you need me! I thought you understood! I *have* to be there! You are in grave danger—"

"Listen to me," she said, and reached out to put a hand on his cold shoulder. His mouth trembled. "Something is not right. I don't know how to explain it, but I just *feel* something amiss. I need you to stand guard for me. If I don't return within one hand of time, you must go for help. I'll be depending upon you, Pondwader. Can you do that for me?"

Tears filled his eyes. He tried to blink them away, but she saw. "*You* listen to *me*," he said in a forceful tone she had never heard before. "The ghosts in the Sacred Pond told me I *must* be with you when you face Cottonmouth!

Glade must be there . . . to help you! I thought you believed me. You said you believed me!"

Panic laced his voice, and Musselwhite gripped his shoulders hard. "I do believe you, Pondwader, and because I do, I promise you that I am simply going to scout the village. That's all. I'll head north to examine the guards' positions, and to see if the council shelter is in fact where I remember it being. Then I'll swim back for you."

"But you said that if you didn't come back—"

"That was just a precaution. I *will* be back for you."

Musselwhite could see the color rise suddenly into Pondwader's cheeks. He stuttered, "Y-you won't. You'll be killed and I'll be to blame! And I'll never forgive—"

"Pondwader," she said softly. "What is the Lightning Bird telling you? Is it trying to warn you?"

He blinked suddenly. "No," he answered with a frown. "No, the Bird is completely silent tonight."

Musselwhite smiled. "If I were heading into a trap, don't you think my son's soul would be trying to warn me? Just as he has in the past?"

Pondwader appeared to be thinking hard. He nodded.

She patted his shoulder. "I'll be back soon. I *promise* you. And, Pondwader? Keep down. Don't stand up or flail about. Your white hair and face draw attention as it is. Use your facemask if you want to get close to shore. Try not to make yourself an easy target for those warriors."

"But . . . ! But what if your scouting takes too long? What if Beaverpaw creates his diversion and we aren't there to take advantage of it? What will—"

"Beaverpaw will be fine, and we will have to find a way of sneaking in without his help. This discussion is over." She set her jaw; Pondwader lowered his gaze and splashed the water with his fist.

"I love you," he said desperately. "Be careful."

"I will. I'll see you soon."

She crawled away, moving quickly at first, then slowed down as she neared the spit of sand where the waves grew more intense, leaping and splashing. A powerful undercurrent tugged at her. Without her heavy coral belt, she'd have had no chance of remaining hidden. The waves would have toppled her and sent her scrambling onto the beach. Laughter drifted from the warriors. She smelled roasting fish, but didn't see a fire.

Reaching down, she untied one of the hollow reeds from her belt, tucked it into the corner of her mouth, and arranged the cord so that it lay just beneath her nose. Then she knotted it at the back of her head. To test the device, she put her face in the water and breathed. About four hands long, the reed stuck well above the surface.

She stretched her legs out behind her, letting the belt weight the lower half of her body down, and ducked her head beneath the water. She found that not only could she breathe, the waves didn't drag at her so much, and she could see fairly well.

Cautiously, she pulled herself forward. As she rounded the tip of the sandy spit, she lifted her eyes above the water and could see the guards clearly. They sat roasting fish over a bed of coals. The crimson gleam wavered. She continued on, following the curving shoreline around until the village came into view.

Tens of shelters crowded the shore, and people packed the spaces in between. She had heard stories of how huge the village had grown, but this . . . ! There had to be two times ten tens of people gathered here!

She untied her mask and placed the turtle shell over her face. Through the small eyeholes, she saw many men and women she recognized. Several of the Spirit Elders sat on blankets in the plaza, throwing bones. Alder looked exactly as she had two-tens-and-six summers ago, her short silver hair braided, her bulbous nose red. She had to be, oh, seven-tens-and-five summers now. Basketmaker, who sat next to Alder, elbowed her in the side and smiled. He looked much older. His hair had been pure black when Musselwhite had seen him last. Now it hung around his gaunt face like scraggly weeds sheathed in ice, and his nose seemed to have grown more hooked.

Nostalgia swelled her chest, bittersweet and potent. Alder had supervised Glade's birthing. Musselwhite recalled how sweet and tender the old woman's voice had sounded as she'd Sung over the newborn baby. And Basketmaker had warned her time and again about how "unpredictable" Cottonmouth could be. Yet she'd heard that Basketmaker had become one of Cottonmouth's greatest supporters.

For moons after she'd left Standing Hollow Horn, she'd missed the Elders, missed the warmth in their eyes and the soft reedy old voices.

Pulling herself onward, she passed a series of beach fires. Young couples sat together before them, smiling, talking, touching each other gently. And after that, she came to the section of shore where racers competed. Two men sprinted toward her, sand flying beneath their bare feet. Spectators crowded around the termination line drawn in the sand and cheered when the runner crossed it. She saw wagers exchanging hands, bets being paid off.

Then . . .

She saw the council shelter. It stood alone on the northern boundary, backed by trees. Four guards crouched nearby, darts lying at their sides as they indulged themselves with a game of dice. A wooden bowl filled with boiled clams sat in the middle of their circle. While one player rolled dice, the others pried open clams, ate them, and tossed the shells into a growing pile beside the bowl.

She crawled forward, getting closer to the shelter, and blood rushed hotly through her veins. There, in the middle, lay Diver. How powerfully she longed to rush to him, to cut his bonds, and fight the whole world, if necessary, to set him free. In all the summers they had known each other, Diver had never shown her anything but kindness and love, and he had risked his life tens of times to keep her safe. Her souls wrenched. The longer she stared at the festering wounds that covered his body, the more a fiery rage rose. Rage that Cottonmouth would inflict his hatred for her upon the innocent. Rage that he would use Diver to force her to come to him when they had nothing left for each other.

Diver stirred, rolling to his back. He wore a beautiful tunic with a blue lightning bolt on the front. She examined him in detail, checking his feet, hands, and face. He—he looked basically all right. If he had no internal injuries, he might be able to run.

But how can I get to him? There are so many people near his shelter. Someone will surely see me.

She truly did need Beaverpaw's help. Could she count on him? Was he even here? She had not seen him, but so many people crowded the village, constantly coming and going, Beaverpaw could be here and she would never spot him.

She dragged her gaze away from Diver, and crawled northward. The trees grew almost out to the edge of the water here. Pine cones and acorns littered the sand.

Camps scattered the forest beyond the village perimeter. The orange gleams of dozens of fires sent shadows climbing through the oaks, pines, and flowering dogwoods. With so many strangers around the village, it would be difficult for anyone, even a warrior who had seen her before, to spot her. Though Cottonmouth would certainly have informed his guards that they had better spot her. Every warrior in Standing Hollow Horn would be fearing for his life, examining and reexamining the faces of each woman her age who moved through the village.

With great care, she slid across the sand on her belly, getting as close to the beach as she could without exposing herself.

A massive thunderhead sailed in front of Sister Moon and the shore suddenly went pitch black. Musselwhite dropped her mask into the water and stuck her head above the water. Removing her breathing reed, she casually rose to her feet.

She tied the reed to her belt, and hummed pleasantly as she unpinned her bun and began unbraiding her long hair. She shook it loose so that it partially shielded her face, and headed for the trail she prayed still existed.

As she entered the wavering firelit shadows, she passed several makeshift "celebration" shelters, constructed just for celebration days and easy to erect and tear down. Thin saplings supported crude lightweight palm frond roofs. Women and children filled the shelters, and, here and there, a few men. The smells of roasting pelican, opossums, and squirrels made her mouth water.

One little boy sat up when he saw her, looked her over carefully, and yelled, "Why did you go swimming in your tunic? Is the water so cold?"

"Oh, it's very cold," she answered with a smile. "I think there's a big storm out at sea cooling it down. . . . Is that turtle in your bowl good?"

The boy grinned, yelled, "Yes!" and tore off another piece of the succulent meat. He stuffed it in his mouth and waved to Musselwhite as she hastened away.

The trail curved around the village, passing about thirty hands from the shelters which formed the last semicircular perimeter ring. She past three men walking in the opposite direction and nodded politely. They paid little attention to her, nodding back and proceeding on their way, as if anxious to find their suppers.

In this last ring, guards filled the spaces between the shelters, leaning against support poles, their anxious eyes moving from the happenings in the plaza to the fluttering forest shadows. The taut young faces told her their guts must be knotted up with fear.

As Musselwhite rounded the trail, a foul odor struck her. No shelters dotted the trees here, but several old clearings did, marking the places where shelters had stood only days ago. All of the celebration shelters had been removed. Why?

Painstakingly, she scanned the mottled shadows and interior of the village, but saw nothing unexpected. She continued around the trail, walking purposefully, her head down, as if she had somewhere important to go.

The stench grew stronger.

. . . Her steps faltered.

Beaverpaw stood against the ancient oak at the northwest corner of the village. Someone had driven a stake through his chest to pin his body to the trunk, and another protruded just beneath his chin, holding his head up so that passersby had to peer directly into his empty eye sockets. Scavenger birds had pecked them clean. The back of his skull did not exist. Vicious blows from a war club had crushed it to bloody pulp.

Musselwhite continued on, but her heart thundered. She had no help here. No one to . . .

"You are still bold, Musselwhite."

She whirled and for a brief instant her eyes met Cottonmouth's, then she saw warriors emerging from hiding places in the brush. They converged upon her from several directions, loping in like hungry wolves.

Musselwhite let out a shrill war cry, twisted sideways, and slammed her elbow into the face of the first man who dared to reach for her. When he cried out and stumbled, she leveled a deadly punch to his throat, and ran for her life—straight into the chaos of the village. People tripped over each other trying to get out of her way, shoving back, and a great dreadful roar rose. Gasps and shouts increased in volume until they drowned out every other sound.

She swerved around the central bonfire, her long legs pumping, hair flying, and headed for the beach. If she could just make it into the water, she might be able to . . .

"Musselwhite! No! Not that way! There are too many guards! You must . . ."

Diver's scream shredded her soul. She glimpsed him on his knees in the council shelter, his face twisted in horror . . . just as she raced headlong into the six armed warriors he had been trying to warn her about. They spread out along the shore before her, looking terrified.

Ripping her stiletto from her belt, she leaped on the closest man, plunged the weapon into his heart and threw his body into the path of her pursuers before she sprinted on. A warrior tripped over his friend, yelled in indignation, and fell. The others jumped over him, shrieking war cries as they pounded after her.

Diver let out an incoherent shout. She jerked to peer over her shoulder, her heart throbbing, and saw three guards leap on him. Despite his bindings, he'd managed to get to his feet and had made it several paces beyond the council shelter before they'd brought him down. He slammed out at them with his bound fists.

Blessed Sun Mother, if only—

A warrior struck Musselwhite from behind. His powerful arms went around her waist, and the force of his attack knocked her to the ground. She screamed in rage as the other guards fell upon her like dogs, grabbing her arms and legs, handfuls of her hair, anything they could hold on to.

Spectators rushed forward, closing in around them, bellowing questions, gasping at the sight of Musselwhite, and craning their necks to get a better view.

Musselwhite wrenched her head sideways, and saw, as if from one of her nightmares, a tall slender man coming through the press of onlookers. A breathless hush fell as people shoved each other aside to make a path for him. The grace of his movements, the sight of his handsome face, struck her like physical blows.

Cottonmouth knelt at her side. He did not say a word. His intent gaze slowly went over her, as if comparing every detail of her face and body with his memory. A strange haunted light grew in his dark eyes.

Softly, he ordered, "Bring her to my shelter."

Dace edged forward, quiet as Mouse, placing his feet with great care so that he didn't snap any twigs or frighten a night animal that would scurry away and draw attention to him. He lifted his dart and nocked his atlatl, concentrating on the voices that echoed from the clearing ahead. Loud. Angry. Diamondback had heard them first, and suggested they all separate and surround the clearing. As Dace sneaked toward a dense tangle of vines, the meadow came into view, and he glimpsed a white face . . . ghostly white.

No. Oh, no.

His heart rose into his throat. At the sound of muted sobs, he fought to restrain himself from charging forward.

Pondwader knelt in the grass, tears drenching his face. Four warriors stood around him, feet braced, stilettos up. They looked scared to death.

"I don't believe it!" a warrior said. Not much older than Dace, he wore a headband to keep his shoulder-length hair out of his eyes. "Cottonmouth told us the Lightning Boy would be here, but I never—"

"Shut up, Wasp," the tall skinny man next to him growled. "Gullwing, you and Cloudfish tie his hands. Wasp and I will search his two packs; then we will take him back."

"Yes, Woodduck."

The two warriors who had to be Gullwing and Cloudfish jerked Pondwader's hands up and began tying them securely with cordage. About the same age, two-tens-and-two or -three summers, both had cut their hair at chin length, but Gullwing was a much more powerful man, broad in the shoulders with long muscular legs. Cloudfish was slight by comparison, with a moony face and flat nose. Pondwader put up no fight. He just bit his lip and yielded.

Dace got on his knees and crept closer, halting behind a thorny bramble of rose bushes. Red fruits covered the stalks and scented the air with sweetness. From this angle, he had a better view of Pondwader. His friend sat unmoving, his expression one of cold defeat, as if he'd lost everything in the world that mattered to him. Dace frowned. He had seen that look on Pondwader's face once before—the day Pondwader's grandfather died. The old man had raised Pondwader, been more than his father, and the loss had left his souls floundering.

Dace sat back. *Where is Musselwhite? She should be here. If she isn't . . . she . . .*

Dace closed his eyes for a brief painful moment. *Dead?* He ached for his friend.

Wasp and the other warrior emptied Pondwader's packs onto the grass, and sorted through the contents. Pondwader tipped his chin, focused on the night sky, as if praying to Sister Moon.

The skinny Woodduck cursed and straightened up. Furiously, he kicked the contents of the packs, sending bags of food, wooden bowls, water gourds, sailing across the clearing to tumble through the grass.

Woodduck crouched before Pondwader and said, "Come along, Lighting Boy. Your death awaits you. We are only its messengers."

He gripped Pondwader's arm and jerked him to his feet. Out of sheer cruelty, he twisted the arm, brutally shoving it up behind Pondwader's back. Pondwader stood still and white.

"Trying to be brave boy?" Woodduck asked. "We shall see how long that lasts under Cottonmouth's torture. He has very persuasive techniques. . . ."

A hiss was followed by the crack of breaking bone, and Woodduck shrieked and staggered. His wide eyes looked disbelievingly at the bloody dart embedded in his ribs. A horrified wail erupted from his mouth. He took three running steps before toppling.

The other warriors scattered, bounding for cover. Wasp yipped when a dart sliced through his chest. He stumbled sideways, fell, and clawed weakly at the grass.

Dace burst from his hiding place and used all the strength in his young body to cast his dart at the warrior named Gullwing. The dart caught the man in side, piercing deeply into him. Blood gushed from the wound and coursed down his naked back in gruesome streams. The man sank to his knees and hunched forward, but Dace knew he had not killed his enemy. He pulled his stiletto from his belt. He would have to plunge it into the man's heart now. He had no choice. His knees shook as he ran. *Kill him while he looks me in the eyes? Oh, Brother Sky, let me do this quickly, so it will be over!*

A war cry split the air. Dace whirled to see Cloudfish leap a fallen log and burst from the trees, his stiletto lifted. Hatred filled his burning eyes. Dace stumbled, stunned at the man's closeness.

"Dace! Get down!" Diamondback screamed.

He threw himself to the ground, and Diamondback's dart sailed right over his head, skewering Cloudfish, slicing his throat. Cloudfish sprawled only hands away from Dace, choking on his own blood. He gripped the dart, holding onto it as he stared Dace in the eyes. It seemed to take an eternity for the man to suffocate. His garbled cries sickened Dace.

Diamondback stepped from the trees, his atlatl nocked and held high, ready for anything. "Come on," he said. "Kelp and Pondwader need us."

"But—but I have to finish killing Gullwing. I only hit him—"

"He's dead, Dace. He bled to death. Let's go."

Dace rolled to his knees. Diamondback grabbed his hand to help him up, but it still took every bit of strength Dace could muster to get to his feet again. When he had braced his shaking legs, Dace looked out into the middle of the moonlit meadow.

Kelp knelt, hugging her brother. She had untied his hands for Pondwader held her in a crushing embrace. His soft sobs carried on the grass-scented wind.

Forty-two

I waited for one hand of time," Pondwader said in an agonized voice. His swollen, red-rimmed eyes peered unblinking into the low dancing flames. "Then I went after her."

A patchy blanket of mist spread around their camp, stroking the air with ethereal fingers, chilling them to the bone. In the moonlight that penetrated the dark branches, the fog slithered around the trunks of the oaks, glittering as though alive, listening, watching, waiting for the opportunity to strike them down. The fire spat and sparked, defending itself against this gossamer assailant.

"Go on," Kelp urged.

As Pondwader's wet white hair dried in the fire's warmth, it began to fluff around his shoulders. "I-I crawled up the shore line—underwater, then I used a turtle-shell mask to shield my face. I never saw her. But . . . she must have been captured. I just don't understand why she lied to me! If she had told me—"

"If she had told you, you would have insisted upon going with her." Diamondback sat across the fire from Pondwader, his brow furrowed. "She did not wish you to go, Pondwader. When the situation looks very bad, she will risk only her own life. It's her way." He heaved a breath. "Though, I admit, I myself have often found it irritating."

Pondwader drew up his knees and wrapped his long arms around them.

Kelp surveyed them both. Diamondback wore a plain tunic, belted at the waist with a braided rawhide cord. She had forced Pondwader to put on his long robe, though he'd insisted he didn't need to. But he'd spent so much time in the cold water his flesh had felt like ice.

She dipped a cup of hot pine-needle tea from the boiling basket hanging on the tripod, and checked the leftover strips of raccoon in the wooden bowl at the edge of the coals. The meat steamed. Running her finger around the lip of the bowl, she found the coolest spot, then lifted it and the gourd cup, and rose to her feet.

Pondwader looked up when she walked around the firepit to crouch beside him. Love for her filled his pink eyes. "Thank you, Kelp, but I think it would come right back up. I'm not hungry."

"I want you to eat," she said. "You're skin and bone. Did you starve yourself on the journey north? Did you think it would make you a better warrior?"

He grimaced. "I doubt that anything could do that, Kelp. It's just not in me."

"Seagull dung," she said. "You're one of the bravest people I know. Now, eat." She put a hand on his shoulder, and lowered her voice. "Please, try, Pondwader."

Diamondback gazed at her warmly, as though touched by the affection she showed her brother. He looked so handsome, his turned-up nose and high cheekbones gleaming in the firelight. Kelp smiled at him. Dace had taken the first watch, leaving the three of them to talk, and Kelp appreciated his sacrifice, especially knowing that Dace longed to speak with Pondwader almost as badly as she did.

"She's right, you know," Diamondback said. "Remember when you walked into the middle of the battle at Windy Cove, Pondwader? I was awed by your courage."

Pondwader's mouth tightened.

Kelp sat down beside her brother and shoved his bowl closer. *"Eat,"* she ordered.

He sighed, picked up a piece of roasted raccoon, and took a small bite. When he swallowed, he closed his eyes, as if waiting. But it stayed down. He finished the first piece and reached for a second. Relief spread through Kelp.

Diamondback waited until Pondwader had finished the second piece and reached for a third before asking, "Did you get a good look at the village, Pondwader?"

Pondwader frowned. "I never get a good look at anything, Diamondback, but I squinted at every blur on the beach. There were many people in the plaza, laughing. I know because I could hear them."

"What about the guards? Did you see any?" Diamondback braced his elbows on his knees and fire shadows flowed into the lines in his young forehead.

Pondwader chewed his bite of meat and swallowed it. "No, I—I didn't. But Musselwhite said there were 'too many' guards. On the south side of the village, there is a sand spit that juts out into the water. She told me that six men were stationed there."

"On the water?" Diamondback said. "That's odd. Unless Cottonmouth fears—"

"An attack from the ocean, yes. Musselwhite wondered the same thing."

Kelp shook her head. "I think it's something else," she said. "The guards may not be out there looking for enemy warriors at all." Pondwader and Diamondback peered at her, and she continued. "Don't you recall Cottonmouth's Dream? The Lightning Birds are supposed to come in with Hurricane Breather. From out at sea. Maybe he has guards posted to keep a lookout for them—not us."

"Hallowed Spirits," Diamondback whispered. "That makes sense." Diamondback did not move. His gaze remained glued to Kelp's face.

Pondwader finished his piece of raccoon and cleaned his hands in the sand. "Musselwhite also said that she thought your father would be in the council shelter on the northern side of the village. I went there and saw many people. One man, the man inside the shelter, stayed on the ground the whole time. I couldn't tell if he were sitting or lying down, but he never got up. And I—I wondered if perhaps he weren't tied up."

Hatred, cold and vengeful, rose in Diamondback's dark eyes. He clenched his fists in his lap, but his voice stayed calm. "If it was my father, and he witnessed my mother's capture . . ." Diamondback glared at the wind-blown flames. "My father will find a way of getting out of his bindings. Even if it means dying, he will make sure the men who hurt her suffer for what they did."

Kelp said, "He loves her that much?"

"More than I could ever tell you," Diamondback replied. "I have been with the two of them on war walks and seen them rush headlong into certain death to save the other. It's . . . unfathomable. And wonderful." Admiration touched his voice. "When she loves, she loves with all of her souls."

"Yes," Pondwader murmured. "She does."

Diamondback tossed another branch onto the fire and the flames crackled, sending a whirl of sparks whirling upward into the swaying tree boughs. In a tender tone, he said, "She treats her children the same way. The entire world could have withered and died, but not her love for us. It was the one constant in our lives. The only thing we could depend on."

Kelp said, "But your father—"

"Oh, yes, he loved us very much, but . . . I don't know how to explain it. Father's love was gentle and warm. Fun-loving. He was our best friend. Mother's love was like a bear in our souls, always ferocious, urging us to leap upon anyone who threatened us. Willing to do it herself if necessary." Diamondback laced and relaced his fingers. Anguish lined his face. "I cannot tell you the number of times I have sought my memories of that love when I thought I might die. And it's always been there. Looking out of my souls at me with fury in its eyes, telling me to get up and fight."

Pondwader had gone silent.

Kelp reached out and stroked his arm. "Are you all right, Pondwader?"

He closed his eyes. "I have to go after her."

"What?" Kelp demanded. "Don't be crazy! You can't just walk into Standing Hollow Horn. Cottonmouth will kill you!"

Pondwader opened his eyes and grimaced into his pale green tea. "Hanging Star told me that Cottonmouth didn't want Musselwhite at all. He said Cottonmouth wanted me."

Diamondback leaned forward. "Who is Hanging Star?"

The darkness seemed to ripple when a gust of wind ran through the forest. Broken shards of moonlight danced over their camp, and all around them oak leaves whipped loose from branches, gleaming like feathers as they tumbled through the air.

"Hanging Star is one of Cottonmouth's warriors," Pondwader answered. "We met him on the trail. Hanging Star, Beaverpaw, and my—our mother were traveling together."

"Great Mouse," Kelp groaned. "You saw our mother?"

Pondwader nodded. "I didn't talk with her for long, but it was during that conversation that Hanging Star said the only reason Cottonmouth sought to trap Musselwhite was because of me. He told me that Cottonmouth wanted me very badly."

"Are you saying that Beaverpaw is in Standing Hollow Horn Village?" Diamondback asked breathlessly.

"I hope so. Beaverpaw and Musselwhite laid out a plan for rescuing your father. Beaverpaw was supposed to create a diversion, tonight, one hand of time after moonrise."

Diamondback rubbed his numb face. "Blessed ghosts. If we have an ally in the village—especially a War Leader of Beaverpaw's skill—we just might be able to beat Cottonmouth."

"Musselwhite thought so, too," Pondwader said.

Fear ran along Kelp's limbs on icy spider feet. She gripped her brother's hand hard. "What are you two talking about?"

Pondwader crushed her hand in his.

"What's wrong?" Kelp asked.

"It's just that . . . well, I see no reason to fight. If Cottonmouth wants me, perhaps the best thing I could do is to give myself up. Maybe I can bargain with him, me in exchange for Musselwhite and Diver."

Diamondback shook his head vehemently. "No, Pondwader. Don't even think about it. Cottonmouth would just kill all three of you."

"But why? If he—"

"Because," Diamondback said harshly. "He hates my mother! He's hated her for tens of summers. He will never let her go. And I suspect he hates my father just as much. Our best hope of rescuing them is to find Beaverpaw and work out a new plan."

"But," Kelp said, "even if we can depend on Beaverpaw, Cottonmouth has ten tens of warriors. How can we ever hope to slip two people through his net of guards?"

Diamondback shook his head. "I don't know. I need to speak with Beaverpaw. You must describe him to me in detail. Then, I think I will go to Standing Hollow Horn for the sunrise ceremonies tomorrow. If I can—"

"No!" Kelp protested, her pulse racing. "You have survived several attacks by Cottonmouth's warriors. There will be someone there who can recognize you, Diamondback. *I* am the logical choice. None of them have ever seen me. Besides, I know exactly what Beaverpaw looks like. I could find him much faster than you!"

Pondwader winced suddenly. Bringing up a hand, he massaged the space over his heart. His face had gone as white as the moonlight. He winced again, and a shudder went through him.

Kelp murmured, "Pondwader? Are you . . . is everything all right?"

With a sad smile, he said, "Music, Kelp. I hear beautiful music."

"Music?"

He nodded. "Do you know how wolves call each other from across the forest? One wolf howling until another answers?"

Kelp wet her lips, glancing down at his hand. His fingers pressed so hard on his ribs that the blood had retreated from his nails. "Yes," she said.

Quietly, Pondwader said, "I'm being called to Standing Hollow Horn Village. The Lightning Birds want me there. I think it's the only way to save Musselwhite."

"Called?" Diamondback asked in confusion. "By the Lightning Birds? What's he babbling about?"

Kelp looked at Pondwader, silently asking if it would be all right to tell Diamondback . . . but Pondwader shook his head. Kelp nodded. She promised a long time ago not to tell anyone about the thunder and lightning that lived inside her brother, and had broken that promise once already. She would not do it again. Not unless Pondwader told her she could.

"He's babbling about saving your mother, Diamondback," Kelp answered, and rested her hand supportively on Pondwader's shoulder. "You're sure about this? It's the only way?"

Pondwader looked at Kelp with his heart in his eyes, and whispered, "Yes."

"Then tell us what the Lightning Birds want us to do, Pondwader."

"Wait a moment!" Diamondback blurted. "I don't think this is wise! We should—"

Kelp silenced him with a wave of her hand. "Go on, Pondwader. Tell us what to do."

Forty-three

The howling wind woke Musselwhite, but she did not move. During the night, her seated body, bound to the shelter pole, had slumped sideways against the ropes, and the rain drumming on the thatched roof dripped methodically onto her right shoulder. Trickles ran coldly down her arm. Her long legs stretched in front of her, and windblown raindrops had beaded upon the flesh. Her feet throbbed and ached. The bindings around her ankles had been knotted with brutal strength.

Singing and laughter rose and fell with the gusting wind. Closer, flames crackled. Fragrant hickory smoke blew over her. Bags hanging from the rafters creaked and bumped each other. The damp floor mats groaned. . . .

Musselwhite clenched her bound fists, knowing that sound as if the years had peeled away like old clothing.

Cottonmouth paced slowly and deliberately in front of her. Her souls remembered: his steps like a man's walking to his own execution—with no chance for salvation. Four paces east, turn, four paces west, turn, four paces east . . . In a lull between gusts, she heard his breathing.

Musselwhite opened her eyes.

At sight of him, gut-tingling terror mixed with remnants of old and powerful love. Her heart pumped.

A halo of silver-black hair encircled his magnificent face. It glittered in the light of the flames in the firepit. Hallowed Spirits, how well he had borne the summers! Lines etched his forehead and the corners of his eyes, but his nose and full lips still seemed carved from stone. His deeply tanned skin had the velvet tones of Deer's winter coat. He wore a plain, everyday tunic, but his ritual garment hung from a peg on the southeastern pole. The rich, blue fabric billowed in the wind, setting the circlets of mica sewn around the collar, sleeves, and hem to winking. Traded from the north, mica reflected light as well as a water mirror. In the brightening gleam of dawn, they flashed like rose-amber tongues of flame.

His presence was like a Spirit plant, beckoning, calling to her, even after all that had passed between them. Part of her longed to reach out to him, while another part recoiled the way the hand did when it accidentally brushed the smooth coils of a poisonous snake.

She tore her gaze away to inspect the sky.

Thunderheads sailed over, leaving patches of stars showing in the wide gaps. Wavering filaments of rain swayed beneath them. The pink glow of sunrise was slowly bringing life to the red and yellow leaves in the forest. Their colors blended with the greenish gray of the hanging moss, and the dark clumps of palmettos. The fresh scents of morning wafted on the breeze. . . . Five warriors, no six, stood guard around the shelter.

Cottonmouth stopped short. He did not turn, but gazed out at the crashing waves where gulls circled and dove, their squeals penetrating the roars of the surf and gale. Already, Snailtoes, the Spirit Elders, and a small gathering of Soul Dancers from around the region were making preparations for the Awakening Ritual of Sun Mother's Winter Celebration Day. Musselwhite recognized most of them. They stood around a large fire on the beach, their faces sheathed with the wavering orange gleam, their bodies little more than black silhouettes against the luminous background of dawn.

"It's curious," Cottonmouth said. "I should be out on the beach with the other Spirit Elders, but I've been afraid to leave you."

His voice echoed through the emptiness that lived in Musselwhite's souls, swirling, coming back as soft and desperate as it had two-tens-and-six summers before. *I've been afraid to leave you. You've been so frantic since Glade caught the fever that I feared you might harm yourself. . . .*

She started trembling.

Slowly, as if with monumental effort, Cottonmouth turned to face her. The deep dark wells of his eyes glistened. "Do you know how much I loved you? What it did to me . . . to lose both you and Glade on the same day?"

Musselwhite braced her head against the pole to keep it steady. Every muscle in her body knotted.

Cottonmouth raised a hand and gripped the fabric over his heart, twisting it with anguished fingers. "I have been thanking the Shining People," he said, "that I do not have to lead the ceremonies this morning. There's a blind panic inside me. A terrifying fear that if I take my eyes from you, you will vanish again. And this time I will never be able to find you."

She narrowed her eyes against the soft timbre in his voice. "What is it you want from me, Cottonmouth?"

"You."

". . . What?"

"I want you."

Old woman Starfish emerged from the shadows of the waking village and walked toward them. She had a bowl of food in one hand and a boiling basket, held by the thongs, in the other. Her toothless, sunken face resembled a winter-killed plum, but her beautiful ritual tunic sparkled, encrusted with polished seashells and seed beads. She took her time, placing her old feet with care. The boiling basket rocked back and forth with her movements.

Cottonmouth turned to greet her. "A joyous Celebration Day to you, Starfish."

"And to you, Spirit Elder."

Starfish knelt and set the bowl and basket on the ground before him. "I have brought you ritually blessed food and tea. Is there anything else you require?" Her toothless gums spread in a smile.

"No, thank you, Starfish. I will see you on the beach soon."

"Yes, Elder."

Starfish rose. "Today is the day, isn't it, Elder? When the Lightning Birds will soar down to free us?"

"It is," he answered solemnly. "Very soon, we will all be together in that shining new world beyond the stars. Prepare yourself."

She beamed. "Yes, Elder. I will." After bowing to Cottonmouth, she turned and walked away, her steps lighter, more buoyant.

People greeted her as she made her way across the village, asking her questions, then casting reverent glances back at his shelter. Mothers rushed to comb their childrens' hair, and get them dressed. Warriors prepared atlatls and darts. Those who already stood carried small packs on their backs, as if for a journey.

Cottonmouth picked up the bowl and basket and walked to the firepit. Kneeling, he hooked the basket's thongs on the tripod to suspend it over the warm coals, then sat down cross-legged, and placed the wooden bowl between them. It brimmed with roasted flounder and tree mushrooms.

"You must be thirsty," Cottonmouth said as he dipped a gourd cup into the basket and handed it to Musselwhite.

She reached for it with her bound hands, and their fingers met around the cup. Cottonmouth flinched. For a long time he refused to let the cup go, seemingly drowning in her touch. Then, finally, he did, and his hand shook.

Musselwhite gulped the drink. Sea-grape tea, sweetened with bumblebee honey. The tartness made her mouth pucker, but the honeyed warmth soothed her raw nerves. She sipped her tea and watched him. He drank a full cup before he reached for a tree mushroom. As he ate it, he gestured to the sky. "Do you see that?"

Musselwhite looked. A pearlescent sheen filled the spaces between the thunderheads. High over her head, the sky glowed a deep blue and mated with the last Shining People, but as it arced downward to the eastern horizon, it faded to purple, and then to an extraordinary shade of lavender, like the rarest of marsh orchids. It lined the drifting clouds with pure amethyst. Just above the ocean, a thin band of pitch black extended for as far as the eye could see.

"See what?"

"The storm," he said. "We haven't much time. A few hands is all."

"Time? For what?"

He tossed a piece of pine onto his fire and flames licked up around the bark. Little pockets of sap boiled out, sizzling and spitting. He moved the wooden bowl within her reach. "Eat. You will need your strength."

"For *what*, Cottonmouth?"

"The end of the world, Musselwhite. When tonight comes, the Shining Eagles will be dead. And so will you and I, and everyone else."

He sounded completely rational. Elated, in fact.

She forced strength into her hands and reached into the bowl, drawing back a large mushroom. He studied her every move, desperation in the black depths of his eyes. He might have been gazing upon an enemy, a warrior braced and ready to kill him . . . rather than the woman who had born his son, the woman who had once loved him with all her heart and souls.

Firelight jumped and danced. The shadows grew slippery, pooling in the hollows of his cheeks, running down his smooth jaw.

"I must join the Celebration soon," he said.

She did not respond, but finished her mushroom, and reached to tear off a large chunk of flounder. She stuffed the flaky white meat into her mouth. *Yes, eat, Musselwhite. Center yourself. Think!*

"Before I go," he continued, voice softening, "there are things I must ask you."

She finished her first piece of fish and reached for another, taking as much as she could wolf down. She might be bound and under heavy guard, but he had not beaten her. Not yet. Not until she lay dead at his feet would she stop trying to save Diver.

"Where is the Lightning Boy?" he asked.

Musselwhite's pulse raced. *Running south for help, as fast as he can! Please—just once—I pray that he's doing what I told him.*

Cottonmouth said, "I sent out a war party last night to search for him."

She had to force a swallow to get her meat down. "Why?"

"He is the one who will kill the Shining Eagles. When he does, that storm out there will grow. It's been waiting for him. When the Lightning Boy calls, it will sweep away the entire world. . . . Where is he?"

"You sent out a war party last night and they haven't returned?" Mind racing, she struggled to read his expression.

"Not yet."

So they had failed to find Pondwader and could not risk returning without him, or . . .

"They're dead, Cottonmouth. You know it as well as I."

"Maybe." He inclined his head ever so slightly. "Though I can't imagine one boy defeating four battle-honed warriors. But it doesn't matter. I will just send out more warriors. Eventually, I will find him. He—"

"No, you won't."

He gave her a sharp glance, and she saw the first crack in his defenses. Fear. Deep. Overwhelming. Panic that his Dream might not come true.

"He's *very* Powerful," Musselwhite raised her voice so that the warriors standing nearby would hear. "I have seen the Lightning Boy do things that would terrify even you, Cottonmouth. With one word, he can call the Lightning Birds from the sky and order them to blast anything he wishes." The guards edged closer, listening with wide eyes. "Pondwader can change himself into Lightning and shoot through the heavens. You'll never find him. He—"

"I do hope he's Powerful," Cottonmouth answered. The crack closed. An eerie light lit his eyes. "After speaking with his mother, I had feared he might not be a Lightning Boy at all—and then, Musselwhite, all of my dreams would have died."

"Dark Rain is here? Alive?"

Distaste twisted Cottonmouth's lips. "Yes, Dark Rain is alive," he said. "Tell me, Musselwhite, where did the pathetic survivors of the Windy Cove slaughter go? South? That's where the Lightning Boy would seek shelter, isn't it?"

He had said the word "slaughter" with no more emotion than if he had been speaking about mosquitoes. Memories from the Windy Cove battle reared: Ashleaf lying with a dart clutched in his withered old hand; children sprawled facedown in the sand; Dreamstone curled on her side in a pool of blood; and the pitiful wails and pain of the survivors.

If only I could get my hands around his throat. "No," she said lightly, unable to keep tremors of rage from her voice. "I'm certain that after 'slaughtering' your best warriors, Pondwader is on his way here." She watched him through slitted eyes. "You still have time. Turn me loose, and I will try to save you."

She glanced at the guards. Was it working? They peered uneasily at each other, frowns lining their brows. If she could keep them anxious, afraid of their own shadow-souls, they might lose their vigilance, and when they did . . .

Cottonmouth leaned toward her. "Yes," he whispered. "I know he's on his way. My Dreams have shown his arrival."

"Is that so? Then why did you have to dispatch a war party to search for him? To drag him back here? You're still a fool, Cottonmouth—desperate to convince yourself and your clan of things you don't believe."

The guards muttered uneasily.

Cottonmouth turned his head ever so slightly to glare at them. Silence followed.

Surreptitiously, Musselwhite studied the men; not one of them bore an expression of reverence, or devotion. Had the recent raids depleted Cottonmouth's supply of loyal warriors? *Yes, there is weakness. . . . I could split this village in two if I had the time . . . but do I?*

Cottonmouth rose to his feet, and went to the southeastern shelter pole where his ritual tunic hung. He removed his plain tunic, and threw it on the floor, standing before her, naked, muscular.

She twisted her head away, closing her eyes, hating the memories of his body, his strong arms around her. . . .

Hallowed Spirits, how could two people who had loved each other with such passion and sweetness come to fear each other so much, to hate each other so much?

"I want you with me when the time comes," he said softly. "When the Lightning Birds crackle out of the sky—"

"Why . . . ? After the terrible things we have done to each other?"

He ran his fingers over the rich blue fabric of his ritual tunic. "I need you, Musselwhite. I always have. *You* are my souls. Without you I am just a hollow shell."

"I won't go with you."

He took the beautiful tunic from the peg. "Oh, you'll be there. I'll see to that."

He slipped the tunic over his head, and smoothed it down over his narrow hips. "When I return, you will answer all of my questions. It will be easier if you tell me of your own free will rather than—"

"I will answer nothing, Cottonmouth."

His gaze slid up to the brightening sky and drifting thunderheads, then scanned the shore. Ten tens of people stood on the shore, their bodies creating a choppy black blanket against the gleaming ocean. Their soft murmuring competed with the rhythmic roar of waves.

"That is your choice, Musselwhite." Cottonmouth tied a rabbit-fur cord around his slender waist and walked back to stand over her. Tall, latently dangerous. He smiled. "Though I am not certain how much more torture your beloved Diver can bear. He's weak as it is. But I assure you"—he reached down, roughly grasped her head with both hands, and his smile widened—"I will enjoy killing him before your eyes, *as you did my son before mine.*"

Her stomach cramped. She twisted from his grip and bent forward, leaning against her ropes, fighting the grief . . . the memories.

Quiet as death, Cottonmouth left. She heard his steps retreating across the sand.

Tears welled in her eyes. She hung her head, seeing with frightening clarity that she had not changed much. Not in two-tens-and-six summers. Musselwhite, the great warrior, still kept a frightened little girl locked inside her, a girl who now stared her terror at the woman warrior. The girl wanted to run, the warrior to fight. Musselwhite had no way of knowing which would prove stronger in the end.

On the shore, men and women formed a single line parallel to the surf. They raised their atlatls as a golden gleam rose above the black clouds and enameled the horizon. Standing erect and proud, they cast their darts high into the sky accompanied by shrill war whoops. *Murdering the Darkness.* People lifted their voices, cheering, praying to Sun Mother, assuring her they had killed the malevolent Darkness which had forced her to seek shelter in the Village of Wounded Souls earlier and earlier each day since summer solstice.

The Songs hushed.

People stood quiet, and still. It took so much longer than usual for the Sun Mother to return that the crowd grew anxious, fidgeting and murmuring darkly in fear.

When a molten sliver of Sun Mother's face finally crested the black wall of clouds, cries of joy laced the wind. People leaped and spun. Dance circles formed up, and the beach became a writhing din of kicking legs, waving arms, and loud Singing.

Musselwhite looked away.

Through the tangled weave of guards, she spied Diver, on his knees in the council shelter, his back to Sun Mother. An aura of gold enveloped him, and though he had turned toward Musselwhite, the blinding sunrise threw his face into shadow. She could not make out his expression.

Not that she had to. She could feel his love, like a warm current, flying across the plaza and into her heart. Sending her his strength—just in case she needed it.

"Hold on, Diver," she whispered. "I'm not finished yet."

She could almost hear his voice, teasing and warm, whispering in her souls, *"I never thought you were. I'm right here with you. We just need our chance. Together, we can whip the world. You know we can."*

Her throat constricted. "Yes," she mouthed the words, "I do. If we can find a crack to squeeze through."

A sudden breathless roar erupted from the people on the shore, and Musselwhite saw Diver whirl to stare. She tugged her gaze away, and saw the Dance circles break up as people shoved and shouted at each other. Women grabbed children and ran for their shelters, while men gripped their atlatls more tightly. Near Cottonmouth, the clan Elders fell to their knees.

Someone yelled, "He's come! He's come at last! The End is upon us!"

Cottonmouth whirled, his tall slender body coated with an amber gleam of sunlight.

The guards standing around Musselwhite gasped and their mouths fell open, seeing something that she could not from the floor of the shelter.

Littlehorn craned his neck. "Hallowed Spirits . . . it's happening. Just as Cottonmouth said it would!"

Then Musselwhite saw Pondwader. Like a ghost swimming out of a vision, he strode up the misty, wind-swept beach, white hair streaming, arms spread wide. Clouds seemed to follow him, rushing in toward shore, gathering over his head. His long robe flapped around his legs. And his eyes . . . those pink orbs reflected the morning with fiery intensity.

To Musselwhite's horror, Pondwader walked straight to Cottonmouth and held out his hands.

Cottonmouth took them.

Heart in throat, Diver watched Cottonmouth and the Lightning Boy cross the village. The crowd jostled, forming into a mob behind Cottonmouth's guards, pushing and slapping each other, juggling for position. Every eye was on the boy. Shouts laced the wind, breathless with anticipation. The Spirit Elders had gathered into a small knot with the Soul Dancers. Their faces glowed as if from an inner fire.

These fools thought this skinny boy could save them, take them to that shining new world beyond the stars. . . .

Something tapped the floor mat at Diver's left, probably another shell blown in by the rising wind. He ignored it, his attention glued to the Spirit Elders, and to Musselwhite.

But when the crowd closed in around Cottonmouth's shelter and Diver could no longer see Musselwhite, he wearily slumped to the floor.

. . . *And saw a hafted chert knife laying there!*

Diver's gaze shot to his guards, still intent on Cottonmouth's shelter, then scanned the forest.

White-hot fear rushed through him.

Diamondback stood in the shadows, watching Diver, his face tense, loving. His son nodded to him, gave him a gripped-fist sign, and casually walked away.

Diamondback must have waited for just the right moment, when the village's attention had been distracted . . . or . . . could it be that the Lightning Boy and Diamondback had worked together, timing their efforts for just this purpose?

Don't be a fool! Too much hope is as dangerous as too little. He concentrated on breathing deeply, evenly, to mask the turmoil that rocked his souls. *You must act as if only you, Diamondback, and Musselwhite are the players here. You can count on nothing else.*

He hunched forward. After days of little food, of wounds and torture, how much stamina did he possess? Not that it mattered. He would fight with every bit of strength he had. Cautiously, he brought his bound hands around and began sawing through the ropes.

Oh, my son, tell me there's a war party out there. That all of this has been carefully planned!

Forty-four

Pondwader walked through the rainy village ahead of Cottonmouth, chin up, steps light. He smiled at everyone he passed, marveling at how euphoric life could be once a man had given himself up for dead.

Guards flanked him, and more guards stood around the shelter where Musselwhite sat bound to a pole. Her dark eyes glinted. She looked at Pondwader as though at her worst nightmare. He tried very hard to project confidence, to show her that everything was all right. From the corner of his eye, he could see Dace, standing outside the village in a group of spectators. So many strangers had come for the Celebration Day that no one paid attention to a few more children—as they would see Kelp and Dace. Diamondback ran the greatest risk here. He had fought some of these warriors.

Pondwader entered the shelter and hurried to Musselwhite. Kneeling, he embraced her tightly. As he kissed her ear, he whispered, "Don't worry. I have a plan." He felt her stiffen. Louder, he said, "Are you all right? Have they harmed you?"

She shook her head. "No."

When he pushed back from her, he saw that Musselwhite's eyes had fastened on Cottonmouth. An emotion filled them that he had never seen before, something stronger than hatred—more like deadly promise. Pondwader sank to the floor mats at her side, just inside the line of drips falling from the thatched roof. From the instant he had walked into the village, he'd started calling the rain. Now, thunderheads crowded together to blot out the sunlight.

He could *feel* their awful Power: a building fury on the verge of bursting loose and destroying everything in its path.

Cottonmouth stood on the opposite side of the fire, arms folded, his gaze on Musselwhite. They appeared to be engaged in a silent struggle of wills.

Outside the shelter, in the pounding rain, guards tightened their circle and threw awed glances at Pondwader. Beyond the ring of guards, villagers crowded together in the rain, pointing, straining to see better.

"The time has come, Musselwhite." Without turning away, Cottonmouth ordered, "Littlehorn, move the people back. This is none of their concern. Not yet."

A very young warrior jerked a nod. "Yes, Spirit Elder."

As Littlehorn trotted away shouting commands, a roar of disapproval went up from the throng. The guards had to whack several people with their atlatls to get them to move. But they yielded, disgruntled, muttering.

Cottonmouth cocked his head, his expression a mixture of curiosity and disbelief. Pondwader could not help but stare into those magnetic eyes. They reminded him of the eyes of a wolf on a blood trail. Standing there in his blue ritual tunic, the circlets of mica glinting in the firelight, Cottonmouth looked magnificent. The silver hair at his temples shone pure white.

He spoke to Musselwhite in a soft precise voice. "Do you know what happened the day I came home from Pelican Isle?"

Seeing Musselwhite's confusion, Pondwader blurted: "Y-you mean, the Pelican Isle Massacre? Two-tens-and-six summers ago? No, I—I mean, I have heard—"

"Hush, Pondwader," Musselwhite whispered. She examined Cottonmouth's face as though logging his expression. Her eyes tightened.

Cottonmouth extended his hands and warmed them over the flames. "Do you?"

"Of course not. I was burying my family," she said in a cold voice. "How could I—"

"*Your family was here!*" he shouted. Then, in a pitiful whisper: ". . . Here! And we . . . we needed you."

Musselwhite said nothing for several moments, then: "What happened when you got home, Cottonmouth?"

His lungs expanded with a deep breath. "I came home to bury our son . . . and found all the Soul Dancers in the village sitting around him, chattering like birds."

"Chattering? About what?"

His fingers clenched into fists over the fire. "They told me not to bother burying Glade. That his afterlife souls *had vanished.* The only soul he had left was the one that stays with the body forever."

Musselwhite sat unmoving. "But—I don't understand. Why—"

"*Don't you?*"

Their gazes held, Cottonmouth's bitter and wary, Musselwhite's bewildered.

In the silence, Pondwader's blood rushed. Dogtooth had said that one of Glade's souls had changed into lightning. He knew what had happened to that soul. He . . .

The Lightning Bird stirred with faint whimpers, delicate, heartrending. Immediately above the shelter, thunder rumbled and boomed and rain shished like a palm-fiber brush on a piece of hide. The baby Bird turned over inside Pondwader, and he felt suddenly as if his lungs had been crushed. Mouth open, he struggled for breath that wouldn't come.

Something Musselwhite or Cottonmouth had said had sent the little Lightning Bird into a panic. Pondwader could feel its rapid heartbeat. The storm had grown deafening. Brilliant lightning flashes brought violent crashes of thunder.

What had happened to Glade's other soul?

. . . Think about this, brainless boy—even you are smart enough to figure it out.

And from the heart of the thunder, words whispered, parts of Songs—about sleeping warmly in drifting towers of cloud, pure white light sparkling in the deepest blackness, the terrifying vertigo of plunging down through vast blue skies . . . living in an eternal flash. Pondwader ached with such wonder that he longed to weep. *Lightning Bird memories.* That's what these were! If only he could—

Musselwhite's question shocked Pondwader back to this world: "Why would the Soul Dancers have told you that?"

Cottonmouth, his face suddenly stripped of the mask of rage, looked incredibly vulnerable. He shook his head. The wind gusted and shoved at Cottonmouth like a hard hand. He walked around the whipping fire and knelt on the other side of Musselwhite.

"I had hoped," Cottonmouth said, "that you could tell me."

"But how would I know?"

Pondwader studied them curiously. As the storm raged, Cottonmouth and Musselwhite changed, their faces relaxing, voices growing softer. They now talked with intimate familiarity.

Cottonmouth spread his hands. It was a pleading gesture. "You are the only other person who might. For two-tens-and-six summers I have been worrying about what happened to Glade. Where his souls went. Terrible nightmares have tormented my sleep. Things too abominable to believe."

Pondwader sat up straighter, bursting to tell Cottonmouth that one of Glade's souls had been living a miracle, soaring across the face of the world in a blinding body—

Musselwhite's voice turned stony. "Tell me what happened the night you were gone. When Glade was so sick. Did you go to see Bright Feather?"

Hair whipped about Cottonmouth's taut face. "I did." He nodded. "He gave me the awl as a gift. He said it could save Glade, that the awl would bring him to life again. Bright Feather—"

"How?"

"By—by acting as a siphon. To drain the souls out of a living person. . . ."

"And instead," Musselwhite surmised with suave brutality, "this *gift* robbed our son of his souls? Is that what you're suggesting? That somehow the awl stole Glade's afterlife souls?"

Cottonmouth sank to the floor mats, and ran a hand through his wet hair. "I don't know, Musselwhite. I went back—after I buried Glade—to see Bright Feather, but the old man could tell me nothing. I don't think he understood it either."

Musselwhite's expression softened. "You buried Glade against the Soul Dancers' wishes?"

"Did you think that I would leave my son to . . . to the predators? No, Musselwhite. Not my little son. He deserved more from me than that. I loved Glade very much. As much as I . . . as I loved . . ."

Faintly, she said, "I know you did."

Pondwader heard the tender echo in her voice, and watched as Musselwhite reached out with her bound hands to touch Cottonmouth's clenched fist.

"Where did you bury Glade?"

"In that small pond behind the village."

"Cottonmouth, forgive me. I should have been here with you that day. To help you."

Cottonmouth looked down at her hands for a long moment, then reached out and touched her fingers gently. In a quick, almost violent movement, he rose to his feet, and went to pick up a small basket which sat at the foot of his bedding. He pulled out a deerbone awl . . . *and Turtle Bone Doll!* He tucked both into his belt.

Pondwader's mouth gaped. She had been here, with Cottonmouth, all along! And she had never told him! She had said only that she knew Cottonmouth, not a word about living in his shelter!

Blessed Brother Sky! His thoughts darted about, collecting clues from here and there. Could *she* have been the source of Cottonmouth's nightmares? Had they been reflections of Turtle Bone Doll's feelings, trapped here, drowning, along with Cottonmouth, in the huge burden of guilt he carried over Glade's death?

Turtle Bone Doll gave Pondwader a bland look, as though surprised, as always, at how long it took him to figure out the simplest of things.

Cottonmouth returned to Musselwhite. He signaled one of his guards.

"Littlehorn, cut Musselwhite loose, then bring her and the boy to the beach. It's time to find out if he truly is a Lightning Boy."

Cottonmouth peered at Musselwhite for a long moment, love in his eyes, then he swiftly turned and strode away.

Guards immediately packed the shelter. One jerked Pondwader to his feet, while another cut Musselwhite's bindings.

Littlehorn could not have been much older than Pondwader. He wet his lips, and his eyes narrowed fearfully when he looked at Musselwhite. "Walk. Both of you."

A hand shoved Pondwader forward and he strode beside Musselwhite across the wind and rain-ravaged village. Her steps were strong, bold. Rain slashed down at an angle, hitting him squarely in the eyes. He turned his head sideways, and saw that Musselwhite's face had gone pale, her eyes hollow, as if looking upon a tragedy too great to be borne.

People crowded around them, leaping to see them, calling questions.

"Are you a Lightning Boy?"

"Have you come to save us?"

One grizzled old man shouted, "Please! We beg you. Call the Lightning Birds so they can carry us away!"

A woman warrior added, "You'd better call them—or we'll kill you for being a fake!"

Pondwader's courage drained away like water in sand as the people lunged and shouted. *Blessed Spirits, please? I'm not ready to die.* Pondwader edged closer to Musselwhite.

When he looked up and saw Cottonmouth standing near the far northern shelter, the Lightning Bird inside him blazed. Pondwader tried to keep his legs from shaking. As he walked toward Cottonmouth, Storm Girl quieted, as if holding her breath, and the raging rain turned into a fine misty shower. That unearthly longing returned. Pondwader looked up at the clouds, and beheld flashes of such wondrous colored light, he could not believe his eyes. Crimsons and ambers, and blues too luminous to be real. They belonged to the skies, to leaps from clouds, and dives through unimaginable silence.

"Pondwader!" Musselwhite whispered, her voice urgent.

"Hmm? What? I'm sorry, what did you say?"

"I've been talking to you for . . . never mind, listen. Do whatever Cottonmouth says. Don't even hesitate. Do you understand? Give him *no* reason to hurt you."

Pondwader nodded. "Yes, my wife."

And he looked back up at the sparkling lights that darted through the clouds like children playing tag. Inside him, the longing swelled and swelled. . . .

Cottonmouth stood outside the council shelter. Musselwhite walked toward him like the lithe warrior-woman he remembered. Beautiful. Confident. Eyes flashing.

Ecstasy filled him at the sight, at the storm, at the shouted exaltation of the people. None of his Dreams had prepared him for the joyous rapture of this final moment . . . or the despair of still not knowing what had happened to Glade. He had truly believed she would be able to tell him.

"Littlehorn?" Cottonmouth called as he raised his arms. "I've told you how this must be. Keep people back."

"Yes, Elder."

Littlehorn trotted down the line, arranging his warriors to form a barricade. They let only the Spirit Elders through. Basketmaker and the other elders nodded reverently to Cottonmouth as they passed, walking inside the council shelter. Cottonmouth returned their nods, and filled his lungs.

As he turned to Musselwhite, mist sheathed his face. Soon, they would be together again. Forever.

Musselwhite stopped ten hands away. Pondwader stood behind Musselwhite, peering over her shoulder at Cottonmouth, his pink eyes huge.

Cottonmouth pulled the deerbone awl from his belt and pointed it. "Come over here, Lightning Boy." Nothing. *"Now!"*

Pondwader flinched. Gently, he touched Musselwhite's shoulder as he stepped around her on wobbly legs and came to stand in front of Cottonmouth. He tried very hard to look Cottonmouth in the eyes, but he was shaking so badly, he couldn't.

"Are you the White Lightning Boy?" Cottonmouth asked. "The one sent to save us?"

Pondwader squinted. "Others s-say that I am."

"Do you believe it?"

"I—I don't disbelieve it. I've just never been certain."

"You've never felt Power moving inside you?"

The boy hesitated, and Cottonmouth saw the truth reflected in his eyes. A joy like spring sunlight glowed inside him. "You have felt it. I can see that. And with stunning intensity . . . Haven't you?"

Pondwader jerked a nod.

"Have you ever used it?" Cottonmouth asked. "To call the animals, or—"

"I called the Lightning Birds once."

Yes. Oh, yes! Soon . . . "I want you to do that again, Lightning Boy. Concentrate on the blaze that lives inside you, and—"

From nowhere, everywhere, Dark Rain's derisive laughter echoed, and she shouted, "Hallowed Shining People, Cottonmouth! Couldn't you have

396 Kathleen O'Neal Gear and W. Michael Gear

found a more convincing savior? You'll disappoint all of your followers. Look at them! They were expecting a grand and glorious hero to come striding into their village. And what do you offer them? A pitiful boy. And a skinny one at that."

Her attack on Cottonmouth sent a wave of nervous laughter among the visitors, punctuated by enraged shouts from his followers. Two men begin shoving each other and yelling, on the verge of a fist fight.

Cottonmouth's brows drew down. *I should have killed her.* About to shout the order, he hesitated. That wasn't in the Dream. He could not take chances now. No. He dared not.

He ignored her, and returned his attention to Pondwader. "Not even your mother believes in you."

"That's not un—unusual," Pondwader stammered. "Even w-worse, here she comes."

Cottonmouth looked up to see Dark Rain pushing through the crowd. She had braided her hair and wore a bright scarlet tunic. Soaked, it hugged every curve of her body. Hate twisted her face. Dark Rain walked up to the circle of guards, and tried to shove her way through. The guards glanced at Cottonmouth, and he shook his head.

Dark Rain shrilled, "You're afraid to have me in there! You know Pondwader is not a Lightning Boy. You are tricking all of your followers!"

"I find it hard to believe that you know anything about holy people, Dark Rain," Cottonmouth called. "Or care to."

"Oh, Cottonmouth!" Hanging Star yelled. "She claims to know intimate details about Soul Dancers! Just ask her!"

More laughter.

Dark Rain propped slim hands on her shapely hips. "If he were a Lightning Boy, surely by now he would have shown it. I assure you, he has not. You might as well let him go. He's just a boy!"

Pondwader frowned his confusion, and sudden terror gripped Cottonmouth. Was this some sort of trick? Some way of wounding or distracting the Lightning Boy so he could not concentrate on calling the Lightning Birds?

Cottonmouth leaned down and murmured, "What's wrong?"

"I just . . . I don't know why my mother—of all people—would be trying to help me."

"She's not. She hasn't changed a bit. She seeks only to embarrass me—helping you is purely accidental."

Pondwader appeared to think about that, then he nodded, and sighed.

"He's my son!" Dark Rain shouted. "I should know!"

"The *whore* is his mother?" An unknown man in the rear of the crowd yelled. "Great Ghosts, Cottonmouth! If Dark Rain gave him birth he can't possibly be a Lightning Boy! We all know the stories. Lightning Boys are born to *good* women!"

"Oh, she's good," Hanging Star bellowed. "She's *very* good. Why, every man here knows that!"

Dark Rain whirled, searching for Hanging Star, and a roar of merriment drowned out the crashing surf. Tens of men in the crowd slapped each other on the backs and guffawed.

Pondwader bowed his head in shame.

Cottonmouth held up his hands for silence. His own unease was growing. As the clamor died away to a series of chuckles and curses, Cottonmouth said, "Dark Rain, you leave me no choice. Many of us here believe he *is* a Lightning Boy. Now, your son will have to prove it."

Pondwader's knees shook so badly Cottonmouth fought the urge to reach out and support him.

In a tremulous whisper, the boy said, "But I—I don't think I can."

"What?" Cottonmouth asked. "Speak louder. I want everyone to hear."

Pondwader forced himself to shout. "I don't think I can! Prove it . . . I mean."

"Of course, you can. I've seen you do it . . . in my Dream."

"H-how?"

In a clear ringing voice, Cottonmouth commanded, "Shoot down the Shining Eagles!"

People in the crowd, outsiders, screamed in shock. He saw several of them backing away, ready to run. Pondwader looked horrified. His desperate fingers knotted and twisted in the fabric of his clothing. "Please," Pondwader murmured. "Please, don't ask me to do that. I—I don't even know how, Cottonmouth!"

"He doesn't know how, Cottonmouth!" Dark Rain mocked. "Which is not surprising! My son has never known how to do anything! Stop this farce. Let me take my son home!"

"If he cannot shoot down the Shining Eagles, then he is not the Lightning Boy promised in my Dreams, and I *will* let him go. But he must prove it first. Pondwader—"

"If you truly wish him to prove it, Cottonmouth," Musselwhite called, striding forward like a hunting lion, "give him an atlatl and darts! Give the boy weapons to shoot down the Eagles!"

Cottonmouth's brows lowered. *With you so close, Musselwhite? And when it will take only five running steps for you to grab them from the boy, and . . . Would you do it . . . ? Could you kill me?*

"Littlehorn?" Cottonmouth said. "Come. Give the boy your atlatl and three darts. One for each of the remaining Eagles."

Pondwader jerked around, breathing hard. "H-How do you know that?" he hissed. "That one of the Eagles already lies dead?"

A hollow sense of fulfillment swelled within Cottonmouth. "Dreams, Lightning Boy. *Dreams* . . . I wrestle with Power every day of my life—"

The boy bravely stepped closer, peering up at him with wide, intent eyes.

"And . . . and with despair, and the waves of solitude that drown you. And you can't let anyone see you flailing, or cry for help. You—you have a rage for pain. For many summers you've been clutching regret to your bosom like a precious child. And . . ." He shook very badly now. "And you would die to protect that agony. Wouldn't you?"

Cottonmouth froze. His heart thudded dully against his ribs. The despair the boy had spoken of crept through him, damping his muscles, weakening his bones. "Did the Lightning Birds tell you that?"

Pondwader's face shone. "No . . . I just knew it."

Littlehorn trotted up with the weapons, and Cottonmouth held up a hand to stop him in his tracks.

"You asked if I would die to protect the agony," Cottonmouth said. "Yes, I would, Pondwader. But what does that mean to you? Why did you ask?"

"Because I think you should want to l-live, not to die."

"I don't have anything to live for, Pondwader. Not here. Not anymore."

"But you do!" the boy stubbornly insisted. He shook both fists at Cottonmouth. "You are a great Dreamer! You could be a great leader. My wife has told me! Make peace with the other villages, then—"

"I can't. I can't do that, Pondwader. Ten summers ago, perhaps, but not now." All his dreams for this world had perished long, long ago. He waved Littlehorn forward. "Give the boy your weapons."

Littlehorn thrust the atlatl and darts into Pondwader's reluctant hands and backed away, resuming his place in the circle.

Pondwader fumbled with the darts, dropping one, tucking another beneath his left armpit while he tried to nock the third. His hands quaked so that the dart wouldn't stay on the atlatl's shell hook. Finally, he did it. He bit his lip.

"Are you ready, Lightning Boy?"

Pondwader shook his head. "No. No, I—I can't do this, Cottonmouth. I can't shoot down the Eagles! All my life I've—"

"Littlehorn?" Cottonmouth called. "Have your warriors aim their darts at Musselwhite. If the boy does not cast on my command, kill her."

Pondwader whirled around to stare in terror. Three of four tens of men stood with their atlatls aimed at Musselwhite. The misty rain had drenched her long hair, slicking it down around her beautiful face. "Oh . . . no, please. Don't hurt her! She hasn't done anything!"

Cottonmouth pointed a finger at the sullen black heavens. "Lift your dart, Lightning Boy. Get ready to cast!"

Pondwader closed his eyes a moment, and Cottonmouth saw the tears that fell from the corners of his eyes. Softly, he answered, "I'm ready."

"Shoot down the Eagles!"

Using all of his strength, he cast the dart out over the ocean. It arced upward and vanished into the glistening rain.

It had been a pitiful cast. Hisses and laughter erupted . . . then a terrifying bolt of bright white streaked the sky. A heartbeat later the crash of thunder pounded the shore, drowning out all other sounds. Cries of awe laced the gathering. Every head tipped up. Through the gray drizzle, Lightning Birds Danced, shooting and leaping, soaring with wild abandon.

Cottonmouth shouted, "Cast another dart, Pondwader. Do it! Hurry!"

The boy wept as he pulled the dart from under his arm, nocked it, and cast.

A Lightning Bird crackled down in violent blue-white fire, and blasted the beach just north of them. The deafening roar of thunder that followed devoured people's screams. The crowd fled, stumbling over each other to get away.

Cottonmouth took two steps after them, yelling, "No, come back! Our time has come! A shining new world awaits those brave enough! Stay with me!"

The Spirit Elders and six or seven tens of young people crowded around the council shelter, their eyes huge with faith, waiting.

"Another, Pondwader!" Cottonmouth said. "Cast another dart! You *are* a Lightning Boy. I knew it! Go on, kill the last Shining Eagle. *Save me. Please, save me, White Lightning Boy!*"

Pondwader bent to pick up the last dart—and a wail went up from the believers. Cottonmouth spun. A swaying black serpent descended from the clouds. The blackness twisted and writhed, driven by tortured winds. Like a hunting snake it dropped its pointed tip, touched the water beyond the beach, and bounced across the frothy swells.

Cottonmouth raised his hands to the waterspout as the wind increased, ripping at his hair and clothing. "The End has come! *Cast the last dart, Lightning Boy! Do it now!*"

Diver gasped when seashells and pieces of coral began falling from the sky; they bounced and tumbled across the sand. The waterspout! It must have sucked them up and now spewed them out again. Believers shrieked and covered their heads . . . and Diver pulled the stiletto from beneath the mat and rose to his feet to stand among them, breathing hard. Diamondback and two other young warriors huddled beneath a pine only two tens of paces away.

The eerie howling, like the end of the world, sent shivers through Diver's souls. When the bizarre downpour ceased, the crowd fled like hunted rabbits. A running man dashed Diver sideways, and he staggered. Weak, he caught his balance, and forced his shaking legs on toward his son. The fury of the wind almost sucked him off his feet just before he entered the trees.

"Father!" Diamondback embraced him in a powerful hug. A girl and a boy were with him. The boy knelt to finger the shells that had fallen from the sky.

"Oh, my son," Diver said, gripping Diamondback's shoulders. "We've no time. Your mother is in grave danger."

"Father, this is Kelp, Pondwader's sister, and her friend Dace. Tell us what to do."

Diver turned. The rain had stopped almost completely now. Here and there, sunlight lanced the clouds. He saw Pondwader stagger, one arm thrown up as he squinted at the waterspout.

Littlehorn shouted, "Run! Everybody, get off the beach! Hurry. Spirit Elders, *run, run!*" He violently waved his arms, yelling orders to other guards, directing fleeing people. The terrible wind almost drowned the warrior's shouts as men, women, and children ran for their lives.

Only the most devoted, a handful, still stood with the Spirit Elders in the council shelter. The structure shuddered in the wind, palm frond roofing flying off to career across the village.

When Pondwader clutched the last dart to his chest, Cottonmouth turned, and the wind ripped the turtle bone doll from his belt. She flew through the air toward the Lightning Boy, somersaulting, flipping, as if *Dancing*. When she hit the sand and started to blow away, Pondwader lunged for her, gripping her tightly in both hands.

"Pondwader!" Cottonmouth shouted. "Throw the last dart! Finish it!"

The boy gripped the last dart, but shook his head. "No. No, I won't!" He watched the waterspout gyrate through the surf just east of the beach.

Musselwhite leaped, ripped the dart from Pondwader's hand. . . .

Cottonmouth reacted instantly. He threw himself at her, grabbing her around the waist, knocking her to the ground. A growl like a raging cougar's came from her lips. Kicking and shouting at each other, they rolled over the sand.

"Now!" Diver shouted, and ran, the young warriors behind him.

Cottonmouth thrust the deerbone awl against Musselwhite's throat—and she went still.

"No!" Pondwader shouted. He shoved the turtle bone doll down the front of his robe, grabbed the dart, and dashed for Cottonmouth.

"Stay back!" Cottonmouth ordered. "I'll kill her! Cast the dart, boy. Do it . . . ! Diver, don't!"

Diver stopped, his legs shaking, too far away to be of any help to her.

"Pondwader!" Musselwhite said. "Do as Cottonmouth says! Cast the dart!"

As Pondwader fussed with the dart and atlatl, Cottonmouth leaned his forehead against Musselwhite's, like a lover letting himself drown in the silken texture of her skin.

"I told you!" Cottonmouth shouted over the wind. "I can't leave you.

Not again. When I go to the shining new world, I'll carry your souls with me. *Inside me,* Musselwhite."

Musselwhite's dark eyes went huge in sudden understanding. She wrenched violently in Cottonmouth's arms. Pondwader took the chance, whirled, lunged for Cottonmouth.

"*Pondwader! No!*" Kelp shouted.

With practiced ease, Cottonmouth slapped the dart from Pondwader's hand, and tried to plunge the awl into Musselwhite's heart. She caught his arm, her face twisted as they wrestled.

Diver ran forward.

Pondwader screamed, "Stop! Stop it!" and dove, reaching for Cottonmouth with his bare hands. His shoulder struck Cottonmouth's, and knocked him off Musselwhite. Pondwader landed on top of him, fighting for the awl.

Cottonmouth saw Musselwhite getting to her feet, and quickly plunged the awl into Pondwader's chest, tearing through the fabric of his tunic, driving it into a hollow between the ribs. He threw the boy away to dive for Musselwhite.

She'd recovered enough to meet Cottonmouth halfway, and slammed him with both fists. He stumbled backward, and she hit him again.

"Musselwhite, get back!" Diver shouted as he grabbed Cottonmouth around the throat, and drove Glasswort's stiletto into the man's stomach. Cottonmouth arched forward under the impact, screaming hoarsely, *"No! No! Where are the Lightning Birds . . . ? Where are they?"*

Diver pulled the stiletto out, and plunged it into Cottonmouth's lungs, then he released the man and let him fall to the ground. The Dreamer curled on his side, his eyes wide with disbelief and pain. He peered unblinking at the wounded Lightning Boy a few body lengths away.

Diver gripped Musselwhite's arm and shouted, "Come on! We have to get out of here. Now!"

"No!" she screamed. Hair whipped around her face as she turned. "Pondwader! I have to get to Pondwader!"

Diamondback, Kelp, and Dace knelt around the Lightning Boy. Kelp was crying, "Pondwader? Pondwader, talk to me!"

Musselwhite shoved between them, dropped by his side, and examined Pondwader's blood-soaked robe. The turtle bone doll's head stuck out above his collar, framed by a white halo of wet hair, as if she were watching, wondering. Musselwhite said, "Pondwader, I'm here. I'm going to carry you. Hold onto me if you can."

"No," he murmured thickly. His open mouth trembled. "No, Musselwhite. The . . . baby Lightning Bird. He—*he's coming.*"

"Let him! I'm going to lift you, Pondwader! We have to get out of here!" Musselwhite slipped one arm beneath his knees and another under his shoulders. . . .

Pondwader's body convulsed in her arms like a clubbed rabbit's. A sharp incoherent cry was torn from his lips as lightning crackled right over their heads, the thunder so loud it deafened.

Musselwhite screamed and fell back.

In the ominous silence that followed, Diver heard a voice—like a whisper from the grave. At first, he thought it was Pondwader, but the Lightning Boy's mouth did not move.

A beautiful voice said, *"Dance with us, Lightning Boy. Come and Dance. You have only to reach out your hand. Come on, Eyeless Boy. It's not so hard. . . ."*

Pondwader lifted his shaking hand. "I . . . I can't . . . reach you."

"Pondwader?" Musselwhite said. "What is it? What's happening?" Frantic, she grasped the awl, tugged it free, and flung it away. "Pondwader, I'm going to—"

"No," he whispered. "No, my wife. Please . . . I have to . . . go."

He reached higher, his white hand like an icy beacon in the storm, and a bolt of lightning exploded on the beach, showering them with shells and sand.

Diver leaped on Musselwhite, pulling her to the ground, shielding her with his own body. From the corner of his eye, he saw Diamondback, Kelp, and Dace dive in different directions.

"Blessed Spirits," Diver whispered. His ears rang. Black spots flickered before his eyes. He rolled to the side and fearfully looked out to sea where the waterspout had been, then back at the village where the warriors had fled. The wind died down to a soft whimper. "Get up, Musselwhite!" he said. "Now!"

Musselwhite did not seem to hear. She remained stone still, her eyes tight with horror.

Diver jerked around, following her gaze.

An eerie luminescent cocoon swelled around Pondwader. Oddly silent. Shimmering. *Foxfire!* Diver had seen it once before during a violent lightning storm—every shell on the beach had burned with this same blue fire. It flooded down Pondwader's arms and legs, following his veins, bathing him in azure light.

Kelp screamed, *"Pondwader!"* and reached for her brother. The instant her hand penetrated the cocoon . . .

Glorious, blinding light engulfed them.

Land and sky had merged. People huddled like mice, ankle deep in rainwater. The heavens had opened half a hand of time ago. Mothers clutched children close, holding blankets, matting, old tunics, or anything else they could find, over their heads. The fury of the storm ripped a blizzard of oak leaves from the branches, swirling them down with the deluge of rain. Even the crying children had been shocked into silence.

Moonsnail glared out from beneath her hood. Dogtooth sat in front of her, morose. Seedpod sat to her left, with Thorny Boy in his lap, a blanket pulled around both of them. Floating Stick crouched on his haunches beside Dogtooth. His sparse white hair lay matted to his freckled scalp.

Suddenly, Dogtooth let out a shriek. *"Look!"* he cried as a monstrous Lightning Bird crackled right over their heads, leaving a trail of pale blue flame. Dogtooth tottered to his feet. "He's beautiful! He's *so* beautiful! Moonsnail, did you ever imagine he would be so magnificent?"

She shouted, "Dogtooth! Sit down before a falling branch knocks your head off!"

The skinny old Soul Dancer cupped a hand to his mouth to shout against the gale, "But I'm so happy!"

"What for?" she demanded. "This is the worst storm we've seen since—"

"But Glade's souls have been reunited at last! He's on his way to the Village of Wounded Souls! Pondwader is taking him!"

Moonsnail exchanged a glance with Floating Stick, then looked at Seedpod.

Seedpod hugged Thorny Boy tighter, and shrugged. "Who knows?" he said.

Floating Stick braced a hand on the oak trunk and got to his feet, announcing, "I'll handle this!"

He slogged through the water, and out into the worst of the downpour to grip Dogtooth's arm, and tug the Soul Dancer back under the protection of the tree.

Floating Stick yelled in Dogtooth's rain-drenched face, "You old lunatic! That was a Lightning *Bird*, not a Lightning *Boy!*"

Dogtooth shook off his hand, and scowled. "You really are demented, aren't you, Floating Stick?"

Forty-five

Twilight fell in a luminous blue veil over the forest. The clouds had parted, leaving raindrops like transparent beads on every hickory leaf, pine needle, and palmetto frond. Through the lacy canopy of branches, the first Shining People sparkled.

Diamondback took a deep breath of the earthy, pine-sharp night, stretched his hands to the small fire, and looked around the clearing. As the storm dissipated, the temperature had dropped, and a biting chill rode the wind. Pondwader lay on the opposite side of the fire under a mound of blankets. His pale pinched face reflected the wavering amber of the flames. Kelp and Dace sat on either side of him. Fear strained the lines of Kelp's pretty face, pulling the corners of her dark eyes down.

Dace sat frowning at the ground. His mud-splotched tunic clung to his body like a second skin, accentuating the muscles in his arms and shoulders. He'd clamped his strong jaw to keep his worry at bay. Atlatl and darts lay within easy reach . . . just in case.

He had become a warrior. And more.

When they'd stopped for the evening, Dace had slipped away without a word, darted a brown pelican, and brought it back to camp. While everyone else had been laboring over the wounded Lightning Boy, Dace had plucked the big bird, quietly skewered it on a long stick, and propped it over the fire to roast. He had seen to the group's needs. Some day, he would make a truly great clan leader.

Diver and Musselwhite knelt a short distance from the fire. His father had an arm around his mother's back, speaking quietly to her. Head bowed, her silver-black hair cascaded around her. Diamondback saw his mother shake her head, heard her say: "This is something I must do, Diver."

His father closed his eyes, as if in pain. But he nodded.

Kelp reached out to touch Pondwader's wrist.

Worriedly, Dace asked, "Does he still have a pulse?"

Kelp nodded. "It's weak, but it's there."

Diamondback rubbed his cold hands together over the fire. "He's very lucky that awl was so short. If it had been just a little longer, it would have pierced his heart."

"But . . ." Dace frowned. "I don't understand. If the awl missed his heart and lungs, why is Pondwader so ill?"

"Sometimes, Dace," Diamondback said softly, "after being wounded, the body goes into shock and doesn't come out for a while." *And sometimes it never comes out.*

His parents rose to their feet, and walked toward the fire. Diver's wide mouth had pressed into a hard line. His round face wore a sheen of sweat. Musselwhite, on the other hand, exuded a confidence and serenity that Diamondback had not seen in over a moon.

When they stopped behind Kelp, looking down at Pondwader, Diamondback said, "He's all right. So far."

His mother nodded and knelt. Tenderly, she brushed white hair away from the Lightning Boy's pale brow. "Pondwader?" she said softly. "I want you to listen to me. I have to go away tonight, but I'll be back tomorrow. Live for me." She bent over and lightly kissed him on the cheek. "Live for me, my husband." Her voice grew hoarse with restrained emotion. "I'm proud of you. You were very brave today."

Diamondback looked up at his father. "What does she mean? Where's she going?"

Diver's mouth pursed. "To Standing Hollow Horn Village."

"What?" Diamondback blurted. "Has she lost her senses! There are ten tens of warriors there. They'll kill her on sight!"

In a barely audible voice, Pondwader said, ". . . Let her go."

He still had his eyes closed, but the lids moved. His lips parted and he took a deep breath.

"Pondwader?" Kelp whispered, clutching his hand tightly. "Are you all right?"

A frail smile came to his face. "I soared, Kelp. I soared . . . and I *flashed.*"

She glanced around, seeing if anyone else understood. Meeting blank stares, Kelp softly inquired, "Where did you soar to, Pondwader?"

"To the . . . the Village of Wounded Souls."

"The Village of Wounded Souls? You mean you died?"

Pondwader wet his lips. "No. That's . . . that's where I came alive. I got my souls back. They were waiting for me . . . sitting on a log by the side of the trail."

Diamondback scratched his neck, lifting an eyebrow.

Kelp's face broke into a broad smile. "Pondwader had lost his souls, they'd been washed away in the Sacred Pond." She said to her brother, "Oh, Pondwader, I'm so relieved."

Musselwhite laid her palm against Pondwader's cheek. Gently, she said, "My heart is glad to see you, Pondwader."

He smiled up into her face. "And mine . . . to see you."

"You saved all our lives today."

". . . Love you, my wife."

Musselwhite bent over to kiss him on the mouth. "I love you too, my husband."

Pondwader's eyes opened. Deep love shone in those pink depths. He worked his fingers to reach for her, and Musselwhite took his hand in a strong grip.

"The . . . people," Pondwader whispered, "at Standing Hollow Horn . . . will not touch him. . . ." He seemed to be struggling to find the strength to continue.

Musselwhite said, "Because they now believe he was a false Dreamer. Yes, I know, Pondwader. That is why I must go."

Pondwader nodded weakly. "I'm glad. He spent the past two-tens-and-six summers alone. . . . You are right to help release him from that . . . my wife."

Pondwader's grip relaxed, and his head lolled sideways in sleep. Musselwhite gently tucked his hand beneath the warm blanket, and got to her feet.

"I'll return by tomorrow night," she said to Diver.

Diver looked at Diamondback. "*We* will return."

"You're not coming with me," Musselwhite said.

"You're not going alone."

"Don't be foolish! You are still weak—and the children need you here. I'll be fine."

Diver slipped his arm around her shoulders. "These are not children, Musselwhite. These are warriors. They don't need either of us . . . not anymore."

Diver stood on the bank of the small pond behind Standing Hollow Horn Village. The trees around them looked bedraggled, stripped of leaves, branches broken to expose the wounded white wood inside the bark. Tatters of hanging moss swung in the capricious breeze. Leaves, branches, and other litter covered the ground, while palmetto fronds hung in the vines where they'd caught.

The sky itself had a tired look, the clouds scattered and wispy in the morning sun. Birdsong lilted in the trees, as if the birds, of all Creation's life, remained undistressed by the storm.

"Can I help?" Diver asked Musselwhite, searching her face in an attempt to read her souls. He struggled with himself, fighting his hatred for Cottonmouth, and all the pain he'd inflicted, and his new curiosity about Mussel-white's response to the terrible man's death. She looked very sad.

"No," she told him.

Musselwhite gripped the blanket she had wrapped Cottonmouth in and pulled his slender body into the water. She picked up the sharpened stakes and tucked them under an arm before wading out. Mist curled from the calm green surface, spiraling up around her. Her beautiful voice lilted, Singing the Death Song.

Diver crossed his arms, eyes narrowed. Musselwhite touched Cotton-mouth very gently. How could she? Memories of hot coals and thorns filled Diver's souls. The dead looked at him with hollow eyes: Morning Glory, so young and beautiful; Blue Echo, full of life and ambition, bleeding in the grass . . . and so many others, all gone because of this man's obsession.

Diver turned away, choking back his building rage. He had to find some way of binding up the ragged tears in his soul, to weave them together like the fibers of a basket into something that would hold the rest of his life together.

Fog shrouded the coastline this morning, thick and sparkling. Tufts clung to the treetops, and roamed the deer trails.

It's over. Power has taken its own retribution. So, let it go, Diver. There is only now . . . and tomorrow. He shivered, and the rage dwindled, replaced by hope.

He filled his lungs with the fresh air, drawing in the damp scents of land and plants.

Yes, retribution. When they had walked into Standing Hollow Horn and seen the devastation, he had been stunned. People moved about like beaten dogs, heads hanging as they hunted for possessions to pack up, or labored to make new travoises. There were no shelters.

The story had come in bits and pieces, told by people with listless eyes. The waterspout they had last seen heading northward up the shore had twisted around and destroyed the village that night.

Villagers had whispered that it was Cottonmouth's ghost, taking revenge upon them for their lack of faith. Others believed the site tainted by witch-craft and accursed. People only wanted to get away as quickly as possible. So great was their hurry, and so powerful their fear, the bodies of loved ones were left lying where the tornado had tossed them.

Musselwhite had found Cottonmouth's body up the beach several hands from where he had died, lying on his back, his wide eyes fixed on the shimmering fog. A serene expression had come over his face.

Diver turned back to the pond as Musselwhite's voice rose in volume, the Song of the dead mixing with those of the birds.

> *Look northward now,*
> *down the pathway of living waters to the*

Wolves in the Village of Wounded Souls.
Hear them call you?
They are calling you,
calling, calling . . .

Diver winced at the ache in Musselwhite's voice.

Musselwhite had pulled Cottonmouth to the center of the pond, her path traced by ripples in the still water. Long graying hair floated around Cottonmouth's handsome face as his head sank below the water. Musselwhite turned him onto his left side, facing north, tucked his knees against his chest, and drove the first burial stake through the blanket to pin him to the bottom of the pond. With practiced skill, she moved around Cottonmouth, driving the stakes to form an oval frame, so he wouldn't lose sight of the tunnel that led to the afterlife.

"May you find peace," Musselwhite murmured. "Glade will meet you on the trail that leads to the Ice Mountains. And I . . . ." As though the pain had grown unbearable, her head bowed. She put a hand on Cottonmouth's shoulder. Very quietly, she finished, "I loved you very much, Cottonmouth."

Silver rings bobbed on the pond's surface as she waded from the water to stand before Diver. She seemed to stare right through him, her face a mask. Water ran down her long legs. From the slump in her shoulders, and the set of her mouth, he knew she felt weary beyond exhaustion.

Diver gently touched her cold cheek. "Are you ready?"

She nodded; tears glistened in her eyes. Hastily, she started to walk away.

Diver gripped her hand, pulled her back, and embraced her tightly. "This is me," he whispered, twining the last of the loose threads of his souls together. "It's all right to cry for him."

Dark Rain walked along the beach south of the abandoned village, her arm linked with young Littlehorn's. She smiled to herself as she watched her slim brown feet splash in the foamy surf rushing over the white sand. A fresh vibrancy filled her, like a fire kindled in her loins that spread to all of her body. The catastrophe had brought about her rebirth.

Lucky enough to have survived the tornado, she'd capitalized on the destruction of Standing Hollow Horn Village; her pack bulged with wealth she'd picked up. Getting some of the necklaces, points, and shells had necessitated the greatest of delicacy, since she'd had to sneak around after dark to loot the corpses. People were so narrow-minded when it came to the dead.

She tightened her grip on Littlehorn's arm. He reciprocated by snaking the arm around her, his hand cupping her breast. He hadn't stopped smiling since she'd crawled into his robes three nights ago, just after the tornado.

She glanced at him from the corner of her eye. At the age of ten-and-six summers, he had little experience—but extraordinary endurance. Not to mention the fact that he had gained enormous status by herding everyone off the beach before the tornado struck. The surviving Spirit Elders of Standing Hollow Horn had declared him War Leader.

She butted him with her hip and smiled slyly to herself as his grip on her breast tightened. He would do. For a time, at least.

"What's that?" Littlehorn asked, pointing with his free hand.

Dark Rain's eyes narrowed. She reached down into the cold foamy surf and picked up the object, ignoring the fact that Littlehorn used the opportunity to feel between her legs.

It gleamed in the wan light penetrating the mist. She turned it over, saw the owner's mark on the back . . . and her heart leapt. She had heard the stories—in fact, from the moment of Standing Hollow Horn's destruction, she'd heard of little else. Cottonmouth and the turtle bone doll. Cottonmouth . . . and *the awl*.

"What is it?" Littlehorn repeated as he rubbed against her buttocks.

She hastily tucked it into her belt, stood, and hugged him. "Just an old deerbone. I'm bored, Littlehorn. There must be a game going on somewhere. Let's find it."

Littlehorn frowned, distracted by her body moving against his. "But what are you going to do with an old deerbone?"

Dark Rain smiled seductively. "Oh, I'm sure I'll find a use for it."

Forty-six

What do you mean, "what happened then?" This is Dark Rain we're talking about, child. Let me see. . . . I think the witch's name was Bog Sparrow. He paid her a huge sum, too.

Hmm?

Indeed, he did. Pondwader lived to a very old age. I sometimes think he may have been the happiest man who ever walked the earth. Musselwhite grew to love him very much, and he never stopped flashing and soaring.

Oh, yes. He thundered, too. In fact, his ability to thunder made him one of the greatest Healers ever. Why people would come for three or four moons' walk away just to have Pondwader touch them, and . . .

Wait. Let me lean forward. Now, speak up!

Naturally, they did. Kelp and Diamondback married the following summer. Kelp became a great warrior woman, even more renowned than Musselwhite had been. You would not believe the things she accomplished.

What?

. . . Do you? How about the rest of you? Would you like to hear that story, too?

Why, of course, I will. Just the fact that you'd ask warms my old heart. That's what I do, after all.

I keep the legends alive.

Now, all of you come closer. This has grown to quite a crowd, and I'm not as young as I used to be. All right, children, sit up straighter. I won't have anybody slouching in my audience. Can all of you hear me?

Good. Let's see . . .

What was that? Something flew by me.

A rock!

Who did that? You! What's your name? You're new here. Well, that was very rude. Never throw rocks at a Storyteller! Stories are sensitive things! You can't just . . .

Oh! Yes, yes. I am Thorny Boy, son of Musselwhite and Diver.

Let me settle myself again, and knot this blanket around my shoulders. The night has picked up quite a chill, hasn't it?

And that's just the way it was when Kelp came home from a war walk to Coral Isle and found Diamondback lying wounded in the brush, and all of her children gone. Why, she nearly went mad with fear. But it all had to do with that wicked awl, you see. Many summers before, Pondwader had tried to purchase it back from Bog Sparrow, but that old witch had other ideas. He knew that one of Kelp's children had grown into a very great Soul Dancer, and he thought that if he could capture that child and . . .

You are *such* a rude boy! What's the matter with you? Here, wait a moment. I don't know how good my aim is these days, but—

Well, you started it! You deserved it. Pay attention, now!

The old witch, Bog Sparrow, had captured little Sandpiper and dragged her deep into the swamps. But he got more than he bargained for, because even at the age of five summers Sandpiper had great Power. She started calling the bears and alligators, you see. And let me tell you, the first time old Bog Sparrow awoke surrounded by tens of glinting reptile eyes, he . . .

Selected Bibliography

Brown, Robin C., *Florida's First People*. Sarasota: Pineapple Press, 1994.

Dickel, David N., C. Gregory Aker, Billie K. Barton, Glen H. Doran. "An Orbital Floor and Ulna Fracture from the Early Archaic of Florida." *Journal of Paleopathology* 2(3):165–70.

Dickel, D. N., and Glen H. Doran. "Severe Neural Tube Defect Syndrome From the Early Archaic of Florida." *American Journal of Physical Anthropology*, 80:325–334.

Davis, Dave D. *Perspectives on Gulf Coast Prehistory*. Gainesville: University of Florida, 1984.

Doran, Glen H., David N. Dickel, William E. Ballinger Jr., O. Frank Agee, Philip J. Laipis, and William W. Hauswirth. "Anatomical, Cellular, and Molecular Analysis of 8,000-year-old Human Brain Tissue from the Windover Archaeological Site." *Nature*, Vol. 323:803–806.

Doran, Glen H., David N. Dickel. "Multidisciplinary Investigations at the Windover Site." In *Wet Site Archaeology*, Barbara Purdy, ed. Caldwell, N.J., 1988:263–323.

————. "Radiometric Chronology of the Archaic Windover Archaeological Site (8BR246)." *The Florida Anthropologist*, Vol. 41, No. 3:365–380.

Doran, Glen H., David N. Dickel, and Lee A. Newsom. "A 7,290-Year-Old Bottle Gourd From the Windover Site, Florida." *American Antiquity*, 55(2):354–360.

Gilliland, Marion Spjut. *The Material Culture of Key Marco Florida*. Port Salerno: Florida Classics Library, 1989.

Hauswirth, W. W. "Ancient DNA." *Experientia*, 50(1994):521–523.

Hauswirth, W. W., C. D. Dickel, D. J. Rowold, M. A. Hauswirth. "Inter- and-intrapopulation Studies of Ancient Humans." *Experientia*, 50 (1994):585–591.

Larson, Lewis H. *Aboriginal Subsistence Technology on the Southeastern*

Coastal Plain during the Late Prehistoric Period. Gainesville: University of Florida Press, 1980.

Lasca, Norman P., John Donahue, eds. *Archaeological Geology of North America.* Boulder, Colorado: The Geological Society of America, Inc., 1990.

Lawlor, D. A., C. D. Dickel, and W. W. Hauswirth. "Ancient HLA genes from 7,500-year-old Archaeological Remains." *Nature,* 349(1991): 785–788.

McGoun, William E. *Prehistoric Peoples of South Florida.* Tuscaloosa: University of Alabama Press, 1993.

Milanich, Jerald T. *Archaeology of Precolumbian Florida.* Gainesville: University of Florida Press, 1994.

Milanich, Jerald T., Samuel Proctor. *Tacachale. Essays on the Indians of Florida and Southeastern Georgia during the Historic Period.* Gainesville: University of Florida Press, 1978.

Myers, Ronald L., John J. Ewel. *Ecosystems of Florida.* Orlando: University of Central Florida Press, 1990.

Nabergall-Luis, Lee Andrea. *Faunal Studies From an Early Archaic Wetsite: The Windover Archaeological Site, Brevard County, Florida.* Master's Thesis, Florida State University, Tallahassee. 1990.

Purdy, Barbara A. *The Art and Archaeology of Florida's Wetlands.* Boca Raton, CRC Press, 1991.

———. *Florida's Prehistoric Stone Technology.* Gainesville: University of Florida Press, 1986.

Tuross, Noreen, Marilyn L. Fogel, Lee Newsom, Glen H. Doran. "Subsistence in the Florida Archaic: The Stable-Isotope and Archaeobotanical Evidence From the Windover Site." *American Antiquity,* 59(2): 288–303.

Watts, William A., Barbara C. S. Hansen. "Environments of Florida in the Late Wisconsin and Holocene." In *Wetsite Archaeology.* Barbara Purdy, ed. Caldwell, N.J.: The Teleford Press, 1988.

Widmer, Randolph J. *The Evolution of the Calusa. A Nonagricultural Chiefdom on the Southwest Florida Coast.* Tuscaloosa: University of Alabama Press: 1988.

Willey, Gordon R. *Archeology of the Florida Gulf Coast.* Washington, D.C.: Smithsonian Miscellaneous Collections, Vol. 113, 1949.